"A richly imaginative and multifaceted collection about grief, inner worlds, what we choose to forget and the responsibility to remember."

Stark Holborn, author of *Nunslinger,*
Triggernometry and *Ten Low*

"In the *Museum* collection, Sutton blends together history, myth and fantasy. There is a fragile and beautiful quality to this anthology, making you question your assumptions about all manner of things."

Allen Stroud, Chair of the
British Science Fiction Association

"Fascinating, intriguing, insightful. Quite simply, a superb collection."

John Houlihan, author of The Seraph Chronicles
and *The Constellation of Alarion.*

"Pete Sutton weaves tale of memory and loss throughout this collection with a style and panache you won't forget."

Shona Kinsella, author of
the Vessel of KalaDene series

"Its halls clustered with abandoned gods and fallen angels, *The Museum For Forgetting* is a timely elegy to memory and identity that resonantes far beyond its pages. It's hard to think of a more relevant collection of fantasy stories from the past twelve months."

Dan Coxon

THE
MUSEUM
FOR
FORGETTING

To Neide

Remember fantasy con 21

Pete W Sutton

Enjoy!

Pete

kristell-ink.com

'The Detective's Tale' first published in Refuge Collection, volume 5 2016

'Sailing Beneath the City' first published in A Tiding of Magpies KGHH 2016

'A Signal in the Dark' first published in The Hotwells Horror & Other Stories 2018

'Twelfth Night' first published in The Dark Half of the Year 2016

'We Do Like To Be Beside' first published in Alchemy Press Book of Horrors 2 2020

Paperback ISBN 978-1-913562-19-9

EPUB ISBN 978-1-913562-20-5

Cover Design by Creative Covers
Typesetting by Book Polishers

Kristell Ink
An Imprint of Grimbold Books
5 St John's Way,
Hempton,
Oxfordshire,
OX15 0QR
United Kingdom

www.kristell-ink.com

Contents

Introduction to
The Museum for
Forgetting

By Aliya Whiteley

As I CAME to the end of this collection I remembered something I haven't thought about in a long time.

We were on a school trip, taken en masse by coach to a public art gallery in order to soak up culture – is that how culture works? I got caught up in a famous painting of sunflowers – those thick bright swirls of paint. I didn't think I'd been standing there for too long, but when I turned around my teacher and classmates were gone. The room was silent; how had I not noticed the absence of their voices? I hurried to the next room, and the next. No sign of them. It seemed to me that I was getting smaller and the rooms darker, the ceilings higher. And the paintings had changed. The expressions on the faces within were worried, anxious. The eyes met mine each time I dared to look up.

They were no longer paintings for everyone. They were just for me.

Then I turned a corner and found the other children and the overworked teacher, and lights and bright, airy paintings that nobody was really bothering to look at. Those oil and watercolour faces receded into the background. I hadn't been missed. We all got in the coach and went home. When I look back on it, thirty years into the future, I wonder if it really happened that way at all.

Peter Sutton's stories are so often about what is recalled, and how those memories change over time. His Museum for Forgetting contains many moments, many emotions. Who is to say if things are what we remember them to be? What matters is how we hold them in our heads, and that changes too – nostalgia, and fear, both play a part.

These stories are filled with people trying to make sense of time. From facing angels to facing death, from loneliness to the clamouring of too many voices, Sutton's characters struggle to find a way to deal with the past, in the many strange ways it presents itself. Spirits and lost souls can be found within this book. Often, we find ourselves anchored in details; of course a Museum for Forgetting would be all about small, weighty items, from 'a beetle-glossy fountain pen' to apple pies from the past containing 'liquid, hot as lava'. Or sometimes we walk in worlds of black and white beauty, from noir to gothic. One of my favourite stories in the collection, Memories to the Flames, is an atmospheric journey into a place of rules and beliefs that stymy creativity, but it seems some experiences cannot be contained. There's a transcendent quality to the realisation that everything must, eventually, change.

Anyway, welcome. Welcome to The Museum for Forgetting. Come in, walk around, enjoy the exhibits. It won't be long until you cease to hear the sounds around you, and get sucked into what you're reading. Each tale here is about your past, and your future. The more you read, the more they come to life for your understanding alone. It's like they've been written just for you.

The Museum for Forgetting

ARABELLA WATCHED SILAS work his broom into the darkened corner. Her lips twitched and she bit down the words of disapproval she knew he would just ignore.

"What," she paused briefly for effect, "is he doing?"

Her assistant, mousey Miss Havelock, jumped. She always did whenever someone spoke to her directly. She glanced at Silas then flicked the single piece of paper on the clipboard, looking under it even though she knew there was nothing there. Arabella, who'd seen her assistant make this nervous gesture a million times, sighed.

"He's removing a bird," Miss Havelock squeaked.

"I see." Arabella pinched the bridge of her nose. Why were there always vermin on lilac weeks? "I shall be in my office. Find Dunster, would you, and send him to me."

"Yes, madam."

Arabella swept past the grand archway leading to the city without glancing out, she avoided looking outside as much as possible, she was happiest when the outside didn't intrude on her sanctum. It was her habit to ignore the city. Vagabonds and wastrels washed up upon the museum's entrance occasionally; visitors, infrequently. Only she and her four staff remained. Once the museum had been a grand place. Its lofty ceilings, grand marble rooms, echoing hallways and majestic stairways were testament to that. People used to come from other cities, other countries even, to donate their items, their memories. Now, few visitors made the hallways echo.

Arabella's stately lilac-enclosed form glided across the main hall, once the reception area for grand openings, one of the few rooms Silas bothered to sweep, and into her office.

At least that hadn't changed. The rows of filing cabinets, holding the card index system for the exhibits, dominated the room, both visually and aromatically. Made from some dark wood, they issued a pungency hard to miss. Like musk and honey. Rare and foreign trees were surely felled for such fine carpentry. A frivolous expense in better times.

She pulled her chair out, wiped the green leather seat and sat with a sigh. Where was Dunster? She required the mail – an intrusion she'd invited, this time. Forced into impatience she glanced around the room. Perhaps she should have Silas investigate the nooks and crannies. Certainly the heavy velvet drapes, once a proud magenta, now vaguely purple, could do with cleaning.

Still no sign of Dunster so she fetched her novel from her personal room. The lodging of a small bedroom and kitchen, a short walk from the office, came with the job of Head Docent. How hollow that title now that she was the one remaining docent. Unless they ever found Spratchett; he was still in the museum, somewhere.

Through a small unobtrusive door set into the panelled wall, she returned to her office and caught Dunster sitting in her chair, his feet on the desk.

"Ahem!"

The front legs of the chair banged to the floor as, with a squeal, Dunster leapt to his feet.

"Sorry, madam. I thought I'd... err..."

"Hear me coming down the corridor?"

Dunster nodded vaguely and turned his cloth cap in his large clumsy hands.

"Where is the mail?" she asked, sailing to her desk.

"There is none, madam." Dunster's rather plain, rather stupid face showed no sign of dissembling.

"No mail?" She expected no answer and cut him off as he started to form one. No mail was unusual, but not unprecedented. Today, however, she had anticipated a reply to a heartfelt missive she had penned the Minister for Arts. None boded ill. Unless he was going to send a personal reply?

"Still no sign of Spratchett?"

"Silas said that certain exhibits are damaged, showing signs of... err... teeth, madam," Dunster said with a grin.

"Teeth. I see." She contemplated the young man, his excessive frame, his child-like simplicity. He had his uses, she supposed.

"Think, Dunster, was there anything else Spratchett said before he disappeared? You were the last to see him."

Dunster went beetroot red and twisted his cap as if he were wringing a cat's neck. "Just what I told you before, madam. That he'd seen the big lie. That the museum were unhealthy. That he'd found the answer but needed time."

All as cryptic now as it had been at the time. She got the impression that Spratchett was somewhere in the woodwork, like a deathwatch beetle. Biding his time. The other docent, missing, presumed, well, missing.

"That'll be all, Dunster."

"Yes, madam."

"Go and help Silas." She dismissed him with a little shooing gesture and decided that tea would calm her. She rang her bell before remembering that Miss Havelock was cataloguing the Gallery of Foolish Desires today at her insistence. The knickknacks and gewgaws that people brought them. Their exhibits, full of unwanted memories, displayed according to type.

She glanced at the little metal safe under her desk. Could she use some of the back pay for Spratchett on a servant? She shook her head at the imprudent thought and went and prepared her own tea.

Blowing upon the straw-coloured liquid, preparatory to taking a sip, she was interrupted as Dunster knocked and entered.

"Post, madam." He thrust a cream envelope at her and stood waiting, a silly smile on his face. "The man said to make sure you read it," he said simply.

"Did he indeed? Well, you can assume I've read it, so run along now."

She used a silver letter opener in the shape of a tiny sword to slice it open. Inside was one piece of government headed notepaper.

Dear Head Docent,

Thank you for reminding me of the annual allotment of funds for the museums of this fair city. It had quite slipped my mind that I was paying you and your extensive department quite so much money in a time of financial uncertainty.

It is with deepest regret that I cannot conceive of increasing your funds, and, furthermore, I find that the budget this year must be trimmed.

Therefore, your department must make a twenty-five percent saving for this calendar year.

She dropped the letter before reading the Minister's name and various titles. Twenty-five percent. Well, that settled it – if Spratchett ever did come back, she'd have to let him go for dereliction of duty. This way she didn't even have to tell the rest of the staff.

A sneaky little internal voice asked if Spratchett wasn't fulfilling the true function of the museum. To become, like the memories attached to its exhibits, lost. Like she had been lost before finding sanctum here. The letter, contact with outside, stirred matters she'd worked hard to bury. She shook her head. Enough. Time to do some work.

It was time for the first tour. She finished the rest of her tea and strode into the grand entrance hall. There were no visitors to take the tour. Just as there were none for the second, third or fourth and final tours of the day.

Out of habit she went through the motions for the final tour, followed only by the echoes of Silas and Dunster mothballing yet another exhibit room somewhere in the bowels of the museum. She realised that they must do it, but wished fervently that the necessity wasn't there.

She remembered her last conversation with Spratchett had been about the mothballing. About how the museum had become perverted. That the museum was supposed to be pupating but had been forced to hibernate instead.

Spratchett had been strange for some time; like everything that washed up at the museum, full of secrets and regrets, disappointments and laments, moments best forgotten. Arabella shook her head again at these unwanted thoughts. She'd worked hard to forget. She closed her eyes briefly, but didn't find peace behind her eyelids. The echo of a scream, the shape and colour of a fading bruise. She shivered. No more contacting the outside. She was safer here. Forgotten, and forgetting. She used her work to drive unwanted thoughts away.

The tour lasted one hour, the effects much longer. The exhibits striking consequences. Each item when held sparking a vivid image.

The baby's shoe tumbling end over end through water, sad little bubbles striking out for the surface in its wake.

The match struck at the same time as a shush, and the sound of many people drawing breath to scream.

The expression on a woman's face at the precise moment her sanity snapped and she lunged, all teeth.

The spastic thrashing of a cat with its back broken by a passing vehicle.

Memories people did not want, tied to the objects that sparked them, immured by the mysterious power of the museum.

The emotions associated with each exhibit still had the power to make the viewer cry out with despair or horror at the world's cruellest vicissitudes.

Later, as she gave each of her staff their week's wage envelope, she wondered if the Minister would forget about them again. Contacting him was a mistake, she saw now. Miss Havelock handed her the report she'd made on the gallery before scampering away.

Silas collected his leather sack, sure sign he'd caught some sort of vermin and was now taking it away for disposal. He merely grunted when she gave him his envelope and stuffed it quickly into a pocket, as if taking money for what he did was somehow beneath him, or dirty.

She waited for Dunster to count the money. At least his counting was improving, and she didn't need to help him anymore. Satisfied, he grinned, said thank you, and left, whistling a tune.

As she locked the door she wondered where Spratchett was. He had the other set of keys, as the museum's only other docent. The museum was large, but they'd searched it all, including the vast draughty attic and the tunnels beneath the cellar.

Silas had extinguished all the lanterns except for the ones in the main hall, which she did now as she passed them on the way to her office, and private rooms. She noted that he'd neglected to fill them ready for the morrow; how annoying it was to constantly have to remind him.

She lay reading a chapter of her novel, but her eyes lost focus as she strained her hearing. If Spratchett was wandering the museum at night she was determined to hear him and direct Silas to wherever she thought the sounds had come from.

As her eyelids drooped and the book became heavy she put out the lights and slept.

***

THE SECOND LETTER came as a shock. The Ministry had miscalculated the cut to the museum's funding, so she had to add a further twenty-five percent.

She'd long since ceased paying herself, being held, forgotten, inside the museum she considered payment enough. She made do with the meagre allowance for museum necessities. What could she do? Take money from each of the employees? Get rid of one of them?

Silas was old. Dunster was simple. Havelock was, was... It had to be Havelock. She'd have to do without an assistant, do Havelock's work on top of her own. There'd be floods of tears, of course. But maybe it would free Havelock to find a boyfriend, or a hobby, or a position more suited to her temperament.

Oh, who was she fooling? Havelock was perfectly fine without a partner, she was never going to take up a hobby and there was no work more fitting for her, unless the library was hiring. Improbable – Ministry cuts rarely wounded only one victim.

In the end there were tears, extra slices of cake to calm themselves and a heart-wrenching goodbye. Dunster had wailed like it was he that was being forced to leave. Even Silas had looked sad.

***

IT WAS LAVENDER week and Arabella was cataloguing the Gallery of Last Goodbyes, while the men were mothballing the Gallery of Foolish Desires. Miss Havelock had taken her clipboard with her so Arabella temporised and withdrew a fat black notebook from stores along with a beetle-glossy fountain pen.

Directly above her she heard running feet. Spratchett?

She closed her eyes and envisaged the museum floor plan. The Hall of Former Heroes. Of course, he'd be gone by the time she got there, but she thought it worth chasing the ephemeral trail the erstwhile employee was leaving.

There was a joy to running in the corridors, one that she'd never have experienced were it not for the missing man. She had him to thank for that, at least.

She skidded into the Hall of Former Heroes and stopped dead.

The great war-horse that stood central to the hall, that had carried some forgotten general into a battle no one recollected, was gone. How had he managed that?

She crept to its plinth, its shocking emptiness rebuking her custodianship, and ran her hand across it – the indentations where its hooves had, until today, fitted, the only clue to what should be on the platform.

The general was upside down in a corner. She stood slowly, chest heaving, straining her ears. The only sounds were the clocks in the Arcade of Vanished Time.

***

IF THE SECOND letter had been a shock the third was a blow. A further cut. She could not take on extra work, she would have to force the men to take a pay cut.

"A cut, madam?" Dunster was the very picture of puzzlement.

"I'm afraid so. Less and less of the museum is working. The minister," she pretended not to notice Silas spitting, "the minister was quite clear on that point."

Silas sucked his teeth, gave her a long appraising look, then took off his apron, folded it neatly and placed it on top of the mop and bucket he'd pushed into the meeting. He turned and without looking back walked from the building. She was too shocked to stop him.

"I can't do it by myself," Dunster said, lower lip wobbling. "I'll go and talk to him." He nodded a couple of times and frowned. "Get him to come back." He rushed after the older man with a shout of, "Silas! Hold up!"

And then there was just her. She couldn't leave, wouldn't leave, would never go back. A fluttering behind her eyes, a memory trying to surface. She grimaced, forced it down, recited a nursery rhyme to make it go away. She would not go back.

By the time Dunster came back there was nothing anybody could do to save the museum.

***

IT WAS LOBELIA week and Arabella had come to no longer expect the men to return. Exhibits went dusty and the lamps in many of the rooms were no longer lit. The fourth letter was a disaster. The minister was going to visit. He'd shut the museum for sure once he saw it for himself.

Arabella, more than once, made it to the great arched doorway onto the street – but she could not face it. Her eyes misted, the street remained terra incognita and she was unable to venture forth. She refused to visit her own abandoned memories, to confront what kept her locked away in the museum, why she'd turned her back on the city.

She did find a bundle of letters on the step. Left by whichever postman still worked, even though Dunster had acted as such for the museum since all those who worked for the government had been laid off. Perhaps Dunster continued to provide that service? But then why wouldn't he come into the museum?

That's where she found the fourth letter. An impending ministerial visit. A disaster.

She did her best, worked from first light till past dark – cleaning, dusting, polishing. But to her eye it all still looked drab and dirty.

The next day a great black carriage pulled up outside the museum. Its birdwing-iridescent lacquered side mercifully blocked the sight of the street from her. She didn't know how long they'd been waiting before she noticed.

Once she appeared on the step, taking care not to step outside, not to lose the sanctuary of the museum, the door popped open and a short man in a smart suit, carrying a tiny pug dog, jumped down. He was followed by a wobbling woman in a cream dress that barely contained her, and two flunkies in matching uniform.

"Head Docent?" one of the flunkies, who'd scurried ahead of the man and woman, asked.

"Yes?"

"Please to make welcome for the minister," the flunky said. She just had time to wonder if the flunky spoke her language or one consisting entirely of officialese when he swept aside and she was confronted with the minister himself.

She bowed a little and held her hand out, which he contemplated for a second and then gave it a sad, limp shake.

"Minister," she said.

The minister turned and gave the dog to the large woman, who immediately started coochy-cooing it. Rubbing noses. The minister turned back to Arabella with a silly grin, which vanished at once from his face. The smile had not reached his eyes.

"I don't have time for the formal tour. You can send your staff home. The museum is to be closed."

"Closed, minister?"

The minister sighed and took from his pocket a golden box, out of which he pinched a twist of snuff onto the back of his hand, inhaling and giving two quick sneezes. "In hard times art is frivolous," he said.

"But without art all you have are hard times," Arabella countered.

"The decision has been made." The minister handed over a buff-coloured envelope, held out his hand, which Arabella found herself shaking, then turned and marched back to the carriage.

The big woman sidled closer, tickling the belly of the pug. "It was the oil," she said.

"Oil?" she murmured, watching the minister being helped into his carriage by a flunky. She wondered how much the carriage cost? How much the minister paid his staff?

"Oil on canvas. The director of the art museum has commissioned a piece depicting the minister." The woman smiled, like the smile of a cat before it devoured a mouse.

"A portrait?" They were shutting her museum because the minister was having a painting made of himself?

"Art is important, but one has to make sacrifices in such straitened times. Perhaps once the troubles are over the museum could re-open? Hmmm?" The lady in the cream dress patted Arabella's arm and slinked down the steps and into the waiting carriage, which pulled off as soon as she closed the door.

Arabella ripped open the envelope and read the thick wad of official papers while trudging back inside. There it was, black and white: the museum was to close. She was entitled to a small amount of severance pay, but there was none for the rest of the staff. No date was given by when she must leave the museum. So, she would stay. She closed and locked the outside door and remembered that her welcoming the minister had been the first time she'd confronted the outside for… well, she couldn't quite remember how long, but a substantial amount of time. She couldn't recall any details apart from the carriage at the bottom of the steps.

It wasn't until she sniffed her calming cup of chamomile tea that the tears came.

***

ONE WEEK LATER and no one had been to insist that she move out. She was running out of some things. Sugar, she could do without; butter, she missed but could live with the absence; flour, less use without butter. The food would run out soon but still plenty of tea. She could survive for some time just on tea; had been meaning to lose some weight anyway.

She'd taken to reading through the index cards; Starting with the ones she'd instructed Havelock to complete, then those she'd compiled herself. Next were those from when docents were numerous and busy, and finally those compiled before she'd joined the museum.

What would happen to the exhibits? What fate awaited those stored in the vast labyrinthine tunnel network below the museum? They obviously couldn't accept any more, not that any had come for some time.

She came across a reference to the Archive of Unfinished

Books. Odd, she'd never heard of that before. It didn't exist on her mental map of the museum. She searched for a physical map; no such Archive. But there it was on the index card. She checked the date: a lifetime before her tenure. There must be older maps then. She scoured the cabinets until she found them.

She laid them out one by one, their brittle rustlings the only sound in the room. Clouds of disturbed dust swirled in the sunbeams from the skylight.

There. A map the colour of old tea, lines scribbled in faded pink, difficult to read. A cramped script. She pulled her glasses out and read the words 'Archive of Unfinished Books.' It did exist.

In a room that did not appear on the later maps. An imperceptible erasure. A kink in a top corridor, a space on one map, not there on the next. Curious.

She determined to explore. No time like the present.

Climbing the stairs, lantern held out before her, she wondered if she should have waited until daylight when secret doors would be easier to find in the light. When she arrived in the right place there was nothing there. The corridor followed the contours of the map that crackled with age. She put it on the floor, and the lantern on top of it and counted out the paces.

They didn't add up. One wall was longer than it should have been. She checked the map. There was an odd triangular space. She knocked along the wall and it sounded hollow. How mysterious. How long had this part of the museum been closed away? She paced it again, knocking, holding the lamp high to search for a join, a handle or button, anything to crack the mystery. She turned to check the map – there was a creak behind her, and a hand clamped upon her mouth as she took breath.

"Promise you won't scream?" a breathy voice tickled her ear. She froze.

She nodded emphatically; the hand that grasped her smelt of chalk. Rough, man's hand, hairy knuckles, she found it difficult to breathe, or calm her racing heart. What to do? She vaguely remembered that you should stamp down on an assailant's foot.

She lifted her leg. The hand opened and moved away slowly.

She spun around and confronted Spratchett. He was dressed in an outlandish collection of garments pilfered from all eras, across the full range of exhibits.

He grinned and held his arms wide to show he was unarmed.

"I wondered when you'd arrive," he said, with a grin full of yellow teeth. "I've been waiting to start."

He'd lost a lot of weight and there was a crazed light in his eyes.

"What are you doing here?" she asked, backing away. Behind him was a room of rotten books. When had he gone mad? Had he discovered this room and something within had triggered it? He'd been going on and on about how the museum had lost its purpose for weeks before he'd disappeared. Never the most stable of her staff, the slow bleeding of money and staff had made him morbid.

"Do you know how the museum works?" he asked, ignoring her question.

"Of course. As do you." She spotted a small camp bed.

"No. How it *really* works." He'd been burning books to cook his meals. "It needs to be free."

"Why don't you tell me? Downstairs?" She'd feel safer downstairs.

"It's time to awaken. It's time for metamorphosis. We need to release the memories. Our country is sick, there are those – men in power, ministers – who'd have the people forget our past. Or worse, remember it incorrectly. The museum was built to hold memories for only a brief period. While those that donated still grieved. An abeyance not an annihilation. An incubation. When the donors are ready the transfigured memories must be released."

"I'm sorry, what?"

Spratchett began pacing to and fro, turning, manic quick.

"I was going to wait until you'd gone, too. I am good at waiting. But you never leave, do you? Never, ever."

"Spratchett, wait, I—"

"Throw open all the doors and windows and liberate the memories!" Spratchett whooped and ran past her, through the door to the first gallery and inside. She rushed to catch up.

Inside, Spratchett struggled to open the large casement window. "Stop!"

He turned and grimaced, grinned perhaps, but he didn't stop. A physical tackle was out of the question, for he was filled with mad power. She stood wringing her hands. With a cry of triumph he threw the window wide and immediately grabbed the nearest exhibit. Whatever power it had – a frown creased his face momentarily – it was not enough to save it. He threw it from the window.

A flash, and the memory dissolved into sparkles. Whoever had brought the exhibit would, somewhere in the city, be revisited by its full force, fresh as the day it was made.

"No! Stop!" She couldn't help herself. She ran and threw her arms around him as he grabbed another exhibit: a dog's lead and collar. Empty feelings of grief doubled her over, horror at witnessing a violent death made her gasp. Spratchett struggled free and ran from the room.

"Too slow!" he shouted as he ran.

She followed but was too late to stop him closing and barring the doors to the gallery. She banged on them as hard as she could. "Spratchett? Spratchett!" She looked for a way to escape and saw none. What would he do?

Crashes came from within the museum. She winced as she envisaged the Boudoir of Unflattering Mirrors shattering. Then the sound of splintering wood – he was in the Index!

She grabbed the window pole and worked it into the gap where the doors met. And rattled it. She brushed the hair from her face, sweat-slicked and distracting. She smelt smoke. Fire! Spratchett was going to burn down the museum. She redoubled her efforts and with some swearing and kicking the doors sprang open with a crack.

Where? She ran down the corridor, listening. There was an almighty crash below her. She sprinted to the marble staircase and took the steps two at a time. Before she reached the bottom she could smell it. Smoke from aromatic wood.

She leapt down the last few steps towards the red glow and skidded on the warm flagstones and confronted a wall of flame. The museum was on fire, beyond the powers of one person to tackle. Spratchett capered close to the blaze, an arm full of exhibits, throwing them one by one into the flames. His clothes smoked.

Arabella backed away until her heel met the bottom step. The back door? That was a level up. She should try to save some exhibits. She ran back up the stairs, and, glancing back once, saw Spratchett dancing in the flames. She swallowed bile and closed her eyes, but the image was still there. She needed to add an exhibit to the museum, something of Spratchett's or something of hers, otherwise the image of him dancing in the flames would haunt her. Her beautiful museum. But she could not, no one could.

The harsh smoke tickled her throat – she didn't have much time. What to save from the vast list of exhibits? Her eyes streamed and smoke stole her breath as the fire shot a hot wind through the building. No time! She entered the nearest room and grabbed those exhibits closest to her. Foreign rage at some perceived slight overcame her briefly when she picked up a pen.

Fleeing to the back door the wind blew through the building like a scream, or maybe it was Spratchett? She stumbled into the courtyard, an armful of memories sublimating, unable to exist outside the museum; she dropped to her knees.

She remembered. The city and the sights and sounds of it now flooded back in. Her voluntary exile, over. Her parents turning their backs on her over her wrong choices. Jeremy's laughing face when she'd told him she wanted to be an artist. His flabby naked body. His snarling face. His fist. Her crawl, the cobbles ticking off every punch he'd landed. The glug and hiss of pouring alcohol, the sweet and bitter smell of it, the glint of his glassy eye.

She would now remember everything.

Memories to the Flames

IT FELT GOOD not to write. Eventide, and all the other scriveners in their cells were scribbling away. Elisenda had followed the ritual, had burned the angel powder in the candle flame, but, tonight, for the first time, hadn't inhaled. Had held her breath, in fact, for as long as possible. The compulsion to write wasn't there. God's words via the angel, distilled into pure inspiration in the powder gathered by the Guardian did not burn in her mind tonight for the first time since she was put in a scrivener's cell.

The light burned overhead, the Inspectoress stalked the corridors and Elisenda allowed herself a secret smile. She'd done it. It had been bubbling inside her for ages. What if she just... didn't?

And now she knew.

It was fine. She glanced out of the little window set high up the door to see the Inspectoress watching one of her fellow scriveners through her own hatch. Elisenda had a little time. She didn't know how to disguise the smell if she burnt tonight's page. And besides, they'd know – a torn-out sheet would be obvious.

She'd have to come up with a plan. She'd used the powder, the usual inspiration, already. She'd just have to make something up.

The link between the ritual, the powder and the words they each produced night after night wasn't obvious. The deity spoke to them and they produced automatic writing. That's what they were told. But Elisenda wondered if it was merely drug-dreams.

She could hear the Inspectoress approaching. She dipped her quill, briefly wondering, as usual, what bird such a massive, night-black feather came from. To work her way within she'd need alliteration. She scribbled something, a snatch of conversation she'd overheard in the halls, aware that the Inspectoress watched. When she heard the footsteps recede, she opened the book at a random place to read what she'd written before, under the influence.

And sad the sea, and dark the waves and cold the shore. And fierce the air, and deep the fall and dry the cave. And tired of wing, and hungry of belly and desirous of shelter.

She'd written nonsense. Never before had she read her drugged writing. It was strictly forbidden. Only the priests could do so. Interpret the words produced to create the scripture. But tonight she was breaking all their rules. Tonight she had broken free of the secret flame.

When the lights flicked out and the corridors were filled with the sighs of frustrated writers denied putting more words on the page, Elisenda closed her journal with a frisson of illicit satisfaction. It felt glorious.

But now she was faced with a new problem. She couldn't sleep. Always, under the influence of the powder, she'd been straight to sleep after evening ritual. But now she was aware of the sounds of snoring coming from the other cells, the cold draught coming from her partly open window, and the regular thump of the Inspectoress's patrol.

Tomorrow, she promised. Tomorrow I'll do it again. And I'll escape.

***

FAVILA PAUSED AT the bottom of the steps, as he usually did. His knees and hips hurt more tonight. Soon he'd have to find an apprentice and initiate a boy into the ways of the depths, just as he'd been initiated so many decades ago. One already chosen to undergo the warden training, like he'd been. Each year the priests collected children from the surrounding villages to replace those that grew too old for the work. Boys to be wardens, girls to be scriveners, a gold piece to the parents. Each year, though, the crop of children was less. The buildings fell into disrepair, the tasks were lessened due to fewer hands at work. They faced decline and fall. Yet, they could, for now, still command the commoners who relied upon the order for indulgences and prophecy.

He plucked the black-iron key from his belt and unwrapped the chain, giving the key a kiss before placing it in the iron-bound oak of the entrance. He mumbled a quick prayer and unlocked the door. As it swung open, he raised the torch, careful to hold it away from his head. He could ill afford to lose any more hair. As ever the sound of small bells filled the air and, despite the underground darkness, there was a hint of summer light and spring flowers in the cave.

He hastened through the door and locked it behind him.

More steps, more strain upon old hips and knees but now he gave it no thought. His heart swelled with love, and awe and pride and fear – the same old mix of emotions. Nearer, my god, to thee.

The black angel lay on the slab as if dead. Its midnight wings thrust out to each side of its curled form. Favila crossed himself and offered up a quick fragment of Psalm: "yea, he did fly upon the wings of the wind."

As he approached, the sound of softly ringing bells became omnipresent and the angel itself gave off a heady perfume. Favila drew forth the other tools of his position. The scraper and the deep-throated flask.

The angel's body glistened in the light of the torch Favila had placed in the sconce beside it. Skin black and oleaginous with ink. The walls of the cave had been filled with writing. Small and large, words over words. The day wardens would puzzle over it tomorrow, as they did every day. But Favila's task was easier. Or harder. He didn't know. He bent to it now and chose the angel's left arm, raising it delicately – even though the angel had never, in all the many decades he'd tended to it, awoken. Like a man in form but vastly larger, some fourteen feet from the tips of its toes to the crown of its head. And the wings – the massive, jet wings – they would stretch from one wall of its cell to the other.

Yes, he thought of it as a cell. Although that was blasphemous. The priest who'd taught him as a boy, carrying the deep-throated flask in awe, had spoken about how the order protected the celestial being from the jealous. From those who wished ill upon them. The order who kept themselves apart from the rest of the population of Newland. The declining order.

But Favila knew they kept the angel here as much to keep it for themselves, as to protect it. Although it hadn't awakened for many decades, more than Favila had been alive, the writings were very clear that when it did wake it wanted to fly. Any creature with such wings would want to fly.

He started at the fingertips and scraped the unctuous black substance into the flask. Later he'd mix it with bergamot and pine resin, frankincense and camphor, as well as many other, secret, substances. Making ink, making powder. Burning the angel's secretions formed the ritual of the dreamers. His was a sacred task, a necessary one, for the order.

Once the flask was full, he pulled his notebook from the pocket of his robe and using a piece of charcoal he drew the arm and where he'd stopped. Scraping shouldn't be too deep, the ritual depended on a steady dose. Each part of it had been developed over many years by the originators of the order.

Favila's role was as prescribed as any of the others. The day wardens who studied for ten years in order to decipher the angel's writings, formed upon the walls using the angel's own blood and feathers as ink and quill from the years it was awake, long in the past. The dreaming maidens, the scriveners, who breathed the angel's fire. Writing the Angel's words one step removed. The Inspectoresses, who'd once been maidens themselves, but who had become immune to the powder over a period of many years. Not all became immune. Some slipped ever further into dreaming, until all they did was sleep and write until they starved.

Once he'd noted the exact position of the scraping, he returned the notebook to its pocket and hung the scraper back on his belt. He grabbed the flask with his left hand and lifted the torch with his right. He turned and bowed to the angel and as he straightened the angel's eye regarded him calmly. He dropped the torch. Its voice reverberated. He didn't know its language, he hadn't the facility. As a child he'd failed that test and been chosen as apprentice to the Collector.

He placed the flask on the floor and retrieved the torch, his mind racing, his heart booming, his muscles trembling. Awe, and fear and flight. The angel had raised itself on an elbow and gazed at him unblinking. He bowed again, mind gabbling, and backed away. The angel asked him a question, but again his mind could not encompass its language. Not many could. He could feel the bounds of his sanity being blown in the gale of its thoughts. Other men had gone mad when confronted by the angel, he knew. He turned and fled, making sure to lock the door behind him. But now he'd seen the angel awake he wondered how it could ever have fit through such a tiny door. Or how a door, no matter how thick the wood and iron, could hold it. Just before he fled up the stairs the room behind the door flooded with light as the angel's fire erupted.

***

ELISENDA WOKE TO the sound of running feet and slamming doors. This burst of activity was unlike any other awakening she'd had here. She glanced at her open notebook. Open to a blank page. She'd been found out. That must be why the Inspectoresses were running. They were about to burst in and drag her away to be punished. She looked around her small cell, searching for a way out, even though she knew there wasn't one.

The door burst open and she dropped to her knees and bowed her head. "Forgive me, Auntie," she said. When there was no response she looked up and Constance grinned at her. "Why, what have you done?" her friend asked.

"Connie! What's going on?" She leapt to her feet, penance temporarily forgotten.

"No idea. The Aunties have all run off!" Connie was positively hopping from one foot to another. Right now they should be standing, head bowed, awaiting the Senior Scrivener to lead them to the feast hall to breakfast. "Come on!" Connie ducked back outside and Elisenda followed. The scriveners loitered outside their cells. Sofia, the senior, stood wringing her hands. When she saw Elisenda, the last to arrive, she drew a breath and became calm, or pretended to.

"We shall proceed to breakfast," she said, as if it were a normal day.

The girls, glancing at one another, unspoken questions brimming, formed up as they would on any other day. From tallest to shortest and oldest to youngest they formed two lines and followed Sofia to the breakfast room. They encountered no Inspectoresses in the short walk down the plain, white-walled corridors, their feet slapping against the darkly polished wooden floor. The smell of breakfast marched them onwards. At least the servants hadn't absconded.

After breakfast they were supposed to attend to their assigned roles. Some of the girls gardened, others did laundry, yet others worked in the library. But there were no governesses to watch over them and ensure they did the work. And yet the majority of the scriveners went where they were supposed to go anyway. A few stayed in the breakfast hall and a couple snuck outside, separate to the gardeners, just to run free for once. Elisenda went to the library. She wasn't supposed to, had never been assigned library duty in fact, but wanted to read the others' books and this might be her best chance.

The other girls in the library watched her curiously as she wandered down the narrow aisles. There was a sweet smell of old paper, dust and the polish they used on the dark wooden bookcases. The light in the library was also the best in the house – a dome of glass acted as ceiling.

Soon the conscientious girls were absorbed in their bookbinding and indexing and Elisenda was free to roam without scrutiny. She climbed a ladder to the upper tier, grabbed a couple of books at random and, retreating to an alcove, out of sight of those below, settled down to read.

Most of the books she flicked through were filled with the same stream of unconsciousness as hers, but the occasional stark passage of unintelligibility stood out. In one book it stood out because someone had drawn a red box around it. She searched and found more.

In each case where a red box had been used the language was that of the angels. Elisenda couldn't read it but Constance could! She had to know what it said – but could she trust Constance? And where was her friend anyway?

***

FAVILA, THE OLD priest and the Head Inspectoress stood in front of the ironbound door. "Will it hold?" the priest asked, a second time. The first had been at the top of the stairs and he'd seemed to accept Favila's assurances. Now, here at the bottom of the stairs, the door in front of him, unearthly fire illuminating all the gaps, he didn't look as convinced when Favila nodded.

"It is a glory this has happened during our watch, Uncle," the Inspectoress said breathlessly.

"Blessed be!" the priest responded. A little less enthusiastically than Favila thought he should. But then the priest was even older than he. Perhaps he had been counting on an easy life.

"Your will, Uncle?" Favila asked.

The pause was so long Favila wondered if he'd been heard, but eventually the priest sucked his teeth. "We need all those who can speak, or read, the angel's tongue. Not just the wardens but the scriveners you have taught to do so, too." Favila gasped, eyes wide – the Inspectoresses taught the dreamers the angel's tongue? "It will enter its hypomania stage and we need to work in shifts to capture what it writes." The priest paused and then made shooing gestures at the Inspectoress, who tutted, gathered her skirts and ran up the steps with an agility and haste Favila would not have imagined.

"And you, Guardian. You know your role when it awakes. You must ensure it cannot escape. It cannot fly." Favila nodded and sighed. He lifted the key on the chain and kissed it. The priest nodded and started up the stairs, much slower and less agile than the Inspectoress.

Favila had read the journals of the first guardian and all who came after. He knew the Gathering by heart having performed it daily for decades. But the Durance? That had been ritually practised, of course, but never needed for many years. He reached out with the key held in a trembling hand. The tools he needed were in the room. With the angel. A ridiculous place to put them, he now thought.

The door swung open to a light almost too bright to endure. The angel burned with a pure fire, without flame. Its bull-like voice formed an enquiry and Favila knew that there was a good reason he'd never been taught its tongue. He wouldn't be swayed by whatever reasons, demands and entreaties it made when he broke its wings. He squinted through the ritual mask he'd pulled over his face until he could see the angel, a black mannequin wreathed in white flame. He closed and locked the door and took a deep breath.

***

"WHERE DID YOU get this?" Constance kept peeking through the branches of the rhododendron, its thick waxy leaves hiding them from view. Their secret place in the garden. Elisenda put her hand on Constance's arm. "No one can see us. You know that. It's okay, please, just look at it."

Constance sighed and sat with her knees drawn up to her chin. "You know how much trouble we'll be in if they find us? With a book? From the library?"

"They're not going to find us, Connie. Please?"

Her friend bit her lip. "El..."

Elisenda opened the book to the red boxed text of angel's tongue. "Please?"

Connie looked close to tears but did glance down and a frown formed. "Angel tongue?"

"It's a scrivener's tome."

"Oh, El. It's beautiful," Connie said, with a tear spilling. "Oh, it longs to fly. Why can't it fly?"

"What's it say?" Elisenda asked desperately.

"It can't be translated, exactly, but the angel is here, and we are part of its dreams and memories. This is blasphemous, El, you must return this and never reveal to anyone that you had it, or that we've read it!" Connie wiped her eyes with the back of her hand and abruptly got to all fours to crawl out of their hidey-hole. "And never speak to me again about this, you hear me, Elisenda? Never!"

Elisenda watched with a frown as her friend exited the bower they'd discovered together when much younger. If it wanted to be free, if it wanted to fly, then what was stopping it? She looked at the house and thought about the Inspectoresses and priests, wardens and scriveners. No, not *what* was stopping it, *why* were they stopping it?

***

THE INSPECTORESSES HAD returned to the halls by the time Elisenda returned to the mansion, the illicit book tucked into her apron, snuggled in a fold of her tunic. If they searched the girls it would be terrible, but they'd never done so before. She thought her face would be a beacon of guilt though and they'd know something was wrong.

As they lined up, she sought out Constance and tried to meet her eyes. Constance looked away. Also looked guilty. But it seemed the Inspectoresses were nervous – some paced up and down the line, others stood in a knot, whispering. The Head Inspectoress, an old priest and a man Elisenda had never seen before walked up the stairs. The girls hung their heads, as they'd been taught to do when a priest was present. But Elisenda tried to watch through her fringe.

The priest wore the same grey tunic they all did but with a crimson surplice where the scriveners wore aprons. The man with him, though, wore a leather tunic that had been scored as if cut with a knife and splashed with some black liquid, like ink.

The Head Inspectoress walked down the line and asked some of the girls to step out, including Constance. "Girls, those of you who have been chosen, follow Uncle. The rest of you are to pray tonight. There will be no ritual. Tomorrow there will be various tasks, and you will have to do the work of these chosen ones as well, as they embark on a sacred task."

Elisenda frowned. A sacred task?

"Choose one, Favila," the priest said. It seemed that was unexpected, as both the Head Inspectoress and the old man in leather turned to him sharply.

"Uncle?" the old man asked.

"We cannot spare any of the wardens, and you need an apprentice at this time."

The man brushed a hand through his sparse grey hair and turned to look at the girls who hadn't been chosen. "I need a strong arm, Uncle. To complete the task."

The priest's mouth twisted. "The task you failed, Guardian."

The old man sighed, and nodded reluctantly.

"Who is the strongest?" he asked.

"I am." Elisenda took a step forward, lifting her head. From the corner of her eye, she saw some of the girls exchanging looks.

"You? But you're a mere slip. Surely one of the older girls—"

Elisenda repeated, "I am!" and scowled at the other girls.

None gainsaid her. None wanted to be singled out.

The old man smoothed his moustache. "Very well. I can only use the tools I am provided. Follow me."

The girls who'd been chosen followed the priest, the old man followed the girls and Elisenda followed the old man. They proceeded downstairs and the priest went down the passageway towards the library, but the old man carried on towards the kitchens. Elisenda caught Constance throw a backwards glance before they were out of sight around the corner.

Instead of the kitchens the old man stopped at a door Elisenda had not paid much attention to in the past. It went to a storeroom, she thought. The old man pulled out a bunch of keys, unlocked the door, painted white, the same colour as the corridor walls. He gestured for Elisenda to precede him into the darkened alcove the door opened onto. She walked past him and squinted, trying to penetrate the gloom. The old man stepped inside, closed the door and there was a scraping sound and a torch burst into life. Ahead, past walls full of shelves holding various household equipment, lay stairs. Going down.

"Why do you need someone strong?" Elisenda asked.

"For the Durance," Favila said, stepping past her and starting down the wooden stairs.

"What's a Durance?" she asked, following him. They quickly reached a landing and a switchback and then they started down stone steps. As they progressed deeper the stone became rougher, less worked.

"Not 'a,' 'the.' It's a ceremonial task. You'll need to hold its wing."

Could she hear bells?

"What wing?"

As they turned a last corner, she saw a thickly bound oaken door set into a blank wall. The door's gaps were highlighted in a cold white light, something bright behind the door. She could definitely hear bells, and there was a perfume she could smell even above the acrid smoke of the torch.

The old man glanced back at her. "The angel's wing."

***

THE ANGEL WAS perfect in a way she would never be able to describe. In proportion, in feature and form. Even if it hadn't been chained to the stout wooden table bolted to the floor. It half-opened its wings as they entered and white flame ran up and down its limbs and body. The sound of bells became all she could hear before it opened its mouth and bellowed words she could not decipher.

"Why's it chained?" she asked. She stared at the silver lettering running along the chain links. Spells to hold it fast. To keep it bound.

"It has always been thus," Favila answered.

Which, she noted, wasn't a proper answer.

The Guardian strode over to a cabinet against the wall. "You have to hold its wings," he said, his back to her.

"Why?" *How*?

Favila turned around and her eyes were drawn to the rusty iron sledgehammer in his hands.

"Weren't you taught to obey your elders without question, child?"

"What are you going to do with that?"

"Get over there and hold its wing. This is in the rituals. The Durance is required when it is awake. It heals when it sleeps."

Elisenda shook her head. It wanted to fly.

"If you do not, I will find another who will, and you will be punished."

She shook her head again and ran over to put herself between it and the man who wanted to harm it. She spread her arms. "Don't hurt it!"

Favila frowned and took a step forward, dropping the hammer into one hand and holding the other out. He moved towards the angel. She couldn't let him and jumped in front of him. He opened his mouth to say something, but she tripped him and he jerked forward. He threw the hammer up in reaction, it hit the table with a resounding smash. The angel crouched and pulled the chain as the table leg that the hammer hit popped out of its metal clasp that held it to the floor.

The angel walked free, but held the long black iron chain that had secured it. Favila recovered from his stumble, Elisenda noting the look of horror on his face seconds before the chain whipped out and smashed his head like a pumpkin.

She dropped to her knees and held her hands over her face. She could hear the angel moving about. Then a clank as the chain hit the floor. The angel said something in its booming voice, and she peeked through her fingers. It held up the keyring and asked a question again. She didn't need to know how to speak angel to know what it was asking. With a trembling finger she pointed to the black iron key that would unlock the door. But the door was obviously too small for the angel to fit through. The angel spoke a single word as the white fire in its fist glowed blue; the keychain and all the keys glowed red then ran through its fingers like honey.

It took a step and crouched next to her and put two fingers on her head. It felt like she stood beneath a waterfall or had fallen backwards off a cliff as her consciousness fled. The last thing she saw, down tunnel vision, was the angel fully consumed in white fire. It sprang upwards from the crouch as a column of flame blasted away the ceiling and the tons of earth above them.

***

ELISENDA AWOKE TO darkness and the smell of fire. She panicked until she could see that above her was slightly less dark. She crawled over to the guardian and the pile of slag that had once been keys. It had happened then. Above, as if someone had whipped away a blanket over the sky, stars suddenly blazed.

She could see, after a fashion, that the door remained locked.

It felt warm and the smell of smoke grew stronger.

There was only one way out. The angel's passage had scored a roughly circular hole from the small room beneath the mansion and through the earth, which steamed and smoked slightly from its passage. There were rocks and tree roots that she could use. Elisenda climbed.

As she got closer to the top, she could discern a red glow and hear the whooshing sound of fire. As she crested the lip of the hole the angel had made, she saw the entire mansion in flames. Knots of scared scriveners and wardens watched as it burned. Inspectoresses wailed and priests stood stunned.

She saw Constance and ran to her friend who hugged her fiercely.

"You look terrible," Constance said.

Elisenda looked down. Her clothes were filthy and her hands were black from the soil. She shrugged.

She tried to say something and only angel tongue came out. Constance's eyes grew round. Elisenda's mind had been touched. The Angel's fingers! She could feel the secret fire spark within. She was glad her friend could understand her, that she could tell her that it only wanted to fly.

She looked up to see the new star ascending.

Sailing Beneath the City

I AM AFLOAT on buried rivers, alone, forgotten, aged. I once had the means of propulsion, of steering, of charts and knowledge, of company. I lost them one by one; they slipped through my fingers like the sightless eels I sometimes catch upon my hooks. There is a mournful bell tolling in the distance. My lamplight casts a circle of lesser gloom. The wavelets lap gently against the sides of the skiff. I once had a purpose. Now I search for the Others, the ones I have lost.

My memories had become a burden. Once they warmed me in the cold lonely nights, then they pained me, filling my heart with spikeful regrets. It is why I developed my memory eating trance. It allows me to forget, to drop the memories like stones over the side of my skiff. I visualise them sinking, throwing small bubbles that slowly rise to the surface as the memory spins end over end forever down into the black water. They cannot hurt me if they remain in the deep blackness.

My waking mind has forgotten, but sometimes when I sleep the bubbles that rise from the blackness pop and release foul smelling, bitter memories. Then I awake fevered and lonely, nostalgic and full of remorse. I don't want to remember. I have to work twice as hard at the trance of forgetting.

Just myself and my dog on the boat. She's a lurcher, a soft ghostly shape often in the distance when we go ashore that at times I struggle to keep up with. I call her Casper. She shares my meals and keeps me warm at night.

I am aboard the skiff, which is the best means of travel in the below, although I once had another boat. The skiff is flat bottomed, sturdy; she's seen me right in this uncertain world. I think the Others may be before me – since leaving the dark sea I have poled, paddled and oared my way along all of these tightly bound passageways. Some open into tunnels, many layered, allowing me to tie up the skiff and explore.

Today I have found the Dome. A confluence of tunnels, a half sphere above the water like an inverted goblet. There are high walls and rusty iron doors, a pier of sorts, and stairs. Somewhere to explore. I tie the skiff, lift Caspar onto the concrete platform and sneak up the stairs. I have an empty dry bag, no telling what I may find. As I reach the top of the stairs I turn to look back at the skiff and my glow light picks out a section of roof from out of the gloom. It is covered in colour, a painting, looking fresh; it is abstract in the gloom, partial. I cannot tell what it is from this angle. I follow the curve of the wall back and forth and see that whatever the painting is, it's not finished on this side. I wonder about climbing up on the other side, the platforms not quite forming a circle, bisected by the large, mostly flooded tunnel I had entered by.

I am enraptured, wandering up and down, glow light held as high as I can. Eating the sight up. It amazes me. The dog, after a while, becomes bored and wanders off. I hardly notice; I know she won't go far. Eventually I grow weary and return to the door and the possibility of exploration. I call for the dog and hear an answering bark echo from somewhere inside. The doors are rusted mostly shut but by breathing in I am able to squeeze inside. I vaguely recognise the tunnels, as if I'd been here before – with my memory eating trance that is possible. I stalk the corridors looking for anything of use. Forgotten machinery stands forlorn, awaiting a spark or guidance it will never receive again. I pay it scant heed. In a storeroom I find crates of tinned food, matches, glow lights, emergency provisions, ropes, lots of useful things. I fill the dry bag and decide that I can come back for more at a later date, no point in overloading the skiff. I call for the dog again, this time there is no answering bark. I fret, although I think it a needless worry.

Later I build a fire on the platform and roast a fish I have caught. The dog still hasn't returned; my throat feels raw from shouting. I hope the smell of food will attract her, remind her where I am. The fish is delicious. I sleep heavily. In the morning there is still no dog. I turn the glow light up and decide to search. I take a piece of chalk and mark my turns, also making a mental note of how many rights and lefts I take. I pass through musty rooms full of rotten and forgotten goods, empty rooms robbed of all meaning, rooms full of mechanical objects dead without the means to fuel them. There is no dog. I may never see her again, it is sobering.

Back at the skiff I prepare another meal. Again, the dog fails to come. I face the fact I am alone. I decide to do a memory eating trance. I forget all about dogs and the concept of pets. I cry myself to sleep. My dreams are often disturbed, I think, although upon awakening I don't remember why.

I cook breakfast and for some reason cook too much. I feel I should share it, but I haven't seen any of the Others for a long time, so who would I share it with? In the end I feed it to the grasping dark deep water.

I spend the day trying to memorise the pictures on the Dome, even trying to scratch them onto the few scraps of parchment I have with a charcoal stick. My attempts are crude; where the unknown artist soars, I flail. I mark this on my ongoing map of the Beneath. I continue with my plan to find the bell. Perhaps in the distance there will be another gate, a populated place, perhaps another sea, more wrecks to plunder. Due to performing a memory eating trance the night before I am aware of an empty place, like a missing tooth, my mind skipping past some memories, affected by whatever I've now forgotten. I have the afterglow of sadness. I check my hands; this time there are no blisters, no soil under the fingernails. This time I have not buried something, or someone.

The Others are few, but important. Now I could add another, the unknown artist, although perhaps it is one of them that has displayed a new skill. There was the blonde couple I had seen on one of the wrecks, who had gone by the time I left. There was the old man whose boat had seemed even more ancient than him. He'd been the one to point the way to the passageways. And there had been the woman I sometimes dreamed of, the one I could not seem to forget. Her red hair like a flag, her quick laughter, her sharing my bed. She'd said she'd meet me on the inner sea. The one I'd wandered round for weeks. Unless there was another one, the old man had hinted as much – that's why I moved from the sea, why I came to the passageways.

I move ever inward, below the city; although I have forgotten much, I remember the names of the architecture I now pass under. Pillars and buttresses and naves and cloisters, foundations for a forgotten world. I see a small platform that follows the wall before turning off at ninety degrees down a small tunnel. On the platform are the remains of a campfire, the detritus of a meal. I paddle closer and feel the cold ashes. The bell calls me on. Once or twice I hear an unearthly wail in the distance. I tell myself it is the wind insinuating down here, moaning to be free. The hairs on the back of my neck stand up and there is a nagging feeling that I should know what this is.

I wind ever further inwards until eventually I come to a vast wall, upon which is a cistern. I travel in every direction I can find but always end up back at the wall. The maze has a heart and ways out but there is no new inner sea. I have been a fool; I should have been more patient.

I sleep and dream. I dream that the woman with the red hair will be waiting for me elsewhere. I wish I could remember her name. I dream of rushing down endless corridors chasing a four legged ghost, of following it, blundering into someone's lair, shouting and recriminations. Beasts with no name, people with no name, a woman with red hair, a child, blurred faces from the past, strange metal vehicles, a vast glowing ball in the sky, the feel of wind upon my face, exotic smells, smoke, fire. I awake to see that the fire has flared up suddenly. I perform my memory eating trance to wipe the memories from my mind. I am sad and disturbed by most of them until the familiar breaths and darkness re-centre me.

I roam further afield; perhaps I have missed something. I pass under the Dome twice more. Both times there are more pictures, I think. I call 'hello' every time I pass. The sound of the bell is a constant lure. Eventually I decide I must return to the sea.

I spend some time doing my memory eating trance, going deeper and more fully than ever before, but since I have forgotten what most units of time are, and have cast away all chronological devices, I am content in my lack of knowledge of how long this takes. I cannot bear the thought that I may dream again – every time I do memories fizz to the surface threatening a volcanic explosion of feelings. I must excise them completely. Once I have forgotten I am ready to move on. First comes the cistern.

Today is the day I take on fresh water. I may as well call it freshwater day. I have forgotten the names of things. I have forgotten the names of days. The cistern is down a narrow canal. Too narrow for the skiff. I take off my clothes, the ones I had found some days ago, and tie the large plastic containers together. The swim is bracing, it cleanses me, I am washed clean, I am renewed. The cistern is open, at the base of a large black wall; here everything is black, I am almost sightless this far from the skiff. I fill the plastic containers; I wonder where the water comes from and what I would do without it. I hum a tune. Once the gurgling and splashing changes in pitch and the containers are full, I make the short swim again, this time weighed down rather than buoyed up by my burden.

That will do me until the current brings me back here under the roots of bridges, the souls of churches, the secret parts of skyscrapers. Having exercised I prepare my meal, cutting the fish thinly and opening a tin of what turns out to be small round yellow fruit that taste like sunshine. I think they're fruit, although I have almost forgotten what fruit is. Forgotten most of the things that grow under the sky.

I will come to the Dome soon. After the Dome I will return to the Arches, then the Gate and finally the sea. I have been foolish to explore this place, returning to the former habitations of the forgotten.

I must prepare for the Dome. There may be more signs there. It has been some time since there were Others though. Some time since I saw Others anyway. Despite all my searching.

I roll the tarpaulin a little at one end to use as a pillow as I wrap the rest around me. I'd better be ready for the Dome. I listen to the bell slowly tolling somewhere in the darkness. I have never seen it. I do not know what it signifies. It soothes me to sleep. I do not dream, or if I do, I do not remember what I dream about.

I think about the time after the Dome. When I am upon the sea. My skiff will meander between the wrecks. I will explore. Life will be good again. Maybe this time one of the wrecks will be inhabited and I'll find the Others. Perhaps there are still Others somewhere upon the sea. Perhaps I'll find the bell. I hope I'll find the woman with red hair.

The Dome is soon; I eat another can. More will be available in the wrecks upon the sea although I have a vague sense that they will not last forever, that eventually the things inside them will turn bad. There are many wrecks and yet the sea is not large. In several sleeps I will be back at the canal ready to take on more water. The bell gently tolls. The wavelets lap against the side. I am forgetting.

Later I check the hooks. I have caught a large fish. I gut it and throw the effluvia of offal over the side. There used to be a time that I would have offered it to something, to some companion. But I have forgotten. The Dome will be very soon. I hear in the distance the strange echoes of it. I can tie up there. Sleep on solid ground. Be secure. I have forgotten why being secure is important. It is something to do with the wrecks.

There is a muffled thud as something hits the side of the skiff. I lean over and stare at the inky water. It is a wooden beam. I pull it aboard and set it to dry near to, but not on, the others. I drink, perform my ablutions and then sleep.

It is time for the Dome, and the skiff speeds up a little then bobs gently up and down, turning slowly as the whirl of current beneath the Dome catches me. I wait until the steps are in sight then throw a rope onto the bollard above me to stop the skiff in its tracks. I am caught. I am secure. Later I will explore. I need some more matches. For now, I am content to stare up at the Dome. There have been no new pictures for a while. This is a shame, and I wonder if the unknown artist has escaped. I wonder if he drowned. I wonder if drowning is an escape. I decide to climb the stairs.

The door is stiff with rust, but it is possible, if I breathe in, to squeeze inside and climb the stairs into the labyrinth where I once knew all the ways but have now forgotten most of them. I take an emergency flare, I hope I will find more. I light it, shielding my eyes which are unused to the brightness, and run the way I still remember, the way to the storeroom.

I spend too long looking at the bundle of rags, and what's within them, on the floor and the flare goes out. I wonder which of them it was. I hope it's not the artist. I move round the room cautiously and eventually find more flares, in the place I would have remembered if I could have seen. There are the remains of a fire here, the remains of a meal, bones of some animal: a long thick skull with sharp teeth, disturbingly familiar. I remember chasing a four-legged ghost in my dreams, for some reason I am gripped by a sharp intense sadness. I am getting hungry, this is taking too long. I grab a couple of boxes of matches and several flares but leave everything else for another time. No point having too much on the skiff. The stuff is safer here.

Back at the Dome I shave one of the pieces of wood and give myself the luxury of a fire and roast the fat fish I caught.

I know I must move on. I know I have to be ready for the sea, but I am tired. I wonder again which of them it was up there and what happened. I decide to do a memory eating trance to forget about them. I am alone. I am better alone. Emotions cannot hurt me if I am alone.

I continue with my travels, my returning. Now there are only the Arches in front, and behind me, the Dome. The first is upon me almost before I am ready. I secure all the belongings as the skiff accelerates silently. I pass the first with only a minor scrape. I try to use the oar to keep the skiff from clashing against the sides. The second Arch passes without much notice. The third gives the skiff a nasty knock and I am thrown to the rough planking floor but neither I nor the skiff are seriously injured this time. I remember being more worried before. As if there was more than just me to be worried about. I shake the nagging feeling from my head as the skiff accelerates in the darkness. I wonder if this signifies that there is a tide; my entry to the passageways was smoother, and I cannot remember having to paddle upstream.

I am upon the sea. My skiff will meander between the wrecks. I will explore. Life is good again. I am alone but I am not afraid. I reach the first wreck and secure myself to it. I get the map out that I had once drawn of the sea, of the wrecks, and scrutinise it in the gloomy light my glow light throws. After I sleep I will explore. Later, I awake with a start. At first, I don't know what woke me. Then I perceive it. The bell has fallen silent. I sit and wait for it to start tolling again. I prepare my breakfast and still no bell.

I plan my day. Perhaps there are still people somewhere upon the sea. Perhaps I'll find the bell, if it starts ringing again. As the skiff bumps gently against the side of the first wreck I wonder what I will find. I throw my rope. I tie it fast. I leap aboard.

The wreck yields a few essential items and many more of a more dubious nature, some that pull my mind towards memories I know are better left beneath the waves. I take what I want and leave the rest. I check my map – there is a series of x's where I'd already explored wrecks. There is a circle around one wreck. I don't remember why it is circled so I make my way there.

On board there are signs of a great struggle, the furnishings a chaos of broken and battered fixtures and fittings. I find them in bed, holding hands, their heads caved in, the murder weapon sat next to them, a golf club. The head of which has tufts of blonde hair glued with once sticky blood, now dried to brown. I hear screaming, I hear myself shouting, I remember the incomplete method of forgetting I used to have, with alcohol. I walk back on deck and sit shivering. I look up into the blackness above. I wonder.

Back on the skiff, I am aware that time has lurched past. I open the map and look for other circles, notes, anything. I see a cross that has been circled. I punt the skiff towards it. The old man's boat reminds me that there were once other people here that I conversed with. The old man is aboard, but would not be conversing again. After seeing his sightless eyes staring at infinity, I perform another memory eating trance. But instead of the sweet darkness I crave I can only see the face of the red-haired woman and the child. I collapse exhausted and dream.

Beneath my hands, which are shiny red and with blisters beginning to show, is the handle of a shovel. I look down and there is a long mound of fresh earth. I drop the shovel and stare at my hands. They are encrusted with black earth. I rub them together, my blisters popping and giving me a delicious pain. Blood wells up under my fingernails and starts to drip onto the fresh grave. The red matches her hair, both of their hair. I walk back to our boat and cast it off: it can wreck itself now. All is lost. I drop our daughter's shoes off the end of the pier. I have weighed them down with stones. I watch them sinking, throwing small bubbles that slowly rise to the surface as they spin end over end forever down into the black water. The dog slinks towards me; it will be a while before she trusts me again. I lean over the side and wash my hands in the water and make the decision to forget.

Benediction

PART ONE – Pilgrimage

I had touched a god once, in my youth. A benediction,
a boon, a blessing. I feel distant from that child, as
if he and I are different people, separate people. He
found the god and now I need to return. I need another
boon. No benediction without sacrifice. I had to walk,
a pilgrimage. Not knowing if I'd be in time, part of the
price. All laid out in the vision I'd been afforded in my
dream quest. I have walked so far, over many days, but
at last I'd arrived at the place of my birth. I will save
her. I'd touched a god once; for her, I must do so again.
The vision told me. I must do what the vision tells me.
So I can save her.

> You first walk the lime tree lined sandy path
> between the Lord's estate and the school. Then the
> road, until the alleyway. One side breeze-blocked
> in grey, the other thorns in green and brown. The
> alleyway opens into the field of grassy mounds –
> the dirt paths winding through them like arteries
> full of poison. The grassy area bound by private
> property. A boundary to the north, another to the
> south. Follow the northern fence and when the

path opens to a woodland the fence takes a sharp
right and ladders up the hill on a dusty river of
wooden steps to the road. Do not take that turn.

The child joined the other children from the village as
they'd played their own games in midsummer. Together
they'd entered the woods; ignored their parents'
warnings not to go too far. They'd played along the
path running up the hill. They'd discovered the jumping
tree and she'd been braver than he had. Climbing the
jumping tree and performing the rite of passage of
leaping from one tree to another. She led. He followed.
He'd always followed.

I reached the lime tree path. I'd shed all modernity in
order to make this pilgrimage. No phone. No transport
but my feet. No money. I'd lost contact, shunned
people. I didn't know if I'd be in time, but the vision
said that was part of the price, part of the suffering
that was necessary to save her. I had to believe. My
course of action prescribed through dream quest,
meditation and prayer, through ritual and instinct. I'd
touched the god once, I needed to do so again.

Ignore the jumping tree and the rest of the
woodlands and come to the crossroads. Here the
path could turn left and back to the village or right
up to the bridge, snaking through it in a tunnel.
Straight on is blocked by thorn trees, but you know
the secret path. To follow the tunnel path into a
cutting and the way, hand over hand, climbing the
steep bank and the old child's fort, woven out of
land flotsam and briar and holly and other greenery.
And here is a way through the fence. Ignore the
trespass and go into the far Lord's estate.

The children had come to the crossroads, one path to
the bottom of the hill, to the village, the other under
the road bridge, ahead the secret way to the top of the
hill. The forbidden route. She'd laughed and tossed her
hair, run ahead. He'd followed. He always followed.
She'd picked him out, in the playground ceremony.
Chase? He'd followed. They'd held hands just that day,
shyly, hesitantly, on the way to the woodlands, part of
a larger group. The others mocked and jeered but he
didn't care.

I'd reached my childhood home, but the village was
no longer a village, it had grown into a town. Houses
had metastasized all along the green spaces, invading
my childhood memories of this place. I found the path
was changed. More of the land taken by developers but
eventually I passed the place I thought the jumping tree
had once stood. I found the bridge. The Lord's estate. I
must go to the top of the hill. Where the god lived.

You must now pass across the Lord's estate.
The undulating feet of the hill. To the top. The
grove. Yew and pine and oak and beech and ash.
The aroma of cleansing pine and the pumpkin
stench of dead leaves. The estate named after the
ancient battle, the hot gates, the three hundred
gods. Summer and heat haze, flower-sweet and
pine fresh, meadow crushed and rolling hillocks.
Remembrance of grass-green clothes and sun-
kissed youth. The pass. The pass and the summer.
And the child. And her.

They walked hand in hand, in the middle of the group.
The hill was steep, and the path narrow through woods,

briar, sloes and blackberry brambles – good picking
come autumn. They'd been forbidden to climb the
hill. And finally the bare grass, waist-high to make
waves through. And at the very top the grove, and at
the centre of the grove, the highest point, the god.
An ancient oak, battle-scarred through melee with the
elements, lightning-gashed fallen limbs lying broken,
asunder. But magnificently and defiantly alive. Despite
their earlier rambunctiousness they approached
carefully, reverently. The god commanded it, irrefutable
atop the crest. She smiled and he grinned. The others
demanded they kiss. So he drew her near and pecked
her on the lips. "Do it properly." She put her arms
around him and placed her mouth on his and opened.
His first proper kiss, hers too probably. The others
made *ooo* noises and then laughing, played catch-me-if-
you-can. But he'd already been caught. Such a moment
required commemoration. She touched his face and
led him to the god. He'd shown her the pocket-knife
earlier. He'd create a love heart.

I patted my pocket to feel my pocket-knife. The same
one; a reassuring lump. My hands bear witness to
years of carrying that knife, small scars reminders of
its sharp and blessed blade. I thought about the old
house. The paint peeling, the gutters full of leaves and
rubbish. The hole the house martins had used to nest
in, empty. The windows grime-streaked. The door
rotted at the bottom. My father's house, now fully
abandoned, it had used to sit at the edge of the village,
near the lime tree path. Now the town surrounded
it. When my father died, I'd moved my mother close.
Maybe strangers had once lived in the old house but
now it looked ripe for development. The village had
grown in size but yet seemed a smaller place, poor

and backward. The children playing in the streets had viewed me with suspicion. Curtains had twitched. But enough of looking backwards. I set my face to the hill and climbed. The Lord's estate was still fenced off, but the rolling hills had been built upon. There was now a wide and dusty road, pocked and pitted and pot-holed. None of this had been here when I took my mother away. Thoughts of my mother, thoughts of home where I'd left her, a woman in her seventies, to look after the children and my sick wife. The tow-headed girl who'd let me catch her upon this hill, with the god watching on. "Be safe," I whisper, thinking of them.

And here is the god of first loves and mock battles, of childhood bravery and guilt, of primary friendships and bonding, the god of your youth. You must touch it to make her well. You must release the magic. Touch the heart. While you are upon your pilgrimage she will falter, but not die. Touch the heart and return to her and all will be well.

Because she'd not said no and because the others looked at him in expectation, he'd have to go through with it. The god stood at the very top of the hill, wind tossing its branches but apart from the susurrus of leaves the summit was quiet. The child swallowed and stepped into the tree's shadow with her. A rich loamy aroma enveloped him, and he reached out a tentative hand and touched the gnarled trunk. Permission, benediction and absolution. He carved his initials and hers within a love heart. Now they would be together forever. The god would grant him that, and luck. He brimmed with luck. They kissed again and returned to the group like heroes of old. She laughed and mouthed 'chase me' and ran off down the hill. She led. He followed.

I stumbled to a halt. Not much further. Come on. But my will to move forward ebbed. I pulled out the precious picture I had of her. Still blonde when it was taken. "For you, anything." A careworn promise, often given. I sighed, renewed my pilgrimage. Up the streets along the hill where once only grass and daisies and clover lay. No waist-high grass to make waves in now. I concentrated on my feet, the hilltop obscured by houses, I pressed on, no meadow-sweetness to accompany me. And then I reached the top. Or as close to the top as allowed. A mansion squatted there now. Where the god had once stood. I slumped to my knees and a sob tore itself out of my throat. A bus careened past on the steep hill road. Where once we had jumped from tree to tree. I had failed.

***

Part Two – Return

A FAMILY WITH a bouncing, bounding dog walk past me and I know I have to pull it together. The adults watch me warily and I know they see a man in sturdy, but weather-beaten clothes, a few weeks' worth of beard, unwashed. Children fly kites from one garden. A family neighbourhood. The thought of my unwelcome visage brings me back to my feet and speeds me down the hill. A bell begins to chime, marking some hour of the day, a church. Perhaps I couldn't touch the god, the lost, but I can ask another for an intercession.

I set my course for the church, ignoring as much as possible the people along the way. Wishing they ignored me in turn. Children watch with curiosity, adults with suspicion.

I arrive at the church, built in the time I'd been gone from here. An oaken lych-gate signals the way into the churchyard. I stop to admire it and there, a little above head height, on one beam, a set of ancient initials carved within a love heart. We'd always be together. I reach out and touch it, wanting the benediction. But all I feel is lifeless wood.

No boon. No absolution. I glance at the church, but it is over. My mother's religion had not saved my father, nor any of her friends. I turn my back on it and know I need to return. As fast as possible. I walk to the part of the village where the shop used to be and am glad to see that there is now a string of shops. I panhandle for coin. "Excuse me," I say to passers-by, "could you spare me some change?" Or, "I'm trying to get the bus fare to take me home, could you perhaps spare me a coin or two?" Most ignore me, cross the road to avoid me, some spit at me, but eventually I accumulate enough coins to at least make a phone call.

"Hello?"

"Hi Mum, it's me," I wind the cord of the phone around my finger. The phonebox smells of piss and mildew. But I am none too fresh myself.

"Where the hell have you been? I've been frantic with worry. You walked out on your wife. Your kids. We phoned the police, told them you were missing. I-"

"I'm coming back, Mum. I just need a way to do so."

"Where are you?"

"I've been home, Mum. To our old house. I thought I'd be able to... to..." To what? What could I tell her? My communion with the god in my youth was mine alone. No one knew. I could hear my children in the background screaming. I miss them more right now than I had for the entire pilgrimage. I interrupt another stream of questions. "How is she?"

"She's dying and you ran away. What sort of man are you? Your father—"

"I need money to come home, Mum."

In among the recriminations, she said she'd send me enough money for a bus ticket to bring me home.

***

When I open the front door, my mother rushes out of the kitchen and gathers me in a hug. Then holds me at arm's length with a wrinkled nose. "Where the hell have you been? And have you even washed since you left? You stink." With screams my children run to me, embrace me. The guilt in leaving them is almost too much to bear. When had my mum gotten so small and the kids so big?

"Go to her, son. She needs you."

I nod, peel the kids off and pass them to my mother, place the rucksack gently down, kick my boots off and approach the stairs. She'd always led. What will I do now?

Our room smells of medicine and underlying old flowers. The dim light from the shaded window just enough to make it to the bed. She lies on her back, wan, exhausted, deep bags under her eyes. Shrunken even more than when I'd seen her last. When I told her that there was something I had to do, and I'd definitely be back. Told her to wait for me. I pluck her hand from where it lies atop the covers.

"My beautiful boy," she murmurs, a sad smile upon her bloodless lips.

"I failed you," I reply, a tear sliding down my face.

"How so?"

"I wasn't here for you. I… I went back to where we began, to see if I could get another benediction. I found our love heart – it was on a church gate, but the tree had gone." I can't look at her while I say this, I stare instead at a picture we'd bought together, of a mighty oak, that I'd put on the wall next to the bed. Our bed.

"Nonsense. You have never failed me." She squeezes my hand and now I dare to see her. To really see her. Skeletal as she is, she is still my life. My heart. My beauty. She smiles again. "Let lost gods lie, we are insignificant to them anyway."

"You knew?"

"Of course. I was there, too, remember? I touched it, too." She grimaces as a spasm of pain crawls through her, knocking down her defences again. "It wasn't just your god. It was mine, too."

"It's all gone. The place no longer exists. The god, our childhood. The developers have chewed it all up. Biting, biting, chewing—" She places a finger on my mouth to shut me up. I gulp down the bile and wipe the tears from my face. "Then what do we do now?" I feel lost, exactly like a little boy again. That lost child she'd led. I'd always followed. Except for the children. I have to persevere for the children.

"I'd like to see the love heart," she says. "Take me there?"

"For you, anything."

I watch her eyes close, her features relax, her chest still. I feel her hand grow limp inside mine. The god was dead, youth and beauty, first love, no longer summer, no grass-smeared clothes, heat haze, flower sweet and pine fresh, meadow-crushed and rolling down the hillocks: no more sun-kissed youth. It was all gone. My soul is torn, and yet she is there still, in my heart. Always in my heart.

The Detective's Tale

THWUNK!

The flick-knife was embedded in the throat of the carefully drawn outline on the corkboard. DC Roger Dickson, slightly stooped and with plenty of grey in his hair, limped over to pull it out. He'd seen Morgan Freeman do the flick-knife thing in the film Se7en and had ruined a perfectly good dartboard before purchasing several layers of cork. His partner, Detective Garrett, often joshed that just because he was a black man of a certain age, he shouldn't model his police career on a Hollywood actor. He did wish he had a job as cushy as the film star's – just turn up in movies for ten minutes, say something Morgan Freeman-y and walk away with a massive pay cheque. His own job sucked, but he knew no other life and it was so ingrained in him, there was – he thought – no escaping it.

The cases kept him awake; often, annoyingly.

Thunk!

The murder of the girl known as Refuge's Angel, under bizarre circumstances.

Thunk!

A missing woman – probably just a domestic taken to the extreme, but whose husband was hounding him for answers.

Thunk!

Around and around.

Thunk!

A man missing in nearby Causeway.

Thunk!

Case after case.

Thunk!

The crossword-maker's apparent suicide which turned out to be a murder.

Thunk!

Over and over, his mind chewed over the cases. When his eyes closed, and he lay still listening to the night noises, it was worse.

The unexpected ring of the phone startled him from his reverie, and he glanced at the clock before answering it. Three-fifteen. AM.

He sighed – only one person would be calling at this time.

"Yeah?" He held the phone lightly, and only as closely as he needed to without it touching his ear, as though it were a turd wrapped in not-enough tissue paper.

"Deeetective!" His partner's excited voice blasted out of the receiver.

"Detective," he replied, biting the word out, low and quick, annoyed again, always annoyed. Their phone calls had achieved the status of ritual.

"We got a gig, so get your lanky black ass out to Marsh Street."

He glanced at the clock again. "I'll be there in fifteen." God, how he hated going up that close to the Maze, a den of thieves and degenerates.

"Roger, Roger and out, out." The click of his partner ending the call came a microsecond before the sound of Dickson sucking his teeth – that stupid old joke.

Detective Roger Dickson… was going to work. He retracted the blade of his knife and shoved it in its specially adapted ankle holster. On the way out, he gave no glance to the bare-walled, bare-floored, bare-of-furniture – apart from a ratty mattress on the floor and a hanger pole holding seven identical shirts – bare apartment. Since Julia left, the house had become strange and empty. He was much more comfortable at the station.

The car felt comfortable, too – his own territory – rather than the abandoned remains of a failed marriage. As he turned to reverse out of the drive, he spotted a mongrel in the rear-view mirror. Dogs were banned from the streets, so this one must have been a stray that had found its way into Refuge from the Maze. It ran across the drive with a human hand in its mouth, its pelt bloody red in the taillights. He shrugged and threw the car in reverse.

It can't have been a hand, he told himself, and if it was… someone else could do the paperwork on it.

By the time he reached Marsh Street – the last street in Refuge this side of the wall that separated the main town from the Maze – he'd had to search for the bottle of generic painkillers, the sciatica a red-hot line down his right side. He grimaced at the chalky, bitter taste and he dry-swallowed, knowing that the NSAIDs would take a while to help, and do little more than take the edge off. He also knew they'd anger his ulcer, but at least he'd be able to walk without crying with the pain. He'd run out of the prescription stuff weeks ago but hadn't managed to get back to the doctor to ask for some more.

He hated doctors, and he'd just get another lecture on how he should be signed off work with a slipped disc.

His partner was on the phone. Garrett threw a quick salute to the car and carried on pacing up and down talking in that rapid-fire, loud way he had. Dickson rubbed the heel of his hand across each eye and clambered painfully out of the car.

"Yes, honey… uh huh… yup. I'll be back as soon as I can. Love you." After putting the phone away, Garrett turned to Dickson. "You look like shit. I mean – the fuck? I'm the one with a new-born and no sleep, but you look like there is a portrait of you as a young man sans blemishes in the attic. Jesus!"

"What we got?" Dickson knew from experience that he'd be best off just making his side of the conversation work.

Garrett – used to this – didn't break verbal stride, "Domestic, wife battered the husband with a frying pan, Betsy has the colic you know, are you taking anything for that?" Each sentence ran on from the last, incessant. Dickson hadn't got used to it since they'd been partners. He was, by nature, taciturn, and suspected that being assigned the younger man – a brand new detective in his late twenties – had been a joke by his former boss. No one had seen fit to change the arrangement since.

He briefly wondered – not for the first time – why Garrett had asked to be transferred to Refuge. And, not for the first time, decided he didn't care. His own journey to Refuge was a fucking odyssey he did his best to forget, although with the ulcer, he could no longer drown it with alcohol. He was an intensely private man and respected others' privacy, unless they were involved in a case. His lieutenant often said that he'd be a great detective if it wasn't for his lack of curiosity. That lack of needing to know everything was what the mayor said he valued most though. He sniffed at the thought of the mayor, wondering if he could afford to join in another poker game. He winced at the memory of the mayor's pet thug laughing like a drain when Dickson had lost a month's wages, pawed into a pile in front of the big man.

Sometimes, in the dead of the night, he fantasised about walking out. Out of the department, the job, the town. There was nothing to keep him here anymore. His wife was gone, he had no friends here, no one would miss him. But something kept him here – he'd fought his way here so many years ago at great sacrifice, seeking refuge from a life gone wildly off the rails, and a complete and utter split with the gang he'd run with and all the booze and drugs. He sighed again – that was literally a lifetime ago. Dickson looked at Garrett, wondering yet again how old the younger man had been when he'd made the break and come to Refuge – had he even been out of nappies?

"You not listening again, Dickson?" Garrett stopped and laid his hand on the older man's arm. "I said, did you want to do the wife and I'll do the kids?"

He hated Garrett calling him Dickson, but no matter how many times he'd told the young man not to, he carried on. The first time he'd met Dick Garrett, Garrett had made the lame joke, "Isn't it odd you being called Dickson when you're old enough to be my dad!"

There was now that special inflection the younger man gave his name, and it grated.

Dickson ran his hand over his stubbly salt and pepper hair and nodded, stalking off before the incessant verbal assault started up again.

***

THE VICTIM'S WIFE was on a ratty sofa in the front room, flinching at each sound made by the team picking over her former husband in the kitchen. A uniform was standing close by. Dickson couldn't understand why the wife was still in the house, why they hadn't taken her to a squad car at the very least. As he got closer, he noted her extreme paleness, apart from a few blood splatters like red paint upon her face. Her mascara had run, accentuating the haunted, shocked expression in her eyes. Her hair was a wild rats' nest and her hands convulsively opened and closed. He was going to get nothing here.

The uniform nodded at him as he approached and gratefully walked off, gone to find coffee no doubt. He made to crouch, but the pain shooting up his leg meant that instead he flopped down next to the distraught woman. She didn't seem to notice.

"Mrs…?"

He'd forgotten the name of the family already – not the worst oversight, but a worrying one for a detective. The woman didn't turn to look at him, but she did start murmuring. It was so quiet that he had to lean very close to hear.

"Why's he late? He's never late. You should punish him for being late! The girls want their bedtime story. But if he's late he'll miss it. Why's he late? He's never late…"

Like lines. He reached out and squeezed her shoulder. "For the girls' sake. Can you…"

The woman whirled upon him, snarling, speckles of spittle at the corner of her mouth as she screamed at him, "He's NEVER late. How's he going to read their bedtime story if he's late?"

Jesus.

"Shhh now, lady," he found himself saying as he recoiled from the rabid woman. All other noise in the room had stopped as everyone turned to look.

"He'll MISS it!" she screamed. A woman in an olive woollen suit hurried over from the other side of the room and started talking smoothly to the distressed woman. With a gentle hand on her elbow, the lady in the woollen suit guided her to stand up, and still making soothing sounds, moved her across the room. As she reached the door, the woman in the suit turned and mouthed something to Dickson, whose eyes weren't so good any more in low light, and so he didn't catch it. He shrugged. The woman nodded and smiled and took the suspect out of the door.

Dickson levered his way up and grabbed the nearest officer.

"Who was that?"

"Doctor Zhan from the Asylum. We called her."

Dickson shook his head. Where were the children? He'd best go and find Garrett.

Instead, he found Eyob Debela – the chief pathologist. He had no love for the man, but fate often threw them together and they had a grudging respect for each other. Sometimes they'd go as far as sharing a couple of whiskies in The Blue Frog – although post-ulcer, that had been very seldom and he'd end up nursing one drink, torturing himself with the smell of smoke in the brand he liked. Far too expensive if he were to drink a lot of it, he'd favoured cheaper brands pre-ulcer.

"Chief."

"Detective."

"What brings you out to this one?" Dickson was intrigued: this sort of banal murder didn't need the chief pathologist.

"The ME asked for my opinion."

"On this?"

"Yes."

"And?"

"We are… collating." The chief ran his hand over his head, tweaking the comb-over that he'd self-consciously cultivated. He rubbed his chest. "These late nights give me heartburn. If you'll excuse me." He brushed past and exited through the front door.

Dickson narrowed his eyes. What was there about this case that needed the chief's opinion? And where the hell was Garrett?

He walked over to the kitchen and popped his head round the door, not wanting to disturb the techies as they did their CSI crap. He quickly spotted that Garrett wasn't in the kitchen, but his eyes were drawn to the blood splatter, which was prodigious, even reaching the white polystyrene tiles on the ceiling. At the epicentre of the explosion of blood was the corpse. He did a double take as he realised that there was no head, as such: it had been repeatedly smashed so much that it was just a lumpy mess on the floor, the first recognisable body part being a partial jawbone.

"Sweet Christ!"

One of the techies glanced up. They all looked the same in their identical paper suits, face masks and safety glasses, with paper hoods covering up the rest of their heads. This one was evidently a woman.

"Christ doesn't enter into it," she said, deadpan. He nodded to her and turned away, shaking his head. The desire to just walk away, never far from the surface, flared. He could just walk out the door, get in the car and drive off. He had enough money to fill the car with fuel several times over, he wondered how far he'd get before the job, Garrett, the mayor, the lack of career prospect in any other field, would call him back…

Garrett grabbed his arm as he walked past an open door.

"In here!" his partner whispered urgently.

"Why you whispering?"

"The mayor has been on at me about the Angel case."

"And?"

"He's getting twitchy."

Dickson sighed. "It's on the list. We have other bullshit to do, too." He gestured behind him.

"This? Open and shut case. Book the wife. Do the paperwork. End of. No one here has had hornets sewn inside their mouths. The paper's not going to be asking difficult questions. No one cares." Whilst talking, Garrett unwrapped a stick of gum. As punctuation, he popped it in his mouth and started chewing. Dickson had always wondered if Garrett had a cocaine habit.

"Have you seen the body?" Dickson asked.

"No, I haven't seen the body, and I don't need to: wifey lost it, battered him round the head with a frying pan, he carks it, leaving their two daughters without a daddy and with mummy off to the big house, end of, tragic tale, blah, blah, blah, onto the next case. Talking of, we should bring that Deacon feller in, he's been sniffing round again."

"Dolan. And his wife is still missing."

"Exactly."

"Okay, tomorrow maybe, let's write this up." His brief flirtation with caring put away due to the sensible words of his partner, he knew the best course of action was to do as Garrett suggested. The mystery of the chief pathologist forgotten, he went through the motions as fast as he could in order to leave.

Later, as he was driving home, he thought he should talk to Debela again, find out what exactly he was collating, just to make sure nothing was going to trip up the open and shut case. As he drove past Joe Dolan's house, he saw that there was a light on, and was sure that a curtain twitched. Perhaps Garrett was right. Perhaps they needed to bring Dolan in.

On the path to his house, an animal had knocked over his bins and spread the rubbish far and wide. His simmering anger threatened to boil over. He stood with eyes tightly shut, trying to take deep breaths, trying to calm down, for a full ten seconds before getting a brush and tidying up. Maybe it was the stray he'd seen earlier. If he saw it again, he'd call the pound. Maybe shoot it, he fantasised. He lay on the mattress for what felt like an hour, but, still unable to sleep, he was soon up again and throwing the knife over and over at the cork.

***

THE NEXT NIGHT rolled round. They had a stakeout to perform. The car idled, the two men sat in shadows, no one outside could have seen their features. Dickson imagined what a passer-by would see, but there were none at this time of night. He glanced at the clock, three fifteen. There were far too many early mornings and late nights on this job – but with the back pain, empty bed and the ulcer which occasionally bent him double, he slept poorly anyway. He glanced at Garrett, who, as per usual, was talking ten to the dozen. About some crap he'd watched on TV, not knowing, or more likely not caring, that Dickson hadn't seen it. Hadn't got a TV even. He could feel the drugs winding down. The painkillers made him zone out, so he'd been cutting them with uppers. He was self-aware enough to realise that he'd started on the long slow spiral, familiar from his youth. He'd have to return to the doc.

He hated doctors, especially now, in Refuge. Couldn't understand the medical system here – how to get things paid for, how to claim back the extras, why they always sent people for expensive tests and procedures no matter how slight the risk – another fucking scam. He ended up paying way more than he probably should just because he couldn't figure out the paperwork. God help anyone who didn't even speak the language.

"How the hell do you go about writing crosswords anyway?" It was the first sentence from his partner that penetrated Dickson's awareness. He grunted in reply.

"Open and shut case?" Garrett asked.

Dickson just nodded.

"Who do we pin it on?"

Dickson rubbed a hand across his mouth. Stubble a pleasant scratch. Blew air through his cheeks. "Does it matter?"

"No, suppose not. We done here? I'd like to get back to my warm bed and warm wife, if you know what I mean."

Garrett sat in the passenger seat and was gesturing at the dashboard. Dickson sighed, slipped the car into gear and drove away from the newspaper man's house. He couldn't help but feel his path on the spiral winding another notch. Christ, he needed something to take the edge off, or give him an edge, he wasn't sure which. How many dead bodies had he seen? He briefly contemplated a visit to the Temple of Bes, but his last humiliation there resurfaced and he shook his head.

Garrett, who thought the shake of the head was aimed at what he'd been saying, replied, "No, really!"

"What?"

"Not listening again, huh? No matter, what I was saying was that it's totally ridiculous how they go about solving cases. I mean, have the show writers ever even talked to a copper? It's ridiculous how…"

Dickson tuned his partner out again, but remembered to grunt at the pauses. Strange how Garrett could repeat himself. He wondered what had happened in his life that made him want to fill any silence with inconsequential chatter. The one time he'd invited Garrett to the Temple, the younger man had turned him down.

"I know it's old-fashioned," he'd replied, "but I'm totally in love with my wife. And enjoying being a father."

Dickson had forgotten what either of those were like. Any reminder of his wife and their bone of contention – and Garrett often reminded him because he was always talking about his own wife and child – left him with a sour taste in his mouth and the ulcer like a rat's jaw, gnawing in his stomach. He dropped one hand to clutch at his stomach and rolled the car to a stop outside Garrett's house.

"We need to go and speak to Joe Dolan about his wife Elspet tomorrow," Garrett reminded him as he skipped out of the car, full of nervous energy.

"I'll pick you up at nine."

"Bring me a coffee," Garrett said breezily, already halfway to his door.

"Fuck sake," Dickson muttered.

***

SAMUEL SPENCER WAS a 'street artist' apparently. Dickson just thought he was a bum. The two detectives sat watching him pan-handle.

"What about him?" he asked the younger man.

"Nah, too obvious," Garrett answered before blowing on his coffee.

"No one would miss him, though." Dickson's stomach grumbled – coffee was another thing he'd given up because it angered the rat-ulcer that gnawed at his stomach lining.

"Yeah, true. But he's not the type, is he? No one would believe he did it." Garrett slurped his coffee and winced: still too hot.

"We can say he did it for drug money?" Dickson wondered how many dead bodies he'd seen. It had been a recurring question lately. He wasn't sure why. He realised that the thought of pinning the murder on a street artist was him getting lazy.

"Do you think he did it?" Garrett asked.

"That bum?" Dickson was confused. Surely his partner knew that he was just casting around for a convenient scapegoat. The mayor was breathing down his neck, no more 'small favours' until he'd put the Angel case to bed.

"Dolan?"

"No."

Garrett turned to show Dickson a raised eyebrow.

Dickson sighed.

"He didn't do away with his wife. But there is something off about him. Not so sure about the brother, too, would like to have a chat with him."

"Ah. Right. Yup, yup. That's what I thought, too."

Yeah, right, Dickson thought, returning his gaze to the street artist. No – Garrett was right – no one would accept him as a murderer.

Garrett's phone rang.

"It's Debela," he informed Dickson before answering it. "A demon?" Garrett replied to something the chief pathologist said.

Dickson frowned at his partner, who shook his head as he said, "Uh huh."

"No drugs. More than human strength. Check… Yes, he's here with me… Yes, of course I'll tell him… Yes… Later."

As Garrett ended the call Dickson asked, "Tell me what?"

"Okay… Our black widow was apparently normal one day, cracked with superhuman strength pyscho-bitch the next. The chief told me to tell you to switch your phone on."

Dickson frowned again. It was on. He pulled it out of his pocket to see that it showed several missed calls from the chief pathologist and one from Julia. The rat in his belly flipped over, twisting the lining of his stomach wall. He'd have to listen to the message. Garrett continued talking.

"Wait," Dickson interrupted. "Superhuman strength?"

"Yeah, we're back to ghosts and ghoulies again. Shit! People go missing all over but when they go missing here, folks jump to the conclusion it's fucking spooks."

It was a well-worn rant by Garrett. Dickson had seen some things that he'd made sure to push far down into his subconscious. He didn't like to think of there being more to the world than the material, but over the years in Refuge, there'd been a few things that weren't easy to explain away. The mayor, Emeritus, was adamant that those things were explainable, that Dickson's own history provided an explanation. Hence why Dickson suppressed things: he didn't know how much the mayor knew about his druggie past and didn't want to rock that boat. One of the reasons he tried to keep on the mayor's good side – not the most important, but there nonetheless.

He realised that his musings had pushed Garrett's reply into the grey realm of background noise.

"Sorry. Repeat?" Dickson asked.

"Not listening again?" Garrett asked without rancour. "I said that Debela suggested we go to the Asylum and question the patient. He doesn't think she could have done it unaided. The husband's head was just mush; Debela doesn't think she should have had either the strength or willpower to do that."

"He wants us to keep the case open?"

"Uh huh."

"Shit."

"Mayor up your ass again?"

Dickson rubbed his hands over the hollows of his eyes.

"Let's get it over with. We'll ask her the chief path's questions and then get the shrink to say she did it, that it was possible due to crazy-person strength, and then write it up."

"Our usual MO, go through the motions, check." The younger man was grinning.

Dickson shook his head. He didn't understand the younger man, what motivated him to go along with the easier path. Usually the young ones were idealistic, but Garrett had slotted right in. Perhaps he had his own understanding with the mayor. Dickson glanced at his phone again. He'd listen to his messages later. He sparked the engine into life and, stomach clawing, hip flaring, joined the traffic. Still on the slow spiral.

***

THEY'D HAD TO drive through the opening in the wall, skirt around the Maze and hit the only road westward over the marshes to get there. There was no traffic by the time they rolled up outside the Asylum. Dickson shuddered as the car coughed one last time before the engine ceased and the various tinkling sounds of cooling metal filled the silence.

"This place gives me the creeps," said Garrett, putting a voice to his own thoughts.

"Yeah? Well, suck it up, son. This is where we'll both end up some day, I'm sure." It was his deepest fear: losing his mind. Worse if he knew it was happening. He thought of his mother for the first time in a long while. She'd walked her own soft spiral before he'd walked his, shedding layer upon layer of who she was. Having to administer her drugs, look after her, clean her, he was too young. No wonder it broke him. No wonder it'd all fallen apart with Julia when... The warning twinge from his stomach made him suppress that thought.

"Let's get this over with as fast as we can," he said, painfully climbing out of the car. It was as if the silence was not silence, as if it were a hundred screaming mental patients, a psychic scream attacking the barrier of his mind. He shuddered again and reminded himself he didn't believe in any of that nonsense. It was better to not believe – easier.

The door opened as they approached and an orderly, wearing the white of purity, greeted them.

"Detectives. To what do we owe this pleasure? Has Homer the firebug asked for you again?"

Dickson shook his head. "Not unless he's out wandering the streets of Refuge?"

Homer, the psycho fire-starter – that was one they did manage to pin on the right person. It took three burned-down houses and an actual death before the man was found, though. Since then, he'd been back a couple of times to talk to him. Homer was keen to confess to many other things done whilst he was sick. And to prove that he was right in the head now. Safe to say, his tales of demons and possession and of cleansing the town had received short shrift from Dickson.

"We're here to see the psychotic saucepan bitch," Garrett said. He used the stupid name the local rag – *The Refuse* – had given her.

"Mrs Sansom. Right. I'll take you to see Doctor Zhan then."

They followed the man inside. The imagined screaming of the patients that Dickson always felt outside cut off abruptly as the door closed and the actual sounds of the Asylum intruded.

Only soft conversations, TVs, radios, disturbing in its banality. As they walked past an old man in a wheelchair, his legs covered by a vomit-coloured blanket, Dickson did a double-take. For a second, the man in the wheelchair was him. Like looking in the mirror. But his second glance took in the fact that the man wasn't even black. It was only his subconscious creating a nightmare image for later, then.

The grey walls, the smell of antiseptic and an underlying hum of misery accompanied them to the doctor's office.

Zhan was waiting for them. The orderly hadn't phoned ahead, so Dickson wasn't sure how news of their arrival had arrived before them. In the light, he was able to study her a little more: she was neat and self-contained, in a blue woollen suit today, closer to Garrett's age than his.

"Detectives. Here to see Mrs Sansom, I assume?"

Dickson nodded, caught Garrett doing the same from the corner of his eye.

"Fascinating case. How does one person suppress so much rage, for so long? She was bound to snap eventually." Zhan's clipped accent was hard to place.

"Just a breakdown then?" Dickson asked.

The doctor narrowed her eyes. "What else could it be, detective?"

Dickson shook his head and smiled disarmingly, but he could tell it failed. "Drugs, perhaps? Or maybe it wasn't her?"

"Oh, it was her alright. Now, did you want to talk to her? We have her on anti-psychotics and tranquilisers, but you may be able to get answers from her if you are clever. You are clever, aren't you, detective?" All her attention was on Dickson. What was she insinuating? He glanced at Garrett, who shrugged: remember the plan.

"Yes, doctor, we'd like to talk to her, and with you again. After."

***

SHE'D BEEN CLEANED up, of course, and her wild hair had been tamed into an Alice band. She also looked remarkably lucid. Especially considering the fact they had her on tranquilisers.

"Mrs Sansom? These are Detectives Dickson and Garrett. They'd like to ask you a few questions about your husband." The orderly showed them in and then went to stand in the corner, arms crossed, ready.

"You want to know why I killed him, don't you?" She smiled, with what Dickson thought was pity. It was not what he'd expected her to say.

"Well, yes." He slid into a plastic orange chair and Garrett dropped into the one next to him.

"You poor man," she said.

"I'm sorry?" Dickson was caught on the hop.

"You are in so much pain."

"I'm fine." Trying to gain control of the conversation, he said, "Now, about your husband."

"She did love you. It's just, well, it all become wrapped up in your son, didn't it? Oh, you poor man; that poor boy." Mrs Sansom appeared concerned.

Dickson could see Garrett's shocked expression.

"We are not here to talk about me. We are here to talk about your husband. You have left your children without a father."

"But you think about him every day, don't you? Little Thomas? So young…"

Dickson didn't know how she knew about his son, didn't want to know, didn't want to discuss it; his ulcer gnawed and gnawed, was suddenly a white-hot pain. He fumbled in his pocket for his pills, and his hand closed around his vibrating phone instead. He pulled it out and saw that it was Julia. He hit the call reject button and placed the phone on the desk. The woman the paper had named 'The saucepan murderess' didn't glance at it, but Garrett did.

"Aren't you going to see what Debela wants?" he asked.

What? Dickson frowned down at the phone – it was a missed

call from the chief pathologist. Why had he seen Julia's name flash up?

"I killed him because he was disrespectful. I had a psychotic break. Nice Doctor Zhan has shown me that. I will be all better soon. I want to stand trial. I know what I did was wrong," Mrs Sansom was saying, but Dickson was staring at his phone. There was a slick of cold sweat on his neck. His stomach, denied the pills he'd been going for, exploded in agony. He clutched at it and coughed.

"You okay, Dickson?" Garrett asked.

"The detective is not okay – the detective is in a lot of pain. Lots... of... pain. Pain." Mrs Sansom's voice descended in register, becoming harsher, more guttural. The lights in the room dimmed and Dickson glanced over his shoulder at the orderly, whose expression was blank. Maybe it was someone getting electroshock? As he turned back, he was hit by the smell of vanilla.

And rot.

"That fucking priest. I told him not to interfere, and now he's fucking dead. Fuck!"

Sansom leapt to her feet, her chair falling backwards to bang on the floor. She made a run for the door. The orderly moved to stop her, but Garrett grabbed hold of her first and she rounded on him with a punch to the gut that drove the air from his body and him to the floor. Dickson winced in sympathy, still bent over his own stomach pain.

As Sansom grinned at Garrett writhing in pain on the floor, the orderly lifted her from behind in some sort of wrestling hold. She shrieked and bucked.

"Let me go! Let me go! I will fuck you up, all of you..."

Her curses descended further until she was growling and snarling like a rabid animal. Dickson helped Garrett off the floor as the door burst open and two more orderlies and a nurse with a long, dripping syringe came in. The orderlies held Sansom steady whilst the nurse injected her. Dickson took his own medicine, watching warily. Within seconds she was limp.

"I hope you got what you came for, detectives," the first orderly said. His face impassive, the white of his uniform now soaking up blood from the many scratches the mad woman had given him.

Dickson grimaced and bent down to pick up his phone, setting off an orchestra of pain in his back.

"Open and shut case," he told the orderly.

As soon as the woman was removed, he phoned the chief.

The chief answered on the first ring. "Where the fuck are you?" he barked. "Father Millar is dead, get your arse here now." The chief ended the call before Dickson could even ask where. The church, he guessed.

Garrett looked a little green but was sucking in lungfuls of breath.

"We have to go. We'll forgo the pleasure of speaking to the good doctor for now. You okay?" he asked.

Garrett nodded, too winded to talk.

Dickson gave the first orderly he saw a message to tell the doctor to expect them back, and the two made their way to the car. Garrett was uncharacteristically quiet. Until Dickson started the car.

"You never told me you had a son."

Dickson sighed and closed his eyes for a good long second. When he opened them and looked at Garrett, at his open, questioning face, he tried to find the right words.

"I don't," he eventually said.

"But I thought she… she said Thomas… I thought… oh." Garrett for once seemed lost for words and stumbled to a stop. Dickson hated to think what the expression on his own face was showing. He put the car in gear and set off, with an inadvertent wheel spin. Garrett remained silent for the whole trip.

There was that, at least.

***

"SHIT!" GARRETT SEEMED even more green than before.

"And piss, and other excretions," Dickson replied, deadpan.

The scene of crime guys buzzed about the room collecting evidence.

"Is he shaved?" Garrett asked.

"Maybe it's a priest thing," Dickson said and shrugged. There was a faint whiff of vanilla in the room, masked by the stronger, more human smells. He had a flashback of the Sansom woman saying "fucking priest". And how had she known about Thomas?

"Hey, someone should check out what's in this bottle," Garrett said, crouching down. He held a hand over his face. Dickson thought he was clutching a handkerchief. One of the white-clad techs took photographs of everything.

"We'd best see what the ME has later," Dickson said, moving to the door. "Oh, and Garrett... let's get uniform to interview the parishioners – seems our priest was playing exhibitionist earlier today."

"Maybe he offed himself?" Garrett asked, before scrabbling round in a pocket.

"Maybe," Dickson answered, but it was too late: Garrett was on the phone; the honey, love, snookums noises alerted Dickson that it was to his wife. He sucked through his teeth. He idly thought about going back to the Temple of Bes. Maybe they wouldn't remember? Maybe the whore hadn't blabbed...

He turned to gaze again at the crumpled, empty vessel that had once been a man. He'd been aware of Millar. How could he not have been? They'd played cards once or twice, when Mayor Emeritus had let Dickson in on a game. Millar had hinted at deeper initiations, at a possible membership to something only vaguely described. Dickson was past feeling much in the way of ambition, though, so he'd played along. But only to a point. Now – perhaps he'd never know.

He gestured to the younger detective and motioned towards the door before exiting, hoping the younger man would follow him. He wanted to speak to Father Mandy and to a couple of the parishioners himself.

***

"WATCH IT!" GARRETT growled.

The car jerked to a stop, throwing the two men forward into the restraints of the seat belts. The same mongrel Dickson had almost run over scooted away from the headlights, with a black, oily coat swallowing the light. How come he hardly saw any dogs in this town, but he'd seen a couple in as many days? As he clambered out of the car, the sudden pain that shot up his leg made him stumble. Garrett, on the other side of the car, didn't seem to notice. Good job, too, he didn't need the younger man's pity. Although perhaps the younger man needed his. They'd been for a belly-buster to prepare for the day, but he suspected the younger man had already had breakfast, because he'd struggled to finish the full-cooked and looked distinctly queasy on the ride over. Dickson had spared no bump or bend. He wondered what Garrett would do if he just walked away from it all. Would the young sleuth come to look for him?

"The chief path here?" he asked the receptionist. She glanced up briefly from her nails and shrugged. They made their way to the morgue below the main hospital concourse, where they were greeted by the ME.

Debela smiled his death's head grin at them and, like a conjuror revealing a trick, he pulled the sheet from the corpse. Garrett, who had looked green coming down, went a very strange shade, turned and fled the room.

"Look," Dickson said in an urgent tone, "this needs to be an open and shut case, we need to determine cause, and who did it, quickly. Far too many damn people are dying at the moment, and we are under a lot of pressure. Give me something good!"

The ME nodded and gestured to the two waiting pathologists as Garrett returned, brushing water and vomit from his suit.

"Feeling better, rookie?" Dickson joked, earning himself

an evil look.

Garrett went over to the body, all professional now, nodding a thanks to Dickson as the older man handed him some Tic Tacs.

"What's that on his cheek?" he asked, his voice rough from calling for God on the great white telephone.

Dickson leant closer, feeling in his pocket for his glasses. He hesitated putting them on – they made him feel old and therefore obsolete.

The older pathologist shrugged and the younger said, "The body is more susceptible to bruising once rigor has set in."

Dickson shook his head angrily – he knew that. Hell, even the younger detective knew that. Damn medical types always assuming they knew more than you. He'd been taking his police exams when this one was still blowing snot-rockets in the playground. He took out a pencil and jabbed at the odd markings.

The ME angled his magnifying glass so the two detectives could see.

"Sar... sarbse? What is that? Latin?" Dickson traced the letters with his pencil. He'd wondered at the signs of the occult he'd seen in the room where Millar had been found but had dismissed them: they didn't want anything complicated here.

"It might be," replied Garrett eventually, "but the word is Esdras."

"How'd you figure?" he asked.

"The impression gets picked up in reverse. See?"

DC Garrett: super-sleuth.

"Didn't you ever play with Silly Putty when you were a kid?" Garrett had a smartarse grin on his face. Just when Dickson had thought that his IQ wasn't so miserable after all.

What the hell was Esdras? He called Dispatch and asked for a search on the term. "I think we might have something here," he said, and caught the ME looking a question at him. "I mean, a possible motive. Tell me how he died, doc."

"Poison. It was in the bottle. Not hugely sophisticated. I don't think he took his own life. Someone spiked the bottle we found at the scene." The ME seemed eager to make things simple.

"I see. So, all we need is a motive and a suspect. Thanks, doc." Dickson turned to Garrett. "Come on, let's see what uniform have for us from the parishioners."

"One more thing, detective," the ME said.

"Yes?"

"There is plenty of evidence that someone else was there. We have fingerprints, blood, hairs, skin in the form of dandruff, and a clear boot print. The murderer wasn't at all careful to conceal himself. Maybe he wants to be caught?" The ME's tone didn't change throughout, but Dickson could see that his earlier request to give him something good was being fulfilled.

As they approached the car, his phone buzzed, then buzzed again. Voice messages and text messages. He glanced at the screen. Julia!

He threw the keys at the younger cop with a, "Your turn to drive!" Garrett almost fumbled them. He wasn't usually allowed to drive.

As the car pulled away, Dickson placed the phone to his ear and flipped the switch for the blues and twos: he didn't want Garrett to overhear…

***

"Roj? Talk to me. We can't go on not talking."

Then why'd you leave, Julia?

"You're being unfair."

You're the one that left.

"Please, Roj. Call me. I miss you."

Not enough to stay!

"Thomas… I… shit, Roj – this is so hard."

It was your fault, your fault! YOUR fault – Roger Dickson jabbed the end call and his wife's sobs were immediately cut off.

He felt the younger man's eyes on him. He turned a warning glance at him. And you can fuck off, too!

Many of the texts were from dispatch – the word Esdras featured in several. They pulled up to the church.

***

ALL THE BUILDINGS were locked and no one came running when Dickson leant on the bell. Garrett jogged his elbow and when Dickson turned to look, the younger cop pointed to an open window.

"Okay, you climb it and then come let me in. I'll phone dispatch."

Garrett shucked off his jacket, folding it neatly on the doorstep, and climbed up the outside of the building.

Dickson's call got through, but the person on the other end was faint. He shouted, as if he were the one that had problems being heard.

"Did you say a book?" the cop on the other end said.

"Yes, a book, dammit!" He thought for a second. "Or something larger, with the word Esdras embossed on the cover. E-S-D-R-A-S."

The next thing the guy on the other end of the line said was garbled but sounded like a question.

"Because it's a vital piece of evidence!" He looked for the younger cop and saw him disappear through the window. Best wrap this up.

"Something, something case?" the man on the other end said indistinctly.

"Yes, it is now a murder case, Godammit…"

"Mumble mumble suit…ase."

What the hell? "Not a suitcase, a murder case!" A suitcase? Who was this guy? What was taking Garrett so long? There was a long, thin howl in the distance and Dickson spun round. The call dropped and, irritated, he saw that reception had given up completely. He put the phone away and drew his service revolver.

The howl came again, drawn out, plaintive. What was it with dogs in this town? There were very few, he knew, but the ones – one – he'd seen seemed somehow… wrong. It appeared to be the opposite of ill. That's the only way he could describe it: bursting with too much life, glossy, at its peak.

There wasn't a third howl.

There was a click behind him and the sound of the door opening, and he got a flash of what Garrett must be seeing: this old, broken down man, jumping at shadows, gun drawn. He forced himself to relax and turned round. That slow spiral was coming along nicely; he remembered the paranoia he got from uppers from when he was a kid, one of the reasons he'd stopped.

Garrett was pale and breathing heavily. "You'd best call the station. We have another murder."

Dickson drew out his phone to show that he had no signal and was surprised to see he had full bars. Damn network.

"I'd best take a look first," he said, and gestured for the younger cop to lead the way. He noticed the faecal stench of corrupted flesh straight away, which only got worse as they moved through the house. It was undercut with the tang of copper, indicating a large amount of spilled blood. When Garrett shoved open the white door to what was obviously a study, Dickson struggled to make sense of what he was seeing.

There was an underlying smell of vanilla, although all the windows were open and the curtains flapped in the wind like some giant bird's red wings. Father Mandy was all over the place. Dickson's eyes narrowed. There was a sense to this tableau, but he couldn't grasp it. It looked like a picture by that guy who painted melted clocks.

"It's getting harder and harder to pretend everything is alright in this town, isn't it?" Garrett asked.

Dickson just snorted and thumbed his phone to call it in. He decided that Garrett probably wouldn't try to find him. He didn't know if that made it easier or more difficult to contemplate walking away.

***

THE NEXT DAY, at the station, Dickson was updating the files on the many cases on his desk when an officer walked up.

"You'd best come see this, detective."

"What is it?" Dickson glanced at the officer, not someone he knew except as a face in the office.

"We have a confession for the Millar murder."

That got his attention. He levered himself up and limped after the officer into the interview room.

"Detective Dickson, this is Jona Mbabwe. He's come clean and confessed to the murder of Father Millar."

"Go fetch Garrett," Dickson said, and stood just inside the door staring at the man in the uncomfortable wooden chair, his hands clasped in front of him on the shiny grey desk. After looking up when Dickson was announced, he now stared at the surface of the table as though it held the secrets of the universe. Dickson threw some pills in his mouth and moved them around with his tongue, trying to summon enough spit to swallow them. He grimaced at the chalky bitter taste of the mixed painkillers and uppers. Round and round we go.

There was a knock at the door and Dickson opened it to let in Garrett. They pulled the slightly more comfortable chairs out and sat opposite Mbabwe.

"So, you're confessing to the murder of Father Millar?" Dickson said once they'd run through the man's rights and started the recording.

"Yes." Mbabwe didn't look up.

"It says here, in your file, that you were brought in for assaulting a police officer."

"Yes."

"Care to tell us about that?" Dickson kept his tone neutral.

"I wanted to get away. He was in the way. So I hit him."

"I see." Dickson slid the file over to Garrett to let him read the incident report.

Mbabwe was one of the parishioners that uniform had interviewed. Halfway through the interview he'd become agitated and tried to run. Very suspicious behaviour – and as he was now the main suspect, damning behaviour.

"Why, Jona? Why'd you do it?" Garrett asked, looking up from the file.

"Millar was an abomination! How could he call himself a priest? He was a fornicator!" Mbabwe's voice had risen so that on the word fornicator he was shouting. He sighed and looked back down to the table. "I'm glad he's dead."

"Glad you killed him, you mean?" Dickson asked.

Mbabwe looked up sharply, a snarl on his face. "Yes!"

Garrett flipped the file closed.

"Give us a full statement," he demanded.

Later, back at Dickson's desk, Garrett fiddled with the pencil sharpener clamped to the edge of the desk, flipping its rotating arm around. Always fidgeting, always annoying.

"Do you think he did it?" he asked the older cop.

"Does it matter? We have enough evidence to convict, and a confession."

"It matters. He can't have killed Mandy. Two priests offed in a day? That's got to be linked!" Garrett flipped the rotating arm again and Dickson found his hand, almost without volition, stopping it and slapping the top of the sharpener. The younger cop drew his hand back as if he'd inadvertently touched a snake.

"I need a break."

"Coffee?" Garrett asked.

"I need something more relaxing. Stress relief." Dickson took out his wallet and winced as he counted the notes. The Temple of Bes wasn't cheap. But he needed something.

"Stress relief?" the younger man asked.

"The temple."

Garrett shook his head.

"You don't have to be such a prissypants. It's perfectly possible to go and just have a spa, although the things the young ladies can do with their hands…"

"My wife would kill me," Garrett said, almost automatically.

"That's different."

"What?"

"Last time I asked, you said how much you loved your wife. Now you say she'd kill you. That's a whole different emotion, means you want to but are afraid. If there were absolutely no consequences, and your wife were never to find out, would you?"

Garrett rubbed the back of his neck, blushing a little. "No... no, I don't think so."

Dickson blew air out of his cheeks. He'd get the young man there in the future, he was sure of it now. But maybe not this time.

On the drive over he saw the same damn dog twice. But in places so far apart it wasn't physically possible. Must be two different dogs. He patted his pocket and felt the reassuring foil packet with its little blue pill. He wouldn't be humiliated this time. He switched his phone off and smiled softly. This would reverse the long spiral somewhat.

***

THE TOWN HAD gone a week without the number of deaths escalating, without falling further down the spiral, with only the ulcer and the sciatica to worry about, without seeing the dog again. Although his bins being upset by some animal was an almost nightly occurrence now.

That's why when he received the phone call about the 'suicide' he felt things starting to unravel again. His hard-won equanimity at the hands of the sweet ladies of Bes evaporated like so much mist. The body floating face down in the river, found by a couple of teenagers, was scarified and emaciated.

At the morgue, he and Garrett had listened patiently as the ME explained that the ancient symbols carved into the flesh were old wounds and the only fresh one was the large eye that stared bloodily from the young man's chest.

"Do we know who he is?" Dickson asked.

"Not yet. We are checking dental records, but to be honest it doesn't look like he's had any work done on his teeth for quite some time." The ME drew the man's lips apart, the rubber of his gloves squeaking a little on the dry gums. "See?"

Dickson leaned close and saw that the man's mouth was a graveyard of mostly brown stumps. None of the teeth that remained seemed to be filled.

"There may be childhood records. But frankly, he could have come from anywhere, and he was fished out of the river naked. His fingerprints are not on file. You'll have to scour the missing person's records." It was hard to read the ME – he was a cold fish, and his dull, monotone voice gave little away, but he did seem to hold some genuine regret that this wasn't going to be one of Dickson and Garrett's open and shut cases.

"It is what it is," Dickson sighed. "Let's get those symbols sent to an expert and hope for a break."

"The Refuse is linking this body to the murdered fathers, you know?" Garrett said, a note of disgust in his voice.

"Well, unless this joker has the book of Esdras inscribed on his skin, I'm going to treat it as unrelated," Dickson replied.

***

WHEN HE STOPPED to think how little progress they'd made over the past few weeks, Dickson was puzzled – why hadn't the chief brought in some big guns from out of Refuge?

They'd spent weeks futilely chasing their tails while more and more bizarre happenings – well – happened.

He had a whisky and was sniffing and throwing his switchblade into the wee hours again. As the clock's hands almost lined up on the number three, it came as no surprise to get the call.

"Deeetective!"

"Detective?"

"We got a bite on the symbols. Professor type, wants us to drive out to his place to discuss."

Dickson glanced at the clock. "At oh-three-fifteen hours?"

"Right now. Yup. Hush, Betsy."

Dickson folded the knife and placed it in its holster.

"Sooner started…" he muttered.

"Roger, Roger and out, out." The click when the younger man hung up was loud in Dickson's ear.

As he opened the door, there was a blur of movement and something low to the ground shot out of his drive. He found himself automatically drawing his gun as one of his bins toppled onto the drive, spilling its contents.

"Son of a bitch." That damn dog was responsible. He righted the bin and swept the rubbish up; he'd watch for that little fucker later, and from now on. A swift bullet to its brain would sort it out.

He waved to Garrett's wife; she held a grizzling daughter. "She still ill?" he asked as the younger man sank into the passenger seat.

"Betsy? Yeah, still got an infection, running a fever." Garrett turned to look at the older cop, who was wincing and popping a handful of pills. "Back still crook?"

"Don't get old, son. It's a bitch," Dickson said with a grimace.

"Live fast, die young, leave a good-looking corpse. Gotcha," the younger man said with a grin.

"So, what's the story with the Prof?" Dickson asked, easing the car out into the road.

"Dunno. The name's Kingstone, odd card by all accounts, on the files as the man to go to for 'occult' shit."

Dickson nodded and tuned the other man out when he started talking about his wife's book club. He paid no attention to the man's wittering until he stopped mid-flow and said: "That's the place."

The large stone house stuck out amongst its wooden neighbours. The professor had some money, it seemed.

As they walked up the path to the scabrous black door there was a thin howl in the distance. Dickson placed his hand on his gun. When they knocked on the door there was a second, louder, closer howl.

"What the hell…?" Dickson gripped his revolver, ready to whip it out.

"Damn strays."

The door opened, and framed within was a bear of a man: long, seagull-grey beard, stout frame.

"Detectives?" he said.

"I'm Dickson, this is Garrett. We believe you have something for us?" Dickson said.

The man rubbed his hands down his belly, held behind a straining waistcoat. There was a third, closer, much louder howl that split the air and made all three men jump.

"Inside. Quickly… quickly!"

The two detectives didn't question, but scurried inside as the professor held the door open. Dickson grimaced as he was forced to push past the man's belly. He disliked touching people.

"What the hell is that?" Dickson asked as the professor closed the door.

The professor ignored the question, striding past the detectives.

"Drink?"

The two detectives shared a glance.

"Just a water for me," Garrett said

"Whisky? Scotch, Islay, if you have it," Dickson said.

"Expensive tastes." The professor sounded impressed.

"Not to put too fine a point on it – why the hell did you drag us out here in the middle of the night?"

There was a sudden, loud scrabbling at the door, an animal's claws scoring the wood. All three men paused and their heads turned towards the sound.

"It wants in," Garrett said.

"Ah, I was… err… afraid of that. That's why I called," the professor said sheepishly.

"What?" Dickson whirled round to stare at the professor.

"I think I inadvertently summoned something. Here to the house, that is. It was already here in town, called from some well of grief, or despair," he said. "You'd best come through to the study."

The detectives followed the rotund professor into his study, which was adrift in paper. Stacks of books leant precariously against each other and the walls, or were propped on, or stacked under the desk. It looked as though the professor had opened half a dozen of them and emptied his filing cabinets, as loose paper littered every surface.

"Make yourselves... well, erm, just wait here. I'll get those drinks." The professor bustled out and the detectives looked around the room in bewildered silence.

"Summoned?" Garrett said at last.

"Ghouls and ghosties, remember? There's a perfectly good explanation, always, remember?" Dickson said, but didn't know if he was trying to convince the younger man or himself.

"Well, here we are." The professor hurried back into the room with a silver tray and on it were three glasses – one short, one long and one fancy. He gave the short one to Dickson with a healthy measure of amber liquid in the glass. The long one, full of water, he gave to Garrett and took the fancy looking one himself; it was filled with a deep ruby liquid that almost glowed within the cut glass.

"Bottoms up!" he said, and dashed off whatever it was in his glass in one gulp. Garrett politely sipped his water and Dickson took a long sniff of whisky, awakening his ulcer which gnawed at him in anticipation. The whisky was smoky, smelling of salty fires.

"Lagavulin," the professor said with a small nod, encouraging him to drink. There was a bang as something threw itself at the door.

"Why don't you tell us what's going on, Prof?" Dickson said reluctantly, putting the glass down on top of a book opened to a drawing of a demonic being that was flayed open.

"Well, that's just it, isn't it? I took the drawings you sent me, the police sent me, and looked them up. They were some sort of summoning ritual that I... ah... that I accidentally read out and—"

There was another bang, rattling the door, and a scream, that surely came from no dog's throat, no animal's throat even. A cold shiver travelled down Dickson's spine.

"What the hell is it?" he asked, all pretence that there was something normal about tonight abandoned.

"It's some form of ghast, I think," the professor said, before steepling his fingers under his lips. The detectives exchanged a puzzled glance. "I don't know for certain, though."

The noises suddenly stopped. Dickson's head whipped round to look at the door. "It's just a hungry dog," he said.

Garrett pulled his gun. "Let's put it down, Roger," he said.

Dickson nodded and pulled his own gun.

"Gentlemen. It's not a dog, it's a creature from... well, that is... it's not from here."

"Should we call animal control?" Garrett asked, with a nervous sideways glance at Dickson.

"Fuck that. I'm going to get this fucker once and for all. Teach him to knock my bins over." Dickson strode over to the door and threw it open. The doorstep was empty. "It's in the garden."

He gestured to Garrett to head right as he went left.

He stuck to the wall of the house as he stalked forward, gun ready. As he turned the second corner, he saw it: it was as large as a man, head down. He didn't hesitate but put three shots into it.

The creature fell, looking more like a man than it should, looking almost exactly like a man. He opened his eyes as wide as he could. They weren't so good in low light. The light from the window didn't stretch as far as the creature, but it was lying still. He crept closer...

Garrett lay on the lawn unmoving, three bullet holes in him. Dickson dropped his revolver in horror and fell to his knees next to the young cop.

"Shit. Shit. Shit..."

He felt for a pulse. He could see where Garrett had slipped on the wet grass, where he'd gone down on hands and knees.

Why had he mistaken him for a large dog?

"Daddy?" A small voice behind him.

He spun round. "What the fuck?"

Like a hole in the night, a shape resolved slowly. It was upright-boy-shaped.

"Thomas?" he said with wonder. How?

"Please don't hurt me, Daddy—" the small voice said. Why wouldn't his son come out of the shadows? He had nothing to fear from his father. "—not like Mummy did."

Tears tracked down Dickson's face and he held his arms out wide. His whole right side was on fire as the slipped disc pressed on the nerve.

Father Mandy's voice echoed inside his head: "Ashes to ashes…"

He shook his head.

"No," he said softly.

His wife's hysterical voice the last time he'd spoken to her: "I swear if you leave this house… If you go to those whores again… I'll make you regret it… Your son is sick, and you've left it all to me to do. I'm the one that has to do everything. If you walk out that door you will regret it. For the rest of your miserable life!"

"No. Please… please." He was oblivious to the seep of liquid into his trousers, the pool of expanding blood he knelt in. He didn't know where his gun was.

"I'm coming, Daddy. Catch me?" the tiny voice said in the same tones his son would have used.

The chief's voice: "She used your own gun. She made sure. The boy first, then her. I'm sorry, Roger."

Sorry. Everyone was sorry. The lieutenant talking of being sorry that he'd have to start proceedings against him. His colleagues muttering sorry, not being able to look at him. The mayor, who'd got him reinstated as a small favour, upon each favour he did in return, saying, "sorry, not this time" when he asked if he'd paid off the debt. No one was sorrier than him.

His own gun.

"Wheeeee!" the creature said, speaking with his son's voice as it ran towards him. He kept his arms outstretched, ready to catch his boy.

As the monster's jaws snapped shut on his neck, his arms came around it, flick knife in one hand. He plunged it into the creature's side, over and over, slower and slower, as his strength fled in great spurts down its throat. Its jaws gaped open and it rolled off him, flanks heaving, its own blood gushing in glistening black arcs. Dickson sensed his own eyes dimming, his vitality waning, the darkness encroaching.

I'll catch you if you fall, Thomas. I'll be there for you, he mouthed, shadows falling.

I will never let you come to harm... ever... again.

A Signal in the Dark

RHEA PLANTED HER feet wide and slammed the beacon into the regolith. The beacon's simple Artificial Intelligence (AI) kicked in as the probe burrowed its way into the planetoid and the beacon's flashing red light became a baleful lighthouse to the void; broadcasting Jianxi's claim to the minerals and providing a homing beacon to the mother mining ship, the *Aphra*.

She recited the company protocol without reference to the little plastic card all scout ships were given. "I claim this solar body in the name of the Jianxi mining corporation in accordance with the laws set under directive 22a. I formally renounce any claim over this land in return for the usual finder's fee."

It was a stupid and pointless piece of bureaucracy but kept claim disputes to a minimum.

Most of the Trans-Neptune Orbit bodies (TNOs) had been found, labelled, claimed and plundered but scouts like her still occasionally came across ones, like this, that neither of the big mining companies had on their records.

Back onboard she heated some slop in a cup. She took the steaming mug and plopped into the drive seat. As she spooned the 'tasty' nutrimeat into her mouth she scanned the nearest TNOs. The Oort was a million miles from Titan (well, thousands of Astronomical Units (AUs) anyway) – arse end of the Solar System. As expected, nothing was happening. She swirled the slop around her mouth; it was bland; but EVA's (Extravehicular

Activities) always made her hungry, it was Pavlovian.

***

"SAFIE, PUT THE ball away!" Always the child made noise.

"Safie, are you listening to me?"

Rhea sighed and clambered out of bed, the sound of the ball bouncing against the hull repetitive and annoying. It almost sounded electronic, the squeak it made against the metal. The ship hummed in sleep and Rhea didn't want to wake too much. Safie playing with a ball would do it though.

"Safie! You know I have to go to work in the morning."

She cursed as she stood on some piece of a toy awaiting her like a caltrop.

"Safie! You stop this instant! If you haven't stopped by the time I get to your bedroom, I'll-" The sound of the ball stopped and Rhea sighed again. She pushed the door open into her child's dark room.

Safie was in the corner, head bowed, long blonde hair like a waterfall over her legs. Her tiny hand clutched a red ball.

"Safie, you should be in bed, come on now." Rhea put on her stern voice and climbed on the bed, fluffed a pillow and then patted it. "It's time to sleep."

"No."

"Safie, don't answer back, it's time to sleep, it's time little girls like you were in bed."

"No." The child shook her head violently, threw the ball against the wall and then caught it.

"Safie, I-"

Safie threw the ball again but this time mistimed the catch. As the ball bounced over to the bed she turned to watch, and Rhea's breath caught in her throat.

The girl's deep, black eyes bored into her, staring from a grey, rotting face set in a rictus grin.

"I don't need to sleep, Momma. I'm dead, remember?"

Rhea sat up clutching her cold, clammy chest, heart stuttering. She clapped the light on and waited for her breathing to calm. Safie had been dead for five years – she usually only dreamt about her when very anxious.

The dreams where Safie was alive were worse, then she awoke feeling happy, but reality asserted itself with a crash. The nightmares were easier to bear. At least that's what she told herself.

It had been a stupid accident that had taken her little girl away. The headmaster of the Vale school had been skimping on maintenance in order to shave extra profit from the obscene amounts he charged the parents. There'd been a seal failure, a slow outgassing, faulty emergency procedures, faulty doors. In all, twelve children had died.

"I see you're already awake," the AI chirped. "You have a message."

Distress signal coming from Orcus, please investigate, she read.

Distress signal?

"Ship, do we have a claim on Orcus?"

"No, that's one of Vale's."

"Fucking Mudders!" Rhea spat. "Can we ignore it?"

"Rules are rules." A phrase the AI had used a few times before with her.

"Fuck." She supposed it made sense. If she were in trouble, she'd accept help from anyone, including Mudders, but she wouldn't like it.

"Okay, set a course." She finished her slop glumly and tapped out a reply. Now to have a rubdown and change out of the suit. Dreaming of Safie reminded her of Titan and the Zone. Full of Vale's bigwig brats. That's why she'd taken a job with Jianxi. Working for the competition was a small revenge every day.

When she got back to the console, she was surprised to see a request for a two-way comm. She thumbed the panel to open the link.

"Rhea, what a pleasure it is to see you up and dressed!" The blond face of Stevenson filled the screen, his clean white teeth set in a stupid grin.

"You're never going to let me forget that, are you?" she groaned.

"Aww, I thought your bed head was cute."

Once, when she was relatively new to the scout business, she'd thought a request for a two-way comm was an emergency and had answered despite just waking up. Naked. Not that he'd seen anything, but it was obvious that she'd been unclothed, and of course he'd said something, and she'd blushed.

She wasn't much of a blusher anymore though.

"What's up?" she asked.

Stevenson sighed and, rubbing his beard, switched to business. "That distress call you're on your way to?"

"The Mudder one?"

Stevenson winced. "The Vale one, yes. Well, it's only the son of the big boss. That's got the brass's knickers in a twist."

"Baxter's precious boy, out here?"

"Seems so. So, act delicately and put on your Sunday best spacesuit. And for God's sake don't call him a Mudder to his face!" Stevenson scratched his ear, sure sign that there was something else. It was one of the tells she used to fleece him at cards when she was aboard the mining ship.

"What else?" she asked with a sigh.

"Well…"

"Yeah, spit it out, man!"

"Joby answered the call, too."

"And what? You think that just because we split and I broke his jaw for cheating on me, we won't be able to be professional?" Wait till she saw that little shit, there was definitely unfinished business there.

The reason she'd been in the Zone in the first place was because of Joby. He'd insisted that their little girl go to the best school on Titan. Together they could just about afford the fees, but if their child's education wasn't important, what was?

When Safie died they split. Badly.

"Just, you know, try not to kill him until after the job is done." Stevenson only knew some of the story; Joby had been mostly absent even when they were together. Safie's death had been the end though. She'd left an uncomfortable pause.

"I'll try."

After signing off she thought she should thank Stevenson for the heads-up. When she got back, she'd buy him a drink.

"Ship, what's our ETA?"

"Four hours, seven minutes and twenty-three seconds."

"Right, I'm going to rest my eyes, tell me when we're thirty minutes away."

OF COURSE, AFTER being reminded of Joby she dreamed of Titan. Of their apartment, owned, like everything in the Zone, by the mining corp. All the facts from that horrible day, a day she couldn't forget no matter how she'd tried to blot it, came rushing back.

Of course the man responsible had got off on some technicality. Although, he'd committed suicide. Couldn't live with twelve dead kids on his conscience. She dreamt again of the vidcast of the news of his death. The awful sinking feeling as she realised he'd escaped.

***

THE BINARY OF Orcus and Vanth filled the screen and a list of facts scrolled down the right-hand side. Rhea could see the mining ship squatting on the planet like a giant leech. The signal was just the standard CQD – All Stations Distress, no other signal or explanation.

Rhea rubbed her eyes then ran her fingers through her stubbly hair. God damn Joby and God damn all fucking Mudders. She took a long slow inhale, held it then blew it out explosively. Time to go to work.

"Ship, can you zoom in on the mining ship at all?"

The image on the screen zoomed in. Everything looked normal. But she could only see one side of the ship, the other being in deep shadow.

"I have failed to handshake with the Vale ship," the AI informed her.

"Neither of them?" Rhea asked, searching the image for a transporter.

"There is only the mining ship there," the AI responded.

Curious.

"Check Vanth?"

"I have done. There are no other ships here."

No other ships. Perhaps her ex had been and gone and never bothered to tell her? But he'd have told the *Aphra* surely?

"Ship, can you do a search for nearby scouts?" Rhea rubbed sleep out of her eyes and slurped the last of her coffee. Time to suit up.

"Scanning."

As the ship approached the landing pad the AI informed her that there were no other scouts in range of her sensors.

Curiouser and curiouser.

Rhea broke out the regulation sidearm and strapped it to her leg. "What do you think this is? High Noon at the Mudder corral?" she murmured to herself. She must be nervous, she only talked to herself when she was nervous.

She asked the ship to ping a message to the *Aphra* to say she'd landed.

***

Little puffs of red dust followed her giant steps across the planetoid. It was rich in iron, which was why she assumed the mining ship was here. She wondered where the Mudder mothership was. And why it hadn't sent anyone to come and rescue the son of the boss.

The airlock was wide open. Both doors, complete

decompression. If Baxter wasn't in a suit this was going to be a very short rescue mission. The power was off, on emergency lights only, the CQD on a loop.

She headed to the control room. She hated Vale ships, so cramped. Their tiny Mudder bodies needed less room than her people. All that gravity crushing them into dwarfs.

She surveyed the wreckage a meteor had strewn across what was left of the control room. Anyone on the ship, and she'd seen no sign of life as yet, would have had seconds to suit up after an explosive decompression. At least there'd been no fire, no oxygen to burn.

This ship was going nowhere. The engines were still sound, but the brain of the ship was dead. So where was Baxter? Did he have oxygen? The ship failed to generate an atmosphere.

She did a thorough search. No one. She found a vid-cube which, from a quick glance, was Baxter sending a message to someone called Madeleine. She pocketed it and made her way to the airlock.

"Ship?"

Rhea listened to her own breathing and frowned. "Ship?"

No answer.

As she thumbed the door release, she spotted a puff of gas coming from her own ship. A hull breach?

She bounced across to her ship as fast as she could. Beneath it lay a jumble of equipment. She frowned. What had he done? "Ship?"

Inside it was worse. The command centre was dark. The AI, dead. The ship was grounded. That fucking Mudder must have been hiding somewhere and took the opportunity to destroy her ship whilst she was searching for him. To rescue him. She turned the air blue. She took a calming breath. She could still fly without the AI, if nothing else important was broken.

Outside, her heart sank to see vital components smashed beyond repair. She glanced across to the mining ship. There might be parts there she could possibly scavenge and jury rig.

She was dead in a few hours if she couldn't get the oxygen generator working.

A shadow passed above her and she glanced up to see another scout ship in low orbit. Joby. So maybe she didn't need to scavenge anything.

"Hey Joby, can you hear me?"

"Yes, I can hear you." Joby sounded flat – angry?

"Well, get your arse down here, that fucking Mudder has wrecked my ship!" She fingered her gun, scanning the planetoid for movement. The dark blotting out of stars that was Vanth stole across the landscape, creeping ever closer.

"No, Rhea, he didn't."

"What are you talking about? He's killed the AI and wrecked the engines, I'm dead in the water here." She continued to scan her surroundings. There were lots of hiding places.

"It wasn't him, Rhea."

That was the annoying thing about Joby. She'd been attracted to his taciturnity, assuming, naively, that still waters ran deep. However, in Joby's case it was all shallows.

"Well, there's no one else here to do it…" Apart from Joby, that is. But he wouldn't, would he?

"The *Aphra* was very sad to hear about your accident, Rhea." He sounded tired rather than angry. "I'm sure that the reward that Baxter senior is offering for the return of his boy will assuage my obvious grief at your predicament."

"You fucker."

"That's what I like about you, Rhea, always so ladylike."

"I'll kill you!" She started bounding towards the mining ship. That fucking Mudder offering a reward? That was just so typical of those grasping planet-crawlers, everything was about money. Fuck Baxter and fuck his son.

"You tried that already, remember? I was sucking my meals through a straw for weeks. I swore that I'd pay you back for that. Getting a reward to do so is going to be so sweet."

"Be a man. Come and kill me. Because if you leave me here, I will escape and will track you down and will kill you." She reached the mining ship and yomped to the engines.

"With Junior here unconscious and no one else going to come rescue you, my version of events will be the truth. By the time anyone comes to collect the scrap you'll be long forgotten." The orbiting scout ship's rockets fired, and the ship moved off. "So long Rhea, and good riddance."

She didn't waste her breath on a reply.

Twenty minutes later she knew she was fucked. The Vale engine design was vastly different from hers. If she'd had specialist tools, and a lot of time, she could potentially jig something together. If her AI was sound, she could possibly have combined it with the mining ship somehow. Think Rhea, think.

She bounced back to her ship, perhaps she could get the communicator working? An honest appraisal of the mess Joby had left the instrument panel in told her otherwise.

She had possibly twelve hours of oxygen. Neither ship would generate an atmosphere; the mining ship's generator was fine, although the hull was breached catastrophically. There was nothing wrong with her hull. Since she couldn't think of how to get off-planet, her problem was how to keep herself alive for longer than twelve hours?

The mining ship had some cutting tools and she had a small maintenance kit aboard her scout. Four hours of cutting, lumping equipment across the surface and soldering later and she had an oxygen generator. It might not have been working at maximum efficiency, but it was going to keep her alive and give her a lot more than twelve hours.

Now to the more intractable problem. Over hot food and drink, thank the stars Joby hadn't sabotaged the micro-kitchen, she puzzled it out. She had a very real problem – people thought that Baxter was saved, so would ignore the CQD, and that she was dead, so not a priority to retrieve her body. She had no next of kin, her folks back on Titan had died years ago, she was split from Joby, and Safie was gone. Stevenson would raise a hip flask to her memory and that was about it. Getting mixed up in Mudder business had fucked her yet again. First Safie, now this.

She was dead on her feet. She had to sleep on her problem, but she needed to fuel her body, too – lots of physical exertion needed lots of calories, needed lots of slop.

***

SHE WAS BACK on Titan, it played in her dreams over and over, toxic memories. The graveyard. She ran her hand over the gravestone, the span of years accorded to her daughter pathetically small, and wiped a tear away. She whispered a prayer, not believing a word of it. He'll be punished, her mouth said, her eyes hard, determined not to cry.

She turned and there was another grave. The Mudder that had killed her daughter. His lifespan many multiples of hers. Even if he'd taken his own life, he didn't deserve to be in a grave, didn't deserve to be remembered with anything but contempt. She found she had a beacon in her hand and rammed it into the grave. Its flashing red light a warning and a message. This is not for you, Mudders. Jianxi, come and strip this place.

The red flashing light.

***

AS SHE AWOKE she remembered the red flashing light. Of course, the beacons, she had about twenty of them. She couldn't reprogram them, but she could put them in an aesthetically pleasing SOS shape for when the *Aphra* came over the horizon; the multitude of homing signals would definitely grab its attention.

She could hardly get the suit on fast enough. Why hadn't she thought of it before? Exhausted from lugging all that equipment, stressed and angry too.

Later, as she stood back and admired her giant blinking SOS, she allowed herself to fantasise about catching up with Joby. She hoped that Stevenson, or one of the other officers, was, even now, trying to contact her. When they couldn't, they'd know her comms were out and send someone.

The signal would take a while to get through, she could add a few more calories with breakfast. As ever the EVA had left her feeling hungry. She was sure she'd soon be burning them off.

Four hours later and no sign of a rescue ship. Yes, the *Aphra* had been days away but there must be another scout out here? She wasn't used to idleness, and it gave her too much time to think, about everything. So, she decided to see what else was salvageable from the Mudder ship. She spent a few hours collecting a pile of things that could be re-used.

Later, back on her own ship, she thought she was too wound up for sleep, but her eyes sagged closed anyway. She hoped she wouldn't dream again.

***

A BRIGHT FLASH woke her and as she stumbled to the porthole, she slapped her hand to her hip to feel the reassuring weight of the gun. If Joby had come back she was going to shoot the bastard.

A ship. A sleek, but obviously Mudder, ship, descended on a pillar of smoke from out of the heavens. She was ready to leave at a moment's notice, so she grabbed her helmet and made her way to the airlock.

She stood outside her ship and watched the two squat figures bound over. Both held firearms. She frowned at that and her hand hovered near her own gun.

"Drop the weapon and put your hands up!" a voice, low, guttural, Earth-accented, ordered.

She shrugged, took her gun from its holster and threw it to one side.

"Now, get on your knees," the voice ordered.

"I'm not a danger. I'm *in* danger!" she protested.

"Do it! Now!" The two figures gestured with their guns. She reluctantly complied. One of them covered her, the other gambolled over, moved behind her and grabbed her hands and tied them behind her back with what felt like cable ties.

"Hey!" she protested, but the figure behind her bundled her to the floor.

"Secure!" A woman's voice.

"Now you'll see what you get for attacking Vale employees and destroying company property," the first, male, said.

"I didn't do—"

"Quiet!"

Rhea struggled and swore and ranted but they bundled her securely and ignored her shouted imprecations so that she eventually fell silent.

The two Mudders frogmarched her to their ship. She wasn't allowed to grab any personal items. The woman had done a cursory search. Rhea got no reply when she'd asked them what they were looking for.

She was shoved into a hastily emptied cargo space, barely enough room to sit, and the door locked. The ship took off, Rhea was jostled and bruised as she wasn't strapped down. Then the artificial gravity kicked in and it pulled at her like none she'd ever felt before. It must have matched Earth's gravity. She had trouble breathing and ached as the G's sucked at her.

The woman, stout, like all Mudders, burst into the room and wrestled Rhea's helmet off.

"Let's see what a would-be murderess looks like!"

As the helmet came off Rhea took a long breath and closed her eyes. Opening them again she stared into a snarling face.

"Murderess?"

"Yes, you lanky bastard, a murderess." The woman sat back on her haunches. Rhea was prone, she'd not managed to get up after launch.

"I'm no murderess, nor attempted one either."

"So why did you attack Baxter and try to prevent your fellow

Giraffe from rescuing him then?" the woman grunted and stood, not waiting for an answer.

Giraffe? That's what the Mudders called people from the outer planets, just because they were naturally taller having grown in a lower gravity. What had Joby told them?

"Whatever Joby said is a lie!" she tried.

"Tell it to the judge," the woman threw back before closing the door.

No matter how she looked at it this was bad. But at least she was no longer on Orcus, right?

***

AFTER A FEW hours they fed her and took the cable ties off. As she rubbed some life back into her hands she tried to get some sense out of them. From what the man said she assumed that Joby had spun a tale of her and Baxter fighting over mining rights, her attacking Baxter and Joby riding to the rescue. The nerve of the man!

She put her side to them. They didn't buy it. But she asked that they contact Stevenson on the *Aphra* who'd back up at least part of her story. That she'd responded to the distress signal.

After they were gone she tried to make herself comfortable and something sharp jabbed her in the hip. The vid-cube! The woman hadn't taken it away.

She took it out and pressed play. Maybe Baxter explained why he'd called for help. If her captors didn't trust her maybe they'd trust him? She placed the cube on the floor as the features of Baxter, a typical Mudder, short, muscular, thick featured, sprang into view. He was helmetless, not the best sign, and he looked tired; perhaps this was before the accident?

"Hey Madeleine. Hey you. It's Daddy. I had to go far away, remember? Well, look."

Baxter grabbed the camera and panned it around the ship. Rhea recognised the one she'd been scavenging from but in pristine condition. He pointed the camera out of the window and the familiar binary of Orcus and Vanth could be seen as the ship approached them.

"Grandpa and Daddy had an argument, honey. That's why Daddy had to go. Had to prove to Grandpa that Daddy could do a good job. That he could provide for his daughter."

The camera swung back to point at Baxter again.

"That's why Daddy is in space. I'll be back real soon, just as soon as I've collected a ton of ore. Love you and miss you."

There was a fade.

The vid clicked on to a scene of utter chaos. A helmeted Baxter sat in front of a kaleidoscope of small flying debris, the command centre far in the background a maelstrom as the atmosphere disappeared.

"Maddy, be good for your mother. I love you! It might take me a bit longer to come home."

Baxter looked off-screen as there was a loud noise, like a tree cracking in the wind. Something fast swiped him away from the screen, then the screen itself tumbled, went black.

Rhea had her hand to her mouth. Baxter knew that everything was going to shit and his first thought was to contact his daughter. She had been gritting her teeth when she first started watching. What advantage could she get with the vid? How could she use it to get one over on those people? But now? She sat stunned.

Baxter was just a father who loved his daughter and was trying to do what was best for her. To show her that he wasn't a good-for-nothing. Her cheeks blazed yet also felt wet. He was just like her. She wondered when she'd started thinking that they were all evil, all culpable, and realised that Joby's casual bigotry had seeped into her soul at some point and put down roots after Safie's death. Caused by a Mudder. The very word one of Joby's...

She banged on the door. Her captors, no longer just Mudders but other folk, needed to see this. It exonerated her, it showed that Baxter was injured in the accident.

The woman was the one that came, her face full of suspicion.

"Here, watch this." Rhea thumbed play and handed it to the woman who reluctantly turned her eyes to the video. When it finished the woman didn't say anything, she just closed the door and took the vid-cube with her.

***

RHEA WAITED FOR her boarding call. The transporter that would return her to Titan was predictably delayed. The Vale base on Neso was where the scout ship that had picked her up on Orcus had deposited her. They'd consulted with Vale head office, as well as the *Aphra*, and by general consensus she was exonerated and freed. No apology.

She'd had to pay for transport herself. The *Aphra* would return to Titan in a few months and she could sign back on if she wanted to. Joby had brought Baxter here to Neso and then left again, destination unknown. Guilt assuaged by the pay-out he'd received from Baxter senior.

Her ship was lost – she'd get a fraction of its cost through insurance, but she was still alive at least. There was some activity at the boarding desk, it wouldn't be long now. She sighed and returned to her book but looked up as a shadow fell across it.

"Hello." Baxter junior seemed younger in person than he had on the vid.

She put the book down and stood, found herself shaking his out-thrust hand.

"Mr Baxter, this is unexpected."

"Rhea, isn't it? Can I call you Rhea?" he smiled, his seeming self-assurance belied by the searching quality of his eyes.

"Sure." She was at a loss. What did he want?

"I thought I'd come and thank you for returning the vid-cube. And for coming to save my life, even if that didn't go to plan."

"You're welcome. How's your daughter?"

Baxter smiled genuinely this time. "Very happy her daddy is safe and not likely to run off back into space alone any time soon. She's looking forward to getting me home."

Rhea smiled in return. The first boarding call was given, people who needed assistance, people with children, gold card members etc. "Good, good, I'm glad. It was nice of you to come and see me off," she said, grabbing her bag ready to join the economy queue.

"I just thought I should come and tell you that the man who brought me here, Joby, he was heading to Mars. He had some plan to spend his money on a little unit there and stop tramping across the Kuiper belt and Oort cloud." Baxter offered his hand again.

As she shook it Rhea asked, "Why tell me?"

"I've read up on you. I'm sorry about your daughter. You didn't deserve what that man did to you. His treatment of me was entirely motivated by greed. I grow tired of people who only ever seek to take advantage of me." He smiled again as they shook hands. "You'd best get on, wouldn't want to miss your flight. It was good meeting you."

"Nice to meet you too," she said automatically. He gave her one last grin then strode off as she turned and joined the shuffling line on its way to the transporter.

Mars! It made sense, she supposed. It had mostly Earth colonies but there were plenty of people from the outer planets that had made their home there too. It was still sparsely populated, the gravity wasn't as crushing as Earth, and it was a big planet to get lost on. They'd even talked about it, gathering enough money to retire to Mars and get a little place. Once she settled in her seat she'd see how much a ticket to Mars would cost.

***

RHEA VISUALISED JOBY waking from the deep dark dream the drugs she'd slipped into his food unit would have put him in. He wouldn't be sure what had woken him, some noise? As she thought about him fumbling in the dark she wondered if he'd realise it wasn't a sound, it was lack of noise. The lights wouldn't switch on. The entire compound would be dark. There'd still be a hiss from the atmospherics but all the other usual machinery noises would be ominously silent. She grinned and checked her chronometer, he'd slumber for hours after he consumed the doctored slop. The hardest part was waiting, motionless, hidden behind the panels, for him to stumble to bed. Sabotaging his pod was child's play.

She pictured him rushing in panic to the suits, where he'd find them slashed and useless, all but one. That's when he'd find her note.

Joby

I did promise that I'd kill you but I've had a bit of a change of heart. So I'm going to give you the same chance you gave me. Give or take.

I've disabled all but the life support. You have no transport. No communications and no portable oxygen.

Unlike what you did to me, one of your neighbours could probably wander past and rescue you. You have been making friends, haven't you? You've not just been hiding out?

Unlike you I don't have a big pay-out to moderate my guilt.

I'll be going back to Titan to visit our daughter's grave.

I consider us to be even. Don't make the mistake of escalating this.

Rhea.

His nearest neighbour was around sixty kilometres away. She hoped the darkness outside of Joby's window would seem very lonely.

***

AS RHEA'S SHUTTLE took off she relaxed back in her seat and took out a photograph of her daughter, letting herself remember the happy memories. Safie was wearing a green party dress, holding a fairy wand and grinning without a care in the world. It had been taken on her birthday – she hadn't seen another one. Rhea smiled sadly and whispered, "I'm coming home, Safie. No more running away."

Thresholds

"JUST YOU AND me, girl, against the world." The cat agreed with him by rolling its head against his fingers and purring. It's what he'd always said to Barbara, his wife, back in the day. The doorbell rang and he rattled the kibble next to the chair to get the cat off his lap. He slept in the chair nowadays, as it reclined. The tablet was connected wirelessly to the door camera and locking mechanism. He peered at the picture the CCTV showed him. A young woman, late twenties or early thirties. Smartly dressed and prepared for the weather. Beyond, he could see an expensive looking car. The route from chair to door control was well-worn, as was the one to the toilet, and the one to the kitchen. He thumbed the intercom.

"Hello?"

"Mr... ah, Randall?" she said, consulting a notebook.

"Yes?"

"I'm Kathy Goddard from social services. Could I come in please? We need to do an assessment."

His finger hovered over the door lock button.

"What happened to Lisa? What sort of assessment?" The cat slinked around his legs.

"Miss Henderson is no longer with us, I'm afraid. You need to let me in. I'm here to assess your needs." She looked directly at the camera and gave a professional smile. He frowned.

"No longer with us? Is she dead?"

"No. No! Of course not. She's no longer with the department."

But she wouldn't have just abandoned him. Would she?

He pressed to unlock the door and shuffled back to the recliner. He remembered what the rest of the house had looked like. When Barbara was alive. Before he'd tried to save her. Before he knew about the threshold. So he could picture the new social worker walking down the corridor, maybe looking up the stairs, maybe looking at the closed door – that led to a bigger kitchen than the one he'd built in this room. Maybe even considering the garden. He wondered if she'd talked to his neighbours. Bound to have – busybody like that. That bitch next door would have complained about his garden, like she did at every opportunity with anyone who'd listen. The cat litter would need changing. He had the one in this room but the others that Lisa had been in charge of hadn't been cleaned all week.

His room – his threshold – stood open and welcoming. He'd removed the door when he'd started on his mission to save Barbara. Lisa had always come to the threshold and no further. This new one came right in and stopped dead and did a slow three hundred and sixty degree turn. He could see that her mouth had dropped open. He'd ceased noticing the smell. He was well used to the files piled up in hazardous stacks that the well-worn paths meandered through. He watched the woman as she took in the fact he obviously never left this room: the toilet he'd had installed, the cooker, the recliner. The fact the floor was covered in lever arch files stuffed with yellowing paper; the walls covered in photographs and newspaper cuttings. The cat, having hidden, poked its head from behind the recliner.

"What is all this?" she asked eventually in a hushed voice.

"I'm saving my wife," he said simply.

"Mr Randall. You can't live like this – trapped in one room. Bathroom facilities and food preparation and cat toilet in the same place. It's unsanitary!"

So. The mask had slipped immediately. She wasn't here to assess his needs, she was here to stamp the state's control over him. She was here to make him cross the threshold.

"Miss. Err…"

"Goddard."

"Miss Goddard. I've been 'living like this' for a considerable amount of time. It's a necessity. Lisa and I had an understanding. She'd bring me what I needed once a week but otherwise left me alone." It had been a most satisfactory arrangement. She'd understood eventually. He'd have to train this new one. He wheezed and reached for his inhaler. He was allowing her to get to him.

"Mr Randall," she started in a schoolmarm voice, "I am here to assess your care needs. Your health and… other needs. Clearly there is some issue here. This property has many rooms – do you find it difficult to access them? Have you got a mobility problem?" She looked around, was she looking for a stick or other walking aid?

"No. There's no problem with mobility. My health is pretty good. I still have all my marbles. I just need to save my wife." He stood and walked over to the kitchen area, filled the kettle and put it on. That'd show her he had no mobility difficulties. "Tea?"

He watched as her mouth made a little twist of disgust. "No, thank you."

"I live simply, Miss Goddard. But you shouldn't mistake that simplicity as being the result of complex needs. I am not," he swept his hand to encompass the room, "a hoarder. Despite what it looks like. That's what they call them, isn't it? Shut-ins, people who collect crap and refuse to throw anything away. I know it's a little cluttered in here," he ignored her mutter of 'a little!' "But it all serves a purpose. It's not just accumulated rubbish!" He'd worked himself up a bit. How could he make her understand about the threshold – if he couldn't even explain the relics?

The kettle boiled and he poured his tea. He only had the two cups – one for himself, stained brown from the tannins, one for visitors, pristine white. He stared into her eyes. "I am not an invalid. I am not mental. I do not need much in the way of care.

I need someone to get the shopping in and take the garbage out, deal with the litter trays in the rest of the house. I'm quite self-sufficient otherwise, thank you."

"Mr Randall, I can see that you think this is all fine, but you must see it from my perspective. The evidence is that you live alone." She opened her buff-coloured notebook. "Your wife died several years ago, you have no children, no living relatives at all, in fact. You don't appear to ever leave this room. There are hygiene issues here. This," she pointed at the lever arch files, "clutter, is a perfect place for vermin to hide. You don't appear to clean this room – there is no hoover and the kitchen area is under a layer of grease. You have one sink. When was the last time you had a shower? I can tell you that there is a smell here that's quite indescribable." As she drew breath to continue her tirade he interrupted.

"Have you ever lost the person closest to you, Miss Goddard?" He shuffled back across the well-worn path to his recliner and sank into it with a sigh as she responded.

"No. I haven't. But that doesn't excuse—"

"It's a terrible thing. But when someone dies they're never really, fully gone, until no one remembers them. Only me and the cat remember her. The poet Robert Montgomery said, 'The people you love become ghosts inside of you and like this you keep them alive' – and so I save her." He smiled, sadly.

"I'm afraid I don't understand."

"This room. Those files. The articles and photographs. The relics. It's what's left of her. It's what I have saved. What I am saving." He saw a glimmer of understanding. Perhaps she'd be sympathetic. Perhaps he could tell her about the threshold.

"Mr Randall. I'm afraid all hoarders have convinced themselves that they are hoarding for good reasons. All shut-ins have a motive for not venturing outside. It's my professional opinion that you are living in an unsustainable and health-impacting manner."

He resisted the urge to shout at her. Resisted telling her to get out. He knew how that would end – she might go away today but she'd be back with paperwork, forcible removal. He'd lose his wife. He'd have failed. He swallowed his anger.

"I am not a shut-in by choice, Miss Goddard. I need to tell you about the threshold." He rubbed his chest and took a slurp of tea. Lisa hadn't understood at first. Maybe she'd never understood? Maybe she'd just been humouring him. He'd never know. It hurt a bit that Lisa had not visited to say goodbye.

"Threshold?" Goddard arched an eyebrow and glanced at the doorframe where he'd quite obviously removed the door. The wood from which he'd used to build the little shelf of his 'kitchen,' which consisted of a kettle, a microwave and a sink. His food needs were modest.

"I'm well aware that this house has more rooms. I've lived here for a long time. Barbara, my wife…" he sighed. "Let me start again. There's a reason I am confined to this room and it's not a medical one. I started too late, you see. To save her – so much is already gone. But it was soon after the funeral. I wish I'd started sooner. As soon as she'd gone."

"I don't understand, Mr Randall."

"I'm trying to explain. When my wife died I was the only one who could remember her. If anyone else thought of her at all, it'd be passing. Her hairdresser perhaps, the GP, the man in the corner shop, none of them knew her, none of them could save her." He stared at Goddard, trying to pass her the knowledge by visualisation.

"And what does 'saving her' actually mean?" She tapped the file gently against her leg. He worried that she was filling in time. But at least she was still willing to listen to him.

"I have tried to secure the time we had together. And even the time before we met. Those boxes over there. They contain her childhood. Toys, books, mementoes, her birth certificate, school photos. These files here contain her letters to me when we were courting, when I worked away. This box holds all her hearing aids and glasses from over the years. I am saving her.

This room holds the ephemera of her life." He wheezed and his chest felt tight. He took another gasp on his inhaler.

"And the threshold?" she asked.

"I didn't know at first. And I don't know how much was lost. I have worked so hard at rebuilding, you see. But, I don't know if it's been enough. When you cross a threshold you forget. It's a scientific fact. It's called 'The Doorway Effect.' And every time I crossed that threshold a little piece of her died. I had all her things in different rooms at first. Some in the attic, some in our bedroom, the kitchen, the front room. And I was slowly killing her memory transiting from one room to another. When I realised I brought it all here. And now I cannot leave. I can't afford to lose any more of her." She had to see now.

"I see."

She didn't see. He watched her glance at the door, the file she'd been tapping against her leg fell motionless. A decision had been made. He knew he'd failed.

"Please." He had to try. No matter the cost to his dignity, he'd do anything for Barbara. Even beg.

Goddard opened the file. "It says here that you have not seen a GP for some years?"

"No. Can we please talk about Barbara, my wife?"

"Your wife is dead, Mr Randall. I'm sorry. We need to look after your needs now." Her gaze flicked from the file to his face and back again. "I've noticed you using an inhaler and rubbing your chest. What are your breathing difficulties due to?"

He sighed. If he gave her what she wanted then maybe she'd be inclined to compromise? "I have asthma. My chest is a little tight right now because I am stressed. This visit is making me stressed."

"Asthma," she said, ticking something in the file. "We need to get you a medical assessment."

"Can it be done here?"

She looked around but he could tell she'd made her decision. "You said you don't have mobility issues. I believe we should book you an appointment to visit the doctor's surgery, don't you? Getting out of this atmosphere of rotting paper will probably do your chest some good."

She hadn't listened. Not really. He had to try again. "I'm sorry. I can't cross the threshold."

"Nonsense. All this stuff will still be here when you get back. Your memories of your wife won't be affected by going outside. When was the last time you had a bit of fresh air?"

"Do you know anyone with dementia?" he asked. He had to try.

"Yes... Well, I have met people with dementia anyway."

"Do you think they're the same person as they were before the dementia? Before the disease ate large holes in their memory?"

Her mouth became a thin line and she frowned. "That depends on what you mean by 'the same person,' doesn't it? Physically they're the same, mentally they're impaired."

The cat chose that moment to make a run for the door, escaping to the rest of the house. He didn't begrudge it its freedom. He wondered if the threshold affected cats.

"Impaired? That's one way of putting it. Wouldn't you say that memories maketh the man?"

"I can't say I've ever really thought about it."

He slurped his tea, to give him time to think of a response.

"I believe that. I believe we are the sum of our memories. And if we start to lose them we start to lose ourselves. Until only the shell is left. But if there is no shell... "

"My duty is to the living, Mr Randall. And I'm afraid your health, your welfare, is my concern. We need to get you assessed and decide upon what support you need."

"The best thing you can do for me is to do what Lisa did for me."

"Clearly Lisa's leaving was the right decision for her, and for the department. I don't know what she could have been thinking, leaving you in such a state."

She breezed through a medical questionnaire and some

more interviewing, poked around the room some more and soon it was time for her visit to come to an end. He could see that he'd failed to convince her. Maybe he'd have time to do so on subsequent visits?

"Goodbye, Mr Randall. Once I've submitted my report you'll hear from us forthwith."

One last try. "Please, Miss Goddard. Please. I will be bereft if I lose her and I'll lose her if you force me to cross the threshold."

"Yes, yes. We've been through all that. It'll all be in the report. Take care, Mr Randall. I've made a note of your immediate needs and will ensure someone brings you some shopping."

He watched her from the CCTV once she'd left. He didn't miss the shudder she gave when she turned to look back at the house before getting in her car.

She was as good as her word though. The next day someone came with shopping and he managed to get them to bring it to the room so he didn't have to cross the threshold. They'd been glad to help until the smell hit them. Then he'd had to offer them a crisp twenty pound note. He wondered if anyone would come and clean out the litter trays. The cat seemed to be using the one in his room all the time. He had to admit that having one near where he prepared food wasn't ideal.

It was the next week that the trouble started. The electrician and the plumber weren't that bad. The health visitor was worse. He could tell there'd be trouble after she'd visited. And there was. Environmental health. A temporary eviction order. He had refused. Now he awaited the authorities who were going to come and forcibly evict him. All he'd wanted to do was save his wife and never cross the threshold. Why couldn't they have left him alone? The cat scrambled from the room when the front door banged open. He remembered when Barbara was the only person the cat would allow close. He wiped a tear and shouted across the threshold, "What happened to you and me against the world?"

Dismantling

"WHO ARE YOU?"

"I am Alfred George Winchester."

Tick.

The murky grey walls close in on me, the steady drip, like a leaky tap, my only companion. I remember Sissy, my wife, could never sleep if there was even an ounce of noise. She's gone now.

"Who are you?"

"I am Alfred Winchester."

Tick.

We were married in the Sixties, a heady time. I wonder if I should say something about the tap? This grey is omnipresent, asphyxiating. I wear an oxygen mask. It was a beautiful day, when we were married, blue skies and sunshine, all our families came. Except for Mum, I wish she'd lived to see the day.

"Who are you?"

"I'm Alfred."

Tick.

We met in '53, or was it '52? We were thirteen and so much in love. Never fell out of love. We met at the big school. White shapes move across the grey, asking questions, calling names, ticking boxes. Grey sludge in, grey sludge out. Where was I? Big school. Mum was so proud.

"Who are you?"

"I'm Alf."

Apples were always my favourite. I remember Mother cooking them up for pie, liquid, hot as lava, with chunks of sugary pith that warmed on the way down. I remember Mother. Mother. I remember. Where was I? The vivid blue of their sheathed hands, a prick there, a pinch there, a wet smear somewhere unmentionable, the high forlorn wail that signals another exit.

"Who are you?"

"Al. I'm Al. Aren't I?"

The Ghost Conspiracy

Introduction by Anthony Fletcher

WITH EACH PASSING *decade your relationship with death changes. I once thought I knew death, as the men and women I looked up to in my childhood and adolescence began to die off. This really did seem to be a generational thing. Thirty to forty years. With each decade since, I thought I knew death. In my fifties, very few of the names I knew and admired had survived. In my sixties, I remembered my own family: parents, aunts, uncles and grandparents who had passed through the veil in their sixties. In my seventies, friends started to be shuffled off by that implacable old skeleton with a scythe. This continued into my eighties so that at the end of that decade I felt I'd won some fabled tontine. And now, in my nineties, I have become intimate with death, a bedside companion even.*

As a young man, I chased ghosts. Now that I am aged they chase me. In a few short months, I will receive a telegram from the queen. It has been some years since I attempted an ambitious work, but I am consumed by the need to tell this.

My relationship with the late Elizabeth Anscombe has been related elsewhere. Her tragic death during the war is common knowledge. I have often, in interviews, expressed the regret that we never got to work together again. She was a formidable intellect and would have had a lasting effect on philosophy if she had only lived.

The fact is, though, that I didn't work with her again, not because of her tragic death — her self-annihilation robbed the world — but because we fell out over the book she was working on after Virtue Theory. I was the one to find her, and I read the notes, the not-yet-completed book, and, God forgive me, I took it and hid it.

I will not try to justify my actions. The ghosts of regret for what you have not done haunt you more than those of what you have. But my actions over this are a regret. If I'd left the notes with her body…

But, and this seems like a weak excuse to me now, I did it to save her reputation. Her book would have seen her labelled as a crank, a kook, a science-denier. I acknowledge now, here in print, in this confession, that my motivation was more selfish. I didn't want to be associated with her abnegation of the ghost phenomena. I was scared what the release of such a book would do to my own reputation. The convenient lie that I'd done it for her has rang ever more false as I have grown older.

Here now, unvarnished, are her words. You may judge me a foolish old man. But I now believe that she was right. I also believe that her self-destruction may have had a more sinister origin. I will let her words speak for themselves.

The Ghost Conspiracy
By Elizabeth Anscombe

Chapter One
The beginnings of suspicion

I AM GOING to start with a controversial statement. I do not think ghosts exist. I do not think our spirits are in the habit of surviving past our deaths. In fact, I would go further and say that I do not think we have spirits at all.

I know what you are thinking. The woman is mad! Picked up a brochure from the Coalition Against the Supernatural. But no. Although I believe that particular association of men is not as looney as the mass media represent them.

Perhaps you are not totally familiar with the scientific basis or history of spiritualism as laid down by those grand old men of the Victorian age, just as I am not familiar with the scientific basis or history of electricity. That unfamiliarity, that ignorance, does not prevent you from living in a world that is pervaded with spirit, nor does my ignorance prevent me from using electricity to power the light I type these words beneath.

The scientific consensus is based on some classic experiments done by Albert Abraham Michelson in the 1800s during his investigations into the aether.

However, I believe these experiments, if they had been conducted prior to when they were performed, would *not* have given the same results. It will take many pages of evidence to establish that this is not a crank theory, and, no doubt, many in the scientific community will seek to debunk it as it invalidates the scientific consensus on spiritualism.

My evidence is that there is a boundary date that marks a fundamental shift in our world. One with profound ramifications for everything we have come to believe. It is no hyperbole to say that this book will change the world.

I HAVE BEEN asked many times why I started to investigate ghosts. Much has been said about my meeting with Anthony Fletcher and his accounts of the experiences of his childhood friend, which led to his fascination with the spirit world. My own non-experience and my belief in that giving both of us an unparalleled objectivity are also well-documented. What is less well documented is that although we met at Bletchley Park it was across the country, near Bristol, where our 'adventures' really began.

A large part of the suburbs of Bristol were built in the Victorian era and this is key to understanding the evidence I will lay out in this tract

It was, of course, in Bristol that Project Spectre was being put together.

As an aside, there was a great battle in the thirties, as I'm sure you must know, between those who saw spirits as inherently evil and those, like myself and Anthony, who saw them as more neutral. Our rather public spat with CS Lewis is certainly on the record. It was our contention, and the War Office naturally concurred, that the dead could be an important source of intelligence about what Germany was up to.

We were called to consult on the Spectre Sessions taking place in building nine at Norton Fitzwarren just down the road from what Anthony jokingly called the 'Neighbour of the Beast' at Cross-Keys.

Cross-Keys is a place for low-security prisoners, mostly Italians. It was virtually empty when we visited. We were to meet a Lieutenant Winthorpe. I have been, and am still, in the habit of journaling my days. In general, this diary tends to turn odd bits and pieces of my day into a narrative. I hope you'll forgive the fictionalisation.

"SO YOU'RE THE ghost-botherers?" Winthorpe said. He was a slight man, in his thirties or early forties, moustache, male pattern baldness, slight accent, but one I couldn't place.

"I prefer the term supernatural investigators," I said, to put him in his place. As usual, Anthony said nothing. His contempt for the military types we often had to deal with was always barely disguised. I could tell it was there, though, and I suspect some of them knew as well.

He barely glanced at me. "This way then, sir. Ma'am."

We were escorted to a Nissen hut with a white painted door and a red number nine upon it. "This is where you'll be working with Doctor Scott. He'll brief you."

The inside of the hut was gloomy and a few boffins messed about with some equipment I didn't recognise. We were introduced rather quickly to Doctors Penrose and O'Keefe and a man just introduced as 'Jones.' Doctor Scott was in his early sixties with a permanent frown, a receding hairline, and rather mischievous twinkling eyes.

"Now then, what have you been told about our little outfit?" Scott asked.

"Not much. Just the basis of Project Spectre. That you aim to raise a spirit using civilian mediums and converse with it to ascertain the potential usefulness of spirits in the war effort," Anthony responded.

I knew more than this. That the boys in the war rooms hoped to place mediums with troops. To coerce foreign spirits to reveal intelligence about the Germans. We knew that the Germans had been working on their own Spirit Officers.

Scott nodded thoughtfully. "Indeed. Indeed. You will meet the civilians in good time. Rum lot if you ask me. But vital to the war effort, what?"

I'd not heard of Scott before we were sent across country and could find out precious little information. Before the war, he was working for Cambridge University.

We'd also been told that they had planned something very similar in the last Great War with Germany but, for some reason our superiors couldn't fathom, had never followed through with the plan.

We were given a little tour, shown the spectraltometers and then taken to the NAAFI to meet with the civilians, a much more colourful bunch than the scientists.

"Mrs Williamson," Scott introduced a little old lady with eyes like moons behind glasses that magnified them.

"Call me Elizabeth," I said.

"Call me Betty then." Mrs Williamson smiled a smile full of dentures. I shook her frail hand and noted sourly that Anthony was being introduced to the three male mediums.

"Is there a reason most of the mediums are men?" I asked Dr Scott. Winthorpe smirked at me over Anthony's shoulder.

"I don't think so. We asked for volunteers from several cities. This is who came forward. That's Campbell, the Reverend Hughes, and Marsh. I'd best introduce you."

"No rush, doctor. I'll just have a little chat with Betty here." I waved the good doctor to go and join the men. Anthony stuffed that foul-smelling pipe he smoked when nervous and two of the men lit cigarettes.

"Shall we go and get some fresh air?" I asked Betty, who nodded.

Outside a brisk wind had picked up, but Betty didn't seem to notice.

"I have met several mediums in my civilian life, Betty, but never one as old as you, if you'll pardon my saying. They say mediums burn out fast, it's a young man's game."

"Mebbe. I only know that they talks to me." Betty's West Country burr was heavy, a pleasant accent.

"How long have they talked to you?" Shivering, I gathered my coat closer.

"Since I were a little 'un. Always." Betty grinned at whatever expression I was making. Polite, but sceptical interest, I'd imagine.

"Mr Pipes was the first 'un. Still has chats with 'im every so often. But that's not who interests these 'uns, is it?" She drew her shawl closer and I wondered if we should return inside.

"No, Mrs Williamson. No, it isn't." My shiver turned into a shudder and, having had enough fresh air, I pushed the door open and gestured her inside.

"That man youse with, he's trouble for you." Betty shuffled inside before I could respond. Trouble?

Back in the hut, I was finally introduced to the three male mediums, none of whom I took to straight off. Marsh seemed the most personable. The Reverend was a nervous little hamster of a man and Campbell was one of those types that always seemed to be suffering. His hatchet-like nose was red and dripping and he was often muffled behind a filthy handkerchief.

Our meeting got underway. Scott chaired, Winthorpe lurked, I let Anthony lead, as we'd discussed. Some men take direction ill when delivered by a woman. Betty was silent throughout, Marsh talked often, and voluminously. Campbell silently suffered. The Reverend talked mainly about purgatory. I scribbled notes – but the essence of the meeting was as follows:

In hut nine our team, including the boffins we were introduced to earlier, who were to record our experiment for posterity, were to summon a spirit from this place and interrogate it. We were to accumulate as many verifiable facts as we could and we were to allow the boffins to check them.

The brass were especially interested in adding details to maps and clandestine observations of men and materiel. Betty didn't look happy but voiced no concern. I made a mental note to talk to her after the meeting broke up.

For several reasons, this did not happen.

The first, and most pressing, was that an air raid interrupted us that evening. The second was that Mrs Williamson lived close by, down one of the warrens of little country lanes that snaked all about the camp, and returned home straight after the meeting. And the third was that Anthony and I argued ferociously and I went to bed angry and without much thought to the issue.

We disagreed on many things, but on the truth, or not, of religion we differed most sharply. Anthony was of the opinion that it was all bunkum, not bothering to differentiate between crackpottery of the worst kind and the established religions such as Christianity.

My contention was that it was obvious, and had been established scientifically, that the spirit world did exist and therefore there was a grain of truth to religion. This was before I reached the conclusion that has led to the writing of this book, of course.

I couldn't see how he could accept the existence of ghosts and not religion.

It was a recurring bone of contention between us. This was its worst flare-up, though. It started with an off-hand comment about the Reverend. Anthony poured as much scorn as he could upon the poor fellow, in that fractious way he has. Belittling and berating. It was obvious that many of his barbs failed to land as the Reverend did indeed seem to be a singularly unobservant chap.

However, I noticed, and I conjecture so did Campbell, if only by the many sideways glances he gave Anthony. Marsh was too self-obsessed to notice anything that didn't relate directly to him and Winthorpe glowered throughout, so it was hard to tell what he thought. He obviously held us all in contempt. Scott did try to moderate Anthony's worst pointed comments, of course. For some reason, and in my notes as well as my recollection, Mrs Williamson's reactions were left unrecorded. She seemed to have the knack of blending into the background.

What we established in the meeting, despite Anthony's best efforts, was that the Reverend would provide spiritual support, Campbell would prepare the ground, Betty would play conduit and Marsh would be the lead, of course.

We'd be working in hut nine and the boffins had all sorts of instrumentation with which they were going to measure a variety of spectral effects.

The very next day, March 31st, we would attempt to summon a ghost.

***

AS DAY BROKE we gathered in hut nine, having scurried there in the pre-dawn light, biting spring winds tossing the daffodils. The wind made the hut whisper to itself. I had the sense that if only I could listen hard enough, the building, new as it was, could tell me the secrets of all that had happened here.

The Reverend had blessed everything and declared the hut inviolable to evil influence. Anthony caught himself in a scoff, and guiltily glanced my way. We hadn't put the argument to bed, but he was obviously loathe to start it up again.

Betty stood serenely unperturbed like she was waiting for someone to bring a chair. Marsh watched the Reverend avidly and Campbell watched Marsh.

Winthorpe cleared his throat. "Once he's finished, what happens?" he asked. Winthorpe was with us yesterday. He should already know, but perhaps he wasn't paying attention. I opened my mouth to speak but Anthony got there before me.

"Mr Campbell will prepare the ground. Give it a psychometric assessment. Then he and Mrs Williamson will attempt to contact the souls collected here and decide which one will be summoned. Mr Marsh will summon it and Mrs Williamson will embody it. Then we can question it."

Unspoken, but discussed with Winthorpe last night, was the fact that the little old lady had been chosen as the vessel for two reasons. The first, and most pragmatic, was that she had done this sort of work before. The second, and the reason Winthorpe was present, and armed, was that being physically the frailest, she was the least danger if the spirit possessing her proved to be hostile. Although Campbell had spoken about how a child had once thrown him twenty foot. The Reverend was on hand to dismiss the spirit if it proved to be – problematical.

"But how will Campbell prepare the ground?" Winthorpe asked. Campbell himself shrugged off his greatcoat and his scrawny frame was exposed to the chill air inside the hut. Not as frigid as outside, but definitely cold. He struggled out of his shirt until he stood, pigeon-chested with pipe-cleaner arms, shivering and goosebumped.

"I think, Winthorpe, you are about to find out."

Campbell closed his eyes, lifted his head and mumbled, his lips moving – in a prayer? Exhortation? – before striding purposefully into the centre of the cleared area at the bottom of the hut. Here the wooden floor had been removed and the dark, ruby-red earth was exposed. It was moist and gave the hut a solid, loamy smell. Campbell prostrated himself upon it, cruciform, and a long low moan escaped him.

Winthorpe unholstered his service revolver, although what good that would do him I didn't know. I watched fascinated as Campbell squirmed around on the soil. The boffins had set their equipment up in a ring around the cleared area. I noted Jones, flat cap describing circles in his hands, watching grim-faced.

"Paul!" Campbell's shout made me jump. Betty calmly wandered out to stand over the prostrate man. "John!" his second, croaking shout, sounded at the limit of his vocal capacity. "Elizabeth!" The name caused a small tingle to pass down my spine like someone had blown upon the back of my neck. I hoped they wouldn't choose that one. "Jacob!" I saw Betty now murmuring – talking to the spirits? I wished, not for the first time, that I could see what they could see, feel what they could feel. Betty's head flipped back and she took a great indrawn breath through her nose that I could hear from twenty feet away.

"Jacob," Campbell repeated, but in a quieter voice, one perfectly timed for the lull in the wind hammering the outside of the hut.

He pushed himself to his hands and knees and, just as he was about to rise, Betty put her hand on the back of his neck. As he bowed his head the Reverend took a step forward, but Marsh shook his head violently and gestured to Jones.

The beefy man shot forwards, grappled Campbell into a fireman's lift and carried him past us to the front of the hut. Campbell looked as though he had been shot, or stabbed, as the blood-red soil had stained his naked chest and face. One of the boffins grabbed a blanket and wrapped him in it, whilst I turned back to concentrate on the matter in hand.

"Jacob?" Marsh asked.

"Yes?" Betty replied, in a deep voice, without a trace of her accent.

"Please tell those gathered here your full name."

"Jacob Andrew Smith." Betty seemed to hang limp, her head lolling, and the possession had left her stooped, in an actor's pose.

"When were you born, Jacob?"

"Fourteenth of February 1855."

We were all mesmerised.

"When did you die, Jacob?" Marsh's high voice cracked a little on the word die. It had been a question we knew we'd have to ask, but opinion was divided in the spiritualist community.

Many believed that ghosts were just people who hadn't realised their physical body had died.

"Fourteenth of March 1911." Betty's posture had not changed.

"How did you die, Jacob?"

Was fifty-six a decent age to die in 1911?

"Coughing sickness."

Well, that could cover a variety of ills.

"Can you see us, Jacob?"

Betty's head came up and jerked through a scan of the room. "Yes."

Marsh wiped his forehead, but a sheen of sweat remained upon it.

"What else can you see, Jacob?"

"Furniture, machines, a gun."

It was remarkable. No trace of an accent, and the voice was in a much deeper register than her own. Yet Anthony and I had discovered charlatans, men and women, who had tried to trick the general public through acting and technical jiggery-pokery. But was Betty such a person? Would the men collude with her to dupe the British Army? No, surely not. We had scientific proof of the existence of the spirit world. But we didn't understand it, or its inhabitants.

"Where did you live, Jacob?" Marsh's reedy voice sounded strained, like he was exerting a great effort.

"At the Primroses. In Fitzroy." Marsh made some sort of gesture. I think he meant for us to write it down. I pulled out my notebook and made notes, although Penrose was already scribbling this exchange down.

"What's your connection to this place, Jacob?"

Betty's head fell further, and she took a couple of great heaving breaths, then seemed to topple in slow motion to the floor. At the same time, Marsh slumped, as though the energy to stand was almost too much.

"It's gone," he announced.

I went to see if Betty was injured by the experience and spotted Campbell looking down on the scene, blanket hanging limply from his sloping shoulders, an expression I couldn't read upon his face.

***

WE MET IN the canteen after the ghost had left, in what became a small tradition amongst us. The bustle of the men eating and the ordered row of tables was a balm to the strangeness we encountered regularly within hut number nine.

I endeavoured, post these meetings, to find out some biographical information from Mrs Williamson. And her experience of the ghost phenomena.

But I will come to that later.

We met that first day, slightly dampened. The boffins stayed to record the measurements they'd taken. There had naturally developed a divide amongst us. The civilians and the military. Anthony and I were given honorary membership of the civilians group, with Winthorpe's disapproving scowl always in the background. Scott, Penrose, and the others mainly stayed in hut nine and ate there.

"Did we learn anything of use?" Anthony asked.

"Jacob is a God-fearing man," the Reverend replied.

"How so?" I asked, glancing at Campbell, who was now dressed.

"Because he was able to enter the consecrated area."

As the Reverend spoke, Campbell's eyelids drooped and his hands trembled.

"Are you all right?" I asked. He jerked, as though waking from a dream.

"Yes, perfectly." A stray gobbet of spittle flew from his mouth and sailed over the table where my fascinated gaze watched it land upon Marsh's lapel.

Marsh himself was oblivious. His lips moved as he stared into the middle distance.

"Anything we can verify?" Anthony asked.

"The address. The name. The dates of birth and death. So yes, quite a lot." The Reverend looked pleased. "I can find those in the local parish records."

"And could have done before today," I muttered.

"I don't see the relevance of—" the Reverend started.

"They think we're frauds." Marsh, when he spoke, squinted, as though he was trying to see something slightly out of focus.

"Oh no, dear. They're just like most people. Unattuned to the spirit world," Betty said, unexpectedly coming to our defence.

"We need to get some information from it, that the brass can't think could be gleaned any other way," I said, smiling at Betty with thanks.

"How would we verify such information?" The Reverend frowned.

"We ask the ghost to go and look at something that's happening whilst we are in the room. Something that we can't possibly see or know about. It has to be double blind, too."

"Double blind?" The Reverend seemed to have become the spokesperson. Maybe because the others were tired.

"Neither the experimenter nor the subject knows the critical aspects, to save against bias. And… cheating." Anthony paused before saying cheating, aware that any such accusation, or the smell of one, could put them against us. We'd seen this before.

The three men exchanged glances.

"We'll agree to the double blind," Marsh spat out before the meeting broke up.

I looked at Anthony and he shook his head.

***

CAMPBELL WENT THROUGH the same rigmarole the next day, and the next and we spoke to 'Jacob' several more times. But we could not coax him into our carefully controlled experiment.

On the fourth day our band, tired and disappointed, met in the canteen once more.

"So, let's summarise what we know," I counted off on my fingers. "One, the ghost can flit about the countryside, but he doesn't want to. Two, he can see perfectly well in the dark or the day. Three, he fears dissolution. Four, we have verified all the facts we can, and they are accurate, but could have been obtained before we arrived." Marsh and Campbell shared a look. I ignored it and continued, "Five, our Jacob is——"

"This is pointless!" The Reverend's interjection was not welcome. Not by me anyway.

"How so?" I asked.

"We all know this. The reason the spirit will not walk abroad is because we are coaxing, not coercing. If you'd let me——"

"No!" Betty seldom said anything at these meetings and had, in the last couple of days, been making her trip home instead of staying in the canteen with us.

"I beg your pardon?" the Reverend said.

"You mayn't have it," Betty responded.

The two stared at each other like cats with their backs up.

"We won't be coercing the spirit," Marsh's high voice was final.

Campbell stood, throwing his chair back with a scrape. He stalked from the room. The Reverend looked like he was chewing over his next words and, at a nod from Anthony, I followed Campbell outside.

He was making a rolled-up cigarette with shaking hands when I stepped outside. It was one of those glorious April days when the sunshine enticed you outside so that the chill wind could stab you and run off with your warmth.

"Is there something we don't know about the ghost?" I asked.

Campbell narrowed his eyes and bit savagely at the cigarette, cupping his hands to light it. I waited, jiggling about and rubbing my hands together.

"We?" he answered.

"The team," I clarified.

"I expect there's lots."

"No. I meant… Is there something you and Betty aren't

telling us?"

At the mention of Betty's name he glanced over my shoulder and I turned to see that Betty stood at the door, looking through the little glass panel, watching us. Betty's eyes drooped in the same way that Campbell had displayed the first time we summoned the ghost.

"Something you are keeping from us?"

Campbell pulled tobacco from his lip, exhaled a cloud of either smoke or steam, it was hard to tell where one stopped and the other began; my own breath steamed in the chill air. He shook his head, flicked the barely smoked cigarette to the muddy ground, cracked his knuckles and stomped off, lost inside his greatcoat.

I looked back at the door, and Betty had gone. Back inside the men had tea. Tea seemed like the best idea in the world suddenly. I fetched a mug and joined the men waiting in line. The tea, when it came, was the brown of tree bark and tasted as thick. The slight chill of standing outside with Campbell had penetrated me to the bone, and the mug was deliciously hot in my hands. I blew the steam off it and noticed that the men had left. All except for Anthony. Time to clear the air.

***

THE NEXT DAY, our fifth at the base, we had a breakthrough, although it didn't seem like it at the time. But before I get to that I should report on the conversations I had been having with Betty.

These took place over many days and are here provided as one long narrative, although that isn't how they occurred. There were many repetitions and evasions before the story came out.

"How did you first come to talk to spirits, Betty?"

"When I were a little 'un. In Bristol," she pronounced it Brizzle, "my mam were a cleaner and my da worked in an office, as a clerk.

"A great big office it was, near the new train station, as built by Brunel hisself. All of red brick it were. I was afraid to go there, but Ma usually went to meet Da, and I'd be taken along.

"One day, Da was late and Ma was worried. For the first time ever she took us inside. Past the great iron gates, down the cobbled path, ignoring the men in their charcoal suits streaming from the doors. We were like two fish swimming upstream. But she was fearful worried. I didn't know why, then, but as I recalled it later, older, it seemed she already knew. How, I don't know, perhaps she were touched with the sight? Perhaps they were just that close.

"A lot of the men had been getting sick, you see. Da said it was something in the water, but he'd been taking a flask with 'im. Ma was in a panic that day. Dragging me along, faster than my little legs could go without running. I didn't understand. I was fearful and cried, earning Ma many a look of disapproval. We crossed the main hall to the great mahogany desks that towered over my child's form. I couldn't see who Ma spoke to and my gaze wandered around the room instead. It was on the balcony I saw him. Standing stock still, head cocked like a bird, staring at me. It's only later I realised that the men that hurried past didn't see him.

"He gestured to me, one thin, pale finger against his lips. His eyes bored into me. Already afraid, he made me gulp down my tears, which must have been a relief to whoever Ma was talking to, and those close by.

"It's a moment that stretches for an eternity in my memory but can't have been more than a second. One moment the man was there, the next I was distracted by birds taking off in a great crowd from a tree outside. When I looked back 'ee was gone. 'Ee should have been obvious to see unless he'd run right fast, but there were no sign of 'im.

"My da had been taken ill. Whatever poison was in that place was not in the water. Ee'd frothed, fitted and fainted. Never the same after that day, never in work again neither. 'Ee'd been a robust man before. After that day all strength were robbed from 'im, and 'is mind wandered. Only thing they saw, that could have caused it, were a rat bite.

"The man on the balcony were my first spirit. But it weren't long before another made itself known. Because my da couldn't work we had to get another place, smaller, cheaper, in a worse neighbourhood. Ma did her best, took on more work, but she earned a pittance. I did what I could. Looked after Da, made sure 'ee was fed, and later, when I were older, took on work of my own.

"In the place we moved to there were another family. They had a little boy, Arthur, younger than me, who were sickly too. I often looked after 'im when 'is parents were out at work. Earned a bob or two for it.

"The room that were 'is was out back of the property. A tiny window overlooking an untidy yard. But there were a pipe, I don't know what it was for, that ran along 'is ceiling and out. It used to bang something rotten occasionally. But this one night there were a clinking and a tapping, and it sounded like code, so I stood on the chest of drawers and tapped back. Something was trying to contact us.

"That first night we got to the stage of 'answer once for yes and twice for no' and asked it a bunch of questions. We were kids playing around. I followed the pipe as much as I could and asked my da about it. He said it was for water for the big sink. I spent some time on my hands and knees under the sink banging on the pipe. But it only seemed to work in Arthur's bedroom."

Why do ghosts only contact certain people? Where do they come from? What are they? Why are there no old ghosts, like ancient kings and queens, or Romans and Celts? Why are they concentrated in this part of the country?

These were questions we will return to. But to stick with Betty's narrative for now.

"We called him Mr Pipes. A silly child's name. I weren't scared, more excited, but Arthur were terrified. People say that children and cats and dogs are more sensitive to spirits. I don't know if that's true, but I saw Arthur years later. He were working as a taxi driver and happened to pick me up once. We chatted some. He'd blanked the whole period from his memory. Or, rather, the specifics of it. He looked so handsome in his grey suit, but my heart was pledged to Mr Williamson by then.

"Anyhow, in his bedroom, when he were a sickly child, we were treated to all the symptoms of the typical haunting. But it were playful. To me. I used to sit on the chest of drawers, a great big pastel blue thing pocked with burns where candles had burned down, and shout out questions, and get yes and no answers. Mebbe it were I that brought it more fully into this world? Writings appeared sometimes, scratches in the walls. There were sudden infestations of insects in the house. They made my father gabble so, he seemed mortally afraid of the little earwigs, spiders, and woodlice. Strange to see a grown-up lost to fear when you're a child. You have this image that all of life's mysteries have been worked out by the giants around you, little knowing that they are as lost as you.

"When the bird got in Arthur's room, we thought it were from outside. A black crow with flashes of white feather when it spread its wings. Did that mean it were old or sick? I don't know. We tried to get the boy's parents to get rid. But when they came into the room there were no bird. They lathered him for lying to 'em and banned me from seeing 'im for a few days. But they soon needed me to sit 'im again.

"The bird was as solid as this hut, bold as brass and twice as shiny, as my ma would say. It either hid or it were a manifestation. Not seen that sort of thing many more times since. It'd join in when we talked to Mr Pipes. Squawking and cawing in time to his answers. We named him Blackie. Not very original, I know, but we were children.

"We fed 'im insects found in the garden and in the rooms we lived in. Earwigs and worms and beetles and flies. He ate anything we gave 'im. There was a solidness to 'im, but he never let us touch 'im.

"One day, when I arrived later than usual, can't remember why, Arthur had been talking to Mr Pipes by hisself. And seemed all bossy when I arrived. Not 'is usual meek self.

"'Mr Pipes dares you to eat Blackie's food,' he said a few minutes after I'd arrived. 'No, he didn't!' I said. But Arthur nodded solemnly. I clambered up onto the dresser and banged the pipe, until there was an answering knock, knock, knock from Mr Pipes.

"'Is what Arthur says true?' I asked. There came the one knock for yes. I sat down on the dresser and crossed my arms, and stuck my lip out. 'Well, I won't do it!' I huffed. Arthur's eyes went wide. 'Mr Pipes said he'd go away if you didn't. And if he goes away your da will go back to being a vegetable.' Arthur passed this news on solemnly, so I knew he wasn't lying.

"It is true that in the time that Mr Pipes had been in the house Da had gotten a little better. Before the ghost, Da had been listless and useless. Since we'd started communicating with the spirit he had picked up. I'd noticed, of course, but hadn't consciously linked the two. I didn't have time to question it right at that moment either.

"I pulled the handkerchief out in which I'd wrapped up the few insects I'd caught for Blackie's tea. The bird flapped down from its place in the corner of the room, where it'd been perched on the pipe. It did that bird look, one eye, a swivelled head, then another eye. I gulped and unpeeled the corner of the handkerchief. The fly was squished, and I knew they ate shit, so I wasn't going to eat that. The worms were all slimy and there was no way I could put one of them in my mouth. The only other thing was a woodlouse, on its back, legs waving in the air. I swallowed a lump in my throat. I didn't want to do it.

"The bird gulped down the worms, picked up the fly and cocked its head at me. It looked like it was inviting me to eat the woodlouse. I picked it up, between finger and thumb. I glanced at Arthur who was watching me keenly, eagerly. I closed my eyes and put the woodlouse in my mouth.

"When I held it on my tongue, I could feel its little legs tickling. I swallowed it whole wondering how long it would live on its journey to my stomach. Blackie flapped an applause and hopped and skipped his way back to his perch. The taste hit me, and I gagged, then rubbed my tongue with the corner of my dress. Arthur passed me a glass of water and I downed it, having to gasp a breath at the end. 'Now Mr Pipes can talk to you properly. Like he does to me,' Arthur told me.

"I didn't know what he meant. But later, when Mr Pipes started whispering to me, it became clear. I had passed his test and now he was rewarding me. As I said, Mr Pipes has followed me since that day and I still get to talk to him about the spirit world occasionally."

***

BETTY HAD TO move out of the house soon after, due to unpaid bills or some such. Her story made it seem as if the haunting was related to her father. I investigated.

The Reverend was a believer, and when pressed, his experiences of the supernatural were of the same sort we had been able to dismiss readily in others.

Marsh came to his calling as a teenager, working in Bristol. Campbell had studied for many years before he got his breakthrough, also in Bristol. I begged some leave and for days six to eight I was in London, studying central records for all the men and women around the country that had declared themselves, or been declared, as mediums.

So many of them had some connection to Bristol, either of themselves or a parent, sibling, or friend, that I jumped to the conclusion that the connection must be there for the others, but just not as obvious.

Why? What was there in Bristol that made it the centre for the spiritualist community? The Michelson experiments had been conducted in the USA after all, proving that the spiritual was present in all countries, that it wasn't a local phenomenon.

But then I discovered that in 1880, Michelson landed in Bristol, on his way to Paris to study at the Ecole Polytechnique. It was only when he returned from Europe that his aether experiments proved the existence of spirits!

***

ON DAY NINE I returned to the camp, full of news for Anthony. But, it seemed, his news trumped mine. They'd had some success. The breakthrough on day five was that Betty had been visited in her home by the spirit. We had agreed that this visit had been interesting, but none of us had realised it meant the spirit now walked abroad. I'm not sure why we'd had this oversight. It is obvious, is it not?

But that meant it could follow a living person. Manifesting wherever that person was. Not totally useful, but if it could roam abroad, and communicate what it had seen between two points, then we had a possible use.

Winthorpe mused upon sending spiritualists out with troops and have the spirits as scouts. But the military application we would leave to others. The very fact we now saw a way to use it was enough excitement for us. Doctor Scott positively glowed with the news. On days seven and eight they'd been experimenting with this new-found facility to travel.

One I had my suspicions of even as Anthony told me. Is this how spirits had spread through the country? I was still, at that time, calling them spirits. What happened on day nine, and my subsequent investigations in Bristol, would make me seek a newer, more accurate descriptor.

As usual, we gathered for breakfast, the civilians that is. The military men always ate breakfast before us. An air of palpable excitement took us as we were near a breakthrough. The spirit, Jacob, had proven that it could see what was around it, even when disembodied. So, we'd set it a task the night before. At a certain time, we'd send the spirit into one of the huts, and we'd bid one of the men to describe in a letter, sealed, sight unseen to any but that soldier, the scene in that hut. If the spirit could describe that scene, as per the soldier's description, then we knew it was real. The letter lay on the table, possible dynamite.

As usual, Marsh drank several cups of tea to everyone else's one; how he could drink the scalding liquid so fast was a mystery to me. Betty had a large appetite, not eating much at home I bet, and the others tucked into the cooked breakfast. My stomach was a little queasy that day so I'd just had some toast and tea.

We scurried from the NAAFI to hut nine to be greeted by O'Keefe. Scott was 'tied up' and the other men were bustling about when we trooped inside the hut.

Amongst us was the usual mix of solemnity and seriousness and the occasional smile or cracked joke. Then we watched Campbell do his usual rolling around in the mud. Jones, as always, grabbed him and moved him out of the way.

Marsh began the interrogation and, for some reason, O'Keefe approached Betty holding some sort of recording device. In his state of enthusiasm, he'd breached the circle of dirt we usually left as the sole demesne of Jacob.

Betty, with her imposing five foot nothing frame, grabbed O'Keefe by the throat. He turned a funny colour, eyes wide, mouth gasping like a fish out of water. Marsh strode into the circle, chanting something in Latin. The Reverend, bible outstretched as a shield, joined him from the opposite direction, his Lord's prayer blending with Marsh's chant.

Betty shrugged and O'Keefe dropped to the floor, immediately curling into a defensive position and covering his throat.

"I will fear no— Erk!" The Reverend's prayer was cut short as Betty took his arm and moved slightly faster than my eye could follow. The Reverend was tossed, as though weighing no more than a bag of sugar, across the room. He landed awkwardly and lay still.

Winthorpe shouted something, his arm out, service revolver wavering; Marsh was in the way.

The Latin chanting reached a crescendo. Betty slumped and Marsh took two quick steps forward to catch her. But it was a lure. She exploded into action and her fist caught Marsh in the sternum. All the life was expelled from him in one detonating breath. I heard a wet crack as he was propelled backwards, skidding across the floor.

Winthorpe smiled without humour and took aim. I was just able to kick out enough so that the bullet, when it came, mostly missed. Betty fell to the floor and a sudden silence fell, bar the whimpering of O'Keefe.

***

MARSH WAS DEAD — the blow Betty struck him stopped his heart. It was a sombre group that stood in the whirling dust outside the hut. Winthorpe, vindicated, seemed to be the only one of us that had any energy. We shuffled nervously, unable or unwilling to return to the hut. To the scene of where it had happened. Betty had been sedated and taken off to the infirmary. And once the medics had taken poor Marsh's body away, Scott had gone to the top brass to make a report. We awaited his return with an impending sense of doom.

Jones, Penrose and the rest of the boffins huddled together and shut us out. Every so often one would throw a barbed glance at us. Campbell shivered and blew his nose. Anthony broke the silence.

"I wonder what they'll tell his family?"

Campbell shrugged, absorbed in making a smoke.

Winthorpe barked a humourless laugh. "They won't tell them anything. Killed in line of duty, blah, blah." He waved his fingers in a typing motion.

"Someone should let his family know," I ventured. Winthorpe blew air from his cheeks. The Reverend nodded and opened his mouth to speak, but was interrupted.

"Here's Scott," Anthony noted. "We're about to get our marching orders."

Dr Scott stomped over to hut number nine, where we shuffled and milled.

"Penrose, take the men inside, we have to secure the measurements and ensure everything is secure. Winthorpe, you're to go to the infirmary, secure the patients." Winthorpe raised an eyebrow but followed orders, stalking off as the boffins jostled through the door, leaving the mediums, Anthony and me.

"There'll be a debrief at oh-nine-hundred tomorrow. But until then I'd like to pick your brains. Let's go and get a hot cuppa and discuss what went wrong." Scott threw out his arm in a gesture of 'you first'. The Reverend shook his head. "I should go and see to poor Mrs Wiliamson," he said apologetically, and trotted off towards the infirmary.

Campbell shrugged and, without looking up, led the way to the NAAFI. He finished making his cigarette on the way over and stayed outside to smoke when we arrived.

"We can't use the same mediums again," Scott said as we sat, three steaming, chipped enamel mugs in front of us. "You and Anscombe will be given some days to find us new ones. Start in Bristol. But we need to be operational again as soon as possible."

***

IT TOOK SOME persuading, but Anthony was cajoled into a brief layover and we communicated our desire to HQ. We were reluctantly given a few days' leave to recuperate before Project Spectre resumed.

Oh yes. They didn't stop it – one man's death was not enough cause. The military was used to experiments proving dangerous. We'd been tasked to bring in new manpower so we'd be able to try again. I was keen to investigate what was the beginnings of a pet theory about Bristol first. And hoped the extra couple of days were going to be enough.

Anthony and I argued as we drove to Bristol. About my pet theory, and about our old bone of contention. But he saw that my instincts were sound. We'd start at the house she'd first made contact with Mr Pipes and then the building Williamson's father used to work at. Anthony was never keen to play Watson to my Sherlock, but this time I felt we were closer than ever to working out something fundamental about the spiritual phenomenon and my eager enthusiasm must have been translated, for he wasn't complaining as much as usual.

The building the Williamsons had lived in when Betty was a child was still there. A filthy early Victorian slum with a black-brick bomb shelter half-built or half-demolished in the garden, like someone had started, then lost the will to continue. The outside of the house was stained, like a fire had once taken it but had also, like the demolisher, given up.

We effected entry by flashing War Office papers and investigated the back room, the one with the pipe. If there'd been anything special about the room, it had left some time previous. The current owner was using it as a washhouse. We had to flip cold, wet sheets out of the way as we poked about the room. I'm not sure what I thought we could find, but whatever it was we never found it. The basics of what Betty had told me were borne out. The bedroom of her childhood friend was exactly as she described it.

The great red-bricked building where her father had worked, and fallen sick, was still there too. No one had ventured inside for some years. The clerk at the council had been unclear, or the papers he'd consulted were. The owners had not wanted the building sold, or even used, and it had stood derelict since the office, and its workers, had been moved elsewhere.

From the outside, it was imposing. A level of grey stone with large arched windows before red brick took over the middle level, with much smaller, squinting windows, and a final level of red and yellow brick with crescent windows. In the centre, where the wall met the overhanging roof, I could see a sandstone plaque, but what it once said was obscured, the only intelligible part being the number eighteen. The year it was built no doubt.

From the road, we could see a wall, twelve to fifteen feet high, with a carriage gate that would give us access. The council had provided a man, who looked a lot like Jones – the same solid, dependable build – to let us in. He wouldn't come inside with us, though.

As we trooped down the path all the birds in the trees took off with a great flapping and cawing. "They know we're coming," I muttered.

"Who?" Anthony asked.

I just shook my head, not able to answer him.

The man from the council, who I mentally called Jones, his actual name long since forgotten, informed us that he'd wait for us on the street.

The front door was oaken, around seven feet tall and studded with iron. Like the gate to a fort. When it creaked open a waft of stale air was exhaled, redolent of mould, which made me sneeze.

"Shall we?" Anthony asked. I had taken an instinctive step backwards.

"After you," I motioned him forward and gave him what I hoped was a brave smile. He pulled his jacket down smart, patted a pocket, where I assumed he kept his firearm and pushed open the door.

The inside was gloomy, and the smell of creatures long gone to rot assailed us. Immediately upon entering there were bird skeletons and pigeon corpses in various stages of decay. Their living brethren added a susurrus that made it feel like the building was breathing.

The antechamber soon opened out into a hall that I recognised from Betty's description. A great desk stood sentinel over a number of exits and above us loomed the balcony Betty had mentioned. I strode over to the desk and, only when I was in the shaft of light thrown from a high window, turned to gaze at the balcony.

Anthony walked the perimeter of the room.

"There." I pointed, and made Anthony aware of the spot where Betty had claimed to have seen her first ghost.

"Perhaps we should have brought the councilman? I'm not sure of the safety of this stairway…" Anthony gingerly crept up the stairs, staring at his feet. I was unable to join him, I felt rooted to the spot. He didn't seem to care that I hadn't followed him. As he reached the top, I heard a creak, loud in the relative silence of the building.

"Careful—"

A cacophonous explosion of cruciform shapes burst forth – pigeons! Anthony staggered, hit the railing, which dislodged a decade's worthof dust, but thankfully held. The pigeons swooped through the room in formation and I ducked as they swept over me and down one of the corridors. They left behind a sudden miasma.

I looked up and Anthony had gone. I stood up on tiptoes and saw his shape, haloed by the light streaming in the window, as he explored some alcove. I wondered. I crouched and made myself young girl height so that the desk 'towered' over me and looked up to the balcony again. Of course, I couldn't see the full depth of it. A man could easily have just stepped backwards out of sight of a little girl. I sighed and stood up, and as I did so somewhere in the building, something slammed shut. Or open.

Suddenly my rationalisation was blown away, like a cobweb on the wind. This building had an inimical presence, even I could feel it. Anthony's suggestion of bringing Campbell with us didn't feel so wrong now. Something crawled over my hand, where it lay on top of the desk and made me jump.

It was some sort of insect, but whatever it was flew through the air as I pulled my hand away from the desk as if it were a hot surface and waved it like my hand was on fire. My scalp crawled and spider-leg fingers of dread played upon my neck. I shuddered.

A door close by sprung open and Anthony was disgorged, dusty, but seemingly no worse for wear. I took a deep breath and tried to forget that the building was only lived in by vermin. That no one had walked these halls for years, and that they'd therefore been claimed by spiders, and woodlice, and earwigs, and silverfish...

"Where should we look?" Anthony asked.

"Where would rats live?"

We both looked down.

"Well, at least access to the basement will be on this floor." Anthony gave me a smile before turning and heading along the corridor the pigeons had flown down earlier. I gave myself the luxury of a final shudder, squared my shoulders and followed him.

The corridor spat us out in front of another door, in a small, enclosed hall. We were not yet at the back of the building. Anthony had chosen correctly, this must have been the way down. I wondered where the birds had gone. Anthony took a couple of steps and threw open the doors. A foetid, stale water odour washed up the stairs, from the darkness beneath.

Anthony had brought a lantern, its feeble orange glow giving us a disc of light to follow down the stairs. The darkness each side swallowed the light, and the sounds of splashing didn't fill me with comfort.

At the bottom of the steps stood an ankle-deep lake of filthy smelling water. We could not avoid getting our feet wet. The room was a cavern, no sense of other walls, the light from the lantern failing to penetrate the darkness.

"Perhaps we should come back?" I asked, trying to keep a tremor out of my voice.

"No time like the present," Anthony replied before moving off.

I could retreat and leave him alone, or I could follow him. I tried to keep close.

Crane flies flitted to the light and danced around us. Somewhere in the darkness things skittered and plopped. I thought that we'd found the rats all right and wished we hadn't.

"Anthony, I—"

"Shhh. Did you hear that?" I turned away from the light and looked at Anthony who searched the darkness.

"Hear what?"

"Sounded like footsteps." He gripped my arm and pulled me with him as he moved with purpose, towards or away from the sound?

"Anthony, I really—" I inhaled a crane fly, I felt its squamous dust explode in my mouth as my teeth, in the process of forming a word, bit down upon it. A bitter, metallic taste burst across my tongue and I immediately gagged. I spat it out, but how much had I swallowed? My stomach roiled.

Anthony stopped dead. Around us, we heard splashing.

"Are you all right?" he asked.

I could only cough and splutter in response. When I caught my breath, I could tell there was something wrong. Anthony stood still, his hand on my arm, the orange disc of light from the lantern cast upon the water.

"What?" I asked.

"Listen."

I strained to listen. "I hear nothing?"

"Exactly. Whatever was splashing through the water has stopped. Or submerged. Or something."

A horrid aftertaste flooded my mouth and I suddenly thought of the crow, Blackie. "Anthony, we have to leave. Right now." I tried to drag him, but he seemed rooted to the spot. In the periphery of the lantern light, I saw a silhouette. "Now!" I stopped trying to pull him away. I turned and ran, splashing my way to the stairs. Something bad was coming.

I didn't stop when I reached the top, I carried on through the building and out the door. As I entered the yard the birds exploded from the trees in a great cawing swarm. The councilman stood just outside and caught me as I collapsed.

***

ANTHONY CAME OUT after a while, of course. I don't know what happened in there to him, but he seemed less affected by it than

I. My life since has become plagued by all the classic signs. I was ill for quite some time after the incident. Anthony and I spent the time at Spectre and writing a thesis. But my heart wasn't in it. I felt it was necessary to put down these experiences before I discuss my supposition. That all ghost phenomena originated in that place. And has nothing to do with the dead.

There is an infection, a contagion, which comes from that place. And I have become infected. All my life I have wished that I could see the things the mediums reported seeing. Now it is happening to me I wish with all my heart that it was not.

For I know that I am a carrier, its insidious presence within me. Ready to come out. When? I know not. How? Again, my ignorance knows no bounds. But I feel it. I must not let it emerge. I feel it feeding from me. From what makes me, me. I have returned to Bristol. I believe the answers to my questions are here.

Why are there no ghosts beyond a certain age? Because what society label ghosts are not the spirits of the dead. They are the effluvia, the cast-offs, the by-product of this *thing's* life. I know this to be true. I have seen it. My own ghosts. Memory leakage. Form and substance spun from the currents of my life. And yet, for me, they are at the absolute limit of my sight, my hearing, my thought. For others, though? For those that have truly imbibed? They must seem more real.

They are more real.

I cannot share this. I must share this. There is a presence. An entity and it feeds upon us. It feeds upon the stories of our lives. It has fed upon me and will continue to do so. Only a small part of it entered me, but it has grown. Oh, it has grown.

I know how to kill it. The part of it inside me. If I no longer exist, if it is exposed to the light, then it is extinguished. The part in me is extinguished.

I have been back to the building, but cannot enter. I am undone. The birds stand sentinel. I may not pass. Its destruction, my desire, unattainable. I may only destroy the part of it that's part of me, by destroying me.

If you are uninfected, by its primary presence or the many carriers, then you must resist. You must excoriate it.

THIS IS WHERE Elizabeth's notes come to a stop. There are other, mostly illegible scribblings that I have kept from these pages. It has troubled me for many years and continues to trouble me. What she has said is true.

I won't disturb the dead (what a hollow thought that has become!) in these notes so will say little of our time in the camp. I will say that Anscombe and I rarely argued, and I do not remember our disagreement about religion rankling her so. Clearly I am an ass!

Our time in Bristol, so elided in her notes, was intense. It took some hard detective work, some serendipity and lots of shoe leather to find out what she glibly describes.

I remember following her out of the red brick building straight away, hurrying to catch her up, unaware then, and until reading her notes, what was wrong.

She reported that she was feeling unwell and we returned to the place the army had placed us. A lodging house, rather than in a barracks with the common soldiery. She gave no indication the next day that anything was wrong. We were due to go back to Cross-Keys. She reported that her obsession had been just that, a fad, a phase, a distraction. Events soon pushed our brief sojourn in Bristol to the back of my mind. Spectre continued, of course, and afterwards there were other experiments in other camps and the periods in Scotland and in France I have dealt with in other books.

It was in Bristol that I found her. In a Victorian terraced house in the suburbs. She had taken a place unoccupied due to death. A common occurrence in those times. The young family that had lived there had suffered. The father, dead and buried in the desert, the mother killed in a bombing raid, the child adopted by relatives.

She'd been talking to them, her notes said, her random scribblings and ravings that I have spared you here. The young woman especially. Her notes were explicit about the pink mist that hung about the widowed ghost.

This is what confuses me. If ghosts are not the spirits of the dead — and I have no reason to doubt her — how had she been communicating with them?

The contagion theory of ghosts has profound ramifications. Diseases can be fought. We have wiped out smallpox, and it looks likely that we will wipe out polio and other killers. Could we eliminate ghosts? Would we want to? I still firmly believe religion is poppycock. In a world without proof of the numinous, would religion atrophy?

It seems likely that there are other presences throughout the world. Other plague-generators and other vectors. I do not believe, in this globalised world, that Bristol is the spiritual prime cause. That argument of Anscombe's is too parochial. It is clear to me, and an abiding shame at my cowardice in not revealing this, in not starting the fight back, that there are others. A species, a race, of entities that can infect humans.

I realise that this is too little, too late, and my life's work has been a sham, but I implore you, reader, you must *fight back.*

Twelfth Night

THE GHOST FLEES across Kochlias and I follow, the city's stygian and labyrinthine streets abetting its escape. All ghosts flee – I wonder where to? If I could collect this one, maybe, maybe I would be ready for Twelfth Night. There is a clatter ahead and, as I careen around the corner, a fathomless cloud of brick dust obscures my view. The ghost's light is lost within the ashen miasma. I yank my scarf, the same colour as the dust, the same colour as my clothes, over my mouth, squint through my eyelashes and slow, to penetrate the gloom of the alleyway.

There is another clangour and my feet are drawn towards the pandemonium. I step out into a main thoroughfare, the mouth of the alley blowing particulates into an already gathered crowd of the Tenebrous.

I have lost the ghost, but the crowd waits expectantly. Here and there amongst the black figures is one in grey, another of the Crepuscular, my own kind. The wide road curves out of sight to both the left and the right, but where the alley has disgorged me, there is a small square. A lone yew tree stands central. Its branches reach to a balcony, upon which profligate light spills.

Fingers of shadow entwine upon the cobbles and the noise of the crowd peaks and is replaced with a hush. There is a flash as a door opens; one of the Illuminated is going to address the crowd.

The white-clad figure, extravagantly lit, contemptuous of the resentment running through the crowd like a contagion, raises its arms and throws back its hood. The blond head revealed, the alabaster face imperious.

"People of Kochlias. Third night is upon us. Who amongst you has the requisite amount of Obol to enter the Lottery?" Hands like marble grip the balcony and the avaricious hawk-like expression sweeps the crowd. None volunteer. None have the Obol yet. It is too early.

The murmuring starts, impossible to pinpoint where in the crowd. Eventually, as it has the other times I have witnessed the Illuminated address the populace, there are cries of "Beneficence, beneficence!" But the Illuminated guard their light jealously. The door opens and closes, the square returns to darkness. The crowd, no longer bound with common purpose, breaks into clots and the Tenebrous scurry to regain their lairs before the Corone enforce curfew.

I share a glance with my fellow grey-clad Crepuscular cousins before we, too, scamper off to our roosts, a step above the Tenebrous, but way below the Illuminated. I turn to where the alleyway was, but it has closed over, the reconfiguration of Kochlias's ways a constant refinement.

I make my way home, but first I must visit the wife and children: a trip to the Tenebrous ghetto.

When the cobbles turn to hard packed dirt and the slate walls turn to raven-black pumice – there is the home of my wife. I do not knock.

"Husband! Have you Bronze for us?" she greets me, as though I was expected. One of the children has espied my approach, no doubt.

"Hello, my wife. There is no Bronze to spare in this, the Twelfth month." I unwind my scarf and clap dust from my ragged cloak.

"Yet you have enough to purchase Crepuscular robes?" she demands.

"We discussed this. Remember?"

She shakes her head. Memories are hard for the Tenebrous

to form; it was not such a long time ago that I was such. The gleam of words, subordinate to what I may command now I have access to some light.

"I am to go first. Only the Crepuscular can enter the Lottery," I state. She nods, in agreement, or submission, it matters not. Soon, one more ghost, maybe two, soon, I may have enough Obol to enter the Lottery.

I share the scraps I can spare, then take my leave whilst they eat, whilst they are distracted, before their pitifulness can stop me, make me spend the Obol on them. Their forgetfulness, when I am out of sight, my only consolation. Their base state disgusts me, disturbs me; I still pity them yet, but less each time I visit. They could help themselves, I sometimes feel.

I return home. The streets of Kochlias are in a playful mood. It must be the excitement of the Twelfth month. It takes me longer to traverse the ways than usual and I stop at the bridge for long moments, hoping to catch sight of the Illuminated maiden once more upon her marble balcony. High above the streets in the airy heights she wanders. I watch and wait, but there is no sight of her. The Illuminated close their shutters and their imprecation of darkness sweeps across Kochlias. I have almost left it too late – I hurry home whilst the Corone are loosed. I make it back just before curfew.

***

THE GHOST HAS nowhere to go. My trap arcs through the air and lands at its base. Its light is snatched out of the air. The gunmetal body of the trap steams gently as I extract the Obol. I am lucky. It is sixth day. The meagre availability of ghosts, hunted to scarcity, means the only way to get the requisite Obols is to take them from another hunter. I watch for other Crepuscular with trepidation now. The few Tenebrous that attempt to get enough Obol to join the ranks of the Crepuscular thin the ghosts even more.

I count the Obol sewn into my robes, one each end of

the scarf, one at the end of the hood, two in the hem, one in the armpit, three in my belt. I contemplate spending one on a weapon, but dismiss the idea. Speed and cunning are my weapons, and my shield. My musings end as I secure the trap back onto my belt. I scan the alleyway in which I have wound up: a part of Kochlias I don't recognise, the sere walls sloping down, the cobbles obscured with filth. I take the path downwards until it winds and limps to the city wall.

I place my hand upon the wall, then rest my head against it and close my eyes. The susurrus beyond scrapes across my listening mind. I grind my teeth and shake my head. Enough! First the Lottery and if, only if, I then am elevated to Illuminated, I can drag the wife and children with me. Before I may even think of the Ferryman.

***

THE FACT THERE are two of them throws me. Two Crepuscular working together, one chasing me into the arms of the second. I stumble to a halt and spin to meet the first, the chaser. The other leaps forward and grapples me, but, as I surmised, has no weapon. The first is more dangerous, armed with a sickle blade.

As he approaches, I go limp, making the one holding me take all my weight. As he adjusts, I spring up and back and arch my head so the crunch of his nose is gristly music in my ears.

My head rings but he has let go enough for me to spin him into the path of the blade. The *shink*, as it scrapes a rib, sets my teeth on edge. I pull the trap, its dull grey body a shadow in the alleyway, and spin it overhead. The stabbed man slides to the ground. The trap whistles through the air and connects, with a crack. The head of the man with the blade blooms a halo of blood. He drops, a puppet with cut strings.

There is a whispering and the ghost that leaps forth from the first body shines brightly, far more brightly than the ghosts I have been hunting. I deploy the trap and the ghost is sucked, screaming silently, within. I crouch over the other, who breathes shallowly. I take his blade.

I extract the Obol, three whole coins, more, much more than the ghosts of the Tenebrous. A slick of blood gathers at the tip of the blade and a drop falls to the cobbles. Him or me, I mutter. I think this night's work has brought me enough Obol to enter the Lottery. I even have enough to exchange one for Bronze, to share with my wife. Enough to tide her over until I can collect the family to me? I tell myself it is. I resent having to pay them now, though. She could help herself.

***

AN EXPECTANT HUSH falls upon the crowd. I grip the handle of the sickle until the grain is imprinted upon my palm. It is the same Illuminated that addresses the crowd, or one so alike it makes no difference.

"People of Kochlias. Eighth night is upon us. Who amongst you has the requisite amount of Obol to enter the Lottery?"

I raise my hand, one fatly gleaming Obol within it, there is shuffling all around me. I pull out the sickle and sweep the crowd with a stare, teeth bared. I turn in a complete circle. They mutter, the Tenebrous; the few Crepuscular move towards me.

There is another Obol held aloft deep in the crowd. The murmuration shifts, roils. The Corone muscle their way through, dressed in their feathered cloaks; knobbed staves prod and poke the crowd out of the way. I endure the avaricious stink of those around me, as a way is opened up for me to the yew tree.

The other Crepuscular with enough Obol is a woman. As she leaves the edge of the crowd, the Corone open a circle keeping the crowd at bay with wood; she is spat upon by one of the Tenebrous. The man, or woman, who spat is clubbed to the ground, the grunts of the Corone administering the punishment loud in the sudden hush.

The ghost that springs up is dim, but worth a fraction of

an Obol. It spins for a brief second, casting ruby, then emerald light upon the front rank of the crowd, but none have a trap. I finger mine but am unsure of the protocol. It leaps away and, from the crowd, two Crepuscular give chase.

We are led up steps carved into the tree, along the wide branch, and onto the balcony. Set against the wall is a model of Kochlias. I glance at its round labyrinthine shape, the steady pulse of changing streets somehow, marvellously, tracked within. I determine to study it later and concentrate on our host.

The illuminated is androgynous, beautiful, icy, imperious. It raises its chin and the Corone that stands near grunts, "Obol."

I spend a minute gathering them into one pile; the female Crepuscular withdraws a bag from between her breasts. We hand them over, their light, bright in the shadows below, barely add to the extravagance displayed here on the balcony.

The Illuminated takes one from each pile and then adds the rest to a cloth bag hanging from its hip, tied with golden ribbon. It nods to the Corone, who bows. Unsure of the etiquette still, I also bow. The female stands contemptuous of any ceremony.

The Illuminated withdraws through the door. I take a step forward and a hand, much larger than my own, clamps upon my shoulder. I turn to look up into the Corone's face. His bushy beard is split in a white grin. He shakes his head. I glance at the female. She is watching with interest.

If there is some signal I do not catch it, but the Corone lets me go, my shoulder burning from his grip. He grunts again. I do not catch what he says, but it is obvious he wants us to follow him.

Inside the marbled residence are many lamps. We shade our eyes; how many Obol does it take to provide so much light? I wonder if I should have tried for one more Obol; I push thoughts of my wife and children from my mind.

We follow the silent Corone, and I marvel at his soundless grace – so large a man, so economical in movement, a dangerous opponent without any doubt. He leads us down corridors, down steps, along more corridors and, eventually, out into a circular room open to the sky. We have walked far, never once having to resort to the streets; the Illuminated have their own ways.

Effulgent torches shine upon something I have never beheld before: a collection of flora, deliberately planted; a profusion of greens, and browns, and reds, and yellows. Nestled within is a contraption that spurts water and the space is full of its tinkling sound.

My eyes, used to the shadows and gloom of the streets are aching, my cheeks wet from a cascade of tears. The other Crepuscular equally affected. The Corone not.

"Rest," his gruff voice commands. "Wait."

He turns on his heel and glides from the courtyard. I turn to the female but she has already scurried off and taken position on a bench. I follow. She watches me through narrowed eyes.

"What do you think will happen now?" I ask.

She shrugs.

"Do you think there'll be more Crepuscular coming?"

She watches me, impassive.

"Here, I mean. More entrants to the Lottery?"

Her expression doesn't change. She hugs herself; the hostility of her gaze makes me smile sadly and shuffle over to a different bench. I finger the sickle inside my sleeve.

There is a sudden burst of piping notes and a bird, small as a starling, drab in colour, hops about and lands in the water. Fascinated, I watch it clean itself. It is so seldom that anything with animation is seen upon the streets. The Tenebrous consume anything that dares.

"Little scamp." The melodious voice shocks me to my feet. I whirl, blade half-pulled. The Illuminated stands an arm's length from me. I hadn't heard any approach.

"I beg your pardon?" I ask, aware that the female Crepuscular has crept closer, putting me between her and the Illuminated.

"The bird. He is a playful one."

I don't know what to say, so remain silent, as does the female.

"You must be weary. You are ahead of most of the

competition, so have a chance to rest before the Lottery on Twelfth Night. Your entry is assured." The Illuminated claps twice and two women, dressed unlike any I have seen – in short olive tunics and beige leggings – hurry into the courtyard. One takes my hand, the other the female's.

"These servants will take you to a chamber where you may rest, be washed and made ready." The Illuminated makes small flicking motions with both hands and we are led away separately.

***

IT IS TWELFTH Night. I am dressed in a loincloth, armed with sword and buckler and brimming with anticipation.

The apartment has a massive bed, a couch, a sunken bath, filled with hot water whenever I want it, and torches, lamps and lanterns. It has learning for the taking. It has no windows and but one door. Which has remained closed.

I have been washed, my robes removed, my sickle taken away, I have slept, and eaten and paced, confined to an opulent prison until now. The servants are solicitous, but uncommunicative. Unable to go forth, or find out more, I have stewed. There are only so many baths you can take. I am mad with silence and inactivity.

Outside the once silent corridors now bustle. I have occasionally heard sweet singing down them, and nothing more. There is now a great activity.

Upon waking I immediately spotted the sword and buckler. I am now armed. I sit and watch the door.

There is a clunk, a ratcheting sound behind me and I turn to see the wall retreating. I stand and face it. Beyond is a large space, dusty ground. No, not dust, something coarser. Sand? I creep to the edge and look out.

In the great round space more rooms are opening, like mine. Above is a great glinting expanse of glass. Behind it, light, the Illuminated.

Lottery.

I tense and relax muscles and stretch so that my back pops and cracks. I stalk into the arena, noting eleven others also making their entrances. Only one will walk out of here, to join the Illuminated.

A bear of a man roars and charges his nearest neighbour. I hear the clash of steel upon steel from another quarter and slowly circle, trying to keep my neighbours in sight.

The nearest, a youngster, first fuzz on his face, stalks closer then takes up a fighting pose, and hop-steps nearer. I am ready. The clash of his sword upon my buckler drowns out the sounds of fighting from further away. I try to look in many directions at once. We exchange a couple of blows. He favours the right. After one such exchange, my sword clattering harmlessly from the boss of his shield, I take a chance and slam the edge of my buckler into his face.

He isn't ready for such a tactic. It scores a deep gash and his head whips to the side, crunching bone loud, spray of blood upon the sand. My following blade takes him high in the chest. He stiffens and drops. I finish him off with a stab to the throat.

A wall rumbles closed. His ghost is child-like and flashes briefly before winking out. This whole arena is a ghost-trap, I realise.

I scan the arena. Near me are two women, seemingly evenly matched. I stride towards them, trying to come up from their side. I guess they'll both spot me.

The first, her grey hair loose, sweat-slicked so that she must wipe it from her eyes, crab-walks away. The other, slimmer, taller, tries to match her, they both try to put the other between them and me.

I reach the first, the slimmer one, and she cannot fight us both off. She tries to skip backwards and catches my blade on her buckler, but the other nips forward and her sword takes the slim woman in the leg.

I feint and the slim woman goes to block, but my blade, that

I fake toward her, goes sideways and pierces her opponent's throat. She topples to the ground. I jump back to avoid the other woman's blade. The ghost distracts neither of us for long. The blood coursing down her leg and soaking into the sand gives me an advantage that I fully exploit.

She manages to graze me, a stinging slash on one cheek that bleeds freely, before I finish her with a stab through the stomach and another through the heart. Her ghost is brief in its radiance.

I am blowing at this point, and hope that I have a little time to catch my breath. There is no other sound of fighting. I have been vaguely aware of other flashes, other walls rumbling closed. I gaze around the arena. The female from Eighth day and the bear of a man stand in the distance. He has made short work of four opponents and the woman has accounted for two more, with the three I have killed that leaves just us.

The woman looks from me, to the larger man, shrugs and makes her way to him; he is slightly closer. I stalk towards them both.

He is massive, muscular, well-fed; may have been a Crepuscular for a long time? He moves with practised grace and I narrow my eyes; it is familiar. Shorn of the ceremonial mask, the leather and the feather cloak, he is nevertheless the Corone. The Illuminated have stacked the competition!

The woman dances away from a charge and I see her glance wildly to me. She's spotted it, too. With no word exchanged, we work in concert. The Corone senses the change, and backs slowly away, his sword atop his buckler, defensive.

I go right, she goes left. I kick the sand towards him, a fakeout. He is not drawn in by it. She drops her sword. What is she doing? He spots it, of course, and moves towards her. I take a few steps, within range of his sword. Still moving towards the woman, he swipes me. I easily block.

He is a few steps away from her, and half-concentrating on me. The buckler she throws slams into his skull with a clang. It is all the opening I need and I hop towards him. Some instinct sees my thrust thwarted. Instead of taking him in the heart, he manages to deflect it enough that it takes him in the arm. A second blade slices, and he somehow manages to block hers too. Yet his sword clatters from his grasp.

As we pull back, readying another blow, he launches an unexpected punch. A massive fist like a boulder catches me and I feel a rib, possibly two, pop. His buckler deflects my blow, but hers takes him through the eye. He topples, like some hewn tree, and her sword is wrenched from her hand. His ghost is like a starling's wing, vast and multifaceted. It sweeps across the arena, before it, too, winks out. I take a breath filled with broken glass and a short step sees my blade slice through the woman's stomach.

She falls. I limp over and raise my sword. I grimace.

"Please…" she says.

I freeze.

"My daughter," she coughs. "Please save my daughter."

A dying wish? I curse it but know I will comply.

I kneel and she whispers instructions. I have no need to finish her off; her blood takes the shapes of wings beneath her dying body. When she has gone, and her ghost spirals and flits away, I stand. My broken ribs, like betrayer's daggers, stab me.

I am ready.

White rose petals shower down. Their cloying aroma sickens me. They turn pink where they touch the blood upon the sand. I drop my sword, fumble the buckler from my arm and trudge back to my luxurious cage.

***

SERVANTS WASH ME, bind my wounds and then leave me. I fall asleep whilst I wait.

I awake to light, and the same androgynous Illuminated sits eating fruit at my table when I get up.

"Welcome to the One Hundred," they say.

"I won?" I wondered.

"Do you not remember? Twelfth Night is over. The One Hundred are complete again. Kochlias is back to normal." Their long slim fingers play over the surface of the ruby-gold apple. They take a delicate bite. "Do you want to see your demesne?" they say.

I nod.

They stand and bid me follow. We take a long walk through the Illuminated's ways. I am still in loincloth only. We meet no one.

"Why is it so empty?" I ask.

They arch a perfectly shaped golden eyebrow. "Why? Because we wish it to be so."

"But all this space," I say.

The Illuminated stops, looks around at the corridors stretching into the distance, the massive, empty room we are passing, a multitude of doors standing open upon it.

"What space?" they ask, then carries on. I follow.

The rooms the Illuminated takes me to are as large as the great square with the yew tree. Seven servants, grey haired, kneel and bow, heads to the floor.

"Why are they kneeling?" I ask.

"You may rise," the Illuminated says.

The servants rise and splinter, moving off in several directions. Two come back immediately and drape me in Illuminated's robes. I finger the soft and silken white material.

"Thank you," I murmur. The servants share a startled look and the Illuminated arches an eyebrow. I curse myself for forgetting my new station.

The woman from the arena was dead, her dying wish binding. My servants seem old; I could clearly use a new one.

"COME," THE ILLUMINATED says and leads me to the floor-to-ceiling window which they push open so that we may walk out upon the balcony.

I look down and see the bridge, where I have spent so long looking up to this very window. Across it, and along the streets, Tenebrous scurry.

"It was her?"

"Who? Oh, this demesne? Yes, it was a woman who owned it previously. Before she accumulated enough wealth to pay the Ferryman. To start her new life."

I nod. It is my plan too, has been ever since I discovered the tales.

"I have obligations," I say.

"Obligations?"

"My family. The daughter of another."

The Illuminated purses their lips and looks a question.

"I need them brought here," I say and turn to look out across Kochlias, to the slums shrouded in constant shadow, filthy with smoke.

"It will cost you," the Illuminated says.

I contemplate the drop below me. I gaze across the city, noticing how clean it is here, how light.

"Of course it will."

I wonder if it is worth it. The wife has enough to live on for some time; I was generous with my last act of charity. Perhaps, with the largess of my demesne, I could still be generous. Pass her word that she now needed to help herself. Put the children to work. My chance of a new life, gathering a Ferryman's fare, that's what's important now. "How much does this demesne make?" I ask.

The Illuminated shrugged.

"What happens now?"

The Illuminated laughs, a high cascading, musical sound. "Now you learn to live." They gently turn me away from the sights and smells of Kochlias. "Welcome to the ranks of the Illuminated," they say.

We Do Like To Be Beside

AND THE DOORS open and we are out and we are running. The dog, Tyr, streaks far ahead. I couldn't keep up with him if I tried. Little God, mother calls him. My sister, older, longer legs, is next, her yellow blouse like the Tour de France jersey; then me. I look back to see my parents getting the things from the car – a brand-new beige Austin Allegro – windbreaks, blue plastic picnic cold box, foldable chairs. And then my feet are on sand and I put my head down and pump my arms and fly as fast as I can to try and catch up with my sister. And there's the sea, the open, blue, glittering sea. The dunes bump against it, and running in sand is hard and climbing the dune is hard and I'm panting.

The dog is barking and my sister has stopped and I'm catching up and that's when I see, when I crest the top of the dune, our dune. There's someone else there, that family – father, massive, glistening in the sun; the mother small, Irish hair; the children, excessive amounts of them. How I hate that family.

The father lies, his bulk in stasis, his hump of a belly proud of the sand. The wife looks up to where my sister holds the dog, straining at its collar, barking. The children don't cease in their tumult but I sense they've seen us. They know us. We live so very near them, after all.

"She's a witch," my sister says. Has said a thousand times. Almost proud of the fact.

And still the mammoth father does not move. They have our

spot in the sand and I look back at my own parents trudging across the beach towards us. I glance at my sister. At the line of her mouth.

"This is our place," she spits out.

"It's public," I say.

"Go and tell the olds they have to set up somewhere else," she says, narrowing her eyes. I've seen that look far too many times.

I take one last look at the family below, the children shrieking, their mother staring at us in open curiosity, the father unmoving. I shudder, they have brought their clutter with them. The sand littered with the same sort of crap they fill their front yard with. Bamboo poles with woven wool dreamcatchers, brightly coloured cloth bags full of God-knows-what, and stacks of curling paper. Do they not want a break from what Dad calls "the detritus of their failed lives"?

"Go on," she growls, her voice blending with the dogs. Tyr's upset too. I spin on my heel and run to where my parents are slowly, too slowly, walking to where we always set up when we come to the beach.

As I get closer I hear them arguing.

"She's your daughter," Mum is saying.

"I'd like to think that by now you'd consider her yours as well," Dad answers back.

Then she spots me and says, "Toby."

"What is it, Toby?" Dad asks.

"There's someone in our spot. It's that family from the corner," I tell them. They know immediately which family, of course.

"Then we'll just have to choose another spot," Mum says.

Dad sighs.

"Can you go and look for another sheltered area please, Toby?" she asks me.

I nod and look back to where my sister still waits at the top of the dune, the yellow of her blouse standing out against the pure blue of the sky. The dog now sits quietly beside her.

"Amy is angry," I tell my parents. They share a look. I put my fingers in my mouth and whistle and see the dog jump up and turn to face me. I whistle again and he races towards me. My sister glances back at us once then walks down into the bowl at the foot of the dune. That's brave of her.

I race off knowing Tyr will catch up. I know that the flat part of the beach will be packed so I have to run up and down the dunes. It occurs to me that another family may get anywhere I find by the time I get my own family back there and wonder what to do about that. I can't think of one thing.

I immediately find another nook with shade for Dad and close enough to the sea for me and out of the wind for Mum and with an area to sunbathe for Amy. It's perfect. It's the next dune to where we usually plonk ourselves anyway. I climb to the top to signal to my sister and parents but they're not there.

Above, I notice that the seagulls are flying in a circle, their raucous cries suddenly loud, as if the lee of the dune I had been in had blocked their noise. Even better. We all hate seagulls. Last year, on this beach, we'd bought chips from the chip van parked by the concrete toilet block and were mobbed as soon as we brought them onto the beach. Mum said that next time we need to eat them near to the van where they had bird scarers. But next to the van smelt like toilets and I wanted to eat mine this year on the beach again but with no seagulls.

I take off my t-shirt and hop-jump down the dune to where I've chosen for us and then place it on the ground and find a few stones to weigh it down. Just to show that someone has chosen this spot.

"Watcha doin'?"

I spin from where I was assessing my handiwork to come face to face with one of the ragged tribe of children from that family. Well, his face is around my chest-height really but chest to face doesn't sound right. Close up my nose wrinkles to the sour milk and biscuit smell of unwashed body. The child smiles a gap-toothed smile. Younger than me, stick legs and baggy shorts, looking like Mickey Mouse. Looking like me at that age but dirtier and with hair that needs cutting.

"Making sure no one takes our spot," I reply. I think a second and take out a lollipop I was saving and give it to him. He smiles shyly and squirrels it away in his filthy shorts.

He puts a finger up his nose and has a good root about. Ignoring the grimace on my face he pulls it out with a slimy green globule at the end which he immediately puts in his mouth. He cocks his head and taking his finger out points behind me. "He sick?"

I frown, and look to where he's pointing. The dog had come back without me hearing, tail between his legs and, as I watch, he heaves, once, twice, and then a thick stream of purplish vomit comes out. What the hell has he been eating? A stench of rotten fish rolls over me, my stomach contracts, and I taste acid.

"Are you okay, Tyr?" I ask and walk towards him. He whines and pants. I need to get him some water. Where are my parents? Amy?

"Can you stay here and make sure he doesn't run off?" I ask the boy and when he nods I run up the dune again. Like before, the seagulls wheel through the bright blue sky, screaming to each other. I still can't see my sister, or my parents.

I jump-skip down the dune. "Does your family have any water?" I ask the child. Again he nods. "Come on, boy!" I call to the dog but he just whines. I have to pick him up. Gosh, he's heavy; a good sheep-chaser Dad had called him when we first got him.

"Come on," I say to the boy and lead him around the front of the dune, past the cleft between their dune and the one I'd staked out. The dog's rancid breath wafts up, his heart racing fast, as he squirms a little in my arms. I look up the small valley between dunes and still don't spot my parents.

The kid remains silent, keeps turning to see if I'm following, his eyes wide. We round the corner, the squealing of the gulls our intro music, and his family aren't there. No, mostly aren't there.

No mother, no horde of children, but there, in the centre of the clearing, the patriarch, unmoved and unmoving, a hillock of pink.

The kid scoots over to a plastic bag and takes out a sand encrusted bottle and holds it out to me. I lay the dog down, my legs and arms screaming from the weight, and grab the bottle. I don't bother asking for a bowl, whatever this family has is covered in grime anyway. I pour a small amount of water into my hand and hold it out for the dog to lick, which he does enthusiastically.

Last year he drank seawater and got sick too. This year he must have eaten something bad. After a few handfuls of water he starts to look a bit perkier. And I scan around. In among the dirt and jumble there's an intricate display of sandcastles and trenches surrounding the man where he lies. I watch the sand flies hover and a glossy black beetle wend its way across the sand.

"Thanks for the water," I say loudly. The kid grins. The bulk in the middle of the maze doesn't move. "Is your dad okay?" I ask and the kid nods vigorously.

"He's dreaming," the kid says.

I stroke the dog's head and he wags his tail a bit. "Ready to get up?" I ask him and he sits up.

"Well... I'd best go find my family," I say. I stand and wipe my hand on my shorts. "Can I take this?" I ask, giving the water bottle a shake to slosh the water inside a bit. The kid nods again.

Not much of a talker.

"Thanks." I turn. "Thanks mister!" I say.

I take a step in the direction of the man and stop, he's asleep, must be to be so still. Best not disturb him.

I scan the top of the dune and only spot a circle of gulls. Time to go.

Back to where my shirt is staked out on the sand. The dog looks done in. "Stay!" I order him and he flops down on the t-shirt and rolls to his side. I give Tyr another cupped hand of warm water and then close the bottle and put it next to him.

"Guard!" I order. He lifts his head but then lets it fall back on the sand.

I go to find my family. It feels like a long time since I've seen them, but I don't have a watch – the strap broke and it's at home on my bedside table. I stride to the top of the dune – three steps forward, one slide back – and stand at the top blowing. Carrying the dog took a lot out of me. There's no one in sight. I march down the side of the dune and up the side of the one we usually camp out on, disturbing the seagulls that all leap to the air screeching like witches, calling to each other like drunken sailors.

Below: the dome of the man's belly, solid, stately, still. The kid is off at the side of the dune, poking at something with a twig.

I try to see the man's features but his bald head is partly covered, his face obscured with a scrap of brightly coloured cloth.

I retrace my path back to the car, which is burning hot in the midday sun, so hot it scalds my hand when I try the door handle.

There's no one inside anyway.

I stand on the wall separating road from beach and turn in a circle. I can't see Dad's red t-shirt or Mum's blue beach dress or my sister's yellow blouse anywhere. I run down the road to the concrete toilet block, ash-black and shaped a bit like a shoebox with a too-large lid. My family aren't here either, nor by the ice cream van. I wander onto the beach and decide that they must have got fed up waiting for me and found somewhere else, maybe even on the flat bit.

I'm a bit worried about Tyr. Maybe I should go back and get him before going for another look? But that would take too much time. So I walk up and down the beach, the flat bit, searching. I walk past families and couples, kids and adults, other families with dogs, and people listening to the radio, a bunch of friends on lilos, and a couple of guys throwing a Frisbee. But not my family.

I'm starting to get real worried now. Where could they be? I know they haven't left because the car is still there. I go to where the sea sucks obsessively at the shore. I like the sea, usually I'm the only one who goes paddling, or swimming, on a day as hot as today. I think the rest of them are mad not to have a cold dip.

I shade my eyes and try to spot who's in the water. Dad

never goes swimming; Mum says he's afraid of the water but he says he's not afraid of water, he's afraid of drowning, which is different. My sister says he saw someone say that in a film once.

I think it's sensible to be afraid of drowning but that it shouldn't stop you swimming.

Dad doesn't like the family down the road, avoids them as much as possible. It was him who first said their mum was a witch, something my sister repeats often. My mum says that he should know, but I don't know why.

I can't decide what to do. I should go back to the dune and find the dog and then go sit by the car. They'll find me at the car. Eventually.

As I walk back, the buzz of music and people talking, playing, laughing, surrounds me but something a teenager says to his friend catches me up.

"What did you say?" I ask.

The young man, first moustache trembling atop flaky lips, gazes up at me. "Huh?"

"Just now. You said someone's been arrested?"

"Uh huh."

"When? Was it here?"

The dude smooths his 'tache and nods. "Just over there." He's pointing to the dunes. To where I've left the dog. To where the family from down the close were. To where I'd last seen my parents, and sister.

"What happened?"

"I don't know, man, they dragged them away, there was a bit of a crowd. Something about it not being natural?" The two youths exchange a glance.

"What's it to you?" The other one asks.

"Oh nothing," I say. "Nothing." I nod a thanks and walk away. Arrested? I'd best get Tyr and then… And then? Do something – surely Mum and Dad would have said something about me. Nah, it can't have been them arrested. Unnatural?

What did Mum mean earlier that Amy was Dad's daughter?

What did Dad mean, she should have accepted her by now?

My mind races as I run down the beach, back to the dunes.

The dog's gone when I return. The t-shirt I took off too. There is a gull eating the dog's vomit. That makes me gag. I need help.

I go to where the man from the corner house is, maybe the family has come back.

Around the corner the girth of the man remains unyielding. I edge closer. There is no child here now. The maze is deeper, the mounds I'd taken to be sandcastles now apparent as just heaps of unburied sand. I edge closer – the bulk does not move. The trenches, narrow and deep, wind around the flat foot of the dune.

I edge closer and venture a "hello" and still no movement. A squirt of seagull poo lands on my foot and soon I'm kicking sand as I try to wipe it off my trainer. I kick a mound of sand over and into the dug-out labyrinth.

There is a sound behind me like air leaking from a tyre. I turn and the wife is there, her children tucked in behind her like kittens. She beckons urgently. I give my shoe one last scrape across the sand and walk gingerly to her. She places a finger, blackened by who knows what, to her wrinkled lips. I frown but keep quiet and when I reach her she places a hand on my shoulder and grips me hard. It hurts a little and I start to struggle.

"Your sister is waiting for you," she hisses.

"Where is she?" I ask and stop struggling.

"Come with me and find out." Her grip does not lessen as she marches me away from the dune. The kids skip in and out and around us. I'm scared, but also really want to see my sister. I hope the woman isn't lying to me.

"What have you done with my sister?"

The woman turns piggy eyes upon me. "Done? Nothing, she wants you to come too. Prevailed upon my better nature, she did."

"What do you mean?" I ask.

"You don't belong. She does. But she convinced me that we can make you belong, too. Once the Dreaming is complete."

The boy I gave the lollipop to skips ahead and looks back at me, smiling. His siblings keep their distance.

"Dreaming? The man, your husband, he—"

"We like living near you, you know," she says.

"What?"

"We do like to be beside you."

"Thanks...?" I wonder why she feels like telling me this. I try to shrug out of her grasp but her hand is like an iron claw. We are heading back to the carpark.

"There's only one problem," she continues. "Your mum's innocent, we don't see that much of you but—"

"But what?"

"Your father." She glances at me and I see disgust in her eyes.

"What about him?" We are getting nearer the cars. She's not turning to go towards our car though. I spot their campervan, dirty-white, battered, leaking oil no doubt, like it does on our road.

"He's... Well, he's always staring. At us."

"Is he?" I'm flustered, the lady from down the road has been walking me at a quick pace, and we are now nearing the camper.

I can hear the dog whining and scratching.

"It's not polite. It's not nice. You're his blood too, that's how she convinced me. Your sister." We come to the van and she pulls a set of keys from the pocket of her tatty dress. The keyring is unidentifiable, a purple blob that might once have been furry.

She fits a key to the lock and pulls the door slightly open, without letting go of me. With her foot she shoves the dog further inside and then opens the door enough to push me in.

Tyr, ready to go for her, jumps ecstatically at me instead. "Wait—" I say, but she's slammed the door behind me and locked it. I try the handle but it won't open, and the van's interior – stinking of old chip fat, soiled, sweaty linen and an underlying rusty, oily odour – has no method of getting into the van's cab.

"Hey!" I shout and bang on the door, giving it a good few kicks. "Hey!"

But nothing doing. She's gone and locked me in here, with the dog, but not with my mum or dad. Or sister. How dare she say Dad wasn't nice. She didn't say anything about my sister at all.

There isn't much room inside – a soot-blackened kitchen, some pots and pans, a couple of bunkbeds and several cupboards locked with padlocks. There is a door to the small chemical toilet, and the windows are high up and thin. I sit on the edge of the bed and wonder what to do next, absentmindedly stroking the dog.

After a while of kicking the door and shouting I realise that no one is going to come and rescue me. I grab a saucepan as a makeshift weapon – I can find no knives or other cutlery – and I sit on the bed to wait. My gaze wanders and alights on an old cardboard suitcase with an advert for laundry on it. Held closed with leather straps. I grab it. Maybe there'll be something useful inside? I struggle to open it. Inside are hundreds of photographs.

Photographs of our street, of our house, of our family, of us on the beach, of our car, our dog, of my sister. Many of my sister. In each one with my parents in, Dad's face is erased. Scratched out.

That's horrible. I spend a long time looking at the photographs.

After a while I lie down, just to rest my eyes. I've no idea how long I've been asleep but I leap up having heard the van's cabin door open then someone climbs aboard. My hand searches the bed until it lands on the saucepan handle. "Ready, boy?" I ask Tyr. He's sat up too, ears pricked.

The door opens a crack and a child eels inside – I leap to the door and try to push it open as the engine starts. The door springs open and I leap out, past a startled dirty child. The whole horde is there but the parents are in the cab. The child I'd talked to earlier gestures from the door and the horde disappears inside. At his command they leave me alone. He raises the lollipop I gave him to his mouth.

I don't wait around. I run, the dog with me. No one raises the alarm. I glance back and all the children have climbed inside. The child who gave me the water bottle waves from the open door, which swings shut as the van lumbers away. As the van turns the corner I glimpse yellow in the passenger seat. Amy! I need to tell my parents they've taken Amy.

It's almost night-time, the light slowly fading into the summer evening. I stop and watch the van pull away. Have I escaped? Now what?

I run over to our car. It's still there. It's still empty. I again go to the chip van. I wish I had some money because I'm starving.

At least I can get a drink at the water fountain outside the toilet block. No sign of my parents here either. I ask the chip-van man if he's seen them, describe them to him, but no. He's also not seen the police arrest anyone. Said that was a rumour passed around by stoners.

The beach is emptying of families. Young couples will turn up soon and walk up and down because it's "romantic". I need to find my family. I hurry back to the dunes and there's no one at the place I'd staked out for us. I climb the hill and look down to where we usually stay and the man has gone and all that's left is the weird maze-pattern in the sand. I sit down and put my head in my hands. I'm going to have to ask a grown-up for help, to call the police.

The dog barks and gallops down the hill. Where the man had lain all day was a smooth circle of clear sand. The dog races across the bottom of the dune to this circle, barks again and runs towards the sea. I watch for a second then start down the side of the dune and I realise something. The weird pattern? It's the street plan of the estate I live on, the central bit being where our house would be – and theirs is blank. Where the man had lain dreaming all day.

I hurry down the dune and see the dog racing towards a figure dressed in blue. The sweat I'd worked up running now cools unpleasantly on my skin. It's Mum! I race to her and grab her in a hug. I've started crying but I'm not embarrassed like I'd usually be.

"Toby. Where have you been, I've been worried sick!" She

strokes my head.

"The family from the corner have Amy!" I blurt out. Mum frowns. "Where's Dad?" I ask through the tears.

"What's got into you? Who's Amy? And your dad... your dad is in our hearts, where he'll always be. He did used to love it here though, didn't he? Beside the sea." She gazes at the sea.

"Amy is... is... what do you mean? Dad is dead?" I'm frowning, it's hard to think, my mind feels foggy – what's happening?

She ruffles my hair. "Wake up, sleepy head."

I shake my head. I had something important to tell her. What was it? I can feel my mind being rewritten, settling into a new groove, history and memory reconfiguring, I try to keep hold of it. Amy is my sister. Dad isn't dead. Amy is... Dad...

The dog barks and runs at the waves and I look up and the sun is sinking into the sea and I wish that Dad hadn't died, a heart attack at forty, and that we'd not buried him last year. I shake my head – falling asleep in the sun has meant I've awoke confused, that's all. "Amy was just a girl in my dream. She wore yellow." I give Mum a quick hug, dry my eyes and run to play with the dog.

Afterword

EVENTUALLY ALL AUTHORS are asked, "Where do you get your ideas?" Our answers are often flippant, dismissive even. I even wrote a story about it – in my previous collection *A Tiding of Magpies: Five For Silver*. But the real answer is that they come from recalling incidents, recalling odd facts and unconnected images and combining such in flights of fancy.

So where did I get the ideas for the stories within this collection?

The Museum for Forgetting itself had its genesis in late 2015, early 2016. It seems quaint now but I was very angry with the Cameron government defunding the arts. I had also read an article, I forget where (no irony intended), about a museum for forgetting in Sweden and I liked the title and it made me want to write a story. For no reason I can now discern I've never tried to sell this one. It was published on the Grimbold Patreon and so has only been read by a select few until now.

Memories to the Flames was written for a North Bristol Writers anthology (*Fire*) – the start of that idea was a combination of images. An aborted story about an angel trapped beneath a library writing books in its own blood. But the story didn't work and I put it aside and forgot about it until I needed an idea for the anthology. Then I remembered the Gabriel Garcia Marquez story – *A Very Old Man with Enormous Wings* – and wondered what would have happened if the people who the angel appeared to had imprisoned him.

Sailing Beneath the City was inspired by a Geoff Manaugh BLDGBLOG post (my first blog – being mainly book reviews was named BRSBKBLOG so it's not the only time I've been inspired by Mr Manaugh). It's probably the earliest of the stories in this collection, written in May 2013. It was the first submission I got feedback on from an editor (who suggested some changes that very much improved the story) and it has been published before. But it fit the theme so well I had to include it.

Benediction was written specifically for this collection. A number of my stories feature the Jumping Tree and the patch of forest that's clear in my own memories of a place of escape while growing up on a council estate. This story was inspired by Werner Herzog's *Of Walking in Ice*. It's had a few different forms before I settled on this slightly unusual way of telling the story.

The Detective's Tale was written on commission for The Refuge Collection – the brainchild of Steve Dillon (from *Things in the Well*) – an anthology in aid of refugees. Steve has very kindly allowed me to reprint the story here. It was written in a draughty castle gatehouse on a wet and windy weekend. Because it was a shared world anthology, most of the characters are not mine and the plot had to fit the overarching story. It's the only bit of my writing that's made it to audiobook so far and it's kind of odd to hear a story written by an Englishman for an Australian anthology being read by an American. If the setting and story intrigue you I thoroughly recommend the collection – it includes a story by Lee Murray which won the Sir Julius Vogel Award. You can see more about the collection on Wikipedia here: https://en.wikipedia.org/wiki/The_Refuge_Collection

A Signal in the Dark was written for an anthology in memory of the Bristol author David J Rodger that I edited. It's in the same story universe as a couple of my other stories – I don't write straight sci-fi often but eventually, someday, there may be a novel in this story universe.

Thresholds was also written specifically for this collection. It has the most prosaic of starts in that I jotted down a list of ideas related to human memory and one of them was the threshold effect. I then wondered about how to dramatise that and in what situation it could be meaningful.

Dismantling was written for performance. Back in 2014/15 I was a regular at Bristol open mic events and had a number of very small pieces that could be performed in less than five minutes. I don't recall where the idea came from.

The Ghost Conspiracy started life as a story within a story in my first novel *Sick City Syndrome*. The editor of the novel thought it slowed the forward momentum of the novel's main plot too much and asked me to remove it – it was around 12,000 words and removing that from the novel was a wrench – but totally the right decision. I realised that with a little reworking it could stand alone and it was published as bonus material – set in the same world as the novel, as a prequel. If you'd like to discover more about that world, I plan to make the novel available to download via my website, once I've given it a bit of spit and polish. There's a nod to Stephen Volk's *Ghostwatch* in there – I asked him if I could and he was happy as long as it was obvious it's not the same ghost. I hope it is obvious.

Twelfth Night was written for another North Bristol Writers anthology (*The Dark Half of the Year*) and I was supposed to be writing a tale around one of our real world holidays that occur in winter like Christmas, Bonfire Night or the like (which was the anthology theme.) Somehow my mind went down a second world pathway and I created the odd city of Kochlias, which I fully intend to revisit one day. My memory of the city is painted in black and white, shadow and twilight. Some time I'll tell the story of the light that was hidden.

We Do Like To Be Beside, the final story, was written for the *Alchemy Press Book of Horrors 2* and is infused with the memories of 1970's family holidays to North Wales.

All of the stories are autobiographical. None of the stories are autobiographical. They are collages of memory, dream, imagination and necessity. I hope you enjoy them.

About the Author

PETE W SUTTON is a writer and editor. His first book – *A Tiding of Magpies* – was shortlisted for the British Fantasy Awards in 2017 for Best Collection. His first novel – *Sick City Syndrome* – was published by KGHH (and is now out of print.) His last novel – *Seven Deadly Swords* – was published by Grimbold Books. He has edited a number of short story anthologies, the latest of which – *Forgotten Sidekicks* – was published in April 2020.

Other Titles From Kristell Ink

A Tiding of Magpies

Pete W. Sutton

One for sorrow...

These deliciously dark tales are themed on the counting magpies songs. Twenty-five tales, ranging from tiny flash fiction to long stories, always entertain and unnerve. Whether it is waking to unmentionable sounds in Not Alone, taking a trip to the land of stories in Five for Silver, the surprising use of a robot butler in I, Butler or competition winner It Falls, Sutton's unique voice shines through.

Forgotten Sidekicks

Edited by Peter Sutton & Steven Poore

We all know what happens when the hero saves the day. But what about their sidekicks?

Too often the hero is held high and celebrated whilst their sidekicks and comrades are brushed to the side; their own battles forgotten, and their actions airbrushed to nothingness from the tales of victory.

These stories didn't make the headlines: but they happened, and they're glorious.

Courtney M. Privett -- Desmond Warzel -- Donald Jacob Uitvlugt
Allen Stroud -- Su Haddrell -- Chrissey Harrison -- John Houlihan
Ian Hunter -- Steve Dillon -- Jim Horlock.

Infinite Dysmorphia

Edited by Peter Sutton & Kate Coe

An anthology of science fiction and speculative stories exploring
how science and technology could change what it means to be
human. Bio implants, cybernetics, genetic modification, age
reversal, robotics and technology...what is the human experience
of undergoing these procedures, and what is the advance of
technology going to bring?

What does the future hold in store for those who are pushing
the definition of humanity?

Ren Warom -- David Boop -- Isha Crowe -- Dolly Garland
Thomas J. Spargo -- Elizabeth Hosang -- Ron Wingrove
Sean Grigsby -- Courtney M. Privett -- Steve Cotterill
Anne Nicholls -- David Sarsfield -- Frances Kay -- Alec McQuay

kristell-ink.com

Lightning Source UK Ltd.
Milton Keynes UK
UKHW012149190921
390854UK00001B/2

The Fox

M. N. J. Butler

CnPosner Books

First published in 1995 by Blackwoods London
Published 2018 by CNPosner Books
Copyright © M. N. J. Butler 1995, 2017
ISBN 978-1718115606

To David and to Beryl and in memory
of I. W. the best of bank managers.

THE ROYAL HOUSES OF SPARTA

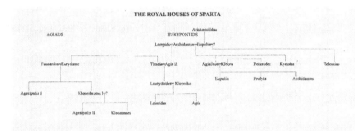

5Glossary of names and terms

Names marked with a * are those of historical figures

Achilles
    legendary Greek hero of Trojan War

Agesipolis
    (1)* Agiad, elder son of King Pausanios, later King Agesipolis I
    (2)* Agiad, elder son of King Kleombrotos, later King Agesipolis II

Agiads
    one of the two royal houses of Sparta

Agis
    (1)* Agis II, Eurypontid King of Sparta, father of Leotychides
    (2) second son of Leotychides and Kleonike

Agisilaos* (Agesilaus)
    Eurypontid, son of King Archidamos and Eupolia, younger brother of King Agis II; later King Agisilaos II

agora
    central public space in ancient Greek city- states

Ainesios
    platoon leader under Leotychides

Alexandros
    (1) Spartan general
    (2)* son of King

	Philippos of Macedon, later Alexander the Great
Alkimenes*	Corinthian, friend of Tolmaios, later member of peace party
Alkmaionids	noble Athenian family
Alkman*	early Spartan poet
alpha	initial letter of Greek alphabet and of Athens; borne on shields by Athenian warriors
Amphytrion	father of Herakles
Amyntas	(1)* Amyntas III, king of Macedon, son of Arrhidaeus, father of Perdikkas and Philippos (2)* Amyntas IV, king of Macedon, son of Perdikkas, deposed by Philippos
Anakos	commander of Spartan cavalry regiment at Lechion
Anaxandros	boy in Leotychides's flock, son of Eutelidas, known as the Magpie
Anaxilas	Syracusan runner
Androklidas*	leader of anti-Spartan

	faction in Thebes
Antalkidas*	boy in Leotychides's flock, son of Leon; later Spartan admiral, ambassador to Persia, and chief ephor
Apella	the assembly of all the citizens of Sparta
Apelleas*	up-country sculptor
Aphrodite	goddess of love
Apollo	god of the sun, brother of Artemis
Apollodoros	Spartan warrior, friend of Pityas
apophthegm	A concise saying or maxim, an aphorism
Archidamos	(1)*former Eurypontid King of Sparta, father of Agis II and Agisilaos (2)* son of Agisilaos
Argileonis	wife of Meleas
Aristeas	Corinthian runner, member of war party
Aristedes	Athenian mercenary
Aristodemos	(1) legendary king of Sparta, father of twin Kings Eurysthenes and Procles, the ancestors

7

	of the two royal houses of Sparta (2) cousin of King Pausanios
Aristokrates	big boy in Leotychides's flock, son of Pharax; known as the Donkey, later as Pointer
Aristomelidas*	Father of Queen Eupolia and grandfather of Agisilaos, later ambassador to Thebes
Ariston*	former Eurypontid king of Sparta, father of Demartos
Aristotle*	sophist from Athens tutor to Prince Alexander
Artaxerxes*	Artaxerxes II, Great King of Persia
Artemis	goddess of hunting, sister of Apollo
Artemision	moon of April
Asklepios	god of healing
Athena	goddess of wisdom
Athenian War, the	the Peloponnesian War, the Long War
Axiochos	son of Alkibiades

Boiotarchs	the seven chief officers of the Boiotian confederacy
Bonehead	name given to boy in Leotychides's flock
Brasidas*	Spartan commander in Long War
Bronze House	shrine of Athena Poliachos ("Holder of the city"), situated on Sparta's highest hill
Cattle Price House	sanctuary of Asklepios of the Cattle Price, hospital in Sparta
Chabrias*	Athenian general
Chairon	elderly and wealthy citizen of Sparta, later Elder
Charmidas*	Eleian, victor in Olympic boys' boxing in 444 B. C.
Chaste Huntress, the	Artemis
Chionis	boy in Leotychides's flock
Cockerel, the	name given to Leotychides
Council (*gerousia*)	Spartan government body, consisting of the two kings and twenty-

	eight elected members over the age of sixty
Dancer	Leotychides's horse
Daphne	hetaira, loved by Anaxilas
Demartos*	former Eurypontid king of Sparta, supposed son of Ariston, deposed on the grounds that he was really the son of Agetus, his mother's first husband
Derkyllidas*	Lakedaimonian general; succeeded Thibron as commander of Hellenic forces in Asia
Dexippas	son of Kallias, cousin of Gorgo
Dinon	father of Doreius (2) and Hekataios, wounded in Long War
Dionysos	god of wine
Diopeithes*	Spartan seer, teacher in Leotychides's flock
Diphridas*	Spartan general in Corinthian War, guest at Menelaos House, later ephor
Donkey, the	name given to Aristokrates

Doreius	(1)* Former Agiad prince, son of King Anaxandridas II; challenged his brother Kleomenes I for the throne, and attempted to establish a colony at Herakleia in Sicily (2) patrol leader in Leotychides's flock, son of Dinon, brother of Hekataios (3) son of Gorgo (2), supposedly by Chairon
Doriska	mother of Dexippas
Dromea	serf, maidservant to Queen Timaia
eiren	boy in flock between ages of sixteen and twenty
Elders (*gerontes*)	elected members of the Council
Elucidates	citizen of Sparta
enomotarchos	Spartan platoon commander
Epaminondas*	Theban officer, later general
ephors	the five principal magistrates of Sparta, elected for a term of one year
Epitadeus*	chief ephor of Sparta,

	said to have made a decree allowing Spartiates to sell their kleroi
Erato	muse of erotic poetry and mime
eromenos	"junior" partner in homosexual relationship
Eros	Cupid, god of love
Eteonikos*	Spartan general, friend of Lysander, later governor of Aigina
Etymokles*	Spartan ambassador to Athens; supporter of Agisilaos
Euagoras	boy in Leotychides's flock; later poet and musician
Eudamidas*	Spartan commander of Olynthian expedition, brother of Phoidibas
Euphron	Argive mercenary
Eupolia	(1)* second wife of King Archidamos, mother of Agisilaos and Teleutias, daughter of Aristomelidas, not of royal Heraklid descent (2)* elder daughter of Agisilaos

Eurydame	Agiad Queen of Sparta, wife of Pausanios, sister of Queen Timaia
Eurymos	Olympic victor
Eurypon	legendary king of Sparta, son of Soos and grandson of Procles; supposed ancestor of Eurypontids
Eurypontids	one of the two royal houses of Sparta
Eutelidas	father of Anaxandros
Euterpe	muse of lyric poetry
Falcon Face	name given to teacher in Agis's flock
flock (*agele*)	institution for the communal rearing of Spartiate children
Galaxidoros*	Theban
General Pentatarchos	name given to Leotychides by the bastards' regiment
General Rhetrae	name given to Leotychides
Geradas	legendary Spartan
Geraistos	Spartan month

Gitidias*	former Lakedaimonian sculptor and composer
Gorgo	(1)* former Agiad queen, wife of King Leonidas (2) Spartan maiden; skilled at spear-throwing, cousin of Kallias
Gorgopas*	Spartan squadron commander
Great Fight	mock battle between two teams of boys
Great King	the king of Persia
Gryllos*	son of Xenophon
Gylippos*	Spartan commander in Long War
Gymnopaidia	yearly celebration during which naked youths displayed their athletic and martial skills through the medium of war dancing.
Hall (*syssitia*)	institution for partaking in common meals
hassock	a padded cushion or low stool that serves as a seat or leg rest

Hekataios	carrot-haired boy in Leotychides's flock, supposed son of Dinon, brother of Doreius
Hektor	legendary Trojan prince
Herakles	Hercules, legendary hero
Herippidas*	Spartiate political leader, advisor to Agisilaos and commander of the Asia Minor campaign
Herodotos*	fifth-century Greek-Asian historian hetaira a courtesan or mistress, especially an educated one
Hidden Thing (*krypteia*)	(1) rite of passage, in which youths go alone into the forest to capture animals or criminals (2) élite body of law-keepers, including the secret police
Hipparchos	polemarch at Lechion
hoplites	heavily armed Greek infantry
Horkios	aspect of Zeus; guardian of oaths

Hyakinthos	legendary Spartan prince, loved by the gods Apollo and Zephyros, killed by discus
Horkios	aspect of Zeus; guardian of oaths discus
Hyllus	son of Herakles, supposed ancestor of Spartan kings
Inspector of Boys (*paidonomos*)	magistrate charged with supervision of education of Spartiate boys
Iphikrates*	Athenian mercenary peltast leader
Iphitos	legendary king of Elis, said to have established the Olympic truce with Lykourgos
Ischalaos	Spartan general
Ismenias*	anti-Spartan Theban politician
Jason	(1) legendary hero, leader of the quest for the golden Fleece (2)* Jason of Pherae; Thessalian, Spartan consul in Thessaly, tyrant of Pherae, son of Lycophron I, allied with Thebes, later ruler

	of Thessaly
Kadmea	the citadel of Thebes
Kallias	Spartan warrior; lover of Hekataios, cousin of Gorgo
Kallibios	Lesser Spartiate, member of the secret police, scribe to Queen Timaia
Kallikratidas*	Spartan grand admiral; succeeded Lysander in that office
Kallipides*	Corinthian exile, said to be finest tragic actor in Greece
Kallistratos*	Callistratus of Aphidnae, brown-bearded Athenian and general, guest-friend of Meleas, uncle of Tolmaios
kanathrum	a fantastic wooden car, shaped like a griffin or an antelope, in which women and children were carried
kappa	tenth letter of Greek alphabet, initial letter of Corinth, borne on shield by Corinthian warriors

17

Karneia	feast of Apollo; competition of poets
Kastor	Brother of Helen of Troy and Polydeukes, one of the Twin Gods
Kerberos (Cerberus)	legendary hound of the underworld
Kinadon*	Lesser Spartiate and revolutionary conspirator
kleiros (pl. kleroi)	land holding granted by the state to all Spartiates
Kleinias*	father of Alkibiades
Kleobolos	up-country sea-captain, commander of the Bellamina
Kleombrotos*	Agiad, second son of King Pausanios, later King Kleombrotos I
Kleomenes	(1)* Kleomenes I, former Agiad king of Sparta, brother of Doreius (1) and Leonidas (1); plotted against Demartos: said to have gone mad (2)* Agiad, second son of Kleombrotos, later King Kleomenes II
Kleonymos*	Son of Sphodrias, lover

	of Archidamos (2)
Kleonike	Spartan chorus-mistress, wife of Leotychides
Kleora*	wife of Agisilaos, sister of Peisander
Konon*	Athenian general in Long War
Kritias*	leader of ruling council of Athens
Kyniska*	daughter of King Archidamos and Eupolia, sister of Agisilaos
Kyros*	younger brother of Great King Artaxerxes II of Persia; raised a rebellion to oust his brother from the throne
Lakedaimon, Lakonia	the Spartan homeland
lamda	eleventh letter of Greek alphabet, initial letter of Lakedaimon, borne on shields by Lakedaimonian warriors
Lampido*	first wife of King Archidamos, mother of King Agis II, grandmother of Leotychides

19

Law-giver, the	Lykourgos, legendary Spartan lawgiver
Leon	(1)* former Agiad king of Sparta, supposed ancestor of Leotychides (2)* former chief ephor, father of Antalkidas (3) name used by Leotychides
Leonidas	(1)* former Agiad king of Sparta, killed at battle of Thermopylae (2) elder son of Leotychides and Kleonike
Leonidia	Spartan games
Leontiades*	Theban official, political enemy of Ismenias
Leotychides	(1)* former Eurypontid King of Sparta (2)* Eurypontid, supposed son of King Agis II of Sparta, known as the Cockerel
lesser equals	Lesser Spartiates
Lesser Spartiates (*Hypomeiones*)	Spartans who have lost their civil rights
lochagos	Spartan military rank,

	above pentatarchos, but below strategos; commander of lochos
Long War, the	the Peloponnesian war, fought by the Delian League led by Athens against the Peloponnesian League led by Sparta.
Lykomedes*	"mad" Mantinean merchant; one of the founders of Megalopolis in Arkadia
Lykourgos	legendary Spartan lawgiver, brother of King Eunomos and regent for his son Charilaos
Lynkeus	legendary hero, famed for his keen sight
Lysander*	Spartan grand Admiral, later vice -admiral
Magpie, the	name given to Anaxandros
Makarios	boy in Leotychides's flock, known as the Monkey
Maro	Spartan cavalry platoon leader
Megabates*	Persian, son of

	Spithridates, loved by Agisilaos
Megakles	Syracusan runner, brother of Anaxilas
Meleas	wealthy citizen of Sparta, lives in Menelaos House, hero of Long War, later general
melleiren	boy in flock between ages of twelve and sixteen
Menelaos	legendary Spartan king, husband of Helen of Troy
Menelaos House	old house in Sparta near racing course, residence of Meleas
Milian, the	Ambassador from Milos to Sparta
Mnassipos*	Spartan, member of Leotychides's hall: later grand admiral
Molobros	successor of Doreius as commander of Leotychides's flock
Monkey, the	name given to Makarios
mora	Spartan military unit, believed to be five or

	six hundred strong
Naktenabo*	Egyptian king, rebel against Persia
Narkissos	son of river god Cephissus and nymph Liriope; falls in love with own reflection
Nikandros	Corinthian, son of Aristeas
Nikias*	Athenian commander in Long War
Nicholochos*	Spartan vice-admiral
Nikomedes	Corinthian boxer
Okyllos*	Spartan ambassador to Athens
owls	Athenian *drachma* coins, stamped with the image of Athena's owl
Pandia	Spartan ephor's wife
Pasemachos*	Spartan cavalry commander at Sikyon
Pasimelos*	Corinthian, leader of peace party
Patroklos	Greek warrior in Trojan war, cousin of Achilles
Pausanios	(1)* Agiad king of Sparta, uncle of

	Leotychides (2)* kinsman of King Perdikkas of Macedon; seized the throne from him
Peisander*	brother of Kleora, later general in Corinthian war
Peitho	goddess of persuasion
Pelles	Spartan cavalryman
Pelopidas*	Theban officer, later commander of Sacred Band
peltasts	light-armed Greek troops, named for their small shields
pentatarchos	commander of fifty
peplos	a body-length garment for women
Perdikkas*	king of Macedonia, son of Amyntas III, brother of Philippos
Perikles*	former Athenian statesman
phalanx (pl. phalanges)	a rectangular mass military formation, usually composed entirely of heavy infantry armed with

	spears or similar weapons.
Pharax	friend of Lysander, father of Aristokrates
Pharnabazos*	Persian satrap of Phrygia
Philippos*	Philip II, king of Macedon, son of Amyntas III, brother of Perdikkas
Philon	Athenian war-captive in Sparta
Phoibidas*	Commander of Leotychides's flock, later Spartan officer, brother of Eudamidas
Phrixos*	Spartan, messenger from Agisilaos to Epaminondas
Pityas	boy in Leotychides's lock
Pleistinoax*	former Agiad king of Sparta, father of Pausanios
Pointer	name given to Aristokrates
polemarch	highest Spartan military rank, commander of army in absence or

incapacity of king

Polyanthes*	Corinthian, leader of anti-Spartan faction
Polybiades*	commander of Spartan army in Macedon after death of Agesipolis
Polydeukes	brother of Helen of Troy and Kastor, one of the Twin Gods
Polydora	Spartan maiden, courted by Sphodrias
Polydoros	(1)* former Agiad king of Sparta (2) name taken by Agis, son of Leotychides
Poseidon	god of the sea and of earthquakes
Praxitas*	commander of Spartan garrison at Sikyon
Prince, the	Alexander, son of King Philippos of Macedon, later Alexander the Great
Prolyta*	younger daughter of Agisilaos
Pronax	boy in Leotychides's flock
Prothous*	Spartan citizen, later ephor and speaker at

	the peace conference of 371 B. C.
rhetra (pl. rhetrae)	clause of the law of Lykourgos
rho	seventeenth letter of Greek alphabet, corresponding to R
rhodibas	boy in flock between ages of eight and twelve
Royal Heraklids	the royal families of Sparta, supposed descendants of Hyllus
Sacred Band	élite Theban military unit, consisting entirely of pairs of homosexual lovers
satrap	provincial governor in Persian empire
serfs (helots)	subjugated population group that formed the population of Lakonia and Messenia
shear-head	rhodibas
sigma	eighteenth letter of Greek alphabet, initial letter of Sikyon, borne on shields by Sikyonian warriors
Skiraphidas*	Spartan statesman, said

	to have opposed the introduction of coins
sktyali	staff used by Spartans to encode and decode messages
Slug, the	name given to boy in Leotychides's flock
sophist	professional teacher of rhetoric and "wisdom"
Spartiates	the military élite of Sparta
Sphodrias*	boy in Leotychides's flock, later Spartan general and military governor of Thespiai
Spithridates*	Persian nobleman and official in the court of Pharnabazos, father of Megabates
stlengis	tool for the cleansing of the body by scraping off dirt, perspiration, and oil; strigil
strategos	general, commander of regiment
Struthas*	Persian satrap of Lydia; replaced Tiribazos
Tachos*	Egyptian king, rebel against Persia
Taurus	aged steward to Queen Timaia

Teleutias*	son of Queen Eupolia her second marriage, half-brother of Agisilaos; later naval commander
Teres	Leotychides's Thracian servant
Terpander	Spartan composer
Theokles	wealthy Athenian populist, friend of Tolmaios
Theoklos	serf, Leotychides's batman
Thermon	Spartan boxer, Leotychides's coach
Thibron*	Lakedaimonian general; commander-in-chief of Hellenic forces in Asia
Thorax*	Lakedaimonian general; said to have been put to death for possessing coins
Thracian boy, the	Teres
Thrasyboulos*	Athenian commander in Long War
Timaia*	Eurypontid Queen of Sparta, wife of Agis II, mother of Leotychides,

	sister of Eurydame; of Royal Heraklid descent
Timandra*	mistress of Alkibiades, said to have been abducted from Asia
Timokrates*	<u>Rhodian</u> Greek sent by <u>Pharnabazus</u> to distribute money to <u>Greek</u> <u>city states</u> and foment opposition to <u>Sparta</u>.
Timolaos* of pro-	Corinthian "rabble rouser", leader Argive faction
Timotheos*	Athenian general, son of Konon
Tiribazos*	Persian satrap of Armenia, later of Lydia, replaced Tithraustes
Tisamenos*	Lesser Spartiate and seer, accomplice of Kinadon
Tissaphernes*	Persian satrap of Caria
Tithraustes*	Persian satrap of Lydia
Tolmaios	Athenian, nephew of Kallistratos
trireme	warship with three decks of oars
tutor, the	Aristotle

Twin Gods, the	Kastor and Polydeukes
Tyndaraios	legendary king of Sparta; father of Helen of Troy, Kastor and Polydeukes
tyro	beginner or novice
Tyrtaios	Spartan composer
up-country people *(perioikoi)*	autonomous group of free but non-citizen inhabitants of Lakonia
vizier	chief minister of the Persian empire
woman, the	Leotychides's Macedonian concubine
Wayfinder	Hermes, guide of the dead
Worm, the	name given to boy in Leotychides's flock
Xenophon*	Athenian mercenary leader
Xerxes*	former Great King of Persia and invader of Greece
Zephyros	god of the west wind

Prologue

Something is going on here.

Something known to none of the Greeks at Court, and few of the Macedonians. Those few look self-important or sly. State secrets often take men this way. In my native Sparta it is almost impossible to keep anything secret. Consequently, few men look self-important. The devious look open, which is far more dangerous.

Last night the King dined sober: an event in itself, but unconnected. Or was it? There is a flower that grows in the mountains bordering this country, which closes whenever the air is humid; during the banquet, the petals of Philippos's face were tightly shot in the mist of secrecy – if such a square, red, bearded face can be likened to a flower. (Antalkidas always said that my metaphors were blurred, and that I carried my analogies too far; but then he said that of everyone except himself).

Apart from myself, the only other Greeks present were some Athenian ambassadors, and the tutor of the king's son. I assumed the pedagogue's presence was intended as a restraint upon the boy's insolent incursions into the conversation of his elders, but the man did not once rebuke him. (How wise the Law-giver was to restrict the teaching of Lakedaimonian youths to none but the best men in Sparta. Slaves and hirelings *are* unfit to mould free men).

This tutor is new at Court. He is considered very learned, having studied at a school of sophists. In my youth, sophistry was not a skill to be learned, like playing the harp or using spear and shield. Sophists simply *were*. I find little to distinguish the new breed from the old – except that the old, having to do as well as talk, occasionally said something wise.

This tutor's talk is preferable to that of the Pella nobles: a euphemism for the hostage chiefs of the tribes Philippos subdued, establishing his rule. These wild tribesmen now wear Greek dress, and decorate their swords and armour with gold inlay; but they have changed little since I first saw them half-starved, unkempt, and clad in animal skins that crawled with as many lice as the wearers. Conversation in the King's great hall

32

is dominated neither by wit nor wisdom, but by the loudest voice. Fortunately for Philippos, he excels in volume.

The hall itself is magnificent. If there are too many gold and silver vases, drinking-cups, and mixing-bowls, it is no more vulgar than the taste of some true Greeks, and less reprehensible in savages than in civilized men. The mosaics are surpassingly beautiful. There is a splendid life-size Dionysos, riding a leopard, on one wall, the god's golden hair falling to his shoulders: his eyes are that striking blue-green colour one sees in so many Macedonians. If one studies the face carefully, one sees that the nose is slightly longer and sharper than the usual depictions, giving Dionysos a somewhat Macedonian look. Perhaps that sums up these people.

To return to that banquet – and return I must, for out of it came this task before me, as well as my awareness of all this secrecy (I rarely note things not intended for me: in Sparta it is considered bad manners) – I believe the king's unaccustomed sobriety was meant to impress his Greekness upon his guests. Macedonian kings claim Argive blood – probably not without reason; many Hellenic armies have passed this way, and armies spread their seed generously. (The other royal boast – that of being Heraklid – should be regarded with greater scepticism, although it is possible. Herakles, the divine progenitor of all Spartiates, was not mean with his favours when he walked the earth as a man, although it was we Dorians he named as his heirs. His posterity through his true-born son Hyllus are the Kings of Sparta, as all Hellas knows). The self-styled Heraklid was at his Greekest that night. He leaned forward on his dining couch, appearing to listen intently to a discussion arising from the tutor's criticism of a book written by his old teacher, depicting an imaginary city. Philippos speaks fluent Greek – a legacy not of that Bronze Age Argive ancestor, but of a boyhood passed in Thebes as a hostage.

He began to look bored. Like many men with great awe of learned books, he rarely reads one. Suddenly his voice boomed out as if he were in the field. Overriding Attic eloquence, he asked me some point or other about the siege of Mantinea, in which I played a small part. This recalled old hostilities, and one of the Athenians referred to Sparta's "cruel destruction" of that city. I thought this description of the banishment of sixty politicians somewhat overstated, and asked the fellow whether he would consider it more merciful to have slain all the men, and enslaved the women and children. (My allusion was to Athens's punishment of Milos, when that island refused to renounce its neutrality and align itself with her. He allowed the incident was regrettable, but reminded me that it happened during the Long War, although many men's lives spanned both the destruction of Milos and the siege of Mantinea. Athenians have flexible memories; their glorious deeds are celebrated in perpetuity, their shameful ones relegated to an insignificant past). Another Athenian informed me that it was a matter of principle. This was too much coming from a man whose city has slaughtered, enslaved and transported entire peoples and, in the reasoned debate of its Assembly, voted to strike off the right hand of every prisoner of war. I replied something apposite, I forget what. I usually forget my apophthegms unless someone quotes them back to me. Generally as his own.

Whatever it was incited a storm of protest from the Athenians. One was even provoked to brevity. "Mantinea menaced no one." Can they really believe themselves?

"Sparta wantonly despised a good, ordered democracy," another intoned with pious conceit.

"No democracy is well-ordered," the tutor murmured.

The first Athenian rounded on the tutor, although I had seen him smile in agreement. It is obviously not safe to be undemocratic in Athens. "So an oligarch would say."

"Define democracy," the tutor gazed at an invisible point in mid-air.

"Another merchants' government Athens supports," I replied. There was fact, if not depth, in my reply.

Having no trade, Sparta has no mercantile party: in Athens, a trading state with little agriculture, the landowners' party is minute. Most other Hellenic cities have sizeable land parties (called oligarchic by Athenian demagogues) and mercantile factions (democratic in Athenian parlance). Sparta favours land parties in the interest of peace and good order. Athens supports the mercantile in her own interest. There is little between the two. The age of tyranny is long past and, with one or two exceptions, the states of Hellas are ruled by elected councils and assemblies (a form of government initiated in Sparta four hundred years ago, when kings still ruled Athens).

A spark of our heat ignited the Macedonians, who understood little of what we were saying and began a noisy dispute of their own. Greek anger is easier on the ears than Macedonian, and wine, rather than blood, stains the tables. We recalled we were civilized men, and moderated the tone.

At this point, Philippos dropped a few comments of his own. He is no lover of Thebes, but many of his views were absorbed there in his youth. His words slandered Sparta and demeaned Athens. It was then I noticed that he was enjoying it all hugely. He exchanged a glance with his most trusted general, a dour man about his own age, who took on that secretive aspect I had perceived previously as he tacitly imposed silence on another Macedonian, whose face immediately swelled with importance. At least I took it to be importance, until his cheeks deflated, as he spewed the contents of his stomach over the intricately patterned mosaic floor.

Philippos is obsessed by siege warfare, but I had already recounted the siege of Mantinea to him privately. A suspicion hardened that his, apparently chance, reference had been calculated to pit us all against another. He may be half-savage, but he is shrewd. I do not know why I say *but*. Civilized men, in their simplicity, wrongly assume that savages are simple, because they are less articulate in their deceit.

Shortly after, the Athenians retreated from the Macedonian din, and the tutor took his charge off – or rather, I should say, the boy took his tutor off. Philippos turned to me, and said somewhat reproachfully "You disagreed with me, and you disagreed with them."

I allowed it was possible to do both.

"I would no more slander your city than I would slander a friend." He frequently slanders his friends.

"If Thebans talked less and Athenians scribbled less, Sparta would be better known."

"No, by Zeus!" He frowned and slammed his wine-cup down. "If Spartans spoke and wrote more!" The creases of his brow smoothed as much as they could. He spoke in careful, measured syllables "Not a single Spartan has told your side of it." Sometimes he states the obvious with great significance. His face lit; the way it does when he is thinking of a new horse, a new woman, a new territory. "You must tell it. Set it down in writing."

I gave him one hundred reasons why this would be to no purpose. He countered my arguments in such a way that I began to feel it my sacred duty. He can be persuasive and, once his mind is fixed on something, he rarely lets go.

I rested my eyes on another beautiful mosaic, in which Polydeukes and Kastor rescue Helen from Theseus. It always pleases me to see the Twin Gods, Guardians of Sparta, and their beautiful, divine sister, in this palace in the far northern wilds. The artist had not made them Macedonian.

"I am the last person to ask." I raised my voice against shouts at the other end of the hall.

Philippos seized upon my words. He misses nothing. "What do you mean?"

"Only that I am a soldier." He was drinking unwatered wine, but he has incredible recall of things said when his speech is blurred and his legs liquid. "Neither sophist nor historian."

"All the better. We might get a few facts." He focussed on two of his nobles – as the one struck the other, who promptly tumbled to the floor, upsetting a number of gold-and-ivory-inlaid tables. I'll give you that house at the edge of Pella... the one I confiscated from...can't remember his name..."

I could. Recently he had had the man stoned to death.

BOOK ONE

At harvest time, Lykourgos sent about the land and saw the stacks of grain standing in equal size, and he smiled and said "All Lakonia looks like a family estate divided amongst numerous brothers."

\- Plutarch

Chapter 1

Leotychides of Sparta sets down these matters of rulers and kings, so that strangers may know of Lakedaimon, and how it led the Hellenes in peace and in war. (Or have I taken this on simply to escape the Macedonian clamour in the hall? Antalkidas believed that most men embark upon great enterprises for trivial reasons).

The flowers of decline blossomed in the season of triumph, the seeds having been sown unaware during the Long War, which was caused by the Athenian blockade of Potidaia.

Potidaia was founded by Corinth: Corinthian citizens volunteered to fight for their daughter city, and were amongst the besieged. Under the terms of a treaty, Corinth appealed to Sparta to force Athens to withdraw.

Potidaia...that small, pleasant Chalkidian city on the sea. Could anything concerning Potidaia *cause* twenty-seven years of war? I smooth the wax and substitute occasion for cause.

I am trying to follow the form Herodotos set for the writing of histories, but Herodotos was Halikarnassan. He reached his destination by long and circuitous routes. Being Lakedaimonian, I am less generous with words, and have no intention of making a verbal journey back into the Bronze Age.

Better simply to say that Sparta and her allies warred to prevent the Peloponnesos from being swallowed into the Athenian Empire, as much of Hellas had been devoured – and, as a consequence of those long years of war, the foundations of Sparta, the model for all Hellas, were cracked.

Once on campaign in the Argolid, I saw Poseidon shake the earth just after the evening meal. The ground parted, tents collapsed, wine-cups and mixing-bowls shattered. It was a relatively minor tremor. The troops were calmed, set up their tents, and rekindled their fires. The earth closed, leaving only minute rivulets of soil where great caverns had appeared. But nothing was quite the same again.

So it was with Lakedaimon during the Long War.

Alas, nothing is less convincing than simple truth, so I shall return to that conference of Peloponnesian allies, where the Corinthians persuaded Sparta to vote for war. One Spartan ephor supported them energetically. This was unusual, as Sparta was always reluctant to go to war, although she had the finest army among the Hellenes. Or perhaps because she had it. Even my grandfather only counselled caution and delay.

Now, I see, I have brought in my grandfather. I think I must give up this mention of Herodotos – as I seem to be doing it, as it were, in reverse. I am not even certain that my grandfather belongs in this narrative. After all, he died before I was born. That was in the nineteenth year of the war. (My birth, not his death). He was a man of his time. (Antalkidas said I was also a man of my time). This raises the question of my own relevance.

Of what significance is my part in the account to follow? Did I cause things to happen the way it seemed to me? Did I cause things to happen? Does any man? (I leave this last to the sophists). No, I do not. Sparta did not just happen. Sparta was the creation of conscient will. Perhaps that is why half Hellas tried to emulate her, and the other half to destroy her. But only Sparta could destroy herself.

I look out upon the Macedonian hills, and think of Sparta held in the embrace of her surrounding mountains like a great basin. The white-capped peaks of dark Taygetos, the clear Eurotas running its serpentine course through the fertile Vale. Spring's breezes, carrying the scent of the golden apple-blossoms. Summer's barley, standing high in the fields, like a green, rippling sea. Autumn, and the aroma of grapes ripening on their vines.

Let me not forget I set this down for foreigners. That foreign cities lie within high, imprisoning walls. Places of narrow lanes and scuttling people, centred about market-places, as if the agora were the city's soul.

O, Stranger, were it not for her fame, you would probably not know Sparta for a city at all.

Look down from a mountain-top, and you will see but fields and fruit-orchards, bounded by straight rows of olive trees. No walls to cage Sparta's sprawling grace. Our dwellings stand in

39

our estates, their door-keepers drowsing in the sun. No gate is closed in Sparta. Else how could friend, neighbour or passer-by step in and borrow his needs, in the absence of master or mistress?

Near the fields stand the small, thatched houses of the serfs, solid and mud-brick red-brown, the colour of the earth of Lakedaimon. Yes, we have our agora, where artisans hammer and chip and make sparks fly: where serfs come to barter food-stuffs grown in their private plots, the rough cloth of their apparel not unlike that proud badge of poverty worn by their masters; only the draping differs. But this agora follows its own winding way and centres upon itself. Not Sparta's spirit. Only an afterthought.

I recall the tent-shaped, wood-hewn dining halls of Hyakinthos Road. I remember dignified elders in their long cloaks coming away from the agora at midday. Fine, crimson-clad, long-haired young warriors stepping aside respectfully, to let the greybeards pass, although the hard-packed earth of all Sparta's roads can easily take the width of two chariots.

In my memory, youths run on the racing course to the melody of flutes; a chorus of bright-cheeked maidens compete in song, a breeze whipping their short peploi about their knees...

All this I recall, but Sparta eludes me. *I* elude myself.

Where is that truth I spoke of so glibly? It changes shape with time and distance. Distorts as I approach it.

I am alone in a forest of memories.

Forget Herodotos. Later I can set this down in proper form. Delete manners of significance only to me. (Delete me if I am of no significance). Perhaps dictate it to that scribe Philippos offered me. He has bought me what he calls a Spartan slave, to whom I can dictate my Doric speech. There are no Spartan slaves: everyone knows it is our law to fight to the death. Nor has any educated Greek difficulty in comprehending another, whatever his native dialect. For that matter, after all that has passed, I speak a number of fairly obscure manners of speech. Yet, I believe I did offer it as a pretext to delay this work until the Macedonian forgot it. It seems that either Philippos is eager for his history, or he believes the slander that Spartans are barely literate. (All Spartiates, King Philippos, can put their hands to sword or lyre or stylus).

40

For the moment I shall dispense with the scribe. Perhaps the fellow is an up-country man. They are not forbidden by law to surrender, although they rarely do. Damn good soldiers. Most of them. I digress...

*   *   *

I was three when I learnt who I was. What I was took longer.

My mother was setting out to perform some religious ceremony. I knew that, from the sort of flowers in the garland she had on her head. Tiny gold lions bit her ears. She turned suddenly to my nurse, her long, dark-green peplos swinging open to reveal her strong runner's thigh. "The Prince will accompany me." (What a strange way memory has. These small matters are clear, although most of that time is quite obscure).

I looked up from under my eyelashes for a glimpse of this personage, having learnt to keep my eyes properly downcast. A bored and lonely child, I lived largely in a dream world peopled with the hero-gods of the tales, and fully expected to see a fine figure in magnificent armour worthy of Prince Achilles or Prince Hektor.

It was only when she added, "He is old enough to appear in public now," that it began to sink in that I was the Prince. My nurse's grim eyes warned me that small boys do not speak until spoken to, so I held my silence until I had the opportunity to question my uncle Pausanios.

Pausanios was Sparta's other king. As everyone knows, Sparta has two kings, the Agiad and the Eurypontid. Descended from the twin sons of King Aristodemos. Pausanios was head of the Agiad line. Apart from this ancient cousinage, we were not close kin; but he was married to my mother's sister, and was the father of my sole companion, my cousin Agesipolis.

I preferred the Agiad palace to our own, although it did not differ greatly in appearance. Like every private dwelling, it was a large tile-roofed wood and mud-brick house, consisting of a series of rooms giving to the inner courtyard. Being lawfully constructed by axe and saw, unlike stone, our houses must be rebuilt every hundred years or so. The new structure is always

41

the same as the one it replaces.

Lakedaimonian architecture is of an austere elegance that does not vie with nature for dominion, but becomes a part of its harmony. Being restricted to simple materials, our artisans created a perfection of line and form that rich ornamentation would desecrate rather than decorate. Again, I digress...

Although my cousin's surroundings were similar to my own (and those of every Spartiate), they were far more interesting. Often visitors came, wearing scarlet war-cloaks. Our way was not barred to the horses of the outer courtyard. Sometimes as we played in the house, Pausanios would step in from the courtyard, seat himself on one of the high-polished wooden benches, take us each on a knee, and tell us stories.

"Am I a prince?" I asked him the next time this happened.

"Yes." His grave young face awaited my next question. I considered him old then. He must have been about twenty-eight.

"Does that make my father a king?"

"More the other way about." He stifled a smile.

"Is Agesipolis a prince also?" I had followed his logic.

"Don't you know anything?" Agesipolis jeered from the safety of his father's knee. Revenge. As a rule, I was the dispenser of arcane knowledge.

A slant of sunlight lit his light brown hair with tawny glints; all he had inherited of Pausanios's deep chestnut. Their clear, bright-blue eyes were alike. A spray of freckles ran across my cousin's nose to his cheeks. He was a few months my junior, and two vital fingers-widths shorter.

"When will Leo' and I be kings?"

"Not quite yet."

"Can we command armies and make war?" Agesipolis was a bit shrill then.

"Some day you will command an army, but you cannot make war. Only the Apella can do that."

"Who is the Apella?" I asked, having accepted kingship as my due.

"The Assembly." Pausanios always replied thoughtfully, no matter how puerile the question. "All the citizens of Sparta."

"Why don't you command an army, Father?" Agesipolis asked.

"Only one king may be absent from the City. Agis is my senior in years and reign."

"What else can kings do?" My singular lack of interest in my father I shall explain presently.

"They can vote in the Council of Elders. The other members must be over sixty and chosen by Assembly."

"When I am king, I shall lead an army against the Trojans," Agesipolis announced.

The blank face among the members of my family (I shall come to the others later) is that of my father. Not solely by virtue of his absence, but because my mother never spoke to him.

I knew only that he had been leading an army to the Dekeleia when I was born, had taken the place, and was still there. That mountain citadel of Attica, only a short distance northwest of Athens itself, commanded the Athenian plain and the direct route to our ally, Thebes, as well as the long island of Euboia; this enabled our warriors to disrupt the enemy's corn supplies. This I learnt from some Elders in the Great Hall of the Agiad palace, where Pausanios let us play as the visitors talked after their midday meal.

One day I asked her, "Why didn't you tell me that Father is the Eurypontid King, Mother."

"I told you."

People forget that children, like illiterates, have excellent memories.

"Why don't you like Father?"

She stopped pacing, to stare at me. I recall that she was pacing the room giving into her bed-chamber, like a caged lioness. The room comes back to me: the opened chests, a table scattered with her ornaments; another, on which lay her comb; a bronze mirror, with an ivory handle carved in the shape of a muse; and pots of the paint she used on her eyelids. Tall and stately, she was considered one of the most beautiful women in Sparta.

Her wide-spaced, green eyes bored through me. "Whose words do you repeat?"

"You never told me he captured the Dekeleia."

"Someone else advised him to." Did a smile touch the

corners of her lips? "Agis hasn't the wit to devise such a plan himself, or he wouldn't have two ephors on his staff."

The first assertion was true, the second coloured by hostility. My father was known for his terse, witty comments. He was also a good general. The two magistrates had been attached to his staff, as a penalty for having agreed a peace during an old campaign in the Argolid, without the city's permission.

"You *don't* like Father!" I accused with more certainty.

The day was hot. She wore her peplos short like a maiden, and her hair was piled carelessly atop her head. It was magnificent hair. Sunset gold. The colour that is called the true Dorian hair, which so few of us have. Perhaps it is because, although our hair ranges from fair to brown-black, it is often touched with copper lights. Not mine. My pale flax was devoid of fire.

She was silent for a long moment. I was uncertain whether she would strike me, or seize me and smother me with kisses. I do not know which I dreaded more.

"Even in Sparta, where women are free, Royal Heraklids have no say in choosing their husbands." She spoke distinctly. "I did not choose Agis. He did not choose me. We were thrust upon each other."

Her voice had taken on the hollow ring that meant she was lying. My mother was a fluent liar, who could be trusted to tell the bare truth when it was calculated to do the greatest harm.

*   *   *

I have been interrupted.

I was writing indoors, as it was one of those overcast days that punctuate the early spring, when an old Illyrian slave hurried in (he must have been taken prisoner early in the reign of Philippos) and mumbled something in his incomprehensible accent, apparently intended to mean that I had a visitor. The tutor was close on his heels.

He declined refreshments, explained he had been passing, (he teaches the boy some distance from Pella) and was pressed for time. He then sat down.

He spoke some half-finished sentences referring to my work, and looked about as if he would find the rest of it in the air. I think he is one of those men who excel in discourse, but find pleasantries difficult.

"Why do you vote by shouting?" His narrow eyes suddenly ceased their journey and challenged mine. "You Spartans vote by acclamation." He spoke incisively and rather slowly, like a teacher to a dullish pupil. "Why do you not use ballots?"

"Is it not possible for one man to write the same name on several ballots?" (Tolmaios once admitted the practice was not uncommon in Athens).

He considered. Emitted a dry sound. I think it was intended as a laugh. "It has happened."

Shortly after, he left.

*   *   *

I suppose I should have begun with Agisilaos, because it ended with Agisilaos; but he made so little impression upon my early years that scant remains. Like the rest of Sparta, I ignored Agisilaos.

Small and slight, he had a pleasant face and agreeable smile (I recall the smile better than the countenance) and was the younger son of my grandfather King Archidamos (I see that I have at last explained who my grandfather was and how he came to be addressing that conference of Peloponnesian allies). Agisilaos was much younger than my father, and they had different mothers.

After the death of my grandmother, Queen Lampido, my grandfather remarried. His ageing eye fell upon a certain Eupolia, who was probably lithe and delicious at the time, but I can recall only as a grey, plump, hen-pigeon of a woman. My mother told me that the ephors fined him for taking a wife so small she might breed Sparta a line of kinglets. Considering the source, I was surprised to learn the tale is true.

I much preferred my uncle Teleutias. ("Teleutias is not your uncle, Leotychides. He is Eupolia's son from her second marriage. He hasn't a drop of Royal Heraklid blood.")

45

Teleutias was only slightly taller than Agisilaos, with a broad brow, bold eyes and the look of a soldier. Agisilaos was also a soldier, and a competent one, but he hadn't a warrior's air.

If Agisilaos was notable for anything, it was his friendship with Lysander; a bond that had been forged in my uncle's youth, when the famous soldier was his lover. (Antalkidas told me this, years later, when we were in the same flock, his pale eyes professing bewilderment, as he pondered why a man already rising great should fancy a boy with one leg shorter than the other.

I forgot to note that Agisilaos was lame, although the limp was his sole memorable quality. Not in itself; a number of men limped from war wounds, but Agisilaos had always limped, and he, too, was a king's son. (This is becoming hopelessly entangled. The written word is a hard-mouthed horse).

For some time I had been aware that people looked at me. Sometimes openly, usually furtively. At first, I attributed it to my royal birth, but no one stared at Agesipolis. Once, as Agisilaos limped across a palace room to retrieve some object my mother dropped (the servant mixing wine could have done it easily), it suddenly struck me that, although deformed infants were exposed, the elders had obviously ordered that Agisilaos be brought up.

Perhaps exceptions were made for kings' sons. The implication was too great a horror to contemplate. Elders were wise and good, and the wise and the good could never be so cruel as to let such a poor creature suffer life. I dismissed the fear, but the dreaded thought raised itself whenever I encountered Agisilaos. Although his limp was slight, it disturbed my dreams. (Is that why I recall his foot better than his young face).

One day, when I had been waving my wooden sword about, playing some lonely game in the inner courtyard, I caught sight of the reflection of a fig tree in the fountain. This fountain was a great, round marble basin, where bright-coloured fish swam.

I knew I was strong, having tumbled Agesipolis into the same fountain, and my limbs were straight. I leaned over the edge, and peered in to study my face.

The bottom of the fountain was slightly sedimented. The serfs were ordered to change the water daily; but, when it rained, they let Zeus do it for them. The top was clear, and a reflection of round cheeks surrounded by long, pale, fair hair peered back at me. A straight nose. Plump lips of childhood, dissolved by a passing fish.

"Do not fall in, Narkissos." A deep voice behind me spoke in a foreign accent. Philon. (How many years since he has entered my thoughts!)

"Narkissos was beautiful." The fish darted in and out of the image. I turned and faced him. "Am I beautiful?"

He raised his eyebrows. "So young to be so vain." I think he sensed the urgency of the question, if not its cause. He passed me a high-polished bronze mirror. "See for yourself."

The image was that of the fountain, only more defined. My chin was slightly cleft. My eyes deep blue, fringed with dark lashes. An altogether acceptable face. Nothing in it to cause all those disquieting glances.

"Do people look at a boy because he is beautiful?"

Have I mentioned that Philon was the last of a group of Athenian war-captives who were quartered in the house while awaiting ransom. The war was draining the resources of a city without a treasury, and the ransom of such men was far greater than the sum they fetched as spear-slaves, most of them being merchants and of little practical use.

"All the world looks at beautiful boys. In a few years, young men will write you love poems, and maidens hide on rooftops to watch you pass – well, in Athens they would. Here, where girls strip stark–"

He broke off and actually flushed. Philon was shocked to see maidens and youths training nude for games in sight of each other. In such matters, he was not unlike Philippos, who would not be so great a lecher if the unclothed female body had been a commonplace in his early years.

Now that I think of it, Philon was the same combination of lecher and prude. I recall seeing a good-looking young serf boy wearing a fine pair of Athenian sandals, and that mirror Philon passed me had been given by my mother to one of her serving-women when my father sent her the muse-handled one.

I thought some of his customs quite as shocking as he found ours. He even admitted without shame to being rich.

Philon was not without vanity himself. His craggy face was

far from handsome, but he had a fine head of black hair that he dyed with a mixture of oil and soot.

"It was the fashion in Athens a few years ago," he explained, when some came off on my fingers, as I tugged his beard to make him tell a story. "Now I use it to put back the years."

Philon told a tale wonderfully well. He knew some that Pausanios did not. I heard the first of these, when the captive declared that I knew the stories of Achilles and Herakles so well I could tell them myself. He offered to recount how Odysseus found his way back to Ithaca. I protested that I did not like Odysseus. I felt he had sullied the Greek victory by winning it with trickery.

Philon made a sign, and told me not to speak disrespectfully of hero-gods. I assured him I had meant no disrespect, but I should nonetheless prefer a tale of someone else. He looked thoughtful. Then he said he would give me a tale of Alkibiades.

I was aware of the war. I knew the names of all the commanders. Our young and brilliant Brasidas, who liberated the cities of the north with only seven hundred serf volunteers, and died in the hour of his greatest victory (I have seen the magnificent monument the people of Amphipolis raised to him, a half-day's fast ride from here. They worship him as a divine hero). I knew of Gylippos, the defender of Syracuse; and my father, who took the Dekeleia.

I also knew the Athenians – Alkibiades, Thrasyboulos, Nikias – but the frontiers of Lakonia had been inviolate six hundred years, and the war seemed as distant as the one against Troy. We revered Trojans like Hektor, who had fought against the Greeks; I saw nothing unreasonable in applauding the feats of Alkibiades, who warred against Sparta.

He assumed the proportions of a divine hero in my mind. Perhaps something of the epic quality of the man came through in Philon's anecdotes about the brave, beautiful, audacious and amusing boy who grew into a valorous, audacious, witty man, and all the rest the world knows so well. (Well, not all. His was a carefully worded version, and hero-gods are not judged by the measure of mortals). So an enemy general casually entered my pantheon of shadow-companions, and caused me to disgrace myself.

Having been told I was beautiful, I accepted the fact of my

beauty as casually as I had that of my royalty.

It still did not explain why people looked at me. If I asked my mother, she would only lie or evade.

"Why do people look at me, Philon?"

He stroked his beard. Some of the black came off on his fingers. "Leotychides, you have asked–" He broke off, as a swirl of skirts and a breath of spicy scent heralded the approach of my mother. "Lady..." He made a deferential gesture. "I was telling your son of beauty."

With a single liquid movement, she bent and took the mirror from my hands.

"Beauty wounds," she said, and ordered me to my nurse.

I would ask Pausanios.

The King took me with Agesipolis to the tomb of Leonidas at the city's edge. The bronze hero-god stood three times a mortal's height from his high-crested helmet to his sandals. At his feet was a stele with the names of the three hundred men who died with him at Thermpoylai.

"Leonidas was Agiad," Agesipolis boasted.

"The Law-giver was Eurypontid," Pausanios told him.

We went on to the temple of Lykourgos. As the King's chariot sped, I sifted words in my head to put to him about those bewildered glances.

"Here is the spirit of Sparta," Pausanios said, as we stepped into the penumbra of the temple and stood before the statue.

"Did Lykourgos slay any monsters?" Agesipolis asked. At that time, the monsters interested him more than the heroes.

"He killed greed and envy in Spartans," Pausanios replied. "Those are the most fearsome monsters of all."

"How?" Agesipolis asked.

"Why?" I wanted to know.

"So that Spartans would live in like manner, and not be envious of one another." It was for this reason, he told us, that men dined in their halls, where the food was simple and the same for all.

("You Spartans with your poverty and your equality!" The tutor scoffs. "Lakedaimon has the best land in Hellas. Lykourgos made you equally well-to-do. Poor men do not enter chariots in the Games." He comes. He goes. I think he finds me a pretext to escape the society of the Macedonians).

Pausanios took us to a part of the temple grounds, where a small, sparkling stream ran. He seated us on a bench, and told us how Lykourgos divided the land of Lakedaimon, so that all citizens would have equal yields of oil, barley and wine-grapes. Like any citizen, Agesipolis and I had each a kleiros, a lawful land-holding, allotted to us at birth for the span of our lives. Being kings, Pausanios and my father also had some private land.

These explanations bored Agesipolis. "When I am a man," he said, "I am going to slay the Persians."

I was in my bath in the Eurypontid palace, counting the tentacles of the squid painted on the bottom, when I remembered I had not asked my question. This was not easily done, as it seemed, for I must not let Agesipolis hear. One had ought to know as much about oneself as others know.

The opportunity came when we visited the temple of Athena, which crowns the Acropolis. There was no chariot. No horse. Our nurses followed behind. Sparta's highest hill does not command a great height. It is the City's sacred way, unfortified, with fine shrines and temples on each side of the road leading to the Bronze House.

Pausanios walked between us, holding each by the hand. Agesipolis turned his head to the temple of the Muses, where a priestess chanted.

"Sir–" I began.

Just then, the King released my hand, to return the greeting of a man who came away from the tomb of Zeus Saviour. The words fled my head. I recalled them and took a breath.

Agesipolis spoke first. "Was Gitidias an up-country man?"

The Gitidias whose songs we still sing had worked the trials of Herakles in bronze for the temple. It was this we were going to see.

"Perhaps," Pausanios said. "Or a god may have given him the gift." We walked the length of a limestone colonnade to the top of the hill.

Inside the temple, a greying woman stood before the portrait of Aphrodite Who Turns Away Old Age. We had the bronze-work to ourselves. A man came in, placed a small clay figure on Athena's offering table, turned to Pausanios, and raised his arm

50

in the greeting that is given to kings.

"Well, Elucidates, have you heard?" Pausanios said, as we came out of the temple together.

"Had the ephors not announced it, sir, Lysander's look would have told me." The man wore the plain, natural-coloured wool cloak of a citizen. Agesipolis and I cast down our eyes, and thrust our arms within our cloaks in a seemly manner. So it is to be Kallikratidas."

"The best of men."

"No man but Lysander would dare to ask a second term as Grand Admiral." Powerful offices may be held for one year only. "I dare say Kallikratidas will have done with this trafficking with barbarians."

As the prolonged struggle took its toll on both sides, Athens and Sparta turned to the ancient enemy Persia – in the persons of Tissaphernes and Pharnabazos, the rival satraps of the Great King's western provinces – But it was Lysander who had literally struck gold, when he gained the friendship of the Great King's rebellious brother Kyros.

"It takes more than Sparta possesses to pay one hundred and seventy rowers for each trireme, Eutelias."

"Hired men," Eutelidas scoffed, "owe their loyalty to the highest bidder."

"So we must bid higher than Athens." A slight breeze moved the folds of the King's long cloak.

The sun that had been low over Taygetos disappeared behind the mountains, turning the wooded slopes black. The peaks lit with a fiery incandescence, as though they had been touched by the hand of a god.

"Do you say Lysander is right, sir?"

"Only that we need not concern ourselves with him any longer."

Agesipolis shifted from one foot to the other. I kicked him. I wanted to hear more, and feared we might be sent back to our nurses. Too late; the King and his friend were saying their farewells. Eutelidas took his leave. I raised my eyes, in time to see that he regarded me with *that* look. Let Agesipolis think what he would; I should ask now."

"When I am a man," he said, "I shall be grand admiral."

"You can't," I laughed at him. "You must be a king."

51

"You, too," he retorted. "We must both be kings when our fathers are dead." Being of an age when we had no comprehension of our own mortality, that of others was meaningless.

(Yes, Philippos, we Spartans speak of death casually. We even bury our dead within the city. It teaches us young men not to fear the common fate of mortals).

The City was bathed in the blue-grey light the hidden sun sends out in the long prelude to night. Smoke rose from the cooking-fires of houses and dining-halls, as though it breathed. Beyond and below us, unwalled Sparta spread out generously into the vale of the Eurotas. Some boys from a flock ran in a field. I envied the youths their strength and their freedom.

Pausanios took our hands. We walked the road downwards, my question unanswered. Unasked.

I forgot the matter entirely, when I was told that I should visit the Agiad palace on the day the Grand Admiral called.

I knew what a grand admiral looked like. He was like the statue of Leonidas in his high-crested helmet. Or the one of Brasidas, which stands in the agora. Yet Kallikratidas had also been a mediator.

When other Peloponnesian cities asked Sparta for troops, she sent only a single man to arbitrate. His ruling was accepted by both sides, because Sparta's just law and good order were accepted by all the Hellenes.

Was a mediator something like a law-giver? Perhaps the Grand Admiral would wear a long robe, like Lykourgos in the temple. I knew no man wears a long robe and a helmet at the same time. When the day arrived, I was certain that Kallikratidas looked like Herakles in the temple bronze. So I set out well-pleased, unaware that disgrace followed me.

Kallikratidas wore a plain citizen's cloak. Neither long robe nor the belted crimson of war. ("Lysander wore his crimson robe the day he was named," Agesipolis whispered. "Father says he sleeps in his armour.") This Grand Admiral was of middling height; a thin, wiry man with grey hair, a short grey beard and iron-grey eyes. A grey man.

My cousin and I played noiselessly in the corner of a pleasant whitewashed room, which gave into a courtyard where flowering almond trees cast shade. A servant passed between Pausanios and his guest, filling their cups with wine. Between them stood small tables of that high-polished wood that foreigners mistake for marble, on which were plates of white cheese, olives and fragrant bread.

"I fear I have had a troubling report." Pausanios rested his weight on an elbow, as he reclined on his dining couch "Lysander sent back the gold he borrowed from Kyros."

Kallikratidas laughed shortly and drily "He was ever a bad loser. Dared to say he is giving me a fleet that is in complete mastery of the sea." He turned his wine cup in his hand "I told him that, in that case, he can deliver me the ships at Samos, as he has nothing to fear in sailing past the enemy in Miletos."

Pausanios laughed deeply, and signalled to the servant, who stood by a large bronze mixing bowl with sea-shell handles. "He *has* damaged the enemy."

"Wins his battle by trickery."

"In his words, 'where the lion's skin will not stretch, it must be patched with the fox.'"

"Spartan lions grow skins to fit Spartan lions." I began to like this Kallikratidas. "He looks hungrily at the islands. In the generations Sparta has led Peloponnesos, she has never taken one finger-width of territory outside her own frontiers."

"Nor will she, whatever Lysander's fancy." Pausanios sliced a pear. The aroma made me hungry. "My dear friend, I beg you, see Kyros. Try to get the gold back."

"Flattering barbarians isn't quite my line of country."

"Athens builds ships with tribute from her client cities. We have no client cities. She pays her rowers with Persian silver. We are poor. If I were to ask you—"

"As my friend, or my King?"

(The King's word being the law here, I should explain that a Spartan king is honoured, but no citizen need heed him).

"As one who is as anxious to see the end of the War as you."

The Grand Admiral smiled thinly. "You would be easier to refuse if you were cunning, Pausanios."

"But being dense—"

"Cunning is not brother to wit." Kallikratidas set down his emptied cup. In its bottom, two hunters readied their spears to attack a boar. "All Sparta knows I have little taste for this war of Greek against Greek." His indifference appalled me. "When we have cured her of empire, I intend to do all I can to reconcile Athens and Sparta, and together drive Persia from the Greek cities of Asia."

I forgot myself and stared at him openly. Everyone knew how the barbarians raided those cities, killed and mutilated their people, abducted maidens and castrated young boys for slaves. Kallikratidas evoked a vision so noble I forthwith resolved to follow him.

"So I can hardly go begging to them now," he concluded.

He was not a grey man.

I remembered myself and cast down my gaze. Pausanios noted it and called us over to present us. Apprehension stabbed my chest. Would Kallikratidas regard me with that disturbing curiosity? Eyes down, we approached silently, and stood straight and still before the Grand Admiral's dining couch.

"Have you something to say, Leotychides?" Pausanios asked. Perhaps my decorum was not all that I assumed it.

"Sir," I asked Kallikratidas. "May I fight under your command against the barbarians." I chanced a swift glance.

He was not a man with a way with small boys, but his eyes were sensitive. As I recall them, unbearably sensitive. "I hope you might be still too young." No *look*.

"Won't you drive the barbarians out of all Asia, sir? That should take a long time."

Again, the thin-lipped smile. "I think we just might let them keep their own country."

Pausanios dismissed us shortly afterwards. I heard Kallikratidas say, "Bright boy."

"Yes... I took them to the temple of Lykourgos recently, and he is memorizing rhetrae. I wish my lazy Agesipolis would show the same endeavour."

Agesipolis heard, too. "Lysander is better than Kallikratidas," he hissed at me.

Years later, even in anger, I never had it in me to recall those words to him.

It had just started one of those late autumn rains as we ran into the courtyard, but the day was soft and pleasant. Still basking in the praise of Kallikratidas, I suggested a game of

Greeks and Trojans. Agesipolis wanted to be the Greeks. I reminded him I could douse him in the fountain. We were riding wooden sticks for horses and splattering mud on our tunics, when Pausanios called us in the steady downpour after his guest departed.

"Leo' said he would push me in the fountain if I were not the Trojans," Agesipolis complained.

"You both look as though you had been in the fountain." Pausanios took in the pools we dripped on the patterned floor. "Go dry yourselves, and I will tell you how Leonidas held the Pass at Thermopylai."

"Then he will make me be the Persians next time. Father, tell us a story we can play and both be Greeks."

I had a sudden inspiration "Sir, tell us a story about Alkibiades." Philon's ransom had finally come through and I missed the Alkibiades tales.

Pausanios's face set "Who tells you such stories?" He hurried on. "Don't you know he is an enemy?"

"So was Hector, sir, and he is a hero-god, too."

"Alkibiades is no hero-god. He's– he's finished. Do not speak his name again."

"Is he dead."

"He is exiled. In Thrace. The Athenians deposed him from his command when Lysander won the sea battle." (Thus did I learn of the battle of Notion. Sparta does not celebrate victory. She expects it).

"Alkibiades lost?" Glorious, invincible Alkibiades!

He clouted me. "I told you not to repeat his name." Never before had he struck me. If he raised a hand to Agesipolis, it was not in my presence. Then, being Pausanios, he went on to answer my question. "Alkibiades was not present when Lysander engaged the Athenian fleet, but their Assembly condemned him nonetheless. Leotychides, it is right to honour a brave enemy, but Alkibiades was a false friend."

"You mean Alkibiades came to Sparta to *betray* us!"

This time the clout set my ears ringing. "Have you not been taught obedience? Alkibiades turned to Sparta for reasons of his own, and turned back to Athens for the same, but that does not concern you." He glanced at the open-mouthed Agesipolis. "Nor you. Just remember, Leotychides, you are forbidden to

55

speak his name anywhere. Any time."

To be certain I would remember, there was no story. He ordered my nurse to take me home. Shamed. Brought low before my cousin.

It was some time before I visited the Agiad palace again.

The occasion was the name-feast of another cousin. I attributed the long exile to my grave misdemeanour.

It really was not that long, but time hung heavy in our house, and Pausanios had been occupied with other concerns, public and private.

I was ignorant of city matters, but I knew that my aunt Eurydame had been very ill. My mother visited her often, and ceased to refer to her sister as "that prattling fool." Now she was recovered, my mother abused her again. Agesipolis had a new brother, and we were invited to a feast.

Royal Heraklid births, deaths and marriages demand the presence of members of both Houses, although the two dynasties have cordially detested one another from the quarrelling sons of King Aristodemos downwards.

My mother and I were the last of the Eurypontids to arrive. A servant already offered the guests their garlands. Some men had taken their places on the dining couches. The women were seated in slant-backed chairs. The great hall was decorated with branches of aromatic trees and of early-flowering bushes. My mother paused in the entry, standing straight in her tightly-belted blue peplos, her sun-gold hair high-looped, with me at her side, my nurse behind us, until all eyes were upon her.

Agisilaos stood beside his wife Kleora, who topped him by a head, and had the look of an unfinished statue. ("Agisilaos is breeding for size," my mother commented when he married her. "It is certainly not for wit.") Poor Kleora's brain was the least part of her anatomy, her intelligence being equal to that of her brother Peisander, who was known as the thickest man in Sparta.

So far Kleora had done nothing to enhance the stature of her husband's prosperity. Their daughter, another Eupolia, was as diminutive as her namesake. ("If Agisilaos wanted to improve his line, he should have married old and asked some tall young man to do it for him.") Around Agisilaos and his wife was a cluster composed of old Aristomelidas, his mother's father, his mother, his sister, his brother Teleutias and Peisander.

"The kinglet is acquiring a courtlet," my mother muttered through clenched teeth, then glided into the hall, turning on them that dazzling smile he reserved for those she despised.

I joined Agesipolis on the children's benches, under the eyes of our nurses. Barely pausing for breath, he said, "I have a new pony and a new brother, and he has a star on his head."

"Your brother?"

"My pony."

The pony could have been a cause for envy, had the Law-Giver not forbidden it. The brother was a disappointment, being only a baby, and a very small and noisy one at that.

As its nurse took it from the hall, I asked my cousin, "Ages', will they expose it?"

"Why? The elders declared it well and strong." He attempted to balance a cup on his head, the way the servants carried pitchers and jars. Agesipolis always had to know the way things were done, and try to do the same himself. "They gave it a name, Kleombrotos."

"But it should have been a girl. One son and one daughter. It's a law."

"I don't know that law. We'll ask Father." Pausanios was making his way to his couch, a wreath of ivy and myrtle on his head. "Later."

Being a queen, my mother had one of the places of honour; only she, Pausanios, Aunt Eurydame, Agesipolis and I were royal. The others were private citizens, the Law-giver having stripped all kings' kin of royal honours – except their consorts and eldest sons – although he was the younger son of a king himself. (Overturns are never initiated by the lower orders, O Shade of Theokles. Lykourgos wrought greater change than any put forward by your Athenian demagogues. Blood and mobs do not a revolution make. Conservative Sparta is the only truly revolutionary state in Hellas; something we, no less than you, deny).

Teleutias, resplendent in his crimson war-cloak, started to share the dining-couch of another young warrior, Agesipolis's fine-looking uncle Aristodemos. Eupolia, her chin and bosom vying for prominence, stepped over to bring her younger son

57

back with the Eurypontid clan.

Eurypontid? No, something else. A circle composed of her own close kin. (Aristodemos was a cousin of Pausanios but, him being only a few years younger than the King, Agesipolis honoured him as an uncle. Royal Heraklid kinship is somewhat entangled, as Herodotos found. Perhaps that is why he made those mistakes).

I saw Teleutias exchange a glance with Kyniska. This aunt of mine was the one of Eupolia's two children by King Archidamos to have inherited his height. A handsome young matron, she so excelled at spear-throw that people said there was little between her and my mother. This did not please my mother.

"I bought that grey," Kyniska's clear young voice reached our corner.

"The man asked too much for it," replied my mother.

"But, Timaia, you said–" Aunt Eurydame began.

An angry flash from my mother's green eyes arrested the Agiad Queen's words.

Eurydame was only a year my mother's junior. Their looks were very alike – the same marble-white skin with bright cheeks and wide-spaced eyes – although my aunt's were blue, and her hair less brilliant. Yet the hand of beauty is capricious, and Eurydame's prettiness was a pale winter moon to my mother's high summer sun.

"And I shall buy its match." Kyniska went on. "Whatever it costs me."

"That is very reckless, Kyniska," Agisilaos admonished.

"Only a fool would not," Kyniska replied shortly. "I have never seen its like. Not even in Agis's stable."

"That is true." Teleutias agreed. He might have agreed more, had Agisilaos not stilled his brother with a glance. Then his eyes were on me, with what I had come to think of as *that* look. *That* look, and something more.

It was one of those late winter months, when the snow-covered mountains shield the Vale from the cruel north-east wind, and a brave sun deludes us that spring has come. After the midday meal, the false spring lured everyone to the courtyard. Agesipolis ran to his father and tugged at his cloak; a long fine, white wool cloak, with the thinnest of purple borders, that he wore well. Tall and lean, his face was too long to please a sculptor, but comely, a countenance of kingly dignity.

"Leo' says we must expose Kleombrotos because he is not a girl." Agesipolis sounded quite enthusiastic.

I explained.

"Leotychides has misunderstood," the King replied. "Over-peopled cities know want, so good citizens have two children only. Some people like one son and one daughter, but such things cannot be arranged by decree, so we make do with what we get."

He kept his face grave, but years later on a bleak, windswept Phokian plain, when our desultory attempts at conversation had given out, Kleombrotos startled our tent-companions by breaking the heavy silence, saying "Is it true, Leotychides, that you wanted to expose me?"

Aristodemos came towards us grinning, his scabbard shining on his sword-belt. He hoisted Agesipolis on to his shoulders and, with his neck wedged between my cousin's legs, began to trot about, tossing his head and whinnying like a horse.

As I watched them, I suddenly found myself flying into the air, when Teleutias swung me onto his own back in the same way. I could smell the scented herbs in his garland. Our crimson-cloaked mounts raced each other around the courtyard, their long warriors' hair flying like horses' manes. Teleutias won. There was a burst of cheers and laughter from onlookers.

The two steeds sat on the ground, regaining their breath.

My mother's laughter rang out into the clear air. She had seated herself in the centre of a small marble bench. Those gathered around her found themselves sitting at her feet. Eupolia cast her a disapproving look, and said something about Lysander's victory.

"Another victory, but no end to this war." Kyniska perched on the edge of the fountain. "What was it like before, Timaia?"

"I could hardly know that." my mother replied icily. She was not more than twenty-five, as the war went into its twenty-sixth year.

"We may soon have peace, now that the fleet is in good hands, Kyniska." Agisilaos said.

Certainly, Kallikratidas would defeat the Athenians, and then free the Hellenic cities in Asia.

59

"To answer your question, Mistress Kyniska..." An old man spoke. (I think he was the brother of my mother's father). "Before this war, Sparta's battles were paid for with booty. Not by borrowing from barbarians. Before this war, no man could be twice grand admiral. Before this war we had Law."

I stared at Agesipolis. "Kallikratidas has been grand admiral only a few months."

"Kallikratidas is dead." He extended me the remaining bite of the honey cake he was eating. "He was killed in a sea battle. Lysander is grand admiral again...sort of. Don't shout, Leo'. They will send us to our nurses."

In my isolation I had been unaware of the battle. Only now I recalled going out one day with my nurse, and seeing a number of men and women with the proud smiles and radiant faces that meant kin or friend had been slain in battle. Agesipolis stuffed the rest of the ignored honey-cake in his own mouth. A man was, and then he was not. There was a hollowness in the pit of my stomach. I comprehended death.

"Lysander is only vice-admiral," Agisilaos corrected the elder deferentially, as he limped about the women and greybeards, seeing their wants, whether they had any or not. (Is it only with hindsight that I see his virtues as vices)?

Old Aristomelidas snorted.

"Father, please," Eupolia implored.

"Lysander acted only in the interest of Sparta," Agisilaos said. Teleutias muttered something. Eupolia silenced him with a glance. He rose and joined Kyniska on the fountain-edge, where they sat with their heads together. "The name of grand admiral means nothing to him," Agisilaos continued. My mother laughed shortly, and raised a languid hand to brush away an unseasonable fly." You have always under-esteemed Lysander, Timaia."

"Dear Agisilaos, you under-esteem yourself." Her voice was a blade dipped in honey.

"It was not well done," pronounced my mother's aged uncle. Grand-uncle? Longevity runs in the Eurypontid line. "Lysander obeys the Law's letter, but he mocks its spirit."

"Sir, Lysander is the simplest and poorest of men," Agisilaos protested. "I think he possesses only two cloaks."

"Why doesn't he have one washed?" Eurydame wondered

60

absently.

Agisilaos smiled tolerantly and went on. "The situation was desperate. Konon has prized a fortune from Pharnabazos for Athens."

Teleutias looked up from his whispered talk with Kyniska. "Konon would be fish food, had Kallikratidas been given the funds from Sparta he was promised.

Eupolia turned on him. "Kallikratidas should not have made an enemy of Kyros."

"It wasn't that way—" Teleutias began.

Agisilaos laid his hand on his brother's arm. He smiled gently. (Yes, I recall the mouth, although the face is dim. It was a small, rather pretty mouth, but it had a priggish set). Their eyes met. The same blue-grey.

"Never was there a finer, nor braver man than Kallikratidas." Pausanios broke the Agiad silence. They had courteously detached themselves from mourning Eurypontid hostility.

"Sir, his courage was beyond question," Agisilaos hastened to assure the King. "Lysander is simply the better Admiral." Teleutias was there. He can tell you that the men were deeply troubled when Lysander left the fleet."

"As he intended," Teleutias stared at the grass. "His followers spread it about that the new man was incompetent."

"You are become fanciful," Agisilaos snapped.

"Then why have such men been raised, now Lysander is back." Teleutias was on his feet.

"Lysander is just."

"When justice profits him." A breeze ruffled his flowing hair. The same light brown as Agisilaos's. "By the time Kallikratidas took up his command, the allies were on the verge of mutiny. Even Spartans were slow to obey orders."

"If he couldn't keep order—"

"He knew who threw the apple of discord. When he called all the Spartans in the fleet together, we were ready for trouble. A real Lysander bellowing. A few floggings..." His feet were planted apart, his thumbs in his sword-belt. "But Kallikratidas only said, 'I did not ask for this command. I am obeying my orders. Are you Spartan enough to obey yours?' Then he turned away without looking back. We were shamed..." He seemed lost in his thoughts. "And there was no longer any doubt as to who was Grand Admiral," he came back. "He went to Kyros then. The barbarian kept him waiting two days, so he came away–"

"Lysander says it is the way of the Persians," Agisilaos spoke patiently.

"It is not our way, Agisilaos. Would that you had only been with us when we stormed Methymna! Once the Athenian garrison submitted, the Methymnians were all too glad to lay down their arms–"

"A minor victory compared to Notion," Agisilaos commented.

"A Spartan victory. Kallikratidas fought like a Spartan. Reminded us that we were Spartans..."

"Good lad," approved one of the elders.

"After Methymna, there was nothing we would not have done for him. There was hardly a murmur when he freed the Methymnian prisoners–"

"*That* I find difficult to understand," Aristodemos conceded.

"He said no Greek would be made a slave while he was in command," Teleutias went on.

"Madness," muttered Peisander. It was the sole word he spoke that day, fortune being kind.

"Then he sent his message to Konon – 'I am going to stop your fornication with the sea.' By the Twin Gods, how we cheered him!"

"What is fornication?" Agesipolis whispered.

"A kind of sea battle," I enlightened him, as Teleutias continued.

"We caught sight of Konon's trireme, and pursued him to Mytilene. Our fleet and the Athenians' entered the harbour at the same time. Kallikratidas ordered the army over from Chios to block Konon from the land side." Teleutias was in his early twenties then. His flushed face looked younger.

"But Konon got away," came the soft, pedantic voice of Agisilaos.

"The Athenians called up every man of fighting age in their city to rescue him. Even slaves. But we could have had him again, if that storm had not come up when he spotted their fires off the Silver Islands," he added quietly. "Kallikratidas took the most dangerous place in the fighting. We urged him to have a care for his life, but he said, "There are many men in Sparta as good as I," and would not be moved."

"Do you consider that finer than victory?" Agisilaos asked coldly.

"To strike straight, and win tomorrow, is better than buying a victory today."

"Well said, Teleutias!" Aristodemos spoke. The brothers' eyes locked. The fiery blue-grey of Teleutias. The icy blue-grey of Agisilaos.

Agisilaos spoke gently. "Perhaps Kallikratidas need not have been outnumbered, had he dealt more kindly with Kyros."

Teleutias's hot temper flared. "And we might have had more ships, had Lysander not used the ephors to his own purpose," he shouted. "'Dice are used for cheating boys. Oaths for cheating men.' Those are Lysander's words. Do you deny it, Brother?"

"You forget you are not yet thirty, Teleutias. You address a citizen."

"Forgive my discourtesy, *sir*. I thought I was speaking to my brother." He turned to Pausanios. "Sir, you told me you had some new horses. I should like to see them."

Pausanios told a servant to take Teleutias to the stables. As if pulled by an invisible cord, I followed him. His angry steps turned up turf. The serf hastened to keep up with him. I followed them to a field at the back of the house. The serf advised him that the chestnut was not completely broken.

The force of his fury pitted itself against the will of the half-wild stallion. I stood in admiration of my uncle, who looked like horse-taming Kastor. He disappeared into a small figure in the distance. When he returned, the chestnut was under control. He slowed to a trot and saw me.

I held out my arms. He leaned over and lifted me on, setting me down in front of him. We rode out, beyond the line of poplars that marked the boundaries of Pausanios's land. He dug his heels into its sides, and we became part of the wind. We galloped far out to the city's edge, where the plain starts the ascent to Taygetos, and turned back only at the beginning of the high, winding road leading to Messenia.

A crowd at the gate awaited our return.

Pausanios, with his brow furrowed. My mother's eyes flashing, as she accused Teleutias of trying to kill me; her

63

strong, angry hands pulling me away. Eupolia holding Teleutias, and reaching up to stroke his hair.

"I may not be royal, Mother," I heard him say, "But I am my own man."

Agisilaos embraced his brother. "Nor am I royal. Nor Kyniska. Only Agis is royal." His face was contrite.

Yes, the face of Agisilaos emerges now. As he was in his early thirties. Light-brown curling hair about a broadish brow, narrowing down to a sharp chin covered by a brown beard. The nose sharp, too.

The eyes, filled with sincere affection. Agisilaos always believed in his own sincerity.

And Kyniska, standing a bit apart, lips parted in a dry smile. Between his mother and brother, Teleutias looked like a prisoner between two guards. Eupolia's gaze fixed on me and held. Once more, *that* look. And the something else I was not too young to recognise as the face of hate.

It was almost six years before I saw any of them again. In a few months, everything changed.

Chapter 2

"My old teacher called your city a barracks."

"When we had the honour of his presence?"

"He never visited Sparta, to my knowing."

"Trust a sophist to judge one city from the distance of another."

"Why do men scorn philosophy?"

"I have seen men from your schools giving out behind the temple of Zeus in Olympia. Men of great learning and little wisdom. They speak of music, but play no lyre; of politics, but rule no city; of war, yet they are not soldiers. They are like athletes over-trained in a single skill. They know one art only. Talking."

"Your people know only the art of war."

"Not so. Sparta's soldiers are her citizens."

"You are splitting hairs." (That, from a sophist!) "Your city is divided into regiments."

"So that every man from twenty to sixty may be mobilized instantly."

"You train for war from childhood."

"Well-trained soldiers live longer. They also win more battles."

"You learn nothing but war skills."

"We are instructed in music, poetry, law, games, horsemanship. Such learning as belongs only to the rich in other cities..." I call for more wine. His visits have become routine. He is as obsessed by laws as Philippos is by sieges, but he drinks his wine as well-watered as a Spartan. "What else do free men need to know? Sometimes we even talk of the ways of gods and men."

"That is to say, you dabble in philosophy, without having had a proper moral tutor in your youth."

"When we are boys, our flock commander puts questions to us. Who is the best man in Sparta? The worst? The wisest? The bravest? And so on. We must reply in few words. Answers that give understanding of values by valuing the qualities of a particular man."

"How old are you when you kill a serf to come of age?"

Another Theban delusion Philippos heard in his youth. "Why would we kill our serfs?"

"Isn't it your law?"

"Our serfs belong to Sparta's land. Land titles lawfully belong to the city. To kill a serf would be to destroy what is Sparta's. It would be punished."

He frowns. Silent. Eyes squinted.

"Why do you play the simple soldier?" He speaks at last.

"Antalkidas asked me something like that..."

"You knew Antalkidas? The son of Leon?"

"As well as anyone could know him."

"How did you regard him?"

"On the first encounter, gratefully. He saved me from a thrashing. I was seven."

"He was an outstanding youth?"

"He was always quick with his replies. He played the lyre rather well. In games he was often second. I recall one time a dispute broke out, concerning which one of two youths had the straightest throw in a spear competition. Antalkidas insisted that the two must throw again to decide it. They all accepted his decision, although his had not been a very good throw. That was Antalkidas."

"Was it?"

*   *   *

Four Elders came to the palace. Elders of the Council, not the Eurypontid elders; although one was both. My nurse flooded me with superfluous instructions on behaviour, before taking me to present me to them.

They were seated in graceful chairs of wood, which shimmered with a silk-like sheen. My mother had appropriated the high-backed one for herself. Her face was death-pale, her lips tightly compressed.

I was duly brought forward, my eyes seemingly downcast, my arms folded within my cloak.

"A fine boy, madam," an Elder commented.

The shadow of a tall vase lengthened on the floor in the

silence.

The Elder rose and approached me. "Leotychides, you are now seven. Would you like to live in a flock with other boys?"

A sharp intake of breath from my mother.

"Yes, sir. Please." I nearly forgot and raised my eyes to him.

"You see, Timaia," said the elder who was an Elder. "It is for the best."

The palm of my mother's strong, long-fingered hand stung the side of my face.

"You little fool! You little fool! Why didn't you tell them kings' heirs are not reared in flocks?"

"Leonidas was."

"Leonidas became king purely by chance. His elder brother died in Sicily."

"Leonidas is a divine hero."

"Be still." She began pacing her chambers. Sweet-scented smoke rose from the incense burning before her statue of Aphrodite. The goddess had a gold neck-chain. A new offering. "Agis has done this."

A sudden surge of gratitude gave substance to that faceless, formless absence of a father.

She stopped pacing, bent, and seized me in one of those smothering embraces. "I'm sorry I slapped you, darling. You are too young to understand." Reproach replaced contrition in the green eyes. "You are all I have. Are you really so anxious to leave your mother?"

Her eyes moistened, not at the prospect of my going from the comforts of the palace to a life harsh beyond reckoning, but because I preferred the company of my contemporaries to her own.

Once she had a maid, a young serf woman with shining black hair, and hands that moved like butterflies as she arranged my mother's hair. The serving-woman lavished upon me all the love that had been her dead son's, but it was not a consuming love, and I returned it freely. My mother banished her to country lands for attempting to steal my affections. It taught me to conceal fondness of anything from her.

My mother loved me exceedingly; but her love was a flawed thing, tainted with jealousy.

The flock was encamped in a plain between two hills to the north of Sparta. It was a world of boys. Boys with shorn heads. Youths with rough-cut hair. All barefoot. Some completely nude. All oblivious to hunger.

The food was watery, tasteless black broth, every evening. The palace cooks prepared meaty, well-seasoned broth to accompany our meals. Here it *was* the meal, and never enough. Life was hunger. Once I bit into a bitter, green, unripe olive that had fallen to the ground. The recollection still puckers the membrance of my mouth. I swallowed it. It was food.

On the plateau of the heights above the camp boys ran, wrestled, and gathered about grey-bearded teachers. Conspicuous by our long hair, good cloaks and tunics, we new boys were at their mercy. Our lot was to do whatever an older boy ordered. Arcane demands. "Bring my jumping stones." "Fetch my oil flask." "You – my stlengis. Make haste!" Where were such things to be found? No one told us. If we were slow about it, we were clouted.

Night brought the sweet forgetfulness of sleep. As it was early summer, we slept under the stars. Morning came too soon. A walk to a deep stream was followed by a plunge into water, still cold from its journey down the mountains. A boy called Euagoras hesitated on the river-bank. Was shoved in. Howled. Pulled out and clouted for screaming. He was a very small boy. Looked more five than seven. I distanced myself from him in the rush back to the camp, where serfs handed out the meagre fare to break the night's fast. We youngest were pushed aside and got none.

The third dawn, as we vainly tried to make our way into the forest of bare legs and feet for something to eat, a shaven-headed boy about ten smiled, and extended a share of his portion. We grasped the kindness proffered, as eagerly as the bread he offered.

There were smothered guffaws when small boys bit into their bread with the full force of their hunger. They reeled back, spitting out pieces of milk teeth. The pale-eyed youth still watched, as a carrot-haired boy followed my example and soaked his in water. Youths meant trouble. I swallowed the bread quickly, before someone could seize it.

That day, youths practised a complex exercise. Arrayed in columns, they wheeled at a command, changed places without missing a step, and re-formed, so that the strongest were always in front. Had I known it, I was watching the basis of those rapid changes with which the Spartan army confronts its enemies, keeping the best men in the vanguard facing the foe, whatever direction he approaches from.

Sometimes the orders were not passed from the commander to the patrol leaders. The boys took their orders from the notes of a flute...but I must say no more. The secrets of Spartan warfare are not for foreigners.

Weapon training was a disappointment. The boys' spears were blunted, and their shields only hollow, wooden frames. The oldest had man-high spears. Their shields were full-sized, but even the commander's lacked the splendid bronze covering of those carried by real warriors.

This exalted personage of about nineteen reclined on the only dining couch in the flock each evening, and put questions to older boys while they served him like a king (a foreign king; no Spartan king was shown such deference). He judged conduct and achievement, meted out punishment and praise. His orders to younger boys reached them only through patrol leaders. Commanders were appointed yearly, although one was dismissed after only a few months by the Inspector of Boys on one of his surprise visits, for punishing boys too severely. Another was reprimanded for leniency.

Our duties were restricted to a simple drill devised (not always successfully) to teach us our left feet from our right. This was because we were seven-year-olds, and seven-year-olds were nothing. Sphodrias explained it, as we took our evening meal of watery black broth sitting under an oak tree.

Only Sphodrias explained things. He had an enthusiasm for explanation. He did not explain why the fat boy, the big boy and that smallest boy Euagoras suffered even more than the rest of us. Nor did he explain mysterious matters such as Passing Out, the Hidden Thing, and the Great Fight. That was not for nothings like us.

He was a gangly twelve then, all knees and elbows, with a short crop of rusty curls and bold eyes. "A boy is a rhodibas between eight and twelve." He spoke between bites. (Where had he got that good bread?) "From twelve to sixteen he is a melleiren." Bite. Bite. "From sixteen to twenty he is an eiren."

"How can you tell a first-rank melleiren from a fourth-rank rhodibas?" Big Aristokrates asked. He was the son of Lysander's friend Pharax, and would have all know it.

"A rhodibas still has his head shaved. I am a melleiren," Sphodrias added importantly.

His own hair was shorter than the rough cuts of most youths.

"I think, Sphodrias," I said, although had I thought I would not have spoken at all, "that you have not been a melleiren very long."

Another melleiren laughed. Sphodrias scowled, seized me by my tunic, and called for an olive switch.

"Leave it alone, Sphodrias." My saviour was that tall, thin youth with the triangular face and pale eyes. "It was a good observation."

Sphodrias still grasped the knot of my tunic. "Nothings must respect melleirens, Antalkidas."

"And first-rank melleirens obey second-rankers, Sphodrias." The pale eyes went to me as Sphodrias reluctantly released his hold. "Has it a name?"

"It is called Leotychides, and it thinks too much of itself."

"Better too much than too little," Antalkidas replied. "I shouldn't mind having it in my patrol next year."

"If you have a patrol," one of his companions said.

"How could I not?" The pale eyes looked skywards, as if he were sharing a secret jest with some Olympian. Perhaps he was. Only the gods knew what Antalkidas was thinking.

I dreaded dire retribution from Sphodrias as the cause of his humiliation, but he continued to treat me with the same good-natured disdain he accorded all the newcomers.

Often we were ordered to gather herbs for the cooking pot. This meant to steal them from the kitchens and storerooms of Sellasia, the nearest town. We also learnt to ease our ever-empty stomachs with purloined fruit, bread, or cheese by the same means. If we were caught, we were thrashed. It was shameful to be caught. Anyone who has seen a Theban straggler spearing hungry peasants knows it is better to forage discreetly, but we were given no reasons. Only told obey. Obey. Obey.

Winter brought the meaning of hardship.

The elders now taught in the plain. Only the hardiest youths braved the windy height to exercise barefoot and nude. The air became too bitter to sustain that interlude of talk after the evening dip, while smoke rose from the cooking-fires into the early darkness. Euagoras groaned and wept without punishment, as he was unconscious most of the time. His eyes were reddened and moist. Although he sniffed constantly, droplets invariably hung from the end of his nose. Some of the boys feared he was dying; some of us hoped he was, for his whimperings disturbed our sleep. Sleep was the only escape from the wretchedness of existence.

"It is a wonder that one survived the wine-bath." Hekataios, the carrot-haired boy, thrust shivering arms inside his cloak.

"Better he had not," said Aristokrates. Older boys did not usually trouble to discover the author of a sob or shriek before clouting for cowardice, and often punished the wrong boy.

Now the flock slept in a large rough hut, but the thistle-down added to our pallets could not keep out the cold. One would turn from one's right to one's left, knees pulled up to chest, yet the icy fingers of winter always found some exposed place to rend the surface of sleep.

One morning, as we crowded about the season's steaming cauldron, holding out wooden bowls, a rhodibas assessed us with a knowing look and asked another, "How many do you think will last the winter?"

"A sorry lot this year! That one might live." He indicated big Aristokrates, "if we let him." One seized the big seven-year-old's bowl, and drank down its contents himself.

I fell into the trap of looking up.

"You–" The rhodibas allowed me no time to hold out my bowl to the serf's ladle. "Go to the heights and feed the boar."

The sky was dark with late dawn. Dark with rain clouds. Even in darkest night, torches were permitted no one. The heights were a black outline. In the distance, snow capped the mountains. Boar? Was this some jest? What did one feed a boar? A bitter wind blew from north, north-east, east, assailing

71

me from all directions. My feet flew pointlessly on the frosty ground. I did not understand what I was to do. Only that if I did not do it, I would be thrashed. My breath formed a frozen cloud's embrace. Tripped. Stumbled. Fell.

I lay in high grasses. My body melted the frost into a damp that seeped into my cloak and tunic. I did not move. The rhodibas was right; I would die. I cared not. I lay on my stomach, my face pillowed in my arms, waiting for the Wayfinder.

By some trick of the landscape, I had fallen in a sheltered place. With first daylight, the sun broke through the heavy clouds. A steady warmth on my back made me drowsy. The sleep that flitted intermittently in and out of the hut now consumed me, the hard ground welcoming as the cushions of my bed in the palace.

Laughter woke me. A short distance away, some melleirens threw the spear. The wind whipped their hair and their cloaks. A burly fellow stepped on to a squared stone, and made a fine, straight throw. The others cheered him. I parted the high grasses in front of me, to watch the competition. Tall, thin Antalkidas was next. His spear veered to the side.

Another seven-year-old plopped beside me. "They are good."

"Some of them." My eyes still on the melleirens.

"I'm Anaxandros."

The fat boy had been called Anaxandros. No longer about. I glanced at my uninvited companion. This boy was as lean as the rest of us, but the wide eyes were the same.

"I thought you were dead."

A tall, slender, dark-haired melleiren mounted the stone, turning his spear by its loop.

"Are you from Sparta?"

"There are no up-country boys in flocks." Raising his arm like the statue of Apollo in the temple at Amyklai, the dark-haired melleiren made a throw as straight as the best. There was grace in his movements. Another cheer.

"We're all Spartiate," Anaxandros replied. "But some of the boys here are from half-way to Amyklai. You have the look of a City man."

It pleased me to be called a man, if only by a contemporary.

72

"I'm from Kynsouria." We call our parts of Sparta by the names of the four villages that formed it in times before memory.

"I'm from Pitane." Anaxandros reached into the folds of his cloak, and withdrew a partially eaten apple.

"My cousin lives in Pitane." The last youth was throwing.

"Is he in this flock? My cousin Pityas is here, but he won't speak to me because he is a rhodibas. Here." He extended half the chewed apple.

I took it. "I'm Leotychides."

"Why did they give you a royal name?"

"I'm the son of King Agis." A dispute broke out amongst the melleirens. I caught my slip too late. "Don't tell anyone."

"I'd tell everyone if I were a prince."

"Not if you had wits. You know that big boy Aristokrates? He talks about how great his father is, and the older boys don't like it." I grasped his wrist. "So you say nothing." I tightened my grip.

"I won't say anything. Let go."

The melleirens were shouting. Antalkidas stepped into the midst of the angriest. He pointed. Said something. They drew back. He motioned the burly youth, and the graceful dark-haired one, to the stone. The burly youth repeated his first straight throw. The dark-haired melleiren mounted the stone. I parted the grasses more, the better to see.

"You–" A melleiren looked my way. "Both of you lazy nothings. Fetch us water for a wrestling-ground."

We ran all-out towards the stream. Anaxandros halted abruptly half-way there. "A rhodibas told me to feed his boar."

"We'll say a melleiren sent us for water. Melleirens count for more than a rhodibas."

We exchanged grins. Complicit. Allied. Friends.

After the time of the olive harvest, Apollo brought up a strong sun in his chariot. Each day he drove closer, as he carried it across the sky to Taygetos. The snow disappeared; the yellow-brown fields became a carpet of green. Croci blossomed, new leaves fluttered on the plane trees, and purple iris shot up amongst the rushes of the river bank.

Gathering herbs one day, I found a large, bubbling cauldron

unattended, and seized the better part of a half-cooked fowl.

On my way back, I encountered the dark-haired spear-thrower, and proudly handed him my herbs, smiling in the euphoria of spring and a full stomach. He was not pleased.

I had thrust the herbs in my tunic as I ate the chicken, and they were denuded of their leaves.

"What do you take me for?" he demanded. "A horse?"

He ordered me back for more. I was careless. Caught. Thrashed.

A few months later, I became a rhodibas. Our heads were shorn. We were assigned to patrols. There was a new lot of seven-year-olds biting into dry bread, gathering about Sphodrias asking stupid questions, and doing any number of ignorant and amusing things. They even believed us and looked frightened, when we hinted they would not last the winter.

Another event of significance took place that year. The war ended.

In a cunning move, Lysander destroyed the Athenian fleet off a place called Goat River in the Thracian Chersonese. Only a negligible eight triremes escaped, led by that Konon whom Kallikratidas had so nearly entrapped.

Athens sued for peace, and a conference of the victorious allies was called at Sparta to agree the terms.

The Thebans demanded that Athens be razed to the ground, which was unsurprising, as Boiotia is a rough country of cattle and cattle-thieves. Ancient, civilized Corinth would have been content merely to enslave all Athenians. But, mercy being the daughter of discipline, Sparta resisted calls for vengeance upon a defeated enemy, and opposed the destruction of a great city.

To be just, it was not revenge alone that moved the cities who called for savage retribution, but fear of Athens. Sparta put forward a means of preventing her from menacing free cities again.

The Athenian Empire has been founded, so to speak, on the long walls linking the city to her port of Piraeus. These vast fortifications could be manned by a few troops of inferior quality, leaving the best men free to sail with the striking fleet that has forced so many cities into submission. Athens, therefore, would be required to destroy those walls, and to limit her warships to a number necessary solely to defend herself.

States that had been denuded of their populations in punishment for rebellion against the Empire, and resettled with Athenians, were to be given back to their original citizens. Exiled Athenians could return to their homeland. Athens was to follow Sparta's leadership in time of war.

The Empire was dissolved, but Athens left free and intact. The conference agreed on it, and Athens accepted the terms. For the first time in the life of every boy in every flock in Sparta (as well as some of the warriors) the Hellenes were at peace.

Anaxandros went to the patrol of Antalkidas, whose confidence in being appointed a leader had not been misplaced. I was assigned to the patrol led by the graceful spear-thrower, who was called Doreius, along with carrot-haired Hekataios, big Aristokrates and Euagoras – who, after all, had survived.

"You're for it, now." Sphodrias demanded our cloaks, sandals, and tunics. "Doreius is the hardest patrol leader in the flock. That's why he gets the best boys and the worst." He obviously included himself in the first category.

We were issued with the single cloak which would also serve as towel and blanket. I was quite pleased with mine; assuming (wrongly) that the coarse stuff would be warmer than the Milesian wool I arrived in. Our patrol leader brusquely ordered us to assemble.

He stood on a slight rise before us, the wind whipping his hair and brightening his cheeks. He had that type of pale, almost translucent, skin that often accompanies very dark hair. His lips were compressed firmly, as his grey eyes scanned us. (Why is it that when I think of Doreius, it is always as that beautiful youth on the hillock)?

"No, don't cast your eyes down. I'm a melleiren, not a man." His young voice was sure and unstrained. "Nor is it seemly to stare." That was for me, and I flushed. "Now listen to me well. You are here to obey. Not to question. Not to argue. Not to complain. You obey me, as I obey the Commander, and he obeys the Inspector of Boys, who obeys the laws of Sparta."

"In your games and your lessons, you must each try to best the other, but if another boy betters you, you must not be envious but glad, for his excellence honours the flock; and, in honouring the flock, casts honour upon you. You may not understand all this now, but you will learn by living it."

"Do not set yourselves up, one against the other, in any manner but excellence. Here there are no ephors' sons, no generals' sons nor kings' sons, no poor men's sons nor rich men's sons. No sons of wise or foolish men. You belong to the flock, and the flock belongs to Sparta. You are Spartiates. Equals. That is the Law of Lykourgos. Sons of Herakles, obey it."

He stood a moment longer; his head tilted slightly back, that ideal youth that every boy dreams of becoming, and then turned away. Had he ordered me to jump from the highest peak of Taygetos, I think I should have instantly obeyed.

Men returned from the war, and an unusual number of visitors came to our encampment. Fathers sought sons they had last seen as infants, or not at all. Brothers found tall youths they recalled as children. Friends embraced and talked simultaneously, trying to fill in the gaps of lives that war had punctuated.

Anaxandros pointed out a grizzled man with many battle-scars as Leon, the father of Antalkidas. Apparently, Antalkidas had neglected to tell his patrol that there were no ephors' sons amongst boys who belonged to Sparta. Anaxandros's own father turned out to be that Eutelidas whom Pausanios had greeted near the Bronze House.

Pharax appeared one day, with a retinue of companions. He was a big man, with florid good looks and a distinctive white streak in his hair, resulting from a scalp-wound. After he left, Aristokrates boasted that his father had been made into a statue. Perhaps he was not far from the truth.

As the warriors returned, men in their prime replaced some of the oldest teachers. We had a new music master. This man was no mean poet, and might have been famous in a city that produced fewer composers of fine verse. It was he who discovered that Euagoras had a voice like a lark.

The small boy's touch on the lyre was true and fine. While we were still learning the simple melodies of Gitidias, Euagoras mastered subtle strings to accompany the words of Alkman.

76

Apart from his amazing gift, he was the same repulsive creature he had always been, with one notable improvement. In midsummer his nose ceased to drip.

As we plaited rushes one day to make new pellets for the flock, a man walked slowly from the road to the camp. Hekataios leapt up and shouted, "Father!" Sphodrias clouted him. He sat down again.

We were in the plain, but the man stopped now and then to rest. He straightened himself before continuing. When he reached us, he was breathing with the sound made by men who survive a spear-thrust.

His hair was white, but his face was not that of an elder, although it was etched with the lines of pain.

He embraced Hekataios, and asked appropriate questions of the rest of us. Sphodrias said, "Go with him, Hek'. We'll finish your work for you." Doreius would not have done that. Father and son walked off together. When Hekataios returned, we had the plaiting all but done.

"That statue of your father..." Hekataios turned to Aristokrates, as he took up some rushes. "You never told us why they made it."

"He was in Athens with Lysander."

Lysander had been sent to Athens, to see that the terms of the peace had been carried out.

Sphodrias laughed. "So it was an entire Spartan garrison. Nor did the Athenians erect it. Some islanders did."

Aristokrates frowned, but did not dare reply to the melleiren. His gaze went to a corner of the field where Hekataios's father was deep in conversation with Doreius. "Our patrol leader seems to have a lot to say about you, Hek' I shouldn't want to be in your place."

"Don't be daft." Hekataios plaited diligently. "They're not talking about me; He's *his* father, too."

Sphodrias exploded. "You'd never know you're his brother when he orders the thrashings."

"He's got to be fair. Father explained all that, when he told me about going to a flock."

"Why didn't you ever tell us that Doreius is your brother, Hek'?" I asked.

"I thought everyone knew." My gaze went to Doreius and his father. I noted the same features in the worn face of the man and the countenance of the youth. "I know I don't look like him," the snub-nosed, blunt-featured, freckled boy went on. "I heard the women say that's because I lay two years in my mother's womb. But they didn't explain how it made me look different," he added cheerfully.

"Through these doors no word goes outside." The oldest member of a dining-hall admonishes each fellow member, as he enters.

Youths, however, do not feel it applies to them when they attend dining clubs to learn civilized behaviour (a lesson they could do well with here); something the men bear in mind, having been youths themselves.

I often picked up intriguing fragments of information, as I was briefly roused from sleep, when eirens and melleirens returned, talking hall gossip, speaking in imitation of the men's terse comments.

One night, the youths came back laughing.

"The Polemarchs fined King Agis for not dining in his Hall, Antal." I recognised the voice of Chionis.

My father was back at last!

"Why didn't he ask to be excused for hunting or sacrificing?" asked some other melleiren.

"He was doing neither. He supped with his wife."

"Who wants to spend his first evening back with a wild boar?" Antalkidas said. "I'd risk a fine for Queen Timaia, too."

"What do you think he will do with the brat?" Owner of voice unknown.

"Forbidden topic." The deeper voice of an eiren.

"Forbidden topics are so much more interesting," Antalkidas again.

"Antal, I have often wondered..." Chionis. "Did you know who he was when you spoke up for him that time?"

"Then? No. He doesn't resemble Timaia. Nor does he look like Agis, for which he may thank the gods, or–"

"Have done!" The eiren commanded. "Or we shall all be thrashed."

Eavesdropping brought the names of a number of famous men to my ears. Gylippos had returned to Sparta, to a hero's welcome. That is to say, the ephors praised him. We do not make speeches and have feasts gloating on our victories.

Lysander, on the other hand, was receiving the honours foreigners accord to victors. Having finished his mission at Athens, he was sailing about the cities that Sparta freed from the Athenian Empire, where he was hailed as a saviour. At that time, a grateful Hellas treated every Spartan soldier like a Games-winner, and for Lysander nothing was too much.

Anaxandros brought me out of a sound sleep with a sharp elbow in my ribs. Some people in the liberated territories raised a statue to Lysander, and he told the people to make a statue of Pharax as well. That is what Hek' meant."

"How do you know what Hek' said?" Antalkidas's patrol had not been planting rushes with us that day.

"Pityas told me." His cousins spoke to him, now that Anaxandros was also a rhodibas. "Pharax isn't a great man like Brasidas or Gylippos. No one would give him a statue here."

"Belt up, Magpie," Pityas ordered. "We're all asleep."

By then, of course, no one was.

Anaxandros Magpie – Diopeithes gave him the name. Wise Diopeithes, who taught us the Law, his sharp nose and bright-hooded eyes giving him the look of an old eagle, his prey the misfortunate boy at whom he would point a bony finger, demanding, "What is the meaning of that rhetra? Don't just repeat it."

Our former master had had us recite the rhetrae parrot-fashion.

"Why did Lykourgos ban the coin from Sparta?" The finger moved and paused at Aristokrates.

"To make the iron ingot our currency, sir."

"The Law-giver had a whimsical liking for iron. Is that what you are telling me?"

"No, sir. He wanted money in big pieces. Gold coins are small." His voice rose in desperation. "And the iron ingot is useless outside Sparta. So traders stopped coming to sell us slaves and luxuries."

"Stop braying, Donkey." Clout. "Admit that you half-know. That is better than not knowing at all."

Diopeithes was lavish with his clouts. His sarcasms stung more, but the hours of his lessons sped as his predecessor's had dragged. "Anyone else? Not you, Cockerel?"

I had earned the epithet by calling out answers unbidden.

"Lykourgos wanted big money to stop theft and bribery," a boy essayed, sensed his reply was inadequate, and sat squirming as the ominous hooded gaze fell upon him.

"Wriggle all you like, Worm, it is as obvious that something too large to be hidden discourages the practices you name as it is that your mind is as sluggish as your body is agitated. But you have not answered the question!" His voice became deceptively gentle. "Perhaps I am not making myself clear. I will give you a hint. It was for the same reason that the Law-giver forbade Spartiates to trade or to learn crafts." The crisp tones cracked like a whip. "The Law does not consist of random measures to impede this or encourage that. It is devised to give shape to a harmonious city. Each rhetra is like the individual note that combines with other notes to create a perfect melody. The banning of the coin is a very important note. Well? Your mouth closed for once, Magpie? No chatter?" The finger found another victim, who simply stammered. "I don't know, sir."

"Bonehead! Anyone? All right, Cockerel, tell them."

"Sir, Lykourgos banned the coin so that men would have to do great things to win honours, and not just be rich."

"Not all men *can* achieve greatness." He tested me.

"But they will be better if they try to *be* something great, instead of trying to *have* things, sir."

After the lesson he detained me.

"You know your meaning, but you must learn to state it briefly. Lykourgos channelled the will of men to excellence rather than acquisition."

"It does sound better that way, sir."

"A graceful admission," he said drily. "Remember this, when you practice running and archery, you do not waste your movements. Now you must discipline your mind as you do your muscles. Cockerel. Cockerel... what is your true name?"

"Leotychides, sir. Son of Agis."

"So...It is a royal cockerel."

Next day he clouted me twice for calling out answers unbidden.

We lost Diopeithes as a teacher when we moved camp to Pellana, but the names stuck. Magpie, Donkey, Worm, Monkey, Slug. Years later, at Leuktra, as I knelt to help a gravely wounded man, he gasped, "By the Twin Gods, it's the Cockerel." I only remembered Bonehead's true name after his life had poured out into the hostile earth of Boiotia.

I daily expected to see my father, after learning he had returned to Sparta. Far away in the Dekeleia, he had thought of me, and had me sent to the flock. (By now I would not have exchanged the worst of its hardships for the boredom of the palace). When the last of the fathers back from the war had called to see their sons, and still he did not appear, my mind went back to that arcane conversation I had overheard.

Had my father been warned by an oracle, like the one that told King Priam that his son Paris would bring destruction to Troy? The other boys whose fathers never came, like Pityas and Euagoras, had lost them in the war. My father neither brought me honour by dying bravely, nor visited me with thrilling tales of battle I could repeat to my friends.

To be different in childhood is hard, to admit it to oneself still harder. I put my father from my mind, and ceased to think of him, except with the vaguest of rancour – and then altogether, when the scandals began, and boys had something other than their fathers to talk about.

When Lysander was in their city, overseeing the peace terms carried out, the Athenians overthrew their government, revolution being endemic to Athens. He restored order by setting up a council of thirty Athenians, headed by one of their number called Kritias. Perhaps that suggested the pattern.

When he made his tour of the liberated cities, Lysander set up councils of ten to govern them, and placed a Spartan governor over each. The governor was invariably a good friend, or a trusted servant, of Lysander himself.

I do not say he imposed them by force. Nor were they freely chosen. Wherever he went, Lysander was paid the honours due only a god. Brasidas was a greater general, Gylippos more ingenious, Kallikratidas bolder, but to the commander who wins the decisive battle goes the credit of victory.

Altars were raised to the liberator of Hellas. Cities gave him talents of gold. One even changed the name of its chief festival to the Lysandreia; a gesture not calculated to please the goddess to whom it was originally dedicated. Poets sang his praises. The likeness of Lysander was carved in marble and cast in bronze. An Olympic winner accepted his olive crown in Lysander's name. The Great King of Persia sent him a copy of his trireme, in ivory and gold.

At last Lysander turned to Sparta, petrified in self-righteousness; wearing his old, frayed cloak like a badge of simplicity, and delivered the fortune of gold coins he had collected into the City's keeping. (He stopped in Delphi, to give Apollo his tithe, but he paid the god's share not from our spoils, but those of our allies).

A great controversy broke out.

Sparta had no treasury. The coin is unlawful. Now Sparta had a treasury, and it was filled with gold. Skiraphidas stated flatly that Sparta must keep to its iron nugget. It was not small, precious pieces of metal themselves the Law-giver feared, but the greed they inspire in men.

His opponents argued that the coins were wanted for the fleet. Respected citizens replied that Sparta had created her fleet to defeat Athens. Now Athens was defeated, we no longer had need of a fleet. If the City broke the law, private citizens would no longer feel bound to obey.

The coins remained in Sparta.

Shortly after the coins came into the city, servants' gossip started a rumour that General Thorax had kept some for himself. The General, a friend of Lysander, but a fine commander in his own right, was unfortunate in that an election of ephors had brought in men who were not open to Lysander's persuasion.

They ordered a search. A hoard of gold coins was found under the tiles of the General's roof. All were imprinted with the owl of Athens, which meant they might have come from any of the liberated states, as the Athenians had forced their coinage on all their subject cities.

Thorax was tried, found guilty, and executed – his crime being personal, while Lysander's was public. Great crimes are always harder to punish than lesser ones. No sooner had the furore died down than Gylippos – great Gylippos, the defender of Syracuse – was discovered to have committed a similar crime and banished.

Lysander, with expedient piety, went to Lybia to fulfil a religious duty. The coins remained in the city.

From the boys who had been attending Dining Hall, I once more heard the name of my old hero Alkibiades. He had fled Thrace after Athens' defeat, and gone to the court of Pharnabazos at Daskilion. Athens was in rebellion yet again. This time, against the council that Lysander set up. The rebels were calling for Alkibiades to lead them. Then suddenly, Alkibiades was dead.

He had been stabbed to death by the Satrap's orders. Another version had the killing done by the kin of a woman he abducted.

"Believe that and you will believe anything," I heard Antalkidas say outside the sleeping hut. "Alkibiades never had to abduct women. All he had to do was smile at them. By Zeus, that man had style."

"A woman was with him when he was slain." Pronax.

"When did he not have a woman with him?" Antalkidas laughed. "This one sold her jewels to bury him. Hardly the outrage of a ravished maiden."

"Pharnabazos was his friend, Antal." Doreius.

"And friend to Lysander. The friendship of barbarians is a double-edged blade." When I quoted that statement back to Antalkidas, years later, he merely smiled.

That same Thrasyboulos who had been a commander in the Long War was leading the rebels. The volatile Thebans, who had recently wanted Athens razed to the ground, aided the insurgents.

The politics of it were very tangled and Athenian. Two parties sent to Sparta for help. Lysander acted with his usual dispatch, and persuaded the ephors to send him to Attica with an army.

Pausanios, however, was able to convince them that the party of Kritias and his council was so small that it could only be kept in power by maintaining a permanent garrison in Athens, and it was contrary to Spartan custom to garrison foreign cities. The ephors gave him an army, and ordered him to put down the rebellion.

The King defeated the insurrectionists at Piraeus. Then he held an inquiry into their grievances. On finding that Kritias and his council had ordered the execution of more of their own compatriots than had been slain in the Long War, he restored their Middle Party, from which Thrasyboulos emerged as leader. (Athenians call this party their Democracy, but there is also another Athenian party that calls itself the Democracy. You see what I mean about Athenian politics)!

Lysander did not take kindly to being thwarted. He summoned enough support to have Pausanios arrested in his absence, charged with disobedience, and put on trial for his life.

*   *   *

The tutor called, just as I finished fair-copying this passage on Lysander. I dictated it to the scribe Philippos gave me, but his written Doric is less fluent than his spoken. He speaks with a foreign accent, and uses idiom that is meaningless to me. He is decidedly not Spartan, neither Spartiate nor up-country man. Not even Dorian. I must ask him what he is, some time.

"Your history progresses," the tutor remarked.

"Slowly."

The scroll was unrolled, so that it ran a good length of this quiet, pleasant room I use as a study. The house is Greek. These people must spend fortunes buying Greek artisans, but Macedon is rich in precious metals since Philippos annexed so much of Thrace. Slaves, too, are even cheaper than they were during the Long War. (The tutor is a paid man. Not a slave).

"The scribe?"

"Worthless. When he is unfamiliar with a word, he invents a spelling of his own. He uses letters that do not exist in the Doric."

He was trying not to look down at that part of the scroll that passed his chair on his haphazard journey across the floor.

84

"Perhaps I would know some of the letters." What he really meant was that he would like a look at it.

"I have removed them."

I passed him the scroll. He was curious. I wanted another's opinion. I cannot trust myself on the subject of Lysander. In writing of one's enemies, hostility shapes one's assessment or, conversely, one becomes over-lenient, so as not to appear vindictive. (Not that truth is always to be found in impartiality).

"You are not one of Lysander's admirers," he concluded the passage.

"I thought I was impartial."

"Was it to balance your criticism that you omitted to tell how he mocked the Athenians?"

"Mocked them...?" Lysander was a strict observer of outward forms. "He would not ridicule a defeated enemy."

"Did he not send flute players to deride them with merry songs as they tore down their long walls?"

"Is that what they say? That it was done to deride them?"

In Lakedaimon, we run to music, throw the spear to music, jump to music, box to music, and drill to music. The thought of expending physical effort without music is inconceivable. Tearing down fortifications is hard work. Naturally, Lysander sent them musicians. I explained.

He absorbed, and then said, "Lysander led the empire faction in Sparta, did he not?"

"There was no empire faction in Sparta. There could be no more be an empire faction in Sparta than there could be a faction opposed to empire in Athens."

In the reign of my grandfather, King Archidamos, there had been a proposal to exact a set tribute from our allies, as most of our wars were fought on behalf of one or another of them. He ridiculed it out of existence, with the terse comment that war does not consume according to rule. The men who advocated treating allies like subjects were heavily out-voted. Sparta was the enemy of empire.

"Lysander believed that Sparta must protect the cities she freed." I extended my moderation to the spoken word.

"A euphemism for empire."

"I doubt whether he thought that far."

"He set up the councils of ten. Appointed governors."

"Favours for his friends. Lysander was a master of intrigue; he was ambitious, but he hadn't a political mind. He never thought beyond his own advancement."

"That *is* a political mind."

"And Sparta withdrew the governors, and dismissed the councils, two years later."

"You understand that I do not necessarily oppose empire. Spartan, Athenian or whatever."

Whatever could it be in Hellas, except Spartan or Athenian?

"After the Long War, it was no longer a question of empire except to the Athenians, who could not accept losing theirs."

"Am I right in assuming that you consider Lysander the cause of what followed?"

"The cause? Oh, not the cause. A link, an important link, in the chain. A reason among reasons. I do not know the cause..."

Hades take moderation! How different our world would be, had Kallikratidas lived and Lysander died.

*   *   *

I learnt that Pausanios had been arrested the day I learnt who I was.

To be precise, I heard a melleiren say that he had heard in the dining hall that the king was to be put on trial. My first fear was that my father had done something to shame me. Then the youth spoke the name of Pausanios.

If, for reasons I have explained, *my father* meant a blurred absence, the word *father* alone evoked the grave young face of Pausanios, telling tales and answering questions. I was not aware that I loved Pausanios, in the way that I knew that I liked Hekataios and despised Euagoras.

Pausanios had always been there, like Agesipolis (whom I suppose I liked), like my mother (whom I supposed I loved), like Aunt Eurydame (who always gave me honey cakes). When he visited the flock to bring me news of Agesipolis, I took his visits for granted. When he stopped coming because he was away with his army, it was not the news I missed, but Pausanios.

I was practising the lyre when I overheard the boy go on to

say that Pausanios was to stand trial for his life. I dropped the instrument, and left it where it lay. The other boys probably assumed I had disappeared behind a scrub-bush, to relieve myself.

I took one of the bows we used for archery and some arrows (a thrashing offence), and went off to bring down a bird to take to Apollo's sacred grounds, which were not far from the camp. I would ask the god to save my uncle.

A group of eirens, wrestling, were too engrossed to see a solitary boy wandering off by himself. I narrowly dodged some melleirens drilling. By hiding behind cliffs and trees, I managed to keep out of sight.

The carpet of summer green was strewn with anemones of every colour, and pale wild violets, as I walked vaguely in the direction of Apollo's grounds. A sparrow lit near a clump of purple columbine that had strayed from the mountains, but such a plain bird was too slight an offering.

I side-stepped a patch of nettles, and frightened a quail cock into flight. Was this prize one of the omens Hekataios was always talking about?

I took aim.

"Leotychides!" Antalkidas made me miss my shot. "Come here, Leotychides."

At seven we had been switched about the legs. Now it was across the shoulders. I approached him slowly.

"Sit down," he ordered. "Where were you going?" I have no reply. It was between Apollo and me. "If you tell me, I might help you."

"The Shrine of Apollo."

"King Pausanios...Is that it?" I looked to the sun Apollo carried towards Taygetos. "No, Apollo didn't tell me. I saw you run off when that fool of a boy blurted it out." Antalkidas had an uncanny ability to read one's thoughts. "Don't you think it might be more appropriate to offer to Zeus for a king?"

"I will, Antalkidas." I would not risk offending the king of the gods, or a melleiren.

"In fact..." The pale eyes scrutinised me. "People might assume that the *son* of a king would also follow Zeus." Seeing that the implication went over my head, he went on. "I always

87

pray to Zeus myself."

"You are not the son of a king."

"Apollo helped the Trojans, but Zeus gave victory to the Greeks."

"Only because Hera made him promise."

He threw back his head and laughed. I did not know why "A sound admonition from a rhodibas! That tongue of yours, Leotychides, will stamp you as much as...well, never mind. And don't worry about Pausanios. He will be tried by the Council of Elders. They are rigid in their observance of the letter of the law. Pausanios is charged with disobeying his orders, which were to quell the rebellion in Athens. He put down the revolt. They must acquit him."

"Then why did they accuse him?"

"The ephors accused him. Not the Council. Believe me, he will be found innocent."

My father was a member of the Council, and Pausanios had once told us kings had a moral influence. They also had only one vote each. Yet Anaxandros believed that Antalkidas was always right.

I promised Apollo the next bird I brought down.

The plain was light in the long summer evening. The sweet scent of the pink blossoms of the matthiola plant became stronger, as the sun lowered and mixed with the smoke of the cooking-fires.

We being of little significance in the present, our talk was of the distant future – when we would win olive crowns, perform spectacular acts of bravery in battle, and such things.

Aristokrates declared his intention of commanding a fleet of triremes. Hekataios sallied that he might better be a friend of Lysander, so he could have a statue like his father.

"Who is that shear-head's father?" came the superior tones of a melleiren, sitting in back of us.

"Pharax," another replied.

"I thought it might have been Eteonikos. He has a statue in the liberated territories, too."

"Who is Eteonikos?"

"You may well ask. They are saying that, when Lysander

dies, the sculptors will worship him as a divine hero, as they have grown rich making statues of his friends."

Hekataios doubled over, in loud laughter.

Aristokrates went red in the face. "Belt up, you stupid little turd. They expose your sort in Athens. I *have* a father."

"Everyone has a father," I told him.

"You *would* say that. Two of a kind."

"Just what do you mean?" Sphodrias intervened. It was more of a threat than a question.

Aristokrates looked as if he would shout again, but retreated before the older boy. "I know," he said. "You know. Everyone knows..."

Hekataios was on his feet. "What do you know? My father was braver than yours. Ask anyone about Dinon of Limnai. He never got a statue. Only a spear-tip in his lung, so that his hair turned white; and he coughs all the time."

"I did not say that Dinon isn't brave," Aristokrates spoke with lethal cool. "Only that he isn't your father. Bastard!"

Hekataios lunged. The two boys became a tangle of arms and legs. A shadow fell. Aristokrates was slung to one side. Hekataios joined him in a gasping heap.

Doreius stood above us, the folds of his worn cloak held as neat as a warrior's by the simple cord. His beautifully curved cheeks flushed with anger. His grey eyes were unrelenting. A wing of dark hair fell on his brow. He tossed it back with an abrupt movement of his head. There was silence all around.

After an interminably long time, he seated himself on the ground with us. Somewhat the way he did when he told those stories that were more in the nature of lessons than tales. Like the one about the ancient Spartan who stood for election as one of the best three hundred men in the City, and was pleased that he was not elected, because that meant Sparta had three hundred men better than he. Or the one of the boy who hid a stolen fox in his cloak, and let it gnaw through to his innards until it killed him without uttering a cry, rather than reveal his theft. That sort of thing. Examples.

Now he told us about another ancient Spartan called Geradas. Some stranger asked this Geradas what the penalty for adultery was in Sparta. Geradas told him there was no adultery in Sparta. The foreigner persisted, and wanted to know what it would be if there *were*. Geradas replied that the penalty would be to sacrifice a bull so large it could lean over the peaks of Taygetos to drink from the Eurotas. He protested that there could not possibly be a bull so large. "Neither," replied Geradas, "could there be adultery in Sparta."

"So you see," said Doreius, getting to his feet, "as there is no adultery in Sparta, there can be no bastards. Nor are there boys without fathers, as all the fathers in Sparta are fathers to all her sons." He turned, and added, almost as an afterthought, "Hekataios and Aristokrates, go to Sphodrias for thrashing. Hekataios for provoking Aristokrates. Aristokrates for ignorance of the ways of Sparta."

The Magpie once reported that Antalkidas had said that the emblem of our patrol ought to be the olive switch. It was known as the best patrol in the flock. We were proud of it.

The trouble with Doreius's tales is that some of them were not directly comprehensible. The unsuccessful candidate and the boy with the fox were easy, but others left us baffled.

"Sphodrias, what is adultery?" Anaxandros asked, as we had our dip in the river next evening.

The setting sun was warm, the water pleasant; and we took our time, splashing and ducking each other as we bathed.

"Stand down the river, Dolt," Pityas ordered. "You're muddying the water. Not you, Magpie. The Cockerel."

(If I quote certain of my flock-brothers frequently, it is because their words have stayed with me, whilst I have forgotten the comments of boys like Slug, whose greatest achievement was being able to piss further than any rhodibas in the flock).

I moved as Sphodrias replied. "Adultery means a woman lying with a man who is not her husband."

"Does that make bastards?"

"Didn't you listen to Doreius, Magpie? There are no bastards in Sparta."

"Like old men!" I blurted.

"What about old men, Cockerel?"

"When men marry too old to get strong sons, they ask a young man to get a son for them. My mother told me."

"That's not adultery." Sphodrias caught hold of some rushes to pull himself onto the river-bank. "That is agreed. Adultery just happens." He picked up his cloak and began to dry himself. "But it is the same in that the husband is the father. The blood-father doesn't count."

I was glad that it was agreed. I had not forgotten Aristokrates's taunt. Now it was all quite clear. I knew my father was much older than my mother. He had asked a young man to get me. I still did not altogether know what adultery consisted of, but I was certain agreed was much better. It sounded very lawful.

"You mean some boys have two fathers?" Anaxandros called from the river.

"Why don't you spend more time with your own patrol? Magpie?" Pityas ducked his cousin.

"Can a boy have two mothers?" Words and water poured from the Magpie's mouth.

"Sometimes. But only the name-mother counts."

"Can he have two mothers and two fathers?"

From the corner of my eye, I saw Hekataios and Aristokrates about to shove Euagoras's head under the water. Their animosity seemed to have been resolved in that mutual thrashing.

"Magpie!" Pityas warned. "Sphod', is it true that they expose bastards in Athens?"

"Sometimes they make them slaves," the Magpie replied for him.

"You travel frequently to Athens, I take it," Pityas said scathingly.

"Antalkidas told me. He likes me to ask questions, so he can laugh."

Hekataios and Aristokrates scrambled up on to the river-bank, shaking themselves like ducks, and wetting a number of other boys like a sudden rain.

"I wish I had two fathers..." the Magpie reflected.

I could have done with one.

Pausanios was acquitted by eighteen votes to eleven. My father voted to condemn him.

Chapter 3

About three months after the trial, Pausanios visited the flock. I could tell it was Pausanios in the distance because he was riding. All the other visitors (except Pharax) walked.

We are not a demonstrative people; I even less so than my compatriots, being early put off excess by the rages and embraces of my mother. (Her public presence was cool poise. Everything about her was contradictory). Yet when I saw Pausanios, I could easily have thrown my arms about his neck had it not been unseemly.

He asked this and that about my lessons and my games. I told them that I was considered the best rhodibas dancer, that my friend Hekataios was the best runner, that Euagoras was to sing in the festival of Karneian Apollo, and spoke at length of the various excellences of Doreius.

"Leotychides– Your speech–" The king's brow furrowed, then smoothed, as I opened my mouth to apologize for wasting words. "Oh, you are losing your front milk-teeth. I feared you were developing a speech impediment."

"I pulled them out myself," I boasted.

"I had to do it for Agesipolis. He keeps them in a box. Leotychides, I have a gift for you." Then he told the first of the three lies Pausanios ever told me. "It is from your father."

"I don't want it, sir. He voted to kill you."

"Is there anything you boys don't know? Leotychides, a man must vote for what he believes just." I think Pausanios, with his way of seeing all sides of an argument, would have established a good case for his execution, had I not rudely interrupted. "I don't want anything from him."

"He is your father."

"The Law-giver said that all the boys of Sparta belong to all the fathers."

"Yes, because–"

"Then I choose you."

I could have told him that, although I suspected my father was purely my name-father, I had seen the fondness between

92

Hekataios and Dinon – who was not his blood-father – so that did not explain my father's indifference. Or, more important, *my* indifference.

But I could not. No more than I could have told him of my wretchedness that first winter. Like the cold, the hunger, the pain of the broken toe, the blisters on hands unused to plaiting rushes, it must be suffered in silence; a hidden thing, like the fox the boy concealed in his cloak in Doreius's story.

"Will you not just look at it, Leotychides?" He held out a hunting-knife with the image of Herakles carved on the handle. Agesipolis has one with an ivory handle, but Aristodemos thought the other boys would mock you if it were too fine–"

"It's not from my father. It's from you!" I was pleased. I wanted the knife.

"He would have sent something, had he the time." He told the second lie.

"It is a fine knife. Thank you, sir."

The third lie was several years later. What a great man Pausanios would have been, had he not been so good.

I did not see him again for two years. Shortly after his visit, we took Pellana in a mock battle. That year we had a bold Commander, who asked permission of the Inspector of Boys to storm Pellana without warning. Not the town, of course, the camp of another flock.

Usually, our mock battles are formal; with each side in phalanges, facing other with shields and blunted spears. This Phoibidas convinced the Inspector that a surprise attack would not only be a more rigorous exercise for us, but test the alertness of the other side.

Pellana lies on a plateau surrounded by dark mountains that were still snow-covered when we set out in early spring. Away from the town, the other flock was encamped around the high hill, where the ancient fortress straddles the river to command the heights. From the hill, there is a clear vista of the north. As the approach from Sellasia is difficult and mountainous, they placed their look-outs facing only the west.

Phoibidas led us over the harsh terrain at night. We caught the other flock totally unprepared, and routed them.

For this exploit, Sphodrias conceived an abiding admiration of the Commander and, forsaking his earlier attempts to

93

emulate Doreius, began to pattern himself on Phoibidas, with somewhat more success. Although I doubt that Sphodrias would have thought to send scouts to ascertain the position of the lookouts before attacking, as Phoibidas had.

We acquainted ourselves with our new camp. The Magpie discovered a spring in a cave. I wondered whether the young Twin Gods had drunk from it, when they were boys. Their father, that ancient King Tyndaraios, had lived at Pellana when his brother drove him from the throne of Sparta, and Kastor and Polydeukes walked these fields as youths.

Pellana was a pleasant place, which was as well, as we were based there for the remainder of my rhodibas years.

The years in which we learned to walk in the moonless night without torches. Saw the bright eyes and swift shapes of nocturnal creatures, unknown to men who fear the dark. The years when I grew to know the terrain of Lakonia as well as I had once known the lonely courtyard.

Mock battles and exercises took us over the narrow defiles of the Parnon range to the east, through scrub-hills, to hidden mountain valleys, where the columns of a temple stood to house the statue of a deity. In our wanderings, we came across altars raised to mark the place where the bones of a divine hero were buried, or where another had performed some great feat.

The Taygetos range is the spine of Lakedaimon, the Eurotas her blood. We trod the spine from foothills to heights. We followed the curving river summer, autumn and spring.

If the poet wants the word for beauty, let him sing of Taygetos; dark Taygetos, where distance is deceptive, and great expanses seem but a step away. Of the bronze moon rising, like a great shield lifted by a hidden hero behind those rounded peaks, and the stars just beyond one's reach.

Let him sing of hills that gods trod, and ground where heroes fought and triumphed. Where heroes fought and bled. Where heroes fought and fell.

Let him sing of Lakedaimon, where men dreamed a noble dream – for what is but a short time in the reckoning of immortals – and, in living their dream, became a little better than men.

Exercises took us to the Skiritis country; scrub-hills peopled by tough, dark little men, who had held their land in Lakonia so long no one recalls who gave it to them. They are guardians of the pass. Not an onerous guardianship, as no enemy had approached for hundreds of years.

The guardianship, like our frontier exercises, was a relic of another age. Like the ancient fortress in the green Bellamina country and the one at Pellana, it recalled a time when Lakonia was vulnerable to encroaching enemies, but that time was distant as the days when gods walked and talked with men, rather than speaking to us only in dreams and oracles, as they do now.

Near the pass at Keryai, some of us broke away from the rest of the flock, to scramble up a narrow goat path to look for wild berries. Chionis shouted that he had found honey, but could not reach it. Pronax hoisted a large rock on his massive shoulder, and called out to him that he was bringing him something to stand on.

Antalkidas leapt in his path. "Put it down, you fool! It is a boundary stone. We are in Argive territory."

We beat a quick retreat.

I cut my foot on a sharp stone, just before we reached the Lakonian side of the border. It was hardly noticeable at first, but on the long march back to Pellana the wound festered. I concealed it as best I could, in fear of revealing our inadvertent invasion of the Argolid. Its throbbing kept me awake nights. I grew inattentive in lessons. I fell behind Euagoras in races.

One night, I woke from a fitful sleep to see Doreius standing by my pallet. He held a finger against his lips, and beckoned me outside.

The thousand creatures of night chirped their song. He ordered me to show him my foot. It was a light night. I asked the goddess to take the moon behind a cloud, that I should not be found out. Swaying on the sound foot, I extended the offending one. He put a hand on my shoulder, and shoved me to the ground, seized my leg, scrutinised my foot, then took up a sticky loathsome mess, and slapped it on the wound.

"Bread mould," he said, as he tore a strip from the edge of his cloak. He began binding it to my foot. "Someday I will show you the statue of the brave boy with the fox." His lips curved softly, when not compressed in his usual manner.

95

He tied the ends of the bandage and rose, "Now go back, and don't wake the other boys."

The wound healed cleanly, leaving only a thin, white scar. I have it still.

"Rhodibas!" Anaxandros shouted, as a shear-head darted past. "Drinking water. Make haste."

The prerogatives of melleirens were still new to us, and we used them whenever possible.

We were splattered with mud, as we broke rushes from the banks of the River Tiasa (one of the penalties of being a melleiren). Our camp was near Amyklai, south of Sparta, the site at Pellana having been requisitioned by the army for something having to do with the campaign in Eleia.

It was five years since I joined my flock. Pausanios's visits had become less frequent, and then ceased altogether. Had my father told him to keep his distance? That father who was still an unexpected absence.

"My hands are bleeding." Anaxandros held them out, as though they were unique. "Lend me your hunting knife, Cockerel."

"We're forbidden knives for rush-breaking."

"Antalkidas will only reprimand me."

"Doreius will thrash me." I passed him the knife.

Sphodrias ran up. As an eiren, he was above this sort of work. "There is the most extraordinary man coming up the road. He wears a cloak with a design in the border."

"My father says they have cloaks like that in Athens," Aristokrates interrupted.

"Those Athenians I saw at the Gymnopaidia dressed like us." Euagoras rarely missed a chance to allude to festivals he had graced with his music.

Some citizens of Athens showed their admiration of our ways by growing their hair long, and wearing plain cloaks with no tunic beneath.

"This man is no foreigner, if you've done chattering." Sphodrias grew impatient when he lost our attention. "He has five slaves following him, all carrying heavy chests. Well, two have something that is covered."

"He must be an up-country man." Some of their artisans are richer than any Spartiate could respectably be. Coins being forbidden, when they work in other cities they take payment in kind, and bring back gold and silver vessels, embroidered cloth, slaves, and other luxuries we do not possess.

"I'm going to see him," Euagoras announced. "If I keep on with this, my hands won't be fit to hold a lyre for the Leonidia." We were to go to Sparta for the Leonidian Games to join in the chorus of elders, men and boys.

"And if you don't, your back won't be fit to sleep on," I warned. The Leonidia was months away.

"I don't play the lyre with my back. Show me where he is, Sphodrias."

"Over there," he pointed. "I have other things to do."

We knew what the things were. Sphodrias was tumbling some farm girl. That was dangerous. The up-country people marry their daughters young, and keep their women close. Aristokrates contented himself with looking. We could always tell when a pretty up-country girl was passing by the sudden rise of his organ. It earned him the name of Pointer.

Diopeithes's "Donkey" had not lasted. Taller and broader than his contemporaries, Aristokrates could beat any boy who used it. He was still larger, but most of us could hold our own with him now. Pointer he remained.

After we washed off the mud, Anaxandros and I sat on the river-bank with our feet in the cool water.

He studied me carefully. "Your hair is the colour of moonlight. His sandy locks had grown out of the rhodibas clip a rich chestnut. Euagoras, too, had darkened. Hekataios was still uncompromisingly carrot. "And eyelashes the colour of soot–"

"Curse you, Magpie! You read that stupid poem." I had received a poem comparing my beauty to that of Hyakinthos.

"Only because you threw it in the river."

"Follow it." I shoved him in, and started towards the place where boys gathered to look at the stranger.

The poem was not the first approach I had. My hair had scarcely lengthened, when a youth about nineteen plopped himself beside me one evening, and planted a wet kiss on my cheek.

"I love you," he said.

97

"Is that permissible?" He was still an eiren.

"If you love me."

"I don't." I wiped off the spittle.

"Then why did you ask?"

"I wanted to know."

That was the end of it.

Anaxandros scrambled out of the river and ran after me. "It was a nice poem."

"It did not scan."

"I have a letter." He held a thin scroll. "You can read it if you want to."

"I don't, but I will if that is the only way to stop you waving it under my nose."

"There was a painted oil-flask with it. I wonder who sent it."

"It says 'Kallias.' The rest only read, "You are very young. I am going to Eleia. If I come back, you will still be very young." I preferred it to the effusions of the poem.

"Do you think Kallias is that young warrior who was a guest in Hall?"

"More likely one of the old members."

His face fell.

Melleirens attend Hall. Tent-shaped, like all the others, the interior of this dining-hall was panelled in plain dark wood. None of the intricate patterns that caused my namesake, the first King Leotychides, to ask a Corinthian host whether trees grew square in his country.

Hall. Flares of lamps on tall, bronze standards, reflecting on wood that has been daily polished for countless generations. Fifteen dining-couches, arranged so talk can be general. Bread, cheese, olives and fruit on small tables. The aroma of well-seasoned black broth, recalling the meals of the Eurypontid palace. Venison or game-birds as well, if a few men have been excused for hunting. Men reclining on couches, speaking of matters of the City, horses, the hunt, each trying to cap the other's brevity and wit. Serfs moving among them, pouring well-watered wine. (Oh, the pleasure of dining where men can differ spiritedly without anger, and become merry without drunkenness).

"He could be a guest." Anaxandros was still thinking of the

writer of the letter. "Guests don't have to be over thirty."

"What matter? He is going to Eleia."

The Eleians had forced the people of Epeion to sell their lands to them. The Epeionians appealed to Sparta. The ephors sent a mediator to Elis, but the Eleians argued that they had paid for the lands, and that Epeion was only a peasant community, not a city, and therefore had no rights.

The mediator ruled that peasants, as well as cities, had a valid right to their land, and that forced purchase was tantamount to outright conquest. Elis refused to comply, and furthermore showed her defiance by invading and conquering the independent cities of Eleia. Sparta was bound by treaty to defend these cities.

It was a minor matter. Purely Peloponnesian. My father claimed the right of command. I heard his name in Hall from time to time, but more of Pausanios. Some of the men praised Pausanios, only to be countered by support of Lysander. For what? Our nights in Hall were so infrequent that the meaning of these pointed comments was beyond us.

I gave Anaxandros his letter back. We joined the group of barefoot flock-boys, clustered about the brightly plumed newcomer. He was young to be a master artisan.

An apprentice approached Antalkidas. "Sir, my master would like to know where the boys exercise."

Antalkidas accepted the honorific no youth is entitled to. "Why is your master here?"

"To make a portrait of a god, sir."

Apollo! I thought. Perhaps the god told him to make it here, near his temple. Antalkidas told the apprentice what he wanted to know. The artisan set up his camp, one luxurious tent and two small ones, on the heights.

The next morning, as we came away from our dip in the river, we saw him chipping away at a rectangular block of marble. His tunic was stained, and as plain as those of his apprentices, but a slave stood by him to wipe the sweat from his brow. He worked directly above our drill ground."

"That's not a portrait of a god," Hekataios said, a few days later. "I looked."

"What is it?" Euagoras asked.

"Grapes."

"Then it is Dionysos," Sphodrias told him. "He carved them in his workshop."

Our patrol leaders ordered us to keep our distance from the sculptor. Staring was discourteous. Being a patrol leader himself, Antalkidas did not stare. He ran up to talk to the sculptor when the Commander's attention was elsewhere.

Euagoras became a person of significance as the Leonidia drew near.

"What are the Leonidian Games like?" Hekataios asked.

"Running, wrestling, jumping, boxing. The Kings and Queens are there. And Prince Agesipolis. The Kings award the olive crowns."

My father! If I could do something splendid! Paris had won all the Games in Ilion. King Priam then knew him for his own son...but my father was away. Leading the army in Eleia.

"How will we know when to sing our part?" Anaxandros looked worried.

"The elders sing first about the great things they did when they were young. Then the men sing of all the brave things they do now. Then we come in with the boys from other flocks, and sing that we shall be greater still..."

Aristokrates shot the small boy a look. Euagoras flushed.

The humiliation of Euagoras had been recent.

We came upon some girls competing in the plain below the high hill. They could not have been older than ourselves, as few had developed breasts or a full growth of pubic hair. (The Pointer did not react. Only clothed females had that effect on him).

One sturdy, dark-haired maid made an exceedingly straight throw. Doreius praised her, and asked her name. Gorgo, as so many girls are called, for the brilliant consort of Leonidas. Then he pushed Euagoras into the midst of the maidens, and asked Gorgo to teach him to throw as well as she. The other girls laughed. Gorgo contemptuously showed him how to manage the leather loop, and where to place his feet for good balance. At last, the red-faced Euagoras, in anger and shame, made the

100

best throw of his life. It was not as good as Gorgo's. With great solemnity, she lifted eyes big and dark as grapes to Doreius, and said, "I'm sorry, I can't make any better of him."

"Nor can I," Doreius told her.

Now Anaxandros persisted "But who tells us when to sing?"

Euagoras brightened "The chorus master. The melody is very simple. It is not like poem singing," he added with a note of superiority. "At the Festival of Karneian Apollo—"

"Is the King there when we sing?" Hekataios interrupted. We had heard, many times over, of the poets' competition of the Karneia.

Sphodrias ran up. "The sculptor has finished." A square patch of even ground inspired him to execute a neat handspring. For all his assignations with up-country girls, Sphodrias could still be exceedingly childish. "I think you had ought to see it, Cockerel."

A group of boys discreetly observed the finished accomplishment. It was the first of the new work we had seen. (Now, even a barbarian would scorn the old stiff style). The sculptor, wearing another splendid cloak, was oblivious to their interest, as he supervised the preparations for his departure.

The marble portrait was in wonderfully natural high relief. Dionysos, looking real as the grapes, stood in his arbour, one arm extended, as though he were inviting a friend to be seated. It was the young Dionysos, a boy about twelve with an oval face, straight nose fair, fresh complexion – and unsmiling lips, curved in latent merriment. Pale gold curls tumbled about his head to the nape of his neck.

His shoulder-cloak was thrown back, revealing the proportioned body befitting a young god. The countenance, like the stance, was calm, poised yet eager, the cheeks round, and the wide, sapphire-blue eyes filled with all the innocence. The artist had captured the precise moment when the man can be seen in the youth, but the child is still present.

Hekataios glanced at me uneasily.

"Leo," Anaxandros said. "It looks like you."

Antalkidas joined us. "What is wrong, Leotychides? It is a charming likeness."

"The god will be angry."

"Don't you know sculptors copy gods from living men?"

101

"Why here? Why me?"

"Would he not find a better model for a young god in a flock than amongst up-country bumpkins?"

It was not without reason. No living man has seen a god. I was still uneasy.

"Will Dionysos send his madness on me?" I asked Doreius.

"Only if you believe you *are* the god. That would be hubris."

I did not see the portrait again for many years. It is in the god's temple in the agora. It was not then he sent me mad.

We walked in loose order along the hard-packed earth road to Sparta. Our patrol leaders were ahead, talking amongst themselves. Antalkidas said something to Doreius that made him laugh. Doreius tossed his head in the way that meant the wave of dark hair had fallen over his brow.

"Euagoras, do all the young warriors in Sparta sing in the chorus?" the Magpie asked.

"Not those in Eleia," I answered for him. "Euagoras, why have you brought your lyre?"

"He hopes someone may ask him to play it," Aristokrates said.

Above the olive trees that lined the road, the tall, rose-coloured columns of Athena's Bronze House came into sight. They looked pale against the dark mountains. On the other side of the Eurotas, the early sun glittered on the blue and white parapet of the towering tomb of Helen and Menelaos.

The leaders halted, turned and faced us, and ordered us to fall into patrols. We had passed Sparta many times, but not one of us had been in the City since joining the flock. The Commander placed our patrol in the van. Sparta would know we were the best.

A crowd gathered at the southern edge of the City, in front of the tomb of Leonidas. The bronze hero-god, in his high-crested helmet, looked down on his people. It was a statue of the old type; stiff, too much chin. His lips turned upward as though he were about to make a battle-jest, to give spirit to three hundred men about to face one hundred thousand.

Doreius showed us the stele where the names of the three hundred are written. I was taken back to the day I stood there with Agesipolis and Pausanios. The crowd parted. Like the shadow of something past, the Agiad King appeared with a small boy at his side. He walked on, solid flesh in his long, white, purple-bordered cloak, the child undoubtedly that Kleombrotos who had been an infant when I saw him last.

"Leotychides..." Doreius motioned. The patrol was moving to the place where boys from another flock took their places for the chorus. "Aristokrates." He halted the large boy, and lowered his voice. "Whisper the words softly. Do not sing."

Euagoras laughed, and nearly tripped over his lyre, getting out of Aristokrates's reach.

At dawn Pausanios, garlanded and in a white robe, made the sacrifice at Leonidas's shrine. His manner was solemn. He moved with dignity. To be a king, I thought, was to be Pausanios. The ceremonies ended. The Games began.

Onlookers took their places on the grass for the wrestling. The bright peploi of the women in the throng looked like flowers. The men's cloaks, plain as our own. Maidens with wild flowers in their shining hair called to one another. Young matrons wafted flower-scent as they looked for a place to sit. Young warriors rose to offer their places. Dark-clad old women turned sharp eyes on this one or that one, and put their heads together. People called greetings to friends and kin.

The wrestlers drew lots. One of the first pair did poorly. The maidens jeered him. Their taunts were as sharp as their faces were sweet.

"That fellow hasn't the shoulders of a wrestler," said the massive Pronax.

"He shows spirit to try." Chionis was as large as Pronax.

"He would show wit not to try," Antalkidas told them.

"He should try harder," Doreius said.

The man who won the wrestling the first day won the boxing the next, and walked up to Pausanios to receive his second crown of the Games. The last day was given over to running and the chariot race.

The racing course stands before a house that has been the dwelling of the Twin Gods when they were men. It belongs to a private citizen now. Everyone uses the racing course.

Many onlookers had already taken their places on the grass around the course, when we came in from our camp in the foothills of Taygetos. It was a hot day, and people brought jars of cool drinks, or baskets of golden apples to quench their thirst.

We stood by the statues of the Twin Gods, which mark the starting point for the runners. Antalkidas suggested that the finishing lines would be more interesting. After standing and giving our seats to countless elders and women, we found ourselves to the back of the statues of the Twin Gods once more.

Twenty-eight long-cloaked greybeards walked to the Elders' benches. Pausanios mounted the steps to the royal dais. More people arrived, and we were moved about again. Our journey took us to the centre of the course, directly opposite the dais.

The King was seated in his high-backed chair. On his left, Eurydame fanned herself. On the King's right was my mother. Her hands were folded and still. Her head turned now to Pausanios, now to the man on her right.

A herald came forward to intone that Prince Agesipolis would initiate an eiren's race. Could that thin youth on the dais be my cousin? Any eiren wishing to be in the lists should come forward.

Doreius stood, turned to me, and said, "Take charge of the patrol, Leotychides." Antalkidas dashed away without giving over his patrol to anyone, followed by Chionis and Pronax. And Sphodrias, who should have known better.

"The maidens will jeer him," Euagoras whispered.

The first race was for men. The runners stood in alignment with the statues of the Twin Gods. The man who took two olive crowns was with them. He was a strapping fellow, but not of the massive build of Chionis and Pronax.

"He asks too much of the gods," Hekataios said.

"He cannot win," Aristokrates agreed.

"My knife to your bow he will," I spoke without thought. I wanted this brave fellow to win.

"Done. I've always fancied that knife."

Pausanios gave the signal. The runners shot forward. Someone at the back pushed between Pityas and me. Pityas glared.

"Remember me?" The intruder turned a broad-browed face towards me. "We broke a fine chestnut once."

"Teleutias!" I remembered him taller. "Stop glowering, Pit'.

104

He is my uncle Teleutias. Should I call you sir? Are you over thirty?"

"Teleutias will do. Do you still ride?"

"Only flock nags. Keep your mouth down, worm!" He really was not talking very loudly, but I wanted Teleutias to know I was in command of the patrol.

The runners turned back at the finish, to begin the second length. My man took the lead, his hair blowing in the wind of his own speed. The day was very still.

"Who is he?" I asked Teleutias. "He won both the boxing and the wrestling."

"Kinadon? That is unsurprising. He is the strongest man in Sparta."

Kinadon won.

"Shall I collect my bow tonight, or did you leave it in Amyklai, Pointer?"

"A wager?" Teleutias smiled. "So now he will use your bow rather than you his."

A large cheer went up for Kinadon, who walked towards the dais. Pausanios stood, and gave him his third crown of the Games.

It came to the turn of the eirens.

Sphodrias was an absurd figure at the starting lines, amongst youths ranging from eighteen to near twenty. He grinned – as if to say he knew he looked a fool, but had got himself into it, and go through with it he would. Doreius stood straight as an unsheathed sword. Antalkidas seemed relaxed, somewhat bored, but he had edged one foot slightly in front of the lines.

Agesipolis was standing. On the dais, he could easily see sitting down. He waved to a runner. Eurydame tugged at his tunic. He sat down. He sat down. The man on my mother's right rose, and gave his seat to a portly, ginger-haired man. I heard Anaxandros ask Teleutias. "Are you the uncle who served with Kallikratidas? Leotychides is always talking about Kallikratidas."

I could have wished him in my patrol long enough to order him to be silent. He made me sound as I had talked at the age of seven.

The runners went forward together. Anaxandros leapt up and down, cheering Antalkidas. A strange youth led. Chionis passed him before the end of the first length. A lead group distanced itself from the others. Antalkidas fell back. Doreius and Chionis stayed with the leaders. We cheered them, as though the power of our lungs could give their feet wings. I clouted Hekataios just in front of him, just in time to prevent him pounding the shoulders of the elder in front of him as Doreius moved forward a few paces.

"That dark-haired youth is good." Teleutias spoke above the cheers for the leaders, and maidenly jeers to Sphodrias, who fell behind the poorest runners.

"He is my patrol leader. The best in the flock."

The lead runners turned back at the starting line for the final length. A fair youth about twenty led, followed by Doreius. Doreius was still better considering the two or so years between them, I thought, as the strange youth neared the finishing lines. Then Doreius shot ahead like an arrow, to win.

My patrol pressed forward. I ordered the boys back.

Teleutias laid his hand on my shoulder. "Do you want a better view of your patrol leader taking his olive crown."

I ordered the patrol to fall in. We followed Teleutias across the racing course, where a few runners still rubbed strained leg muscles. Doreius approached the dais. Something was wrong. Pausanios did not rise. The ginger-haired man got to his feet. Teleutias scowled.

I was distracted by the sudden appearance of Agisilaos. He always appeared suddenly, as no one thought of him unless he was present, and sometimes not then.

"Teleutias, Mother would like to leave."

Teleutias stared at the dais. "What in the name of all the gods is Agis doing here? Why is he not in Eleia?"

"Poseidon shook the earth. It was an omen. Agis turned back. Teleutias, kindly see to our mother and Kleora."

"Cannot you?"

"I am in company."

He indicated a square-faced man with red-veined cheeks. The rest of his face was hidden by an untrimmed beard, the same faded russet as his hair. The hair itself was long, and so roughly cut one could not tell where beard began and hair ended. He stood as if staking dominion over the piece of earth on which he had planted his feet. Anyone who has seen Lysander's statues knows the stance.

"Teleutias..." Agisilaos's soft voice grew insistent.

"As you will." Teleutias ruffled my hair, and lowered his voice. "You have got an extra lad in your patrol, Acting Leader."

Anaxandros had fitted himself in behind Aristokrates. I barely took it in, for it struck me that the ginger-haired man on the dais was my father.

My father! The gods intended it this way when they sent him back from Eleia. Had Priam not known Paris for his son when he won all the games? I won none, was not in the lists, but I was acting leader of my patrol. Commanding boys older than myself. "Who is that boy?" he would ask Pausanios and...

I observed him closely. He was not truly portly. His weight was the hard muscle of a soldier. He was only middling height, but he stood straight. His eyes were bright blue and his face ruddy. Rising sixty, he had the look of a man in middle years, although there was more grey in his hair seen closer.

He gave Doreius his olive crown. His voice was clipped, as he advised the youth to enter the lists for the Pythian Games. Pausanios leaned forward to tell my patrol leader that Olympia was something no gifted runner could deny himself. My father made a terse comment to the effect that Elis's land was better than its people.

"They organize the Games fairly," Pausanios told him.

"It is easy to be honourable once every four years," my father retorted crisply.

Doreius saw us standing in good order. He saluted the two Kings, and then said, "Well done, Leotychides."

Clearly, he spoke my name. My royal name. No other boy in the flock had a royal name. My father had not exposed me, but neither did he call me to him.

He looked at me; no, through me, with those cold blue eyes. Then, before Doreius, before Agesipolis, before my flock-brothers, with all Sparta looking on, he turned away to give a command to his servant. I stared at the turned back. My mother's green gaze intercepted mine.

The unseen glances of my patrol behind me fuelled my anger.

Their unspoken thoughts. I wanted to call out, "You were right, Mother. I understand. This man who would make me nothing *is* nothing."

I ordered the patrol to fall in, and led the boys off the course, concealing the fire of rage and shame.

Doreius had put a name to it. My fox.

Chapter 4

Sparta made no claim to the Greek cities of Asia that she liberated from Athens, so the Great King of Persia claimed them for himself. These cities appealed to Sparta.

The ephors called upon all the Hellenes to contribute troops for their defence. A certain Thibron was appointed commander-in-chief of the Hellenic forces. He was a singularly unfortunate choice, as he had previously commanded only Spartiate regiments.

As equals may differ in rank but not in status, the Spartan army is an army of officers commanded by other officers, making it a self-disciplining force as well as a disciplined one. This has played no small part in Sparta's fame in battle.

In Athens, generals are elected! That is to say, more often than not, their tactical skill is political, and the objectives of commanders conflicting – a weakness that helped lose them the Long War.

No, don't set that down. It is a comment. I am dictating this to the scribe, who assures me he will use no letters that are not unquestionably Doric, and set down everything precisely as I say it. Precisely. That is an order.

The choice of Thibron was an unusual one. Spartan practice has always been promotion by merit. Thibron had shown no exceptional qualities except an agreeable manner and a sensitive touch on the lyre.

Some of the foreign regiments he commanded were composed of the dregs of Hellas, mercenaries unable to distinguish the just spoils of war from brutish attacks upon friendly cities. The people who had hailed the Hellenic army as saviours soon fled from it in terror.

Unable to impose discipline, Thibron was recalled to Sparta, tried, and banished for one year. In his place, the ephors sent out Derkyllidas.

Derkyllidas was a general who demanded the impossible, and got it. A hard disciplinarian, he was also a great favourite with his men – although not with Lysander, who was never over-fond of commanders of quality; unless, like Brasidas, they were safely dead.

First, Derkyllidas got the army back into control; then, by clever diplomacy, he induced the satrap Tissaphernes to let him pass unhindered through his territory to that of Pharnabazos, where he took nine cities in eight days by persuasion alone.

His success frightened the rival satraps into burying their differences. They joined their armies and threatened to expel Derkyllidas from Asia. As the sole purpose of his being in Asia was to protect the Greek cities, he replied that he would quit voluntarily if the satraps would guarantee their independence.

Their forces far outnumbered the army of Derkyllidas, but they were reluctant to take their chances in the field against Greek fighting-men led by Spartans. Tissaphernes and Pharnabazos agreed to guarantee the freedom of the cities if the Spartan governors were withdrawn.

Derkyllidas did not interpret his orders as being the protection of the posts and perquisites of Lysander's creatures, and agreed. Whatever his private feelings on the matter, Lysander kept his own counsel. He had always known how to bide his time. When he had the opportunity, he ordered Derkyllidas to stand guard, like a disobedient junior officer. The greatness of others was ever an offence to Lysander.

In the event I have not made it clear – and I think I have not. – no, you need not write that... it was just a passing comment...all this took place over some years. Since my encounter with my father at the Leonidia and the conclusion of the Asian matter, three years had passed.

Another campaign had forced the Eleians to restore the independence of the cities they conquered, and to return the lands to the Epeionians. Doreius, Antalkidas, and the other eirens of their year had gone into the Hidden Thing, and passed out of the flock. We were now proud fourth-rank melleirens.

We fought the Great Fight, setting out at night, the sky bright with stars, the dew on the tall grasses wetting our feet and ankles – You are not writing all that! I was thinking aloud. I know I ordered you to write precisely what I said, but—

I have dismissed the scribe. The Great Boys' Fight... How clear it is...

Marching through the night to Therapine, to the shrine of Achilles, to make our first sacrifice... the torches of the priest flaming through the dense growth of plane-trees surrounding it...the solemnity... how different from laying those small private offerings on the offering-tables of the gods...The sacrifice goes willingly...a good omen.

Owls call through the many-voiced night, as we go the short distance to the shrine of Ares Enyalios. The second sacrifice. Those snarling small dogs the war-god likes. Do I imagine a smile on the lined face of the priest, as we set off again on the route followed by files of torchless fifteen-year-old melleirens since the day of the Law-giver?

Birds awake. As they know of all things before men, so they know the coming of dawn before the first paling of the sky. We draw lots, and become two teams. The two teams draw lots for the fighting boar. It is said the team whose boar kills the other will win. Sometimes it does. Our boar loses.

A hidden sun lights the sky. Mist rises over the lake. As it clears, the island in its centre is green and shining from the morning dew. Again lots are drawn. Our team will cross to the island by the Bridge of Lykourgos, the other team by the Bridge of Herakles.

At midday on the island, the two teams draw up facing each other. Sphodrias grins. The solemnity is gone. The Great Fight begins. Our object is to tumble our opponents into the lake.

Shoving, pushing, using our bodies as hurling-javelins, we are in the midst of the mass – moving forward, backward, pushed and pushing. I am going back. Steadily back. It is my luck to be facing the Pointer! I lunge. He reels. Steadies himself. I am going back again, until I strike something cold and wet.

There are already boys floundering in the water...I am not the first to splash. My head, caught in a wrestler's grip, slowly goes under....Have done, Pointer! You have had your laugh. My head is lifted up long enough to see the hatred in those eyes... feel it in the relentless grasp between neck and shoulder, as the water fills my mouth and nostrils...Apollo, don't let me die like this!

111

All over the island, boys sit on the ground, tending bruises, sprains and fractures. Why, Aristokrates? It is said the Law-giver devised the Great Fight to replace a very ancient and savage rite, when an enemy had to be sacrificed to Ares Enyalios. Had Aristokrates – I could no longer think of him as my flock-brother Pointer – reverted to those times? Was I his enemy?

"We've won," The Magpie beams.

I cough water and mucous, noting that he is dry. Hekataios is fascinated by a thumb that dangles limply. Slug and Worm are engaged in a pissing competition with some boys from another flock.

"Our boat wasn't worthy of us." Sphodrias grins, although he, too, is dripping.

"You mean the other boar had the misfortune to have Euagoras on its side." Someone laughs.

The small, slight form is prone but breathing.

Why had Aristokrates tried to drown me? What had he called me? The word – words? – that explained the half-remembered whispers, the furtive glances of my childhood. My father's hostility. *That* look.

For a brief instant, it had all been clear. Or was this simply the illusion of a half-drowned youth at the moment he thought himself dying.

After my father's scorn, my reach towards excellence changed its nature.

I had always enjoyed being best, and for that reason expended my efforts, as much as possible, on those activities in which I naturally excelled. I was a good boxer, and a good dancer, but, despite my long legs, a middling runner. I had neither the steady pacing of the long-race runner that Hekataios displayed, nor the unbelievable spurts of speed Doreius could summon in a short race. (The mother of those brothers must have been magnificent on the course). It had long been my habit to avoid the racing events in our flock competitions. I did not wish to become another "Antalkidas-always-second," as his contemporaries called him. I would be first or nothing.

All that changed.

I no longer sought individual excellences, but the essence of excellence in its totality. As one of the qualities of excellence is endeavour, I not only entered races, but put such an inordinate amount of practice and determination into winning that I twice bested Hekataios. It did not happen again, but at least I was not "Leotychides-always-second."

My obedience was impeccable. So much that I went nearly a year without a thrashing. But I never acquired the reputation of a prig. Perhaps because I was less concerned with my rightness than determined to out my father in the wrong.

This in its way, was contradictory, as I had assigned him to oblivion.

He who had disdained me all my life was to be banished from my mind. He who had shamed me publicly was to be

shamed by my lack of shame. "All Sparta's fathers are fathers to all its sons." All but one. That ginger-haired man with cold blue eyes who turned away from me. Let every father who visited the flock be more to me.

This, too, he had made impossible.

When fathers visited the flock, they showed an interest in the achievements of boys other than their own sons. As one of the outstanding melleirens, I was often singled out. Yet a fear that concealed pity might have prompted the kind comments; the interested and interesting enquiries of these fathers made my replies simply courteous and distant.

In one way, my confused and contradictory determination succeeded. When Doreius went to the Hidden Thing, I was made patrol leader. Now I must be the best patrol leader in the flock. The resolve was not entirely a stratagem in my war against my father.

Under the command of Doreius, our patrol had been the best in the flock. It was the new commander who appointed me, but new commanders often consult good patrol leaders. Had Doreius suggested that I replace him? I did not know. Yet I regarded the reputation of the patrol as something like a sacred trust. It must not shame Doreius.

A patrol leader's duties consist of more than teaching obedience, keeping order and discipline. Even when he seemed most remote, Doreius was aware of the needs of every boy under his command. Constantly together, flock-brothers learn to respect one another's inner privacy. Foreigners often remark upon the good manners of Spartiates. Perhaps it is only the sensitivity of the flock-bred to the invisible boundaries of the spirit. The hand of comradeship is always there; but one must know when, and when not, to extend it. Particularly when it holds the wand of authority.

This is the most difficult duty of the patrol leader.

Euagoras lost his voice with its changing. He plucked his Aristokrates, I knew, was torn between pride and shame of his father, but our mutual hostility precluded any speech from me. I would have asked Hekataios to have a word with him; but Hek', too, had lost his cheerful grin and become somewhat prickly. A youth? A girl? With melleirens, love-sickness is a common complaint. And one of the most delicate.

I would make a start with Hek', I decided. Before I could, the Monkey disappeared.

We were again at Pellana. The Polemarchs ordered our return there. A flock had been displaced by the exigencies of the Eleian campaign. The Eleian campaign was concluded. The same flock must go back. Antalkidas called it army logic.

I noted the Monkey's absence at night – and assumed that he had slipped away to a lover or a woman, and would creep to his pallet before dawn. This was a thrashing matter, but a patrol concern.

There was no sign of him next day. I should have to report his absence to the Commander. A far more serious matter for Monkey, and it would look bad for the patrol.

To leave no stone unturned, I decided to go up to the cave under the hill; a place where our patrol met to discuss private matters. Perhaps Monkey had confided in one of the other melleirens.

I recall the damp smell of the cave, the trickling water of a hidden spring, and Euagoras plucking his lyre, as I asked about the Monkey.

"Maybe he drowned," Hekataios suggested. "Like that boy last summer." Not in my patrol.

"His own fault," added Sphodrias, who had nearly died in a similar accident.

"Maybe–" Worm began, but I silenced him as running

114

footsteps echoed in the cave. The Magpie appeared, followed by some boys from his old patrol. When Antalkidas went into the Hidden Thing, Anaxandros had somehow managed to get himself transferred to mine.

"Kallias has seen *her!*" he said breathlessly, as he squeezed himself into the gathering.

"You wouldn't have seen Monkey, would you, Magpie?" I asked. He replied with a blank look. The Monkey was forgotten by all, as they turned eager eyes on Anaxandros.

No one had to ask whom he meant by *her.* There was only one *her.* All over the camp, boys gathered in small groups to discuss her secretly. For *her,* words carried to the privacy of the dining halls and spread from flock to flock, like fire.

She was a certain woman in the town of Aulon, near the Messenian border. None of us had seen her, but she was thought to be very beautiful. Yet it was not her reputed beauty that inflamed the imagination, although it undoubtedly helped, but her fiery rhetoric about justice and the equality of Spartiates.

"He rode to Aulon last night–" Anaxandros went on.

"What does she look like?" someone asked.

"Kallias said she has auburn hair and violet eyes. Beautiful as a goddess. She had an apple in her hand."

"Eris?" Bonehead laughed.

"Belt up. Go ahead, Magpie..."

"She asked the warriors at the meeting for a sword. Kallias was quickest, so she took his," he added proudly. "Then she said 'You see this apple? It looks perfect from the side you see, but there is a worm in it.' Then she took the sword out of the scabbard. Kallias said she did it like a soldier. She cut a chink out of the apple, and said, 'Now it is clean.'" He paused dramatically. "She told them that, if the worm had stayed, it would have eaten through to the core, so that it would have been necessary to cut it like that–" He mimed a slash. "She cut it in half then, and said, 'It is better to cut out the worm before it has time to corrupt the whole.'"

Aristokrates made a sound of admiration under his breath.

"Leave Pellana, and you'll have no skin on your back," I threatened.

"Belt up, Cockerel," said a boy who was not in my patrol.

115

"Tell us the rest, Magpie."

"He has a spare cavalry horse, but his cousin made him take her instead of me. That girl Gorgo, who taught Euagoras the spear. She's a dreadful girl. Everyone is afraid of her. Kallias says—"

"Never mind Kallias. What happened at Aulon?"

"I can't remember everything, but she asked them, 'Who are the criminals? Those who make mockery of a just law, or those who put them down to restore it.' Kallias said they all cheered then. That's a nice melody, Euagoras. What is it?"

"It hasn't got a name." He spoke in the sly voice that told us it was his own composition. "But you know that statue of the beautiful goddess Justice, beating the ugly goddess Injustice. I thought to call it the Beautiful Goddess."

We all knew that the Beautiful Goddess had auburn hair and violet eyes.

*   *   *

"Makarios is no longer in your patrol," the Commander said, Makarios being the Monkey's true name. "Makarios is no longer in the flock."

Patrol leaders do not question a commander's decision.

"With respect, Commander. May I know whether I am at fault."

"The order came from the Inspector of Boys, Leotychides. Consider yourself free of blame." He hesitated a brief instant. "Makarios is base-born. He was returned to his mother yesterday. Keep this to yourself."

The Monkey a bastard? But there were no bastards in Sparta. In any event, his father had been slain in the Long War. How could he disown him so many years later? And I was still in the flock, although my father had denied me. Or had he denied me? Ignored me, yes. But never had he said, "Leotychides is not my son."

Had I merely assumed my own bastardy? I thought back to that long-ago fight between Aristokrates and Hekataios. Had it been planted in my mind then? But if it were not true, then why...? Why? Why?

Hekataios climbed the long, stony incline of the high hill, to

116

pick his way along the narrow path leading to its dangerous north face. It had become his habit to stand alone and immobile, looking out across the vast expanse whenever he thought himself unobserved.

"Hek', Hek'." I called softly, so as not to startle him into a fatal fall.

"Hek', what is so fascinating about the mountains of Arcadia?" Although we were not certain whether they were across the northern border. Pellana's terraced landscape is deceptive.

He did not smile. "I was looking at something else."

"The sky? Goats? Fowl?"

"If you must know, it is my father's kleiros."

Why did he lie? With a word, he could have stopped my probing.

"That lies in the Vale."

"It was. It isn't."

"Hek', there are no kleroi up here. The land is richer in the Vale."

"Why else would it have been stolen?"

"Kleroi cannot be transferred." I quoted the rhetra.

"Hades take your rhetrae, Cockerel. *She* says they can. Now." The woman in Aulon.

"What else did she say about it, Hek'?"

"The Magpie couldn't remember."

"Then he doubtless misspoke her."

"Does that explain why my father's lands are here?"

"Why don't you ask Doreius about it?"

"Doreius!" he exploded. "Doreius didn't even think to ask Artemis to help Father."

"Hek', you talk senselessly. What has a goddess to do with it?"

"Doreius gave Artemis the olive crown he won in the Pythian Games. Now she has chosen him. *That* is what he asked of her."

Who but Doreius could it be?

Before he passes out of his flock, every youth in Sparta participates in a ceremony, in that most holy of temples; the one belonging to Artemis Orthia, in the hollow at the east edge of the City. One group of youths attempts to steal cheeses from the altar. Another group defends it in a fight of olive branches.

There is no greater honour for an eiren than to lead one group or the other. Doreius was leader of the defenders. Could Hekataios be touched by that ugliest of vices, envy?

"The Inspector of Boys chose Doreius," I told him. "Because he is the best in Sparta."

"That is all he ever thinks about. Being best. I don't understand him, Leo'."

I did. It is the nature of the eagle to soar, of the swan to swim, of the lark to sing. To be anything less would be false. Untrue to his nature.

Yet his brother's anger was a clean anger, if unjust. That ancient Spartan, who came away, rejoicing that there were three hundred better men in the City, is hard to imitate. Only a few, like Sphodrias, can effortlessly do so. For the rest of us, it is the reward of relentless discipline. But envy did not speak with the voice of Hekataios.

"The finest thing Doreius can do for your father *is* to be best. You too, Hek'."

He smiled lightly. That was a good speech, Cockerel. I heard Doreius make it when we were nine."

"I must contrive one of my own. I shall also look into this land-stealing matter, although I think you imagine it."

No one but a deserter could lose his kleiros. Dinon was awarded a prize for valour in the Athenian War. Would Antalkidas know? Pausanios? I would ask Pausanios, if only he would visit me.

"Cockerel!" The Magpie ran up. "Do we attend Hall tonight?"

"Tonight you are waiting on the Commander." His face fell. "That is an honour, in the event it escapes you."

"But Cockerel, Kallias is guesting in Hall tonight."

Kallias was the giver of the oil-flask, and the writer of letters. The young cavalry officer was known to be brave, and of a forthright nature; a good man for a youth to emulate. Nonetheless, the Magpie was becoming absent-minded, and off-hand about his duties.

"No doubt he can get himself invited another night."

"But I told–"

"That is an order, Anaxandros." The Magpie, not having been schooled in the rigorous regime of Doreius, sometimes forgot that one does not argue with a patrol leader. "Get back to those shear-heads, and see that they don't gouge or bite. Send any bad losers to Aristokrates for a thrashing."

Hekataios laughed shortly as the Magpie dashed off. "Some of the boys thought we would have it easier when Doreius gave over the patrol."

"You must allow the Magpie wants discipline."

I, too, liked attending Hall. The talk of the men. The torchless walk back under the stars, singing of Justice and the Muses walking the broad streets of Sparta, and other songs of Tyrtaios and Terpander. But the dining- hall, although at the very end of Hyakinthos Road, was still a very long walk, and it was a season when we older melleirens were exceptionally busy supervising the younger boys. Perhaps tomorrow...

"Whatever you say, Cockerel, Antalkidas knew how to lead. That patrol of his was second only to ours."

The cloak hung from the branches of an apple tree. I stopped and smiled. The Magpie had rinsed it in the river to look his best in Hall. Eyeing tree and cloak, Antalkidas stood.

We saw less of these eirens now. Those who had passed out of the flock, but lived on its peripheries in tents, too old to participate in its activities, too young for a regiment. Still under the authority of the Commander, but no longer a matter for his attention, they lived with us, but apart.

"Would you say that cloak is ripe for picking?" he mused.

"It's the Magpie's."

"Oh yes. You have him in your patrol now. I found him amusing."

"It shows."

He leapt up for an apple, and bit into it. "Time passes, Leotychides."

"What is your latest scheme?"

"Have I spoken of a scheme?"

"You never pass meaningless comments without reason. It is only your reasons that have no meaning."

He laughed "Shall we sit down?"

"I was on my way to the river," I said needlessly. We had poured too much water on the wrestling-ground, and I was

119

bespattered with mud.

"A brief pause only." Seated on the grass, he played with a twig, drawing designs in the red-brown patch of earth between his feet. "Time passes. Boys join the flock. Leave. Commanders go; or, more to the point, new commanders are appointed.

"And you would like to be next year's."

"I am not of the stuff of a flock commander, but, being a good Spartiate who always obeys, I prefer to choose those who give the orders... I think Chionis would do well."

"Why?"

"The alternative is Pronax. I detest prigs."

"Doreius is not a prig."

"He is not in the running, having had the poor taste to choose a father who came out of the war with nothing but ruined health and a red-haired cuckoo in his nest."

"Doreius can't be passed over."

"Things change. Even in Sparta. Wise men change with them."

"What is the point of this, Antal? The Inspector of Boys doesn't consult melleirens."

"Men advise the Inspector." He threw away the core. "Beauty is a powerful influence. You need only say a few words here and there. *Words* only, I assure you. Men can be moved by beauty without their own knowledge. Not I..." he added, although it had not occurred to me to think of an eiren as a man. "I keep my mind quite distant from other parts, and, on the whole, I think I prefer women." I tried to envision the erudite Antalkidas, like Sphodrias, tumbling up-country girls. With that uncanny ability to read thoughts, he said, "Not peasants smelling of milk and manure."

"Spartan maidens?" Not even he could so much as think it.

"Women. Not maidens. A woman reaches her peak of beauty at thirty, just as a boy reaches his at fifteen. Really, Leotychides, you should learn these things for yourself... You are fifteen, and I'll wager you have known neither man nor woman."

My urgent, formless desires were not things I wished to discuss with Antalkidas, or even put into mind-words, lest they take the form of the unattainable.

His pale eyes regarded me coolly. "Have you ever asked

yourself why a man already rising great should fix his affections on a boy with one leg shorter than the other?"

"There is no boy like that in the flock."

He told me about Agisilaos and Lysander.

"That would have been years ago. Agisilaos is nearly forty-five. And he has never been of any matter."

"You do not take my meaning. If the rumour I heard is true, you cannot afford to mistake it." He grasped my arm. "Are you listening to me, Leotychides?"

"Antal, the next commander–"

"Hades take the next commander! Particularly if it is Pronax, although it won't be if it means throwing my own support to the too perfect Doreius. You were always clever in your lessons. I want you to think carefully on King Demartos."

"Why? He left Sparta and exiled himself in Persia."

"Because he was deposed."

"King Kleomenes conspired against him."

"The conspiracy succeeded because King Ariston had divorced two wives for barrenness, when he married Demartos's mother. Married her the day after she was divorced from her first husband."

"As you say, I know my lessons, Antal."

"Don't play the fool. It is not convincing. When the Queen gave birth to Demartos seven months after she married Ariston, he said some stupid things about the boy not being his. Quite sensibly, he soon saw qualities that convinced him he was his own son. I say sensibly because Demartos was a bright lad. He became King when Ariston died, and reigned well. But his enemies were able to depose him, because his father never formally *recognized* him."

"No man does. These things are understood."

"We are speaking of kings. The direct descendants of Herakles through Hyllus."

"He was brought up as the heir."

"So he was..." He let the words hang in the air. He could say no more without touching on that which could not be spoken.

"My father wouldn't do it, Antal. You were in Sparta that Leonidia. You saw it."

"He had only just seen you. The resemblance–"

"Resemblance?"

"He might have wished you had resembled him more," he finished, too smoothly.

I got to my feet. "If he could be persuaded, my mother would have done it."

"There might be nothing more calculated to turn him against you."

"Everyone knows–"

"That King Agis is besotted with his wife? It must run in your family. Ageing Eurypontid kings and their young wives, Archidamos and his Eupolia, Agis and Timaia; although with her it is understandable, if idiotic. Beware of it in yourself, Leotychides–"

"Then you believe he is my blood-father?"

"By the Twin Gods, *you* had best believe it."

Anaxandros's voice preceded him. "Cockerel! Cockerel!" Antalkidas muttered under his breath. Anaxandros halted, panting from his long run. "Cockerel, Prince Agesipolis is here on a fine horse – a grey – "

"Why?" Antalkidas snapped.

"To see the Cockerel. I mean Leotychides."

The pale eyes met mine. Antalkidas lowered his voice. "Whatever you do now, think on what I have told you."

Agesipolis was tall. If there was a finger-width between us, it was in his favour. He wore a cloak of fine wool, carelessly. He was too thin for his height, but his arm muscles were well-developed. Pausanios had not neglected his heir's weapons practice. The spray of freckles across the nose was all that remained of my old playmate.

(At Torome he gave me a description of myself that day. Barefoot and caked with mud, nude except for a rag of a cloak slung over one shoulder, holding another, the Magpie's, in my hand).

The gangly young prince and the muddy melleiren looked at each other, and were strangers.

"Leotychides, your father is very ill."

"I thought he was in Delphi, giving Apollo his tithe of the spoils from the Eleian campaign."

"He had started back into Sparta, but he collapsed during the journey. They took him into Herea. It was the nearest city."

"I shall offer to Asklepios for his recovery."

"It is a bad fever. He is not young."

So the stilted conversation went on.

"Leotychides, we are cousins. I think – I believe–" He looked like a boy who has forgotten a rhetra. Then the words rushed out, disjointed. The old Agesipolis. "Talk...matters of state... Go to Herea...Lies, of course..." His very freckles flushed.

"Agesipolis, what message has Pausanios for me?"

"You mustn't say – his enemies. He has so many, Leotychides, there are many tales about you...slander..."

"Yes, Cousin, everyone says that I am not the son of my father."

"I wouldn't say that."

I raised my voice. (He told me, in the hills of Aphytis, that I had roared like Derkyllidas in the field). "Pausanios thinks that if my father does not recognise me, I may not succeed him. Not so?"

"Yes. Well–"

"Then perhaps you will tell me how I am to go to a foreign city, when no boy may leave Pellana."

A sharp look in the round, bright, blue eyes. "Is a boy ever denied permission to go to his dying father?"

If I did not undeceive him, the Commander would assume that my father had sent Agesipolis to call me to his bedside. My cousin was childish. He was not a fool. It was quite typical of him to forget to leave me his horse.

Anaxandros offered me Kallias's spare mount. Sphodrias suggested we borrow some horses from a nearby farm he knew (too) well. Hekataios reminded him that you cannot borrow things from up-country people whenever you need. They consider it stealing.

We discussed the journey to Herea in the cave. The Commander welcomed my friends' request to go with me. One can ride alone in safety anywhere in Lakonia, but he thought it better if we were several when we crossed into Arkadia.

I chose Anaxandros, Hekataios, Sphodrias and Pityas to accompany me. We would have to make do with the flock-ponies. Although they would be winded along the narrow, curving, mountainous north road.

123

We ceased talking at the sound of footsteps echoing in the cave. It was Aristokrates, come to ask a word outside with me. I stepped out into a night bright with stars. The swine is going to ask him who I am naming acting leader, I thought. And it must be him, because, after Hek', he is the best.

"Leotychides, my father has a stable full of horses near Sellasia."

"Why, Aristokrates?"

"After the death of General Thorax, he considered it wiser to change his owls into horseflesh." (Pharax was an admiral now. Quite a good one).

"What I am asking is why you try to drown me, and now offer me your father's horses." Was he trying to buy a chance to be acting leader? I would name Euagoras first.

"I thought about that. I really had nothing against you."

"A nice time to think of it."

"Well, I did pull you out."

("You did not break your teeth on the dry bread," he said many years later on, on that dread day when we all said what we could never say before, or nothing at all. "When they taunted me about my father's statue, I blamed you. King Pausanios visited you, and I thought it was from him. At the Leonidia, Doreius put you in charge of the patrol, and it was 'Voice down, Aristokrates.' 'Head up.' 'Fall in.' 'Fall out.' As though you were the Commander himself. I hated you.")

"Thank you, Aristokrates. Is there anything else you wanted?" There was not. He started away. "Wait. You are acting leader. I'll tell the Commander."

"Leotychides..." He half-turned. "Will you please take the horses. If you must beat a fast retreat, you'll cut a far better figure well-mounted."

"Is it because you tried to drown me? That doesn't matter. I've forgotten it."

"Then stop talking about it. I'm not riding a flock-nag, so we all might as well have decent horses."

The gate-sentry challenged us as we drew rein at the walls of Herea. Before I could reply to his challenge, Sphodrias called out, "Prince Leotychides of Sparta and his honour guard."

124

We were let past, and told the way to the house where the Spartan King had been taken. I was glad that I suggested stopping under the plane trees, to wash off the dust of the road in the River Alpheus. We were presentable. Our bare feet and shabby flock-cloaks would arouse no suspicion. Everyone knows Spartiates dress simply.

"I should hate to live in a walled town," the Magpie said. "It makes one feel closed in."

"I believe the purpose is to keep enemies out," I told him. "And Sphod', even Agesipolis hasn't got an honour guard."

"I know. But foreigners expect that sort of thing."

"All the same, I shall say what is necessary."

A Lakonian sentry stood outside the house. He was one of those freed serfs who are trained as light-armed foot soldiers.

"Leotychides, the son of King Agis." I gave my name curtly.

He did not move. "Young Master, the King has not told me of your coming."

"Does the King require your permission to receive his kin?" The voice of authority is usually respected. Nearly three years as patrol leader had shaped mine. "Out of the way, fellow. Tell the servants to inform their master we are here."

The walls of the house were brightly painted with scenes from the Trojan War. Sphodrias gasped. The Pointer told him foreigners often decorate their houses this way. There were a number of silver vases, a gold-handled krater, and intricately carved chairs inlaid with ivory.

Indeed, there was altogether too much carving on the chairs and tables. Although some of the objects were quite beautiful, the line was lost in over-adornment. I had heard that ordinary Lakedaimonian articles fetched enormous sums abroad. Now I understand the reason. It was the first time I had seen anything that was *not* beautiful.

Herean servants brought us refreshments. The house was large by Arkadian standards. It seemed cluttered and stifling. Shortly, our host appeared; a dark man in a cloak with a wide border. He wore two large finger-rings; one the type that can be used as a seal. He was a Herean of wealth and standing.

"Sir, I am Leotychides, the son of King Agis. These are my friends. I thank you for giving my father hospitality. Is he improved?"

"The fever comes and goes. You will find him much changed, I fear." No doubt, after four years.

As we exchanged courtesies, the door of a room opened. My enemy stepped out. A white-haired old serf, who had probably been a boy of twelve when my father was playing with wooden swords. *He* would know I came unbidden.

My host ordered an upper servant to take me to my father. My friends followed. The old serf stood against the door like Kerberos, but he would not be appeased with cake, lyre or lies. His very black eyes told me that he would kill and be killed to protect his master.

I leaned down to his ear, although I had not yet my full height, and said in a low voice, "Do you want my father to die with no son to commend him to the gods?"

After a long moment, he stood aside wordlessly to let us pass. Then he took up a post at the open door. One call from my father, and the hue and cry would be raised.

The dim room smelled of sweat and illness. A brazier burned, despite the warmth of the night. My father's sword was laid across his shield in a corner of the room, with his parade armour. It must have been what my father wore to dedicate the spoils at Delphi, for an ordinary travelling cloak and broad-brimmed traveller's hat were folded and laid on a chest. A silver-bound chest with a design of nymphs and flowers; undoubtedly Arkadian. On a table by the bed stood a cup of wine, half-empty. A wooden cup, painted with a hunting scene. Lakonian.

Had it not been for my host's warning, I might have thought myself in the wrong room. The sleeping man on the bed had white hair. The once-ruddy face was touched with colour only by the lamp-light. The jaw had gone slack and the skin was fashioned to fit a fleshier countenance. Two cushions had been cast on the floor.

Sphodrias sneezed. My father made a sleep sound, snorted, sat bolt upright, and said, in a surprisingly firm voice, "What is this gaggle of youths doing here?"

The cold blue eyes had not changed.

He cleared his throat. His hand went out to the wine cup while his gaze went over us. A general sizing up an unexpected situation. His eyes fell on Aristokrates. Had my old adversary given up his chance as acting leader for some malicious prank of his own?

"You are the son of Pharax, are you not?" my father asked crisply.

"Yes, sir."

"Does your father know you are here?"

"Not yet, sir."

"Are you being impertinent?"

"No, sir."

"I think you are impertinent."

I felt ashamed of my unworthy suspicions.

My father turned to Anaxandros. "And you?"

"Anaxandros, the son of Eutelidas."

A ghost of a smile stretched the dry lips. "Eutelidas...well, your father and I haven't always seen eye to eye, but he is a worthy man. Are you the younger son?"

"Yes, sir."

"Let us hope the elder has more sense."

It was the turn of Pityas. This time, there were no sarcasms. "I knew your father. He served under me in the Dekelian campaign. A brave man. His name is written." He skipped over me to Hekataios, with a reference to Dinon's valour, and then came to Sphodrias. "You look familiar. Who are you?"

"Sphodrias, the friend of Leotychides." he replied steadily.

"Then you are a fool. Now you have all come. You may all go. Dismissed."

They looked towards me. I told them to leave. My father looked into his wine. "Can you not obey as well as command?" After a long silence, he spoke in a voice like burning ice. "Did you not hear me order you to leave?"

"I'm sorry, sir. I thought you were speaking to a wine-cup."

"By Zeus, you are insolent."

"No, sir, you ordered my friends out. You did not speak to me at all." I was suddenly seized by all the years of pent-up rage. I would have my say if I were flogged for it, but I would not waste my words. "There are things to be said between us. I'll not go until I have said them."

"Did she send you? Or was it that meddling fool Pausanios?"

"Agesipolis told me that you were ill. I took it upon myself to come."

"Pausanios. And you hoped to find me dying."

"No, sir. That would be a cheap victory."

He took a long breath. "You hate me as much as I do you."

"I have greater objects for my hate." The grandiose statement rang absurd in my ears. "I mean I find personal hatreds petty."

"You give a good imitation of a fine hater."

"You misunderstand me, sir. I meant only that the victory of death over life is a mean thing, unless it is a life taken in battle at the risk of one's own."

"You are a good talker. It may have impressed Pausanios, but there is nothing less calculated to incline me to you."

"I'm not trying to. Whether you like me or not matters not at all."

"Then it is not your intention to persuade me to recognise you?"

"Of course it is. You are a king. I am your heir. May you live many years, Father. I should prefer to be a man before I am King. But I *am* your heir."

"What did he say, Leo'"

"Why have you come out? Did he order you out?"

My father had attempted to pitch his voice as he would in battle. The effort had been too much. Sweat broke out on his brow. His next words were so feeble as to be embarrassing. I pretended not to hear. The appearance of strength was illusive.

I stepped to the door, and asked the old batman to send for the physician, as much to win his trust as to extract a promise from my father that I would be permitted to return when he had rested.

I cannot recall what words he used, but he gave it. Most probably to have done with me, but the draining of his strength had recalled to him his mortality. A man with death hovering over him does not give promises vainly.

I finished the last of the meat, and sopped up the rich sauce with my bread. "Do you think our host would give us a place to sleep tonight?"

"He has already shown us our rooms."

The warmed bath-water the servants brought us took me back

to my childhood.

"Sphod', you risked a lot with what you said. I think I am fighting a losing battle."

"What did I risk?"

"He is a king. Kings are bad enemies for men who plan to be generals."

Sphodrias had often stated that intention.

"I can still choose my friends. This water is scented!"

"Mine isn't." Anaxandros splashed some under his nose.

Nor was mine.

"I think the gold basin was meant for Leotychides," Pointer suggested.

"Keep it, Sphod'." Even in the palace, we hadn't scented water. "He's quite set against me, you know. It isn't as if he knew nothing of me. I think Pausanios has kept him informed."

"Get some sleep, Leo'," Sphodrias said. "You'll need your wits about you tomorrow."

"I don't think I can."

I lay on the floor, threw my cloak over myself, and fell into a deep sleep.

Only Anaxandros thought to make use of one of the beds.

"Agisilaos," my father said, "is a good brother."

"A good brother is not the same as a good king."

His back was propped against the cushions. He was not feverish. His voice was firm, but his night-battle with the fever had drawn greatly from him. "Agisilaos is Royal Heraklid," he replied. There had been a subtle change. He appeared to accept that he *owed* me. Not recognition, but something in the way of an explanation.

"Eupolia hasn't a drop of Royal Heraklid blood." My mother had repeated this phrase so often that I heard her voice in mine. We might have shared a silent smile, had we been friends rather than enemies.

"There are other considerations."

"What consideration could outweigh making a king of Lysander; all Sparta knows that Agisilaos is simply his creature."

"Lysander is my friend."

"A great friend! Do you think they say the coins came in the reign of Pausanios? No, it is the reign of Agis!"

"I had nothing to do with that." My words jolted him, so that he defended himself to me.

"You bear the blame."

He recovered himself. "You are aware of affairs of state, no doubt, of which I am ignorant."

"You are right, Father. But I do know that when a great man like Gylippos can be corrupted, something is wrong. And if I were king, I would make it my concern to speak out against it."

"Are you enumerating my failings?"

"No, sir. I was saying what you had ought to do."

I expected him to strike me. He burst into laughter.

"You are an insolent cub," he said finally. "You might even make a good king. But it is something that cannot be."

"You really had ought to have these braziers removed."

Was it the night of the same day? Or the next? The lamps were lit. The old batman gave my suggestion a look of approval. The over-heated room in the cluttered house, in this closed town of narrow lanes, could do little good to a Spartiate, accustomed to spacious rooms and broad streets.

"That fool of a physician says they will sweat out the fever."

"Master," says the batman, "he also says you must not eat solid food."

"It is this Herean slop that makes it worse. Black broth would put me on my feet again. Why are you back, Boy? I only promised to see you once."

"You went to sleep while we were talking."

"*You* were talking."

I do not recall all I had said. My reasoning was my own, my arguments hybrid, culled from the Aulon woman, from men in Hall, from discussions with boys whose information was also second- and third-hand. Small wonder he had chosen to sleep.

"I'm sorry if I wasted words. This time I shall listen."

"I think we have said all that needs to be said."

"No, Father."

"I think we can drop that pretence, too."

"Very well. I have no father. You have no son." Only two small oil-lamps burned on the table. The small noises in the other parts of the house made the room more silent. I pulled up a hassock, and sat near the bed. "Who is he, if you are not?"

130

At last the words came. "I cannot tell you."

"Is he alive?"

"Dead." The syllable came through tight lips.

"Who killed him?"

"Barbarians." I was glad I had not let the shadow of the thought cast itself across my mind.

"Was he brave?"

A long silence. "He was brave. Ask no more."

Having spoken the unspeakable, we were less constrained.

"Sir, foreigners might have believed those romances Demartos told them about his birth, but Spartans knew—"

"It is not the same thing."

"In Hall, they say Lysander already acts with more pomp than a king—"

"I have told you he is a friend of my youth."

"Then you know him for what he is. He holds no office, but can raise men up and cast them down. And he raises none he can't rule. He even made governors of some of his own serfs—"

"You have been listening to disgruntled men. Or is it Pausanios?"

"Pausanios does not talk to me on matters of state."

"Pity. He might learn something. One advantage of dying will be that I'll no longer have to dine with the man."

"Is that why you voted to kill him?"

"I voted for his conviction, you young fool, because I knew he would be acquitted. It had to be the Middle party...that is why the ephors sent him to Athens with an army. But he had not got the authority to restore it without referring back to Sparta. That was a political matter. I made the same mistake myself once... that's how I got lumbered with two ephors on my staff... not that I let them interfere in military matters. Pausanios had to be taught that he can't go setting up governments."

"Lysander did."

"Lysander was Grand Admiral."

"I thought he was *Vice*-Admiral."

I expected another outburst, but he spoke quietly and thoughtfully. "Lysander has his faults, but he is not the monster you assume. It was a political error to think he could force Kritias and his council back on Athens. I let him know he would have no help from me, by disbanding my army in the Dekeleia.

131

But it wasn't simply stubbornness on my part. He knows the danger of Athens."

"Athens is defeated."

"The nature of a people is not changed by defeat."

"Kallikratidas wanted to reconcile us. Kallikratidas–"

He interrupted me. "How your eyes shine when you speak his name! Is it Kallikratidas you try to emulate? Kallikratidas you admire?"

"Above all other men."

"I have done you an injustice. I thought your coolness to Lysander had other origins...Kallikratidas was a fine man, but he died before the Athenian Assembly passed its decree ordering that the right hand of every prisoner of war be struck off. Only one man voted against it. Would any other Hellenic city be capable of such cruelty? Even in the heat of battle, we do not mutilate our prisoners. It is a barbarian thing. It was after that that Lysander and I made a pact to destroy Athens when she was defeated. Not in vengeance, but because she would always be a threat to the peace of Hellas. The ethics of Hellas."

"You did not press for her destruction."

"I withdrew from the pact, because some of my reasons for entering it were personal – but that is not your concern. Lysander's were not. Try to understand...when the Persians invaded, we were war-leader of all the Hellenes. Under our leadership, Xerxes and his millions were defeated. When the barbarians withdrew, we retired to the Peloponnesos, and concerned ourselves with our own city. But Athens saw our withdrawal as an opportunity to rule Greece. She had learned from the Persian wars what could be done at sea, and built a powerful fleet. A fleet is a striking force. Things could never be the same. Unless Athens was destroyed."

"We defeated Athens."

"And secured peace for how long? A generation? Two? Lysander feels that, as Athens was not destroyed, we must be powerful enough to prevent her from ever rising again."

"If we must emulate Athens in order to contain her, then she has won, not Sparta."

"Sentiments worthy of Kallikratidas. But we must be practical."

"Does being practical mean setting up Spartan governors

over free cities? Cities that *we* freed. Brasidas would not have done that. He fought to put down empire."

"Lysander overstepped himself with his decarchies. I agree. He was always ambitious, and all the adoration went to his head. He is a great commander and practical man. He is not perfect. Nor am I. Nor any man. Even Pausanios, as you will someday learn. But enough of this–""No, sir, I'm sorry to have interrupted. I want to understand Lysander. I must, I dare say."

"*Must*, why *must*?"

"For when I am king."

His hand shook with anger, spilling drops of wine on the coverings. "Can't you understand? You are not to be king. Did you really think I would put you, who are nothing to me, above my own brother?"

"No, sir. Only your duty."

He was sinking. Light food was set out on tables in his room. For two. This time the old batman had come for me. The King did not touch his food.

"I have sent for you because, although I cannot name you my heir, I feel it just that I make some provision for you. No, that is not entirely true. I am dying in a foreign place; and you are clean, with the cleanness of the flock on you, the cleanness of Sparta before the Long War tarnished her. Don't interrupt. I can promise that you will command a regiment when you are thirty. I shall leave you enough of my private property to live as befits you."

"My kleiros is sufficient, and I shall rise in the army by merit."

"And you wanted all..."

"Because it is my *right*."

"By Zeus, you are Spartiate if nothing else."

"What happened, Cockerel? You were there a long time."

The King had called for my friends. Perhaps he wanted youth about him to counter death. They came with well-rehearsed praises of me, bored him, and were sent out again.

"We talked of the Long War...He told me that the Athenians

133

claim they have the shield of Brasidas...they thought they killed him at Koryphasion, you know. They struck him down with so many wounds. But that was during a pitched battle, and there was no time for taking trophies.

"Then, when Brasidas became famous in the north, they hung up some dead Spartan's shield they had fished out of the sea, and said it was his."

"When he asked you stay, I thought..." The Magpie's sentence expired.

"He talked about my grandfather, too. Did you know he was a great friend of Perikles?"

"King Archidamos!" Hekataios exclaimed.

"From before the Athenian War. Even after the war began, my grandfather halted with his army at the very borders of Attica, and tried to talk Perikles into a peaceful settlement. Perikles refused. He thought my grandfather would spare his estates because they were personal friends."

"He warms to you," Sphodrias said.

"He thought my grandfather over-cautious in his youth...It's odd. At times I almost liked him."

"He hasn't—"

"No. And he won't."

"Did he order you out again?"

"He said he wanted to rest."

And so did I. I was simply seeing it out to the end. The weariness of defeat. The King took a bad turn the next day, and I did not see him. He had seven servants with him. Except for the constantly present old batman, they worked in turn.

We were taking the air in the courtyard when the batman came to tell me to hasten to the King.

The room was filled with Arkadians. Only my host and the physician were known to me. The braziers had been removed. The sick man's face was waxen, but he wore a fresh tunic and sat up in bed, his back against the wall. The cushions were gone. On the table beside the bed lay a short Lakedaimonian sword. On either side of the bed stood three servants. The old batman told me to go forward.

Despite the presence of all the foreigners, the room had taken on a more Lakedaimonian aspect. I cast my eyes down as I approached the King. Not before I had seen the apprehension in

Sphodrias's face. Was the outcome of all this to be a public repudiation?

The King made a motion. The servants withdrew a few paces away.

"Sir?" I presented myself.

"Give me your hand, Leotychides."

I stretched forth my arm, thinking he wanted help to rise. He took both my hands and turned them palm upwards.

"Young hands, but hard," He withdrew a ring from his forefinger. A seal ring with the face of King Polydoros carved in carnelian. An Agiad King. Pausanios had one like it.

"Put it on." A consolation prize? Well, I would not argue with a dying man. The ring fitted. He ordered a servant to hand him the sword. "It belonged to my father. You will find it long enough to reach the throats of your enemies." Son but not heir. Was that the meaning of these things? I had rejected his property and his preferment. This was to be his bequest. He lowered his voice. "Listen to me, the Long War would still be going on if divided leadership had not brought Athens down. Do you understand? Factions and divisions create wars and lose wars. I charge you; do not let the kingdom divide."

He called for undiluted wine to pour a libation to Zeus, and then raised his voice. It was still weak. The low hum of voices ceased. "Men of Herea..." He took a long breath. "I have learned that, like King Ariston, I have made some foolish remarks that have caused confusion regarding the succession." He paused to gather strength. He choked, and then marshalled his vocal powers. When he continued, it was with the voice that had commanded armies. "Should I die before I am able to do so myself, bear witness to all Lakedaimonians that Leotychides is my son, my true son, and true heir to the Eurypontid throne."

The babble that broke out covered his words to me. He spoke softly, as he tested the royal ring on my finger. "It fits. Is it an omen, do you think?"

"My hands are the size of yours."

"Long-fingered, like your mother. Mine were always too small for a man." I had not noticed the small hands and stubby fingers before. "Leotychides, remember the first duty of kingship. Keep the realm united."

"Yes, Father."

"We might have been friends, had we known one another."

In panic, I felt my eyes moisten. As if I were a small child, he raised his hand and brushed away the tears from my cheek. "And get those bleating goats of yours out of sight if they can't control themselves," he ordered.

My friends had pressed in closer, their heads hidden in their cloaks to cover their wet cheeks.

"Leo – Prince Leotychides..." Aristokrates began.

"Have done, Pointer," I snapped.

My father turned to the old batman, and told him to start packing. Seeing the question in my eyes, he said, "We've work to do in Sparta."

"Cockerel, what–" Anaxandros's words were blurred, as once more he turned his head into his cloak.

"Any more tears, and I'll have you all thrashed for shaming us before foreigners," I threatened, and then knew the futility of my threat. Kings' heirs are instructed privately. I would not be going back to the flock.

Our host tried not to look relieved that his royal guest was departing. Even a dead king would pollute his house. How superstitious foreigners are! But I need not have feared their disdain.

The Hereans were looking only at a king's last farewell to his heir, a father's last words to his son, youths grieving the passing of their king, to them a natural part of the pageant of death.

Only we Spartans conceal that which must not be seen. Those things that can only be demeaned by demonstration.

BOOK TWO

Chapter 5

A clamour of lids beating against cauldrons entered my dream. King Pleistinoax was dead. Agesipolis showed me his Grandfather's statue. The statue died.

Coming fully awake, I looked on my father's face and knew.

He was unaware when we crossed into Lakonia. For two days and two nights, I sat by his bedside in the palace with the old batman. I must have dozed. It was the white-haired serf who knew when my father's spirit went out of him.

While I slept off the vigil's weariness, my mother arranged the funeral.

A Spartiate is buried simply in his cloak. Kings and slain warriors are borne on a shield and honoured with an olive crown. A Spartan funeral shows death neither fear nor awe. Only women beating cauldrons to herald the death of kings survived from our obscure past in Doris.

My mother performed the ceremony well, and made a mockery of my father's funeral to frame her performance.

His body, in a rich robe he never wore alive, lay on a bier pulled by four white oxen. It was painted with his accession to the throne, the death of Hyllos and the trials of Herakles. Given more time, she would have taken our line back to Perseus. The bier moved slowly to the Eurypontid tombs, accompanied by flute, lyre and harp, and a Dorian lament. Dark-clad women lined the way, throwing white flowers as they raised their voices in praise of the dead king.

I led the Eurypontid men. Agisilaos limped a few paces behind me, beside his mother's father, old Aristomelidas – who was neither Eurypontid nor kin but was, surprisingly, still alive. Kyniska headed the women kin, whose ranks were swelled by Eupolia's and Kleora's relations. Behind them, the Agiads. Then came the Elders and ephors. Lysander was in the forefront of the private citizens and young warriors. Following them in this seemingly endless cortège came the two mourners from every up-country village, as is the custom.

In front of the bier, in stately solitude, paced the severe, dark-clad figure of my mother, with the wine for the libations.

Now as the kin, Eurypontid and Agiad, poured into the great hall for the funeral banquet, that stark Alkestis-like figure drew me into a side-room, threw back the end of her peplos that covered the bright hair and laughed.

"Leotychides, you do well to wear that old cloak." Her white face was flushed and still beautiful. Black always became her. Her eyes sparkled. "How the people will praise your simplicity!" She seized my hand and scrutinised the seal-ring. "Agis gave you this?"

"Do you think I would take it from his dead hand? Why an Agiad king, mother?"

"Polydoros." Her smile was like one who quenches thirst after a long march over parched ground. "It is the seal of Sparta. You cannot use it until you are twenty. You must have a regent." Her brow creased. "Agisilaos will expect to be named...Go and change for the banquet. You are a king. You must look a king."

"We are given only one cloak a year."

"Dromea has had the women weaving since Agis was brought in dying. He was so long about it that they shall have woven three cloaks by now."

Dromea! The name brought back long, loving dark eyes, shining black hair, and hands that moved like butterflies. A gentle voice that never reproached, nor demanded love, and so was returned it in full measure. "Dromea is here?"

"Where else?"

"But you sent her away. On account of me."

"It did not concern you. Dromea wished to remarry. I released her." That was a lie. Dromea's lover was a palace servant. Because of her banishment, they had to wait four years to marry.

"A new cloak today would be unseemly, Mother." I strapped sandals on feet that had not known the touch of leather for years. I was King. Not my mother.

People milled about the great hall, talking. My friends started back to Pellana after the funeral. My kin were strangers. I was alone. Phrases drifted to me. "Disgrace..." "Ostentatious..." "The young King was seemly enough..." "Well, Timaia had passing dignity..." My mother had a way of emerging unscathed from the havoc she created. One of the men standing by the

Herakles statue moved. I saw the chestnut hair of his companion. I was not alone. I made my way to Pausanios.

"Leotychides, we must not be seen to be too close," he warned, after the exchange of courtesies. "Do not add my enemies to yours."

"Your enemies are my enemies." I meant it as an avowal.

He mistook my words. "Some are the same. There are also men who believe I was wrong to restore the Middle Party, now Athens is intriguing again. Konon–"

"Should have twice been consigned to the deep." Teleutias joined us, a young boy with him. "A god must protect the man, the way he escaped both Kallikratidas and Lysander." He glanced at the boy. "Pausanios, before he goes to the children's benches, this lad wants to pay his respects to his cousin."

Bright, Agiad, blue eyes looked up at the melleiren, recalled the melleiren was now a king, and cast them down.

"What rank are you now, Kleombrotos?"

"Second rhodibas. Our flocks fought last year, Leotychides. My flock brothers think you are a fine fighter."

"Tell them you are the sort of boy I should like to have had in my patrol." I had learnt to size up a rhodibas quickly. This one was hardy, quick-witted and obedient. Those eyes were kept down by discipline, not want of spirit.

"Father, must I sit with Eupolia and Prolyta?" Agisilaos's second daughter was as small and plain as his first. His son Archidamos, being only an infant, was the sole member of the brood missing.

"They are your kin," Pausanios told him.

Kleombrotos looked towards a pretty, bright-haired girl of about eleven. "She, too, is kin. I would eat with her." Teleutias laughed. "Let him. My nieces are not lively company, sir."

The servants were bringing in food. Kleombrotos withdrew to the children's benches. Two king's chairs stood on the dais. Agisilaos edged his way towards the one that had been my father's. Should he try to use it, I should forcibly dislodge him, but there were decorous ways. I invited Pausanios, audibly, to take the place next *mine*.

Eupolia glared. Kyniska lifted an eyebrow. Kleora looked vaguely distressed. Peisander ate. Agisilaos called Teleutias to him. My mother's smile was dazzling.

When the eleven days of mourning had passed, Agisilaos claimed the kingdom.

My mother stood, mirror in hand, pulling and pushing at the same strand of her high-knotted hair. Finally, she ceased and began shaking a small, flat, ivory scent-bottle carved with roses.

"I wish it were the Bronze Age, so I could challenge Agisilaos to single combat," I said. There were more than twenty days yet before the monthly meeting of the Apella, when the succession would be decided.

"Be glad you cannot. You may be taller, but he is a seasoned soldier." She muttered an expletive as the stopper came out, splashing her with too much spicy scent, and called for another peplos. "The sea-green."

"Mother, will you receive them dressed so gaily?" A deputation of Elders was coming for her statement.

"Hypocrisy won't further your cause." She played with that strand of hair again. "I leave that to Agisilaos."

Aphrodite's bronze statue stood in its niche, as I remembered it. The altar was bare.

"You have forgotten Aphrodite," I said, when she returned in the sea-green peplos.

"There is nothing more she can do for me. Where is my lion brooch?" she asked herself aloud. "It belonged to King Eurypon's wife." That to me. "Find it!" to her serving-women. She rummaged through a chest herself.

Dromea ran in with the brooch, rubbing the ancient gold with a soft piece of leather. Two upright lions, holding a bud between them. She raised it high to affix it.

"Leotychides..." she placed her hands on my shoulders, and looked up. It still seemed strange to be taller than my mother. "Will you not tell me how you made Agis recognise you?"

"I cannot. I don't know."

"At least tell me what you talked about. What do you owe a man who ignored you for the whole of your life?"

"Sparta. Surely respect of his confidence is little enough for that."

"Confidences...?" The lioness poised for the spring. "What lies did he speak of me?

141

"Nothing. I have told you, Mother." She was playing with her hair again. "It looks very well, you know. You didn't sacrifice much." Her mourning lock had been one small curl.

She turned to me. The long-fingered hands raked through her neatly-looped hair, pulling it loose until it fell like fire to her waist. In the front was a wide, white streak that had been concealed by careful arrangement.

"*That* I cut in a true mourning lock." Her voice rang. "It grew back white." She held up the mirror to her face, and continued in a flat monotone. "I am almost thirty-four; I am told I look younger. Inside, I am as old as that." She touched the white lock and called for Dromea to bring her comb. "You may have Dromea if you wish. I know she goes to her rooms at night."

The workings of my mother's mind were unfathomable.

"Dromea? She is like a mother to me."

I felt the sting of her strong hand against my cheek. "I suppose you tell her how you made Agis recognise you. What a cruel, ungrateful boy you are."

Four Elders waited in the small audience room, taking wine and refreshments. The scribes stood, their writing tablets hanging on leather thongs about their necks.

Agisilaos had produced witnesses supporting his claim to the throne. My father's old batman and his other servants swore that he had owned me as his son and heir, but serfs' words weighed less.

For the same reason, I was barred from speaking on my own behalf before the Assembly, while Agisilaos could speak for himself. The Hereans were summoned, but had not yet arrived. Everything rested with them and my mother.

She seated herself with a single liquid motion, and permitted the Elders to finish their wine. Her peplos gave her eyes the colour of the sea. In shallow waters. The lion brooch that fastened it was of the same very old Lakonian work as her arm-ring. Sun shining in from the courtyard reflected on the brighter gold of the lions in her ears. They were neither old, nor of the same shaping.

She was required to swear by certain deities. They were very solemn oaths and I thought, Apollo, let her tell the truth for once if it cost me the kingdom. The most aged of the Elders turned to the recorders and dictated, "Queen Timaia to the citizens of Sparta."

"Timaia, Queen of Sparta, mother and widow of Spartan kings," she corrected him gently.

"In reply to Agisilaos the son of King Archidamos..." The Elder did not like his work, and wanted it over quickly. "Son of King Archidamos and Eupolia the daughter of–" she hesitated. "Aristomelidas, is it not?"

There were one or two smothered smiles at this veiled reference to Eupolia's undistinguished ancestry. The Elder, a man nearing ninety, shifted his feet like a rhodibas. A second elder came in. "Madam, Agisilaos claims that your son is not the true son of King Agis."

"He has called his late King and brother a liar?" The green eyes registered profound sadness on learning of this outrage, but implied no better might be expected.

Three of the Elders hastened to implore her to understand that only duty forced them to repeat such an assertion. Her warm voice reassured them that she knew slander was as distasteful to men of honour, like themselves, as to her.

Her tone became crisp. "Pray continue. We must do what is required of us."

With a trick of voice, she took command. Like a king taking the most dangerous place in battle, his life the sacred blood-price of his kingship, Queen Timaia assumed responsibility for this sacrifice. She was Alkestis again, herself the heroic sacrifice. No actor could have played it better.

A hard-eyed man, a young sixty, was not beguiled. "Madam, there are sworn witnesses who heard King Agis say that your son was not his. That Poseidon shook the earth to warn him from your rooms, and that he did not take the husband's rights for nearly eleven months before your son was born."

A suspicion of mirth touched the green eyes. "When men are in wine, the earth is sometimes unsteady beneath their feet."

"It is not unsteady for eleven months, Madam."

"When a man is in wine, he often cannot recall, the next day, what he has or has not done."

"Madam, King Agis drank his wine in the lawful dilution of four parts water to one wine."

"Without doubt. In his Hall." Outside in the courtyard, a serf fed the fish in the fountain, while another rested against a bench he should have been polishing. How long could my mother continue to parry these questions, without the lie that would bring down on her the consequences of those terrible oaths?

"Madam..."The hard-eyed man persisted. "Some of your husband's body-servants swear that he did not approach your rooms after the earth shook."

I burst out "Sir, are you refuting a queen of Sparta with the word of serfs?" My indignation was real, its cause spurious. No few serfs were more truthful than my mother. Almost anyone was more truthful than my mother.

"Madam, we could continue another time." One of the Elders glanced reproachfully at his colleagues. "When your son is not present."

"The King chooses to remain," she said. "We shall continue." she looked straight into the sceptical eyes of the hostile inquisitor. "Is nature consistent as the moon? Are there no men amongst you whose mothers carried them more or less than a full term, yet are the true-born sons of their father?"

Like many a soldier, my mother fought best with her back to the wall.

Neatly side-stepping those solemn oaths by generalities, and answering questions with questions, she created an illusion of baring her breast to the verbal arrows, and forcing them into her flesh.

Aware that every Spartiate knew of Geradas and the stranger, she reminded the Elders that, through her, I had as much of the blood of Herakles as the half-royal Agisilaos and, while refuting his accusation, she told the people of Sparta that it mattered not a jot if it were true.

She was magnificent.

When they were gone, she laid her hand on my cheek, where she had struck. "I'm sorry I slapped you."It was one of our moments of harmony. I think if I had asked her, then, the name of my blood-father, she would have told me. I did not. My father was the man who had owned me as his son, and that was an end to it. The moment passed.

She kissed my brow "Forgive me?"

"How not, Mother? And this time I am old enough to understand."

She frowned. "This time? I never laid a hand on you before."

Fortunately, the oaths applied only to the testimony.

The Hereans came to Sparta. One by one, these Arkadians of high blood and repute swore solemnly before the Council of Elders that my father, in clear mind and firm voice, had declared me his son and heir. Their statements were recorded to be read out in the Apella when it met.

One Herean went into detail about the touching farewell between father and son, tears and all. I dare say that is what started that idiotic tale; that my friends and I influenced my father, by weeping and begging him to recognise me. Had we done so, he would have sent us out before any of us could utter a word. But the poor fellow was a foreigner, well-intentioned, and knew no better.

Antalkidas came to see me. He had walked by night from Pellana, arrived in time to break fast, and stayed for the midday meal.

"I should have liked to have seen Lysander when Agis sprung his surprise." Antalkidas examined his wine-cup. "I understand he squealed like a stuck boar."

"Lysander bellows."

"True. Agisilaos squealed."

"Agisilaos whimpered."

He raised an eyebrow. "You are developing style. The short-sleeved tunic is right, too. Plain but fine. I like a king with style." "I hope the Apella shares your good taste."

"Agisilaos – that is to say Lysander – has been mustering his forces." He swirled the wine in his cup. "Queen Timaia has been building up her own for years; but as she could not have foreseen recent events, her front-line troops consist of Agis's enemies – so her army is somewhat disarrayed."

"Antal, Assembly is not a battle-field."

He sighed "I fear the style conceals an innocent, still. I must take you in hand. And, I dare say, be more respectful." His thin face froze in solemn lines. "Excellent wine, sir. Is it Chian? Pity the King dilutes it so lawfully. Unlike his father..." So my mother's statement had reached the dining halls. Your friends are very close-mouthed about what happened at Herea, Leotychides..."

"Who is the new flock commander?"

He laughed. "A few years more, and you will be as adroit at evading questions as any king. The new commander is Doreius."

"The best...despite your intrigues."

"This year's Inspector of Boys is a Spartan of the old type. Have you been riding recently?"

146

"Riding...?"

"You sit a horse well. It would do you no harm to be seen about the City. On reconsideration, stay in the palace."

I assumed he meant riding would appear ostentatious.

Antalkidas brought me bits of news from time to time. Friends of Lysander recalled a slight earthquake about ten months before I was born. Others laughed them down, saying earth-tremors were so frequent in Sparta no man could put a date to one fifteen years past. That sort of thing. When the sun dipped behind Taygetos each evening, I thought of the smoke rising from the cooking-fires at Pellana, the scent of the matthiola plant, and the talk in that quiet hour. Who was now leader of my patrol? Who carried Doreius his food as he reclined on the commander's dining couch, asking questions, testing the boys?

I sat on a bench in the courtyard on a shimmering afternoon, watching a bird fly deep into the fountain to drink from the bottom. The servants still forgot to fill it. How quick and sharp and deep my replies would have been. And Doreius would say...

A man stepped from the shadows of the covered colonnade. I did not question his presence. Citizens come and go, borrowing their wants. His features were agreeable, but not striking. Unknown and faintly familiar.

"A horse? A chariot, Kinadon? Be welcome."

"You know me."

Only as I spoke did I know him. It was the soft, fairish hair I recalled blowing in the wind of his own speed. The compelling eyes I had not noticed at the Leonidia.

"I saw you win three olive crowns in the Leonidian Games."

"What year was that?" He was older than I thought him. Possibly thirty-three or so.

"You must win often. Won't you be seated?"

"Don't you want to know why I am here?"

"I assume you will tell me in your own time."

He sat on the ground, with his back against the fountain. "We wanted to know more of you." His voice was soft but incisive.

"I see only one of you."

"We are an army." His smile was not a smile.

"What army is this?"

"The dispossessed. Someone is trying to dispossess you.

147

That is why you interest us." He picked a blade of grass and chewed it. "What will you do if the Apella decides for Agisilaos? Go into exile, like Demartos? Found a city in Sicily, as Doreius did?"

Had Agisilaos sent him to learn my mind? "It is something I do not consider."

His laugh had an edge to it. "You need not. Your kin are powerful and wealthy. You would be an ephor or grand admiral. The consolation prizes are rich for deposed kings."I stood. I did not like him after all, but I was certain he had not come from Agisilaos. "I don't think we have anything more to say, but I will tell you this. Should Assembly decide for Agisilaos, my kleiros is sufficient for me."

His words were a lash of bitterness. "How not? No one will take *your* kleiros." He drew himself up like a soldier coming to attention. "Forgive my blunt words, Young King. I think you have had too many of them." He turned on his heel and walked away.

"Kinadon! Wait!"

The man was disagreeable, but unusually outspoken. Since becoming King, I had tried to learn why the Monkey was taken from the flock, why Dinon the father of Doreius and Hekataios had left Limnai for the north, why the coins had remained in the City, but all I received were evasions. If anyone would give me a direct response, it would be this blunt man.

"The decree of Epitadeus," he replied almost carelessly.

"What is that?"

"In the last year of the Long War, when Epitadeus was chief ephor, he permitted men to sell their kleroi."

"That is unlawful and impious. Sparta is sworn to the Law of Lykourgos. If this Epitadeus would change it, the other four ephors would not.

He smiled. "Two were in the Dekeleia to prevent your father meddling in politics again. Epitadeus needed to persuade only one."

"No man would give up his kleiros."

He perched on the edge of the fountain. "Let me tell you of a man I know. He was born Spartiate; he went to war. He won two prizes for valour. When he returned to Sparta, he found his father had given up his kleiros.

148

"You see, this man's father had been passed over several times for men of less merit. He was offered a governorship for his kleiros. He agreed. Governors become rich quickly, and since it was possible to buy a kleiros, he thought it would be simple enough to acquire another.

"He did not become rich because, although he was a foolish man, he was a good man. He returned to Sparta without wealth. He no longer had a kleiros to provide his share of the food for his dining club, which meant that he ceased to be a Hall member, and not being a Hall member meant that he had no place in a permanent regiment, which meant he also had no vote in Assembly. He had become a not-quite-Spartiate. A lesser equal, it is called. There is even a term for such men now, although you won't find it in any of the rhetrae."

"What happened to the son? The one who was commended for valour?"

"He, too, is a lesser equal, being the son of one. The City took back his kleiros, so he hasn't the means to pay his dining-club share, and so on."

"Kinadon, you are the son, are you not?"

His eyes became dangerous. "If you are going to offer to intervene for me – do not. I warn you. Do not." I had been. "They have already tried to bribe me." He got to his feet. "A fool who thought I would use my allies for my own gain."

"Allies?"

"I stand with the dispossessed. To stand with them, I must be one of them." He came away from the fountain, and walked about as he spoke. "Now, as to what happened to the boy in your flock...his father was disenfranchised, no doubt...reduced to the ranks of lesser equals. This can happen in a number of ways." He spoke like a patrol leader. Probably he had been one.

"If a man will not sell for gain, he can be persuaded. No promotion for his son. No husband for his daughter. If he still refuses, he can be bastardized if his father is not alive to own him. Or he can be fined on false charges, so heavily that he must sell to pay."

"Who is the criminal? Those who abuse the law, or those who destroy them to restore it?"

His eyes blazed blue with a strange radiance. He joined me on the bench. "You understand!" (Poor Kinadon, always too

149

ready to believe in anyone who appeared to share his fervour).

"Another's words."

"Who?"

"A woman I do not know."

"The firebrand in Aulon?" He frowned. "She concerned herself only with Spartiates. Many are lesser but Spartiate."

"Do you not?"

He seemed to be looking at something very beautiful in the distance. "I want justice for everyone. Serfs. Up-country men. Everyone. True equals."

"Kinadon, you go too far. Let us concern ourselves with the equality of Spartiates."

"Us? Are you an ally, then?" His mockery was not unkind. "I think I have learnt why they want to set you aside, Young King. It is dangerous to walk with Justice in Sparta's broad streets now."

Kinadon taught me to wrestle. Not as he could, but better than I was. My mother raged when we dug a hole in the courtyard. I dare say we should have used a field at the back. I think she would have liked to consign Kinadon there altogether. Wrestling lessons always ended in an argument.

"Kinadon, the serfs are tillers. They could not have defended our frontiers six hundred years."

We scraped the earth of the wrestling-ground off us as we talked

"I commanded serfs in the Athenian war. They were good fighters."

"Chosen for their warlike natures. Like the men Brasidas commanded. Who were freed."

"What became of the men *I* commanded?"

"They serve with Derkyllidas in Asia. As free men."

He tipped up the water-jar and drank deep. "In Messenia, I heard that we honoured all two thousand of them. And then killed them."

"Kinadon, could a tenth part of that number be slain without all Sparta knowing of it? Would two thousand warriors quietly let themselves be slain without fighting?"

"The story was put about by Athenians during the war," he

allowed.

"Who tried to incite the Messenian serfs to rebel."

It was the closest Kinadon ever came to a smile. "I never truly believed it."

"But you tell it."

"It has its uses. I would free all the serfs. Not the fighters alone."

"Who would till the land? Slaves?"

The discussion had been good-natured. Nothing was ever light-hearted with Kinadon. He sat quietly and still. "Not slaves. When I was with the garrison in Athens I went about Attica. I saw the silver mines at Laurion and the quarries of Piraeus. And the slaves who work them. Once they go into the mines and the quarries, they never come out. Never see the light of day."

"How did you see them?"

"A friend and I went into the mines. Spartans went wherever they wished in Attica in those days. An upper slave showed us about. The mine slaves sleep on shelves. The stench... Excrement. Decaying corpses. The dead lie amongst the living dead. One man died when I was there. A spear-slave, Corinthian or Sikyonian. A Peloponnesian. Once he had been a warrior. I took him to be about sixty. He was twenty-five. Not slaves. Never slaves." His eyes took on the glow again. "Our army will free all slaves."

"There are no slaves in Lakedaimon, except a few owned by up-country artisans. They are in neither mines nor quarries."

"There are no frontiers to justice. I am Lakedaimonian. I will start with Lakonia."

"And put unwarlike serfs in arms to be taken by an enemy, and sold as slaves to join the poor wretches in the mines?"

Another time, we argued about the up-countrymen.

"They are Dorians like ourselves." Kinadon reached up and took a golden goblet from the tree. "Why deny them a place in Assembly?" He divided the sections of the fruit.

"They do not live under our law, nor wish to. Think you that they would take their sons from the fields to be reared in flocks? Or cease to marry their daughters too young? Or even trouble to walk the distance to the City on Assembly Day?"

"They must be forced to."

151

"They would not divide their land into equal portions. Nothing will stop their buying and selling."

"Young King, Spartiates also buy and sell land now."

"So you say, Kinadon. But you also tell Athenian tales you heard in Messenia."

"This is no Athenian fancy." He finished the golden apple, and wiped his fingers on his cloak. His eyes blazed into mine. "I know."

"I believe you were wronged. I think one or two other men also have been cheated of their birthright. It is a thing I would right. But that Sparta has foresworn her Law, I cannot credit."

One had to be with Kinadon in all things. He ceased to call. I was alone the day Assembly acclaimed Agisilaos King.

"The Apella was divided," Antalkidas said.

I was in a small, pleasant reading room when he arrived. The servants were accustomed to his coming and going, and showed him in.

"How can you know? Do you spend all your time between the Babykon and the Knakion?" It was easier to speak of trivia.

"Diopeithes spoke. He was your teacher once, was he not? He recalled to the citizens an ancient prophecy that Sparta would be destroyed by a lame king. Everyone thought Agisilaos was finished then."

"Everybody but Agisilaos, it seems."

"Lysander, whose knowledge of oracles is as limited as his ambition is limitless, had his own interpretation. He claimed the oracle referred to a bent sovereignty – that is to say, a king who is not unquestionably Royal Heraklid." He came close to saying what could not be said, and gulped down his wine, forgetting to savour it. "Lysander swayed them. I still regard you as my King."

"Assembly does not."

"Assembly reached a twice unlawful decision. Sparta did not send to the prophetess in Delphi to ask Apollo the meaning of the oracle. Nor was he consulted regarding the succession. The vote was taken before the god had spoken."

"The Council may set aside unlawful decisions."

"Be quiet and listen." He forgot I was his King. "Lysander

152

has a following in the Council. Now that Athens grows ambitious again, there are Elders who blame Pausanios. Do not look to the greybeards. What are you going to do?"

"I will not go into exile and raise an army."

"Quite right. No deposed king who took up arms against the City has ever been recalled." The pale eyes conferred with the gods. "But there are men who would take up arms for you here."

"Who are these men who would raise armies, but not their voices in a vote?"

"Those with arms, but without a vote. It is best if you do not know."

"Do *they* know?"

"Sometimes men need a cause to give direction to their just grievances. So I ask you again, what do you intend to do?"

In the bottom of my wine-cup, Achilles bent his knee and steadied his spear. "I don't know, Antal'; there is something I must know first."

Pausanios treated me as a son when I was a child. He was only a few years older than my mother, and one of the few people for whom she had good words. Yet he was not a man to lie with another's wife unless the man asked it of him, and my father clearly had not thought himself too old to beget a healthy son.

Once I had played with the idea that Kallikratidas was my blood-father, but that was childish dreaming. Like Pausanios, it was not in his nature, nor would his blood have rendered me unfit for the kingdom.

Had I been sired by a criminal? But sons are not guilty of their father's crimes. I knew it was not a serf. I hadn't the look of one. Although the Messenian serfs were Dorian, we had none here. An up-country man? The sculptor? Of all the boys in the flock, he chose me as his model.

Unlikely. At the time of my begetting, he would have been a grubby apprentice, and not the imposing figure who appeared on the heights. A deserter...What else? Deserters and their get were outcasts. I had seen one once, and backed away in repugnance from the foul-smelling creature dressed in bright rags; half his face bearded and half clean-shaven, as the Law decrees, so that their appearance will be as loathsome as their cowardice.

Had such a creature been...but my father had said the man was brave. And my fastidious mother would not have taken such a one into her bed. This was madness. A lunatic! Had they feared I would lose my wits like Kleomenes, who went mad from drinking uncut wine and chopped himself to bits? It had to be a lunatic.

"Who was he?"

Dromea's room under the eaves was small. My head brushed the drying herbs that hung from the ceiling.

I seated myself on a rush pallet, covered with a dry sheepskin and faded cushions that had once belonged to my mother.

"I am forbidden to tell you." She offered the wine-cup again.

"You know I would keep my silence."

"It was the doing of the gods."

"You, too, say Poseidon warned my father."

"Poseidon!" she smiled with gentle contempt. "Mistress made me put a poppy potion in Master's wine, to give him early sleep. Once, she told me to prepare it twice the strength. It took him unsteady on his feet. He thought the earth shook, and believed it an omen. How Mistress laughed."

"Why did she hate him?" I took the wine-cup. Set it down. "Was she truly an unwilling bride?"

"I was undressing her for bed the night her father told her she was to marry the king." Dromea leaned against a plain wooden table, searching the past in memory. "She was not unpleased to become a queen."

"Why then did she betray him?"

"Do not blame her. The man had Eros on his shield—"

His shield. A warrior at least. "This was not the work of Eros."

She tested one of the drying figs on the table with the point of a sharp knife. "I thought he was Apollo when I first saw him—"

"Another god! How did my father learn of it?"

"It was those prattling maids." Her gentle face showed a rage of which I thought her incapable. "Mistress said your name was Leotychides, but that it should have been – his."

"You will not tell me what that name is?"

"We must not speak of it." She pulled up a three-legged stool, seated herself opposite me, and took my hands in hers. "They say it shamed the City, but I know not why. He was like a god." Her eyes softened and glowed.

"Did she tell anyone other than her women?" Perhaps I might learn more there.

"Her sister. The other Queen."

Eurydame! My aunt babbled without a thought to what she was saying, but Pausanios would have secured her silence now. "She might as well have shouted it from the top of the acropolis!"

"She was young and mad with grief when he left."

"I am going mad with wondering. Was he a lunatic?"

"Never such. He was a guest-friend to the King."

"Guest-friend? A *foreigner?*"

"He looked a man of Sparta after he shaved his beard and grew his hair long, and put away his fine robes. Folk said he was a true son of Lykourgos."

No foreigner was hard enough to earn that name. "What was his city?"

"Athens."

"Athens!" I leapt up at the word. Apollo, this was too much. "By all the gods, why couldn't I have been left unborn?" We were at war with Athens at the time of my birth. The ransom prisoners who were quartered in the palace! It would be one of them. "Philon!" That lecherous old man, with his dyed beard and his hero-tales. "A merchant..." I do not know when I seized the knife. Nor whether I meant to turn it on myself.

"Not so. Not so. He was a great man in his city."

"Then another of the captives. What matter?"

Dromea was on her feet. "Have I not told you the man was gone before you were born?" She tried to prise the knife from my hands. "He was a ruler or a grand admiral or something great." Her hands were strong. Mine stronger. The knife point pricked my chest. "My little Leo', don't. Don't. He was the one called Alkibiades."

155

My mother sat, motionless. Her arms rested on the ram's-head arms of the chair. She was alone in the room opening to her bed-chamber. The only sounds came from outside; cicadas, birds crying their farewell to day. The pots of eye-paint on the griffon-legged table, the ivory comb, and the muse-handled mirror were idle, as the last rays of the departing sun struck Aphrodite's statue in its niche.

Her hands – those restless hands, always gesturing, playing with an arm-ring, rummaging through chests –lay folded in her lap. "You know." It was not a question. "Dromea told you." No anger sparked her toneless voice.

"All Sparta knows. Dromea is loyal to you."

"Forgive me, Leotychides." The blue-grey aftermath of the sunken sun made her a dark silhouette.

"Let blame pass with the past."

"You have his beauty, but not his magic. His one flaw the gods transformed into a gift."

"Flaw?" Was there still more to know?

"He could not speak the letter *rho*. When he said krater, it came out kwater." The shade of a smile touched her lips. I recalled the creased brow of Pausanios when I lost my front milk teeth. "It was charming, and other men copied it."

"Mother, I have forgiven you."

A touch of the old fire kindled the toneless voice. "You think I ask your pardon for giving you, for a father, the most beautiful and brilliant man among the Hellenes!" The old evasiveness intruded itself as well. "It was for some thoughtless words that may have harmed you."

(I learnt later that Alkibiades, too, had spoken quite openly of the matter. It is a wonder that, with the blood of such a notorious pair of chatterers in my veins, I am known as a man of few words).

"They said that he loved wine and luxuries too well," she went on quietly. "But he took to our ways, as though he had been born to them. Whatever the strongest men in Sparta could do, he did as well or better, and none would deny it."

"That does not concern me." But I listened.

"He was of the highest birth in Athens," she went on.

156

"That is of no interest to me."

"His cousin Perikles was guest-friend to King Archidamos."

"He betrayed a guest-friendship."

"Did Zeus not take the place of Amphytrion?"

Could she see herself as Alkmena? "Alkibiades was no god. And no god who loves this city brought him here."

"He came to Sparta because his enemies in Athens were jealous of his youth and brilliance, and laid false charges against him. Sparta did well when she followed his counsel. It was Alkibiades who persuaded the ephors to seize and fortify the Dekeleia."

"And to send out the Eurypontid King as commander?"

"He was ever a man who could achieve many purposes with one." The eyes, the voice, remembered things, not of my knowing. "And he could have been ours."

"Where was his friendship to Sparta when he intrigued for Athens with Tissaphernes?"

"It was Agis who turned him from us." Her voice hardened on the name. "Alkibiades gave us wise counsel. Agis opposed him. Alkibiades won great battles for us. Agis hated him. Alkibiades was becoming the greatest man in Sparta. Because of Agis he had to flee the City. Agis turned his love of Sparta back to Athens."

"Better had he remained a lover of his own city."

"He had the Athenians on his knees, begging him to return." Was she even speaking to me?

"They banished him after Notion."

"Such a people are unworthy of a man like that. The Thebans were right. Athens should have been destroyed."

Even today, there are men who debate whether Alkibiades was devoted to his city, or solely to his ambitions; but surely his love of Athens must have been great to arouse this violent jealousy in my mother.

Servants came in to light the lamps. I saw she was weeping. Her hands remained folded. The servants withdrew. "I have long wanted to tell you these things. To let you know the nature of your true father." The two small rivers continued their silent flow down her passive face, undisturbed.

"My true father is Agis, the son of Archidamos, who owned me his son and heir." I, the fruit of a liaison that had caused the husband so much pain, the King such shame.

She misunderstood. "To the world you must be that." At last, the hand moved. Brushed the wet cheeks. She became brusque and practical. "You need not trouble yourself about Lysander. The darkest gods of the underworld will seal his fate."

"What are you saying?"

"I invoked them when he had my lover murdered."

"Alkibiades was slain by barbarians."

"Pharnabazos had reason to please Lysander, and Lysander to dread Alkibiades. Yet I believe, above all else, he knew he could never be the greatest commander in Hellas whilst Alkibiades lived." She rose in a cloud of spicy scent. Her face assumed the fearsome beauty of the Furies. "Lysander, who would be great above all other men, shall be cast down." She chanted like a priestess. She was a priestess. Both queens were royal priestesses. "He who lives for glory shall die a little death." Light from flickering lamps played across her upturned countenance. "His bones will lie in foreign earth."

"Mother, you brought no death-curse on my father? Did you?"

Her strange smile played with me. "Of which father do you speak?"

"Madam, I speak of your husband."

She made me wait. The green eyes bore into mine. Then she gave a small, dry laugh. "I would rather Agis had lived until you were of age." She began her lioness-prancing. "But what do we do about you *now*?"

Had it been only today Antalkidas put that to me? I had hoped to find an answer in my blood-sire's name, but that uncovered only more uncertainty. Apollo, tell me what to do. Give me a sign.

"I had despaired of Agis owning you, and made my friends among his enemies." She paused briefly. Her long nails tapped against a bronze-bound chest. "This year's ephors are Lysander's, but we shall see better men elected next year."

"What men?"

"Those who oppose him in principle. And those of no principle who will oppose him for gain. I can buy men as well as he. I have been acquiring land for years against this day."

A thought played across my mind, like a dimly remembered

chord. "Land? What land? Where? In the Eurotas Vale?"

"Where else? Would I buy scrub-hills?"

"How did you buy land, Mother, when none may be sold?"

"Epitadeus changed the law. You are too young to remember." It had not been Kinadon's delusion. "You must visit guest-friends...The King of Macedon – no, remain in Hellas. The Archon of Syracuse? The Prince of Pherai? Nearer. The Peloponnesos. Tegea or Corinth..."

She went on, while my thoughts beat like bird's wings inside my head, until I felt I was drowning – as I had the day Aristokrates held my head under the water of the lake, and shouted "You *foreign* bastard." The word so carefully buried by my unaware will burst through the years.

"Mother–" She whirled about. "Sparta might suffer a bastard on the throne, but not a half-Athenian bastard."

"That–" She made an airy gesture. "Do you think the men who voted for you are unaware of that?"

"They believed my father."

"Some, perhaps. *Agis* knew."

That much was certain. My father had known, yet he left the kingdom to me. Aware of the wild and reckless blood that came to me from both sides, he had passed over Agisilaos for me. Whether as the better of two bad horses, or for some quality of my own, he had given me the throne of Sparta.

"The Agiads will support you," she continued. "And my close kin amongst the Eurypontids. Agis's friends. Lysander's enemies. And his false friends. Once-bought men can be twice bought." Triumph lit her eyes like the flickering flames in the lamps. "Leotychides, our faction will swell and shake Sparta like a trembling of the earth."

The god had heard me. He sent his sign. "I charge you, Leotychides, do not let the City divide," my father had said. The half-Athenian bastard was a better Spartan than Agisilaos. He knew how to obey.

Halfway to Pellana, I threw my sandals in a wood.

159

Chapter 6

Frowning with concentration, my scribe quick-marches his stylos across the fair copy of this account.

The king wishes to see the work as far as it has progressed. Now the tutor arrives, and asks whether I might have the scribe set down the whole of the rhetrae for him! (There are not many; where there is good law, there is no need for a clutter of laws to confuse men's minds, and bring on a plague of pleaders).

I recite the rhetra forbidding the writing of the Law, Lykourgos having decreed that it be committed to memory, so as to shape the spirit and not become dead words on dusty scrolls. He reflects a moment, and is on his way. I had reached Kinadon's plot and its aftermath – how compelling the past becomes – and might have drawn some conclusions, had it not been for the intrusion.

As it now stands, I have briefly summarized those events in the last years of the Athenian War. Of which I had no personal experience. I considered excluding them altogether (although such scruples did not deter Herodotos), but to omit these matters would be to present a fact without a reason. If there is such a thing as a fact. Perhaps there are only many reasons which make a truth. Sometimes.

One might do better to say that, for four hundred years, Sparta gave Hellas a model of dignity, good order and freedom and then... But it is the *and then* this purports to recount. And that leads back to facts and reasons.

161Of my own part in these events, I find I have done nothing as yet except lose the kingdom to Agisilaos. Of this, I merely set down that, after a succession dispute, the son of King Agis was passed over for the King's brother unlawfully.

Philippos looks grim. Perhaps the plot was an unfortunate

note to end on. When I read out the passage concerning the trial of Pausanios, he looked offended. Pausanios was not offended.

"Have kings of Sparta no power whatsoever?" the Macedonian demanded.

"Most certainly not," I assure him.

The dinner is not in the great hall tonight. Only the King, his son and a few of the younger, more civilized nobles are present. Is it to keep down the din? Or discretion concerning the secret endeavour they are planning? In Sparta, where men talk less, everyone would know about it.

"The plot to slay the Kings..." Philippos begins.

"Not the Kings alone."

"The leader of the conspiracy – he was guilty?"

"He was guilty and innocent."

"Perhaps–" The tutor is silenced by a motion of the King's hand. Philippos does not want to pass the night defining guilt and innocence.

"Kinadon was condemned solely on the word of an informer."

What do such niceties matter here? Philippos arbitrarily convenes an Assembly whenever he wants to execute a man. The man speaks. The King speaks. The tribesmen vote to please the King.

"But you believe him innocent?" The blue-green eye bores into mine. He recently lost one in battle.

With that sublime trust he had in everyone who agreed with him, Kinadon took another man into his confidence. Everyone knows of the notorious informers of Athens, the first, always, to be torn limb from limb in any of that turbulent city's overturns. How could there be such a creature in Sparta, where the Apella meets in the open, and men are taught to speak their minds?

Yet that was what the man proved to be. He reported that Kinadon took him to the agora one day, when the Council met, and pointed out the Elders, the two Kings and a few rich men, and called them enemies. The other men who happened to be there – citizens, up-country artisans and serfs – he named his allies.

The spy claimed, further, that Kinadon told him that soldiers, like themselves, would use their war weapons on their victims on the appointed day; that with them were serfs and up-country

162

men, who would turn their scythes and sickles and axes into effective killing instruments on unsuspecting men. But he would say no more. Only that he had his orders. The invention of a police agent? Yes and no.

Every village had its troublemakers, generally men without land or craft. When men trade and sell their birthright, there are always those with nothing. In Athens, they are the majority.

So some drunken serfs and up-country louts inspired by greed, blood-lust, or the fiery invective with which Kinadon drew attention to himself in the first place...hardly more than that, except in the mind of the informer and that of Kinadon himself. A few strayed seeds of truth...but that attention to orders, the careful delineation of Kinadon's authority, bespoke a Spartiate design.

Kinadon planned a rebellion, but not the blood-bath reported by the informer and made public by the ephors. That was no part of his vision. After a neat dispatching of the enemy, Kinadon would have expected his followers to quietly put down their sickles and axes, and disperse. Champion of serfs and up-countrymen, Kinadon was Spartiate. He assumed they would obey.

Philippos is still awaiting a reply.

The ephors acted without consulting the emergency Committee of the Assembly. There was nothing written in Kinadon's hand. No man accused him except the spy. No man had been brought to trial before solely on another's accusation. But it served its purpose. People talked about the trial. Not the succession.

I have touched upon another sore point. Philippos was not next in succession when he seized his kingdom.

"Surely the matters were connected."

I cannot but laugh. "Kinadon would not take up arms on behalf of any king. Although the manner in which the succession was decided may have hardened his resolve."

"But he did conspire," the King's son insists. He is a bright lad. By Macedonian standards his manners are good. His Greek is flawless.

"He never denied that."

He implicated only himself. The ephors gave out that he revealed everything when he was questioned, but they were never able to learn the date set for the rising, or the names of his colleagues. Given Kinadon's nature, he undoubtedly shouted his own part defiantly, but nothing more.

Months of arrests turned up only some frightened serfs; and a few up-country louts – who knew little, and that from someone well down in the hierarchy of the conspiracy. Finally, the names of a handful of the leaders emerged. Distinguished names like Tisamenos...

Tisamenos, descended from Eleieans who had been the only two foreigners ever to be given Spartan citizenship. Tisamenos, who had the gift of prophecy. What dark future had he seen, that caused him to cast his lot with the conspirators?

"If he wasn't the other King's man, why did he plot?" Philippos demands. Macedonian successions are usually decided by one claimant murdering the other.

"The ephors asked him that. He replied that it was in order to be equal to the best man in Sparta."

They do not understand.

"The rulers cannot have been very certain of their strength, to send a cavalry regiment to arrest a few rebels," the King's son declares.

"Did you see the woman?" the King asks, his eye glittering. What an incurable lecher he is.

I think of three wagons in the Pellana road. The dust raised by horses' hooves. The setting sun. The prisoners standing. The woman in the lead wagon; tall, small-breasted and willowy, like those maidens who are such good jumpers. She was very, very beautiful.

"I saw her once from a distance. I doubt if Kinadon ever spoke to her."

"Then these people from – what was it – Aulon? They were not part of the plot?"

Kallias had thought not.

It was one night when we were coming away from a dining-hall. The talk had all been of Kinadon. I glimpsed Antalkidas, and ran towards him to ask him this or that. He might not have been the mover of events he fancied himself, but he had a way

164

of knowing things other youths did not. At my approach, he hastened his steps, and immersed himself deeply in conversation with a companion.

Someone called my name. I turned back. Kallias motioned to the edge of the path. I thought he meant Anaxandros, but he broadened the sweep of his arm to include us all. His regiment was ordered to arrest the Aulon party.

"I cannot believe they were involved," he said. "She is of good family. There were no ruffians at her meetings." He ruffled Anaxandros's hair. "Keep this to yourself, Little Magpie."

The King repeats his question.

"Does it matter? They died. At least the Aulon leaders were permitted the dignity of the poisoned cup."

The tutor's voice reaches me from a spears-length behind. Again I have thoughtlessly stridden ahead, while he keeps pace with the torch-bearers.

"The King's nephew concerns him." He lowers his voice, although the Thracian slaves cannot understand us. This nephew Amyntas is the rightful King, whom Philippos deposed when the young man was a child.

I reply this or that.

"The Prince picked up the point concerning the cavalry regiment quickly." He is inordinately proud of his pupil "Not many boys of his age would recognise the overplay of strength as a sign of fear."

"That was not my meaning."

"Two guilts do not add up to an innocence."

"Two...?"

"You did mean to infer that the man Kinadon was condemned by men no less guilty than himself?"

"Oh...yes...that..."

Sphodrias disappeared the day Kinadon died. He returned to Pellana just after the evening meal, his face pallid in the light early-autumn evening.

"I saw it," he said. "They lashed Kinadon through the streets of Sparta. There was a large crowd. Even the deserters were out, and no one bothered to beat them. *They* jeered him more than any of the others. His hands were stuck through a wooden yoke about his neck, and his cloak was blood-red from the lashes. It made it look like a warrior's cloak. And he walked like a soldier. He didn't even try to duck the lashes." I could picture those compelling eyes blazing through Sparta like a flaming sword.

"I think people felt ashamed after too much of it. Everyone started going quiet. Even the women. When the deserters saw they were the only ones still shouting, they melted away before anyone turned on them...Hades take it, Kinadon made you feel he was the best man there."

I could not sleep that night, and stepped over the rows of sleeping boys to take my tangled thoughts to the river.

The light step of bare feet pressed the dew-wet grass. A shadow fell across the rushes. Doreius sat down beside me, and threw his arm across my shoulders. Artemis lifted the bronze-shield moon above the mountains.

We sat silently, listening to the chirping things of night, as the star-flecked Eurotas whispered between its rush-strewn banks.

When the waking birds announced impending dawn, Doreius said, "Go to bed, Leotychides, and do not wake the other boys."

I stood, my muscles stiff from sitting so long motionless, and waited. When Doreius did not rise to come with me, I walked towards the sleeping place. I looked back once.

Doreius was still sitting, elbows on knees, staring into the river...

"Who was responsible for the manner of the conspirator's death?" the tutor is asking. "Lysander?"

"Lysander had his faults. But he killed clean." I halt on the path. The pedagogue's sigh of relief is covert and amusing as he catches his breath. "Kinadon's conspiracy came at a time when there was a land seizure such as few cities have known." Greed had infected Lakedaimon, like one of those fevers soldiers pick up in Asia. The locals are not affected, but it ravages those who have always breathed clean air. "The odd thing is that, after the executions, no one seemed to link the trials to it...rather as if the blood-letting had purged Sparta of its ills. Two months later it

166

was all forgotten. Although the flesh had not entirely rotted off their bones in the Kaidas, conspirators and conspiracy might never have been. Sparta had forgotten. I had forgotten...

"You must have been very young."

Atop the acropolis, between the Bronze House and the temple of Aphrodite of war, at the very edge of the steep incline overlooking the blue-white limestone dancing-floor, is a seat fashioned by nature of two stones.

Hekataios plopped on the ground beside my "chair." "Has it started?"

"Just."

The rounded peaks of the lower mountains of Taygetos separated from the highest, snow-capped ridges, as the sun rose and struck the new, bronze shields of the dancers. Harps and lyres and flutes intensified. The dancers stepped forward, swung their shields in unison, and locked them.

A hired dance master, Athenian naturally, won a prize for a dance copied from our dance for Apollo. It was quite good, but no paid dancer can capture the splendour of young Spartiates dancing for the god before they became warriors.

Patterns formed, changed, re-formed in different shapes, all in perfect symmetry, to the stately vibrance of the music. It seemed a very short time before Apollo brought the sun directly overhead. The new warriors raised their shields to salute the god. The dance ended.

"Doreius was the best."

"He wasn't, Cockerel."

"His back was straight as a spear."

"That fellow with the Dorian hair leapt higher."

"You are not to leap higher than the others."

"Then why are you considered such a fine dancer for your leaps?" The heel of my palm went forward to shove him. I recalled the steepness of the incline an instant before tragedy.

"Antalkidas was second-best." he continued, as we got to our feet.

"Do you find that surprising?"

A priest scowled at our too-loud laughter, as we passed the

Bronze House of Athena.

"Cockerel, do you think the war will last long enough for us to be in it?"

"What war?" We ran through the limestone colonnade, between the Victories Lysander raised to commemorate his triumphs at Notion and Goat River; two young goddesses, wings outstretched, and held up by eagles. "It's all rumours."

There had been talk that the Great King of Persia was secretly building war-ships.

"Haven't you heard?" The Persian triremes have been sighted afloat. A great barbarian fleet."

Like the sun on the new, bronze shields, the vision of Kallikratidas shone before me. Kallikratidas was dead, but Pausanios would realize the noble dream. Pausanios, at the head of an army of all the Hellenes, joined in friendship to march against the barbarians. How small were other concerns in comparison.

Yes, we were very young...

*   *   *

Pausanios was cheated of his command.

With the Persian fleet menacing Hellenic waters, it was no longer a question of if, but when, a confrontation would take place. Sparta hosted a conference of the cities of Greece, which voted to send an army to Asia on the sound principle that, if war is inevitable, it is better waged in the enemy's territory than one's own.

Sparta was, as always, war leader. My father had claimed command of the Eleian expedition. It was the turn of the Agiad King. Pausanios had reigned more than ten years, Agisilaos less than one. Lysander spared neither effort nor influence in securing the command for the junior king. That is to say, for himself.

The Hellenic forces assembled at the port of Geraistos in Euboia. Every city was bound by treaty to send a contingent. Athens, that self-proclaimed champion of her Ionian brothers in

168

the cities of Asia, declined. The Argives and the Corinthians also refused to commit their troops.

The Argive default was unsurprising. Argive hostility to Sparta goes back to the end of the Bronze Age. The Achaian kings of the Argolid ruled most of the Peloponnesos and the Dorian Argives fancy themselves heirs to their empire. Sparta's leadership of the peninsula has always been a bitter draught in Argive throats.

The defection of Corinth was another matter altogether. Corinth was an old ally. A proud and fiercely independent city, which had voted against us more often than any other in those conferences of Peloponnesian allies.

Sparta and Corinth were like two old friends, whose frequent and spirited differences of opinion only strengthen ties based on mutual respect. But since Lysander paid Apollo's tithe from the spoils of our allies, the amity had cooled.

In the dining-halls, men muttered that the Corinthians were being accursed petty about their spoils from the Long War, considering that we had become involved in that struggle on their behalf. Self-righteousness is often the first resort of the shameful.

Then Agisilaos had a dream...and Thebes withdrew as well.

In his dream, a voice spoke to my uncle, and told him that he was the first king since Agamemnon to lead a force of all the Hellenes against Asia. It was a somewhat absent-minded voice, as it forgot the absence of the Athenians, the Argives and the Corinthians.

The vision of himself as Agamemnon inspired Agisilaos to further emulate the Bronze Age King, and he decided to sacrifice at Aulis in Boiotia, as Agamemnon had when he invoked divine intervention for a wind to blow his ships to Troy.

Well, not precisely. Agamemnon sacrificed his virgin daughter. These being more civilized times, Agisilaos substituted a hind. There were current jests that his daughters were unacceptable, but Eupolia and Prolyta were far too small and plain to inspire any man to illicit defloration.

The royal dreamer arrived in Boiotia, bringing his own priests. Like a great king amongst subjects, rather than a guest in foreign parts, he set up an altar, and prepared to sacrifice without consulting either the rulers or the priests of the land.

Thebes sent messengers hot-foot to Aulis, to order Agisilaos to desist. They arrived to find the altar set up, with the sacrificial animal already smoking upon it. Showing remarkable restraint for that volatile people, the Theban emissaries simply requested him to halt the ceremony. Agisilaos-Agamemnon, Great King of Dreams, with imperial disdain, ordered his priests to continue.

At this, the Thebans were so offended that they seized the hind from the altar, and scattered the burning pieces on the ground. Having estranged another ally, Agisilaos limped off in high dudgeon and, putting Boiotia behind him, set sail for Geraistos – having conceived a deep and abiding hatred of Thebes, for which Sparta and all Hellas were to pay dearly.

Had I been told the name of my blood-father in my childhood days in the palace, I should have been proud as Polydeukes or Herakles on learning they had been sired by Zeus. The poets do not tell us the feelings of their name-fathers on the matter, but their verses would lead us to believe that neither Tyndaraios nor Amphitryon were disquieted.

The days were long past since I confused Alkibiades with the divine heroes. He was a mortal, a foreigner, the most talked-about man of his day – and my feelings were ambivalent, their ambivalency not the least distressing aspect of them.

I could never entirely suppress a certain inner excitement when men spoke of his courage, his brilliance, and his wit; and – dead though he was – men still spoke of him, still do. It is difficult to envisage a time when people will not talk about Alkibiades.

On such occasions, I blamed myself for disloyalty to my father. When the other side of Alkibiades was discussed – Alkibiades the devious, the luxurious-living Alkibiades, the empire designer – I assured him that, as the son of Agis, it touched upon me in no way whatever.

On my return to the flock, no one questioned. No one commented. I reported to Doreius. He ordered me to take charge of my patrol, and turned to his other concerns. It was as if my brief reign had never been. But it had.

I could not look at a flock-brother without asking myself "Does he know?" Aristokrates's "foreign bastard," of course, came from Pharax, who had it from Lysander. Gossip, not certainty. Yet while I laughed with my friends, and exchanged gibe for gibe, the unanswered question was ever in my mind, like a shade between us.

When I fell under suspicion during the Kinadon matter, the true showed the depth of their friendship – and they were the many, not the few. Would they have been, had they known? And in some confused, obscure manner, Kinadon himself came into it. Although we did not speak of it any more.

We were digging the earth for a boxing-ground, when I received a message in my mother's bold handwriting. Agisilaos had seized my private inheritance. He gave half to Peisander, so as not to appear acquisitive.

Wealth has no meaning to me. In the days I was king, I never troubled to learn how many running-horses, chariots or whatever, my father had owned. I still had my kleiros. My father's recognition ensured that I was legitimate and full Spartiate.

The loss of the kingdom I accepted as the will of the citizens of Sparta; this petty theft enraged me. Often it is trivial injustice that causes great upheavals, while great injustice provokes mere apathy. As I read the message, they finished digging and watering the ground. Pityas called out to me that he had drawn my name in the lots.

I remember throwing the message down. I remember walking to the boxing-ground. I remember facing Pityas. Then all memory ceases, save Doreius shouting, "Stop, Leotychides! Stop this instant. You are killing Pityas."

As the Law-giver forbade submission, in games as in battle, Lakedaimonian boxing is straightforward. Fell your opponent, and you have won. My mind cleared. I found I had deliberately kept my friend on his feet so that I might continue savaging him.

That day I recalled the other inheritance. The unspoken, unspeakable one. I determined to conquer this angry, defiant mixture of my mother and Alkibiades, and truly be the son of Agis – even before Doreius had me thrashed.

171

The next time I faced an opponent on the boxing-ground, it happened again. Doreius matched me with eirens to the age of nineteen. I savaged them all. In the end, he forbade me to box with any youth but himself. I could never best Doreius.

Doreius finished his year as Commander, and became a young warrior. By this time, the Asian expedition had been decided. Every young Spartan wanted to be part of it, although there were few places for young warriors on Lysander's staff of thirty officers. It was the King's staff, but everyone referred to it as Lysander's.

It was no surprise that Doreius was one of the few selected to go to Asia. Neither, on reflection, was the inclusion of Antalkidas.

I turned sixteen in the month of Artemision, and became an eiren. With the appointment of the new Commander, the ban on boxing was lifted. I resolved to restrain myself, but again lost all control. Like Doreius, the Commander intervened and challenged me himself. He was an even better boxer than Doreius. I bested him.

Unlike Doreius, he did not re-impose the ban. He kept me on as leader of my patrol, but told me to take all the time I wanted to train in the gymnasium, in the City. Perhaps it was because he was of a different turn of mind from Doreius. Perhaps it was because we were approaching an Olympic year.

I was no longer the best boxer in the flock. I was the best boy boxer in all of Sparta. And I would take this unconquered, all-consuming rage as a gift of the gods, and forge it into an olive crown.

Thermon was a big, square, ginger-haired man in his thirties. He had won a laurel crown boxing in the Pythian Games, and taken prizes in the Isthmia. It was he the Commander approached to gain me permission to train for Olympia.

"It is against custom," Hekataios grumbled the first day I set off to the City, in the still-dark dawn.

"Winning is a Spartan custom, Hek'." Sparta had many

172

winners when men of all cities trained only the two months in Olympia.

"Foreigners train a year ahead of an Olympiad now," Anaxandros joined in. "In their own cities. That is why they win."

Hekataios pointed meaningfully. Clouds obscured the last paling stars. "An omen! No good comes of breaking custom, Leotychides."

Like many boxers, Thermon had a squashed nose. So many that I took the precaution of attaching a nose-guard to my boxing helmet.

I was convinced that my special gift was all I needed for Olympia. Thermon challenged me to a match with his left hand tied to his side, to balance the disparity in years and weight. He bested me swiftly. All the young warriors who were gathered about us roared with laughter.

I was the only Spartiate boy boxer training for the Olympiade, although there were some up-country boys who prepared in their own villages, if at all. Again, the Athenians were to blame. They produced a new type of boxer, trained from early childhood for the Games, although he might not be good for much else in life.

Surrounded by mocking warriors, I felt rather like a seven-year-old in a flock. Thermon had not meant the lesson unkindly. It was well-intended – like advising me to wet my straps, so that the leather would harden and give better support to my wrists and hands.

He was showing me some tricks the boxers in Olympia try on their rivals one day, when the man Meleas came up.

I was under some obligation to this person for saving my helmet from some young men, who were offended by the nose-guard. He had come into the changing-room just as they were about to take it apart, and ordered them to give it back to me.

"Why shouldn't the boy protect his beauty?" he asked. "It is beauty, in all forms, that brings men to what is good."

Someone asked whether that was a poem. He replied that it was something an Athenian wrestler said. "A good wrestler," he added.

Meleas was a thin-faced, dark, wiry man, who boxed with the boxers, wrestled with the wrestlers, ran with the runners, but

173

was entering a chariot in the lists. It was from overhearing him that I learnt that the Asian campaign was not an outstanding success. Nor was it a failure.

174Agisilaos appeared to be covering a lot of ground, and achieving little except a few skirmishes. To do him justice, we were weak in cavalry, and the barbarians are strong in horse.

He brought his forces into Ephesos for winter quartering and, in that Ionian city, called up more men for the spring campaign. To build up the cavalry, he excused any man from war duty who would supply a mounted substitute with full panoply. Again, Agamemnon...?

This Meleas was remarkably well-informed, and men always asked for news. He was also respected. They asked his opinion as well.

Now he invited Thermon to the midday meal the following day. In an afterthought, he included me in the invitation. It was the house near the other racing course, he told me. By the statue of Herakles.

He swerved his spirited mount about, his thighs gripping it tightly, his back straight.

"He rides well."

"Meleas? He is one of the best soldiers in Sparta. Commended for valour in the Long War. Pausanios gave him another prize for bravery in action at Piraeus. His chariot never wins in the Games. Good fellow. But a deadly bore when he gets on to politics."

I stood by the statue of Herakles, thinking myself the victim of another jest. Here was nothing but the walls of the Menelaos House, and the racing course in front of it. Then it struck me that he had meant the Menelaos House, and I knew who this Meleas was.

One of his ancestors had brought the house with spoils from the last Messenian war. His was a family that had produced a fine soldier in every generation. Meleas owned more running-horses than any man in the city.

A very dignified old servant opened the gate.

The ancient palace was centred about a great square room with patterned marble floors, overlooked by a gallery on an upper level. The walls were painted. Unlike the house in Herea, these paintings were dim with age. I recognised Apollo by his golden hair, as he threw the discus with Hyakinthos. An almost invisible Eurydike followed Orpheus from the House of Hades.

The heroes of the Trojan War lived when this house was built. Helen had lived there. Perhaps the Twin Gods stood in this very room, when they called upon their beautiful sister, the walls ringing with their laughter, as Kastor recounted how he had tamed a wild horse, or Polydeukes told her about besting his opponents. Polydeukes the Boxer Twin, Polydeukes, son of Tyndaraios, son of Zeus...

"They seem to grow dimmer every year." Meleas came in. I had been staring at the outlines of an old fifty-oared galley. The Argo? "I considered having an artist restore the colours. But the hand would not be the same. Perhaps it is better to let things fade untouched in their purity..."

Meleas often spoke as if his words had a meaning within a meaning, I found as we took of the midday meal. That is, when Thermon let him talk at all. Whenever Meleas touched on matters of the City, Thermon turned the talk to Games. When Meleas regretted the waste of keeping a commander like Derkyllidas in Sparta, Thermon contrived to link it to his own single-handed slaying of a boar! It was an interesting tale, but I fancied Meleas had heard it before.

The sun flowed generously into the room. Soft-footed servants filled our cups the instant they emptied, without the slightest gesture from their master.

The meal laid out on the tables looked the usual; bread, cheese, olives and figs. The taste was anything but ordinary. So subtle was the seasoning that it surpassed anything served at Corinthian banquets, although I knew nothing of Corinthian banquets then.

Thermon warned Meleas that the Athenians would ruin the chariot racing next. Meleas considered that it was harder to over-train horses than men. Thermon regretted that Lykourgos had not foreseen this practice when he founded the Games with Iphitos. The Athenians, Hades take them, were imposing their ways on the Games, as they had once forced their customs on half Hellas.

It was Meleas, this time, who turned the talk back to Games. His comments were so pointed that, for all their subtle meanings, it was obvious that I had not been invited as an afterthought. I was present so that he could dissuade me from entering the lists for the boxing.

"Let our youths run in the stadion," he said. "No boy has ever died from losing a race."

"Would I train a lad who would not win?" Thermon burst out.

My heart leapt. I knew by this time how much I had yet to learn, but Thermon had never indicated that he would consider training me. Thermon, the best boxer in Sparta, believed I would win.

Thermon was here to be discouraged as well. Who was this Meleas to intervene? What right had he? As in the succession dispute, and the seizure of my inheritance, my youth precluded me from speaking on my own behalf, as the two men argued it.

Before I left, Meleas took me into the courtyard. Rosemary, basil, mint and other sweet-scented herbs grew in the corners amongst plants that flower in summer. A straight row of pomegranate trees gave shade to marble benches. Everything was so arranged that the very shadows fell in perfect symmetry. Helen's courtyard. I have always thought of it that way.

"Why do you disdain the stadion race?" Meleas asked.

"Sir, I am nothing great as a runner."

Sunlight reflected on the fountain, I was certain the servants remembered to change the water every day.

"There is almost a touch of spring in the air today," he said. "Spring is the beautiful season in the year...and in a man's life. I believe Lykourgos set the age for war at twenty, so that every youth could have his spring." His voice lashed like a whip.

"Why do you want to throw yours away on a boxing ground?"

"To be equal to the best man in Sparta, sir."

He looked at me long and enigmatically. "Are you certain you do not wish to be better?"

Whatever Meleas may have said to him after I left, Thermon undertook my training.

It was all too clear that, had I entered the lists unprepared, I should have been eliminated before the second lots were drawn, or at most the third. Polydeukes, son of Tyndaraios, might have vanquished all comers endowed only with his own strength, but Polydeukes was the son of Zeus. I was the son of Agis. Solely.

Sphodrias was in love.

He had still some months before he turned twenty, became a young warrior, and was permitted to marry. His beloved was sixteen, and not of lawful marriageable age until her seventeenth birthday.

"Twenty is young to marry," Kallias told him.

"Her father will refuse you," said Pityas, who had a sister. "She will go to him and smile, and say in a sweet, soft voice. 'This man's father was an ephor.' or 'That man was commended for valour.' It will be years before you have the use of your kleiros, Sphod', and no maiden wants to live with a husband's kin, unless she is so small and ill-favoured that no one else asks of her."

Sphodrias dismissed all these obstacles with a wave of his hand, and declared his intention of marrying the girl the first day he saw her.

A chance comment in Hall punctured his assurance. Someone mentioned that senior officers were in from Ephesos, to discuss the appointment of the new staff for the spring campaign in Asia. Sphodrias recalled that the expiration of the old staff's year coincided with the month of his Polydora's seventeenth birthday. His days were haunted by visions of the return of splendid crimson-cloaked warriors with tales of exotic lands and the aura of distant battles.

Sphodrias brooded for a time; then, ever a man of action, resolved to fortify his position for the enemy assault. In this case, the resolve was his. The action ours.

Hekataios was sent to stand on the path leading down to the hollow of the temple of Artemis Orthia, when the maidens went to dance for the goddess. Aristokrates, who was tone-deaf, had the task of attending a competition of maidens' choruses, in order to waylay the girl at the finish with some new tale of Sphodrias's daring, and so on.

It was in this way that I found myself watching a score of wrestling maidens, wondering in what not too preposterous manner I might detach Polydora from the rest long enough to tell her that Sphodrias had single-handedly disposed of a pack of wolves. Aristokrates, Hekataios, and I had been with him; but we did not count, not having passed out of the flock.

177

A fair number of men gathered to watch the competition. The indomitable Gorgo was wrestling. Her prowess at games often drew onlookers. While all eyes were on Gorgo, I sought a girl with hair the colour of an autumn leaf and iris-blue eyes, who sat with the losers. Sphodrias, being Sphodrias, had fixed his affections on the most beautiful maiden in Sparta.

"Someone catch your eye," I replied shortly

"Ah, the lovely Polydora..." Antalkidas wore his crimson cloak well. His hair had not grown to full warrior's length; but, being straight, it almost touched his shoulders. He was still too thin for his height, but he held himself with an air. He made a passing soldier.

Polydora moved. Was she leaving? No, only reaching for her peplos to cover her body against a chill breeze.

"Let me be the messenger," Antalkidas offered, as the girl stood to brush off the caked mud. "You are not betraying a confidence, Leotychides. Everyone is laughing about Sphodrias and his vain hopes."

Before I could halt him, Antalkidas made his way to the girl. Soon they were talking. Suddenly she smiled. I wondered whether he was betraying Sphodrias, and what he was doing in Sparta when he should have been in Ephesos with the army.

He returned with a rather muddy flower. "A love token." He gave it to me. "For Sphodrias. You see, he has been sending all of you to bore the girl with his various achievements. I told her, in some detail, his opinion of her charms. She found that much more interesting." He linked his arm through mine. "Now to serious matters."

I withdrew my arm and started away. "I am training."

"I saw your trainer setting off to the hot baths with his friends."

"I know where I am going."

"I doubt it. Leotychides. I am not going to do a sprint on this racing course to keep up with you."

"Hades take you, Antalkidas! You were content enough to keep a safe distance between us when Kinadon was arrested."

"That was dangerously close to the succession dispute."

"A friend is closest in danger. Or a craven."

The pale eyes drained of expression. "Never mistake me for a coward, Leotychides," he said quietly. "I'll risk my life for a

178

reason. But I'll not ruin my career for a gesture."

"Sometimes a gesture is a reason."

"I have never pretended to believe in everything we were taught in the flock. Had I been I born Athenian, I would fight for empire. Had I been Theban, I'd raid cattle. I am Spartiate. I act within the customs of my city, but I am still the same man I would be wherever I was born. Whatever that is, it is neither coward nor hypocrite. And, should you accept my friendship with all its limitations, your friend."

Replacing the memory of the hastily retreating figure was another, of a youth who came to the palace the day everyone else turned away.

"I cannot place limitations on friendship, Antalkidas."

"You must learn, my dear boy. You must learn." He grimaced and held up his forearm in front of his face. "Might we not stand somewhere out of this rain?" A downpour threatened to bring back winter with a vengeance. The slopes of the upper ridges of Taygetos were still white with snow. "The Persians would have a sheltered pavilion, but that great oak over there will do."

"I thought you were fighting barbarians. Not consorting with them."

"Diplomacy, my dear. We had to pretend to believe in that truce Tissaphernes offered, although we know he has secretly sent to the Great King for reinforcements."

"Why?" I shouted against the beating rain.

"To buy time to bring our cavalry up to strength." He sat down in the shelter of the wide-branched tree. "Some barbarians are quite pleasant. Tiribazos is an excellent fellow. Only a few years older than I, and definitely a rising man. One could tell that from the banquet Tissaphernes gave in his honour, when he came in from Susa." He went into some detail about the variety and tastiness of the food. The splendour of the eating and drinking vessels, the wine, the singing-girls and dancing-eunuchs. "With one of those petty, indirect phrases the barbarians use, Tissaphernes let us know the human delicacies were ours according to our tastes. That fool Doreius declined, and some of the other Greek officers followed his lead."

"Were the pleasure slaves Greek?"

"How not? But such scruples appeared a calculated insult to

our host. One cannot decline so much as a cup of wine without offending barbarians. I told the interpreter that the Sikyonian general was impotent, and that the Spartans, being unused to drinking wine, were temporarily incapable."

"What a rotten thing to say."

"Then the imbeciles made a liar of me, by going to the nearest brothel, and buying what they could have had as a gift."

When I stopped laughing, I said, "So your barbarian friends thought less highly of you when they found you lied."

"Not so. They esteemed me for saving everyone's face. I cannot think why those six fools preferred dear goods of inferior quality."

"I can," Perhaps a god told me that pity kills desire.

"You!" Amusement shaped his face. "What would you know of such things? You, who return men's gifts with cool, polite messages, and beautiful women's glances with indifference. You are sixteen. At your age I– but never mind my lurid youth."

"Would you have me another Euagoras?"

Since his features settled, Euagoras had become quite pretty, in his frail way, and his beautiful voice made him not a little sought-after. Usually, not in vain.

"There are other extremes. Really, I sometimes fear for your health."

"Antal, why are you in Sparta?"

"I am the wits the gods forgot to give my general – you remind me, if I leave him too long, he will commit some unspeakable blunder – but I had to speak to you before we return to Ephesos. Are you aware that Agisilaos is the most unpopular man in Sparta? People are saying the wrong man was made king."

"They had ought to have thought of that when they voted."

"Sulking is a futile policy."

"Antalkidas, we both know Agisilaos is nothing. It is Lysander who reigns."

"Then you don't *know*. Sit down, Leotychides. Sit *down*, Eiren. A warrior commands you." I obeyed. "Lysander and Agisilaos have quarrelled."

"Quarrels can be mended."

"A quarrel of that nature...I'll begin at the beginning. Agisilaos was brooding about the incident at Aulis when we set out. He left decisions to Lysander, as always. Wherever he went, there were crowds waiting to see the great Lysander: men seeking promotion; petitioners asking for this or that. Lysander received a constant stream of visitors, granting requests in the King's name – he has certain presence, in his wild-looking way. I often think the greater Aias must have looked like that. Even our own men said Lysander looked the King, and Agisilaos his servant.

"Was it ever different?"

"In the past, Lysander was the great man, and Agisilaos nothing. Now he is king, and his regality had already been affronted at Aulis." He found a twig in the wet grass, and started one of his aimless designs in the mud. "Agisilaos dropped Lysander a few hints of his displeasure. The first was a polite suggestion that petitioners speak to him directly. Lysander ignored it. To press the point further, Agisilaos began to refuse requests that came to him through Lysander. Anyone who approached him by that quarter came away empty-handed. Those who came to Agisilaos got what they wanted, and sometimes more." Rain effaced the pattern. Antalkidas tossed away the twig. "Lysander eventually understood, and warned his friends that his intercession did them more harm than good. Still, few took Agisilaos seriously. So he appointed Lysander his meat carver."

"His meat carver!"

"I didn't think he had it in him. Whenever Lysander's friends came to him with a request, he would say, 'Go ask my meat carver. See whether he can help you.' The master has taught the pupil too well. Lysander asked for an audience of Agisilaos – the old friendship had come to that. I made it my concern to be the junior officer on duty." The downpour slackened. Droplets fell from the leaves on to our heads. "Agisilaos was seated at a large table piled with scrolls. Shortly before Lysander was due, he asked me to have all the chairs removed." Antalkidas mimicked the soft, meek voice "'My dear Antalkidas, this room is cluttered. Would you have the servants remove all chairs but yours and my own?' He is always very polite to his subordinates, and he can be charming."

"You were charmed."

"Leotychides, I told you I detest prigs, and Agisilaos is king

181

of prigs, if nothing else. When Lysander came in, he started to greet Agisilaos warmly. But all he got was a cold glance, which froze him where he stood. And stand he did. Agisilaos tossed me a scroll and ordered me to draft a reply immediately, so that I would be unable to give Lysander my seat. Then he read two or more of the things on the table. You know how red in the face Lysander becomes. This time he was quite purple. Agisilaos finally looked up, and stared at him without a word. Lysander said 'Well, Agisilaos, you certainly have a way of putting your friends down.' 'Only when they would raise themselves above me.' Agisilaos snapped back. Then it was on. The reproaches, accusations, excuses. Lysander, the fool, reminded Agisilaos of all he had done to make him king. The last thing a man new to honours wants is to be reminded that he owes it to another. I think only then Lysander knew that the Agisilaos he raised up had become someone else."

Had he? In Thrace there are creatures that change the colour of their fur with the seasons, but it is the same animal inside.

Antalkidas went on. "The result was that Lysander fell back on self-righteousness, and asked Agisilaos only to send him somewhere he could be of use to Sparta. So Agisilaos appointed him ambassador to the Hellespont. A meaningless honour that sends him into obscurity. Sun broke through the lightened clouds to shine upon the acropolis, touching the gilded eagles supporting Lysander's marble Victories. "But he certainly stirred a hornet's nest in Sparta when he made an enemy of Lysander. The number of men who would fight for your rights–" It may have been my face he read this time. "Not Kinadon's rabble–"

"Those good men with just grievances?"

"That was rash of me," he admitted unabashed.

"Leotychides, the Lysandrians are calling for Agisilaos's blood."

"You think I would make common cause with Lysander?"

"When he dies, his cause dies with him. He is old. You are young, and your reign will be long."

"Let the Apella proclaim me king, and I'll be king." I got to my feet. "I must go."

"Not before you hear me out. Timing is the larger part of success. Agisilaos is despised now, but there is nothing better calculated to raise a man's popularity than a few victories. And he knows it. He has even passed over his friends, and appointed Derkyllidas and Herippidas to commands for the spring campaign; as well as that mercenary general – what is his name – Xenophon, who knows the terrain of Asia as we know Lakonia. He has taken on the whole of the fellow's army as well. Ten thousand men seasoned in fighting barbarians. With commanders like that, he cannot fail. And the kinglet is not incompetent himself. Leotychides, come to terms with Lysander, before Agisilaos has his victories."

"How little you know me, Antal."

He leapt up. "I know you too well. I only hoped you had grown up. I wonder why I bother with you."

"I, too, wonder."

He read my thought again, threw back his head, and laughed. "Not so, Leotychides. I don't need my friends to advance me. My enemies will do quite well."

"Antal," spoke Thermon's obedient pupil. "Political matters do not interest me."

"My dear Leo', you *are* a political matter." As he turned back to the City, he looked over his shoulder and called out, "You cannot outwit Fate, Leotychides."

Two days after Sphodrias was enrolled in the army, he was betrothed to Polydora. Usually, the wedding follows the betrothal in a month or so. Sphodrias married the girl seven days later.

Kallias learnt that Sphodrias was guest in a certain hall on the night of his wedding. Now that he was a warrior, Sphodrias sat with the men, but we could still enjoy the jesting. A young man must be quick to slip from his hall to his wife at any time. The Law-giver knew that desire thwarted is desire enhanced.

Sphodrias bore it all with his usual good spirits, although we knew his thoughts were on Polydora, who waited with a woman friend in a secret place – her hair cut short as a youth's and disguised in men's clothes, as is the custom for a mock elopement. I have never understood why, in foreign cities, weddings are made to appear an abduction. I have never really understood foreigners.

Even old Chairon, who was rising fifty, joined in the gibes, and warned Sphodrias that impetuosity had lost many a battle. Another man replied that delay lost more. Chairon had been paying his unmarried man's fine for nearly twenty years.

"Why was Sphod' in such haste?" Hekataios asked, when a gust of laughter was loud enough to drown the forbidden talk in the youths' places.

We found out a few days later. A ship docked at Gythion, disgorging the soldiers returned from Asia.

There was no training that Assembly Day. That morn, Sparta's citizens and the onlookers streamed towards the Assembly place, between the Babykon Bridge and the Knakion Stream. From my seat atop the acropolis, I watched them. The crimson cloaks, among the worn, looked like the first anemones of spring that dotted the fields.

The greatest victory so far had been diplomatic. And it was Lysander's. He had turned his appointment as ambassador to the Hellespont to effective use, by persuading the satrap Spithridates to desert the Great King, and ally himself to us. If Agisilaos thought he could discard his patron so easily, he had been mistaken.

The warrior passed the Bronze House without stopping. I leapt to my feet as he approached. "Doreius!"

His hand on my shoulder pulled me down again. "Hek' said I would find you here."

His short sword hung jauntily on his belt. His grey eyes were startling in a face golden from the Asian sun.

"This is a good place you have found." He seated himself on the ground.

"Hek' is a patrol leader, too, now," I told him.

"I know. My father told me it several times." Something below captured his attention briefly. "Hekataios is the best of brothers, but he lacks the will to excel."

"Hek' is good at everything."

"It is not enough. One must burn to be best. Like you. Like Pityas."

A bird flew to the ground, sang three melodious notes, paused, repeated them; and then, like a poet ignored, took flight again.

"What of Euagoras?" Doreius asked. Our thoughts crossed.

"He plays and composes his own poems."

He was speaking to me, more as patrol leader to patrol leader than as warrior to eiren. I picked a wild mint leaf to chew.

"Tell me about Asia."

"Asia..." He looked towards distant fields of young, green barley, parted by the soft breeze. "Too many people. Too little land. Mendicants and slaves. Even the greatest are slaves. That is Asia. What of Aristokrates?"

"Poor Pointer. He loved Polydora, too. But he was truly glad when Sphodrias won her. Of course, he was wretched."

His laughter rang out. A man's laugh. No longer a youth's

"I'm not laughing at the poor boy's distress. I was your paradox of an explanation. Although I couldn't name it better."

A bee buzzed about the mint. We talked of this boy and that. When the sun was directly overhead, men streamed onto the streets below, towards their midday meals. Thermon would be glad to be done with speeches, and on his way to the gymnasium for my training. I struck out at the bee.

"If you don't want the bee, throw away the mint," Doreius said, and got to his feet. "I have a thirst for the waters of the Messeis spring." He looked towards the high bluff above the City, on the other side of the river. "Walk with me to Therapine, if you have nothing better to do."

"Nothing." My lie spoke itself.

"I have some bread and cheese we can eat on the way."

As we passed the tall, smooth columns of the Bronze House, Doreius stopped and laid small offerings on the altars of the brother gods, Sleep and Death.

"Death is the friend of men captured by barbarians," he answered my unspoken question. Two hard lines appeared at the corners of his mouth. Then his eyes returned from wherever his thoughts had been. He added with a slight smile, "And Sleep is no enemy of soldiers after a long march."

We followed a roundabout route to the river bridge. Anyone seeing us might have thought we were not making for the bridge at all. We stopped by the racing course beside the statues of the twin gods, to watch some youths running. We diverted to the hollow, to see garlanded maidens dance for Artemis Orthia. We would have observed a rhodibas drill, but the boys broke off

185

at a melleiren's command.

No wind disturbed the silver-green leaves of the olive trees in the grounds of Athena, leading to the bridge.

"What a stupid man Aristogoras was," Doreius laughed shortly.

"What Aristogaras?"

"Have you forgotten the tale?"

"Oh, *that* Aristogoras..."

"Foreigners think the Council declined his proposal to take Persia, because they feared a three-month march. Even I once thought that the meaning was that riches are not worth a day's march, let alone three months."

"Isn't it."

"In Asia, I came to believe those Elders were still wiser. They knew you cannot hold a corrupt thing without being corrupted by it."

"Was Antalkidas on the ship with you?"

He cast me a quizzical glance. A faint stirring of the air carried the scent of the flowers of the citron trees. Wild cherry blossoms fell like snow.

"Antalkidas is still in Asia. He has made himself indispensable. He is learning the barbarian language, and they say he understands the barbarian mind."

Our feet echoed hollow, as we crossed the wooden bridge over the Eurotas. We turned, and started up the incline. The breezes of the higher ground set yellow flowers dancing in the fields. The sun burned hot. Sweat poured from us.

"We will stop and eat just beyond the sanctuary of Polydeukes," Doreius said.

The sanctuary stands on a plateau half-way between the plain and the high bluff where the tomb of Helen and Menelaos stands. The path to the bluff and Therapine is steep, and strewn with white rocks. It is said that the temple was built where Kastor fell, and Polydeukes pleaded with Zeus to let him share his immortality with his mortal brother, as they had shared everything in life.

Had the Twin Gods set the pattern for this sharing of Spartiates, even to life and death? Had Zeus, in letting his son share his divinity, become father to Kastor also? I turned to Doreius to ask him of these things, but the matter of blood-

186

fathers and name-fathers was too close to the bone. Instead, I spoke of Asia.

"Is it true that the barbarians wear armour like fish scales under their clothes?"

"Yes. The golden apples will ripen well with this early spring."

"They say Agisilaos had the prisoners stripped."

"So the troops would see what poor creatures they were, and not fear them in battle. What a splendid spring this is."

"Are their horses really so fine?"

"Big. Better than their fighting men."

Far places call to youth. My questions inflamed my own imagination. Or perhaps I had absorbed more of Asia from the silver-tongued Antalkidas than I had thought. I went on about the banquets, those gardens the barbarians call paradises, and I don't know what else.

Perhaps it was the heat and the effort of the climb – although there had been steeper climbs in high summer with the flock – but Doreius lost his temper, and I learnt that day that I had never seen him truly angry before.

When he appeared furious because we broke some rule in the flock, it was because he chose to. This was none of that cold, measured rage. The sides of his mouth whitened. He paled under his tan and shouted, "You want to know about Asia? All right. I will tell you about Asia."

And he did. My questions had awakened many phantoms, and they all poured out. There is not a boy in the Hellenes who had not heard tales of the cruelty of the barbarians; but hearing these old stories – horror-filled and sickening though they were – and being there and witnessing their truth, were far apart.

I doubt whether he knew, any longer, that I was there, as he described the terrible things. There was rage in his spirit, as there had been in my mind the day Kinadon died. Then Doreius had come out and sat with me, and calmed the rage, while the river whispered. Now he was alone with his furies, and I could do nothing.

Far, far below, the silver-shining river ran through the curves of its rocky bed.

"Doreius..." I touched his arm.

He looked at me as though I were a stranger, and then said, as

187

if from a distance "I ought not to have spoken to you of these things."

It showed me that you have a fierce temper, I thought. That you had to will yourself to be what you are, and what you are is everything I want to be.

"Doreius, let us swim. We can walk to the spring later."

Sun sparkled on the Eurotas. Clean. Cool. Clear.

"Yes," he said, still far away. "Let us swim."

Did he start running down the incline? Did I? Perhaps both of us. It is habit to run to a dip. We stopped at a place where the river curved about a level space of green grasses, sprinkled with yellow and purple and red anemones.

Doreius threw down his belt and scabbard, flung off the crimson cloak, plunged in, and disappeared under the water. I was running towards the river-bank when he emerged.

"Bring me my pumice and my sponge," he shouted. "They are in the box."

I searched amongst his things, and found a dark-wood box, intricately carved with roses and nightingales, and inlaid with nacre. Inside were compartments where he had placed his comb, sponge, pumice and stlengis. A large piece of bread and some olives overflowed the top of the two divisions they had been stuffed into.

I removed the comb and the food, and carried the box to the river-bank, where iris pierced the rushes like blue torches. Doreius swam idly. The tightness was gone from his face.

"Here is your box," I called as I waded in. "I'm using some of the pumice."

I stood calf-deep, rubbing the pumice over me. It was an odd sort of pumice, unusually fine-ground. When I wet it, it became slippery. The box slid out of my hands.

"Doreius! I have dropped the box. The river took it."

"Let the river have it."

"It is beautiful."

"A barbarian thing. No – don't go after it! You'll rinse the pumice off."

He swam to the shallower water, and waded up to me. "You have got enough on you for a regiment." He scooped it off my back and shoulders on to himself. "You don't need much with that sort of pumice."

We covered one another with the slippery stuff. Suddenly Doreius shoved me in, as if I were a reluctant Euagoras of seven. When I cleared the water from my eyes, he was leaping about in the deeper part of the river, like a dolphin.

I swam out to him and ducked him. He came up spluttering, then submerged himself and disappeared so long I began to fear for him, until I felt a tug on my ankle pulling me under. When he came up, he was laughing.

The warm sun was good on water-cooled flesh, as we pulled ourselves up on to the river-bank. We rinsed our cloaks in the water, spread them out to dry, and threw ourselves down on the resilient spring grass.

"So you defeated Molobros," Doreius spoke first. "I never could." Molobros was the flock commander who had succeeded him.

"I could never win with you."

"You never tried."

"I always box to win."

My other opponents became impersonal objects of an inarticulate anger. Doreius was always Doreius.

"And now you look to box your way to an olive crown."

I turned my head to read his face, but his eyes were closed. "Thermon is training me. He is a fine boxer–"

"I have heard of the best boxer in Sparta."

He wouldn't train me else he thought I could win. He's got me some hard leather hand-straps from abroad. And a helmet made to measure. His friend Meleas tried to stop him training me. Not that it is his concern. I don't like Meleas."

He opened his eyes and threw his arm across them to block

"Not Meleas? He did that for Thermon? I didn't know they were such great friends. Never have I known two men less alike."

"Sometimes men are drawn into friendship when they love the same boy."

"You think it is that? How very unrewarding for them both."

"Don't be frivolous." The patrol-leader tone made me open my eyes. I could not see his eyes, covered as they were by his arm. "Worthy love becomes whatever the boy wants. It transforms itself into the love of a father, or a brother, or a teacher. It can even take the form of not appearing at all..."

I sat up and pulled his arm back, away from his eyes. "And you, Doreius, what of your love?"

"Oh, that..." he said, trying to make his voice light. "Since a small golden boy, with chicken fat on his tunic, offered me a fistful of bare stalks, you have had my love."

"And you mine, Doreius."

Chapter 7

In the Messenian Gulf small, swarthy men in fishing boats looked up, and waved to the shipload bound for Olympia.

Pityas and Aristokrates were with us. Hekataios was not. He was a long-race runner, and the stadion race is short. The thrill of being at sea had dispelled for them. They hung their heads over the sides. Other boys lay groaning on pallets on the deck, although the summer sun had not yet set.

Thermon sat surrounded by a group of up-country lads. He had found a new audience for his tussle with the boar. Meleas was on a different ship with the chariot men. Doreius tossed me an apple over the heads of some other runners. Meleas persuaded him to enter the lists when he saw how things were with us.

I stood at the ship's rail, chewing my apple.

A man beside me said, "You are a born sailor." It was spoken in the manner of high praise. I recognised him as the son of a fleet commander; an up-country man famous in the Long War. He was to run in the race with the shield that ends the Games. "Have you been on a ship before?"

"Never."

"You are fortunate. The sea likes you. The greatest men are those who master it. Lysander. Alkibiades..."

He would have named his father but for good manners.

I searched his eyes for *that* look. They were innocent when he spoke the name of Alkibiades. Was I heir to Alkibiades's brilliance as sea-commander? I was ashamed of the thrill of pride in my veins.

That night, as men and boys lay sleeping on the deck, I remained awake.

"I know my being caused you shame," I told my father's shade. "But I shall bring honour to your name in Olympia.

191

When I walk in the procession of winners, and the herald calls 'Leotychides, son of Agis,' you will be as happy in the underworld as Achilles was when Odysseus told him of his son."

The swaying of the ship seemed to sweep it up into the night sky, and I reached out my hand to grasp a star. He was sleeping, and had not seen this shamefully childish gesture.

Olympia was waking from its four-year sleep when we marched the short distance from the Eleian coast. Only a few cities had as yet set up tents in the hills above the sanctuary grounds, where athletes and their trainers live for the two-months training. Those were largely other Peloponnesians, having the shortest distance to travel.

The men who knew those hills found us a good site, near a stream under the shade of some oaks. While our servants unloaded the donkey carts of huge baskets of barley, amphoras of oil, vases of wine and great clay jars of olives, we crossed the Kladeos to the sanctuary grounds.

Who forgets his first sight of Olympia?

The valley lies in a triangle, where the course of the River Kladeos meets that of the Alpheos, and looks to the wooded slopes of Krannion. It is pretty country. The green is not so vivid as in Lakedaimon, nor the flowers so many, nor the mountains snow-capped, but it is...Olympia. The temples, the altars and the thousands of statues in the sanctuary grounds are from all ages. Supported by warmly painted Doric columns, the temple of Zeus was immense in the near-empty grounds. A slave sweeping the ramp leading to its entrance looked no larger than an ant.

Some foreigners passed us on the paved path.

"...and that Corinthian boy boxer is all they claim." One was saying. "But not a word to Bolkon, lest it dishearten him. Ah, the Spartans are here." His voice faded as they walked towards that very old, very beautiful temple of Hera. "They may dress like beggars, but they walk like kings."

"Philasians?" Apollodoros asked. He was a young warrior with a ready smile, who had become acquainted with Pityas on the ship. The two were constantly in each others' company.

"Sikyonians." Doreius had learnt the look and accents of foreigners in Delphi and in Asia.

192

"What Corinthian boy boxer?" Pityas wanted to know.

A slant of sunlight struck the temple's west pediment.

Lapiths and Kentaurs fought one another across its frieze. Apollo stands in the centre, his arms outstretched, commanding them to cease. Apollo was noble, but it was old work; the god's hair in stiff curls, too much chin.

Let me win, Apollo, I prayed to him silently, and I shall give you a beautiful new portrait. Some day. Lest that be too vague, I added that I should also give him my olive crown after the winners' banquet. There was a rumble of thunder, and I hoped Zeus was not telling his son to dismiss my plea. In the god's holy grounds here, his voice is powerful. Awesome. Frightening. Nowhere else does one hear it so.

Even a barbarian ignorant of the gods could not doubt that Zeus is king, when he sees the statue of the god enthroned in the great temple. Two men had preceded us there, and laid rich gifts on the offering table. In the penumbra, their faces were obscured. They left as we did. We stepped aside to let them pass, and I saw that one was a boy about my age.

They were both fair-haired, and their light tunics were of a linen finer than any my father sent my mother from the Dekeleia. They wore more jewels than a Spartan going into battle. The young man looked at Doreius and his gaze held. Unsurprisingly. The beauty of Doreius caught many men's eyes.

"Well, Doreius, you might remember me." His smile was wry. "Having robbed me of my laurel crown."

"Anaxilas!" Doreius seemed pleased by the encounter. "I did not think the Syracusans would be here this early."

"The trainers thought us best away from the pleasures of our city." He turned to the boy. "Megakles, but for this Spartan, your brother would have brought back a crown from Delphi."

"Your trainer always tells you not to look behind you," the boy replied.

"Nor did I. The finishing line was only a spears-length ahead... Then suddenly, as a god appearing, this man was between it and me." He laughed. "Do you recall that Theban, Doreius? The one who came in third...what was his name? The

Syracusan and Doreius talked of Delphi. The boy fell into step with me.

193

"Are you in the stadion race, too?" His belt was embroidered in shining greens, reds and blues, with touches of gold in the weaving, and depicted the whole of a boar hunt.

"I am a boxer."

"So am I." There was something familiar about the belt. That hunt and twin hunters. He scowled. "My father forbade me to box in Olympia."

Anaxilas looked back over his shoulder. "Have done before you start, Megakles. Father is right. Let the Athenians kill fools and each other in the boxing and wrestling. Aristokrates made a sudden movement. So as not to burden him with concern, the Syracusan continued smoothly. "Of course, a very big boy has nothing to fear."

But Aristokrates had heard, and I had heard.

"Elders are too cautious," Megakles muttered. His blue eyes owned open envy. "You Spartans are lucky, to live with other boys and have no one telling you what to do."

He was a foreigner, so we choked back our laughter.

Smoke rose from the cooking-fires, when we returned to the hills in the light summer night.

"Anaxilas seems a good fellow." Pityas dipped into his black broth. "But Megakles is a liar." The Syracusan brothers gave us a cup of wine in their tent on the way back. "He claims his father will give Anaxilas an olive grove if he wins."

"I doubt he lies," Apollodoros said. Syracuse is the richest city in Hellas. All Syracusans are rich."

"He won't win." Aristokrates reached for another hunk of bread. "He lives too soft. That tent!"

"Anaxilas is not soft." Doreius stacked tinder tent-shaped, for a fire. The night was warm, but the sun was setting and the sky darkening. "See him run if you think so." "Gylippos had to win their battles for them." Pityas supported Apollodoros.

Doreius cast him a scathing glance. "Do you think he defeated an Athenian army with one regiment of Sikyonians?"

A shadow moved across us. "You are right." The shield-race man from the ship halted in passing. "The Syracusans knew nothing of the sea, when Athens sent the greatest fleet in Hellas to conquer their city. They took their ships out and engaged them each day. They learnt as they fought; and when Gylippos

194

arrived, they were standing the enemy off smartly. So father told me, and he knows the sea."

"Who is his father?" Aristokrates asked when the man was gone.

"An admiral in the Athenian war," Doreius told him. He fell silent.

For some reason or none, I recalled why Megakles's belt was familiar. Those twin hunters and their boar-hunt were painted in the bottom of one of the two-handled cups in the palace! Perhaps it was not so wonderful. Syracuse was founded by Corinthians. Generations before the first Olympiade, the herds of our ancestors gazed together in windy Doris.

The fading sun made shadow-patterns through the trees. Euagoras reached for his lyre. He slipped the straps of the lyre over his shoulder, and turned to Doreius. "You sing." Euagoras still did not entirely trust the sounds that came from his own throat.

Doreius did not have the sort of voice that makes men famous, but it was true and sweet. I think it was only in his rare smile, and his singing voice, that men glimpsed Doreius as I knew him. Others saw only the patrol leader, the commander, the warrior.

Night fell. Fires burned. A swell of voices joined in the singing. Between songs, voices carried from the Argive camp. Once it was the same melody as ours, although the words differed. The cattle of their forefathers had also grazed in Doris. How many cities Doris had begot. How many and how unalike. Or perhaps, not all that unalike. Beneath their finery, the Syracusans were warriors and men.

Being tone-deaf, Aristokrates never sang. Tonight he was locked in his silence. At some time he shook himself out of it to say, "When that boy said he was forbidden to box here...I mean, his brother said – I thought they were just soft, but if they are not–" He swallowed the rest of it. "Leotychides, if an Athenian wrestler kills me, tell my father I was not afraid."

"Megakles is right. Elders are too cautious," I told him. I told myself, and believed it.

The days became longer and hotter. The night-fires many and closer together. From central Hellas came Thebans and other Boiotians, Athenians and Euboians; from the north the

Phokians, Lokrians and Thessalians; from the far north Olynthians, Amphipolitans and Potideans. From Greek cities of barbarian lands they came – Asia, Thrace, Macedon, Sicily and Italy. Dorians, Ionians, Aeolians. All. From the mainland and the islands. The seas of the east and of the west, until the fires of Hellas filled the hills like stars.

Training began. We took our midday meal in a room of the Eleian magistrates' hall, where the sacred flame burns day and night. One day, I arrived late and walked about the hot, noisy room, looking for a place at one of the long trestle tables. The benches were packed with bare men and youths, but I noted the long hair of some Spartans and started towards them. Older men. I should have to be silent with downcast eyes. I hesitated.

The Syracusan boy Megakles called out to me. And shoved into some Naxian or Mytilinean to create a free space. His damp hair was straight. The curls must have been contrived. Megakles found the food dull. I found it rich. We both fell on it ravenously.

Across the table, a man raised his voice above the din. "Spartan women can neither spin nor weave, and know nothing of the kitchen." It was a black-curled young man. A Corinthian. I knew him by sight. A runner, about twenty or so. His eyes met mine directly. "Is that not so?"

"Why should our women learn the work of serfs?" I tore a chunk of bread in half.

"What will they do if your serfs rebel again?" He had a handsome face, but he was ignorant and almost discourteous.

"Our serfs never rise."

"Not after the earthquake?"

"That was two hundred years ago." I washed down the bread with wine. "And in Messenia." Would the fool not be quiet and let me eat?

"Those Messenian serfs, who love your city so well that some turned to Athens in the Long War?"

"All men would rather be free than unfree. When my father took the Dekeleia, twenty thousand slaves ran away from Athens to him." I had not intended to reveal my father's name until I brought honour to it.

Alkibiades cast a long shadow here, where he had entered seven chariots in the games, taken three prizes with them, driven the first prize chariot himself, and then given a banquet for over one thousand guests. Not a day passed on which one did not hear the name of Alkibiades.

The Corinthian's dark eyes sparkled. "A strange city, where the women rule the men, and the warriors fear to leave their own frontiers."

Fear is not a word used to Spartans. "We have left Lakedaimon often enough to defend Corinth, when Corinthians could not."

My arm was caught from behind and held in an iron grip. "Say no more." The man who held me prisoner was Cretan. They are strong, tall men who are reared in flocks and, like us, keep many of the old Dorian customs. "For your own sake." He spoke with authority. It was training to obey.

"This is not a good place to sit," Megakles said.

We finished our meal quickly and left the hall.

The Cretan waited by the entrance. "That Corinthian Aristeas taunted you deliberately," he said. "He hoped you would strike him."

"Why? I do not know him."

"He loves a boy boxer from his own city. Draw his blood in this holy place, and you will be sent back to Sparta. In disgrace."

"Does he do this to every boy boxer?"

"If he might take an olive crown for Nikomedes."

So I was well-considered. "Does he affront the Athenian?"

I had seen this boy. He would have had some claim to beauty, had his body not been thickened and ungainly from over-training. Here, amongst the flower of Hellas, he must have felt shame. I regarded him with pity, although I might better have thought of him with concern.

"That boy's trainer is always about him, like a nurse with a child." Some other Cretans called to him. "Keep your distance from Aristeas. He is a wild fellow." He caught up with his friends as they walked towards the Altars of Herakles.

I avoided the Corinthian that day. The Cretan seemed a man of good will, and he had no reason to lie.

The evening meal was done. Aristokrates played knucklebones with Euagoras. Pityas and Apollodoros had found

197

an acorn, and were planting an oak. In the hills above, the torches of walking men moved like fireflies. Thermon's voice boomed out. "And its tusks were..." I exchanged a smile with Doreius. He held out his hand to me. I followed him away from the camp. Often, when we explored the heights, pursuing old paths or making new ones, we passed faces briefly illuminated by torchlight, and caught scraps of talk in foreign accents.

"...horses have a Nisaian strain..."

"The Halikarnassan," Doreius said.

"...Spartan's greys are good..."

Meleas? We saw little of him, as he spent most of his time with his horses, or with friends from other cities.

"...boy boxer from Athens...quite lethal..."

I was silent.

"...all purple and fairly slithering along the ground..."

We turned off the path, and speculated upon the possible nature of that purple creature in the enigmatic fragment overhead. We had exhausted ourselves of possibilities, when we reached the higher ground, with its density of laurel, wild olive and cypress trees. Raised voices drew our attention downwards.

A number of torches illuminated a group of young men, who stood in a thinner clump of trees. Slaves held the torches; this was a good thing, as the movement of hands in heated debate would have set the foliage afire.

"Argos is Argos and Corinth is Corinth." It was the soft, sibilant Doric of Corinth.

"In union there is strength." Another Corinthian. Tall, in a sky-blue tunic. Black hair. Aristeas. "Are we a client city, that Lysander dedicates our spoils in Sparta's name?"

"Aristeas, Sparta fought three wars for us."

"And measures her reward in our shame."

"You listen over-much to that rabble-rouser Timolaos."

We might have moved off, had not a tall, fair youth in a patterned cloak said, in Attic cadences, "The Lakedaimonians are becoming high-handed, Alkimenes." That from an Athenian!

"Spartans have a charming reluctance to leave their own city," the one called Alkimenes replied.

"I think that arrow was aimed at us." Another Athenian spoke. He was small and dark, like an Ionian islander.

198

"Let Alkimenes make his point, Theokles," said the fair youth. "It may be an insignificant little point, but he seems to be the only man here who can keep to one."

"I wasn't shooting in your direction, Theokles, although the arrow appears to have found its mark," Alkimenes replied. "Athens might like to find a calling for her excess citizens in our city, but she lacks the force to do so."

"Sparta does not," an Argive interrupted.

"Sparta had no appetite for foreign lands. So I ask you again, Aristeas, what have we to gain by merging with Argos?"

"Numbers. Are you peace-party men unable to count?"

"Sparta – that city you fear so much – is the least peopled city in the Peloponnesos."

"What have you to lose by merging our cities?" The Argive demanded.

"Ourselves."

A branch was nearly set aflame, as one of the group stumbled against a slave. He looked older than the others, but in no manner distinguished, apart from his mode of dress.

"My thwoat is parched with all your talk." At least I think that I what he said. A speech impediment made his foreign accent incomprehensible.

A youth stepped forward. He had been standing in Aristeas's shadow. "For once, Axiochos makes sense."

Doreius and I continued our upward climb. At least I knew now what was purple and slithered along the ground.

"Did you see that youth who was as bored as the wine-soak in the purple cloak?" I asked, as we picked our way along a narrow cedar-scented path. An owl hooted. Something moved in the leaves above. "His name is Nikomedes. He is a boxer. He is very good."

We talked about him as though the Athenian boy did not exist.

The path gave out. Somewhere near, a stream whispered over rocks. Its fresh scent rose from the damp earth. Low-hanging branches swept our faces. Doreius held one back to let us pass. A small animal turned shining eyes on us, scuttled for cover, and said, "Spartan, you are standing on my foot." It was not the animal, of course. A man's dark cloak had concealed him as he sat on a rock under the trees. "I take it that you are Spartans, for

199

no one else can see in the dark and tread new paths with bare feet."

"The dark does not hinder you," Doreius said.

In reply, he held up an extinguished torch. "I am hiding from unwanted company."

"We'll not disturb you, then."

"You mistake me." It was too dark to see his face clearly, but his voice was familiar. "I couldn't bear an evening in the company of Axiochos."

"I think we heard you earlier on. Are you called Alkimenes, sir?"

"I fear everyone heard us. They are good fellows, albeit noisy. Except Axiochos. He is unusually disagreeable when he is in wine, and that is usually."

"Sir, why does he wear cloaks made for a god?" I asked.

"His father wore purple cloaks and looked like a god. Axiochos was worn by the cloak. And would you mind omitting the *sir?* Your Spartan manners make me feel a greybeard at twenty-five."

Doreius recalled his Spartan manners, and introduced us.

"Come share my rock, companions of the night, and look at the spirit of Hellas..." Alkimenes turned his head towards the camp-fires in the hills. "Diversity! How each city differs. There is life in diversity. Competition is its spark. Is that why this air affects me like wine? Olympia is everything that separates us from the barbarians."

"Many things separate us from the barbarians." Doreius spoke softly.

Alkimenes followed his thought. Or part of it. "Yes. Reason too. The barbarians believe their Great King rules by the will of his god, and so become his slaves. Our gods are inconstant. Zeus holds the balance, and tilts it where he will. It is not good for men to be too certain of their gods."

"I heard you spoke for us," I told him. "You spoke well."

"My young friend, if I may call you that, I spoke *against* Argos. Not *for* Sparta. Like Aristeas, I opposed sending Corinthian troops to Asia."

"You have not been in Asia," Doreius said.

"Perhaps I shall yet. You dedicated our spoils in Sparta's name. We shunned your Asian campaign. Let it be forgotten."

"It is not solely our campaign," Doreius reminded him.

"Sparta is war-leader, and many of my countrymen are still angry. You know the jest about portioning out duties..." We did not. He went on. "Well, it was proposed that the Eleians, who arrange the Olympic Games so well, should arrange all the games in Hellas; the Athenians, being masters of ceremonies, should be put in charge of all festivals, and the Lakedaimonians be thrashed whenever another city does wrong." Only the night creatures chirped their answers. "Spartans never understand that one."

"There is diversity in laughter, too," Doreius said.

"It spoils a jest to explain it, but I shall try. If a pupil fails to learn his lesson, his tutor is thrashed, is he not?"

A vision of the Commander thrashing one of our honoured elders flashed across my mind, and I laughed aloud.

"Yes, laughter has its diversity also," Alkimenes agreed drily. I explained. "Just so. I should have remembered that your teachers are never slaves. Perhaps I can put it this way. At the last Olympiade, I saw an old man arrive late in the stadion, and there was not a place to be had. He wandered about, looking for a seat vainly, until he reached the Spartan section. There, every man stood as one to offer his place. And the old man – I remember him shaking his fist – shouted at the onlookers, 'All Greeks know what is right. Only the Spartans do it.' You see, we exact a fuller measure from the teacher of Hellas."

Corinthians have a charming turn of speech, which is natural to them as the sudden lighting of their vivacious faces.

"I do not know," said Doreius, "whether we have been praised or abused."

"Both?" Alkimenes laughed. "In any event, I am throwing myself upon your mercy to show me the path. I know not where I am. But at least it is where Axiochos is not."

"Alkimenes, who is Axiochos?" I asked.

"The son of Alkibiades. He mimics his father in every way; but where Alkibiades lavished his fortune with splendour, Axiochos flaunts his with vulgarity." Son of Agis, I warned myself, this has nothing to do with you. My ears listened on. "Drunk Alkibiades was wittier still. Drunk Axiochos quarrels or vomits, or both." Alkibiades was inescapable. This Axiochos gave it all a terrible immediacy. Axiochos, who in blood bore

201

the same relationship to me as Hekataios to Doreius. No. Dinon was name-father to Hekataios, and Hekataios was the favourite of his father. I forced it all from my mind, to hear Alkimenes saying, "...Why, his speech is normal as yours or mine. But Alkibiades had a charming lisp, so Axiochos must lisp and make himself unintelligible, for which one can be thankful at times. It is strange...Alkibiades was the most dangerous enemy Corinth had, yet one cannot but admire him. Great men ought never to have sons."

The two months passed. There were times it felt as though we had been forever in Olympia, but when we walked in procession, city by city, to take our oaths before the altar of Zeus Horkios under an open sky, the training months seemed hardly to have been at all.

The sanctuary grounds were filled with more than twenty thousand people. Barbarians, as well as Hellenes, stood amongst the onlookers – heavy-browed Phoenicians with sea-weathered faces, slender Egyptians in long, striped robes, bright-cheeked Macedonians with jewels fine as the Syracusans – but they were coarse, loud men, seen close. There was even a Persian, wearing trousers and a long high-necked coat with sleeves, although it was the hottest month of the year.

It was into this throng that Euagoras disappeared.

"The heralds' competition," Pityas suggested. "Maybe he has gone there." I think he wished to watch it himself.

"No. He went towards the Temple of Zeus." Apollodoros pointed. "Perhaps to hear the orators speak at the back."

"Not Euagoras," Aristokrates declared.

"He will have gone to the poets' competition." Doreius spoke with assurance.

"Let him go," I said. "He is not in the Games." He was the pentathlete's responsibility here, and Megakles beckoned to me.

He had been observing the Athenian boxer for me. This boy's trainer kept him a secret from other stadion boxers. Being a runner, Megakles aroused no suspicion.

"Anaxilas wants to talk to you," I told Doreius.

The Syracusan brothers detached themselves from a loose group of their countrymen, and stood in the shade cast by a statue. Doreius spearheaded a way through the crowd. Syracusan athletes had worn all their finery for the oath-taking, and an onlooker paused to turn to a companion and remark audibly. "Ostentation!" then, taking in our shabby cloaks and bare feet as we approached, added, "More ostentation!"

Anaxilas looked unusually grave. He was a lively fellow, more often with a smile and a jest than a serious word. I wondered whether the onlooker's insolence angered him, and hoped he would not desecrate the sanctuary grounds with a thoughtless blow. Tempers were short now; the Games were upon us. He sliced the air with his hand. "Let us leave this rabble!" It is impossible simply to walk out of such a press, but it seemed to be carrying us towards the paved road leading out of the grounds. "That Corinthian Aristeas–" Someone shouldered past, cutting off his words.

"A good runner," Doreius allowed. "But I am not concerned."

"In the race only I need concern you." A smile touched the corners of Anaxilas's lips, then faded. "Aristeas's father is guest-friend to my father. He has played upon that to make me his messenger. His friend Nikomedes wishes to speak to Leotychides."

"I would not go," Megakles spoke up.

"Have done, Megakles. You were not asked." Anaxilas scowled and fell into the uneasy silence of a man arguing with himself. "You have drunk my wine in my tent, Doreius." He spoke finally. "I have shared your black broth." He had lied politely that he liked it. "My father's guest-friend is my father's guest-friend, and I honour the gods, but are we not also guest-friends of a sort?" He turned to me. "Megakles is right, Leotychides. Do not trust Aristeas. He is of good family, but he is a hot-headed fellow who follows nothing but his own will. He cursed an islander who stepped on his foot."

We shouldered our way through to the paved path, where we walked with less difficulty, as there were more people going in than coming out. Having said what he had to say, Anaxilas was in better spirits, and talked with Doreius about horses. It was I who first saw Aristeas. He stood at the edge of the sanctuary grounds in his sky-blue tunic, with a shoulder cloak of a darker blue. As we approached, he sauntered down the road, and came to an abrupt halt before me.

203

"You are standing in my path," I told him.

"Anaxilas, have you not passed on my message?" The Corinthian pretended astonishment.

"He has." I had decided what reply I should give. "Nikomedes is welcome in our camp."

"But he awaits you under the Zeus-struck oak. Now."

"Let him," I replied.

"He wants a friendly word with you." Aristeas's eyes looked amber in the bright sunlight. "What do you fear?"

Fear. The word burst in my head.

"Remember what the Cretan told you," Megakles whispered.

An athlete in Olympia is a too-taut bow. The bow snapped. I forgot the olive crown, my father, the Games, my companions. "I fear the gods, but not you, nor Nikomedes. Tell him I will go to him."

Aristeas inclined his head in a movement that looked polite but bespoke anger, and turned away.

"We had all best go," Anaxilas said. Whether a formal guest-friendship existed between us or not, the brothers were true friends.

"No, I told them. "He would think I feared."

Small in the distance, I could see the blue tunic of Aristeas, as he sped with the steady pace of a good runner.

The oak stood between the Corinthian camp and our own. Its greater branches were blackened. Green leaves sprouted on a few slighter ones. The boy boxer leaned against the lightning-split trunk, one sandal on, the other in his hand. He was a pleasant-faced youth with light brown hair. Aristeas was disputing with him. I heard him say, "I told you he would not be alone."

"Nor am I," Nikomedes replied.

The Corinthians stepped forward. The four of us stood, wordlessly facing one another; Aristeas by the side of his friend, as though he held an invisible shield over him.

"Aristeas, leave us," Nikomedes spoke finally. "We're both boxers."

Aristeas looked at Doreius. They withdrew, walking together without speaking. They were of a height. Runners. Rivals for an olive crown. What did one know of foreigners? Was it all a trick to lure Doreius here? I would have called out to him, but that

204

would make me look fearful, and shame him as much as it would me. They halted out of hearing distance, about a spears-length apart.

Nikomedes seated himself under the tree. I took a place opposite him on the ground.

"Sorry I had to send for you in this way," he began. "My trainer would be unbearable if he knew." He had lively blue eyes. "Aristeas heard some talk about a boy boxer who refused a bribe. He knew I had been offered one, and was concerned."

"That you would take it? Or that you would not?"

"He knows no fortune is large enough to buy my failure. But that boy is in danger." He lowered his voice, although only the birds could hear us. "Something in his food..."

"What is this to me?"

"I thought it might be you. I know Spartans do not take bribes."

"No one approached me. Have you warned the Athenian boy?" Did I want him to?

"The monster? He is safe enough. The great wagers are on him." He fingered his broken sandal-strap. "He has been training for this since he was six. Make your cook taste everything you eat. Aristeas orders his cook to taste all his food."

"We eat from a common pot."

"Then it could be your wine. Make the server taste it."

"Our servants belong to the City. I'm not certain it would be lawful to use one that way." I pulled up a tuft of grass. "Why do they let barbarians watch the Games?"

"It need not be a barbarian." He followed my glance. Aristeas and Doreius sat watching one another like fighting cocks. "Not Aristeas." He laughed "Asian Greeks have learnt some tricks from their swift Corinthian neighbours." His face became grave, with one of those swift Corinthian transitions. "I know Aristeas tried to anger you, but he would do no worse. And what he did was for me, although I did not want him to. He would not do it for himself." He wanted me to think better of that disagreeable fellow. "He risks his father's rage if he makes a valuable slave eat tainted–" He laughed. "But, of course! If your server poisons himself trying to injure you, you cannot be held to blame."

"Nikomedes, you are not a fool."

"Did you take me for one?" He was a merry boy. "It was Aristeas who reasoned it. His father's cook, you know."

"We are the only boys who matter. You and I and the monster."

Nikomedes meant well. "That Athenian is slow to think." This much, I could return his good will.

"So Aristeas says, but he is a runner."

"I have a friend who has seen him training. A stadion runner–" He waved this away with a hand motion. "He is a boxer in his own city." He listened. "Nikomedes, that Athenian could fight us together, and still be on his feet." One had never ought to discuss such matters with rivals. How often Thermon had repeated that. "But he is slow to move and slow to think." Forgive me, Thermon. "He is powerful, but I am quick. And so are you."

"He grinned. "You have watched me train."

"How not?"

"I have observed you, too."

We laughed and grasped one another's arms in the grip of friendship. It was to be a friendship for life.

"He takes an eye-blink to think. We can use that eye-blink."

"You are like me, Leotychides. You want to win it right."

"I intend to win it right."

"I told Aristeas you were a true boxer. It is something runners don't understand. But you are wrong about one thing. I'm the one who is going to win."

There is no greater bore than the man who relives his feats in the Games at every opportunity, so I will not set down such an account, although that Olympiade is clearer to me than anything that occurred a sennight past. The day of the boxing, the onlookers, tight-packed, seated on the natural incline of the valley within a valley that is the stadion. The heat of the sun beating down in the boxers' square, as the lots were drawn each time for a fresh match...

The Athenian surprisingly submitted to a brave young Sikyonian, who was unable to continue. (The boy died on the journey back to Sikyon). In the end, it was Nikomedes I faced

206

on the boxing ground for the olive crown. I remember Nikomedes, assured, alert, his sturdy body oiled and sanded: his lively blue eyes challenging, taunting and smiling in a way that was not smiling; his light-brown curls darkened with sweat just before he put on his helmet. I have held the memory far longer than I saw him thus. When the first blow was struck, he ceased to be another youth – and became that nameless, formless enemy on whom I vent the rage of years. Thermon had taught me to use that anger – not, as he thought, to master it – for it was something that came and went of its own volition. I could no more subdue it than I could summon it at will.

I remember the noise of the onlookers...I remember Doreius, Thermon, Pityas – the entire Spartan section – crowding round...but I am becoming a Games bore.

The next day I woke late, in a tent. Why? The tents were for trainers. We slept in the open, on the ground. My friends tell me that the first thing I did was to feel my nose. Doreius assured me that it was intact, that I had taken the blows on my body and not my face – but again, according to my comrades, I continued probing until Doreius asked Euagoras to pass me the mirror the slight youth always carried with him. It was the touch of deference that gave me the courage to ask Doreius, "Did I win?"

The next question when, talking all at once, they described my victory, I kept to myself. "Is that all?" The elation that I felt so often in anticipation came later in the winners' procession, when the herald intoned, "Leotychides, son of Agis, of Sparta." But it was a cloud's passing only. The high points of achievement are always but a cloud's passing; the rest, the strong wine of anticipation and the mellow draft of recollection.

Doreius told me that a runner knows his glory when he crosses the finishing lines first; the boxer is too sore and fatigued and must wait: but, for all, it is but a cloud's passing; boxer, runner, ruler, victorious general – "Is that all?" To be sustained, it must be surpassed. Only the most torpid man will not ask "Is that all?" And set his foot on the path to the higher peak.

Had Lykourgos asked it of himself, or had a god told him that it is necessary to shape the aspirations of mortals to achievement rather than acquisition, when it is in our nature to ask, "Is that all?"

"How is Nikomedes?" I asked.

"That Corinthian nearly bested you, my lad." Thermon frowned. "Lucky you caught his left eye, and left him with sight in one side only."

I sat up. My muscles screamed. "I put his eye out? Doreius, did I–"

It was Thermon who replied. "You closed it for a few days only. You won't go far in the men's boxing if you are so tender-hearted about your rivals.

Doreius gave me the belt before the winners' banquet. It was the same work as the one Megakles had worn. An ancient battle, warriors in chariots with golden shields and gilded armour. I had thought only to find this finery interesting. Doreius saw I admired it.

"I wagered my barbarian dagger on the Thessalian chariot." We stood on the tent I had abandoned. "Anaxilas thought too much of the Halikarnassan's large horses."

"It is beautiful." I started to fasten the belt about my cloak.

"Would you shame us?" It was his commander's voice. "Or do you think you are going into battle? Put it away. It can be made to hold a sword." He straightened the olive crown on my head.

"Doreius, did you forget to offer to Artemis? Hekataios says she refuses you nothing."

"Is my brother the confidant of gods now? She did not refuse me this time. You have an olive crown, have you not?" I was shamed. I had asked Apollo only for my own. When I gave him it, I would pray for one for Doreius. (O, be careful what you ask the gods). "There will be other races," he went on, but I knew Doreius ran to win. That was in him.

I removed the Polydoros ring, and was going to place it with the belt. I never wore it in the flock, where adornments are forbidden. Doreius passed it back to me. "Wear your father's ring. You have honoured his name."

I might have spoken then, but Pityas, Apollodoros and Aristokrates rushed in.

"Are we going now, Cockerel?" Pityas asked.

208

"I wasn't aware you were winners." Doreius took in their neatly combed hair and immaculate cloaks.

"Nor is Meleas, but he is going."

"Meleas is going with a guest-friend," I told them. "Some important man." Meleas had arranged a place for Doreius. It was the only time Doreius accepted a privilege not earned by merit. This, too, was a gift.

"We are flock-brothers," Apollodoros protested.

"Eleians understand nothing of flock-brothers." Apollodoros rested a hand on Pityas's shoulder. "Come along. The Philasians have offered us a cup of wine, and the Syracusans are revelling. We'll not be dull."

Aristokrates glanced about. "Where has Euagoras gone?"

On the way to the banquet, Doreius and I called at the Corinthian camp to see Nikomedes. His left eye was yellowing around the edges. He talked about his plans for the Isthmian Games, the Pythian Games and future Olympiades. Aristeas betook himself elsewhere. We heard him say, "Oh it is the Spartans, here to gloat," in a voice meant to be overheard, so we kept the visit short.

There is a touch of sadness in the merriment of the winners' banquet. The next day the tents will be struck, friends say farewell and go back to their own cities, as Olympia returns to its four-year sleep, peopled only by priests and their servants. These days the sad note dominates the merry song, for most of the friends will be going to war against one another when the truce of Zeus ends, but Hellas was at peace with itself then, and it was only the sadness of farewell. Of something past and passing.

The distinguished men's dining couches were apart from those of the winners; food and wine the same, but ours tasted of undying fame. We knew that all eyes were upon us, because we were the best in Hellas. We spoke of the Games and of valiant rivals. When I protested that there were many boxers in Sparta as good as I, a Thessalian laughed and told me to keep them there.

Someone on the other side of the room dripped a wine-cup with a loud clatter. I looked in its direction, and saw what I hoped not to see. Euagoras shared the couch of a foreign poet, the pentathlete forsaken. I glanced across the room to Doreius, but he was talking to the tall, fair Athenian called Tolmaios. Tolmaios was the nephew of Meleas's guest-friend, a brown-bearded man named Kallistratos. No doubt he owed his presence at the banquet to his uncle. It was his friend Theokles who sat with us and wore an olive crown.

The meal ended. Guests and winners mingled. Doreius came over, perched on the end of my couch, and presented me to Tolmaios. His Corinthian friend Alkimenes was not present.

A lyre sounded. A familiar chord. Surely Euagoras would not have had the effrontery to sing before crowned poets.

I looked hard at him, trying to convey, "I shall thrash you when we are back in Sparta." If he saw me, he took no heed. His poem was about the death of Hyakinthos. The melody was not unlike The Beautiful Goddess. Happily, Theokles's voice drowned the singer's in an oration about poor men.

"You never spoke to a poor man unless he carried your torch," Tolmiaos laughed.

"I dress to the left," Theokles protested.

"The poor man enjoys your handsome right shoulder." Tolmaios took the cup from his friend's hands and drank. "The left would please him equally."

He made way for his uncle, who approached with Meleas and some other men. Doreius and I rose for our elders. Perhaps I should not have been noticed, had the foreigners not remained seated. Perhaps it was inevitable.

Theokles appealed to Doreius. "In your city, all citizens have a vote. This oligarch would deny it to poor men."

"In our city all men are poor," Doreius replied.

"You know I am no oligarch, Theokles." Tolmaios drank and returned the wine-cup. "I would not limit the Assembly to landed men, but to Athenians of good qualities and learning."

"The rich and tutored." Theokles turned to the older men. All but Meleas had given their attention to Euagoras. "I say, let us have an equality of citizens."

Meleas smiled. "Equality is the journey, not its end."

"And the end?" Theokles demanded.

"Excellence."

Tolmaios raised his hands in imprecation. "Meleas, have done!" You will have him Lakonizing. Remain a demagogue, Theokles. Better a bare right shoulder than bare feet."

The song ended. Kallistratos wiped his eyes. "That boy is a fine poet."

Some noise at the entrance caused a welcome distraction.

"The revellers are here," Tolmaios sighed.

A group of men carrying wine-cups came in, laughing loudly, led by an unsteady Axiochos. He leaned upon a flute-girl and looked to trip over his trailing cloak. Some Eleians barred his way. His voice rose in slurred protest. It was nothing to me, now that I wore an olive crown and was equal to the best man in Sparta.

The Athenian uncle and nephew glanced scornfully at their compatriot. Kallistratos started to turn back to Meleas. His eyes stopped at my face. Not long, but long enough for me to see the naked curiosity, before a veil of polite disinterest fell over *that* look.

Everything went hollow. Whatever I achieved, I was what I was. Bare to the thousand eyes that bored through to my bones. No number of olive crowns could equal me to the best in Sparta. I was what I was. And what I was shamed Sparta. Shamed my father. Shamed Doreius.

He had told me to wear the Polydoros ring. But he had not known. How could he? I never spoke of it to him. It was not in his nature to think me less open than himself. The talk went on around me. I did not hear it. I would go from Lakedaimon. Found a city in Sicily. I must seek out Anaxilas. Ask a likely place.

Doreius laid a hand on my arm. "Let us walk in the Victors' Road while it is still light. We can come back later."

The summer sun had dried the grass of the grounds, but there were still small flowers growing about the trunks of the row of poplar trees that shaded the statues of Games winners. I bent and picked one. It had the shape of an unturned vase.

Doreius said this or that. I replied this or that. We fell into silence.

"What Euagoras did was a small thing...I brought more shame...I wanted to be king because it is my right...had I known, I would not have gone to Herea – I do not think I would..." My words spoke themselves.

"Leotychides, there are times when you have made more sense. Sicily? Euagoras? Herea?"

211

"It is *true*." I burst out, as we passed the statue of Demaretos the Hereian shield runner. "I have it from my own mother. It is true. I told no one what was said between my father and myself in Herea. I wanted to tell you, but no great things were said..."

"Have you been drinking too much wine?"

"You know better." I had barely touched my wine. "I still do not know why my father gave me the kingdom."

"The same reason I gave you a patrol. You were the best."

"You loved me. He did not."

"Knowing that love can confound judgement, I would have passed you over, had another boy been as worthy." He pointed to a statue. "Look...Charmidas..."

I dutifully studied the famous boy boxer. I had crossed my own forbidden boundary of inner privacy. Doreius had pushed me back within it. I should have preferred...What?

"My father was not unfond of Agisilaos."

"He knew him."

"Teleutias knows him."

"Teleutias is not a king." He examined a very old statue of a man whose name could be made out as Eurymos. It was not very interesting. The features had disappeared into time. But once that man had walked in a winners' procession, and placed an olive crown upon his head. And asked, "Is that all?"

"This is fine work." Doreius called my attention to yet another statue. Rather, he ordered it, for he spoke in his patrol leader's voice; his commander's voice. He drew back, to leave me alone facing Apollo in a charioteer's robe. His hair was still bright. His eyes cleverly made of pieces of sapphire, so that they seemed to be looking at you however you turned. He held the reins of four spirited bronze horses; lightly, yet masterfully. It was not Apollo, of course. The god's face is serene gravity. A charming whimsical smile, tending to one side, played on the lips of this mortal charioteer. "The world is mine," it seemed to say. "And if it knows it not, then its folly shall amuse me." His features were familiar to me, having seen them often enough in my own reflection. Considering the years separating a man of thirty-two and a youth of sixteen, the resemblance was remarkable. It did not need the letters carved in marble to tell me that Alkibiades, the son of Kleinias, had won that race.

"When we were in Asia," Doreius spoke quietly, "Agisilaos

212

had a friend on his staff. A friend of his youth. The man came down with a fever. One of those Asian fevers that strike suddenly and fiercely. Men often recover, but whilst the fever rages they are helpless. A scout rode in and warned that the enemy was near. Agisilaos gave the order to break camp. As he mounted his horse, his friend called out to him. Stretched out his hand, asking not to be left behind. Some of us went to him. Others started making a litter. Agisilaos ordered us to desist. There was no time, he told us. One officer protested, but Agisilaos snapped, "Obey your orders. One cannot always be kind and practical too." And he left his friend to the barbarians. At least he might have finished him off. That is the man your father passed over for you."

"You knew. You always knew. That man Axiochos is—"

"A fool," he finished for me. "Leotychides..." The voice was a commander's "When did you see that bull stretching over Taygetos to drink from the Eurotas?"

I allowed that such a bull could not possibly exist, and turned my back on the statue of Alkibiades.

Doreius was smiling, his arms outstretched. "Then come here and stop talking nonsense."

Chapter 8

There is a place where a number of laurel trees stand. The shower of their silver-grey leaves creates a roof over a soft, even grassy, place, where a stream takes a wilful way from the river. Nearby, the Bridge Road separates into two paths: one leading back to the heights of Sellasia, where my flock was encamped; the other to the barracks quarters, where all young warriors between twenty and thirty live, each in a plain but pleasant room.

The trees were our private meeting-place.

"I forgot to thank the Cretan," I caught a long, pointed leaf before the stream carried it away. "The one who warned me of Aristeas."

"He will be in the next Olympiade."

"I shall not. I am not going to box again." I would always be good, but the rage that made me great had gone out of me. "Well, only in Lakedaimon," I amended. "So I won't be in the Games again until I enter a four-horse chariot."

"The chariot race!" Doreius tossed his head back, clearing his brow of the wave that always fell forward. His grey eyes sparked with amusement. "Are you not somewhat young?"

"Not until I am old. Twenty-five or thirty."

He glanced towards the low sun. "We must go."

"It is not late."

"Have you thrashed Euagoras?" He took the leaf from me and turned it in his hands.

"I ordered Anaxandros to." The Magpie laid the branch on lightly. Lenience had been misplaced. "Euagoras grows insolent. I think all that praise at the banquet went to his head. But his poems are exceptionally fine."

"Praise the poetry and punish the insolence." The sun sank below Taygetos. Again Doreius looked vast. "Leotychides..."

"I am posing for my statue. Am I to blame if I am kept overlong?" Meleas had commissioned it. Doreius, Sphodrias, Kallias, Apollodoros and other young warriors also contributed

214

to the cost. My contemporaries could only offer enthusiasm, as eirens have nothing of their own, but many more donations flowed in from citizens who wished to honour a Spartan Games winner. "Doreius, a few of Lysander's friends have given payment towards it."

"They have not forgiven Agisilaos." The blue prelude set in. Doreius rose, and brushed leaves and twigs from his short-sleeved tunic. "Come. Even games winners can be thrashed, and warriors made to stand guard with shield for disobedience." We walked to the shrine of Hermes, where the paths separate.

"Antalkidas once said that Lysander's friends would turn to me. I think he believed I should court their favour."

"Will you?"

"You know better. Let Lysander seek another client-king." Even Agisilaos was sufficiently Royal Heraklid to baulk at that.

We parted. I ran back to the flock faster than I had run any race, in order to be amongst those coming out of the river when the commander counted heads.

It was in the sculptor's workshop that I first heard the name of Timokrates. Hellas had forgotten it now. His deeds will be cursed by our sons' sons.

Agisilaos and his gifted commanders were winning victory upon victory in Asia. The satrap Tissaphernes fell into disfavour with the Great King, who appointed a man called Tithraustes in his place. Tithraustes beheaded his predecessor, and pledged to protect the Greek cities in his satrapy; a promise exacted by the presence of the Hellenic army, and one which he had no intention of keeping if that army could be got out of Asia. Persian arms had failed. He sought another method. The Great King was becoming short of patience with his underlings, as Hellenic warriors penetrated deeper into the Median Empire.

In appreciation of Agisilaos's victories, the ephors gave him command of the fleet as well as the army. It was another break with the Law of Lykourgos. My uncle used his new powers to appoint that dimmest of men, Peisander, grand admiral – giving him command of Sparta's one hundred and twenty triremes, as carelessly as he had given him one-half my inheritance.

Sphodrias sat on the ground – legs propped on a tool-box –

giving out on these matters, as the sculptor added details to the wax-covered clay model of my statue. It was his opinion that our armies would reach the Great King's royal city of Susa by the Karneia; barbarians were notoriously poor seamen, no threat even to an admiral as witless as Peisander, and so on.

Meleas arrived to see the statue, before it was covered with the outer layer of clay, to ready it for the kiln.

"Apelleas, are you certain all this is not a distraction?" he asked the sculptor, as he took in Sphodrias expounding, Hekataios, who intently watched the apprentice at work, and Pityas and the Magpie wandering about the large yellow clay figures, which stood in iron frames, as yet uncovered with wax. I had been standing an eternity looking into the distance, as the artisan posed me placing an imaginary olive crown on my head.

The sculptor was the same man who made the Dionysos. He gave me no sign of recognition. As soon as he finished a work, he lost interest in it. When it came out of the kiln – the outer layer of clay picked off, the bronze burnished – he would examine it, and then turn away, as though it no longer had anything to do with him. Did he ask "Is that all?"

Sphodrias sprang to his feet. "I just stopped in passing, to invite these youths to my son's naming feast."

Meleas examined the features and form of the waxen likeness of me. "It will be a fine bronze. Have you entirely given up working in marble?"

Apelleas motioned towards a number of smooth-faced, god-sized, mortal-sized and smaller wax-covered forms – awaiting his hand to give them features, sex and stance. "I could do one marble in the time it takes to do these." He called for a chair for Meleas.

"Perhaps one of your sons will love marble as you once did."

"My sons! One dreams of commanding a fleet. The other has an inclination to sophistry, and longs to travel. I blame that tutor I bought them. I have apprenticed my nephew. He has the hand and the eye."

Hekataios ran up. "The heat melts the wax between the core and the outer layer," he said "That is how they get the hollow, where they pour the bronze–" He saw Meleas. "Excuse me, Sir. Leo', come look. Sorry, you've got to stand there, haven't you?" He ran off again.

Apelleas called for wine. "But I am to make a marble in Corinth. Artemis Huntress."

"An offer from Corinth is a sculptor's olive crown," Meleas said. "Corinthians are born knowing what is best."

"And Rhodians know what is biggest."

"Did you encounter a certain Timokrates when you were in Rhodes?" Meleas asked.

"The merchant?"

"The same. Is he a man of immoderate wealth?"

"For Lakonia, yes. By Rhodian standards, middling."

Artists measure the purse-depth of their patrons surpassingly well. He shouted at a young apprentice, who picked the remaining bits of clay from a fired statue. The nephew?

"Does his trading take him abroad often?"

Apelleas laid down his tools, and took up his cup of wine. "Meleas, you are looking for facts about this man. All I know is that he trades mainly with the barbarians of western Asia. His affairs prosper, and he is ambitious. His competitors say he would sell his mother if the price were right, but they are competitors." He took up a large blue stone – translucent, and both dark and bright – held it up to the light of the sun, and then rested it at the corner of my eye.

"Good match," he said to Meleas. "I can do the iris in one piece. This youth has good lashes. I shall make them separately, with bronze wire. That cannot be done in marble." He regarded me again. "He has a familiar look." He turned back to Meleas. "Now, what do you want me to learn about Timokrates?" Sudden awareness struck him. "I know who the boy resembles. A portrait I made once. A young Dionysos."

I put him in mind of *his* portrait!

At one time I had not savoured the thought of giving over my patrol to another boy, when I passed out of the flock. Now I envied Pityas his freedom to ride and hunt with Apollodoros. I had spent much of the day with Doreius when I was posing for the statue. The work was completed, and our time now restricted to stolen meetings, or walking back together from a

217

dining-club where he chanced to guest, and I sat apart with the eirens.

Sometimes Meleas gave us an opportunity to meet, by inviting us to the Menelaos House to share the midday meal with himself and Thermon, who had at last forgiven me for forsaking all but Lakedaimonian boxing. Poor Thermon. He deserved a pupil as dedicated to the discipline as Nikomedes. Had Nikomedes been Spartan rather than Corinthian...but this idle speculation is pointless. And painful.

On one of the days when we were invited to the Menelaos House, our host had quite forgotten us. Those swift, unobtrusive servants quietly introduced the extra dining-couch, and certainly Meleas revealed nothing, but the other guests were men of thirty and more, full citizens. It was not a gathering for a youth and a young warrior just twenty-two.

Aristodemos was one of the guests. I had not spoken to him since my father's funeral banquet. Lysander was enemy to Pausanios, but now he was hostile to Agisilaos also. I did not know where this placed me with regard to the Agiads, although I had no part in it. I recalled Antalkidas saying, "You *are* a political matter, Leotychides."

Aristodemos greeted me in a kindly manner, and called me Cousin. We were both Royal Heraklid, and the meeting passed with ease. I took the meal with my eyes downcast. Doreius spoke only when one of the men remembered to address him. This was either Meleas, Aristodemos, or a certain Diphridas, a man of charm and ready wit.

The talk was of the war between Phokis and Lokris. There had been some discussion of this in Hall, but the squabbles of distant northern states aroused little interest. Phokis had levied taxes on a territory it disputed with neighbouring Lokris. The Lokrians retaliated by invading Phokis itself.

Meleas and Aristodemos felt that the Thebans had a hand in it. This was confusing, as Thebes had persuaded the Phokians to tax the disputed territory; and had then incited the Lokrians to invade Phokis, as well as sending warriors to lend a hand in the invasion.

Sparta had a number of distant allies; states that had attached themselves to the Peloponnesian alliance, for protection in the Athenian War. Phokis was one such, and now sent to Sparta under the terms of an old treaty. Thebes was another, although she had cooled to us over the matter of the spoils.

"Most of our allies have men serving under Agisilaos in Asia." Aristodemos opposed sending troops to rescue Phokis. "Our freed-serf regiments are with him, too. The up-country men are getting in their crops, and would have little enthusiasm for this expedition."

"Are you speaking for yourself or the King?" someone asked.

"Pausanios will speak for himself in council." Time had dealt lightly with Aristodemos. He was as lean and bright-haired as he had been at Kleombrotos's name-feast, but the laughing young warrior had given way to a man of crisp authority.

"Our Peloponnesian allies have no quarrel with Lokris." Diphridas included Doreius when he addressed the company. "Nor have they treaties."

"We have," Thermon objected. "An ally is an ally, and that's an end to it." He set down his wine-cup, as though that settled the matter. A servant promptly refilled it.

"Thermon, the old glory hunter is hot for war, and doesn't care what it costs us," Diphridas replied bluntly. Lysander was back in Sparta. "A pity Agisilaos won't have him in Asia. He might be of some use to that fool Peisander. Lysander does know the sea."

Aristodemos dipped his bread in some oil that had spilt over the cheese. "The Phocians ought not to have taxed a disputed territory without sending for a mediator, if they are going to look to us to keep the wolves from their goats." Only then did he eat the bread.

Aristodemos never spoke with food in his mouth. Neither did Meleas, Diphridas or Doreius. I resolved to swallow before speaking in future. (Can one truly remember such trivia while the fate of the Hellenes was being decided)?

"It is a matter of honour," Thermon protested. "As much as the war in Asia."

"This matter of Phokis and the war in Asia may not be unconnected." Meleas spoke softly, but everyone listened. "There is a Rhodian named Timokrates, who came to the mainland with gold worth fifty talents of silver." He had spoken of this Timokrates with Apelleas the sculptor. "He gave it to faction leaders in three cities to provoke war with Sparta."

219

"Meleas, you are become fanciful."

"Would that I were!" Meleas countered Thermon's outburst. "In Thebes the money went to Ismenias, Androklidas and Galaxidoros." Could the sculptor have told him all this? Or had he asked questions of others?

"Ismenias is ambitious and Androklidas is avaricious," Aristodemos reflected. "All three are foes to Sparta."

"In Corinth," Meleas went on, "payments were made to Timolaos and Polyanthes. I had heard that name. Alkimenes called him a rabble-rouser. Aristeas admired him.

"I'd credit Timolaos with anything that might make him leader of Corinth," Diphridas said. "But I know Polyanthes, and he is not venal."

"A man can justify himself taking a bribe if he uses it to enrich his faction," someone said.

"Well, there is certainly a war party in Corinth now," Aristodemos confirmed. Alkimenes was a peace-party man. He had disputed with Aristeas, who must be of the war party. No, it had not been something about merging with Argos. I really had not paid much heed to these Corinthian matters.

Diphridas was thoughtful. "This has the sound of an Athenian intrigue."

Meleas disagreed. "Athens has lost none of her old ambitions, but the Athenians are Greeks and would not need to hide behind a man like Timokrates. The faction leaders I have named would think well before taking gold from barbarians while a Hellenic army is fighting in Asia."

"The Great King..." Diphridas courteously masked his disbelief.

"To be precise, Tithraustes. On behalf of his royal master." Meleas rose from his couch and faced his guests. I had always thought him like Antalkidas, a man with a liking for knowing what other men do not. I began to suspect in it something more serious of purpose. "A year or two of the sort of success we are having in Asia, and Persia will be driven out of Ionia. We could even be in Susa. Divide us in Hellas, and we are weakened in Asia."

"What has this to do with Phokis and Lokris?" Thermon demanded. "You stray, Meleas."

"There are Theban regiments in Phokis–"

220

"All the more reason—"

"Theban regiments whose purpose is to provoke Sparta into firing the first shot, in order to justify Thebes, Argos and Athens warring on us."

"The Lokrians fired the first shot."

"First shots are frequently a matter of interpretation. But wherever the rights lie, a general war would mean that in time we must withdraw our army from Asia, and leave Ionia to the Great King."

"If all this is true, Meleas, what would you do?" someone asked.

It was Aristodemos who replied. "The Thebans sent emissaries to Athens, to remind Athenians of their grievances against Sparta. I would send an embassy to Thebes, to remind the city that, but for Sparta, its citizens would be Athens' slaves."

"Little that would mean to the Thebans," Thermon scoffed.

Diphridas disagreed. "The Thebans are a volatile people. Rough. Hot-headed. Undisciplined. Act before they reason. They are still smarting about their spoils, and Agisilaos offended them by his behaviour at Aulis. But they cannot have forgotten what they suffered from Athens."

"So we woo the Thebans, and Hades take the Phokians?" Thermon challenged.

"Would you have us wear to please the Great King of Persia?" Meleas came near to anger.

"An ally is an ally," Thermon thundered "And a treaty is a treaty."

Diphridas rose and went to Meleas. "I believe you," he said. "And I am with you. But I fear we have just heard the voice of Sparta."

The Apella voted for war.

The ephors ordered a general mobilization.

Pausanios was in command of the Peloponnesian regiments that were to assemble across the border in Arkadia at Tegea. Lysander was ordered across the border with a staff of Spartan officers to muster the Phokians and other northern allies.

Doreius was ordered to march with Lysander. He confided

that the two armies were to rendezvous on an appointed day for an assault upon Haliartos, on Boiotia's northern border, just south of Phokis. As Haliartos was a town subservient to Thebes, it seemed the plan was to draw the Thebans out of Phokis, by threatening their own territory. Lysander would be second in command to the King who deposed the Council of Thirty he set up in Athens.

"Lysander will not like that," I said.

"Lysander will obey his orders," Doreius replied.

Sparta was filled, like a late-spring field of poppies, with the crimson cloaks of warriors. Young soldiers ran down the path to the hollow, carrying garlands to Artemis Orthia. Kallias, with a face shining brightly as his scabbard, announced that his company of cavalry had been chosen as honour guard to the King.

He looked like a hero-king in his plumed helmet and burnished bronze armour, riding a splendid chestnut. Pausanios had a partiality for chestnuts. I wondered whether the grave-faced man had a secret vanity for horses that matched his hair.

Behind him rode the honour guard, in single file, on the narrow road. Their leather armour was decorated by the bronze of the Agiad device. After them came the heavy-armed infantry, the hoplites' shields slung across their backs. O, to go with them. A warrior...They were followed by batmen, cooks and other army servants, urging on donkeys laden with all the baggage of an army on the move.

The Magpie stared longer than the rest.

I left whatever I was doing, and ran up to him. "Go and wave to him. I'll relieve you here."

His feet barely touched the ground.

"They are splendid!" A melleiren gazed at the dusty road.

"Continue your drill," I ordered.

They *were* splendid. I looked up every now and then, as the curving road took them out of vision and brought them back again, until they were small black figures against the sun, indistinguishable from the trees atop the peaks of the mountains.

News came in slowly. Lysander, we heard, had persuaded the Boiotian Orchomenians to declare their independence of

Thebes, and to join his force. Then there was silence from the north.

One night, while sleeping under the stars, the Magpie startled the flock awake by crying out in his sleep. He woke, stepped quietly over the others, and walked towards a copse. Had he gone to the river, I would have followed him to see whether he was troubled. As he made for the trees, I assumed it to be a cramp followed by an urgent call of nature, and went back to sleep. The next day, Agesipolis turned up.

We had just come out of the river after an evening dip, and were drying ourselves with our cloaks. The Magpie wanted to talk to me. The others ran off towards the cooking-fires. My cousin rode up, and flung himself off a fine horse.

"You looked like having great sport in the river," he said. "I wish I had come earlier. I would have joined you."

"Join us some time in winter. What brings you here, Ages'?"

He gave me a look that meant he would tell me privily, and said, "Good evening, Anaxandros."

It should not have surprised me that he recalled the Magpie's name. Kings' heirs are taught such things. Anaxandros invited him to sit down. Agesipolis looked about. For a chair? He joined us on the ground.

"It is dull in Sparta," he complained. "My dearest friend is gone on duty."

"So is our most tiresome teacher," the Magpie said cheerily. His smile faded. "Agesipolis, is there anyone who can explain the meaning of dreams?" That cry in the night.

"Priests," my cousin replied promptly. "Tell me your dream and I'll ask for you."

"I have a friend in the King's honour guard–" The Magpie began.

"*My* friend was rejected for it. My father's friends say he is using me to advance himself." Agesipolis turned to me. "That Meleas is one of them. Aristodemos is no better. My friend will blame me for his being put on border duty."

"He would not be such a fool, Ages'." I said, but if he is, I thought, you are well rid of the fellow. "Go on, Magpie, what was your dream?"

"I dreamt that a spear went through my thigh, but I couldn't feel it."

223

"You never feel things in dreams," I told him.

"That wasn't the reason. I looked and saw that it was Kallias who was wounded. Not me. He was lying in blood."

Agesipolis surprised me by the gravity of his expression. He almost resembled his father. "I shouldn't worry, Anaxandros. I have offered to Zeus Saviour to protect my father. One had always ought to pray to Zeus for kings."

"Ages', Kallias is not a king."

"Zeus will no doubt look after his honour guard as well, Leo'," he replied lamely, and turned back to the Magpie. "Ask one of the gods who helps mortals to look after your friend. Apollo or Artemis or the Twin Gods – no, Polydeukes and Kastor are more helpful to men at sea–"

The Magpie was on his feet. "I'll ask them all. Thank you, Agesipolis."

"Kallias will be the best protected soldier in the king's army," I remarked as the Magpie left us. "What was the other reason you are so certain he is safe?"

"Father's army wasn't really involved much in the fighting." He smiled and looked very young. The fierce joy in his eyes was not that of a child. "Leo', Lysander is dead."

The great bronze-shield moon looked over the mountains. My old enemy was dead. I surprised myself by feeling nothing.

"How?"

"It's still a state secret, so don't tell anyone."

"If it's a state secret, don't tell me."

"You are Royal Heraklid. Leo'; you don't know the trouble that man caused Father."

"You haven't told me how he died. Was it an illness?" Had one of Apollo's arrows taken him? A sudden fever like my father's? Lysander, too, was old.

"I do not know everything, but he didn't wait for Father to arrive with the Peloponnesians, and attacked Haliartos with his own army alone. He was killed – and most of his army with him, I believe."

I leapt to my feet. "Most of his army slain, and you sit there grinning!" Apollo, let this be one of my cousin's fancies. Let Lysander and all his malice live, but don't let the unthinkable be true.

News trickled in. The bodies of the Spartan dead had been recovered under truce. That meant it was not a victorious army that was marching back to Lakedaimon.

"The dead are buried in their war-cloaks," a rhodibas chattered, "with olive crowns on their heads."

"That brat has a loud voice," the Magpie said.

How long it was before those far trees on the mountain-tops thickened in the distance, and became files of men marching south to Sparta. How many tricks the light played on strained eyes, as the trees stayed fixed in their places. It was the Worm, who had eyes like Lynkeus, who definitely sighted the army on the road.

The men above thirty, the full citizens, would go straight to their houses; the young warriors to their barracks. Making up some pretext, I begged leave of the Commander to go into Sparta. Perhaps he believed me. I ran to the barracks quarter of the City.

The men marched in columns to their barracks. Their faces were grim under the sweat and dust of the road. Their eyes were fierce. Their steps seemed to ring with anger. It was not a victorious army, certainly. Neither had it been defeated.

I intended to wait only until I saw the face I searched for, but Doreius's eyes lit at the sight of me, and I was rooted to the spot. He returned in less time than I thought he would. He had washed his face hurriedly.

It looked like a white mask against a rim of grey.

"Come along." he threw his arm about my shoulders. "Meleas invited me to take a cup of wine after I reported back. I can use it."

"Has your enomotarchos dismissed you?"

"I am my own platoon leader, and I have dismissed my platoon."

"You've been promoted?"

"Because every man over twenty-four is dead. My platoon consists of the five of us still living."

"Where is Sphodrias?"

"Wounded. Not gravely. Kallias is in a bad way. One of those freak things. Meleas knows more about it than I do. He was with the King. It is a wonder that imbecile Sphodrias is alive; but, by the Twin Gods, he is a splendid man to have at your side

225

in battle!"

"Where are the wounded, Doreius?"

"A strange thing. The King's son, Agesipolis, rode up to meet his father on the road. He asked for Kallias, and ordered that he be taken to the sanctuary of Asklepios of the Cattle Price. When he saw Sphodrias, he had him sent there, too."

The priests of Asklepios at the god's sanctuary near the Cattle Price House are the finest healers in Sparta.

"Lysander thought he could talk the Haliartans over to us, as he had the Orchomeneans." Thermon stood by a wall where ancient penteconters fought a faded sea-battle.

"With a Theban garrison inside the city?" Meleas asked drily.

Thermon affected not to hear. Lysander could do no wrong. Like many another good man, he rarely confounded opinion with reason. "They refused. He ordered the assault."

"He was like a dog with fleas all morning," Doreius quaffed his wine. They had already talked their way through the battle, and were back at the start.

Lysander had led his men up the walls. When the Haliartans were unable, or unwilling, to strike for their freedom from Thebes, he assaulted the city fortifications. The main body of Thebans outside the walls, hoplites supported by cavalry, attacked.

"First rule of war. Don't get caught between two enemies. Old dogs forget old tricks."

Thermon glared. "A Haliartan spear brought Lysander down. He stood closest to the wall." His utterance was in some way a challenge.

"We tried to fight our way through to his body," Doreius said.

The northerners made for the hills. Thebans ran after them, shouting victory cries. They pursued too far. Thermon and another Spartan officer rallied the allies. They turned and rained spears, rocks and any other missiles that came to hand, down upon the enemy. About two hundred Thebans were slain that way. The rest fled. The Spartans near the city wall fought on, to recover Lysander's body. Most were slain.

Thermon held out his wine-cup. "Our brave northern allies slipped back across the border into Phokis, during the night."

Meleas might have recalled Thermon's spirited defence of the Phokian alliance.

"If Lysander had waited for us, it would have been a victory." Meleas looked as though his fine wine tasted bitter.

"I came down from the hills in the morning, to fight for Lysander's body. But Pausanios had asked for a truce." Thermon's face flushed with anger. "And asked for the bodies of our slain. Like a defeated general. Why did he not fight for them?"

"We considered it in the King's war council." Meleas restrained himself with visible effort. "Thermon, Lysander wasted an army. Our strength was halved." His patience was wearing thin. "The enemy were strong in cavalry. We were weak. We could not recover bodies so close to the walls without taking Haliartos, and Thebans held the city and its fortifications. An Athenian army arrived to reinforce them–"

"With Thrasyboulos at its head," Thermon growled.

"Why, in the name of Athena of Victories, didn't Lysander wait for Pausanios?" Meleas leapt to his feet.

Had Lysander tried to snatch the fame of a single-handed victory? Or had the iron nerves of the victor of Notion and Goat River cracked?

"Why was Pausanios a day late?"

"Our allies. The Peloponnesians. Lysander knew they cannot mobilize as quickly as we do. And we waited for the Corinthians." Meleas returned to his chair, but stood, one hand resting on its slanted back. "We waited. They did not come...Pausanios is a brave man, but he never wastes lives."

"He hadn't ought to have asked for that truce," Thermon insisted. "I tell you, Lysander is an angry shade."

I recalled my mother's fury-face as she cursed Lysander. "Where is he buried?"

All three looked at me as though they had forgotten I was there. I became aware of what I had done. Spoken without being addressed. Broken into the talk of warriors and citizens. It was too late.

"In Paonia," Meleas said shortly, "with full honours."

"Disgraceful," Thermon muttered. I did not know whether he spoke of my inexcusable behaviour, or Lysander's burial place. "You would have fought to the death, wouldn't you, Doreius?"

227

"Had I been ordered to." He turned to Meleas. "The King was right. But I'll not forget those Theban bastards jeering us out of Boiotia. By the Twin Gods, it cannot be left there, Meleas."

"No," Meleas spoke with quiet certainty "Athens wouldn't let it even if we would." Strange! He did not say Thebes, but Athens.

Doreius and I left the Menelaos House together. When we reached Hermes's shrine at the parting of the paths, he made a sign of respect to the god, and turned towards his barracks. I waited for him under the laurel trees the next day, and the next, but he did not appear.

Apollodoros had been fined for setting a bad example, because Pityas threw down his balancing-stones in anger, after coming second in a jumping competition. Apollodoros never lost his temper when disappointed in a game, but nor did Pityas after that. When five days passed and there was no sign of Doreius, I concluded he had been punished for my unseemly interruption into the talk of grown men. I had shamed Doreius.

I clouted a rhodibas for disputing a melleiren, and caught sight of Agesipolis running up the path to the heights. His horse grazed below, in the plain.

"Are you thinking of joining this flock, Ages'?"

He did not smile. "I thought it was over now Lysander is dead, but his shade is worse than he was living."

Some melleirens stopped a ball-game to look towards us. I motioned Agesipolis to a hill, where we could be private.

"They are going to try father for his life."

"Ages', it is not easy to bring a man to trial. The ephors could not try the traitor regent, even after seeing his letters to the Great King."

"Everybody knows Father recovered Lysander's body under truce."

"It was not a submission. He broke no law."

"It isn't law," his voice cracked. "It is Lysander's friends."

"Ages', why don't you talk to Aristodemos?"

"He considers me frivolous."

"Then talk to your friend."

He picked a thorn lodged in his ankle from a prickly weed.

"Now there is trouble over the house, he avoids me."

"That is no reason. You did not shame him."

My cousin shouted. "I tell you, they are going to kill Father."
I rose. "What are you going to do, Leo'?"

Sometimes a god whispers silently in one's ear.

"I am going to see your father." I had not known until I spoke
the words.

The gates, the courtyard, the rooms of the Agiad palace
awakened memory. I walked with assurance to the king's
reading room. Perhaps that is why the servants let me pass
unhindered.

Pausanios sat in a tall-backed chair, holding a scroll thick
enough to be a book. He was not reading it. Atop a lion-legged
writing table, a stylos rested against a wax tablet, as if
abandoned. The King's short beard did not hide the lines in his
face. The sun's finger touched a bronze mixing-bowl with fire.

He looked up. "Leotychides! How kind of you to visit me."

"Sir, there is talk of a trial," I blurted.

"So it would seem." He called for wine, as though I called
upon him daily. Placed the scroll on a small table near his chair.
"Even poetry declines now..." What poem had he been reading?
We drank from cups painted with Herakles slaying monsters.
He turned to the servant. "Leave us." His slight gestures barely
moved the folds of his long, narrow-bordered cloak. He had
looked a hero-king riding to war. Now he was wise
Rhadymanthos, or some other great king of ancient days. Why
had Lysander hated him so?

"Sir, no sane man would ask you to order warriors to die for
Lysander's body when you could never recover it."

"Fervour is no friend to reason. It did not help that
Thrasyboulos led the Athenians." He smiled. I thought, I am
become as fanciful as Agesipolis.

Pausanios had been pondering some matter of the City when
I imposed my company on him. I felt foolish. Having shamed
Doreius in the Menelaos House, I now intruded upon the King
as though I were an elder or a king. Or worse, a child. Had any
boy in my patrol behaved with such audacity, I should have
thrashed him until his skin broke. "Were it not Thrasyboulos, it

would have been another general, sir. Athenians will always want what is not theirs."

"Attica is over-peopled." He rose. I got to my feet. Assuming he wished me to leave. With his customary kindness, he put me at my ease. "Once, Athens had a law-giver who bought them time to make craftsmen's helpers of their free tillers. Those men who must give over four-fifths of their crops. But the craftsmen grew rich and bought slaves in great numbers, and peopled Athens still more. The tillers stayed poor, or became rowers who can only prosper in war. A mob." Pausanios was no hero-king. He would not have slain those monsters. He would have heard out their minds as they devoured him.

"Do you mean, sir, that Lysander was right. That we should have destroyed Athens as the Thebans wished?"

He sat down his wine-cup on the writing-table. "Sparta did not become famous by doing wrong. We live with earthquakes and storm. It must be our destiny to live with Athens as well." He returned to the chair.

I carried his empty cup to the krater, and began to mix fresh wine. "Sir, the trial–" I cut off my words. It was clear the King did not wish to speak of it.

"Say your mind, Leotychides. It is your right. I am going to beg a favour I would ask of a man grown."

"It was nothing, sir." This calm, thoughtful King, who knew so much of men and cities, would know how to reply to the accusing Elders. It was not my place to ask him how.

"Agesipolis is a good boy, but young for his age..."

"Only because he has not been flock-reared, sir."

"Leonidas was reared in a flock. Perhaps private upbringing of Kings' heirs is no good thing."

"You are a good king and not flock-reared. Agisilaos was, and he is the worst of men."

"He was not without good qualities. He is mindful of the well-being of his men in war." I thought of the men left for the barbarians. "He lives more simply than the least Spartan." He was too good to know what his words implied; I too young. "Leotychides, be a friend to Agesipolis."

I knew then. He was to die. At forty, he was meeting death with the dignity in which he lived his life. Birds sang in the courtyard. Horsemen galloped the rim of the krater, as they had

230

in my childhood when Pausanios struck me to stop my prattling of Alkibiades. His gaze fixed on something in the courtyard. He seemed already to be waiting to cross the river to the underworld. The dead do not reckon in time. I studied the bronze grooves of the sea-shell-shaped handles. "Fight them, sir. Fight Lysander's friends."

"Would you have me disobey my orders?" He took the wine-cup from me. "Be careful of such words. Enemies could turn them against you." His spear- and shield-hardened hands grasped my shoulders. "Men will try to use the son of Agis–"

"They already have, sir. I am not easily used."

"Lend Agesipolis your strength. I leave him an uneasy heritage. Will you give me your word on it?"

I took my place at the feet of this man who had the face of my childhood's father, as a gnawing fox tore wild words from me. I told him of those who had urged me to fight for my kingship, of my mother's plots, of how I kept my word to my father not to divide the City; but that I should gladly take up arms to fight for him against his enemies, and any manner of things.

His hands cupped my face, and turned it to look into his kind, bright-blue eyes. "Why, Leotychides, no harm will come to me. This trial is nothing. Like the other."

Pausanios, what a poor liar you were, for a king.

I went directly from Pausanios to the Menelaos House.

Meleas stepped out, before the servant had time to show me into a room where men's voices were raised.

"They were my father's friends," he explained. "I am trying to calm Lysander's storm."

I told him of Agesipolis's fears, and how I had found Pausanios. He made an angry gesture. "Fool boy! Why didn't he come to me? Why bring you into this? They have moved more swiftly than I thought." He reflected only briefly. "Don't go to Pausanios again. Avoid Agesipolis. Do not come here until I send word it is safe. Warn Doreius as well. The endangered are dangerous."

Another old man was being shown in. Meleas sent me out with a servant, by a hidden passage in the ancient palace. A cold north wind of a thought blew through my mind. The absence of

Doreius had another explanation. I was endangered, therefore dangerous. Some dark fate had befallen him. Because of me.

"You know, that girl Gorgo is really not unpleasant," Anaxandros said, as he scraped the oil and sand off my back. "She walks up here every day to let me know how Kallias fares."

"Magpie, what did happen to Kallias?" He has been with the King. The King's army had not fought.

"A wild Theban threw a spear at him before the truce. It struck his thigh. He bled a lot. Like my dream."

"What did the healing priests say?"

"The gods told them that, if he lives, he will not limp. It was very good of Agesipolis to look after him. When you see him, thank him for me."

"Thank him yourself. That looks like his horse on the road."

Avoiding Agesipolis was not as easy as Meleas thought. This time my cousin had not come lightly. Anaxandros noted his distress, and left us. The wind blew down from the heights, as Agesipolis dismounted. The horse was restive. I stroked its neck to quiet it.

"Father is safe," Agesipolis said. "He got over the border to Arkadia."

"Arkadia!"

"The sanctuary of Athena in Tegea. They have given him asylum."

"Pausanios a suppliant?"

The wind blew the long cloak about his thin legs. "Aristodemos is to be my regent. I do not like Aristodemos. I don't want him as regent. Leo', what am I going to do without Father? What am I going to do?"

He looked to me as though I, five months his senior, would tell him all he needed to know.

King Agesipolis!

Chapter 9

A few days after Pausanios fled, Doreius stepped into my path as I was coming from the river.

"I waited for you by the Wayfinder's shrine," he said. "I had ought to have remembered you would be setting the melleirens to breaking rushes—"

"Meleas said you must not go to his house." A dash of boys sprayed us with water as they rushed past. "I think he helped Pausanios run."

"Is the King safe?"

"Safe, but not king, Doreius. Nor fit to be. He ran." No matter how I turned the fact, it showed me the same face. Pausanios had run away to save his life.

"There must have been reasons."

"Kings do not run. He could have fought. Or stood trial."

"The Polemarchs kept us for days with their questions..." He absently picked a sprig of columbine, which had strayed from the mountain. "About the King...Mostly about the King..." A melleiren ran up to ask something. "We will talk of this another time."

"Doreius, I cannot meet you again. You must not seek me out."

I took his meaning, and could not leave him with the misapprehension. "You do not understand. I am in danger. Nothing that touches me is safe."

"I see." The mask fell. "You know me to be such a weakling that I am unable to protect myself. Such a coward that you must shield me. Is that your opinion?"

"Of course not, but—"

"Leotychides, once you asked me whether you could stand at my side in battle. You must think me a craven warrior if you consider that a safe place." The commander called my name.

"Under the laurels," Doreius said quickly. "When the boys are asleep."

The moon was high and silver. Frogs croaked. The dark peaks of Taygetos were black against the moon-washed sky.

"When I left you at the Wayfinder's shrine, I was so drowsy I felt the ground coming up to my face," Doreius said. "The next day the Polemarchs sent for the survivors. Why were we still alive when the others were dead? I explained that the fighting stopped with nightfall as usual. We intended to resume in the morning, but the King arrived and arranged a truce. Then it was how many men had he? How many the enemy? Where did Lysander's body lie? Some of them simply wanted to know the facts of it. Others wanted us to condemn the King. That I could not do. He acted in every way honourably–"

"Until he ran. Once I thought, if I patterned myself on Pausanios, I would be the best of kings. My father was a good king. I honour him, but when I looked at Pausanios, I thought, *that* is kingship."

"Leotychides, sometimes we make statues of those we look up to. And blame them for being only men." The frogs sounded louder in the silence. A nightingale sang somewhere. "Lysander need not have died, but for his own impatience."

"Lysander died under a curse."

"If curses could kill, men would not need spears."

"Doreius, a priestess cursed him. A royal priestess. I do not remember the whole of it, but she doomed him to die a small death. His bones to lie in foreign soil. But first, he should be shamed. It was before he went with Agisilaos to Asia."

Doreius spoke thoughtfully. "Lysander was not shamed. Agisilaos shamed himself when he named Lysander his meat carver. Lysander was the elder. He was loyal to his bond with Agisilaos. He was angry, but not shamed."

"But his death–"

"He was an old man. Testy. Short-tempered. No man who dies bravely in battle dies a mean death."

"He does not lie in Spartan soil."

"Sometimes that is the fate of fallen warriors, but it is no dishonour," he smiled slightly. "The gods are not so easily used. Not even by – a royal priestess."

I thought of Aphrodite's bare offering table. How often my

mother had importuned the goddess, but she had not brought Alkibiades back to her. "Hekataios once saw a red fox outrun a hound. He took it as an omen that he would win his next race. He did. But he usually wins long races."

He laughed. "My brother sees omens in the leaves of trees."

"I mean he was no more a fool than I." He did not dispute it. The star-touched stream whispered over its mossy rocks, as it had in the days of the Law-giver, but two kings had been unmade by one old man. "Doreius, whatever honours are paid Agisilaos, unless Apollo says I am not, I am King. And I shall not run."

Argos and Corinth openly joined the alliance of Athens, Thebes and Lokris against Sparta. Between them, the enemy raised a force of twenty-four thousand heavy-armed infantry and fifteen hundred cavalry, as well as a large body of light-armed infantry from other cities. In all, an army of fifty thousand.

The ephors ordered Agisilaos and the Lakonian regiments back to Greece. Agisilaos signalled that he would obey his orders. He assembled the allied contingents, and asked whether they would return with him or stay in Asia. The men voted to accompany him, and wept as they voted. Perhaps some tears were for the rich spoils of Persia, but most grieved at leaving unattended the dream of over two hundred years when victory was in sight.

It may have been simple loyalty to Sparta that decided some votes. Others were undoubtedly influenced by the thought of enemy armies devastating the lands of their own countries. Or perhaps it was the fear that without Sparta, the war-leader of Hellas, that invincible army would disintegrate into many significant bands in the vastness of Asia.

The barbarians had not spent their gold in vain.

When I was called to the Menelaos House, I thought to find Doreius, and perhaps Thermon, for the midday meal. I was shown a room I had never seen before. Meleas was alone.

He sat at a writing table, a stylos in his hand. "I have sent for

235

you to thank you. Pausanios would not have been acquitted this time."

"Leonidas did not run away, sir."

Meleas smiled wryly. "That is what Pausanios said, when we urged him to slip out of the city. It must be hard to have so recent a divine hero in the family."

"Agesipolis need not worry about that." A servant filled my cup.

"Leonidas died in obedience to the Law. Would you, a king's son, have a king dignify a traitor's malice by his death?"

"Lysander was my enemy, but no traitor."

"He plotted to make himself king."

"He was not Royal Heraklid, sir."

"There was a certain speech found amongst his effects." Meleas held out his hand for a scroll. "It argued that the kingship should go to the best of all the sons of Herakles, and not to the god's descendants through Hyllos."

There may be some merit to that."

"It was a complex conspiracy that would have put lies on the lips of Apollo, to prove Lysander to be that man. Blasphemy as well as treason."

"Sir, did Pausanios know of this plot?"

"He did when we told him."

"Why did he not refuse to stand trial?"

He struck the writing table with the scroll. "Kings cannot *refuse*. A king, above all, must obey."

"He did not obey. He ran."

"The trial was unlawful. Can you not understand?"

"I shall try, sir."

"Try harder."

"Doreius thought there might have been reasons."

"Then consider that, loving Pausanios less than you do, Doreius might know him better."

"Pausanios could have fought his enemies."

"Take up arms against his people? Is that your notion of a king?"

Finally, I spoke into the silence. "There was nothing but to flee, was there?" He let my question be its own reply. "Have you seen Lysander's speech?"

"I wrote down the substance of it, while it was still fresh in

236

my mind." He passed me the scroll.

I unrolled it and read it through. "I had not believed Lysander so thoughtful."

"Someone else wrote it for him. A foreigner who lives by the art."

Anaxilas had spoken of men paid to make the worse cause sound the better. Many men would have been moved by this speech. Good men, like Thermon. Lysander's enmity to Pausanios had not arisen solely from their differences about Athens. He intended to replace the Agiad king. He could not have foreseen that Agisilaos would turn against him. It was for this that he had contrived to make Agisilaos king. Would Sparta retain a king made by such a man? "What will happen when this is known?"

"As it is a royal matter, Agisilaos must be consulted before it is made public." He placed the scroll in a box painted with Herakles slaying the Hydra. "A many-headed monster..." He spoke in that double-meaning way of his.

"But you know."

"You will be going into the Hidden Thing soon. I have just come out."

I thought he was evading a reply; then the implication made me forget the question.

In ancient times, youths went into the forest to search out thieves and robbers before coming of age. Under the Law of Lykourgos, crimes became few; an eiren is fortunate to find a runaway serf to bring back to Sparta, or an up-country apprentice who has stolen from his master. Most must be content to take a wild beast to prove strength and courage.

Law-keeping passed from youths to men who could stand against a robber band come over the frontier or, as it happened two hundred years ago, quell a rising in Messenia. This body of men retained the ancient name. The Hidden Thing. Meleas was known to be one of them; it is no hidden matter when a man is out on the roll. It is a proud thing to be reckoned the strongest and bravest of warriors.

"I have withdrawn," Meleas answered, the many conjectures rolling about in my head.

"Why, sir? It is such an honour."

237

He told me about a secret body within this police that had been formed to snare Kinadon, who was himself a law-keeper. "I was asked to gain Kinadon's confidence. When I told them I could not deceive a man who had fought by my side in three campaigns, they found another informer."

"Who ordered this secret force? Who brought informers into Sparta? Was it Lysander? Agisilaos?"

"It is very simple to give many wrongs the name of one man." He turned the Hydra box in his hands.

"Did you warn Kinadon?"

"I told myself that if he were blameless, he had nothing to fear. Nor would he have heeded me. This house, my running horses and chariot made me the enemy." He stood and came around from the writing table, to lean against its edge as he spoke. "He was not the brute men think him now, but a thoughtful man. Our tent-companions complained that our talk kept them awake until dawn...but that was before bitterness twisted him. Before he was wronged, and added all injustices to his own, and made a god of it. Anger can be a cleansing thing, but bitterness distorts the spirit. No matter. It is done now. But that secret body was not disbanded when it was over. Monsters are easier created than slain."

"Who commands these secret law-keepers?"

"In law, the ephors. In practice, themselves. Who knows who they are? I think not a few are unknown to one another. The monster is self-generating."

"Sir, how many Spartans know of this?"

"Very few. I tell you because Agisilaos may be popular with the foreign troops, but Lysander's friends hate him. If you find yourself King, you should know." He smiled wearily. "And because Pausanios is in Arkadia, Aristodemos has enough to do as Regent, and I have lived too long in a silence with it. So it appears that I have unburdened it all on a youth of seventeen."

The war was moving south to Peloponnesos. The ephors ordered a general mobilization. Four thousand heavy-armed Spartiate infantry, and six hundred cavalry, were put under the command of Aristodemos. Peloponnesian allies contributed ten thousand more fighting men.

Timolaos of Corinth actually proposed that war be waged in Lakonia! The saner of the enemy commanders convinced him of the impossibility of breaching frontiers that had been inviolate six hundred years but, while the generals argued, Aristodemos moved quickly and invaded Corinth itself. Doreius was with our army of fifteen thousand that was going out to engage fifty thousand. This time I did not watch the warriors marching on the road.

I was in the forest.

I slaked my thirst in a thin trickle of a stream, and studied the leaves of the Taygetos flower that some call the king's flower. There was no blossom; its white flower appears only in midwinter, before its leaves.

I wondered why its blossoming was contrary to nature, and why it was sometimes called the king's flower, and any number of things that had never entered my mind. It is that way in the Hidden Thing.

It was day, but the foliage is thick in this part of the forest of the Taygetos range, and it shut out the sun. In the darkness of the forest, the war seemed very remote. Life becomes simple when it is reduced to survival.

I gnawed a cold piece of the hare that I had snared and cooked the previous night between forked twigs. It had taken time to learn how not to set afire the small bird or animal brought down to stave off hunger. To bury food, so that no animal might make off with it during the night. There had been so many charred meals, and many of berries, and days of none at all.

It takes time to learn the ways of the forest. The snap of the twig that signals the danger of boar. The rustle of leaves alerts one to the presence of a prospective meal. The type of plants that indicate the proximity of a stream or spring. I had learnt the ways of the forest. That was the easy part.

I thought I had known what it was to be alone. That was before I lived on the slopes of Taygetos, apart from human kind. Always I had been able to turn to a flock-brother and talk of commonplaces. Or look in silence to a friend, whose presence is a sort of armour of the mind, when unbidden thoughts arise.

239

Having mastered the way of the forest, my mind woke. The I-aware part that had been dormant when the survival-aware took over. And I was alone. Cut off from my flock-brothers, unbound by duties, where nothing could hide me from myself. Why is it so painful to know oneself?

Before a youth sets out in his lonely life in the forest, he thinks mainly of the ferocious beasts – the wolves, boar, or even the lions – that await him, although there are not so many lions now. And he dreams of the wolf, boar or lion he must kill and bring back in token of his self-mastery. But the most ferocious beast is that knowledge of self. Then self, and knowledge of self, become one. And the knowing is no great thing.

I am giving away no secrets if I say that a Spartan army drawn up in battle array resembles a bronze wall bristling with spears. Our enemies are familiar with the sight. The hoplite, in his heavy bronze armour, stands legs apart, feet firmly planted, his helmet protecting his head, neck, cheeks and nose. His right hand grasps his iron-tipped spear, pointing it directly at the enemy; his left arm is thrust through the great round shield that covers him from chest to thigh.

As the order to advance goes down the line, the feet come together in marching step. The shields lock, so that each man's shield covers his own left and the right of the man next to him. The wall moves towards the enemy in a slow march. Step. Step. Pause. Step. Step.

If a man is of valorous spirit, his nature impels him to rush forward and fling himself upon the enemy. If he is timid, he is inclined to fall back. The Spartiate hoplite does neither. Discipline keeps him in place, and in step with his fellows. I doubt that is a secret either. If it is, it matters little that I disclose it, as foreigners cannot imitate it. It is a discipline that begins at seven, and cannot be acquired by weapons training alone. It is the reflection of a mind that is disciplined in all facets of life, manifesting itself on the battlefield.

Faced with the slow, steady advance of that lethal moving wall, a brave enemy will often rush forward rashly, in a futile attempt to crack it. Not a few have impaled themselves in this way. Another wave follows more cautiously.

The Spartiate hoplite is an expert at close fighting with his short thrusting sword.

The wall of shields holds. The enemy's spirit ebbs. He turns, presenting his unshielded, vulnerable middle to Spartan spears. Seeing his comrades fall with little damage to the Spartans, the battle-fury drains from the enemy, and he flees in disorder. A fleeing man is always at one's mercy; a timid foe doomed at the outset.

Level ground and a formal battle, with both sides drawn up facing one another, favour Spartan warfare, but there are methods of standing off surprise attacks and other contingencies. Most of them.

In late summer, when the bluff above the city is yellowing, the Messeis Spring at Therapine spills over the rocks in a silver spray, and sends down a slender stream that keeps the grasses green under the plane trees and gives the earth a pure, sweet, scent.

A blue butterfly lit upon a red lily, closed its wings, and opened them before flitting off again. I picked an arbutus berry.

"That is not ripe," Doreius said. It wasn't.

The army retreated a few days after I came out of the Hidden Thing, carrying my wolf – a large, shaggy one – slung across my shoulders. Taking the wolf had been no great thing, either.

"Your hair is too long for an eiren," Doreius tugged a lock. "Your commander is lax."

"I have passed out of the flock."

"Cut it. You are not yet a warrior."

"We shall have won the war before I am."

"Would you rather we lost?"

A brown-winged, yellow-breasted bird sang its three melodious notes on a branch above us. The sun was strong, and we were protected from the breeze that blew the wilting petals from the last of the wild violets.

"In every other city, men are warriors at eighteen."

"They are not warriors. They are only landowners, merchants and artisans in armour. That is why we win. Don't be impatient of the next two years of your life. The army has first claim on the next forty."

"Tell me of the battle."

"We engaged the enemy near Nemea. Faced the Athenians. Defeated them. Routed the Thebans, and sent the Corinthians running back to their own city. We lost twelve men and three horses."

"Was Aristeas with Timolaos? I should like to see him run."

He sat up, his head thrown back in sudden laughter that brought me out of my lassitude. "It was a battle, not a banquet. Or do you think we stop to give our names and ancestors as though it were the Trojan War?"

"What is Aristodemos like in the field?" I picked a twig from his hair.

"He thinks quickly. Acts. We did not know we were a spear's-throw away from the enemy until we heard their battle-hymn. The trees are thick around there. They were advancing for a surprise attack. You know the rest. Aristodemos ordered us into battle array. He led the charge. Athenians are brave, but they cannot stand firm and hold their line. Aristodemos is a fine commander.

"Better than Agisilaos."

"Agisilaos is no mean general. But I'd rather serve under Aristodemos. It's getting late." The sun's brightness had softened. "We had best start back."

"It is still early, and there are apples on that tree." I ran to the tree, shook it, and returned, tossing apples to Doreius. "I promised Pausanios I should protect Agesipolis." A pleasant aroma rose from the white flesh of the red apple, as I bit into it.

"Are you better able than Aristodemos?"

"I have thought on that." The birdsong was less, and the unclouded sky became sombre. "Ages' will no longer have a regent in two years. I shall be twenty also. If I reigned now, I should only have Agisilaos as regent, but if I send to Delphi when I am of age, and Apollo names me lawful king...Pausanios could only have meant that."

"Did he?"

"I don't know. Anyway, it must be my decision. And Apollo's."

"Yes. Let it rest with the god."

I leaned back against the tree trunk. "So the war is all but over."

242

"The battle is over, but the Thebans and Argives have holed up in Corinth. The Sikyonians are frightened. We left them a garrison, but...No, it is not over..."

Our voices were the only sounds now. The bird-song and chirping of insects had stilled. The sky was darkening without any intervening blue prelude.

"How quiet it is. Like that poem of Alkman's." I began to quote and Doreius spoke the lines with me.

> *All things sleep,*
> *the beasts sleep,*
> *the bees, the mountain*
> *creatures that creep*
> *upon the dark earth sleep,*
> *the monster drowsing*
> *in the crimson seas,*
> *and birds fold*
> *swift wings*
> *sleeping*

"Doreius, the sun is turning black!"

"It is only an eclipse."

"An eclipse! An omen...An omen for Sparta!"

"The sun will be black at Athens, at Argos, at Corinth and Thebes, too."

"How do you know?"

"I talked to old soldiers, who saw the same eclipse from different cities on the same day. The omen could be for any of our enemies, as easily as for us." He turned me to face himself. "First rule of war, my love. Don't panic."

"I thought it was don't get caught between two enemies."

"Some rules are two-parted."

It was a two-parted omen, also.

That wily Athenian Konon, who escaped Kallikratidas and evaded Lysander with eight triremes, took his ships to Cyprus and put them in the service of that island's Tyrant. In time, the exile became the Tyrant's chief minister, and in that office persuaded the satrap Pharnabazos to merge his strong fleet with the Cyprian fleet in the war against Hellas. Athens, that great

243

defender of Asian Greeks, was silent on the matter. Athens, like Persia, was at war with Sparta. Nominally, Pharnabazos was admiral of this combined fleet, but as barbarians are notoriously bad seamen, Konon commanded it.

Grand Admiral Peisander sighted Konon's fleet off the Karian promontory of Knidos. The Cyprian fleet alone equalled ours in number. Any melleiren would have known to avoid an encounter. Peisander engaged the joint fleet in its full strength. I shall say no more of his stupidity. He died bravely. So did his men. With the Spartan fleet sank the hopes of Ionia.

Agisilaos had swept down from Asia through Thrace, Macedonia, Thessaly and Phokis, and reached Boiotia, when his wife's brother lost our fleet. The King was preparing to engage a large force of Thebans and Argives near Koronaia, when messengers reached him, telling of the disaster at sea.

The troops had seen the eclipse, and were already downcast at the bad omen. With uncommon good sense – no, I must be just; Agisilaos was always quick with a retort, or a great decision. – he gave out that the messenger brought news of a great sea victory.

The men went into battle in high spirits, and defeated first the Argives, and then the Thebans in a spectacular victory in the plain. Agisilaos was quite badly injured in combat, but he had himself carried about on a litter after the battle, to visit the wounded.

Was there still something of the flock in my uncle? Or was he thinking of the hostility of those Lysandrians in Sparta, who had already deposed two kings?

Sparta greeted Agisilaos with less acclaim than my flock-brothers accorded Euagoras, when he came out of the Hidden Thing with a runaway serf. (Doreius told me that such runaways would rather a beating in Sparta than a second night in the forest with wild beasts, and thought that Euagoras and his captive helped one another find the way back to the City). Now the small youth sat under an ash, picking a melody to his newest poem, while Hekataios and Anaxandros skinned hares we had taken earlier.

"Agisilaos has been seen riding around his courtyard on a wooden stick." Anaxandros wiped his knife on the grass. "Playing horses with his son. What manner of king is that?"

"Agisilaos is no king at all," Aristokrates blew on the tinder, to hasten his fire.

"We all know that," Hekataios said. "But who will tell Agisilaos?"

"I shouldn't be surprised if someone did." Aristokrates spoke meaningfully. His father owed his statue to Lysander.

"No one said anything when he named Teleutias grand admiral," Hekataios challenged.

He could have made a worse choice." I attached a new string to my bow.

"Haven't you got that fire going yet, Pointer?" Anaxandros held up the skinned hare by its legs. "Teleutias is a good man, Cockerel, but he is Agisilaos's brother."

"He can't help that. Sing your new poem, Euagoras."

"It doesn't scan, Leotychides."

Nothing scanned. Lysander's friends in the Council of Elders were old, and moved slowly. Honest citizens, like Meleas, might be pleased to see Agisilaos deposed, but they would do nothing to overturn the Apella's decision.

"Pity Peisander didn't leave Teleutias much of a fleet." The Magpie tossed the hare to Aristokrates. It hit him. He threw it back with a true aim, flush in Anaxandros's face. A scuffle broke out. Hekataios and I tried to separate them, and became part of the fight. Hekataios slipped on the skinned hare. Anaxandros laughed. Hekataios lunged. Anaxandros backed off, and slipped himself. His look of surprise set us laughing. We forgot why we fought.

Doreius and I set out after dawn one morning with spear, knives, bows and arrows, for a day's hunting. Spring had come round again, but snow still covered much of Taygetos, forcing game down to the lower peaks.

The sun cast its morning light on the mushroom-shaped roof, under which the assembly meets, as we reached the Babykon Bridge. Men streamed from its open sides. People lined the path leading to Knakion stream. They cheered loudly, when a tall, white-haired man stepped forth. A newly-elected Elder. I knew him for a friend of Lysander. A woman walked up to him, extended a plate of food as is the custom, and spoke in a ringing voice, "The city honours you with this meal."

We might have tarried longer, had we not caught sight of our flock brother Pronax. This time, he saw us and bounded over.

"Have you seen Chionis, Doreius? He was to meet me by the Babykon." No, we had not seen him. "I thought he might have come here in error. He may not have attended properly, as he seemed in great haste when I met up with him coming out of the barracks." Doreius and I smothered our smiles. "I remember saying tomorrow is Assembly Day, and a new Elder is to be elected..."

So he went on, until Doreius took advantage of a brief pause to say, "Pronax, we are going hunting." We set our spears against our shoulders.

"I shall go with you." Pronax brightened. "Wait until the Elder comes down from the acropolis. I understand the King will be here." It would not occur to Pronax that such an encounter was not to my liking. "To be elected an Elder is an olive crown for excellence." Pronax often solemnly stated what everyone knows.

I could see the new Elder leaving the shrine of Zeus Saviour, followed by youths and garlanded maidens. He crossed Acropolis Road, and went into the temple of the Muses.

There was a stir amongst the people waiting at the foot of the acropolis. They made way for twenty-eight long-cloaked Elders, headed by a light, grizzled man with a wimpy beard. His wife was amongst some women. She must have been there all the time, but Kleora never was a woman to draw the eye, despite her height and flesh.

"Spare your greetings," Antalkidas pushed his way between Doreius and myself. "Watch Agisilaos." My uncle had something white draped across his arm. "Have you seen his house? The gates look as though they were built in the reign of Aristodemos. Our first king, not our good Regent."

"You go too far, Antalkidas." Pronax towered above Doreius, and Antalkidas, although they were tall men. "Have some respect for the King."

Antalkidas's pale eyes met mine, as he replied, "I always

respect the *King*."

The Elder and his procession started a leisurely way down Acropolis Road, to the street leading from the agora. He halted as Agisilaos stepped forward and approached him. "Now," Antalkidas whispered. Agisilaos presented the white thing to the Elder. A fine robe, even and pale in colour. He looked up to speak to the old man. We were too far to hear his words.

"Note the deference. I wonder that he doesn't cast down his eyes. How old is he now? Forty-five? Forty-seven?"

"Explain yourself, Antalkidas."

"To you, my dear Pronax? That would be a task beyond Herakles. Ah, here comes the ox. Not Kleora. The animal." The crowd parted to let a servant pass. He led a fat beast. "Agisilaos will most respectfully beg the Elder to accept it. See how he turns away to avoid being thanked."

"Such deference from a king, the good Elder will think. A poor king who gives all his spoils to his troops. Surely Lysander, great as he was, must have sorely offended this good, gentle man." Antalkidas linked his arms through ours. "Come, my friends, the comedy has ended for today. Now you see how Agisilaos is winning over the council of leaders. Long life to you, Pronax. We shall meet again, I dare say."

We walked west towards the mountains. Antalkidas with us; for that matter, in Sparta, when he was supposed to be at sea with Teleutias.

"I wonder how many of the good Elders know of a certain speech that was shown to Agisilaos..." he mused.

"Do you think Agisilaos fool enough to let it be public?"

He raised his eyebrows. "You are developing your own sources of information, Leotychides. Do you know as much about his adventures in Asia?"

"They were worn fairly thin in Hall, Antal."

"I do not mean the field of battle. Do you recall Megabates, Doreius? No, he was after your time. Beautiful boy, Spithridates's son. Agisilaos was in love with him. One night the boy tried to kiss him. Barbarian courtesy to a king. Agisilaos misunderstood. He turned away; and declared that he would rather be master of himself in such matters, than see all the things before his eyes turn to gold. Gold! Interesting metaphor for such a simplicity-loving Spartan."

247

"That, too, reached the clubs," Doreius told him.

"But, I wager, nothing about the other pretty boys who slipped from his tent, in the early hours of the morning. Agisilaos must have an audience for his virtues. By the gods, there is no one vainer than a modest man."

The road took us through a sea of green barley, as Antalkidas regaled us with tales of Agisilaos's love affairs. Serfs worked in the fields, singing a song their ancestors sang in the same fields, before Dorians came to Peloponnesos. A few slept in the sun, their sickles abandoned.

Antalkidas mopped his brow. It was not wet. "Let us sit down."

"That always means a scheme."

"Surely I am owed an ear for rescuing you from Pronax."

"Most surely," Doreius agreed. "But Sphodrias, Kallias and Anaxandros are waiting for us. There is a house ahead. Borrow a spear and some dogs, and come with us, Antal."

"The barbarians – I must stop saying that – hunt on horseback. Civilized custom. That is a rather fine house...Do you think there might be a training-chariot about the place?"

"For yourself?" Doreius did not disguise his incredulity. It stretched the imagination, not so much to envision Antalkidas controlling four horses, as wanting to.

"Tiresome. But one must do what one can to annoy Agisilaos. He considers running horses ostentatious. The word is that he has persuaded his sister to enter a chariot in the Olympiade. He thinks a woman in the lists will put the men off racing."

"If he thinks anything will discourage them, he doesn't know Spartans," Doreius said.

Neither, I thought, did Agisilaos know my Aunt Kyniska, if he thought she wanted persuasion. "I thought you were with the fleet, Antal." He halted in front of the gates.

"I learnt all I needed to know from Teleutias."

"And Teleutias thanked you for honouring his trireme with your presence, and dismissed you?" Doreius leaned on his spear.

"Agisilaos always gives his friends what they ask for. Why should his brother not send me back to Sparta, if I wish."

"Teleutias is not Agisilaos," I told him.

"He does know his way about ships," he conceded "A man who makes the most of a small fleet is a useful teacher, if I am to be grand admiral before I am thirty-five."

Doreius smiled. "You speak so kindly of Agisilaos that he will disappoint you, despite your youth."

"I shall be indispensable. I told you in Asia, Doreius, one must be indispensable."

"Antal, why are you in Sparta?" I asked.

"I thought it would be interesting to see what the Lysandrians would do to Agisilaos. But I fear I was mistaken." The pale eyes turned on me. "I find Agisilaos is doing it all."

Konon prised a great deal of gold from Pharnabazos for Athens. The Athenians built ships and intrigued in Ionia. Sikyon cast uneasy eyes across the Nemea River to Corinthia, as Argos and Corinth merged, and Athenian regiments passed through Corinth as they pleased. The Sikyonians asked that the Spartan garrison remain in their city. Well before the Long War, Perikles attacked Sikyonia, and the Athenians only withdrew when forced to by Sparta. The grain-rich countryside of Sikyonia whetted the ever-hungry appetite of Athens for conquest.

The shipyards of Gythion hummed with activity, building triremes to replace some of the ships Peisander lost. With Pityas and Apollodoros, Doreius and I walked down to the port, to see new triremes launched. We stood outside the town; under olive trees, dipping their silver-green leaves towards the silver-green sea. The oars beat the water like wings, as the long, proud, beaked ships with their huge eyes and billowing square sails disappeared, much as the war had receded to a word within tranquil Lakedaimon – although we were still at war with Persia, and in Hellas.

Our days were filled with running and ball games, and throwing the spear. With hunting and cooking the day's bag on the slopes of Taygetos, as one or another of us played the lyre, and we joined voices in song. I had a fine new bow and quiver, which Doreius gave me. Had he guessed that I sold the bow I won from Aristokrates, to buy him a box to replace the one I dropped in the river? It was made by a fine artisan and had the portraits of the Twin Gods carved on the cover.

Antalkidas contrived to have himself posted to the garrison we left in Asia, where he frequently hunted with his barbarian friend Tiribazos. On horseback, no doubt. Sphodrias was seen about the city with his son Kleonymos. One could excuse him his excessive pride in the boy – who had Polydora's autumn-leaf hair, iris-blue eyes, and the promise of her great beauty. Meleas married his cousin, a neat-featured young woman as poised and composed as himself. Aristokrates fell in love with her at the betrothal feast. In the Olympiade, Sparta had won a spectacular victory.

Kyniska's chariot took first prize.

Many years before, the Eleians unjustly banned Sparta from the Games. That year, the four-horse chariot race was won by a Spartan who entered in the Theban lists. When the judges learnt he was Lakedaimonian, they disqualified him. Sparta had not had a chariot win since. Now the City hailed both win and winner with an especial fervour.

Kyniska commissioned Apelleas to make a statue of her chariot and horses, to set up in Olympia. The City raised her another in Sparta. If Agisilaos had thought to decrease the running-horse population of Sparta, his scheme badly misfired. Women, as well as men, were now choosing horses to train for the next Olympiade.

"Kyniska was lucky," Sphodrias said.

I suppose, because we were looking at horses, her win came to mind. They ran wild and free, in a field near Amyklai green with late spring – manes and tails flying, perfect in their kind. The servants warned us that some of them had not been broken.

"It wasn't luck," I told him. "Kyniska always had a better eye for a good horse than her brothers. And Teleutias is no mean judge of horse-flesh."

"I like that white..." Doreius had not taken his eyes off the stallion.

"You can tell at a glance it hasn't known a rider," Kallias spoke with cavalry authority.

That was enough for Doreius. He was into the field, with the speed that won him his laurel crown. Grasping the white's

250

mane, he hoisted himself onto its back.

"He'll be off in less time than it took him to get on," Kallias said.

Doreius's sprint acted as a signal. At once, we were all dashing out after horses. A good chestnut nuzzled my shoulder. As it seemed to like me, I was going to choose it when I saw the black stallion. Its hooves rang, as it trotted up, lifting its forefeet as stylishly as a fine dancer. Then it came to a dead halt, its coat shining in the sun, its mane long and silky.

Its neck arched. It looked at me sceptically with large, liquid eyes. I stretched out my arm towards it. It backed off and – lest I think its retreat a nervous one – raised those elegant forelegs as if to say, 'If you think I shall have a man on my back like those other fools, I have a lesson for you.'

Doreius still clung on to the white, looking like Horse-taming Castor. I thought of imitating his sudden leap, but it was not the right move for this horse.

"Well, my fine dancer," I spoke to the young stallion aloud. "We must become acquainted, for you are the most beautiful horse I have ever seen." As I spoke, moved closer to it, very slowly. "And that broad back of yours was made to support a man in comfort on a long ride. Really, men are not just flies too big to switch off, and I could take you many interesting places you cannot go on your own." He was about to turn and be off in contempt. "But I think I must convince you of that." I grasped the mane, pulled myself on to the broad back and, gripping tightly with my thighs, held on for all I was worth. If I let this horse throw me once, I should forever forfeit his respect.

I cannot say that I mastered the black that day, but I held on. A moving speck in the distance grew larger, more distinct, became Doreius returning with the white under control. Kallias had not been in this flock, and had not reckoned on his will. Apollodoros claimed to have encountered no difficulties with a piebald mare, but his backside was the colour of the red-brown earth.

"Those were splendid horses," Sphodrias said, as we rinsed off the sweat and dust in the River Tiasa. "I wonder whom they belong to."

We took different paths after the midday meal. Sphodrias

challenged Kallias to a wrestling match, and the others went north with them to Sparta and the gymnasium. Doreius and I continued on the Amyklai Road. Ahead, the great temple of Apollo crowned the heights above the town, its tall columns shimmering in the heat.

"You could give Apollo another gift." Doreius spoke quietly. It was your father's to you."

"A king's gift. A king's ring." Our steps raised dust in the road. "To keep it and not to wear it would look as though I have no right to it." Next month I would be twenty. "If men see it on my finger, they will call it a claim to the kingdom. Some will rise."

"And you do not wish that." A slight smile expressed his doubt.

"Now? When Sparta is at war on two fronts? Divide the City? My father's shade would not let me rest."

Could I risk men to come reading in the Lakonian records *In the reign of King Leotychides Sparta divided against herself to the gain of her enemies*. "Let it be as you said. Leave it with the god."

Doreius halted. "I-I said...?"

"By the Messeis Spring. When you came back from Nemea."

"Leotychides, I am neither king nor king's son. I cannot give good counsel on such matters."

"Perhaps Apollo spoke to me in your form."

He smiled. "It was not Apollo with you by the Messeis Spring."

"Well, I have decided."

A warm wind ripples the grasses of the hilltop. I thought of jealous Zephyros watching Apollo and Hyakinthos throwing the discus.

"I shall keep the sword," I told Doreius. "That was a father's gift to his son."

I wet my hands and face in the purifying waters of the sacred spring, before going into the temple. It was cool in the penumbra. The god's ancient statue stood – bow in one hand, spear in the other – upon an immense throne covered in beaten gold. Hyakinthos is buried beneath its base.

I laid the royal ring of the Eurypontids upon the offering-table and raised my arms to the god.

"Apollo, I am the son of Agis, and my royal father gave me this ring. Without consulting you in Delphi, the men of Sparta voted to make my uncle king; although it is the son, and not the brother, who succeeds him, and my father declared me his heir before witnesses. If the citizens of Sparta call me to be their king, I shall take back the ring, and wear it as my father bade. If not, it is yours, Apollo. It is no unworthy gift."

Doreius waited for me outside the temple. "The anemones are many this year." He, too, thought of Hyakinthos. Up here the anemones are all red, as they spring from the blood of the beautiful youth who died in the Olympian's arms.

Coming down the steep descent from the plateau, my spirit was light. We talked about the horses, and laughed when we recalled Sphodrias nearly breaking his neck to display his horsemanship.

"I wonder who does own them...."

"Doreius, I did not want to tell the others then, but they are mine." My mother's brother died, childless, of a wound taken at Nemea, and left his possessions divided between Agesipolis and myself. "That black stallion would make a fine cavalry mount." We were back on the road to Sparta. "I think he was training it. It understands cavalry commands."

"Leotychides, if a warrior points out a cavalryman who is not all he should be, he gets his horse as well as his place in the cavalry."

"A cavalryman had ought to have a spare." A blossom fell from a wild cherry tree. "Kallias says there is a man in his company who cannot control his mount in a charge...You are a fine rider..."

"My regiment suits me well enough."

"Kallias says that there are always men who are good for nothing but pointing out the failings of others, but do not better themselves. I could replace one of these men when I am twenty. Kallias tells me that a weak cavalry can cost a battle."

Leotychides, is this all concern for the cavalry? Or do you simply like the feel of a horse under you?"

A breeze moved the branches of the olive trees that line the roadsides; not cruel Zephyros who killed Hyakinthos, but a gentle god who carries the scent of flowers through the Vale.

"It doesn't matter. A hoplite regiment will do as well. And the armour is more splendid."

He halted and looked me in the eye. "Then why have you been practising vaulting on horses with your spear, cavalry-fashion, since you were sixteen?"

"You saw me?"

"It would have been harder not to."

"I'm sorry. I was not straight-spoken."

"Nor was I." He smiled. "I, too, have talked to Kallias."

The sun struck the bronze of an old statue, almost hidden between the olive trees.

The first time I saw the statue of the boy with the fox, I had been disappointed. It was smaller than I anticipated. Now I saw it was a very fine work. Perhaps watching Apelleas sharpened my eye. Or was it life that honed the perceptions of the spirit?

A few of the old sculptors had known what they wanted from bronze and marble, and tried for it, although they lacked the skill. Yet their work had an intensity of feeling that penetrated its shortcomings. Once in the south, I saw a grave-marker of a youth, mourning a dead friend, which had almost brought tears to my eyes. The boy with the fox was the same sort of work. One felt his concealed pain, as he sank to the ground dying.

"Wait, Doreius. I didn't see it properly before."

"The boy with the fox? That always takes time."

Chapter 10

Sikyon is a busy trading city. Like all foreigners, Sikyonians prize objects of Lakedaimonian making. We men of the Spartan garrison bartered pitchers, oil flasks, and such things for coins: to buy sweet plums, or a cup of fine Sikyonian wine in a wine shop; or a place in the upper part of the theatre, where it is carved out of the rock. Once glancing down, we saw Euagoras between two senior officers, in one of the best seats.

Army logic sent Euagoras on garrison duty, and left natural soldiers like Hekataios and Aristokrates in Lakedaimon. Yet, sometimes army logic has a rhythm of its own, and Euagoras was useful at devising games and music competitions, to keep the men occupied. Tedium was the only enemy that seriously threatened us.

I had set out with dreams of adventure and glory. I was a warrior. The day I left Sparta, my mother turned out to see our company set off. Her beautiful face was set and grave, as she told me to come back with my shield, or on it. It earned her a cheer. She had a way with crowds. After a year on garrison duty, I felt I was more likely to fall in the field of boredom, and be carried back on a discus.

All over the compound, men threw the discus or played knucklebones. I had just come off duty, and been to see Dancer (so I called the black horse). My groom was a serf from my kleiros. I did not know the fellow – unlike my batman, who was the son of the old man who had kept vigil with me at my father's dying bed.

I wandered down to the infantry section to pass the time of day with Pityas and Apollodoros. Then I saw Praxitas, the garrison commander, drilling hoplites. Some Sikyonian troops stood idly and watched.

The garrison consisted of two regiments of heavy-armed infantry – one Spartan, one Sikyonian – and a company of

255

Spartan cavalry. We had, as well, about one hundred and fifty Corinthian exiles; young men who opposed the union with Argos, and had come in with their weapons, asking for a place in our army. They elected a fellow of about thirty as their general.

I had no wish for my own company, having been in charge of a punishment detail. We were only fifty horse, and the talk would be of nothing else in the cavalry section this day. Pelles, the man who had been flogged, was a friend. We had danced for Apollo the same day, been enrolled in the list of warriors, and taken our horses at much the same time. He fell foul of Pasemachos, the cavalry commander, shortly after we were posted to Sikyon.

The first month, his groom let his horse lame. Pasemachos boomed at him, demanding to know why he was in a cavalry regiment at all. Poor Pelles stammered that he was here to die for Sparta.

"By the Twin Gods, you are here to make the enemy die!" Pasemachos thundered, like Zeus in Olympia.

Pelles gave his mount careful attention after that, but when he became enamoured of a hetaira in Sikyon, he began to be heedless and inattentive. Once he misunderstood an order, and earned himself a full night standing guard with his shield for disobedience.

This is humiliating; I know from experience...but that is another story. Pelles took advantage of the darkness to slip away to his mistress, and was punished by a flogging. I had rather another than I had ordered the army serfs to bind him and wield the lash.

I turned, and started back to the stables, to tell the groom that I would exercise Dancer myself, when a black-haired Corinthian stepped into my path. Ask me how I could tell him from a Sikyonian before he spoke, and I can only say that Corinthians wear their cloaks with a certain air.

Some of the exiles had arrived with only what they had on their backs, and no servant to look after them, but even the men whose cloaks were becoming shabby still sported those elegant folds. This one looked at me as though I should know him.

"Leotychides, the son of Agis." He looked amused at my bewilderment. "You do not remember me, do you."

As he spoke, I did. It was that he was the last man I thought to see amongst the exiles.

"I know you, Aristeas. Where is Nikomedes?"

Anger sparked his eyes. "In Corinth, with the traitors." He linked his arm through mine, as though we had been old friends in Olympia, rather than enemies.

"How long have you been there?" Most of the exiles had come in when the boundary-stones separating Corinthia from the Argolid were removed.

"Since the bastards changed our feast-days to Argive feast-days. Timolaos betrayed us. It is conquest, not union. Corinthian citizenship is abolished. Well, by Zeus, I will die a Corinthian before I live an Argive!"

"So you are in accord with Alkimenes."

"Alkimenes wastes his time with Pasimelos and his peace party." He lowered his voice. "There has been a massacre. On the feast of Artemis. Half the peace party are slain."

"No man would shed blood on a holy day."

He laughed bitterly. "There is nothing our rulers would not do, if their Argive masters ordered it. I told my father – We quarrelled when I left Corinth – Being a good peace-party man, he disbelieved me." Exiles always exaggerate, I thought. He kicked a stone. "The Argives are organizing the Isthmian Games. The Isthmia has always been Corinthian. Those Games of yours in Sparta – you don't even let foreigners watch them..."

"The Leonidian Games."

"What would you do if foreigners arranged them?"

"It could not happen."

"Because you would kill them. Or die yourselves. Peace party!" He spat the words. "The only way to free Corinth is with the spear."

"Aristeas does not use a knife when a sword will do," Doreius said, as we walked towards the infantry section. He retained his rank of platoon leader when he took his cavalry horse. In a short time, our platoon was the best in the company.

Some hoplites threw the discus in the fading light of the sun. In front of another garrison hut, a man sang and played his lyre. It was a song of Alkman's about the simple pleasure of making

257

soup on the wooded slopes of Taygetos.

A number of Corinthians were also singing as we approached their section of the compound. The exiles had songs of their own making: bitter, stirring songs about their city's rulers; defiant, stirring songs about the victory to come. News of the massacre in Corinth had spread like wildfire, and new words were being put to old melodies. One rumour had it that the survivors were on their way to Sikyon. Another had no survivors living.

A small group of Corinthians huddled together on the ground, talking in their soft, sibilant Doric. Amongst them, I recognised the black curls of Aristeas. When he saw Doreius, he leapt to his feet, and embraced him as though they were reunited brothers. I recalled how they had sat in hostile silence as Nikomedes gave me his warning in Olympia.

Aristeas motioned with his head towards his companions, who sat in front of the hut. "They have just come in. Those five." Five! Was that the army they expected? "They were there when it happened. Come..."

It was not a pretty tale the new arrivals had to tell. The peace party had been swelling in numbers with each Argive affront. Pasimelos received frequent warnings that his life was at risk. The Feast of Artemis neared. The warnings became threats.

"Pasimelos told us to meet him outside the city walls at Kraneion, in the gymnasium, on the morning of the festival," one of the Corinthians, a soft-spoken man in his thirties, explained. "The young men came, but our fathers and grandfathers could not credit that anyone would commit so great an impiety as to shed blood on the goddess's festival."

"They will be punished," Doreius spoke with certainty.

"My friend," the Corinthian said. "The gods move in their own time, and we must move in ours."

Another man spoke. "We heard the screams. Outside the city walls, we heard the screams still..."

"Some men were standing in small groups, talking with friends, when they were slain." The youngest newcomer spoke. He was no more than eighteen. "I stayed in the city with my father, you see. He holds with neither peace nor war party. We were in the theatre. My father was talking to a friend, a peace-party man. When he slumped over, my father thought it a seizure. It was I who saw the blood seeping through the back of his cloak."

"Theatres are sacred to Dionysos," I spoke stupidly as Pronax. "He will send them mad."

"Can mad beasts be maddened further?" he went on. "I saw the killer running. I saw him take a dagger he had concealed in his cloak, and stab a man. Or perhaps it was another. They all had daggers hidden in their cloaks."

"That is why they chose the festival day," the eldest explained. "They knew we would be without weapons."

"The theatre was all confusion. Women screaming. People scrambling over seats to get away. Slipping in blood and falling. One of the judges stood, and called out, "Stop this. You will bring a curse on Corinth." He had a white beard. A killer plunged a blade into his throat. All the peace-party judges died. We fled from the theatre. I saw the old judge lying where he fell. His beard was soaked red. I don't know why, but that seemed the worst of it."

"Men were stabbed in the shrines and sanctuaries as they made their offerings," another man said. "That is how most of the old died."

I no longer disbelieved in the massacre. These sober men of the peace party were not hot-heads like Aristeas and Kallipides, could not have acted the depths of their quiet outrage.

The eldest man spoke again. "The men of middle years were speared, as they fled into the side-streets."

Aristeas looked up. His hands clenched. His cheeks were wet. I doubt he knew he wept. The other exiles hid their tears in their cloaks. He forced his voice through his throat, but when he spoke it was firm. "Does my father live?"

"He came to us in the gymnasium, Aristeas. All the men who escaped the massacre came to us. We knew we would no longer be safe there, so we made a run for the Acrocorinth." That small mountain of a citadel. "Argive troops attacked us on the way."

"My father..." Aristeas repeated.

"He was wounded."

"What is the name of the man who shed his blood?"

"It was an Argive, Aristeas. His wound is not grave."

"Then where is he?" Aristeas demanded. "Where are the others?"

259

"We crossed into Sikyonia, before we stopped to rest for the night. In the morning, our mothers and sisters arrived. Timolaos sent them, to persuade us to come back."

I wondered at the stupidity of these women. Doreius told me later that foreign women are kept close and know nothing.

"I should think Timolaos would be glad to see you gone," Doreius said.

"The best men of the city were with us. They would have made it known, in every corner of Hellas, that Corinth wants no union with Argos."

"And not before time." The fire was back in Aristeas's eyes.

"Timolaos and his underlings swore solemn oaths that Corinth's constitution will be restored. Pasimelos put it to a vote. They voted to return to Corinth. But we have little trust in the vows of men who desecrate a day sacred to a god. We think it a trap baited."

I glanced at Aristeas, and thought of a day when I stood in the barracks quarter of Sparta, searching faces. Surely there was a question in his mind that pride and anger forbade him to ask. If Doreius – but in Sparta, such things did not happen to come between friend and friend, father and son, brother and brother. It was simpler to be Spartan than Corinthian. I put the unvoiced question for Aristeas. I asked about the safety of my friend Nikomedes.

"Nikomedes the boxer?" someone passed the wineskin again. "He is training for the Games."

Aristeas was alert. "What Games?"

This time there was a false note in the reply, but the evasion was kindly intended. "The Pythian Games. The next Olympiade. Who knows? Nikomedes is always training."

Doreius stood on the high fortifications, looking down into the compound, a strong autumn wind whipping his hair about his face. I climbed up to join him. In the infantry section, Praxitas looked on while both hoplite regiments drilled.

He kept the Sikyonians turned away from the Spartan regiment, as it practised that movement that allows men to fight and regroup simultaneously. Something that foreigners are not intended to study.

The Sikyonians responded smartly to the commands of their officer. Directly below us were the ragged columns of the exiles. They were, for the most part, well-born young men like Aristeas, who knew nothing of hoplite drill. In foreign cities, where citizens are divided into men of good family and those of common origin, the well-born are cavalrymen. They had come to Sikyon with cavalry armour, soft leather cavalry boots, and cavalry weapons.

"Will those Corinthians never learn to keep in step?" Doreius watched them. "With allies like that, it is a wonder we won the Athenian war."

"They show enthusiasm."

A sudden cloudburst sent the Sikyonians scurrying to their huts. The Corinthians, like the Spartans, continued exercising.

"Discipline would serve them better." Something in the distance caught his attention.

A sentry halted two figures. Doreius eased.

"Are you on duty, Doreius, or hiding from Pasemachos?"

A man stood guard with his shield. "I am to see that he doesn't move a muscle."

"Is it the fellow in Maro's platoon, whose horse shied on parade?"

"It is Maro," he replied.

We stayed in the battlements until the sun had sunk, releasing Maro, who walked off with stiffened gait. Then we started down and collided with Euagoras, who was on his way up. He held a letter in his hand. The scroll meant news of Sparta; each commonplace like a piece of red-brown Lakonian earth.

"Old Chairon..." The wind carried the rest of his words away.

"Has paid his unmarried man's fine for the twentieth year." Doreius finished for him.

Euagoras caught his breath. "Better than that. He has become enamoured of a maiden."

"Then he'd best marry her quickly, before he's fined for marrying too old," Doreius said.

"She refuses to have him. She says if it is unlawful for a man to marry for wealth, it is dishonourable for a woman to do the same."

Doreius approved her sentiments. Euagoras ran on. "And Konon is rebuilding the Long Walls of Athens, with the gold

Pharnabazos gave him."

Doreius stared at him in disbelief.

"That being, in your estimation, of less importance than Chairon's troubles."

"Perhaps in Chairon's, too, Leotychides. Oh, I nearly forgot. Praxitas wants to see you. Immediately. It was an order."

The polemarch was an iron-faced man in his middle years. He bore a resemblance to Pasemachos that was in no way physical. Pasemachos was lean. The cavalry commander had a full head of greying brown hair. Praxitas was pale red and thinning. Yet they were men of a stamp.

Both had risen, slowly and steadily, by merit. If Pasemachos was still but a pentatarchos, a commander of fifty, it was because the cavalry is a very small part of the Spartan army, and there were far more good men than promotions.

Praxitas was seated at a table in his hut. Two oil lamps flared in their standards. Senior officers were with him; a strategos and a lochagos. And two Corinthians. Their accents named them. Damp soaked the elegant folds from their cloaks. The autumn rains had started, but there were none today.

They were telling very much the same story that I heard from Aristeas's companions. I started forward to report to the polemarch. A lochagos halted me in the shadows. Army servants brought wine and dry cloaks for the Corinthians. They stood to change. One was Alkimenes. The lochagos silenced me. When I heard, the other man addressed as Pasimelos, I studied him carefully.

I had thought the leader of the peace party to be older. Pasimelos had grey-touched hair, but his face was of a man not more than thirty-five. The two Corinthians draped their crimson cloaks with the elegance of Corinth. Although they were Dorian like ourselves, they could never be mistaken – even silent and in our garments – as Spartans.

I recalled Alkimenes talking about diversity, although I had forgotten much of what he said at Olympia. A flock of goats is a flock of goats, whether it is in Sparta or Sikyon; but men create their cities in their own image. It is that diversity which separates us from the beast, as well as from the barbarian. Those Corinthians who fought for the freedom of their city also fought for their being as men.

"The massacre was an error, as well as an impiety," Pasimelos said. "Timolaos knew he had gone too far. When we returned, there were no further attempts on our lives." He sipped the Sikyonian wine, in the manner of a guest silently complimenting his host on a vintage of quality.

"They foreswore all their vows." Alkimenes spoke with controlled intensity. "Our constitution had not been restored. Our laws are still Argive. Our festivals, Argive. We are absorbed into Argos still."

"I have never believed in taking by arms what can be gained by persuasion." Pasimelos's voice had a resonance to it. "But the Argive garrison in Corinth has been strengthened. Athenian regiments come and go as they please. You will agree that, against this, persuasion is powerless. There is only one way. That is what we have proposed to you. If we fail, we are ready to die with honour, as one cannot live with honour in Corinth today." It was spoken quietly.

Praxitas clasped his hands in front of his chest. "Gentlemen. Don't think us unmoved, or ungrateful. But there are hazards in your plan."

"Not so." The flickering lamp-light played on Alkimenes's animated face. "If you march by night, you could be any army. If you are seen at all. And, knowing how quickly Spartans can form into battle-order, I doubt whether any Argives will be over-anxious to come out and engage you."

"You seem to forget I am responsible for this garrison."

"Send to Sparta for reinforcements."

Praxitas looked somewhat taken aback. Spartiates in their forties are not commanded by men in their twenties.

"Then..." continued Alkimenes, oblivious. "With the garrison secured, you march to Lechion on the night Pasimelos and I are on gate duty. We open the gate. And you have Lechion."

"I thought I saw Praxitas suppress a smile. "You make it sound all very simple."

"But it is."

Pasimelos silenced Alkimenes with a hand on his arm. No," he said. "It is not simple. There is a Theban garrison in the harbour, an Argive garrison in Corinth; and, if the Athenians hear of it, they will send a regiment or two on the double. There are also the Corinthian troops in the citadel. They may turn a blind eye if they see you on the march, but that I cannot promise. They will not be permitted to disregard your presence in Lechion. They will fight. You will be outnumbered, sir, but in all the many years Corinth and Sparta were allies, and in the few we have been enemies, I have never known Spartans to be put off by numbers."

"You are a clever politician, Pasimelos," Praxitas replied.

"Had I been clever, I would not have relied upon reason. Those young Corinthians who came here with nothing but their weapons were wiser than I."

"Praxitas leaned forward. "Gentlemen, let us be blunt. You are both Corinthian officers—"

"Would we have crossed a swollen river, if we hadn't to leave and return secretly?" Alkimenes demanded heatedly.

So it went on, until the two Corinthians had to leave in order to return under cover of night. They put on their own dried and cleansed cloaks. Praxitas promised to send on his decision to them at Corinth. How, I could not fathom.

Only then was I required to present myself to the polemarch. "Did you recognise either of those two men?" Praxitas snapped.

"Yes, sir. I know Alkimenes. We met in Olympia when—"

"Euagoras!" He cut me off. "Send in the man who knows Pasimelos."

"Euagoras is—" one of the senior officers began. Praxitas cut him off to dismiss me.

It was only later that I learnt that Euagoras had been going into Corinth to gather information, posing as a Messenian poet. His slight stature aided the deception. No one thinks of Spartans as small. If he were discovered, he would be tortured and executed. I had thought his hair simply refused to grow to warrior's length.

Discipline was suspended. No drill. No duty. No orders. No punishment. Doreius, Maro, Apollodoros and all the men who had been in battle knew this meant we were going to see action.

Sharp words were sharpened. The ashen shafts of spears tested. The garrison smiths kept busy perfecting already flawless iron tips. Our batmen collided with each other as they left burnishing shields to bring us arm-rings and other ornaments. Mine left a thumb-print on my helmet.

"Do you intend to use that as a mirror?" Pelles shouted across to me, as I polished the jutting brim.

All over the compound, we donned our crimson cloaks, and adorned ourselves for battle. Doreius combed his hair, and twisted it into those handsome curls that look so fine hanging from under a helmet.

"Not that way," he said, as I struggled with mine. "Here, I'll show you." The ivory comb slid easily through my hair. "Keep it," he said, when he had done. "It was for you anyway. I have another." It was a beautiful comb, with a trireme carved upon it.

Pityas and Apollodoros arrived in their gleaming hoplite armour, holding their high-crested helmets. Apollodoros provoked a gust of cavalry laughter.

"What tender hands the man has!" someone called out.

"What *have* you got on your hands, Apollodoros?" Doreius asked.

"Gauntlets. I took them from an Athenian I killed at Nemea. That's a fine sword-belt, Leotychides."

It was the Syracusan belt Doreius had given me in Olympia.

"Do you think we shall march on Corinth?" Pityas asked.

"Unlikely, with two regiments and fifty horse," Doreius replied.

"Don't forget the mighty exiles," Apollodoros joined Pelles and Maro in mimicry of their ragged drill.

Pasemachos appeared from nowhere. He stared at Pityas and Apollodoros in their hoplite armour.

"What are these," he boomed "Brassed batmen?"

Our two friends melted away.

The commander's shield was almost plain as mine. Only a simple design encircled the letter lamda, for Lakedaimon. He cast his eyes about us, and then said to Doreius, "If I fall, you are in command."

More men from Sikyon were mobilized for garrison duty. Some of the light-armed Lakonian servants also stayed with the garrison. The new regiment came in from Sparta to replace us. We were ready to march.

We decorated our horses' bridle with bronze ornaments.

265

They, too, were going to war. Our batmen stood by, holding our helmets. I vaulted on to Dancer's back, and leaned across his smooth neck to look at Doreius. His cheeks were flushed, his grey eyes shining.

"What is it, Starer?" he smiled.

"I was thinking that foreigners are right when they call us the finest-looking men in Greece."

"Let foreigners say it."

We started out just before sunset. The Spartans led, section following section, marching in columns, a sea of shining brass,crimson cloaks and crested helmets, shields slung across their backs; step, step, pause, step, step, to the music of lyre and harp and flute.

The Sikyonian regiment marched behind us. After them, the little band of Corinthian exiles. They were in high spirits. Praxitas was not. The foreigners lost us time, being unused to marching torchless in the dark.

We halted at the River Nemea, which separates Sikyonia and Corinthia. There Praxitas sacrificed the goat to Artemis, before we crossed into Corinthian territory. He ordered the music stilled. Only Spartans march to war with all three instruments.

The long, high walls linking Corinth to her port of Lechion loomed up, black against the transparent black of night. We marched up to the east gate and waited. That is to say, the hoplites did. Praxitas ordered the cavalry near the Sikyonians on the assumption, no doubt, that if the enemy appeared, they would be the first to bolt.

There seemed to be some sort of trouble. Maro, who had eyes like Lynkeus, said he could make out Praxitas and some others. I was ordered to report to the polemarch.

Praxitas stood with two of his senior officers. Pasimelos and Alkimenes were there in armour and carrying spears.

Praxitas turned to Pasimelos. "Is this man acceptable?"

"If you will take his word," Pasimelos snapped back.

"He is a Spartan officer," Praxitas said shortly.

I was ordered to change my crimson cloak and cavalry leather for the clothing and armour of one of the Corinthian exiles. Alkimenes checked the details.

"Hide your hair under the helmet, Leotychides. Only Spartan

warriors still wear it long."

"If there are questions—" Praxitas began.

Pasimelos came close to losing patience. "Alkimenes and I are on guard duty at this gate. It is we who ask questions."

Praxitas drew me aside, his hand on my arm in an iron grip. "If this is a trap, try not to be taken alive."

The gate closed behind us. Within the walls, it is a morning's walk from Corinth the port. I was cut off from other Spartans. Alone in an enemy city.

Some distance south on the heights, the lights of Corinth flickered. We walked what seemed an endless path across a field. It was a quiet night. A breeze carried the faint notes of a priestess singing a hymn to Aphrodite.

We came to a road. Cattle slept under the stars in the fields on either side. The peasant hovels were dark.

"We always seem to be companions of the night," Alkimenes broke the silence.

"I was thinking of what you said. About diversity—"

"Don't talk," Pasimelos ordered. "That Lakedaimonian accent will betray you."

We turned our backs on Corinth and walked towards Lechion.

The buildings of the ship-works stood black against the dark sky. Silent as shades. There were many tones of black that night. On the road, we encountered a few men in toque-shaped Theban helmets, wandering about in groups of two and three. I reminded myself that Alkimenes had been not unfriendly to Sparta in Olympia. I remembered that men could change. Had Aristeas not changed?

Huts glowed dimly as we approached the port. The fires of the Theban troops reflected on the waves of the harbour, where small boats at anchor swayed gently. The garrison troops were drinking, singing, playing knucklebones, and doing the things men do to pass the monotonous evenings.

The two Corinthians insisted upon showing me everything. Praxitas had irritated them by his caution. Pasimelos was leader of the peace party. Such a man would not be party to treachery.

Yet men who would shed blood on a sacred day could also hold a man's friends, sister, mother, hostage to torture and death. Who knows what a man might do in those

267

circumstances? Was this all a hoax to draw us to destruction?

A Theban stumbled out of a wine-shop, and jostled Alkimenes. A signal? Discovery? The Corinthian helped him steady himself and set him on his way with a jest. A chariot clattered to the port.

When we came outside the walls, Praxitas questioned me about what I had seen. The harbour? The Thebans? Were the wine-shops full? Empty? When he had done, he ordered me to give the exile back his clothes.

Alkimenes helped me lace the pieces of my armour together. My batman had it all to do over.

The gate opened to let us in.

Praxitas deployed the cavalry between the harbour and the main body of our army. There was a danger of attack from the Theban garrison. A sudden cavalry charge can often break a battle-line of infantry. We formed our square near an olive grove I had passed with the two Corinthians.

Our army, that crimson sea with foam of brass, that had seemed so great on the march, looked petty and lost in the vast expanse between the walls. Praxitas must also have been uneasy. I heard Pasemachos tell Doreius that the polemarch had sent a messenger to Sikyon for reinforcements.

The polemarch set troops to work digging a ditch in front of our lines. Others cut down trees. Praxitas ordered them to do it quietly. An impossible order. They obeyed as well as they could.

The men worked through the night, building an enclosure. By dawn, a stockade was erected. The hoplites filed within. The line stretched so long that the far left was unaware of what happened on the far right. We seemed more. We were not.

Daylight. The peasants came out of their huts. A few gaped, and then went about their work. Pasemachos ordered us to mount and form a square. Our platoon was in front, facing the harbour.

Apollo drove the sun up to the centre of the sky. Neither the Thebans in the harbour, nor the Argives and Corinthians in the city, appeared to have noticed a Spartan army within the walls.

The sun lowered behind the west wall. The enemy seemed as

unconcerned as the grazing cattle. My eyelids became heavy. Whatever I had expected of war, it was not drowsiness.

"Why do they not attack?" I asked Doreius.

Only his eyes and mouth were visible below the helmet; his head, cheeks, nose and neck covered in bronze. "They, too, have probably sent for reinforcements."

"We are so few."

"We are Spartiate."

"They would do better to attack before our reinforcements arrive." Sweat ran down my cheek. My right cheek itched. I could not scratch it under the cheek-pieces of my helmet.

He smiled wearily. "Perhaps we neglected to tell the enemy we sent for them."

I no longer envied the hoplites their gleaming armour. Cavalry leather is more comfortable if you have got to live in it.

Pasemachos let us sleep in relays that night. In the morning, we drew up once more in battle array. Praxitas deployed the Spartan hoplites on the extreme left of his battle line, the Sikyonians in the centre, and the Corinthian exiles flanking the east wall. Once more, Apollo began to carry the sun across the sky. I thought of Pityas and Apollodoros with the hoplites, protected by the stockade but open to the sun's assault. Dancer nuzzled the ground, vainly searching for fresh grasses.

Then it happened.

Like a brass comet, a large body of Argives rushed the stockade, brandishing spears and shouting war-cries. At the same time, another enemy force ran down the northward incline from Corinth, and rushed the east wall. A strange type of light infantryman.

Instead of armour, they wore linen corselets. Their shields looked as small as toys, but their spears were twice the length of ours. Their swords were double most Greek swords, still longer than the Lakedaimonian thrusting blade. Cowardly weapons that kept a man distant from his enemy. Light and fast on their feet, they were a full regiment. Only the Corinthian exiles faced them.

Pasemachos pointed to the leader, a wiry man in an Athenian helmet, and shouted across to Doreius, "Iphikrates!"

"Who is Iphikrates?" The name meant nothing to me.

"A captain of mercenaries." The grey eyes behind the helmet-slits were disdainful.

Often men tell of battles they have fought, as though they saw everything sitting above the field, with the gods. It is not like that. Ask a man who has slain a few enemies how goes the battle, and he will say we are winning. To badly wounded men we are losing.

The Argives broke through part of the stockade, and hurled themselves upon the Sikyonians. Corinthians from the city joined them in the attack. The Sikyonians fell back. They Corinthian exiles fought desperately against the mercenaries. We were too far to help them.

The Sikyonian line broke. The men ran in disorder. Most fled the field and made for the sea, casting aside their shields to hasten their flight. A few stood. And fought. And fell.

Pasemachos spat an obscenity. He drew rein even with Doreius. "Praxitas cannot see what is happening from his part of the stockade." The commander subsided into thought, and then continued in a lowered voice. "If those bastards..." he gestured toward the harbour, "ever decide to fight, a charge of thirty could do for them just as well as a charge of fifty. They're only Thebans."

He dismounted abruptly and faced us. "I'm calling for volunteers." He raised his voice. "I'll not give odds that a man comes out alive."

The entire company dismounted smartly, and stepped forward to volunteer. Pasemachos chose his volunteers indiscriminately, to hasten the operation. "The rest of you remount and keep your eyes on the harbour."

He recognised the face of Doreius behind the helmet, as he stood with the men he had chosen. I could read the commander's eyes. "I meant you to replace me," they said, between anger and regret. It was too late.

"Tie your horses to the trees," he ordered, and sent young warriors to collect the shields the Sikyonian deserters had cast aside, while he explained his plan.

We were to attack the Argives on foot, from behind the foreign shields. The enemy, seeing the sigma for Sikyon, would think us easy work. The surprise impact of Spartiate warriors would throw them into confusion.

The men returned with the shields. Pasemachos thrust his arm through one, and stood before us. "Do I make a passing Sikyonian?" he demanded, and grinned. His lips returned to their usual lines of stone. He ordered us to take up the shields. "Well, gentlemen, tonight we shall dine in Lechion or Hades' Hall," he laughed grimly, and fixed his gaze on the enemy. "By the Twin Gods, you'll find you have made a mistake about these sigmas!" He roared as he led the charge.

We rushed the Argives. They fell like grain under the sickle, at the first impact. More of their fellows joined in. It was spear to spear, shield against shield. Sword against armour, swords against sword; sword into that something soft that means it has found its mark. Sword against bone. Sword against tendon. It was the noise of metal upon metal. Shouts. Screams. Grunts. It could have been an instant. Or a day. The Argives no longer fall back. They were amongst us, and around us.

I saw Pasemachos fall, and come up again, sword in hand. My own sword-hand was empty. I lay in something hot and sticky, in a moving mesh of sandalled legs. I saw the sky. Blue. Clear. Untouched. The sun. A splinter of its brilliance touched my throat. It blotted out the rest, and Death covered me with the smell of horse and leather.

When Praxitas saw the Sikyonians give way, he brought the Spartiates out of the stockade, keeping the enclosure to his left. The Argives saw that deadly, slow march of locked shields to their rear, turned and ran. The extreme right of the Argive line fell to Spartan spears. The rest fled in disorder towards Corinth.

I was unaware of all this at the time.

Apollo had taken the sun behind a cloud when the sky returned. The battle was still going on, although it was quiet in the field where I lay. Choked. Doreius removed the wine-flask from my lips. His palm supported the small of my back.

I was a shade, and so was he. We were not yet in Hades's Hall, because in the underworld the dead do not know those they have known in life. As we waited for burial to release our spirits, I asked Doreius how he died, and told him how Death had descended on me.

271

It had not been Death. Doreius saw me fall, and covered me with his body. Soon after this, Praxitas led out the Spartan hoplites, and the Argives surrounding Pasemachos's volunteers dispersed.

Other men lay in the yellow field. Spartan and enemy. Wounded and slain. My shield! My honour!

Doreius knew what I was looking for, and showed it to me. "You were still clutching the knots when I carried you over here. It would have served you better covering yourself rather than a dead Argive."

"Pasemachos...?" I asked.

"Dead. He fought like a lion. Pelles brought down the Argive who killed him. There are only Pelles, you and I, now. We are cut off from the rest of the cavalry." I touched a cut on his chin. "An Argive spear," he explained. "The wound was my doing. I was in a hurry to deflect the tip from your throat."

All about the field, men tended their wounds. The sounds of battle reached us from other areas.

"It looks like the island in the lake after the Great Fight."

My comment provoked more mirth than it was worth. The sun is good on living flesh. We clung to one another for support, as we choked on our laughter. Doreius sobered first.

"The spear barely touched the muscle," he said. "I think you slipped on blood, and knocked the wind out of yourself." I noted that my leg was bandaged. "Stand and walk on it, or the leg will stiffen."

I stood. My fine sword-belt hung loosely, nearly severed in the centre. "My belt!"

"It is no disgrace. The slash is in front."

"It is ruined." He laughed shortly. "Better that than a speared gut."

A large body of Argives was fighting it out with the Corinthian exiles. Argives? Had the light-armed mercenaries been a phantasy, like my death?

"You told me the Argives ran back to Corinth."

"The exiles appear to think they do not belong there." The Corinthians fought like Achilles avenging Patroklos. "After they defeated the peltasts, they interrupted the Argives and halted their retreat."

"Peltasts?"

"Iphikrates's mercenaries. They are called peltasts for their small shields."

"The exiles defeated them?"

"They fought like madmen. Or heroes."

Cowards' weapons had been no match for raw courage.

The Argives were being forced back towards the Spartan lines by the ferocity of the exiles. It was an orderly retreat. They broke when they saw where it was taking them, and ran to the wall. The exiles were close on their heels. A number of Argives seized scaling ladders, and leaned them against the wall to make their escape. Exiles dragged them down. Those who were not speared were trampled and suffocated by their own countrymen pushing for a place.

The exiles shook the ladders. Argives fell like olives beaten from a tree. The Corinthians speared them as they fell. Very few made it over the wall. A joyous shout went up. The Spartan hoplites saw the main body of Argives fleeing towards their line.

They fell on the Argives. A wild exultation seized my spirit. Something new. Something old as time. I looked at Doreius and saw it reflected in his eyes. He thrust his arm through the handle of his shield. I seized a spear from a dead man. We rushed forward to join in the kill. So many Argives fell that the bodies piled up, pressing one upon the other like stones in a wall.

The pipe sounded the note to regroup. The Thebans from the harbour garrison marched towards us.

Doreius and I fell in with one of the Spartan companies that formed columns, as if we had drilled together for years. We had. In our flock. In their flocks. We locked shields.

The cavalry intercepted the first Theban assault. A few brave Thebans tried to attack the horses. The music of harp and lyre joined the advance note of the flute. The Thebans panicked at the sight of our slow-moving wall bristling with spears, and broke in disorder. They fled back towards the harbour. We were after them in fast pursuit. They tried to climb on to the walls. We dragged them down and put them to the spear.

"Cockerel! Look!" someone shouted. Pityas pointed to the roof of the ship-works, where a number of Thebans had climbed for safety. Their toque-shaped helmets were silhouetted against the sinking sun. We scrambled after them.

I placed my foot on a dead Theban's chest, pulled out my spear, and turned to face another Spartan with his spear raised. All around us were Spartans holding weapons at the ready, but there was no more work to be done.

"What in the name of Hermes are you two doing with those Sikyonian shields?" Pityas lowered his spear. "Why are you not with the cavalry?"

"Because hoplites have a better war." Apollodoros flicked one of the larger pieces of gore off his armour, as he replied for us.

The Argives and the Corinthians from the city sent a herald, requesting a truce to recover their dead. Praxitas granted it without conditions. Lechion was ours. Doreius recalled that he was acting commander of the fifty, or rather of the thirty-odd that was left of it. We rejoined the cavalry. He named me acting leader of his old platoon.

The songs of Tyrtaios rang out from the harbour to the rooftops. Doreius inspected his company, sent Maro to have the spear-tip cut out of his shoulder, and tended the men with minor wounds himself. Myself he made walk, to keep my leg limber. We led our mounts, and fell behind our comrades on the way to the port and the victory songs, eating some dried apricots I had requisitioned. I gave an apple to Dancer; consolation for having missed the battle.

On our way to the port, we encountered a party of Argives collecting their dead. It was heavy work reducing those stacks of bodies. They went about it silently and methodically. One man broke the rhythm and stopped short, remaining still as the dead himself, as the work went on around him.

The dead man was no more than a youth. And beautiful. His friend was not yet thirty. Two young Greeks. Dorians like ourselves.

I hadn't known I halted until Doreius said, "That, too, is war."

Our reinforcements arrived the next day. Praxitas put them to work tearing down a section of the western wall large enough to let an army pass through. The new men were to garrison Lechion. He was taking us with him across the Isthmus of

274

Corinth to march on the fortress of Sidos. A victorious army always fights best.

The exiles stayed behind. They knew their own countryside, and planned to raid the estates – reasoning that, where patriotism failed to move, burning crops might.

The night before we set out. Aristeas came to say farewell. Doreius had his work cut out to convince him that an assault upon Corinth itself would be futile with our numbers. Aristeas reasoned that, if two regiments, fifty horse and one hundred and fifty exiles could take Lechion, nothing was beyond us. Hope tinders high in the dry dust of exile.

"It is like trying to make a cock swim, to make you Spartans war," he said. "But when you fight, you are artists."

"You didn't do badly yourselves." None of us would ever mock those ragged columns again.

"We left slightly fewer Argives to plague our city." Aristeas had a gash above his left eye. Several on his right arm. "I have a mount now. I don't think I was cut out for a foot soldier."

"The peltasts would not agree," Doreius said.

"We taught the shoemaker's son that it is unwise to fight gentlemen. Iphikrates's father is a shoemaker of Athens, you know. Iphikrates formed that band of mercenaries, and patterned their weapons off the savages of the north. No doubt fashioned by shoemaker's tools." His face underwent one of those swift Corinthian transitions from scorn to quiet gravity. "We lost half our men."

"On parade, you looked full strength."

"Those are new men from Corinth." A smile flashed "They joined us during the battle."

"Is Nikomedes with them?" I blurted out heedlessly. Aristeas would not have been alone, had Nikomedes joined the exiles.

He kicked a stone. "Nikomedes is in the citadel guard."

"Perhaps called up–"

"Every man over eighteen knows he can be called. Never speak of Nikomedes, Leotychides. I know no man of that name. Better for Corinth had you killed him on the boxing ground."

We marched on Sidos just after daybreak. The governor refused to surrender the fortress. Praxitas sacrificed the goat to Artemis. The omens were good. We formed columns. The line of command. Doreius named Maro his successor, should he fall.

I felt hollow. My nostrils filled with the feral smell of the battle that had yet to come. I willed the music to stir me, as it had in Lechion. It remained distant and apart.

Images flashed across my mind. A man with his stomach ripped open, screaming. Another, grappling with a spear sticking in his side. Pieces of gore on armour, which had been the flesh of men. The glazed, staring eyes of the dead. I longed to wake in our tent at Sikyon. To stay transfixed forever where we were. The enemy frozen in place in its line of battle, facing us.

Doreius looked at me. He had looked at me an instant before we charged the Argives with Pasemachos. Before we engaged the Thebans. I stared straight ahead. I dared not look at Doreius, and shame him with my shame. That much I could do. I would not shame Doreius.

Doreius gave the order to charge. Dancer carried me forward. Training took over. I hacked the enemy hand that held the spear that fell with its owner. The rest was mindless. Metal clashed on metal. The hot blood rose.

The fortress fell to us. I did not recall my shame until after we had taken Sidos, and were marching on Krommyon.

We bivouacked nearby, and sat about the circle of fires; our weapons stacked in the centre, so that they were at hand in case the lookouts sighted an enemy.

Pelles was in high spirits, and was fighting the battle for Sidos again; his face clean where the helmet had covered it, mouth and eyelids begrinned. Like all of us. I was silent, the fire-light weird in the mask-like faces. I remembered my shame.

Pelles laughed loudly, and called for more wine. Doreius said quietly, in a moment of silence, "There are no battles less alike than a man's first and his second. In the second, he knows what to expect."

Pelles started his feverish boasting again, then his voice subsided. He reached for his lyre. The phantoms had visited him, too. And Doreius *knew*. There was only one way he could know. They had touched him at some time with their dark wings. Perhaps in Asia. Knowing this would happen to me, he had named me acting platoon leader.

Shame changed its face to pride. I was ready to take on my

phantoms now. Perhaps that is why they did not trouble to approach me, when we took the fortress of Krommyon.

It was there that Apollodoros fell. I wanted to go to Pityas. Doreius held me back. "He will come to us when his smile honours Apollodoros."

Praxitas left garrisons in both Sidos and Krommyon; and led us east, to fortify the heights of Epidikaia, which command the vital pass to Sikyonia. The campaign that started with two soaked Corinthians at Sikyon had given us control of Corinth's port, and the surrounding country.

He joined us, as we were having our evening meal of crushed corn and dry bread.

"I hunger for a bowl of black broth," he said. "And you could all do with a dip in the Eurotas." He turned to Doreius. "How old are you?"

"Twenty-nine, sir."

"When will you be thirty?"

"In a month and a few days."

The polemarch nodded. "Your company can wait a month for a new commander."

Chapter 11

Athens sent envoys to Sparta to negotiate a separate peace. When the gains of Praxitas brought the war closer to Attica, she was ready to desert her allies and cut her losses. Athens was playing for higher stakes.

Konon gave her use of the joint fleet of the Cyprians and Pharnabazos, with the knowledge of the Great King. Had I been asked, I would have said, reject the peace offers. Call up contingents from all our allies. Invade Attica, and tear down those long walls that Athens swore never to raise again.

Sparta welcomed the prospect of peace. Too often we have trusted, only to be deceived. My mother shared my misgivings.

I called on her, to give her a rather pretty silver dish with turned-up edges, which I had found in a Theban garrison hut in Lechion. She told me it was a Corinthian work of a master silversmith.

She had kept on the palace, which was hers by widow-right, although the wives of dead kings usually sold their royal residences. My mother still lived like the wife – or was it the mother – of a reigning king.

My father's army servants were not hers by widow-right. By law, they passed to Agisilaos. When they showed a reluctance to serve their old master's brother, my mother had them listed as palace servants. When I called, they treated me as a king.

Kleora had assumed the duties of the Eurypontid queen, but my mother was no less busy in the City. Agesipolis being unmarried, she appropriated the religious and ceremonial duties that would have gone to his wife, as well as some of Eurydame's. My aunt was little seen since Pausanios was deposed.

My mother was popular with the people of Sparta. She was their beautiful, outrageous Timaia, who might lie with an enemy general, but saw her son off to war like a traditional Spartan mother. Who went everywhere on foot that other queens went to

278

in a litter. She enjoyed walking, but her simplicity was praised so highly that Agisilaos ordered Kleora to put away her kanathrum and walk.

"We should have destroyed Athens after the Long War." My mother held out her white arm, and studied the underside of it. It was a new habit. Graceful. But new.

News had come in that Athens had sent a virtual army of stonemasons and carpenters to repair the section of the Lechion wall that Praxitas tore down.

Of course, it is the right of the victor to raze a defeated city, and to enslave or slay its people; but all Hellas knows it is better not to do so. "We need only seize Piraeus, garrison it, and force the Athenians to tear down their long walls."

"But we shall do none of those things. We shall listen to Athenians talking of peace while they plan war. Aristodemos believes we would do better to talk to the Thebans."

"Because it is too unimportant?"

Her laughter rang out. "Because the Thebans interrupted that absurd ceremony at Aulis." Again, the scrutiny of her arms.

"What does Agesipolis say?"

"Agesipolis!" She took my hands, and drew me to a chair facing her own. We were in a pleasant room giving into the courtyard. Changes had been made since my father's time. "Agesipolis and Agisilaos are constantly together."

"The Kings must dine in the same hall."

"Men do not dine in the afternoon. Then it is Agisilaos and his latest boy, and Agesipolis and his handsome young men. All hand-picked by Agisilaos. My dear, there is only one king in Sparta. Do you know that Agisilaos has made old Aristomelidas an ambassador?"

"His grandfather still lives?"

"And Teleutias is still grand admiral in all but name."

"He is competent."

"My dear, would he be the most powerful vice-admiral since Lysander, were he not brother to Agisilaos? Eupolia's brood are doing well." Kyniska was not mentioned. Her chariot win made her unthinkable as well as unspeakable. "The kinglet will go too far—"

"Put away the dream that Sparta will beg me to be king."

There was an acceptance of Agisilaos now. Even the

Lysandrians had been won over, beginning with Eteonikos, who had been immortalized in bronze on Lysander's orders. Pharax was often seen in his company, too.

"If you had *his* charm, it would be on its knees." I had forbidden her to speak the name of Alkibiades to me. She cheated by saying *he* and *him*. "No matter. You are handsome. You are admired. Everyone knows of that very brave, very silly thing you did at Lechion. We must seize the advantage."

"I have been just promoted."

"Platoon leader." Her hands fell away. "You, who were born to be a king." She rose in a spicy scent. "You must journey with an embassy."

"Aristomelidas will name me, no doubt."

"Antalkidas is to lead the embassy to Sardis. There is a place for you. And your Doreius."

"Antalkidas dared approach you!"

"He paid his loyal respects to his queen."

"Doreius would no more accept advancement by patronage than I."

A slant of sun set a ring of fire about her sun-gold hair. "Trust you to attach yourself to a young man as ambitionless as yourself."

"He is a pentatarchos and just turned thirty."

"Is Antalkidas not the same age?"

"His father was once chief ephor."

"Antalkidas will be greater than Leon."

Doreius was not without ambition. He must always win, be best. His rise was assured with his early promotion. Nor was I meant for obscurity.

I took those restless, long-fingered hands in mine. "I am a warrior, Mother. A good warrior. I think I can be one of the best." Had I not willed myself to be a patrol leader. A games winner. "How many of our kings would be remembered, if we had not to commit their names to memory in the flock? But that of Brasidas will be sung forever."

"So will that of *King* Leonidas."

"Because he obeyed his orders. As I do mine."

She sighed. "If only you had had your accession rites, you would understand."

"I saw Agesipolis celebrate his." Surprisingly, the gangly

youth had performed the sacrifice to Demeter, and other rituals, with a serene dignity that belied the absurdity of the bony figure in heavy ceremonial robes. "It is not worth setting brother against brother, friend against friend, father against son, to decide whether this man or that shall have the honours paid to a king."

"Sweet Aphrodite! I hope you are not basing your notions of kingship on Agesipolis! I cannot understand how he can have so little of Pausanios in him. And his fecklessness certainly does not come from our side."

"Well, a man cannot have three sides." I spoke without thinking. She smiled. Her green eyes laughed what I would not hear. I quickly asked. "How does Kleombrotos? Where is his flock?"

"He is of little importance. A younger son."

(I did locate his flock. Kleombrotos was a sturdy melleiren now, with bright hair and the Agiad blue eyes. I had to take Lechion again for him and his flock-brothers).

My mother studied her arms again, and said irrelevantly. "I am glad that the dead do not know each other in Hades's Hall. I would not have *him* see me old."

So that was the meaning of the new gesture. She was searching for signs of age.

"Mother, time is a stranger to you," I said truthfully, despite a wayward piece of the white lock of hair. "Although I liked your hair the old way."

"It is that new woman from the secret police. Useless!"

"Secret police? In the palace?"

"My dear, all Royal Heraklids are watched now."

"Can't you protest?"

"Aristodemos did. They removed them. And replaced them with others."

"Who are they? What are they? Where are they?"

"Serfs. Lesser Spartiates. Whatever is suitable for their place. We make jests about it."

"How do you know? If they are secret?"

"Old servants are loyal. Serfs know everything. As for the others, I think it started with Kallibios. A new scribe. Lesser Spartiate. His father, poor man, was quite destitute. I let him farm some land of mine. Kallibios is so grateful he tells me

281

everything they ask him. He is supposed to be reporting on our talk this afternoon."

"How do you know he is not?"

She pointed to a distant corner of the courtyard, where a young Spartan was giving all his attention to a pretty serf girl. "Kallibios," she said. "He asks me what I want him to say."

"You trust him?"

"I do not trust any of them. Although I think most of them trust me." She touched her hair. "But I must have someone more skilled for this."

"Where is Dromea?"

"I have made her husband a steward."

"Is old Taurus dead?"

"Not *that* estate." Her gesture was impatient.

My mother's land purchases were making her one of the richest women in Sparta. But she went on foot...

Not long after I spoke with my mother, Antalkidas put himself in my way.

Doreius and I had been in the temple of Artemis Othria to place two finger-length bronze cavalrymen upon the offering table, in thanks for victory and a safe return from foreign lands. Amongst bronze and clay hoplites, of the same size, was one holding a lyre in its spear-hand. "Euagoras," Doreius said.

At the top of the path leading to the hollow where the temple stands, Antalkidas waited for a chance encounter. We exchanged greetings. Doreius had to see his father. This time he did not ask me to come with him. I assumed he did not want Antalkidas along, and accompanied him only as far as the stables.

"I dare say Euagoras told you where we were," I said, as Doreius rode off.

Antalkidas did not deny it. "I wanted to speak to you. You have heard that I am an ambassador to Sardis?"

"And then what, Antal? Will you borrow Lysander's speech, and bribe an oracle to make yourself king?"

"I really don't think I should like being a king. The Persians have a board game. The pieces are kings, queens, generals, cavalrymen and hoplites. The King is the most important piece. But he must only move forward in a straight line." The pale eyes shared a jest with a god. "Now, can you see me moving in a straight line?"

"On a curving road, perhaps."

"Leotychides–" He tried to look as though a sudden thought struck him. "A cavalry officer has a horse. And an ambassador goes mounted – so I have just decided. We could ride to my kleiros, and be back before I must be in Hall. Not the least advantage of being a citizen is that one can offer a friend a cup of wine under one's own roof." He knew well that his hospitality could not be refused without offence. His kleiros was at the edge of the vale in Pitane, well beyond that newly-cleared quarter of the City where rich citizens were building second houses. Workmen ceased hammering and sawing to look up as we rode through.

"Sparta grows greater," Antalkidas said.

"It grows more houses."

We had to wait for a servant to take our mounts. Serfs become lazy in the absence of master or mistress. The house was not as neglected as that of some new citizens. Nor was it as well-maintained. The wine was excellent. A present, Antalkidas said, from Tiribazos. We took it in a somewhat overgrown courtyard.

"I really must grow a beard." He fingered his chin. A beard would give him years. He was still too thin for his height. "In Persian courts, only eunuchs are beardless."

"I hear your friend Tiribazos has replaced Tithraustes as satrap."

"I have spoken of you to him. He was most interested. Not least, that you are still alive. Succession disputes are settled simply in Asia. A dagger...Poison..."

"You will cease to discuss me with barbarians. I am not king."

He raised his eyebrows. "What a splendid royal command from a not-king."

"Sparta's disputes do not concern Persian satraps."

"Ah, but they do. The Persians despise Agisilaos–"

"I heard differently."

"Persian insult is offered with exquisite courtesy and rich praise. Agisilaos spent two months in Pharnabazos's palace. He sat on the ground to vaunt his simplicity. His appearance, as well as his manner, lost us respect. I explained that he was not true king. They, too, have had their usurpers."

"This has nothing to do with me."

You are tall. The Persians expect a king to be tall. You ride well. All Persian gentlemen ride brilliantly. You have looks. They prize beauty in their kings. Their king is a sacred being to them. A god."

"Are you trying to make me Great King of Persia, now?" I sipped my wine.

"Only a king that a Persian king can treat as a king without losing his dignity."

"Antal, why this embassy at all? We are at war with Persia."

"A war we have no hope of winning." He was unusually grave. "When Peisander lost our ships and those of our allies, we lost the Asian war."

"You go to Sardis to ask terms?"

"By no means." The pale eyes consulted Olympos. "I shall merely turn a disadvantage to an advantage. And, in the words of Kallikratidas, I shall stop Konon's fornication with the sea."

The changing room was full. The Leonidian Games approached. I was telling the Magpie about the battle for Lechion. (*again*, he would say if he were here).

"We all knew you would be the first of our year to be promoted, Cockerel." He scraped some skin off my back, along with the oil and sand.

"He wasn't first," Pityas grinned "Euagoras made platoon leader in Sikyon."

"Euagoras!" The Magpie dropped the stlengis. "Hek', you always wondered how he survived his wine bath."

"Euagoras survived because Euagoras is as tough as old cavalry leather," Pityas told his cousin.

From another bench came the voice of Sphodrias, talking about his son. Kleonymos was going to his flock the following year. If Sphodrias was to be believed, Kleonymos performed greater feats than the child Hermes.

"Have you seen the boy?" Pityas asked. I allowed that it had been more than two years. "He is as beautiful as a young god."

284

The talk stilled as Kallias strode in. Without a word of greeting, he said, "Well, the bastards have done it. The cavalry is ruined."

Pityas and Aristokrates stared.

They were his latest recruits. Pityas found it strange to have another man in Apollodoros's place at his right in his hoplite regiment, and the poor Pointer welcomed any distraction from his hopeless passion for Meleas's wife. Kallias was quick to seize upon any man who might be induced to take his horse, and uphold the regiment's reputation.

Agisilaos persuaded the ephors to implement the same decree that he had applied at Ephesos, exempting a man from war duty if he provided a mounted cavalryman with full panoply in his stead. The device had been successful in Asia; but this was the first time, since Lykourgos made us Equals, that a Spartiate could be excused a citizen's first duty – unless he was holding public elected office.

By vigorous recruiting, Kallias and officers like him had kept our regiment free of these substitute cavalrymen, whom we regarded as little more than mercenaries. Now, he sat down on a bench, and told us all cavalry regiments were to be broken up, and the cavalry enlarged by taking in more substitutes.

"Why?" he asked.

"Teleutias says Agisilaos wants a large cavalry to pursue the war in Asia, when we make peace with Athens. Antalkidas says some of Agisilaos's friends wanted out."

"Who are the substitutes?" Pityas dipped into the oil. "Up-country men?"

Kallias moved his head in a negative gesture. "Lesser Spartiates," he replied. "Landless men."

Pelles leapt to his feet. "By the gods, I'll not serve with them."

He had taken his flogging like a Spartiate at Sikyon. An Equal amongst Equals. To be punished before inferiors was more than any man could be expected to take.

"What is to become of *us*?" the Magpie asked.

"We will be the officers. The substitutes are private soldiers."

"Like a foreign army..."

Kallias noted the Magpie's stricken face. "You will have your own platoon."

285

"I dare say that's one way of getting a promotion. Pity Leo' had to blood his spear for his." Anaxandros walked out.

"I didn't mean–" Kallias began.

"He knows it. He's angry, too. Does Doreius know yet?"

"Then I'll hear about it from him in Hall tonight."

Hekataios paused by us on his way out. "Speaking of my brother...Was it you two who put him up to it?" He glared. "Perhaps not. It was just the sort of story that would appeal to him."

Sphodrias looked at his retreating figure, and turned to us with open bewilderment. Kallias glanced at me, and said, "Let us walk to the racing course." Sphodrias knew it for a private matter, and muttered something about his duties.

It was one of those spring days that the gods give only to Sparta. The flower-drenched breeze brought us the sweet sound of a maiden's chorus, practising under a plane tree as their chorus-master led them.

"Do you know what Doreius intends to do about Gorgo?" he asked. "I am *her* cousin. And her father hasn't been himself since his head-wound in the Long War."

The girl who refused to marry old Chairon turned out to be Gorgo. Her mother had turned away other suitors, hoping to force the girl to change her mind, but Gorgo swore she would wear the short peplos of a maiden for life before she would marry riches.

Doreius, who would pay an unmarried man's fine when he reached thirty-one, promptly made an offer for her. The sturdy little girl was now a tall, handsome maiden, who drew the bow as well as some men, and was worshipped by the girls she trained in games. She and Doreius were well-matched.

It was all very simple, until Dinon took a strong stand against his elder son marrying a maiden of twenty-two. Unreasonably, I thought. Had she been a widow, Gorgo would not have been considered old.

"Dinon will not be moved," I told him. "Nor will Doreius." The flutes from the racing-course drowned the maidens' chorus as we neared it.

I have sometimes seen great bitterness between fathers and sons in foreign cities. In Sparta, there is usually fondness. I have always considered the reason to be that we owed our land to the City, rather than our progenitors. Unasked obligation is a burden hard to bear generously.

"I had thought to have married the girl myself," Kallias said. "But she always seemed more a sister than a cousin. It never occurred to me. Hek' seems somewhat unfriendly."

"Hek' always sides with his father."

Hekataios, also, always underestimated his brother's will. Doreius would not affront his father. Neither would he take any wife but Gorgo. If necessary, he would pay a fine until he was sixty.

Some men did. Even a fine man like Derkyllidas. Such men were subject to much jesting in Hall, and Doreius set as much store on being the best citizen as he had on being the best youth in the flock.

"Hipparchos has been appointed garrison commander at Lechion," Kallias said presently.

"Isn't he the brother of an ephor's wife?"

"Be grateful he is not Thibron."

"I thought Thibron was banished."

"He is back and promoted." Kallias chewed a blade of grass. "As Agisilaos can refuse his kin nothing, I dare say the ephors reckon theirs deserve something, too."

I found my mother in the courtyard. She was standing by the fountain, looking at the reflection of the moon in its still water. It was a clear night, the black sky scattered with stars. The soft moonlight made strange beasts of the shadows of the trees.

"When I was a little girl," she said. "I thought I could dip my hands into a fountain and capture the moon. Perhaps I did, for a short while." She looked up at me. "Have you ever captured the moon, Leotychides?"

"I think I have."

It was one of our rare moments of sympathy.

Her wry smile broke the strand. "Young men usually slip away from dining halls to a bride or a lover. Rarely to mothers. What do you want?"

I told her.

"Really, Leotychides..." She walked away, and seated herself on a bench.

"You could do it, Mother."

"My dear, queens have some privileges, but even kings cannot interfere in the private concerns of citizens."

"Doreius saved my life. It would be simple courtesy to receive his father." I sat beside her. "Talk to Dinon. You can charm the scales off a serpent when it suits you."

"I seem to have failed with you."

"You are a popular queen."

Her laughter rang out. "In other words, my high-minded son would have me use my influence. Oh, Leotychides, in one way we are alike. When we love, it is unmeasured." She took my face between her long-fingered hands, and kissed my brow. "And, for that, I will do as you ask." She rose. "Let us go inside. I have some fine wine from Chios. We shall drink while you tell me of this serpent to be de-scaled."

By the fountain, she stopped and placed her hand on my arm.

"Leotychides, before I do this... think. Are you certain you would not prefer some other maiden for Doreius?"

"Yes, Mother. He is set upon Gorgo."

"That is precisely what I mean." She ran her fingers through the water, and scattered the moon.

There was a fondness between us, my mother and I, but no understanding.

Doreius was betrothed to Gorgo eight days before our regiment was ordered to the Lechion garrison. Hekataios recovered his good nature sufficiently to see a favourable omen for the marriage. I hoped, for Dinon's sake, for the wedding to take place before the bride was an ancient crone of twenty-three.

Chapter 12

For days the skies had been a mottled grey. The colour of the spear-tip cold that pierces to the bone. The allied troops kept to their tents, or warmed themselves in the wine-shops of Lechion. Some Corinthians, back from a raid, searched the rubble of demolished wall section for firewood.

Only Spartans exercised. Hoplites, bare under their cloaks, willing themselves against the cold. Fifty cavalry braved the weather. Our company. Doreius and Kallias had a competition going between them, as to which one would have the smartest company. They had their work cut out.

We had arrived with a full regiment; five companies, each consisting of six Spartiate officers and forty-four untrained men. The young substitutes were bitter and rebellious, the older men obedient but spiritless. Doreius and Kallias offered to exchange any man over thirty-five for any man under twenty-five.

The other commanders of fifty responded readily, and traded off their trouble-makers. Such an exchange would have been unthinkable in the days of Praxitas; Hipparchos did not interfere with the cavalry regiment and its commander Anakos. The older officers liked Anakos for his charm and witty speech. His easy-going ways made his pentatarchoi unsure of him.

Doreius and Kallias drilled their rebellious troops unmercifully. They would order them into battle-array at midnight, and severely punish any laggards. A show of drowsiness meant a day on shield guard. Disobedience, a flogging. After a time, they began to take on the look of Spartan cavalry.

At last, the fierce weather forced Kallias out of the competition. It was snowing lightly one morning, when Doreius kept his company vaulting on and off their horses, until

Pasemachos himself would have proud of their smart mounting. There was more to it than show. If a cavalryman cannot mount front to back, he can get a spear in this back. If he cannot make the turn instantly, an enemy may rush up to take him in the throat. That was the day I heard one of the troops say. "Wait until we see some action. That bastard Doreius will get my spear in his back."

I was meant to hear. There was bad blood between the troops and the officers. The matter of the helmets had exacerbated it.

The rich men who equipped their substitutes had not, in the main, taken full panoply to include the open-faced helmets. Anakos thought it looked ragged to see a few parade helmets among the battle helmets, and ordered that only officers were to wear parade helmets. The troops hated the helmets and the men who wore them. It was a visible difference between us, and these men who might have been full Spartiates and Equals.

The man who voiced the threat was in my platoon. I had him flogged for insubordination.

"Would you have ordered that flogging, had he threatened another officer?" Doreius asked me.

"I do not know."

"You will stand guard with your shield the rest of the day," he snapped. "Next time you give an order, you will know the reason."

The sympathy of the men swung to me, not to Doreius, who punished me for ordering the flogging of one of their fellows.

"Look how the bastard treats his eromenos." "The lad is nearly frozen." "I'd give him some of my wine, if he would take it." And so on.

They did not know how tenderly Doreius wrapped me in his crimson cloak after my punishment duty, and held warmed wine to my lips, nor did they see the wretchedness in his eyes, as he aid, "I had to do it, Leotychides, because you are the best. You always were the best; I cannot let you be less."

I knew without his words. There was rare need for explanations between us. We had known spring together, smelt the stench of battle side by side, and felt death brush us with its dark wings. Sometimes, now, months passed between those times that Eros whispered to us. I could even believe in a time when only our spirits would love, the rest burnt away, as the mortal part of a hero is burnt away to make him a god. But then, is love not a god?

The new men saw action when Agisilaos led a force through the Pass of Tenet to Corinth, and tore down the portion of the Lechion walls the Athenians had rebuilt. Teleutias, who supported him by sea, captured the ships and dockyards, although he commanded only twelve triremes.

The garrison cavalry played such a small part in this action that it is not worth setting down. Doreius was dissatisfied with the look of the men, and took his company on exercises almost as soon as we returned. The distractions of Lechion were not good for discipline, and with Agisilaos's army encamped here, it was livelier than usual.

"Argos was good." Hekataios sat on a three-legged stool, warming himself with a cup of wine. His regiment was with Agisilaos. He soon searched out the tent we shared with Pityas, Kallias and Anaxandros. "I do not think the Argives knew they started a war until we set their crops afire."

"Teleutias did it all." Aristokrates spent more time with us than with his own tent-companions.

"I don't like Agisilaos any more than you, Pointer, but he is a good general." Hekataios set down his cup. "Some Theban envoys came in today. Agisilaos has sent to your father." Pharax was consul for Thebes in Sparta.

"First Athens. Now Thebes wants peace." Pityas lay back on his pallet, studying the clouds of his breath.

Hekataios winced, as tone-deaf Aristokrates reached for a lyre. "The Athenians did not look very peaceful in Arkadia." Iphikrates and his peltasts attacked Mantinea. Its defenders sent to Sparta. "The peltasts took to their heels as soon as they saw our columns," Hekataios laughed. "They are as frightened of Spartans as the Arkadians are of them."

"The Corinthian exiles gave them a bloody nose, when we took Lechion." Pityas rose, took the lyre from Aristokrates, and laid it back on the table. "Have you seen them, Hek'?"

"There were some Corinthians with us at the Isthmus."

"Who?" Pityas demanded.

"Hoplites. Some cavalry." Hekataios turned to me. "Where is

291

my brother?" Pityas took a cup of wine, and returned to his pallet.

"He thought his men needed some night-riding."

"Doreius hasn't changed since he was a melleiren." Aristokrates lighted a wick from the fire-pot, and set it in the oil of the lamp. "He took our sandals and tunics a *month* before the other patrol leaders."

A great guffaw brought Pityas upright. "Poor wee Tok. Wants his sandals and his tunic."

"Don't play the fool," Aristokrates snapped. "You can't blame those poor bastards for hating him."

"When you have blooded your own spear, Pointer, you will understand."

"By the gods, Pityas, I have told you often enough not to call me by that ridiculous name."

Aristokrates took offence easily. Pityas grew short-tempered. I knew why.

Hekataios grinned. "Had you remained a hoplite, Aristokrates, you would have had a better war."

"Pityas goes too far," Aristokrates said, as we rode towards the harbour.

Agisilaos and his army were in the old Theban garrison huts. Pharax had arrived and sent for his son.

"He jests."

"I asked him to desist."

"His mind is uneasy." In the distance, slight figure limped towards the wounded huts. "Aristokrates, I am turning back here. It will do you no good with Agisilaos to be seen with me." A horse neighed in the harbour stables. Dancer pricked up his ears.

Aristokrates regarded me levelly. "I want no favours from Agisilaos."

"Do not set him against you. Promotion comes slowly in the cavalry."

"Agisilaos may do as he pleases. Look. There is my father."

Pharax stood outside a garrison hut, a fine-looking man, large like his son. He smiled when he saw Aristokrates. The smile faded when he recognised me.

"I forgot to inspect the company horses," I lied. "I must go back. I have no wish to stand guard with my shield again."

Agisilaos stepped out of the wounded hut. He walked to some men who gathered about a small brazier, spoke to them, and called to a servant to bring wood for a fire.

"Doreius did not order you to inspect those horses twice, Leotychides." Aristokrates dismounted smartly.

Pharax stepped forward. Agisilaos regarded us directly.

"Your father will want you privily. I am going back."

"You are very stubborn, Leotychides." Aristokrates took two steps back. Then, before Pharax, before the men, before Agisilaos, he raised his arm, and gave me the salute that is given only to kings.

Winter would not loosen its grip on the season that rightfully belongs to spring. The anger between Aristokrates and Pityas deepened. They were flock-brothers, friends, but it took little to set it alight. A few skirmishes were all that was needed to stop this bickering.

There were Theban troops massing around the Piraeum. They already held that fortress. Rumour ran through the compound like a river in full spate.

Pityas warmed his hands over the fire pot. "The exiles have never been away this long."

"Some Corinthians came in with Agisilaos." Anaxandros polished his scabbard. It was something he did daily.

"Hoplites."

The exiles had liberated enough horses to form their own cavalry. A large number of artisans and their sons had joined the well-born young men, and formed a hoplite regiment.

"He means the men who were with us in Sikyon," I explained. Aristokrates opened the chest that stood by Doreius's pallet. "Where is that silver tankard Doreius won from the Corinthians, Cockerel?"

"He traded it for a silver arm ring for Gorgo."

"The tankard was valuable."

"She can't wear a tankard, Pointer." The Magpie's breath came out in clouds.

"Wine is tasteless in silver," Pityas said. "Gold, too."

"Your cups are gold, I take it?" Aristokrates laughed.

"The exiles took some when they raided Polyanthes's estate. He filled his wooden cup from the half-full krater left over from

293

the evening meal. "I think we had ought to look for them." They could be cut off somewhere."

"Hipparchos would call it deserting," Aristokrates stated, looking through the chest.

"We're off duty."

"Pityas," I said, "We cannot search all Corinthia."

"We need not. There is a man in the Kraneion, who will know where they are. He takes messages in and out of Corinth for them."

Aristokrates looked back over his shoulder. "If Spartan officers call upon that man, Timolaos won't give him an easy death."

"I know how to get a message to him. Leo'?" Pityas looked from me to Anaxandros to Aristokrates. "I'll go alone, if I must." He would not be swayed, however we reasoned it.

I sat on the edge of my pallet. "We'll send to this man. Meet him separately, or whatever you do. If our friends are in trouble, we'll report it to Doreius. Go back with a platoon. Or a company, if need be."

"Doreius won't order a company to search for some Corinthians."

"They are his friends, too," I told Aristokrates.

"Thank you, Leo'" Pityas fastened on his sword belt. Anaxandros searched for his boots.

"We haven't permission to leave Lechion," Aristokrates insisted. "We'll be disenfranchised for desertion."

"Really, Magpie? Leo'?" Pityas asked. "We're better off without Aristokrates if he fears so much."

"You say I fear?" Aristokrates demanded.

Retract, Pityas, I thought, knowing that he would not.

Pityas strode across the tent to face him. "I say you are a craven."

Aristokrates lunged. I caught his arm. "Cease this instant." It was a patrol leader's voice. He heard a king. He froze, although he was trembling with rage. Too late, I recalled that royal salute before Agisilaos.

Anaxandros stood by his cousin. "All Sparta knows what to call a wrestler who returns from Olympia alive and without an olive crown." he taunted.

This time I did not restrain Aristokrates. It was not my right.

The table, chairs, lyre and cups went flying in the scuffle. Aristokrates fought the two cousins at once. I moved the fire-pot out of the way. The krater trembled. I seized it and doused them with wine. It would not have stopped them more than an eye-blink, had the tent-flap not lifted. Cold air pierced the smell of smoke, meat, horse and leather.

Aristeas stuck his head through the opening. "Is this a private battle, or may I join in?"

The flock brothers untangled themselves. We hauled Aristeas the rest of the way in.

"We were going to look for you," Pityas told him.

Aristeas slapped his own brow. "I should have sent a message with the hoplites." The scar over his eye had whitened. Those on his sword arm were red. He was shabby and very lean. The exiles were becoming hard as Spartans. "We were in the Isthmian Games."

"I thought Argos organized the Isthmia now." Anaxandros collected cups from the ground.

"So did the Argives," White teeth flashed in the Corinthian's bronzed face. "I took an olive crown." He balanced a wreath on his forefinger. It was dry. Most of the leaves gone. "It was an olive crown. Keep it for me."

Pityas took it from him. "The long race?"

Aristokrates went to his pallet. Apart. This was no boys' fight that would end in laughter.

Aristeas seated himself on the three-legged stool. The only piece of furniture still standing. "We watched Argive priests dedicate the animals for the sacrifice to Poseidon. Judges, priests; every one an Argive." His dark eyes sparked fire. "I walked up to one of the judges as soon as the ceremony was done. I wore this cloak–" He fingered a well-draped fold of the coarse, blood-stained garment he took from a dead Argive. "'Move off, Fellow.' he said 'You don't belong here.' 'Not so,' I told him. 'It is you who do not belong here.' He looked at me more closely then. 'Who are you?' he asked. 'A citizen of Corinth, Argive' 'What is that?' His mouth opened to deepen his affront. No sound came out–"

"You speared him?" Anaxandros broke in.

"How could I? We were in the temple grounds." Aristeas fell into his own thoughts, then came out of them. "No, he had caught sight of Agisilaos, and a Spartan army drawn up in battle-order."

"We heard you were with him at the Isthmus." Anaxandros called for wine.

"We let Agisilaos know we intended to take back the Games," Aristeas explained. "He promised to support us. The Argives ran so fast they left the beasts they dedicated for the sacrifice. Their Corinthian lackeys fled with them." Nikomedes would have been in the lists. Hate is stronger where there has been love. "We dedicated some new animals, and held the Games." He examined a graze on Pityas's arm. "Put some wine in that."

Anaxandros's servant passed around the cups. Aristokrates set his down, untouched.

Aristeas picked up the lyre from the ground. He played softly and absently. Something the Corinthians in Olympia sang. "Considering we had no training, Corinth did well."

"War is good training for a runner," Anaxandros said.

"For Argives," Aristeas replied tersely as a Spartan. "We invited Agisilaos to judge the Games. He said it was a Corinthian matter."

"Well done, Agisilaos," I thought. "If you must be a king, be a good king."

"Did Agisilaos say what he intends doing now?" I asked.

"We told him the traitors in Corinth will eat well, as long as Piraeum feeds them." The people of that fortress at the foot of Mount Geranaia had more than enough cattle within their walls to keep Corinth supplied.

"There are good men in Corinth." Alkimenes and Pasimelos would also go hungry.

Aristeas's hands stilled on the lyre. I recalled the elegant young man in the blue tunic disputing with Alkimenes. "It was they who told us how the cattle are coming into Corinth." There was no longer any division between the exiles and the peace party. "They also say that some of the men who took part in the massacre are in the Piraeum. By all the gods, I hope Agisilaos gives them to us." No few of the exiles had kinsmen among the slain. Blood dues to be paid.

"Will he take us?" Pityas asked.

"I don't know. He has our cavalry and some Philasian.

Aristeas met his eyes. "I hope so."

Aristokrates looked up, but did not move from the pallet. "Aristeas, you were in Olympia. Did I submit?"

"I doubt you could have," Aristeas did not comprehend the import of the question.

Anaxandros leapt up, and walked to his flock-brother. "I oughtn't to have spoken so, Pointer. They all thought you dead in the Games, before you came around." Aristokrates remained silent. "We know you'd die rather than submit."

Pityas joined him. "I spoke in anger, Pointer, and wrongly. I ask your pardon."

Aristokrates regarded them both. Slowly he took up his cup and drank Anaxandros's wine. The quarrel was reconciled, but it was not an easy silence.

"Why do they call you Pointer?" Aristeas asked.

"Because they are careless of their lives," Anaxandros growled, but the anger had gone from his voice. He busied himself going through Doreius's chest, to hide his loss.

"Try Kallias, Pointer," Anaxandros suggested.

"He has nothing. We have bartered everything."

"And you are always cheated," Aristeas laughed. "Spartans know the value of nothing. The traders are aware of it."

"We do not pay for many things in Sparta." Anaxandros's explanation was cut short when Aristokrates held up the box, with the Twin Gods carved on the cover, that I had given Doreius. "Take that, and let me be far away when Doreius discovers it gone," he warned.

Aristokrates returned the box to the chest. Aristeas rose, drank down his wine, and gave the lipped cup to Aristokrates. "Barter this." He told him what it would fetch. Anaxandros's eyes widened. "Ask the double." He threw his arm about Pityas's shoulders, and the two left.

Anaxandros's eyes followed them. "So that is why Pityas has been in such a foul temper."

"That is not your concern, Magpie."

Aristokrates slipped the wooden cup into his cloak. Anaxandros quickly righted a chair, as Doreius came in. His face was reddened from the cold, lips set tight against the weariness his eyes could not conceal. He took the cup from my hand, and drank the wine in one draught. "I think the men will be too tired to make it to the wine-shops tonight."

Aristeas was here. He says we are going to march on Piraeum." Anaxandros recounted, not quite accurately.

"Agisilaos is sending the Amyklaians back to Lakedaimon." Doreius warmed his hands over the fire-pot. "We are to escort them past Corinth."

"Your company or mine?" the Magpie asked.

"I rather thought it was Kallias's company." A weary smile touched the corners of Doreius's mouth. "The regiment entire. The hoplite regiment as well."

"Two regiments!"

"To give Anakos his due, he tried to convince the Polemarch it was excessive." Doreius stretched out on his pallet. "Hipparchos was adamant." The garrison commander had Lysander's bluster, but not his brilliance.

"Why has Agisilaos dismissed the Amyklaians?" Aristokrates choked as a contrary wind blew down the smoke-hole, filling the tent with smoke. Anaxandros waved a cloak, making it worse.

"I dare say he doesn't want them walking off in the midst of a battle, to sing the hymn to Apollo at the Hyakinthia."

Aristokrates looked as though he envied them this pious duty. He got to his feet. "I think I'll see whether I can find a game of knucklebones in the wine-shops."

"I'll go with you." Anaxandros followed him. He did not see us signal to him to remain. We laughed. Aristokrates had a woman in Lechion. The last thing he wanted was the Magpie following along.

"Where is Kallias, Doreius?"

"On duty."

"Do you think we'll see some action?" I opened my cloak out, and folded myself into it lengthwise, then threw my fine new crimson over me as a blanket. We both kept one cloak fresh for the battle.

"Not likely."

The cold still found its way in. I wrapped the second cloak about me, cocoon fashion.

Doreius laughed. "Do you intend to come out of all that a butterfly?"

"A butterfly on an iris, on the banks of the Eurotas."

"Why is it always spring or summer when we think of Lakedaimon?"

"Because it *is* always summer in Sparta, even in the coldest winter."

"A green field with yellow flowers in spring."

"The slopes of Taygetos in autumn."

"The Halls in winter."

"A walk to Amyklai in the hot sun..."

The fire burned low. It was too cold to rise and refuel it.

"Doreius, my mother once asked whether I had ever captured the moon. I thought of the day we rode side by side, victorious from Krommyon, and told her I had. But it wasn't that time at all. The moon lives over Lakedaimon."

"You were up amongst the stars on the ship to Eleia."

"A stranger voyaging."

He pulled his cloak over him. "I remember once when you were first a melleiren... I saw you take a shining pebble from the river, and hold it up against the night sky. As if you were testing it, to see whether it was a piece of the moon."

"I was too old for such fancies."

"When it dried and dulled, you threw it away. Perhaps it wasn't such nonsense." He stretched out his hand, and I reached to clasp it. "We have grasped the moon, Leotychides."

The cold fire warmed our clasped hands. His went slack and heavy. I rose and covered him with his extra cloak. The thin lines at the sides of his mouth no longer smoothed in sleep.

We rode slowly, keeping pace with the hoplites, under a morning blanket of clouds. We had passed Corinth, and kept on going northwest. Crossing into Sikyonia, thin sun broke through. We halted while Anakos and the polemarch had a brief discussion.

Anakos rode back to us. Hipparchos ordered the hoplites to about-face. I was so certain of our orders that I pulled the reins to turn Dancer about. When it was "Forward," I tugged so hard that he turned his head, and gave me a dark look of equine reproach.

Doreius went white with fury. With abrupt decision, he dug his heels in his horse's sides, and rode towards Anakos. I went with him.

"Sir!"

Anakos turned. "I know what you are going to say, Doreius. I agree with you." The sun grew strong. Spring touched the air. "But our good Hipparchos is a bit overwhelmed by a direct order from the King."

Doreius stood firm. "Sir, the King's order was that the Amyklaians were to be escorted as far as they wanted an escort. They are in friendly country now."

"Alas, Hipparchos has interpreted it in his own way."

"Sir, one of my platoon leaders has a friend amongst the exiles, who tells him that Corinth is on the verge of rising. The rulers will have sent to Athens for reinforcement."

"And I have a Corinthian guest-friend, who sent me word of the same."

"The hoplites will be returning past Corinth without the protection of cavalry, if we escort the Amyklaians further."

"I am not unaware of that. But I know how to obey my orders, Pentatarchos. Do you?"

They glared at one another. Anakos, with his charm and dinners for senior officers, could not have been like less like Praxitas and Pasemachos, but there was no trace of that sparkling smile on his face now. His anger reflected that of Doreius. The anger of intelligent officers at an imbecilic order that rendered them both helpless.

Doreius turned his mount. We rode back to our section.

We escorted the Amyklaians at a speed dictated by the pace of foot-soldiers. It seemed an age. When we neared Sikyon, Anakos spoke briefly with the Amyklaian commander. There we left them, turned back, and rode as if the Furies were after us.

We reached the Isthmus road. Anakos halted abruptly and held up his hand. Doreius stared, as if transfixed by something ahead.

Spartan hoplites ran in loose order up an incline. Bodies lay in the ground, with long spears sticking out of their sides. Twice-long spears. To avert bad luck, I tried not to think of carrot-red hair under one of those helmets. The dead were Spartan...

A glance told the story.

The hoplite regiment had been marching in column, section following section. Iphikrates and his peltasts spotted them unprotected by cavalry. When the enemy appeared, the hoplites had deployed to the left throughout the columns, until the battle line stood, shields locked, facing the peltasts.

The exiles had taught the shoemaker's son the folly of using his peltasts in frontal assault.

The men on the extreme right are always in the position of greatest danger. Their shields cover their own left side and the right of the men next to them, but their own right sides are exposed. Seeking to protect their vulnerable sides, these end men in foreign armies often move to protect themselves, sometimes causing armies to turn in on themselves. Spartan armies do not turn in on themselves. The men on the right stand firm. These hoplites had stood firm. And died.

The light-clad, mobile, mercenaries dashed down from a rise, struck at the unprotected sides of the hoplites, or simply hurled their javelins and scattered.

Hipparchos ordered his men to pursue the peltasts. Weighed down by their heavy armour, they were too slow. On the slippery, uneven ground, the wall of shields broke. When the hoplites turned, the peltasts halted in their flight, wheeled around and hurled spears at their backs. The bravest ran along their flank, aiming at their sides.

Even before Anakos gave the order to charge, Dancer flattened his ears back. He was made for war, that horse. Hooves battered terrain that had bested good men. Then the flute sounded. Cavalry, halt!

Anaxandros kept on going, leading his platoon in the charge. Anakos shouted. Doreius shouted back. "He's tone deaf." And rode after his errant platoon leader. I went with him.

The peltasts ran wildly from Aristokrates's charge. More dispersed and ran into the covering bush, as Doreius and I followed him. We caught up with our flock brother. Doreius ordered him back.

The peltasts kept their distance. That inadvertent rush should have shown Hipparchos what a cavalry charge could do.

Hipparchos and Anakos conferred with sweeping gestures. Anakos remounted, and turned his horse with such fury that the startled beast reared. The Polemarch had ordered the cavalry to keep a continuous front with the hoplites!

Each advance cost the enemy nothing. They struck and dispersed before we could retaliate. The retreat cost our hoplites dearly. From a safe distance, the peltasts would reappear, and hurl their javelins at the unprotected middle of their backs. At some time, an Athenian regiment of heavy infantry appeared and stood in battle array, blocking the road past Corinth.

The slaughter went on. I relive the sounds, the smells, and the sight of that battle forever through the years. Like a sore tooth, one keeps probing despite oneself. With each retreat, the peltasts became more confident; they swarmed about us like mosquitoes, the tinny, resonant voice of Iphikrates urging them on.

A horse screamed, as a long spear pierced its side. Still, the cavalry could have driven off the peltasts, had we been permitted to charge them. By Apollo, I say it to this day!

Hipparchos gave the order to regroup on a hill, as if a rise would prove a deterrent to the ever-bolder peltasts. Rather, it gave them better targets for their javelins. The Athenian hoplite regiment advanced. Marching steadily for the kill.

Hipparchos opened his mouth wide, to bawl an order. It never came. He died bravely, I will give him that. Some of our hoplites broke and fled towards the sea. An unusual number of boats sailed along the shore. Boats! Allied troops had left Lechion to see what was going on. The port was unguarded.

Cavalry squares became shapeless. Ours held, and covered the remaining hoplites, as they collected the bodies of the dead. In a voice as loud as Menelaos, Anakos ordered us to charge the Athenian hoplites and ride flat out for Lechion.

Our company led the charge. That makeshift cavalry was holding. Our ruffians were fighting and riding smartly. The Athenian line broke. I glanced towards Doreius, to tell him silently of my pride in what he had done with them. To share his pride in his company. He was not there. Only his mount rode beside me.

I turned Dancer back towards the Athenian lines.

Ask me how I knew where I would find Doreius, and I can

302

only say a god whispered to me. Or that when two spirits draw close, they speak without words. The Athenians were regrouping. Two delayed. One held his spear raised. I rode him down. The other fled.

I lifted Doreius from the ground. There was no time to bring him around with a sip from my wine-flask. A fleeing hoplite seized his mount. I lifted him on to Dancer, and took up his shield. Doreius would never forgive me if I left his shield in the field of battle.

Dancer fell in with the cavalry rush towards Lechion. Hoplites clung to the horse like apples on a tree. We did not push our passengers away, but there was nothing we could do to help them.

The quiet of Lechion after the noise of battle. A peasant played a flute, passing his winter idleness. I lifted Doreius down, gently, from Dancer's broad back. Tipped my flask against his lips, carefully, so he would not wake choking, as I had the day we took Lechion. How long had I taken to come around?

Aristokrates knelt beside me. I said, "Bring me uncut wine. From the tent. Doreius is stunned." And when he did not move, "By Apollo, Pityas, that is an order." Because Pityas was there too. And the Magpie. Standing about like imbeciles.

Pityas said, "He is dead, Leo'."

"He is stunned. He hit his head." How pale Doreius was. Marble-white.

"Leotychides. Look at me. He is dead." Kallias.

"I thought I was dead, too, the other time."

"Leave him alone. He's a little mad." The Magpie.

"A man's eyes are closed when he is stunned, Leo'"

"By Apollo, Pityas, you are a fool. He isn't even wounded."

Pityas unlaced the leather armour. Placed his hand on the warrior's cloak, which is crimson, to conceal the blood of battle. His palm came away red. But the dead are cold, and Doreius was warm.

I held him to myself, so that his warmth would give the lie to their words. The congealed blood broke afresh, and flowed in a crimson stream, over my arms and chest and face, into his dark curls, as a fox with spear- sharp teeth began to stir.

O deceiver fox, I know better. Can blood flow hot when a man is dead?

"Pentatarchos!" I knew that voice. It was Command. Command penetrated the benumbed lacerations of claws and teeth, like one of those wounds one does not feel until the battle has ended. Claws and teeth pierced the numbness with the voice of Anakos and, far away in Lakedaimon; a beautiful youth raised his arm like the god to throw a spear...

"Pentatarchos!"

I looked up. "The pentatarchos is dead, sir."

"He named you next in command. Stand up, Pentatarchos." Spartan muscles obey when the spirit is elsewhere. "Take command of your company."

My legs followed the order. My voice called men to attention. My eyes saw that we were still sound. My mind said, "Do you know that you are all alive because he made cavalrymen of you, when you cursed him for it?"

"Pentatarchos!" It was the acting garrison commander. I do not recall his name. A greying man. "I need a senior officer to ride to the King." I looked across the gulf to Mount Geranaia. "You will find him at Piraeum. You are to tell him what happened. In detail. Leave nothing out. You understand why it must be a senior officer?"

My groom led Dancer. "Sir, will the dead be returned to Sparta?"

"The bodies should keep in this weather." What was hardened like water into ice. "Who commands your company in your absence?"

"Pityas."

"Don't spare your horse, Pentatarchos."

"Yes, sir." I mounted.

"And, Pentatarchos – I will do everything I can to see that your friend is buried in Sparta. Damn fine officer."

I hated none of the Argives I killed, Uncle, I said to the face of Agisilaos in the wind. Not the Thebans. Not even the Athenians. That was war. Once I thought I knew what it was to hate. I did not know its shadow. You showed me its true face.

304

You, who gave careless orders to a fool. You, who advance your friends; it is you who set fools above men who know not how to disobey. You killed them, Uncle, as you killed the men who sailed with Peisander. But you are not a fool. You stand condemned by your own cleverness. I am your executioner.

It was morning when I reached Piraeum. Agisilaos had captured the fortress the day before. One of his regiments had taken the port of Oenoe. The early sun glistened on the sea. Mist rose from a small lake in the countryside. Near its edge, Agisilaos sat in a graceful rose-coloured pavilion.

A long line of captives, hands bound, heads bowed, was paraded before him. Spoils, like sleek cattle, that army servants guarded for the King. The people of Piraeum had submitted without asking terms. Yesterday they were free men and women. This spring day, they were slaves. A man tried to comfort his wife or sister. A hoplite prodded him. A boy, about twelve, held his head high, defying his bonds. Kallikratidas, how right you were! No Greek should be made a slave.

Agisilaos looked in high spirits, talking with the men to his right and to his left. Pharax and the Theban emissaries waited outside the pavilion. The Thebans had worried brows.

My senses were preternaturally sharpened. Without taking my eyes from Agisilaos. I planned my moves and took in the talk of the troops nearest me. Report in detail. He must know why he dies. My orders agreed with the wish of the god. It was all clear now.

Zeus had willed that Patroklos die by Hektor's hand, so that Achilles would slay Hektor, and Troy fall. Doreius had died so that I should kill Agisilaos, and rid Sparta of unlawfulness.

"The King will divide whatever the slaves bring." An old hoplite spoke to a younger man. "They should fetch a good price." I thought I must cry "For Sparta" as I plunge the sword into his throat. Men must know why he dies. "Agisilaos always looks after his men. Remember him sending fire up to us on the heights that fierce night." No more will you make Spartans greedy, Uncle, and make them soft. "But Poseidon's temple caught fire from the sparks. The god is angry." I was the instrument of Poseidon. I had thought it to be Apollo or

Artemis.

Dancer was covered in foam. At his mouth, it was red. Only a little further, Dancer, and it will end. For us both. I urged him past the slaves and other spoils. A platoon leader shouted at me to halt. There were foreigners with the King. Emissaries seeking terms of surrender. The King received them generously. But he was making the Thebans wait. They'd get no easy terms. The war was won. Over.

Dancer felt my impatience, and moved a foreleg. The platoon leader seized the reins. I ordered him to let me pass. I was a company commander. He obeyed.

O, Dancer, best of horses, only you could make this gallop, after all I put you through.

I halted in front of the pavilion. Pharax approached the King, accompanied by two Thebans. The Spartan with the white streak in his hair leaned to the King, for a private word. Agisilaos gave some terse reply. Turned his back on the Thebans. A public affront. Pharax flushed.

Two hoplites tried to turn me away. Platoon leaders. I snapped at them. Told them to obey a senior officer. Shook them off. Dancer was as still as a horse of marble.

"Sir!"

Agisilaos looked up at my voice. Rose. Limped towards me, past a group of Corinthian prisoners. Guarded by Corinthian exiles. Aristeas leaned on his spear. The captives looked as though they knew they would not live to see the sun set. Agisilaos and I were face to face. He had become weathered. The sharp eyes and prim mouth unchanged.

"Yes–Yes–" Anxious. No. Greedy. Thirsting for another victory. Another success to grind in the face of Thebes.

"Ambush near Corinth, sir." I spoke as to a stranger. Doreius, your spirit is bound to the earth until you are buried; so wait for me. We shall not know one another in Hades's hall, but we shall journey there together. "The hoplite regiment of the Lechion garrison is lost."

"Lost?" A trick of the king's voice shrilled his shout into a howl. "How lost?"

My hand dropped to the hilt of my sword. My voice told him clearly and precisely, leaving out nothing, while Reproach spoke to me with tender irony, saying, *Achilles acted by his own will. When the gods choose men as their instrument, they do not take them into their confidence.* I ignored Reproach. It spoke firmly, *Achilles did not know what the gods intended. Nor do you.*

"And Lechion? Lechion?" Agisilaos drowned the voice of Reproach. My hand tightened on my sword. *Leotychides, it is hubris to assume you act for a god.* "I am asking you, do we still hold Lechion?" *Hubris, Leotychides.*

The Theban emissaries stared and strained to hear. The sword felt good in my hand. *Not Poseidon, Leotychides. Not Apollo. Not Artemis. If you are touched by a god, it is with the madness of Dionysos. Will you shame Sparta? Shame your father? Shame me?*

My hand dropped to my side. "Secured by cavalry, sir." *Do not fear, I will not shame you, Doreius.*

Agisilaos shouted orders. Men ran this way and that. Struck tents. A few gave commands still holding bowls, as though they had interrupted their breakfast. The Thebans smiled. Pharax appealed to them. They walked away. Laughing. Agisilaos returned to me. "You are done in. Have some wine and rest."

"I have orders to take charge of my company."

"I will assume responsibility." That charming smile in the leathery face. "You have done your duty."

"I must obey my orders, sir."

"Good man," he approved. "Change your mount. That one will never make it back to Lechion." He ordered a hoplite to bring me one of his own horses.

Three riders making for Piraeum passed me as I rode out on a mount from my father's stable. I laughed wildly without mirth. Agisilaos had not known me.

Hekataios was in our tent. He had survived the fighting to help collect the hoplite dead.

"Anakos looked like Herakles in anger when he heard *you* had been sent to Agisilaos, Leo'," Anaxandros said. "He sent three other men to turn you back."

"Be quiet, Magpie." Aristokrates spoke sharply.

"It's all right. I have my wits."

307

Pityas filled a basin with water. I removed my helmet, and rinsed my face. The water darkened with dried blood. Not my blood. More than blood. The blood of my soul. I dried my face on my cloak, as I had thousands of times before.

Hekataios laid his hand on my shoulder. "We left Doreius's gear as it was."

I walked to his pallet, and began to sort out the few possessions of a Spartan officer. Soft leather boots. A new crimson cloak. He would be buried in that. An olive crown on his brow, as they covered him with the red-brown earth of Lakedaimon. Apollo, this was not the olive crown I asked for him.

I got on with it. Sandals. Spear. Sword. He was lying on his shield now. Somewhere in the compound. A box of Lakonian wood with the Twin Gods carved on the cover. A comb. Sponge. Stlengis. Gorgo's silver arm-ring. Pumice. Oil-flask. Drinking-cups. An ornament for a horse's bridle. Some hard, dry bread. A pebble that a boy of twelve had thrown away, because it was not a piece of the moon.

My fox clawed and bit and tore. O, Boy of the Statue, you can bear the pain, for you are bronze. But I am flesh, and this, my fox, too cruel.

I seized a handful of hair, and hacked off a mourning lock with my sword. Stilled my fox. Turned to my flock-brothers, and honoured Doreius with the proudest and most radiant of smiles.

BOOK THREE

Chapter 13

The secret is out.

Philippos is going to war on Persia. The Macedonians are going to free (and no doubt pillage) Ionia. I cannot contain my laughter. The tutor does not smile. He is a sophist, not a soldier.

"Philippos has a standing army of forty thousand," I explain. "It is a good army." A disciplined army to any but Spartan eyes. "It gives him command of Macedon and Thrace. The Great King has millions. The barbarians are not great fighters; but, by sheer numbers, they could destroy his forces."

"Sparta put smaller numbers in the field against the Mede."

"And could have defeated him, had we not been forced to abandon the campaign by the intrigues of Athens. But we had almost the whole of Hellas with us."

"Why should not all the Hellenes follow King Philippos?"

Is this dry man jesting? No city in Hellas would accept these savage Macedonians as war-leaders. I recall the tutor is from Stagira in Chalkidiki. His years in Athens may have given him an Attic accent, but he still thinks like a provincial Greek. "Not a single Hellenic city would follow any but Sparta or Athens. The Thebans, who are true Greeks if nothing else, were rejected. If they were unable to command sufficient respect, I don't fancy Macedon's chances."

"The Prince shows great promise." Ah, the adored pupil. "He will some day be King."

"A king is no more than his people. Although he can be less."

"A vigorous, powerful king, imbued with the spirit of Hellas—"

"The spirit of Hellas does not love powerful kings."

"Such a man might make Hellas as one." Again, his sense of humour fails him. "We have the same tongue, the same gods."

"And the same appetite for freedom."

"The ferocity of our freedom has cost us dearly."

"It is not our freedom that has cost us, but our foolishness."

"You, too, believe in the cause of Hellas in Asia."

"Some day, when we have done fighting one another, our

sons, or our sons' sons, will free Ionia. Is sophistry not intended to teach patience?" This time he smiles. "If you are kindly intentioned towards Philippos, spare him mockery. Urge him to be content with the leadership of his own kind."

"The prince burns to free Ionia."

"Let him."

"He loves Hellas."

"Leave Hellas to Hellenes." The boy is bright. Better than his father. He could be a good king, if this man does not lead him to folly. I speak bluntly. "He will never lead our cities freely. If he would do so forcefully, every one of them will hate him as no man since Xerxes has been hated." The tutor looks distressed. Why do I bother to dispute his preposterous dream? I say, more kindly, "The Asian cities would not bring him all he believes. They have been great trouble to us and little reward."

So it goes on, until he asks for what I have come to think of as his routine rhetra.

Since I explained that the Law is not written, he regularly calls to ask me to quote another rhetra, which he picks at like a bird pecking at a grain in search of the kernel, then goes off repeating it to himself.

Could he be setting it all down?

The King has returned from the Pythian Games in great high spirits. He sent me a message, asking whether I would give a reading of what I have set down so far. Again, there is a dinner. Again, it is limited to Philippos, his son, the younger, more civilized nobles, and the tutor. There is coldness between the King and his son, but that is of no matter.

It is Asian matters that provoke the most interest. I conclude the reading in telling how Konon and Pharnabazos threatened and coerced the cities on the Ionian coast, and in the Aigean islands, into submission.

"I heard it that the Athenians were welcomed," Philippos says.

"They would tell it that way in Athens. Our reputation, as much as our garrison, protected those cities. After the disaster in Corinthia, they feared we were no longer able to do so."

The shoemaker's son followed up his success at the Isthmus

311

Road, by pressing on to capture Sidos and Krommyon – as well as an important fortress on the border dividing Attica and Boiotia, which Agisilaos had taken. All that Praxitas had won – except Lechion itself, which we still held.

The Thebans immediately withdrew their suit for terms. Athens broke off those prolonged peace negotiations. The Corinthian exiles no longer had the freedom of the land for their raids, but they persisted in sailing about the coast, to land at night and lay waste to the estates of the traitors.

"How could one unimportant battle in the Peloponnesos affect the Ionian cities?" the King's son asks "Only a single Spartan regiment was lost."

"No Spartan defeat could be considered unimportant. It was the first time Spartans had been defeated by equal numbers. Konon and Pharnabazos used the incident to destroy belief in Sparta's invincibility; but, when Derkyllidas persuaded Abides and Sestos that we could protect them, those key cities remained loyal." Again, that great man had used words rather than force of arms to effect his persuasion.

"So you still controlled the Hellespont...?" The king looks thoughtful. He knows what Athens would do to capture the long strait between Europe and Asia.

The Prince tilts his head. "I once saw a copy of the Iliad that ended with an unfinished sentence "There came an Amazon queen..." You have finished your account with the words, "And then Antalkidas undertook his mission to Sardis.""

"Antalkidas devised a plan to win the Great King's allegiance from Athens, and bring him over to us." When had Antalkidas not had a plan? "Tiribazos had replaced Tithraustes as satrap, and it was through him that he hoped to accomplish it."

"But you have told us that it was the Great King who created the alliance against Sparta, and promoted the war in Greece," Philippos interjects.

"His creation had served its purpose, and got us out of Asia. It was beginning to threaten him. Konon and Pharnabazos virtually controlled the sea off western Asia. As for Pharnabazos, the Great King does not like his satraps to become too strong." The Prince looks up sharply. "Athens had rebuilt her long walls, and was building ships. In brief, Artaxerxes's allies threatened his own dominions. So Antalkidas went to

Tiribazos, with the proposal that all the cities of the Hellenes should be set free. That would be to the advantage of the Great King, because on their own neither Sparta nor Athens could trouble his territories.

"What had Sparta to gain?" A shrewd glint lights the King's small blue-green eye.

"Our allies were all free, so we had nothing to lose. But Athens would lose the client cities she had regained, Thebes would be stripped of the Boiotian cities subject to her, and Argos would have to free Corinth. Our enemies would be considerably weakened."

It is the Prince who comprehends the audacity of Antalkidas's plan. "And his strongest argument was Sparta's comparative weakness at sea! He deserved success for his daring."

"Men seldom get what they deserve."

News of Antalkidas's journey got out, and he arrived at Sardis to find that enemy ambassadors had preceded him. Konon openly represented Athens at Tiribazos's court.

"What happened then?" someone shouts from the end of the room. I can tell that the King, his son and the tutor know the rest, so I make it as brief as possible.

Antalkidas brought Tiribazos around to his way of thinking, but the Satrap hadn't the authority to agree to the proposal without the consent of the Great King. He secretly gave Antalkidas gold to raise a fleet, and did us another favour as well. He threw Konon into prison for having diverted the Great King's money for the advancement of Athens."

This last provokes gusts of laughter from the nobles and even the King, who have heard it before. I still find it amusing. So had Antalkidas who, in his own way, had done for the slippery Athenian who had deluded Kallikratidas, Lysander and Teleutias.

"I cannot look upon the presence of a Greek in a barbarian dungeon as a source of amusement," the tutor said quietly.

I frequently find his conversation engaging, and have acquired a certain respect. It takes courage for this little hireling to speak up to us, as he often does.

"Nor would I," I reply with gravity "had Konon not done so much to prevent Sparta freeing Greek cities from barbarians forever."

"And after that..." The Prince returns to the point.

"Tiribazos travelled to Susa, to put Antalkidas's proposal to the Great King. Shortly afterwards, news came through that he had been detained on account of some court intrigue."

"I know that. I meant in Hellas."

"Oh, the war continued."

*   *   *

For a while, the balance tilted towards Athens.

The Athenians had moved from the position of ancillary allies of Thebes in the Lokrian squabble to leaders of the war against Sparta. Perhaps they could not forgive us of the debt they owed us for saving them from destruction. More likely, it was their old dream of making all Hellas an Athenian empire.

The great King replaced Tiribazos with a satrap called Struthas, who hated Sparta. The ephors anticipated his first move, and sent an army commanded by that same Thibron who had been fined and banished for being unable to control his troops. He was a charming man, and had many friends.

So was that pleasant fellow Diphridas, whom I had met at the Menelaos House just before the outbreak of war. But Diphridas has enemies. He had recently been elected an ephor, and fiercely opposed the appointment of Thibron, but could not carry a majority of his fellow ephors with him.

Early on in the campaign, Thibron died bravely and unnecessarily, as did most of his men.

I do not know whether men had come to appreciate Diphridas's astute judgements, or whether his opponents simply wanted him out of the City, but when his year as ephor expired, Diphridas was appointed commander, in Thibron's place. Sparta's fortunes began to turn.

Athens sent out Thrasyboulos. The ageing general brought the strategic city of Byzantion to heel by putting its mercantile party in power, as Athenian warships waited in its harbour.

From Byzantion he sailed to Lesbos, where he raised the towns who refused to submit to him. After plundering Lesbos, he sailed around the southern coast of Asia, exacting tribute from the Greek cities with his old mastery of bribery, threat and force. At Ayendos, he was offered money voluntarily. By night, Ayendians forced their way through to his tent, and killed him.

Thrasyboulos. Alkibiades. Konon. Those names had been the Long War to me. The new war was bringing new men into the struggle for those most coveted of Athenian offices: those of the three generals elected to rule their city. Timotheos, the son of Konon, had the support of his father's followers. Iphikrates had become famous for his work at the Isthmus Road. The shoemaker's son was raising that tinny voice in speeches, wooing the extreme democrats in an attempt to become a ruler-general. A man called Chabrias had been noted for his competence in the field, and was gaining a reputation in the Middle Party.

Names changed. The enemy was the same.

Agesipolis sat at a table in the room where Pausanios had received Kallikratidas. He wrote lists. Studied maps. Moved armies on tables. I had seen it all before.

The previous year there had been a campaign against the Arkanians that was admirably suited to a fledgeling commander. That, too, inspired lists, maps and armies on tables. When the time came to claim his right of command, Agesipolis allowed Agisilaos to dissuade him. The Eurypontid King led the army himself.

It was Meleas and his wife who had involved me in his attempt to make my cousin assert his rights as King. Mistress Argileonis made a pious journey several times a year to the sanctuary of Athena in Tegea, each time returning with a letter from Pausanios to his son. Once, Meleas asked me to be his wife's letter-bearer. Agesipolis was pleased to see me. Meleas urged me to renew the childhood friendship.

Agesipolis was not afraid of Agisilaos, as they thought. He simply did not wish to displease him. I think few people appreciate how lonely my cousin had been most of his life. I had had a taste of being a child constantly among my elders. Agesipolis endured years of it. By the time he was a youth old enough to compete with other youths in the gymnasium and on the racing course, he had become a stranger to youth.

315

Agesipolis had the gift of laughter. Pausanios had condemned his friends rightly for sycophancy and wrongly for frivolity; and sought to surround him with solemn young men intended to set an example, who had the practical effect of boring my cousin to exasperation. If the defection of his friends at the time of Pausanios's trial taught Agesipolis anything, it was to put no trust in friendship. Which made him lonelier still.

When Agisilaos returned from Asia, he made a point of cultivating the solitary youth in their dining hall. If he chose, my uncle could be a witty companion. He spoke to the young Agiad King as an equal. He never criticised my cousin's attachments, as Pausanios had done, and Aristodemos after him.

My mother's assertion that Agisilaos had hand-picked his lovers was untrue. But the one or two young men who had shown true affection, and urged Agesipolis to assert himself as King, were swiftly posted to distant places. Agesipolis soon forgot them. Where there is no trust, there cannot be love, and Agesipolis trusted no one. No one except his exiled father...and Agisilaos.

I did not learn these things in a day or a year. They came out in chance references, wisps of conversation, in anger, in triumph, in resignation. My own place in my cousin's life was unique. I belonged to a time when life was simple, and we played with wooden swords.

There were times, I believe, when he would have liked to return to those days. Sphodrias had called upon him, to thank him for looking after him that time he was wounded. He found him with Agisilaos and Agisilaos's young son, Archidamos. Not wishing to pass time in the company of the Eurypontid King, Sphodrias paid his respects and left.

He called again with his own son, Kleonymos, before the boy went to his flock. Sphodrias never missed a chance to show the boy off. Archidamos was there, this time, without his father. Sphodrias told me Agesipolis spent most of his time being the enemy, while the two boys ambushed him.

Agesipolis liked Sphodrias. Sphodrias, too, had the gift of laughter. I frequently asked him to join us hunting, or trying our hands at racing chariots. If my cousin showed any sign of rebellion, it was being seen in my company. Agisilaos was too wise to reproach him. Perhaps he, too, had seen the stubborn lowering of the head like a goat, that gesture retained from childhood.

Agesipolis always asked after the Magpie, so Anaxandros and Kallias were drawn into the circle, and through them Pityas. There was still the influence of Agisilaos, and whoever might be the current favourite, but now there was a cross-current.

We planned the Arkanian campaign with him, and he showed a grasp of strategy astonishing in a young man who had never blooded his spear. His enthusiasm was boundless. After one evening in Hall with Agisilaos, he changed his mind.

Now, a year later, he showed the same initial enthusiasm and subsequent procrastination about leading an expedition against Argos.

"There is a great deal to recommend an invasion by way of Nemea," he began as I came in.

"You have claimed command?"

"I shall."

I settled in a chair. "Which means you have not."

"I think, two companies of horse–"

"Ages', are you not bored with playing Spartans and Argives? It has gone on nearly as long as Spartans and Arkanians."

His round blue eyes were reproachful. "That is cruel, Leo'."

"I am too old for games, and so are you."

"It is not as easy as you think. Will you dine with me tonight?"

"You know better."

"It is as much my Hall as it is that of Agisilaos. I know Assembly treated you shabbily on the succession vote–"

"You think that is why I won't dine with the man?"

"Leo', he was kind to me when my father went into exile."

"Your father's friends were loyal."

"To him. Not to me. Agisilaos understands me."

"By Apollo, I do not!" The chair fell backwards as I leapt up. "I cannot understand a king of twenty-four, who has not faced the enemy, when his city has been at war seven years."

His face paled. The freckles stood out on his nose. "You bastard–" He flushed. That was his undoing. What he called me, any man might call another in anger. I had done so more than once. The flush robbed the word of its innocence. He had

317

spoken what could not be spoken, and he knew it. "Leo', I did not mean–" Horror-struck, he backed off as the apology made it worse.

He took refuge in childhood. His head lowered. He stared at the floor, as he had when he was six and Pausanios threatened dire punishment. "I will learn my letters, Father." The time he broke Leonidas's cup playing ball in a forbidden room. "I will practise the lyre every day." When he laughed at an Elder's bad memory.

"I will claim command, Leo', I swear. By Zeus, I will tell Agisilaos tonight."

I pressed my advantage. "You tell the *ephors*, Ages'. Agisilaos is not the law in Sparta."

I had seen Agisilaos about the City a few times, since that day I had nearly committed the great impiety of shedding my father's brother's blood: when the son of Agis had been possessed, not by a god, but by the wild, hot, blood of Alkibiades and Timaia.

Leaving the seats of honour with Agesipolis at the Hyakinthia, I had, for an instant, come face to face with my uncle. We did not speak. But there was a recognition in his eyes there had not been when a mad-eyed, blood-stained cavalry officer told him of the lost regiment.

Agesipolis kept his word. The next argument was to prevent him giving me a ridiculous promotion.

"I am young for pentatarchos, Ages'. Raising me higher at twenty-four would render us both absurd. And before giving the Magpie a company, I should consult his immediate superior."

"Who is he?"

"Kallias."

He laughed. "I took you to be serious."

"I am. Ages'; only a bad commander, and the worst of kings, places an unproven officer over men trained to obey. It is for that I will not break bread with Agisilaos." I cut off his reply before he could utter it. "Let me see that list."

"You cannot object to Sphodrias."

"He is a good soldier. He has served under Eudamides. Phoibidas speaks highly of him. The list, Ages'."

He destroyed it. "You would not approve. But I must have a

staff."

"Choose generals of the quality of Meleas. Aristodemos is the obvious polemarch."

The goat look. "They will treat me as a youth."

"They will respect you as their king and commander."

"I'll not have them as tent-companions."

"The king can hardly choose his tent-companions from platoon leaders and commanders of fifty."

He started another list. "You choose my staff," he said. "I shall choose my tent-companions." I saw my name written. "You are kin," he said shortly. "Sphodrias will rank high enough. And the two of you had best be damned good company, if I have got to look at those two long-faced old men every night."

Aristodemos and Meleas were both younger than Agisilaos, but there are times in which a battle can be lost by prolonged pursuit.

I passed the task of picking the staff of thirty officers to Meleas. The Polemarchs agreed his selection. The generals all approved Agesipolis's plan of invading by way of Nemea. Once on the march, Agesipolis was in sole command.

The Argives have a way of pleading holy days whenever they are threatened with invasion. The same holy days do not prevent their shedding blood when they are the invaders. As we approached the frontier, two Argive heralds arrived carrying garlands, and solemnly proclaimed a holy truce.

Agesipolis coolly and truthfully told them that, before setting out, he had visited both Olympia and Delphi to consult the priests of Zeus and Apollo, and that both gods had agreed that a deceitful truce was not binding.

We crossed into the Argolid.

The first day in Argive military territory, we found a place to bivouac in a pleasant plain, with good, wooded heights on which to post outward-facing lookouts on all sides. In the last light of the day, army servants set up the great circle of tents, while the troops stacked their weapons within it.

Someone found a stream, The Spartans ran towards it, like boys in a flock, to wash off the dust of the road. Agesipolis plunged into the cold water without hesitation, along with the rest of us. Pausanios had not reared him soft.

Two men compared battle-scars, and it became a competition. The Magpie had come out of three campaigns with nothing to show for it but a sprained finger. The older men who had been in the Long War had the best collection, but they were upstream. Sphodrias and I argued as to which of us had more scars. Sphodrias called upon Agesipolis to judge. He studied us both carefully and pronounced Sphodrias the winner.

"He lies, Ages'! He has only three, and I have four."

Sphodrias stared at me. "I see only one on your arm, one on your thigh, and a scratch on your left leg."

"And the one on my foot."

"He got that in the flock when he stepped on a stone, Agesipolis," the Magpie shouted.

"And Sphod' got that mark on his shoulder when he jumped off the hill at Pellana."

Agesipolis laughed, pronounced us both liars, and declared in favour of Kallias. Then Meleas appeared. My cousin's laughter silenced.

Aristodemos and Meleas were discreet, but Agesipolis knew they were assessing him. Conversation was stilted. We sat in front of our tent, as smoke rose from the cooking fires. I took my lyre, and began to play.

When I had done, another lyre a few tents down the circle struck the notes of a rousing melody. Pityas was singing one of the exiles' songs, a fitting one for this campaign, as it mocked the Argives. Agesipolis asked what it was. I told him about the exiles and how they defeated Iphikrates and his peltasts. I found myself talking about Pasemachos ordering us to take up the Sikyonian shields. Soon we were all telling our favourite battle stories.

I do not think Agesipolis knew what a witty and amusing companion Meleas could be on campaign. My cousin relaxed enough to tell a few anecdotes of his own. Inspired strategy fascinated him. He had read or listened to a great deal about warfare.

"I should like to take Argos," he said, as we had our evening meal. His face, illuminated by the fire, was animated. I thought "Let Meleas hold his tongue."

"It could be done," Agesipolis went on. Aristodemos looked on the point of interjecting. Meleas frowned. "If we call Teleutias up with the fleet, while we attack from the land side."

The fleet was strengthened with ships paid for by Tiribazos's gold, but it was not what it had been before Peisander lost it.

"Do it, sir!" Sphodrias grinned with enthusiasm.

Agesipolis smiled. "Another time."

Aristodemos eased. The meal ended. Agesipolis called for uncut wine to pour to the gods. Servants filled our libation cups. Agesipolis stood. A sudden jolt sent me to my knees. The krater that held our dinner wine tumbled. Sphodrias fell forward on his face. The King stumbled. The deep, red wine spilt over our hands.

Poseidon had shaken the earth.

It was a minor quake. The earth stilled. The rents closed, leaving only small rivulets of soil where cracks had appeared. Men dashed about, dousing fires where they threatened to spread. The foreigners who had thrown themselves flat began to rise. Others ran aimlessly.

Meleas stood, feet apart, like a hoplite about to engage an enemy, threw back his head, and raised his fine voice in the hymn to Poseidon. Aristodemos joined him. Agesipolis took it up when Sphodrias and I added our voices. Voices from all the Spartan fires swelled the hymn. Men from the allied contingents walked away from the circle of fires and stood about in huddles.

A Tegean officer came to us, and explained that he had been elected spokesman for the allies.

"Speak then," Agesipolis said.

The Tegean pointed to a fallen cup. "The gods have refused the libations, Sire."

"On the contrary," Agesipolis replied. "They were so pleased they took them from our hands."

The Tegean was not convinced.

"Assemble your troops," Agesipolis ordered.

Meleas glanced at Aristodemos. When a sizeable number of foreigners had gathered, Agesipolis turned his back to us without a word, and walked towards them. He wore his goat look.

Aristodemos ordered us to follow the King. He led. I

understood. He was polemarch. If a king is slain in battle, the polemarch takes command of the army. And if a king is rendered unfit. Such misfortune has been provided for since King Kleomenes went mad. If Agesipolis knew we were behind him, he gave no sign. Meleas knew he was disliked, and kept the distance discreet. Only close enough to appear to be escorting the King.

Some of the troops murmured amongst themselves when Agesipolis halted.

The only foreigners my cousin had known were guest-friends of Pausanios, ambassadors, and similar dignitaries. This army contained peasants and artisans – not all pleased at being at war – as well as common mercenaries, the dregs of many cities.

Agesipolis waited for the mumbling to cease. When it did not, he spoke with some impatience.

"When you have done buzzing," he said conversationally, "I have something to say to you." His unusual manner quietened them, and sparked their curiosity. "I understand some of you think Poseidon is angry," he went on, and explained his interpretation of the omen, as he might have to a group of acquaintances.

Many seemed to accept his explanation quietly as it was given, until one man spoke up. "King Agis turned back from Eleia when Poseidon shook the earth."

Defiance hardened. Such groups usually find a leader, often self-appointed.

"As you saw me tell the Argive heralds, the gods approve this invasion," Agesipolis replied.

"Maybe Poseidon doesn't, King," the spokesman suggested.

There was some laughter. Agesipolis broke into it. "Hear me–" he said sharply. "If you thought your sons or your friends planned wrongly, would you warn them before or after they acted? Poseidon shook the earth *before* Agis went into Eleia to warn him not to do it then." He paused and raised his voice to declare decisively, "We *are* here. We have already crossed the frontier. The god shook the earth to show that he is pleased we are here." He started away and then looked back. "I am going to sacrifice now, to thank Poseidon for his sign. Any of you who don't credit yourselves with more wit than the gods may join me."

322

As Agesipolis ordered the setting up of the tripod, Meleas said, "I think there is something of Pausanios in the boy, after all."

We penetrated deep into Argolis, putting fields of barley, ready for harvesting, to the torch, cutting down olive trees, tearing up vines, burning villages and towns, and taking everything of value we could carry. If the men came out to fight, we put them to the spear. We did not take women or children as slaves.

It was not our intent to annex Argolis, or force her to pay tribute; only to keep her fighting men occupied rebuilding their towns and villages when we launched a major offensive in central Greece. We could not attack Attica and Boiotia with a strong enemy on our own border.

Agesipolis's enthusiasm, and his daring, inspired the men. He was not one of those commanders who could join in barrack-room talk, and be at ease with them in their own way, but they liked the young King.

Then I glimpsed him one night, standing still as a stone, as if transfixed, watching a particularly fine town burn. I dismounted beside him, as troops ran out of the town loaded with valuables.

"Is it always like this, Leo'?" He did not shift his gaze. "Was it this way in Sikyonia?"

"By Apollo, no. Sikyonia is friendly territory. It would have been a flogging offence. He said nothing. "Ages', don't pity the Argives. This is what they do in other countries. It is the way of all armies in enemy territory. Let them see how it feels. They voted for war."

A woman screamed.

"*She* did not."

"Maybe her husband, or her father or her son, will think before he does so next time."

He turned at the note of impatience in my voice. "*Your* men are the worst looters in the army."

"I certainly hope so, Ages'. They are desperately poor."

A good number had been in my company at Lechion. Doreius's training was permanently ingrained in them. They were good mounted fighters.

323

Agesipolis looked to the direction of the screaming woman. "I suppose their poverty excuses them that."

"That is the doing of some foreigners. I ordered my men to make the whores do a free night's work, if they couldn't contain themselves. In any event, I think they are busy looting."

If he continued in this mood, he would lose his popularity. "Ages', you said you wanted to take Argos..."

"I was thinking of it only as a tactical possibility."

"We could pay a call there, if you could devise a way to do so without heavy losses." It would be a blow to Argive spirit to feel their chief city threatened.

One could almost see the maps and troop markers forming in his mind.

"Pentatarchos! Look!"

One of my men rode by with a burning brand. I vaulted on to my horse, and rode after him; just in time to stop him setting fire to a grain store we had ear-marked for our own provisions.

On the opposite side of the trenches around the city walls of Argos, we waited in battle order. Agesipolis's face was peeling from sunburn. His eyes were distant. He said, "I am going to lead the charge alone."

He himself had been planning the assault upon Argos. His enthusiasm returned, after the short lapse before the burning town. Now he spoke in that remote way again. He rode out a few paces, and halted. Then I knew.

It had taken longer than is usual for the dark-winged phantoms to brush him. Now he was going to meet them in single combat. I looked at Sphodrias, but caught no response. I think he was one of those few men who never felt the eerie flutter of those wings.

A regiment of Boiotian cavalry approached from the countryside. Agesipolis did not so much as turn. I told Pityas to take command of my company, rode up to Agesipolis, and drew rein at his side.

"Agesipolis, I claim my right."

"What right?" He only came back a short way from some place distant.

"As a Games winner. To fight at the right hand of my King."

He swallowed in anger, and gave the order to charge.

We crossed the trenches. Some Argive troops came out to meet us, changed their minds, and went back into the city. Agesipolis led us so close to the walls that Argive troops rushed to close the gates, in desperate fear that we were coming in. The Boiotian cavalry regiment came thundering towards us, pursued by our two companies of cavalry, and Sphodrias, leading his hoplites. They ignored our presence in their haste to reach the safety of the city.

The Argive guards shut the gates in the faces of their allies, so great was their haste. The terrified Boiotians parted from their mounts, and clung like bats to the walls under the battlements.

At that point, Agesipolis threw back his head and laughed. The troops started laughing, too. We all did. I cannot recall another action that ended with an army in laughter.

In every place, in every way, on that campaign Agesipolis surpassed Agisilaos's achievements in the same territory. Years later I was to hear an Argive mercenary reckon his age by saying he was born in the year Agesipolis invaded. At the time I remember watching Agesipolis laugh, his face flushed with victory, and thinking, "He will never be subject to Agisilaos again."

Agesipolis drained his wine-cup. The afternoon sun moved along the colonnade outside. "Pityas wants to return to a garrison at Sikyon or Lechion."

"He has a friend among the exiles."

"I have told him I will see to it. No one can call garrison duty showing favour." My cousin spoke defiantly. "I still think we should have fortified the pass at Mount Kalama."

We had fought the campaign again while we wet our throats in the Agiad palace, the dust of the roads still on our cloaks. I said something about the coming campaign in Attica.

His face fell. "Agisilaos will have command of that."

"Claim it for yourself. He has usurped your right of command often enough."

He spoke with difficulty. "Leo', I know he has his faults, but I would not permit *him* to speak against *you*."

325

"But I have no faults." I got to my feet. It was not the time for argument.

He smiled "So you always fancied. My mother would be pleased to see you." He meant that I should have a chance to greet my wife, before setting out to the hall where I was dining with Antalkidas. He had left urgent messages for me at my barracks, the Agiad palace, and the houses of a number of friends.

My wife lived in the Agiad palace, in my aunt's quarters. My mother was implacably opposed to the match, having herself selected three maidens of impeccable Royal Heraklid blood, from among whom she graciously allowed me a choice. Having seen all three, I chose none.

Shortly after, I saw Kleonike practising for a competition of maiden's choruses. For that rehearsal, she took the place of the chorus master and sang his part. Her voice was unusual. It was a haunting voice, low and vibrant, with a touch of the careless insolence of an up-country boy herding his goats. Her looks were as pleasing as her singing.

I saw her on the running course, and watched her throw the spear. She won no race, but was amongst the front runners. Her spear went straight. She would have strong sons. Her nature was agreeable also. Her father was lochagos in a fine regiment, and decently poor.

Being under thirty, I could not speak on my own behalf. Nor would I ask any woman to live seven years with my mother's displeasure. Aunt Eurydame declared she would be delighted to have Kleonike with her. She and Agesipolis approached Kleonike's father for me. I do not think my aunt was entirely displeased by an opportunity to annoy her beautiful elder sister.

Anyone would have mistaken her as the elder now, as she sat with her women companions in a room opening into the courtyard. Her prettiness faded when Pausanios was deposed, and she was becoming rather plump. The women excused themselves when I came in.

These companions were widows of Royal Heraklid lineage and small means. One or two had once lived with my mother, but such companions rarely stayed long in her favour. My aunt dismissed the servants.

326

"Tell me, Leotychides, will Pausanios be proud of him?"

"More than proud."

"That young man is with him. I saw them just now coming in from the courtyard."

I nearly said, "It has been a long campaign. He has earned it." I recalled I was talking to my aunt, and muttered something about the fellow being harmless enough and short of wit.

"Agisilaos is the wit," she replied shortly. "Leotychides, will that man rule my son again?"

"He feels a certain gratitude to Agisilaos."

"Agesipolis is so easily led."

"He is not weak. Gentle–"

"Pausanios is not gentle. He was never led." she smoothed her hair. "Kleonike is selecting maidens for a chorus. You can see Leonidas."

I had been out of Sparta when my son was named. The royal elders had given him as fine a name as I could have wished. Had I been present, he would have been called Agis. His nurse brought him in.

"How like Timaia he is," My aunt took him from his nurse. He had changed from a rather unappetizing bit of flesh to a handsome child, who looked at me with large green eyes and fair hair that was brightening to sunset gold. "He has the look of our family. Kleombrotos has it a little. Agesipolis never had. I wonder why it is always boys with us? Timaia and I. Sons and a grandson. I must find Agesipolis a wife who–" She broke off, as Kleonike's voice preceded her.

"Tell a false note from a true, and simply because she is an ephor's daughter–" Her face was flushed; and small, dark curls had escaped to frame it becomingly. She treated me with seemly dignity. I gave her a sign that meant I would try to steal away to her the next night. One is always watched closely, the night of one's return.

"I was telling Leotychides that Leonidas resembles our side of the family." Eurydame babbled on, as though she were bestowing the highest of compliments. "It must miss a generation. Agesipolis resembles Pausanios, although I don't think him as fine-looking. Leotychides, also, is like his father–"

"Dear Aunt–" I interrupted her train of thought before she took it further. "I must go, or I shall be unpardonably late."

327

I waited for Antalkidas by the Cattle Price House. He came out of the Agora, accompanied by an ephor and a polemarch. He talked. They listened. He saw me. Took courteous but brief leave of his companions.

"You received my message."

"How could I not?"

"You are in luck." His short, neat beard was darker than his garish hair. "Two members of my Hall were excused for hunting. There will be game tonight."

"What is so urgent that it cannot wait until I have been in Sparta a full day."

"Venison."

He was not downcast by the failure of his mission to Sardis. Mere delay, he assured me. "I have put a stop to Konon. Tiribazos bought us a fleet."

"And was recalled to Susa."

"Unfortunate for him, but he can do us more good where he is."

"His successor will not."

"Disagreeable fellow, Struthas. I must put a stop to him, too. Patience, my dear Leotychides. But not too much."

Antalkidas was in high spirits all evening. The talk in Hall centred on the Argive campaign, and turned to the coming invasion of Attica. Antalkidas praised Agesipolis lavishly, and waxed enthusiastic on the autumn offensive.

"Of course," he said as soon as we were outside, "there will be no invasion."

All the creatures of summer spoke as we walked back from Hall. Boys behind us sang a song of Tyrtaios. The sky was splendid with stars. Moonlight outlined the rounded peaks of Taygetos. The sights and sounds and scents of Lakedaimon.

"You, no doubt, will persuade the Athenians to surrender without a battle.

"Something like that. You heard about Teleutias?"

"No, Antal. We had no news of Teleutias in the Argolid."

The boys' voices grew fainter, as they turned off the path towards their flock encampment.

"It seems Agesipolis put Agisilaos's little skirmish in the

shade there. Or was it really Aristodemos?"

"It was Agesipolis. What about Teleutias?"

"The Athenians were sending help to the Tyrant of Cyprus."
Cyprus had rebelled against Persia after Konon's demise.
"Teleutias sighted them with his squadron of triremes, and
destroyed every enemy vessel."

"Teleutias knows the sea."

"My dear Leotychides, you have missed the point entirely.
Cyprus is at war with our enemy, the Great King. The Athenians
were helping *our* ally, who is the enemy of their ally
Artaxerxes. And Teleutias stopped them. Now do you
understand?"

Both sides had acted against their own interest. Athens and
Sparta were becoming like two tired boxers striking out
aimlessly. I said something to that effect. The analogy pleased
Antalkidas. He asked my permission to borrow it.

"But, Antal, a boxing match ends only when one boxer is
defeated."

"Never carry an analogy too far. We have a few new ships of
our own. I intend to command them."

"The Magpie will be pleased."

"By Zeus, Leo', I tell you that I may be appointed grand
admiral, and all you say is that it will please Anaxandros."

"He has admired you since you were his patrol leader."

Surprisingly, he seemed quite gratified.

"Well, if he and his friend want to join my fleet, they are
welcome. And you, Leo'."

"We are cavalry officers, Antal."

"You haven't heard? A number of cavalry troops – those who
lost their kleroi for illegitimacy – are to be given a permanent
regiment of their own. A hoplite regiment. The officers will be
full Spartiate, of course."

So others have seen the potential of these men. In more
respects than one.

"This will not be good for the cavalry." Most of the younger
men fell into this category.

"I don't think you understand, Leo'. There will be no
permanent cavalry regiments. Don't worry; there are places for
all of you in hoplite regiments at your present rank."

"By Apollo, Antal, you must have it wrong. Such a cavalry

329

will be useless in battle."

"It has always been a small part of the Spartan army."

"Numbers do not matter."

"I quite agree. But I am not chief ephor...yet. Leo', when I take command, I will need good officers at sea. Men I know. Flock-brothers. You, the Magpie, his friend Kallias. Not a flock-brother, but a sound man..."

I thought of Pelles, the garrulous Maro – excellent cavalry officers – as Antalkidas went on talking about the war at sea.

It was my first night back in Sparta after a hard campaign. I was overwhelmed by the disbanding of my regiment. It was all those men with whom I had ridden into battle. Alive and dead. There was also the sea.

The sea beckoned – and I forgot that Antalkidas had a way of telling only half a story, and agreed before I learned that Tiribazos was back in the favour of the Great King.

That barbarian had an uncharacteristic consistency in his friendship for Antalkidas. Perhaps he respected the insincerity of its reciprocation.

Chapter 14

A tall woman left the temple of Artemis Orthia, as I entered. Her head was covered by the end of her peplos, her face shadowed as we passed one another between the two columns. I laid my finger-length bronze cavalryman on the offering-table. There were many such small helmets; swords, shields, mounted warriors, and hoplites in full panoply for the Chaste Huntress after the campaign in the Argolid. So few, after Corinthia. Was the goddess elsewhere then? Or was she angry because she had no sacrifice before the battle on the Isthmus road?

I turned to the rose-marble portrait of Artemis and Apollo: divine sister facing divine brother; doves at their feet.

"Daughter of Zeus, we had no time to make the sacrifice. You must know that, you who protect Spartan warriors in foreign lands. We have always honoured you. Why did you turn from us?"

I left the temple, and stepped out into the quiet. The hollow is still as a mountain peak. The bird-song, clear in the laurel trees that bound the grounds sacred to Artemis, Huntress and Mistress of Wild Things. Beyond the holy grounds, the grass is greener, – where the nameless dead of Sparta lie, before the honoured place where limestone grave-markers bear the names of priestesses, and warriors slain in battle. The tall woman walked among the marked graves, followed by her maid. I wished her gone.

"What should be carved upon it?" Dinon had asked me. (He died two months after his son).

"Warriors with shields."

That day, we followed the bier with radiant faces, smiling proudly. Hekataios, at his father's side, ready to give him his arm; but the white-haired man did not falter. His wife had been a very pretty woman in her youth, and still had the ways of beauty. She, too, smiled; but her pretty ways died with her elder son. Gorgo, head high, a slender silver ring on her arm, a proud smile on her lips. Her maiden's peplos black, her face stark white.

Warriors followed us to the shrines and sanctuaries, Anakos amongst them. Some I did not know. Men who had fought near Nemea. Served in Asia. After the funeral feasting was done, in the house on the stony land, the last guests gone, Dinon asked, "What should be carved on the grave-marker?" and I replied, "Warriors with shields."

A shadow fell across the patterned shadows of the boundary trees. The woman had come back from the graves.

"Leotychides." She halted.

Her long peplos was so simple I would not have noted its richness, had I not been the son of my mother. Her dark hair, centre-parted, fell in two wings on her temples; and was gathered in a high loop, showing earlobes weighted by small bunches of gold grapes. A heavy gold ring circled her left arm.

"Mistress Gorgo."

On her right arm was a slender silver ring that had been exchanged for a tankard, I had already recognised her by her walk. In a city where women are known for the pride of their steps, hers was still exceptional.

"I married Chairon for peace," she said in her rich, low voice. I had not seen her since the day we followed the bier.

"You owe me no explanation, Mistress Gorgo."

"There is no other to whom I would give one."

"Have you found peace, Mistress Gorgo?"

"If peace is an absence of pain." Her brow was smooth. The bold-arched eyebrows static. The frowning, sturdy little girl, the defiant maiden, had disappeared into this handsome, poised woman. The eyes were the same. Large and dark as ripe grapes.

"Are you at peace, Leotychides?"

"It is not in my nature."

"I envy you."

"My pain?"

"Only the living know pain." Her eyes were fully on me, like two dark suns. "I have seen your son. I, too, would like a son named for a hero."

I understood her. "Your husband is an honourable man, Mistress Gorgo."

"Nor would I dishonour him." She walked away with that firm, proud step.

A few nights later, as I neared a dining hall with a brother

332

officer, Chairon drew me aside.

He complimented me on the fine appearance of my son, and confided that it was his great regret that he had married too late to sire strong children. He also made it quite clear that his friends would be detaining him late in Hall that night. Very late. Between honest men that is how such things are arranged.

Gorgo was a fever that raged in my blood.

Between us there was fire. No laughter. No tenderness. Few words. Only that tinder fire that had been lit the first night I slipped past the servants sleeping under the eaves, and into her rooms. Felt her strong limbs, as the moonlight flooded over those parts of her face and body not hidden by the long mass of her heavy dark hair unloosed from its high knot. Kleonike was like a refreshing stream, smiling and gentle. Gorgo was a storm of thunderbolts.

The rest of that summer I lived in a fever of Gorgo.

I would find myself thinking of her in dining-halls where I guested, her image compelling me to slip away to her on nights when I intended no visit.

It happened so frequently I wondered that no one noticed my departures and returns. Perhaps it was because Kleonike was again with child, and no one looked for me to slip away.

I stayed so late in Gorgo's rooms that I had to go directly to my barracks, the hall having emptied. Another time I encountered Pronax, leaving the barracks quarter at dawn, as I returned. I muttered something about hunting. He said he would go with me. I had to endure his company the whole of the day.

Sometimes Gorgo's servants were stirring when I left her. The cook saw me on his way to the cook-house to prepare breakfast for his master and mistress. I stumbled against her maid outside her door.

There was another night when I reached my barracks room against a paling sky, only an eye-blink before my batman came in with a bowl of black broth to wake me. The night we truly talked.

We started remembering small things in the after-quiet. The time she taught Euagoras the spear. The Magpie's fury when she took Kallias's cavalry horse to ride to Aulon. A sharp, premature breeze blew in from the courtyard. She rose and picked up some garment, hers or mine, to wrap about her, and stood outlined against the dark light of the sky.

"Do you think of them? That woman from Aulon and her followers?" she asked in her rich, low voice.

"Rarely, We were very young then, Gorgo."

"My husband is of an age to remember Sparta when she was pure." She turned, partly facing me. "Men no longer speak freely in the streets and the gymnasium, and the hot baths."

A chance word overheard by a gymnasium servant or a bath attendant, or even a by-passer, had cost more than one man advancement. Only in Hall, where no word goes forth, could men speak easily.

"That is true."

"Did Doreius know?"

"He knew. But he was of a metal that could not be corrupted."

"That I know. Perhaps it is one reason why I have followed him into his grave. I wish he had not known."

"I too, thought I had died, Gorgo. It was only my youth."

"Many boys were."

"But it was you he loved," she went on relentlessly. "You he fought beside. You, who were so close to him that you cannot know how much of you is yourself, and how much Doreius. That is a trust, Leotychides. Never betray that part of you that is Doreius."

"I kept his company of cavalry what he made it. Now it has been disbanded–"

She rounded on me. "There is more to Sparta than one company of cavalry."

"It was his. It was mine. It is finished."

"Your pain is the price you pay for living."

"You live, too, Gorgo. You speak too passionately for one dead."

She wrapped the garment about herself more closely. "I think of many things, but it is as though someone else thought them."

"In myself, I call it wisdom."

Did I fancy the wry smile illuminated by the moonlight? "Yes, I must learn the language of the old."

"Age is said to bring tranquillity."

"It is a long season between spring and winter."

Thus we talked. We who, at twenty-four, would never be young again.

I went to her only twice more. The third time she sent me away. The purpose had been accomplished. The fever still burned in Gorgo also; but she, too, was Spartan.

I sailed to Aigina in the Grand Admiral's ship. Antalkidas put in only long enough to pick up a squadron of triremes to escort us to Ephesos, where the rest of the fleet lay. Upon reaching Ephesos, he disappeared. If Vice-Admiral Nicolochos knew where his commander went, he told no one. Anaxandros, Kallias and I occupied ourselves seeing Ephesus.

It is a city of splendour and squalor. So many people in the streets that one cannot walk without being jostled. The great temple of Artemis is beautiful, but the statue it holds is that of a barbarian goddess who stole the Chaste Huntress's name. The Ephesians, also, looked more barbarian than Hellene, although they speak our tongue. Wherever we went, vendors hawked baubles, sweets, brocades, fowl, women, boys, eunuchs, virgins. Clearly, they were unaware that Spartans have no coins.

Antalkidas returned and summoned me. He looked at ease in the grand admiral's quarters of his trireme, leaning against his writing table, tapping a scroll against his palm. "Gorgopas is concerned about Aigina." This was the commander of the escort squadron. "Eteonikos is governor. Need one say more?" He dropped the scroll, and waited for me to be seated before taking his own chair behind the table. He always showed me these small courtesies due only kings and elders.

"Well, Leotychides, let us have some wine. Tenedian. Our Sikyonian did not travel well." He added lightly, "Nicholochos will be in command in my absence."

"You have just returned."

"I have some business in Susa."

"Antal, if you leave the fleet again, it will appear–"

"That I was given command to please Tiribazos? Let it. By the time I am done, I shall have shown all Hellas what I know of the sea."

335

(Of course he did. Brilliant. Daring. Original. His feats at sea are too well-known to want repeating).

"You will accompany me to Susa," he went on. "Anaxandros and Kallias, also."

"They are here to fight barbarians. As I am."

He looked into his cup. "I may have hinted to Tiribazos the King will be with me." He was still too thin for his height. Young-looking for his high office. "The true King. Set aside in a court intrigue. One does not confuse Persians with councils and assemblies." He leaned back in his chain "The Great King can be very helpful in your cause."

"I was not aware that I had a cause." I rose. "Nor will I play king in a barbarian court."

"By Zeus, you are King when it suits you." He struck the table "Sit down. If you are not King, then remember that I am Grand Admiral and I have not dismissed you." I obeyed. "Very well. You do not want the Great King's friendship. But Sparta does."

"You will not move the Great King with a rival to Agisilaos, Antal. He hates Sparta. He was our enemy before Agisilaos led an army into Asia."

"His younger brother Kyros raised a rebellion to usurp his throne. Sparta was friend to Kyros. Surely *you* understand how that would vex him." He filled our cups. "Athens bartered the whole of Ionia for gold to pay their rowers. We freed it. Do you wonder that he hates Sparta and loves Athens."

"Take care you do not join Konon in his dungeon."

"Konon made Artaxerxes look a fool. Kings do not like being mocked." The pale eyes met mine. "But you know that."

"How do you plan to turn him from Athens?"

"Plans must never be so fixed that one cannot change them. Leotychides, if you will not be friend to yourself, be friend to me."

Long ago Antalkidas told me that, within the limitations of his nature, he was my friend. I must remember those limitations. "You are grand admiral. You command."

"It is your co-operation I want. Not your obedience."

"Sir."

"By the gods, Leo', you try a man's patience."

336

So it went, until he said coldly, "You prove more hindrance than help."

"Return me to Sparta."

"To cause more talk than you already have? I think not."

"I do not take your meaning."

"Discretion, Leotychides. Chairon is a citizen of standing. You will accompany Gorgopas and his squadron back to Aigina, and remain there as long as you are needed."

"Anaxandros and. Kallias will not willingly go to Susa."

"You are dismissed." He did not rise.

Anaxandros and Kallias were on deck. I joined them at the side. Fishermen hauled in nets filled with a shining, squirming, catch. The air smelled of salt and fish.

"Did Antalkidas tell you where we go next?" the Magpie asked.

"He is going to Susa." Anaxandros's eyes widened. "I am ordered to Aigina with Gorgopas."

"The sooner he returns the better," Kallias said. "Eteonikos is hollow as his statue."

"Agisilaos named him governor of Aigina." Anaxandros turned at the sound of dogs barking.

Antalkidas came on deck. At his heels were three of the finest hunting dogs I have ever seen. "Good evening," he said pleasantly.

"What splendid dogs," Anaxandros gazed at them.

"A gift for the Great King. Tiribazos assures me he has none of our breed." His manner gave no hint of the cold words that had passed between us. "What does one give the richest man in the world? Something of one thing Sparta has best."

"Have we only one, sir?" Kallias asked.

"I can hardly give him a few of Sparta's women." He put the dogs in an officer's charge, and joined us, leaning companionably on the rail. "The King keeps strange beasts from his Indian provinces. Elephants. Tigers. Water horses."

"Have you seen an elephant?" the Magpie asked.

"They are great, grey ugly creatures, like monsters the heroes fought." Antalkidas had once told me Tiribazos had pictures of these beasts. I doubt he had seen one himself. "The

337

tiger is fierce and beautiful. Larger than a leopard, with stripes instead of spots. But elephants can be used in war. Horses fear them, Anaxandros. They create havoc with the chariots if not kept well apart."

"Chariots?" The Magpie hung on his words. "Do the barbarians still use chariots in battle, Antalkidas?"

"The Great King has a regiment of them. With scythes on their wheels."

A red-gold sun sank towards the sea, and set the crests of the wavelets afire.

"Even the sun looks different in Asia," the Magpie said.

"This is the very beginning of Asia. When you see the interior–" Whimsy shaped Antalkidas's smile. "But I forget. You will wish to accompany Leotychides to Aigina." Anaxandros caught his breath. "Will you not?" Anaxandros cast a pleading look on Kallias.

"With your permission, sir," Kallias replied. Anaxandros's face fell. He looked from Kallias to me and back to Kallias again. I had not seen him so close to tears since that first winter in the flock. Antalkidas still faced the sea. There was the briefest silence before Kallias went on. "But Anaxandros was just saying how much he looked forward to seeing Susa."

Antalkidas turned his face to me. The pale eyes were amused. He always enjoyed moving men in a private game of his own.

A generation after the Persian Wars, Perikles of Athens *punished* Aegina for surrendering to the barbarians. Athens seized the island, expelled the Aiginetans and settled it with Athenian citizens.

The Aiginetans were given asylum in Peloponnesos. After Athens was defeated in the Long War, Sparta turned out the Athenian settlers and returned Aigina to its own people. Now Athens threatened again. Aigina sent to Sparta. We sent them the garrison they asked for. Agisilaos gave them a military governor they did not request.

From Aigina, a good naval commander can put considerable obstacles in the way of Athenian merchant vessels.

"If you want to make Athens come to reason, disturb her trade routes," Gorgopas said, as we sailed a smooth sea westward. "Now the Grand Admiral has given the order we can get something done."

Gorgopas was the sort of commander who would never be grand admiral or vice-admiral, but would always know what was needed, and do it without hesitation. He had been having trouble with Eteonikos. "With Lysander commanding him, he looked competent – but, on his own, he can't keep control."

"You served with Lysander, did you not?" Kallias asked.

"In the Athenian war. When I was young. Pharax was my commander. Good man." He talked about Notion and Goat River. "A spy brought news that Alkibiades had ridden down to warn the Athenians a Spartan fleet was in the waters. Lysander put all his ships on alert. When we had news that the Athenian commanders turned him away – by the gods, how we laughed. He was the only man on the sea a match for Lysander. Well, there will never be another Lysander or another Alkibiades. None like that now. Unless it is the Grand Admiral. You haven't got to tell him a thing twice. Or even once." He did not know the Grand Admiral was sipping wine with the Great King. If he was not in a barbarian dungeon. "His year will be worth seeing."

He did not see it. We fell into an ambush shortly after we stepped ashore. The Athenian general Chabrias landed his hoplites by night, and set the clever trap that caught us. It was my first encounter with him, although it was not the last.

The fighting was fierce and close. Gorgopas was a lion. It is thanks to my batman that I live. Perhaps the enemy were unaware that Lakonian army servants are armed.

Kallias and I came out of it with minor wounds. Only enough of us survived to carry the shield on which lay the body of Gorgopas.

Eteonikos, cast in bronze by order of Lysander, governor of Aigina by the patronage of Agisilaos, listened thoughtfully as Kallias recounted the facts of the disaster. The governor was a tall, silver-haired man, with a grave and dignified manner. His eyes rested on me longer than on the others. A good protegé of Agisilaos had ought to speak to me coolly. Yet, as Lysander had fallen, so might Agisilaos. If I were to become king, unfriendliness now might be to his disadvantage later. He seemed to weigh chances whilst Kallias told him how we had been taken unaware. How Gorgopas fought to the death.

The governor voiced appropriate words. He assigned us comfortable quarters. His physician saw to our wounds. A badly wounded man died. The governor buried him with honour. We awaited orders. None came. The governor invited us to dine. He addressed me with something like deference. Or it might have been interpreted as distance. Eteonikos was a survivor.

We went for a walk in the town. Triremes at anchor looked in want of paint. A number were beached. One trim ship was guarded, and well maintained. Seamen spilled in and out of wine shops. Singing. Brawling. Others leaned against buildings, eyeing pretty Aiginetan boys and girls who passed. A few played knuckle-bones on the narrow streets. About twenty of them gathered about a cock-fight. Making wagers. Urging on their favourite.

A fat-bellied merchant ship sailed in sight.

"Athenian," Kallias said. "We could take her with one trireme."

The seamen continued their pursuits undisturbed until a captain strode into the street. He heaved two of the cock-fight crowd to their feet. He called others by name, cursing and threatening. It was the trim trireme that gave chase to the merchantman. It took the angry captain so long to gather crew and fighting men that the Athenian ship escaped.

I told Eteonikos of the incident, when we dined with him that evening. "The captain did what he could, but some of them flagrantly disobeyed him."

"The truth is that I have nothing to pay the fellows," he confided. "The coffers, gentlemen, are empty."

"Lesser Spartiates are subject to war duty as we are," I said. "Up-country volunteers must serve under whatever conditions prevail."

"These men were promised pay." He did not name the

promiser. "I cannot risk a mutiny. Eagerness is fine in young officers, but we learn discretion with age."

"Of course you know best, sir. I was only concerned that Athens might send triremes next."

This touched him. To be known as the governor who lost Aigina would be a sorry end to his career. "You think that possible?"

"My father always said that opportunity is the god of war."

"I must consider sending to Sparta for funds."

Later, Kallias said, "He will *consider*! What was that King Agis said about opportunity?"

"Something I never knew he said."

A deputation of Aiginetans called upon the governor. No doubt they wondered where they would go when they were punished this time. Eteonikos received them privately. Something must have passed to stir him from his inertia. One of his officers told us the governor had sent a desperate message to Sparta, pleading for funds.

If there was news from Susa, it did not reach Aigina. Kallias was concerned that the Spartan embassy might have met with ill-fate. I argued that Anaxandros would have hazarded more in the ambush, but it lay heavy on him that he had not accompanied him, or stayed him from going.

There was little to do but wander about the town. The Aiginetans were ever courteous, their questions and their apprehension silent, as Athenian vessels sailed unmolested about their coast. After a time I avoided their eyes by keeping to the harbour, where I encountered largely the men from the garrison and the ships.

A woman's scream turned me into a side street. A wall blocked its end. A girl struggled with three seamen. One seized a basket from her hands and dashed it to the street. Another shoved her against the wall. She was little more than a child, and looked to be the daughter or young wife of a poor artisan.

"Let her go," I ordered.

The seaman barely bothered to turn his head. "You can have her when we're done."

I struck him for his insolence. He fell. His companion still held her prisoner.

"Do as he says." A bearded man stood beside me. "She is not

a whore."

"Can't pay whores until we're paid, Captain."

It was the captain of the trim trireme. He seized the two seamen and knocked their heads together. They released the girl and fled, leaving their friend in the street. The girl snivelled, and babbled about her basket and her mother and her brother. The captain told her to go, and to keep away from the harbour.

I touched the prone man with my boot. "Did I kill him?" If he had kin on the island, I had best watch my back.

The captain gave the man an experienced prod. "You did him *less* damage than you did the Corinthian lad in Olympia."

I looked at him closely. The beard was fuller. The face sea-weathered, but I knew the up-country man who ran in the shield race nearly ten years ago. "Kleobolos!"

"I saw you at the cockfight, Leotychides. No time for greetings."

"Yours was the only ship to go after the merchantman."

"She's a fine ship, the Bellamina. Deserves better. I got command of her the day she left the ship-works at Gythion. My first command." He smiled ruefully "There is a wine-shop nearby. Come share a cup."

It was a seamen's wine shop of the better sort. Chairs, not benches. Tables separate. I had seen its like in Lechion and Ephesus. A half-full cup stood on Kleobolos's table. He must have run out when he heard the scream. The old proprietor himself brought a jar of wine and two fresh cups. "From a friend," he said. The wine was strong, one part to one, the way up-country men and foreigners drink it.

"Is there often trouble with the men and the Aiginetans?"

"Nothing a few floggings wouldn't cure. And before you ask, I ordered it, but–" He hesitated, uncertain how much he could say.

"Eteonikos countermanded your orders," I finished for him.

"They are not bad lads. All this started when they didn't get their pay. Took their time about manning the triremes. They'd row out only a short distance from the harbour, come

342

back, and report that the enemy escaped, Escaped! A
merchantman moves so slowly you could swim out and
catch it!" Kleobolos leaned forward. "Gorgopas was going
to speak to the Grand Admiral."

"He did. Antalkidas gave him authority to override the
governor's orders, but it died with him."

"There might be no Spartan garrison here, for all the good it
does. Athenian ships sail along the coast as though they
owned it." He filled our cups again. I drank only a sip of
the strong wine. Kleobolos drank deep. "No friend sent
this. It is that old man himself. Always does. Because I
take my ship out. These Aginetans are good people. You
are a Games winner, Leotychides. You know how it is when
men know your face. Buy wine for yourself and your friends.
Honoured to do it."

"Sometimes it was like that in Sikyon and Lechion."

"When we came here we might all have been Games winners.
We're Lakedaimonians. We'd look after them. Now...I can't
take the way they look at me."

"I know."

"Son of Agis, you do not." He grasped my wrist, "You are
young, but you are a king's son. The Grand Admiral is your
friend–"

"He is in the east."

"King Agesipolis could speak for us in the Council. He tore up
the Argolid. They'd take heed of him. Tell him Athens is
going to take this island, and make slaves of these people.
Sparta's name will be dragged in the mud. Help us."

How could I tell this decent man that Agesipolis
would not raise his voice against Agisilaos in Council? I
was spared an evasion when a grey-bearded seaman came to
our table.

"Kleobolos, Eteonikos has a message from Sparta."

Deep in wine and his own thoughts, Kleobolos
muttered a suggestion for the governor.

"Kleobolos!" The man spoke sharply. "Teleutias is on his
way here."

It took an eye-blink or two to sink in. Kleobolos tipped a
few drops of uncut wine from the jar on to the table, in a
libation to Poseidon. "No better man on the sea than

343

Teleutias. A current of excitement ran through the wine-shop. "I hope he knows what he is coming to."

Eteonikos had sent to Sparta for funds. The ephors sent him Teleutias instead. With the impending arrival of Agisilaos's brother, the deference the governor had shown me could clearly be discerned as distance.

The seamen placed lookouts to watch for Teleutias's trireme. The sun was setting when it sailed into the harbour. A large crowd of seamen gathered at the pier. Some carried bread from a dinner interrupted by the lookout's call.

Standing at the back of the crowd with Kallias, I saw Kleobolos at the very front, and made my way through to him. He looked uneasy. Teleutias leapt ashore. The seamen gave a great cheer. He was followed by a servant, who carried a large, bronze-bound chest. It brought a still greater cheer.

"Hades take it!" Kleobolos growled. "They think it contains their pay. I know that chest. Teleutias always has it with him."

"We must warn him, Kleobolos. Or Eteonikos will have his mutiny yet."

The cheers subsided, as the servant with the chest proceeded on his way. The crowd at the pier lapsed into silence. It was the dangerous sort of silence, which the spark of a single incendiary phrase can ignite into mob madness. We stepped forward. Kleobolos called out. Teleutias saw him. Called him by name. Acknowledged me briefly.

Since Agisilaos seized the kingdom, if I met Teleutias in the street or at a festival, we greeted and went our separate ways. The shadow of Agisilaos always fell between us.

Kleobolos wasted no time. "Teleutias, the men think you have their pay in that chest."

Teleutias's colour rose, "Pay?"

"I think Eteonikos promised it." I filled him in as shortly as I could.

"Eteonikos thinks that by doing nothing one can do no wrong." Teleutias called to his servant, "Follow me with the chest." The men heard him, and thundered an ear-splitting cheer. Teleutias turned back to the pier in silent fury.

"Poseidon, I hope he holds his temper in."

Kleobolos grasped his sword-hilt.

Teleutias faced the crowd. An expectant silence greeted him. The seamen towered above his short, sturdy frame. Arms akimbo, he scanned their faces, matching their silence with his own.

His voice rang out, "Comrades in arms! I think you would like to know what is in this chest." A roar of approval. The look on his face silenced it. He ordered his servant to open the chest. One by one, he held out a cloak, a battle-helmet, the usual paraphernalia of a soldier on campaign. "Well, that is all I have brought, and if you want it, you can have it. A number you have served under my command. I think you know I would go without food for two days, rather than see you go without for one. You know that, when I am in command, your lives are more important to me than my own..." A heckler started to interrupt. Another man cut him short, Teleutias went on. "I know you, too. And I know you were *once* all good men." A beginning of a murmur. He pitched his voice higher. But I think you have forgotten that Spartans do not beg favours from pay-masters. Greek or barbarian." He spat the last word. He knew of the mission to Susa. "We make the *enemy* supply our needs." A few men started to cheer. He cut into the cheers. "It is not by *begging* that Sparta won fame in war."

The many-throated laughter was better than a cheer. They were with him now. He sat on a mooring-stone, and spoke of the hardship ahead. And the rewards. I do not recall all the speech. I was looking at his face. Despite the deep lines on the broad brow, and the grey in the brown hair blown by the sea-breeze, he looked a young warrior. In Sparta, he was a man of middle years. Now, Teleutias was happy.

When Eupolia bound her family to herself and to each other with such unnatural closeness, she cut Teleutias off from the brotherhood of Spartans. Only at war could he be an equal amongst equals, a comrade amongst comrades. Himself as he was meant to be. Agisilaos called his separateness kingship. Teleutias, if he ever put a name to it, would have called it loneliness.

When he finished his speech, they cheered, much as the young Teleutias and his shipmates must have cheered

345

Kallikratidas when he sent his message to Konon. A seaman stepped forward smartly, and asked for his orders. Teleutias told the men to finish their evening meal, pack a day's rations, and come armed to the ships.

Then he stepped into the crowd, greeting this man, jesting with that one, listening gravely to another as he walked on. He halted when he came to us, thanked Kleobolos, and threw his arm about my shoulders. "Well, Young Leotychides, I thought you were with the Grand Admiral."

As he had his loyalty to Agisilaos, I had mine to Antalkidas, "He thought I might be useful to Gorgopas."

"I need not ask whether the Bellamina is ready to weigh anchor. Kleobolos. Leotychides, you'll sail on my trireme. Time you learned something of the sea."

"What are we doing, Teleutias?" Kleobolos asked.

"Keeping the promise I just made those men." He grinned, "And I think it's time we gave the Athenians a bloody nose."

That night we sailed.

"You may think I'm out of my wits making for Piraeus," Teleutias said as we stood on deck, the sea lapping the sides of the trireme.

"No, Teleutias," one of the officers laughed. "What chance has the strongest fleet in the Hellenes against our twelve triremes?"

"What I'm reckoning on," Teleutias replied, "is that the Athenians have grown lax since they've had the freedom of the Aiginetan coast."

"They still have their long walls."

"Manned by poor troops."

"The harbour will be full of warships."

"The ships' captains will be at home in bed." Teleutias spoke with confidence. "And the crews asleep or drunk. Remember, ten of those Athenian triremes at sea are more dangerous than twenty in the harbour." He gazed at the glistening, black-rippling waves, and turned to me. "The sea, Leotychides, can be as beautiful as a fine horse. And, like a horse, you must love her to master her."

This is the way I like to remember Teleutias.

346

A short way out of Athens' port, we dropped anchor.
Teleutias called all the men on deck and explained his plan to
them. We were not to capture the port, but to damage the
warships lying in the harbour. Merchant vessels were not to be
attacked, but taken in tow and captured with their cargoes. From
those merchant ships we were unable to take, we had to carry
away as many prisoners as possible. The order went down the
squadron. We waited for dawn.

"Can he do it?" Kallias asked me...

"If he cannot, it will not be our worry. Nor anything else."

The harbour was quiet. Some richly dressed merchants and
ship-owners stood on the wharf. A few drunken seamen and the
usual port rats lounged or slept. No one gave us more than a
passing glance as we rowed in – taking us, no doubt, for an
Athenian squadron returning.

They turned about sharply at the sound of shrieking wood.
We rammed the long triremes. Their bare masts creaked as they
crumbled. It was as sudden as a cavalry charge.

Kallias leapt off the deck, seized a fat man, and carried him
aboard. I took a fellow in a fine cloak for my prize. Men leapt
from other ships. Soon only the wine-soaked spearmen and port
scoundrels were left. There would be a small fortune in
ransoms.

When the merchant ships were tied to our triremes, Teleutias
gave the order to withdraw. We slipped away with our squadron
intact. I heard later that the Athenians sent down an army,
thinking we had captured the port.

Teleutias sent back four triremes to Aigina with our takings.
We sailed to Sunion, where we captured more corn ships. We
brought these back to Aigina as well.

Teleutias had shown Hellas that Spartans could do at sea
what we had always done on land; damage an enemy of greater
numbers with a small, disciplined force.

Athenian ships ceased sailing past Aigina.

Chapter 15

"In my youth," said a Royal Heraklid elder, "if a man did not take a wife by the time he was thirty, the women married him to the ugliest maiden in Sparta."

We were in the great hall of the Agiad palace, witnessing the marriage of my younger cousin. "I find the bride quite comely, sir."

"That was not my meaning." He glanced towards my beaming aunt. She and my wife had had their heads together, choosing a wife for Kleombrotos before he was twenty. He had not yet turned twenty-one. "When does the King marry?"

I was spared a reply, as Kleombrotos agreed to the maiden and her dowry in a firm voice. Agesipolis caught my eye.

"What was he saying?" Agesipolis straightened his garland.

"That it is strange that a younger brother should marry before the elder."

"My mother told him to say it."

"It is something most kings do, Ages'."

"There is time." He began to move amongst our numerous kin.

Teleutias and I greeted briefly and turned away, our pretended coolness as false as my mother's and Kyniska's pretended warmth. My mother also made a fine display of fondness for her sister, for me, and Kleonike; although she spoke privately to none of us since my marriage. Agisilaos avoided Aristodemos. I have since learned that mutual hostility is common to all royal lines. Eurypontid and Agiad antipathies might be reckoned near affection in most dynasties. We only hate. We do not kill one another.

Eupolia looked as though she regretted this, when Agesipolis seated me next to him for the wedding feast. Aware that Agisilaos and I were not on good terms, my cousin placed himself between us, thus flanking the Agiad king by two Eurypontids. Agesipolis frequently created such situations.

When the bride left the hall to meet her husband in some

secret place, I overheard one guest whisper to another, "Is the Eurypontid King to preside at the Conference?" Another replied "Which Eurypontid king?" I determined to seek out my cousin, and make it clear that this incident would be the talk of every dining club but his own. This went out of mind when two kinsmen halted me, to ask about the conference.

I had recently returned from Aigina. The only conference I knew of was one almost three years past, when Argos refused to agree to a peace treaty because Sparta proposed it.

I detached my cousin from a conversation.

"What is this conference they talk about?"

"A conference." he smiled at someone behind a flower vase. "Something about peace in all the Hellenes, the Asian cities and – oh yes, peace with Persia."

"Is that all?"

"You know I have no head for these things."

"Will you preside?"

"Agisilaos always does that."

"Yes. Always."

"Don't plague me, Leo'. It is my brother's wedding."

I left the palace with Aristodemos. It was the time of lamp-lighting. The days were still short. Men set out to the dining-halls. We spoke of the conference.

"Antalkidas has not set out the terms in full." The Grand Admiral was presently writing his name upon the sea.

"Does he know himself, Aristodemos?" I had assumed that, at most, Antalkidas would have soured the Great King's friendship with Athens.

"He seems confident." Antalkidas always seemed confident. He commands the sea sufficiently to divert the trade of the Euxine from Athens to the ports of our allies. It could bring Athens to terms."

"Is the Great King of Persia aware that he has agreed to peace?"

"So it would seem. You look doubtful, Leotychides."

"It is only that the other conference failed."

"Antalkidas has spoken to the great King himself, this time." We reached Hyakinthos Street. "Will Agesipolis preside?"

"He may."

"That means he will not." Aristodemos turned off to his

dining-hall, I to my barracks.

When the days lengthened and the sailing season began, calls to the conference went out to cities large and small; enemy, ally and neutral. Elders and ephors readied their houses to lodge the emissaries. All Hellas awaited Antalkidas. Agesipolis was at ease with the grey-bearded ambassadors in the Agiad palace. He had known the Philasians since his childhood. The Milian was an excellent man with sad eyes that had witnessed the destruction of his city. Agesipolis listened with sweet patience as he praised Lysander – who had freed it, freed the Milians, and returned them to their island.

My cousin called me to dine one evening.

"Leo', you must help me. The Argives have arrived a day early."

"They are under your roof?"

"It was either them or the Athenians. We could not ask the Milian to suffer that. One of them might have known him as a slave."

"You are right. Ages'. But I cannot meet the Argives." That much I owed to my exiled comrades. "You will be excused from Hall to greet new arrivals."

"If I can hear Lysander praised, you can break bread with an Argive ambassador."

"You are a king. I am a private citizen."

He wore his goat look. Our words grew heated. I left the palace and returned to the cavalry barracks. Aristokrates was not in his room, nor was Pelles. I called to my batman to bring me something to eat, and went to my own room.

Anaxandros was searching through my chest.

"Magpie! When did Antalkidas come in?"

"He is not here. He sent me ahead to see that apartments are readied for Tiribazos. Where are your wine-cups, Leo'? Someone borrowed all mine."

"Tiribazos is in Sparta?"

"Leo', I saw the tigers and the elephants and the chariots with scythes." My servant brought in the food and wine. Anaxandros and I set to it. "Antalkidas named me his secretary for secret matters he wanted known. Where is Kallias?"

"In his club, no doubt. You recall that citizens dine in Hall?"

350

"Tiribazos sets a fine table."

"I apologize that mine is less. When did you reach Susa?"

"It was a very long journey. I did not know there was so much land in the world. We could never hold it."

"Was that Antalkidas's intention, or yours?"

"We had been more than a month out in the journey. Antalkidas said. 'Had Susa fallen to us, we could never hold all this without making Hellas a slave to it.' Leotychides, the Great King rules Egyptians and Babylonians and other peoples. Not just Persians and Medes." He washed down his bread with wine. "He owns the lands of Upper Asia, Baktria and India, almost to Encircling Ocean."

"Did you see his palace with walls of gold?" Maro and Pelles stood in the door.

I would have asked Anaxandros more of Antalkidas's meaning, but Pelles and Maro filled cups with wine, settled themselves on the edge of my bed, and talked at once.

"What is Tiribazos like?" Pelles made himself heard.

"Quite pleasant, for a barbarian. We were his guests."

"The whole of the Spartan Embassy?" Maro asked.

"He has a large house. More a palace. And one of those parks they call paradises. The trees are beautiful, and planted in wonderfully straight rows. Wherever you go, there are sweet-scented flowers. And peacocks with fan-tails of a thousand eyes." He turned to me. "He has the most splendid horses, Leo'. Giant horses. Horses for gods."

"Did you ride one?" Maro wanted to know.

"I often hunted with them. Tiribazos presented me with a fine grey for my own use. And he gave Antalkidas a Syrian concubine–" His brow furrowed. "I don't think I had ought to have told you that."

"Is she beautiful?" Pelles sat forward. "Is she here?"

"You will forget it, Pelles. That is an order. Magpie, might you tell us what passed with the Great King?"

"Tiribazos has to prepare the King to hear Antalkidas. There were Athenian agents at the royal court who poisoned his ear against Sparta."

More young cavalry officers came in. They seated themselves on the table, perched on the arms of chairs, crowded on to the bed. Whenever there was space, Anaxandros had to

351

begin again.

"Antalkidas was playing a board game with Tiribazos when the summons to a royal banquet came. We all dressed in Milesian wool cloaks, never worn. The finest of simplicity." Anaxandros spoke. The words had the ring of Antalkidas. "I thought the Grand Admiral uneasy. Another would not have noted it, but I am his flock brother. He was my patrol leader."

"So you have told us," someone said.

The wine gave out. Pelles's batman brought in a fresh jar. Anaxandros answered questions about the splendour of the Great King's palace; the silks and jewels of the courtiers.

"The King's table faces the hall. No one may turn his back on Artaxerxes. Nor touch his person with so much as a finger. A Persian would die for it. He is like a god to them."

"What does he look like?" Maro asked.

"Very tall. Quite old. With a long red beard. Henna. He wore a garland of rare flowers, drenched in precious scents. He has great dignity. A fat man sat next to him. The Vizier. We do not have them. The most powerful person after the King. A kinsman of the King was on the other side."

"Where was the Grand Admiral?"

"A few places down. Being his secretary, I was at the King's table, but further away. I had my own interpreter. He stood in back of my chair."

Men were sitting on the floor now. At one point I saw Anakos standing in the doorway.

"Antalkidas was placed between two courtiers. One was a friend of Athens."

"Did he know?"

"Tiribazos had told him whom to beware, but he gave no sign of knowing, and talked easily. The King took no heed of him until after the first courses were taken away. Then he said something, and Antalkidas replied."

"What did he say?"

"I don't know, Cockerel. They spoke Persian. The King passed a comment to the Vizier. The interpreter said it was, 'He speaks our tongue well.' More food came, on great silver platters. I lost count of the courses. They do not eat everything on the plate as we do. We were wiping our fingers on those

352

warm, scented cloths they bring between courses, when the King spoke to Antalkidas again. They spoke longer this time. Again the King made some comment to the Vizier. I asked the interpreter the meaning. It was 'What good manners he has for a Hellene.' Whenever the King talked to Antalkidas, there was a change in him."

"He became friendlier?" Maro rose and filled his cup.

"He is so old and dignified one could not say friendly, but – no longer bored. Although I had not noted he was bored before he ceased to be. He sent a servant with some food from his own plate to Antalkidas."

"What?" someone asked.

"Poison," another surmised.

"I think it was larks in honey. The interpreter said, 'Lord, the ruler of the world honours your master.' He always called me lord. The king talked more and more to Antalkidas, until he was talking to no one else. Near the end of the banquet, he took off his garland and sent it to Antalkidas. The interpreter said there was no greater honour. I told the man to translate everything.

"Antalkidas spoke about the flowers. The interpreter said it was so graceful a speech it could not be translated into Greek. The King asked him if he liked the perfumes. Antalkidas replied. The Persians all went silent. Tiribazos looked worried. My interpreter was pale. I had to order him to speak; when he did, it was a whisper. 'He says, lord, that the flowers' own scent is better.' I forgot I was not supposed to look directly at the King. When I did, I saw he was laughing." Anaxandros wet his throat with wine.

"What happened then?" Maro wondered.

"The King sent for Antalkidas next day. They talked a long time. The next time, we hunted with the King in his game park. And I saw the tigers and the elephants."

"Antalkidas is a brave man."

"Everyone knows that, Maro. After he agreed a treaty with the King–"

"He *has* agreed a treaty, Magpie?"

"Did I not tell you?" Antalkidas said, "I have persuaded the King to peace. Now we must persuade Athens." His face glowed. "We captured enemy ships, enough to bring the fleet up to eighty triremes."

Tiribazos and his retinue were Antalkidas's guests in the Grand Admiral's fine new house in the new quarter. He was a black-bearded man, in a heavy sash with turned-up toes, and a flattened cap that came over his ears. A strange sight in the broad streets of Sparta. Wherever he went, he was followed by his retainers and slaves. Few Spartans had seen trousers and long sleeves before, but even children were too courteous to stare.

Hekataios, Aristokrates and I watched from the acropolis road, as he rode towards the agora.

"Is that a general holding a sunshade over him?" Hekataios wondered.

"A slave," Aristokrates told him. "The Magpie says some of their slaves wear jewels."

"They are all the Great King's slaves." I pondered the fate of those who barter freedom for luxury. "I wonder what he will make of the Persian colonnade." Each column is carved in the likeness of one of Xerxes's defeated commanders.

"Have you seen Antalkidas, Leo'?"

"He sees only ephors and Elders."

"And his secretary," Hekataios laughed. "The Lord Magpie."

A few days later I received a message from Antalkidas, inviting me to the midday meal.

A servant showed me into a sun-filled room. A splendid lion-footed writing table, topped with green marble, stood in its centre. The tall-backed chair was vacant. Scrolls in fine leather tubes of green and red and blue were slotted along a wall. Lakonian scribes set words in wax. They looked up as Antalkidas strode in. He embraced me as a friend, and turned to the servant. "I told you the small writing-room."

"You said only the writing-room, Master."

"Go tell Cook there is a guest."

"Cook is angry. The barbarian's servants were in the kitchen again."

"Tell him the barbarian thinks I must have you both beheaded for insolence."

The man grinned. "We will keep our heads and our insolence, Master."

Antalkidas was no longer too thin for his height. Success, too, gave him substance. He always had presence. Now it was a commanding presence. "Come, let us walk in the colonnade. I have had enough of squabbles and scribes and petitions." He stood back to let me precede him. I was to be shown the courtesies of a king.

The tiled roof extended over rose-painted columns. Ivy climbed half their height. Serfs planted young saplings in the courtyard.

"Date palms." Antalkidas followed my gaze.

"Quite." He shouted across to the serfs. "That last tree is not in line." The man went on digging. "The fleet obeys me. My servants please themselves."

"Perhaps a wife would order such matters better than a Syrian concubine."

He laughed "I had to leave her in Halikarnassos. Pity. She is exquisite. Would the Elders like her here, do you think?" We strolled the colonnade.

"So you have become the Great King's friend."

"The Great King has no friends. His subjects are his slaves. The Greeks at court are petitioners. Exiles. Sycophants."

"Anaxandros says you charmed him."

"I do not fear him. Nor envy him. I want nothing of him for myself." He paused to arrange a fallen vine on its upward climb. "He can laugh with me on an equality. Poor Artaxerxes. Perhaps I am his *only* friend. Within limitations."

Two serfs set up a fountain on a twisting stand, the bowl held by marble maidens frozen in dance. A strange, sweet aroma wafted towards us. "What sort of ivy is this, Antal?"

"The fragrance comes from the jasmine in the corner. A gift from Artaxerxes."

I glanced at the fountain. "Another gift?"

"Won with my sword." He met my eyes. "This house and everything in it was paid for with honest spoils. Wealth is not my ambition. It is too easy."

"What is your ambition?"

"I don't know. Would it not be dull to know what one will do next?" A glance skywards. "Has Anaxandros spoken to you of the treaty?"

"Amongst tigers and banquets and battles on the sea."

"He is a good warrior. And fortunate. He did not take a single wound. I believe he was disappointed. But let me not forget. I invited you to a repast."

We stepped in another entry, to a room of entirely Spartan beauty. The furnishings were sparse and graceful, the high-polished floor in a pattern of pale and dark woods. Dining-couches, cushioned in glowing colours, stood either side of small tables with food for two. A servant mixed wine in a fine bronze krater, with a warrior donning greaves on its neck.

"No, Leo'. You will not be forced to take bread and salt with barbarians. Tiribazos has brought his own cooks." He gave me the couch of honour, took the right, and waited for me to be seated before himself. He pleaded a delicate stomach, although he has a hearty enough appetite in Persia.

"You like the barbarians too well, Antalkidas."

"Do I?" he reclined on one elbow. "Tiribazos is an amusing companion. We share a taste for good wine, fine women and games of wit. But as a people...No, I do not like them. They are cruel." With his free hand, he poured a drop of oil on his cheese. "Is Euagoras in Sparta? I should like Tiribazos to hear him sing."

"Euagoras will not sing for barbarians."

"Euagoras sings for Euagoras. Whoever listens." His wine cup paused half-way to his lips. "Again, he might refuse. Doreius had the moulding of him, too." The pale eyes held a steady gaze on me.

"Antal, surely you are great enough now to admit that Doreius had the best patrol. Was first in everything."

"Doreius was a good officer of quite extraordinary beauty, and nothing more. No – hear me. Had he lived one hundred years ago, he would have risen to polemarch. Today he would go no higher than he was. A commander of fifty. I am sorry he was slain. I miss him. Not least because he would be totally unimpressed by all my glory. He would not have envied it. Nor would he have despised it. As you do." He held out his wine-cup for refilling, without removing his eyes from my face. "Stop trying to be Doreius, Leotychides. You do it poorly."

"One may aspire."

"A king's aspirations should differ from those of other men. Had I been your patrol leader, you would reign now, and it

356

would be the peace of Leotychides rather than Agesipolis."

"I do not take your meaning."

"I need a king to swear the oaths and sign for Sparta," he said casually. "The peace of Agesipolis. How amusing to see Agisilaos swallow that!"

"Does Agespolis know he is to sign?" My cousin had not spoken of it.

"I thought you might persuade him."

"It is you who are Peitho's favourite."

"My gifts of persuasion seem to have failed with you."

"Antal, what is this treaty that everyone speaks of, and no one knows?"

He gave an order to a servant who brought in a bronze casket. Antalkidas withdrew a scroll and took it from a red covering with gold lettering. "You need only read the end of it." The rest is all Artaxerxes's titles. He passed it to me.

It was quite short. So brief that a Spartan might have written it. I wondered whether he had.

King Artaxerxes says that the Greek cities in Asia and the islands of Klazomenai and Cyprus belong to himself: but that all other Greek cities, small and large, must rule themselves; with the exception of Lemnos, Imbros, and Skyros, and these should belong to Athens as before. If any of the parties refuses to accept this peace, King Artaxerxes will make war against it in alliance with those who agree to it; by land and by sea, by ships and with gold.

"We had to concede something to Athens," he said, as I passed back the incredible document.

Had his success unhinged him? "Artaxerxes orders us as though Hellas were a Persian satrapy."

"Artaxerxes can barely order his own empire. Babylonia is disquiet, Egypt on the verge of rebellion and–"

"You give him Ionia."

"Less than Athens gave him."

"We freed it."

"How many Peloponnesians must we send to die for cities that are only a name to them? Persia will always take it back. The barbarians are too many for them. Asia too vast."

"You are winning at sea."

"Until Zeus tilts the balance to Athens again. Leotychides,

we need peace, and so does Athens. It wanted a generation to recover from the Long War. In less than half that time, we are at war again. Neither tired boxer will submit. It is time the judges step in and declare the contest finished."

"We defeated Persia when Xerxes invaded."

"In our own territory," he snapped. "Xerxes was a fervent fool. Persia cannot take Hellas, and does not want it. It is not the King's earth, as he calls Asia."

"Persia gains by your treaty–"

"Only what he holds."

"Athens gains. What does Sparta gain?"

"Triumph shaped his smile. "Sparta is arbiter of the peace. Sparta will enforce it." He unrolled the scroll and read, "*All other Greek cities, large and small, shall rule themselves.* Think, if it does not pain you too much. Thebes must release the Boiotian cities; Argos withdraw from Corinth..."

I had seen the exiles gaze longingly at the lights of their city. They had not seen their fathers, mothers, or sisters for years. Inside Corinth, the lives of brave men hung on cobwebs. And yet...I remembered Kallikratidas saying "And we shall join together, as we did in the days of Leonidas..."

"Thebes and Athens will not agree."

"Athens will agree the peace, as will Thebes."

"And the Asian cities? What of their freedom?"

"Ah, the Sirens' song!" The pale eyes beseeched Olympos. "All any ambitious tyrant or demagogue or king need do is cry 'Free the Asian cities' and Hellenes will follow him to Hades' Hall." He rose and paced the floor of dark and pale woods. "What is there in that call to lure otherwise sensible men? Glory? Fear? Spoils?"

There was no little reason to his words. I searched for the flaw. "You have said it. The barbarians are cruel."

"We told the Hellenes of Ionia, one hundred years ago, that we could not protect them unless they removed their cities from Asia."

"If it is all good reason, why do you want a king's voice added to your own?"

He raised it. "Because there are too many stubborn, dreaming Spartans, like you." He returned to his couch and reclined on an elbow, his free hand resting on one knee. Impatient finger-tips tapped the knee, belying his easy manner. The sea is calm, but the seamen sense a strong current beneath the smooth surface. "What is, *is*, Leotychides. Not always as one would have it."

Teleutias standing on the pier. We do not beg favours from Greek or barbarian... "No good can be bought with the Great King's gold."

"Far better to spend it to buy peace in Hellas than to stir war."

"To what purpose of his own?"

"To end Hellenese adventurers raising revolts in the Western Province."

"The Western Province!" It was the Persian name for Ionia. Rage stirred in my veins. Against the flaw? Against reason? White froth appears on the waves; the sky darkens.

"Can you not understand? If we wish Persia to stop meddling with the mainland, we must cease meddling in Asia."

"I would not persuade Agesipolis if I could. Nor would Pausanios." My cousin corresponded openly with his father now.

"So I shall."

"He will not hear you."

"Then I must make use of Agisilaos. Although it galls me to make his name great."

"You could not."

He swung his long legs over the side of the couch, planted his feet firmly on the floor, and faced me. "I would do even that before I risk the peace."

"Betrayal." The word spoke itself.

"I told you my friendship has its limitations."

"You mistake my meaning. It is the Hellenes you betray."

His eyes narrowed as they had the day I nearly called him a coward. "Do not go too far, Leotychides." He spoke with tight control. "Let the Asian Greeks move their cities to Thrace or Macedon or Sicily, where barbarians are fewer and poorer."

"Hades take the Asian cities! It is a betrayal of Sparta."

"I am giving Sparta command of Hellas."

"That *is* betrayal."

"You talk wildly."

"Withdraw the treaty."

"Peace."

"Submission."

"I warn you, Leo'. Say no more."

"How much did Artaxerxes pay you?"

"Fool!" He knocked over a small table as he leapt to his feet. "Traitor!"

"Sparta has changed since our fathers were boys!" He kicked away the table. Blood-red wine stained the patterned floor. The pale eyes lost expression. "But I forget," He added quietly. "Yours was a boy in Athens."

Agisilaos presided.

The conference was stormy. Or so I gathered from Agesipolis. Being under thirty, I could not attend, but my cousin called me to the Agiad palace after every session, to pour out the day's events. Often he kept me long after the blue prelude had descended over the city, as though he were delaying...what? Sometimes he repeated himself as the time approached to set out to the dining-halls, or recalled some detail of small importance.

"The island delegates were very heated when it came to giving over the Asian cities," he said. It brought Asia closer to them. "The Athenians supported them, but allowed themselves to be persuaded that it was inevitable. The Peloponnesians did not appear greatly concerned." There were enough Peloponnesian bones buried in the distant East. "The Thebans objected to giving freedom to all the cities of the mainland." That would end their dominion over Boiotia. "They had a long consultation with the Athenians when we broke for the midday meal. I think the Athenians must have either refused them support, or made some promise. They were silent after that. The Argives spoke for the Corinthians as well as themselves. They oppose the peace most strenuously."

"Did no Spartan speak against it?"

"Teleutias scowled all the time, but he won't speak against Agisilaos."

"Sphodrias was never one to hold his silence."

"Leo', I don't think Sphodrias opposed the peace. Many men are weary of war."

"There is nothing Sphodrias likes as much as a good skirmish."

360

"A skirmish, yes. He dislikes being long away from Sparta."

As I left the palace one evening, I collided with Kleombrotos coming in the gate.

"Leotychides! Is my brother ill? My mother?"

"They are both in good health. I just left Agesipolis looking forward to your guesting in Hall with him."

"My brother had me recalled from garrison duty to dine with him?" He made an angry gesture. "Leotychides, there is nothing but talk of this conference at Sikyon. Have I misunderstood the terms of the treaty?"

"I fear not, Kleombrotos."

"And my brother?"

"He will not speak for it."

"I would fight it."

"You would lose."

Ceremonial duties took Agesipolis to Amyklai for the Gymnopaidia. As always, he would have me with him in the royal palaces, my presence causing comment. A large number of delegates were present, as well as other strangers who had made the journey solely to attend the only Spartan festival open to foreign onlookers.

When the boys finished dancing, my cousin and I somehow became separated in the departing throng. Foreigners never move in an ordered manner with their jostling and pushing. I started back to the city alone.

A tall, fair man in a cloak of a subdued pattern fell in step with me. "I think we met in Olympia...Leotychides, the son of Agis, isn't it."

Tolmaios had accompanied his uncle to the conference. We fell into step, talking of Olympia.

"I saw Nikomedes in the Isthmian Games," he said. "He took an olive crown. It would have been his second, if those Corinthian rebels had not disrupted the Games two years before."

"The Isthmia belongs to Corinth. Aristeas won the long race."

It was a touchy subject. We let it go.

"How is your friend?" he asked. "The runner who was crowned in Delphi."

361

"He had the honour to be slain in battle."

"Theokles, too. On his way to Cyprus. Damned silly battle. Damned silly war. Where are the wine shops in Sparta?"

"You are in Amyklai."

"How does one know where Sparta ends? The agora seemed to have contrived its own shape."

His eyes went to Kyniska. She stood in a chariot she had taken to using in the City, and was surrounded by admiring youths, young warriors and women. "What a splendid-looking hetaira. Not in her first youth, but—"

"There are no hetairai in Lakedaimon. You are staring at the daughter of King Archidamos."

"My dear, what a fool I am. She would be your aunt. By the gods! It is the famous Kyniska! I saw her statue." Apelleas tactfully omitted certain lines from her face. "Strange. In Athens—"

"In Athens, women are neither seen nor heard."

"Best not even spoken of. You know Athens?"

"I stepped down briefly in Piraeus once," I replied literally. "There is a spring. Drink your fill if you are thirsty, and I will escort you back to Sparta before some woman does you an injury."

Foreigners are scandalized by our women, yet complain of the dullness of their wives and educate only their whores. I was angry. I would have been angry had he criticized Spartan youths, elders, wine, wasps or rocks.

"Every city has its own ways." He sensed my mood. His tone implied that, as a reasonable Athenian, he humoured me.

"Yes, and if Athens had not disturbed them, there would be no war. No trafficking with the Great King."

Surprise shone through his complacency like a weak sun. "I did not know there was a Spartan party opposed to the peace."

"We have no parties, nor do we abuse one another before foreigners."

"We have. We do. But every Athenian opposes the treaty."

I gazed at the heart-shaped cyclamen leaves about the spring. Agisilaos had persuaded the Council to agree the treaty. Antalkidas swayed Assembly. The move would not come from Sparta.

"Your uncle has a following in Athens, has he not?" I asked

tentatively, as an uneasy balance swung in my mind.

"He hoped to be elected a ruler-general, but Chabrias is the rising man in the Middle Party, and has stolen much of his support. The shoemaker's son is the coming man amongst the extreme democrats. Iphikrates a ruler of our city! Oh well, perhaps one of your men will run him through first—"

I let him prate on about his disorganized polity while I tried to reach a decision. Hades take it, let the credit go to Athens as long as the treaty was not agreed.

I raised my eyes to Tolmiaos. "Athens could break up this conference simply by withdrawing."

"Any ruler who failed to agree a peace that freed our trade would fall tomorrow."

"I thought you said that all Athenians oppose the treaty."

"In principle."

"Much good your parties and disputes do you."

He did not take it up. "What has happened to us? Our ancestors threw Xerxes's ambassadors in the Pit with condemned criminals, when they asked us for submission. I believe yours tossed them down a well. Not terribly civilized, our forebears; but, by the gods, it was better than this." He got to his feet. "I should like to get drunk. Will you join me?"

"My drunkenness would change nothing."

"Theokles always says—" His voice broke. "Said—" he corrected himself "that madness is the only sanity in madness."

I took him to the Menelaos House for a cup of wine. Meleas got on well with Athenians, and Tolmaios was not a bad fellow.

"Antalkidas to Leotychides. Forgive words spoken in anger, and my friendship will be without limitations."

"Leotychides to Antalkidas. The only unforgiveable words are written in the treaty. Dissociate yourself, or there is no friendship between us."

The end of a friendship is like a little death.

Meleas told me that when the Athenians signed the treaty, Tolmaios turned his head into his cloak and wept. One white-haired old Eleian did not trouble to hide his tears. I have heard it said that we Lakedaimonians were all well-pleased that day, but they forget that Spartans know how to conceal their foxes."

"When Agisilaos signed for Sparta," Agesipolis recounted, "someone called out. 'Alas for Hellas, when we see our Lakedaimonians Medizing.' Agisilaos heard it, and retorted, 'Not at all. You see the Persians Lakonizing.'"

A flock commander would have punished so facile a reply.

Chapter 16

I would not trouble to set down the happenings at Mantinea, had the Athenians not made so much of that quite insignificant and purely Peloponnesian matter. The number of cities that Athens destroyed, enslaved and despoiled are a matter of record; yet, with their eternal scribbling and high-flown speeches, the Athenians have created such an enduring legend of Spartan crimes that I have heard it mentioned by Pella nobles, who do not know where Mantinea is.

Arkadia is a territory consisting mainly of small peasant communities. Its few cities are ancient, and stronger in history than in fighting men. Except one. Mantinea, which had ought not to have been a city at all.

It had been created at the instigation of the Argives, who wanted a base in Arkadia. They persuaded four villages to merge, erect walls, and declare themselves a city. Thus, Mantinea was born.

Its mercantile rulers were aggressive, as is the way of mercantile factions, hostile towards the other cities of Arkadia, and possessed the only army of any significance amongst them.

After a series of hostilities that belong to another account, we had signed a thirty-year truce with Mantinea. Less than two years after Antalkidas's peace was agreed, that truce expired. The ephors sent to Mantinea, requesting its rulers to tear down their walls as an earnest of peaceful intent.

Certainly, no Arkadian city was going to attack them. Nor were we a threat. Sparta could have conquered the whole of Arkadia many times over in the past four hundred years, had she territorial ambitions. The Mantineans refused to destroy their fortifications. We sent out an army to do it for them.

Agesipolis led the army, because Agisilaos waived his right of command. I suspected his reluctance to leave Sparta was linked with the imminent election of new ephors.

It was a younger campaign this time. Meleas was in

Athens, visiting guest-friends. It was too unimportant an expedition to warrant a polemarch of the stature of Aristodemos. Most of the foreign contingents consisted of very young men who needed to blood their spears for the first time, although many of the former exiles of Corinth volunteered as a gesture of gratitude.

Although Argos, too, had signed the peace, we had to threaten the Argives with invasion to force them out of Corinth. Pityas had gone up from Lechion with Aristeas, for the celebrations. He talked of it so often most of his friends could have recited his description of Corinth in the joy of freedom: the dancing in the streets; the people singing the exiles' songs, words they had sung secretly in Argive times. Pasimelos was cheered wherever he went. The exiles were treated like kings.

Some of the people called for the death of the traitor rulers. Free Corinth banished them instead. They went into exile in Argos. (Years later they pushed their luck and tried to recapture the city. They failed and killed themselves, rather than fall into the hands of their compatriots).

Aristeas was not with the Corinthian contingent that marched on Mantinea. His father died just before it set out. At least the old man had lived to see his son return alive, whole and honoured.

It seemed strange to see the toque-shaped helmets of Thebans in our ranks. They were rough, crude, rustic fellows – apart from two young officers, a very tall man and his friend, who were notable for their quiet speech and pleasant manners.

A short march from Lakonia, it was the sort of campaign Sphodrias liked. We were no longer young warriors dreaming of glory in distant lands. War can be good, but I had seen enough of it to know that peace is better.

It would be a quick victory, and then back to Sparta; to the game-filled slopes of Taygetos, the gymnasium, the dining-clubs, and telling Leonidas stories of the heroes of the Bronze Age. My second son, Agis, was still too young to understand.

We laid waste to the country around Mantinea, hoping to bring the enemy to terms. They sent no heralds. Agesipolis ordered us to march on the city. He sent in his own herald with our terms. They returned – having been treated less than courteously, and told to warn the Spartan King that, if he wanted Mantinea's walls torn down, he must do it himself. I believe Sphodrias would have been grieved had they given in without a battle.

Agesipolis deployed his army in a long battle-line, to give the impression of being more than we were. Spartans took the dangerous extreme right, the Corinthian section the place next to us – and so on, city by city, to the extreme left flank, where my cousin placed the disciplined Thebans.

Sphodrias was pissing when the Mantineans sent their army out to meet us. The thin yellow stream retained its steady arch as they advanced. He grinned. "Nothing like a good piss before a battle." Then he took his place with the hoplites he commanded.

Flute, lyre and harp began the hymn to Kastor. Agesipolis led the singing. The two armies advanced towards each other. The Mantineans avoided the Spartan section, and attacked the further allies.

When a battle-line is very long, it is impossible for the right flank to know what is happening to the left. The music of war played. We sang on, undisturbed. It was not until we saw a number of toque-shaped helmets fleeing in disorder that we knew the Thebans were in trouble.

Agesipolis snapped an order. As it went down the line, he turned his mount and rode towards the combat area. His horse reared. He controlled it with a firm hand, and galloped so swiftly his own horse guard was left behind. The hoplites followed. As the only Games winner at hand, I was at my cousin's right, urging my mount to keep even with his on his solitary dash.

The Theban columns had dissolved. More lay dead or wounded than fighting. The pleasant young Theban officer lay on a heap of bodies. His tall friend stood in front of him, shielding him with his own body and fighting several Mantineans simultaneously. Blood flowed from his wounds.

Agesipolis dug his heels into his horse's ribs, and rode down the enemy who had the tall Theban at bay. The Mantinean was trampled by hooves. I deflected a blade from my cousin's throat, as he brought down another. A smart thrust of his spear finished a Mantinean who went for his chestnut. The others fled, as the horse guard closed in.

The main body of the Mantinean army retreated towards Sphodrias and the hoplites. He grinned; as he did when the twig snaps, signalling the rush of a boar. They changed direction when they saw the lamda shields, and ran to the safety of their city. The hoplites pursued them. Sphodrias would have followed them, had Agesipolis not seen Mantineans rushing to close the gates. He sharply ordered them to halt.

The Mantineans did not venture forth again.

Agesipolis decided to force the walls. It was not the most inspired of his plans. His siege engines and battering rams were of little use against the strong fortifications. Muttering that siege engines had not changed since the Persian wars, he called a council of war.

He came to it with some designs of his own. There were artisans amongst the allied troops. He would have them construct better engines. Sphodrias said this would take too long. Kallias reminded him that the artisans were only young apprentices. My cousin lowered his head, in the manner that preceded the goat look. His physician came into the council tent. My cousin's wounds were superficial.

Agesipolis had sent him to the two Thebans. The physician reported that the tall officer would recover. His friend took seven wounds. He would die.

"He is an excellent man," Sphodrias protested, as though that mattered to the war gods.

Agesipolis forgot his siege-engines. "I shall sacrifice a cock to Asklepios for him."

"I dare say every obscure Theban will now expect the King of Sparta to risk his neck for him," Kallias grumbled.

"That sort of courage is never obscure," Agesipolis said softly.

The next day, Agesipolis ordered his army to dig a trench around Mantinea, and the other half to stand guard in front of them while they dug. The trench, he explained, was to protect our men as they erected a wall around the city walls."

"Why are you laughing, Leo'? It is not unusual."

"I was thinking that we were sent here to bring down the walls of Mantinea. Not raise more."

So it was to be a siege. Agesipolis had held another council of war with himself during the night.

That evening, a party of Mantineans came to us after dark. They were in rags, although most had cultured voices. They asked to see the King. We kept our hands on our sword-hilts. They told him it was futile to lay waste to the country. Mantinea was ruled by a council comprised of sixty merchants, whose wealth was in the city.

It was also a waste of time to besiege the city. The harvest had been good, and there was enough food in Mantinea to last a year. They urged us to act quickly, as the rulers had sent to Athens for troops. (The Athenians refused them, but neither they, nor we, knew that).

Kallias did not trust them, but the foreign commanders were against a long siege. Their troops already muttered amongst themselves, anticipating rations of crushed corn. Agesipolis listened to all, replied to none; and, wearing his goat look, spent a day alone strolling along the River Ophos, which runs out from the town.

Kallias, Anaxandros and I passed time throwing the discus. The Magpie noted the tall Theban walking towards us. He carried a stick, but did not lean on it. He halted and stood a few paces away, so as not to disturb our game. When it finished, he came closer.

"I am told the King saved my life." He was still pale and haggard. "I should like to thank him. I fear I was only aware of a crimson cloak, and knew it to be some Spartan. And after–"

"It is that way with some wounds," Kallias said. "I was out of my wits for days from a wound I took at Haliartos."

They spoke of Haliartos. We talked of Lechion. The Theban was bewildered as to why Lysander did not wait a day for Pausanios and his army. I never understood why the Theban garrison in Lechion did not advance.

"Agesipolis will be pleased to see you," I told him when he took his leave. "How does your friend?" I regretted the words as soon as they were uttered. The physician said the man would die

"He takes water and broth without knowing it. And he is strong." He started away and then turned. "You must let me know if any of our troops are disorderly."

Kallias watched him go, "I am glad that I shall never have to kill that man."

Agesipolis came back from his solitary stroll just before the evening meal. Beaming.

"It is all too simple," he announced. "We'll dam the river."

We dammed the river. Each day, at dawn's first light, Agesipolis went to the trench and looked at the walls of Mantinea until midday. I began to wonder whether he thought he would stare them down. He repeated this performance at sundown.

"What are you looking for, Ages'."

"I'll not tell you. You will argue."

He confided to Sphodrias that the walls were mud-brick. This was something we could see for ourselves. One day, as we stood in the trench, staring witlessly at the walls, Agesipolis pointed and cried, "It is darkening."

"A shadow," Kallias whispered. "It is the time of day for shadows."

The following morning, the darkened part was higher.

"The river is rising," Agesipolis smiled. "Not a shadow, Kallias. It is unwise to build a city on a river."

His dam stopped the outflow of the Ophos, and caused the water level in the city to rise and seep into the mud-brick walls.

"By the gods, Leo'," Sphodrias exclaimed. "Your cousin is the wisest man in Hellas."

The entire army watched as the damp rose to the top of the walls, and cracks appeared.

One day the tall Theban came out from the wounded tent, talked with Agesipolis, and watched with him. Agesipolis walked a way back with the Theban. When he rejoined us, he was smiling. "Pelopidas spoke, and took some food. The physician says he will live."

"The gods must love that Theban," Pityas said. "What is the tall one's name, Agesipolis? I can never remember it."

"Epaminondas."

When the walls were about to collapse, the Mantineans sent a herald and surrendered the city.

Agesipolis banished the sixty members of the council. They were pleasantly surprised, as they expected to be put to death – which is undoubtedly what they would have done, had our positions been reversed.

We divided Mantinea into the four villages it had been before the Argives made it a city. The landowners were pleased, as it meant they could live on their estates near the villages. The landless were also pleased, because we divided the estates of the banished rulers between them.

As the sixty set off into exile, we had to post a guard of Spartan troops along both sides of the road, to protect them from the wrath of their own people. Agesipolis disbanded the army. We all went home.

Thus ended Sparta's cruel destruction of Mantinea.

"You have become older, Leotychides," my mother said. "It makes you still more like *him.*" Her invitation – summons – had reached my barracks that day.

"Unlike you, I am not timeless."

I lied. The years had thinned her face, and she very discreetly coloured her cheeks. I dare say she thought *he* might look in from Hades' Hall. Yet this honing down intensified her good looks. If she could not defeat time, she would cheat it.

She toyed with the heavy gold arm-ring she wore. "You must resolve your differences with Antalkidas."

"He has dared speak to you on the matter?"

"He paid his respects to his Queen, when we met at a festival. He asked about you, and feels that in some way he may have offended you."

"I should rather not discuss it."

"You do not recall the Long War. The peace had to be." So much for that casual greeting at the festival.

"Antalkidas still loathes Agisilaos. He used him because that

371

silly boy would not see reason."

"Agesipolis is not a boy. He is a brilliant general."

"Let him use his brilliance to restrain Agisilaos." She started her lioness pacing. "The Great King wrote to the kinglet asking for private friendship. A barbarian courtesy." Those extended loyal respects. "Agisilaos replied that private friendship is sufficient. Oh, he is sly. Sly. Sly, All Sparta knows the contents of that secret reply. The fools say, what a good Spartan he is. But he is friendly enough with barbarians. One of his circle was in trouble in Karia. Agisilaos wrote to the Prince and asked him to acquit him whether he was guilty or innocent. The favour was granted."

Knowing the punishments inflicted in Asia, I could not blame him. Still, there was that other friend left for the barbarians...

"Mother, what do you expect me to do? I am not even a citizen yet."

"Antalkidas is. Make your peace with him. Let him guide Agesipolis."

"Agesipolis has his own mind." Could that mind ever be turned on matters of the City?

She looked into the courtyard. "I saw your wife – what is her name?"

"You know her name is Kleonike, Mother."

"She was going up to the Bronze House with your sons and their nurse. They are handsome children." With an almost imperceptible glance, she added, "The third boy is quite pretty, too."

"I have only two sons,

"Indeed!" She turned to face me. "If Chairon could get a boy like that, the ephors fined him too heavily for marrying a young woman," My mother removed her arm-ring.

"Give this to your wife from me. Tell her she may call upon me. With my grandsons."

Meleas was full of some book his Athenian wrestler friend had written. He read me portions of it. I half-listened.

"It is nice poetry," I said when he had done.

"It is philosophy."

"Poetry can be philosophy," Mistress Argileonis pronounced. "Although philosophy may not always be poetry. Actually, Meleas, that is rather more like a play."

Meleas's neat-featured wife was neither tall nor beautiful, but had quiet presence. Fully five years my junior, she treated me as though she were something between a mother and an aunt. She was that rare creature; a woman with a sense of humour. I have known many witty women, but few with the gift of humour.

"Your mind is elsewhere," Meleas roiled up the book. "Both of you."

"That is two minds," corrected Mistress Argileonis. "Or do you credit us with but half a mind each? Leotychides was talking about Agisilaos when you brought out that book.'

Their two children were in that tranquil courtyard I always thought of as Helen's. The girl was studying her letters; the boy, two years her junior, stalking a butterfly. They made a pretty scene.

"Yes...Agisilaos..." Meleas said. "Anyone who stands up to him is swiftly found a post abroad–"

"And the men of Sparta do nothing," his wife interrupted, "including my husband."

"My dear, two wars tire a man."

"There can be another, if Agisilaos continues bickering with the Thebans."

I reassured her about our friendship with Thebes.

"Thespiae and Tanagra have sent to Sparta for protection against Thebes," she said softly, "The ephors are considering their request."

Meleas stared. "My wife," he said, "would be invaluable to the secret police. But I cannot believe that Boiotian cities keep her informed of their needs."

"Pandia's husband is an ephor, as you know," she replied.

In the courtyard, the girl knocked her brother's elbow, just as he was about to pounce. The butterfly escaped.

"Have we treaties with these Boiotian cities?" I asked Meleas.

"We are bound by the peace to protect the independence of every city in Hellas," Meleas replied. He looked shaken.

And weary.

Mistress Argileonis kept her silence. She never overstated a point.

Agesipolis, wearing an old barbarian helmet, cowered behind a chair. A small boy waved a wooden sword and challenged him to fight. I watched them a while unobserved before I spoke.

"You wouldn't be the barbarians for me, Ages'."

"How could someone called Leonidas not be the Spartans?"

My son seized the advantage of his inattention to strike him with the flat of his wooden sword. I clouted him, and noted with satisfaction that no tears misted his wide green eyes. He was five and should have known better.

"Cast your eyes down before men," I told him. "Now go to your nurse. That is an order."

"He is lonely," Agesipolis said. "You tell him stories of Kallikratidas and Pasemachos and Praxitas. He wants barbarians and Athenians to fight."

"Where is his brother?"

"Aunt Timaia sent for him again." I had thought my mother would be taken with Leonidas, who so resembled her. Of course, she favoured Agis – who looked like me or, more to the point, like Alkibiades. "You are hard on the boy, Leo'."

"His flock will be harder. He ought not to have struck when your head was turned."

Agesipolis grinned. "Spartans win. As you told my father when you shoved me in the fountain. Why do you look so severe, Cousin? Are you going to bully me again?"

"*Bully* you?"

He laughed. "You won't have the opportunity. I hear my guest coming." A whimsical smile played across his lips. "My royal guest. Royal Heraklid, according to his own account."

A stocky man with blue-green eyes, dark brown hair and beard stood in the entrance. He had the jaw of a strong man, but his mouth was weak. The hilt of his sword was inlaid with gold. He wore more ornaments than we do going into

374

battle.

Agesipolis presented me to King Amyntas of Macedonia.

Amyntas was a king without a country, but he was very careful of his royalty. I think the familiarity with which Spartiates treat their kings offended him. It was only when he learnt that I was cousin to Agesipolis that his royal dignity permitted him ease. (Apart from the weak mouth, Philippos resembles his father. His Greek is far more fluent).

Olynthos, the greatest city of Chalkidiki, had persuaded a number of other cities of that far northern peninsula to join her in a league, to fight for some territory it disputed with Macedon. (Most territory in these parts is disputed. Or was until Philippos swallowed it all).

The Olynthian League defeated Amyntas and forced him out of the disputed territory. It then went on to seize the Macedonian cities as well – including Pella, his capital, where I set this down.

The Macedonian King had come to Sparta as a petitioner to ask us to recover his cities for him, but the peace only bound Sparta to protect Greek cities. Amyntas was treated with courtesy and offered asylum. The King of Macedon would simply have been another exile living in Sparta, had his fortunes not taken a turn for the better, in no way owing to himself.

Akanthos, a Greek city on the isthmus of Akte in Chalkidiki, and Apollonia, a Greek city of Thrace remained aloof from the league, and were under threat. They, too, sent embassies to Sparta, calling for protection. Despite their Greekness, there were cogent arguments put forward in Assembly for keeping out of the far northern embroglio, but they presented convincing evidence that Athens and Thebes had made a secret alliance with the Olynthian League.

This put it in another light altogether.

Between the northern border of Boiotia and the far north lay Phokis, Lokris and Thessaly; countries that could easily be squeezed into submission by a strong Olynthian confederacy to their north and an Attic and Boiotian alliance to their south, making a powerful, geographically contiguous league of the whole of central and northern Greece linked to the far north.

The Olynthian League had already made incursions into grain-rich, gold-rich Thrace, and the resources of that territory would be at the disposal of such an alliance. Thebes was still smarting at losing her dominion over Boiotia. As for Athens…had the tired boxer refreshed himself with a sip of wine and started to flex his muscles again?

Representations were made to Olynthos, demanding that it quit the Greek cities it had taken, and cease its assaults upon the rest. The Olynthians did not comply and, much to the delight of Amyntas, we decided to war upon the league. It would be a quick victory. The far northerners still fought as though they were in the Bronze Age. We called on the signatories of the peace for fighting men.

Had there been any doubt about the complicity of Athens, it dispelled when the Athenians refused to send troops. In Thebes, that same Ismenias who had taken a barbarian bribe to start the war in Greece forbade any Theban citizen to volunteer.

The Akanthians and the Apollonians made a particular request that Eudamidas command the expedition. Perhaps it was not surprising. The spectacular daring of Phoibidas had made Sphodrias his great admirer, and there was more than a touch of it in the elder brother, which appealed to these far northerners. It was not a campaign of sufficient importance to be led by a king, so they had their way.

Eudamidas asked to have his brother Phoibidas put in charge of the allied contingents, while he went ahead to Thrace with the Lakonians. I had never liked this; brother asking preferment for brother, friend for friend, but Sphodrias said it was not like that at all. The brothers were simply accustomed to fighting together.

"Leo', do you know whether Agisilaos told Phoibidas to leave me out of the Olynthos expedition?" Sphodrias asked.

We had spent a pleasant day visiting his son's flock. Kleonymos had fulfilled his promise of great beauty. He was a quick-witted melleiren with charming manners, who excelled equally in music and games.

"Agisilaos doesn't confide in me, Sphod'. He, no doubt, heard that you once called him Lysander's little general."

"I'd say it again. Fancy Antal throwing in his lot with

Agisilaos."

"I've meant to tell you, Sphod'. You needn't shun Antalkidas on my account. You spoke for the peace and have no quarrel with him."

"He is too thick with Agisilaos." We stepped out of the way of some very small shear-heads beginning a race. "I thought Agesipolis might have told you something."

An eirens' boxing competition caught my attention. "Keep your head down, Lad ... Sorry, Sphod.' You were saying."

"About that talk Phoibidas had with Agisilaos."

"I wasn't aware they talked." Since my cousin asserted his right of command, there was no further point in tormenting him with a conflict of loyalties, "We rarely discuss Agisilaos."

I daresay Agesipolis wouldn't know either. Agisilaos speaks more to him than bare civility demands, since–"

He broke off. A flash of an autumn-leaf-coloured head sped towards a cliff. Sphodrias was fighting to control himself from calling to his son. It was from that cliff that the melleiren had fallen when we were boys. The melleiren fought death valiantly for three painful days, before he died.

The youth veered away from the cliff, his flight taking him in another direction.

"Sphodrias, are you saying Agisilaos is cool to Agesipolis?"

"It started when Agesipolis claimed the Argive campaign."

"They made that up."

Polydora's uncle is a member of the Kings' Hall. He told her that Agisilaos became friendly again when he tried to win Agesipolis over to the peace. When he failed, he told Polydora's uncle that he wanted no private friendship with his fellow King.

Kleonymos halted as he reached his destination. Another youth. The older youth turned. Archidamos, the son of Agisilaos. I doubt whether Sphodrias saw the face from where he stood. In any event, it meant nothing. The boys had liked one another as children. And kings' heirs are lonely.

"Go on, Sphod'..."

"That's all. Good riddance, I say. Agesipolis is twice the

King Agisilaos is."

I recalled all those times Agesipolis had pleaded with me to guest in his Hall, as he suffered the blandishments and displeasures of the man who had been father, brother and confidant to him. And my mother called him weak.

"Have you come in hope of finding me playing war again?" Agesipolis asked, putting down whatever he was reading.

"No. To accept your invitation to dine. Now that you no longer need me. Forgive me, Cousin."

That is how I happened to be in the Kings' dining-hall when Agisilaos received the news that Phoibidas had seized the citadel of Thebes.

"Come off it, Sphod'. Kallias said, as we settled ourselves in a corner of the gymnasium, "Taking the Kadmea is an act of war."

"There were strategic reasons." Sphodrias mopped his brow. It was a hot day, and we had been running. "Thebes is in the direct line of march to the north. The Thebans could have used the citadel to block supplies and reinforcements."

"We are not at war with Thebes."

"Ismenias should have been tried long ago for taking bribes from the Great King." In argument, as in battle, Sphodrias never hesitated to defend an indefensible position.

Ismenias had been co-ruler of Thebes, with Leontiades his political enemy, but the hostile faction of the former was firmly in the ascendancy. When Phoibidas stopped outside the walls of Thebes on his march north, Leontiades approached him with a proposal that he seize the Kadmea. While the Council of Thebes was meeting in the agora, and most people were taking the midday meal in their houses, Leontiades opened the gates to Phoibidas and led him into the citadel. Then he returned to the Council, told them that a Spartan garrison held the citadel, and ordered Ismenias arrested. Three hundred of Ismenias's followers immediately fled to Athens. The new Theban rulers executed Ismenias for taking the Great King's bribe.

"Phoibidas didn't really invade," Sphodrias temporized. "Leontiades invited him in. Rather like Pasimelos, Leo'."

"Corinth was occupied. Thebes is a free city."

"If Phoibidas were not your friend, Sphod', you would put him on trial for his life." The Magpie laughed.

Phoibidas was recalled to Sparta to stand trial for acting without orders. Agesipolis confided that, in Council, Agisilaos persistently maintained that Phoibidas should be judged solely by whether or not his action was in the interest of the City.

He was sentenced to pay a staggering fine. It would have beggared him, had he ever been pressed to pay it. A Spartan garrison was left in the Kadmea.

Teleutias was in my seat atop the Acropolis. The place of solitude and reflection. I acknowledged his presence with that briefest of greetings that marked our encounters in Sparta, and was going to take my thoughts elsewhere. This time he prolonged the exchange.

"I have been ordered to Thrace," he said when we ran out of nothings.

He was to take command of the army fighting the Olynthian league. I think we talked awhile about the campaigns of Brasidas in the same territory. The sun dipped behind the mountains, and the peaks glowed with that unearthly fire. The City was bathed in blue.

"Ismenias was as guilty as Ephialtes," he said, "but his punishment was long in coming." Our talk had taken us to Boiotia.

"Theban politics have always been like that."

"All the Hellenes took the Great King's bribe, in one way or another, when we signed the peace," The darkening sky outlined the trees like files of marching men, "The gods are not mocked, Leotychides."

Men were setting out to their dining-halls. We got to our feet. Lyre, harp and flute floated from the temple of the Muses, as we passed the Bronze House by the statues of the brother gods – Sleep and Death – and descended the hill, talking of this and that. At the bottom of the hill, we parted.

"Teleutias–" He turned back... "Aigina. It was good."

"The sea is clean."

The following year Phoibidas was appointed a governor in Boiotia.

I permitted Agesipolis to persuade me to enter a chariot in the Olympiade. It was a mistake. I have found it is usually a mistake to permit oneself to be swayed by others. Obeying an order is a duty. Bowing to persuasion is an abdication of reason, and that is why I rarely do so. My friends call it stubbornness. They also claim that reason is the name I give my own arguments when I attempt to persuade them.

I was moved not by my cousin's arguments, nor by force of his will. It was something close to pity. Pity is the very last thing that should move one. Mercy is a noble mover of men. Pity is contemptible and contemptuous.

Agesipolis was no longer the lonely, suspicious youth-man he had been. Born to be a king, reared to be a king, in becoming himself he had become a king; and in becoming a king he became himself.

He was at ease now with his contemporaries and near-contemporaries, a friend amongst friends. But he could not share our common past with us, never be part of those boyhood talks at evening when the cooking-fires sent up smoke, never be Magpie or Cockerel or Pointer, never recall the Great Fight or any of the thousand triumphs and humiliations that bound us together. Denied the comradeship of the flock, I thought the comradeship of the athletes' camp his due.

In Olympia he was a king amongst competitors. My cousin could no more put aside his kingship than the lark can change its song. He was never a pretentious man.

If Agesipolis tasted the comradeship of the fires in the hills, above the Kladeos it was less in our encampment than in that of the Corinthians. He found their sparkle and ease congenial. Moreover, he was not king of Corinth. Certainty he took to Aristeas when Pityas presented him.

There was little of the shabby exile of Sikyonia in

Aristeas now. He was a man of standing, who often spoke for the land-owners' party in the Corinthian assembly. Agesipolis had brought with him a king's seven servants. Aristeas had that many slaves to attend him and his horses. He, too, was in the four-horse chariot race.

We were coming away from the hippodrome after a practice run, when Aristeas said, "Do you remember Anaxilas the Syracusan? He has invited us to take a cup of wine with him."

"With pleasure."

"He is a strange fellow. Had some fancy that you and I were cool to one another."

The change in Anaxilas was less of person than of presence, He still laughed easily, but there was a certain gravity beneath the laughter. His fair hair had darkened somewhat, his short beard a shade darker than his hair. He had entered two chariots in the lists; one he would drive himself. "I shall lag well behind my charioteer, but I thought it would be amusing."

Megakles did not share the lavish tent this time. Something about a grain cargo detained him in Syracuse. The younger brother had little time for Games. "I have little time for anything else," Anaxilas declared, "unless it is the fair Daphne. That is why he is rich, and I am poor. I am eternally frivolous." One knew he was no more the one than the other.

It was not the best of Olympiades. Agisilaos coerced the organizers into slipping a grown man into the youths' race in the stadion; the Athenian lover of some barbarian friend of his. The incident embarrassed the Athenians as much as ourselves, and infuriated the Eleians.

The chariot Anaxilas drove himself only narrowly missed a prize. Aristeas did well, too. I was an inexperienced charioteer unworthy of his horses. Agesipolis's chariot was all but last. Our poor showing did not trouble him. That was the difference between us.

He was invited to the winners' banquet. He said he had not won, and joined his friends for a cup of wine at a table outside a wine-shop, in that village that sets itself up on the other side of the sanctuary ground during the Games.

381

We talked of winners and losers. Of other Games.

"I ran in the last Pythian Games," Anaxilas said, "Again I was second. I have done with running. Perhaps my second son will take a crown."

"I know of no race for boys of eight," Aristeas laughed.

"He shows promise. I am thinking of sending him to Lakedaimon for a Spartan rearing." Did he think of Doreius coming from behind him to win his own first Pythia?

"Some strangers do." I recalled Anaxilas's tent, the hangings, the vessels, the food, and the wine, "Life in a flock is hard."

"He will learn good manners. He may even grow into a man like Antalkidas." Anaxilas brought his hand down on the table. The nails were lightly tinted. The palm calloused with spear and reins. "By the gods, there is a man. He bartered the Great King what Persia already held, and received all he asked for. My brother would envy such a trade."

Agesipolis smiled. "If you wish your son to be a great trader, Anaxilas, do not send him to Sparta."

Aristeas sipped his wine "Anaxilas merely wants his son to be a Games winner, an admiral and perhaps the most brilliant man in Hellas."

"Antalkidas is a poor man, Anaxilas." Agesipolis told him "He gave all he received from the barbarians to the city."

"He took fine spoils in the war," Pityas added. "But it all went on a house and running horses."

"What better?" Anaxilas called for more wine. "Spartans and Syracusans are less sensible of wealth than any men in Hellas," Aristeas said, "Syracusans because they are the richest, Spartans because they are the poorest."

"Pay no heed to this absurd fellow." Anaxilas squinted against the glare of the shifting sun. "Next he will tell you we throw gold cups into the sea after we have used them."

"No," Aristeas agreed. "They keep them to use once again."

He regrets his ancestors did not go to Sicily with the wisest Corinthians. "Well, Leotychides, may I send my son to you? Will you arrange what must be done?"

"It is done, Anaxilas. If that is what you wish."

"Let him go young. Before the war triremes set out to sea."

Agesipolis looked up sharply "Do you not believe the peace will hold?"

"We see the mainland from a distance," Anaxilas told him.

"Distance lends a clearer view of the terrain," Agesipolis persisted,

"Agesipolis, in every mainland city but yours there is a war party and a peace party. A faction that supports Sparta and a faction that supports Athens—"

"No more," Aristeas interrupted.

"Then it will be democracy or oligarchy. Horses or bulls. Apples or pears. Ambitious men rise upon factions. Factions must have a cause, if not a reason. The apple men will call for war upon the pear men. The triremes will put to sea."

"Agesipolis, I thought you opposed the peace strongly as Leotychides," Pityas said.

"Only that we gained too much by it."

"Nor do I dislike peace, Pit'. But we abandoned the Asian Greeks."

"If Persia did not hold them, Athens would seize them. Her greatest crimes wear a noble face," Anaxilas smiled wryly. "And never have Asian Greeks cried, 'Rid Sicily of Carthaginians'."

Agesipolis was going to reply when something in the street caught his attention, "By Zeus! There are Pelopidas and Epaminondas."

Pelopidas looked in fine health. There was a spring to his step as he walked with his tall friend. Pityas cast a look that was as meaningless to me as it was to Anaxilas, but was returned by Aristeas. Agesipolis rose and started towards the Thebans.

Aristeas stayed him. "It could be awkward."

"Agesipolis saved their lives," I told him.

"That is possibly why they have chosen not to see him." He spoke with such forbearance one found it difficult to credit him the hothead of another Olympiade.

"No man would be such an ingrate," Anaxilas argued.

"Don't be dense," Aristeas snapped, eyes blazing. He was still Aristeas. "Agesipolis is a king."

Agesipolis wanted to know what it was all about. Aristeas explained that those two Thebans were known to be exiles living in Athens.

"With Ismenias's faction?" I could not credit it.

"I doubt they were his followers, but–" Aristeas completed his sentence with one of those airy Corinthian gestures.

"But what, Aristeas?" Agesipolis demanded.

"The matter of the Kadmea turned many Thebans against Sparta."

"Ismenias could have blocked our supply route when we held the Kadmea." Agesipolis always thought in tactical terms. "His death was none of our doing."

"That is known."

"But you think we acted wrongly," Agesipolis persisted.

"I think you had good reason. And they have reason. Sparta is not Argos and you have no intention of annexing Thebes, but it is a question of pride."

Agesipolis was silent a long moment. Then he said, "Thank you, Aristeas, for telling me what my other friends would not."

His reproachful gaze fell on Pityas.

I knew why there had been silence on the matter. A man tends to have an affection for a life he has saved. Agesipolis often spoke fondly of the two Thebans. His friends had not wished to hurt my cousin's feelings.

While we broke camp, as the tents were struck, the servants packing our gear into chests, my cousin, wearing his goat look, insisted that I accompany him to the sanctuary grounds.

Once there, he took a planned route leading past the six altars of Herakles and the temple of Hera to Victors' Road, where Charmidas still glowed in his triumph, and old Eurymos stood worn and featureless. Abruptly, Agesipolis turned left and halted.

My cousin had found that bronze boy of seventeen placing an olive crown on his head.

"How does it feel, Leo', to know that you will be there for

all time?"

"Someone I was will always be there."

He motioned. "Another admires your glory."

I turned and saw Nikomedes. He stood two or three paces away, looking at the statue. He had to have been somewhere in the Corinthian encampment, but kept his distance whenever we were there.

"Nikomedes." I strode toward him. "Nikomedes, my friend..."

The welcome in his face was tentative.

"Have I a friend I would have for a friend? Or haven't you heard that I am no longer a favourite in Corinth?" His eyes dared me to pity him, challenged me, defied me as they had once done on the boxing ground.

"The war is finished."

"My countrymen have long memories." He had the same rounded face and brown curls, and was only slightly taller than he had been as a youth. Time had not changed him greatly. Only the merriment was gone. "You know, I was thinking, but for you, that would be my statue standing there."

"That is good sense. I'm glad the beating I gave you hasn't damaged your brain."

We tried to bridge the years with jests and banter, talking around sensitive matters like soft-footed seven-year-olds stepping around nettles.

"Are you still boxing?" he asked me.

"Only in the Leonidas Games."

"Lakedaimonian boxing!" he scoffed. "It is nothing."

"What would you know of it? Foreigners can't attend the Leonidia."

"Corinthians saw the Spartans boxing amongst themselves in Sikyon." He stepped dangerously close to the nettles, and retreated. "I dare say I would have quit, too, had I won that," He pointed to the statue's olive crown. "I lie. I would have gone on and on, until everyone said, 'Poor old Nikomedes. Why didn't he retire while he was still great?'"

"How did you let a Sikyonian take the crown from you this time?"

I could have bitten back the words. My horses had kept

me from the boxing, but I heard from some Milians that the Corinthians cheered the Sikyonian who was fighting their compatriot. Of course, it had been Nikomedes.

"My own fault. I let something distract me. It is hard for a man who has known his city's cheers to endure its jeers." He grinned. It was a self-mocking grin without self-pity. Nikomedes always had been game. "A beginner's error." Deliberately, he stepped into the nettles. "It was all for nothing, that war. In the end, you Spartans had to drive the Argives out for us."

"Not for nothing…" The Corinthians had fought and resisted. A matter of pride, Aristeas would have said; Alkimenes would call it being. But I could no more explain that to a man whose pride and being lived on the boxing ground than I could explain Nikomedes to his fiercely patriotic countrymen. "Not for nothing," I repeated, my words dictated not alone by loyalty to my Corinthian battle-comrades. An implied acquiescence could only diminish Nikomedes. Alkimenes would have understood, perhaps. Alkimenes, who talked of diversity in men and in cities. "Do you ever see Alkimenes?"

"I don't move in such exalted company these days."

"Your friend Tolmaios was in Sparta. He's not a bad fellow."

"He was Aristeas's friend. Not mine." He refused to move from that nettle-patch. "Rum, isn't it? It was Aristeas who filled our tent with Argives and Athenians. I could never stick Argives. I'm not over-fond of Athenians either. I seem not to have much time for anyone…"

"Spare some for one friend at least."

"Hades take you, Leotychides! You don't give up, do you?"

"That is how I beat you, isn't it?"

For a brief instant, the mockery and the self-mockery left his eyes, "They may have robbed me of an olive crown at the Isthmus, but it was *mine*. That Philasian they crowned… I could have beaten him with one hand. Nothing can change the fact that I am the best in Corinth."

"I know."

"That is why I tell you. Old Friend, you had best go, or

the hero and his pack will be searching for you. And your friend there is beginning to look restless."

"He's only a cousin."

Talking to Nikomedes had taken me some years back. It was Olympia, where winners are kings and kings...only kings.

I waved Agesipolis over. For once, his royal tact failed me.

"Another valiant Corinthian exile?" he asked gracefully.

"They are no longer exiles, Ages."

"A man may be an exile in his own city." Nikomedes smiled in that wry, charming, Corinthian manner, muttered some courtesies, and excused himself.

Chapter 17

As the month of Artemision approached, and with it my thirtieth birthday, Meleas told me that a member of his dining hall had recently died. He suggested that I ask to be admitted.

This was about two years after Agesipolis pushed me into that chariot race, and I was determined not to act against my better judgment again. I politely declined. It was a good hall. That is why only a death could leave it short of a full complement of fifteen members. It boasted the great Derkyllidas. But Antalkidas was a member also.

As a citizen dines in Hall the whole of his life, the acceptance of a new member is a serious matter. It takes but one enmity to mar the harmony, the congeniality and good conversation that is more important than the food on the tables.

That is why it takes but one vote to turn an aspirant away.

I could envision Antalkidas exchanging a glance with some god, as he flattened the ball of bread in his palm, signifying a negative vote, before he dropped it into the kaddichos; the bowl the servant balanced on his head, as he passed amongst the members collecting these bread ballots.

I have always preferred declining to being declined. There were other halls I knew would have me. Why was I standing outside Meleas's hall on my thirtieth birthday, waiting for the door to open and a servant to turn me away?

The reason was that Meleas knew how to argue a point.

Or rather he did not argue it. He changed it. At some time in our discussion of the matter, it had become a challenge. He had given over trying to convince me of his certainty that Antalkidas would not kaddich me, and left me with the conviction that to turn away from the risk of being refused would be an act of cowardice. Not that he would suggest such a thing. Meleas was far too polite, but the thought had not lodged itself in my head on its own. It was easy to see why Meleas got on so well with Athenians.

Night had fallen on the City. A three-quarters moon rose from behind Taygetos. Still I waited before that closed door. I recall thinking of the youths inside. Remembering how it always amused boys to see an aspirant turned away. If he seemed a particularly brave-looking fellow, we regretted it. I hoped the youths would regret my rejection, and then wondered why I cared for the opinion of some imbecilic boys.

The door opened. The servant stepped to the side. A white-haired elder stepped forward and pointed to the door. "Through that door let no word spoken here go outside," he admonished. I had been accepted.

The elder's grave face dissolved into a thousand lines as it broke into a smile. He was the first to welcome me, as the eldest member of the hall. Next came Derkyllidas, the most distinguished of the greybeards.

The tables were laid with bread, cheese, olives and figs. Two servants stood by great cauldrons of black broth, waiting for us to be seated before ladling it into our bowls.

With my membership of the hall, I became a full citizen of Sparta. I could vote, put myself forward for office, and don the citizen's cloak that Kleonike had secretly set her servants weaving several weeks previously. My sons had not yet learnt to keep secrets.

On the walls of the hall hung shields, spears, and swords; each one taken from an enemy of great valour or renown slain by a hall member. One spear was so old that it had a bronze tip. All these things I had seen before, when I dined with Meleas – or, in the days of our friendship, Antalkidas – but now that it was my hall, I found myself particularly moved by them. Would I add such a weapon of my own making? The thought of giving the long sword of Iphikrates to my hall was pleasing.

On two of the walls, the dark wood panelling was covered by beaten bronze – this luxury acceptable only because the bronze had been melted down from shields taken from the enemy, in two famous battles commanded by members of the hall in times past. The flickering flames of the lamps in their tall standards reflected against the bronze, and illuminated the face of Antalkidas. The faces of the men occupying the couches nearest him were turned in his direction, as he gave forth. I wondered again that he had not voted against me.

389

Some other members stood to welcome me, as I made the slow progress to the couch that would be mine, accompanied by the old polemarch who was senior member. A fellow called Mnassipos said that he understood I was a good man with my bow, and that the hall tables could do with some game. Another man chided him, saying that he was surprised that a man with so delicate an appetite would notice.

Mnassipos was always watched carefully to see that he consumed every bit of his food, which meant that some of the members suspected he was supplementing his evening meal with delicacies at his house before setting out. Often men would insist upon having their share of this or that, so that if the fellow were doing some unlawful stuffing of himself he would pay the price in discomfort. It is only on becoming a member of a hall that one knows that, as a young soldier guesting, one's understanding of the jests has been superficial.

When we came to Antalkidas, he rose and welcomed me with the customary courtesy.

Since the signing of the peace, Agisilaos held Antalkidas in high esteem for his agile mind, and often looked to him for advice, which he sometimes acted upon and frequently ignored. Antalkidas, on his part, openly criticized the King in terse, witty comments, which were widely circulated, as he intended them to be.

I reflected that, perhaps, he had refrained from kaddiching me simply to annoy Agisilaos. The pale eyes told me nothing as we exchanged civilities. The disinterest in them was not that rage that forced out all expression. Between us there was no hostility. Nor was there the shadow of past friendship.

A few days after I took my place in the Apella, I called at the Agiad palace, to see when Kleonike would be ready to move to my kleiros. I had inspected it, and the house was in good condition. I had not reckoned with my usually gentle aunt, who tongue-lashed me as if I were a particularly bad-mannered and troublesome child.

Kleonike managed to silence her briefly "Eurydame, we will visit you often, but my place is on my husband's estate now."

My aunt clutched Kleonike and Leonidas to her, as if I

390

intended banishing them to furthest Asia, and renewed her complaints. Into it all strode my mother, like an avenging goddess. Agis followed her with his nurse, his long, pale curls and dark-blue eyes giving him the beauty of a child-Dionysos.

Without a word to her sister, my mother passed a scroll to my wife. "Kleonike, I have transferred everything." Kleonike appeared to know what she was talking about.

"Mother, what have you transferred?"

"Your share of wine, barley and oil to your hall."

"From whom have you transferred it?"

"The City, of course. How do you think you have been eating the past ten years?"

"In my barracks. Or guesting in halls."

"Do you think Sparta can feed all its young warriors eating like horses?" She turned hack to Kleonike. "Speaking of horses, he has far more than any three men could use for war or the Games. He must sell some–"

"Mother–"

"Be quiet, Leotychides, Men do not understand these things." I started to tell her that foreign men managed their own estates, but I recalled a number of foreign officers who would have cut short a campaign at a vital point, because of their concern for their crops. Such matters were best left to women – whose administration, being uninterrupted, was better. She continued. "And build a second house near the agora."

"Are you trying to take them from me even when they are in the City?" my aunt demanded.

My mother ignored her "The steward is honest but ageing. A serf of the old type. These younger ones keep back more than their half of the harvest, and sell it if you don't watch them. With all these landless men about now, they have a ready market. Agis will live with me until he goes to his flock."

Kleonike's face set. I intervened, "Mother, it is not good to go to a flock directly from a palace."

"You did. The Syracusan boy went from better."

"Agis will go to my kleiros with his brother."

"I won't," Agis announced. "I want my pony and my grandmother." Pony?

His nurse slapped him. He turned a reproachful sapphire gaze on her, and said, "I won't like you if you do that again."

These up-country women, mistakenly called Spartan by the foreigners who hire them for great sums, are nurses specially trained to discipline children. They are grim and rigorous. If they ever knew how to smile, they are taught to forget the art. I was amazed to see the woman's granite face soften. Had neither Kleonike nor I been present, I am certain she would have begged the insolent boy's forgiveness.

My mother turned to my aunt. "He has the charm," she said, as if there had been no silence between the sisters for seven years.

Agesipolis called for wine "Citizens of standing keep houses in the new quarter now."

"Then it is the houses that have standing. My kleiros is only a morning's walk out. Ages', have you rescued me from the women to plague me yourself." He seemed uneasy "In any event, I am a very new citizen, as Etymokles reminded me when we met by the Knakion."

Putting on the cloak of a citizen had inevitably turned the speculative glances on me again. Looks that I had learnt to interpret as asking, "Will this man be King? Will Agisilaos fall?" I dare say Agisilaos had had his fill of them, too. As time passed, and Agisilaos became entrenched in his kingship, the silent questions all but ceased. Even renewed by my new status, the glances were brief and pale reflections of the past.

"Etymokles!" Agesipolis exclaimed. "He is a friend of Agisilaos." The hostility between the two Kings was deep and open now.

"He was quite agreeable. Told me how not to make an ass of myself." As many tyros did.

"He is his friend. Not a sycophant. Leo', the Council met today. To discuss the news from Olynthos."

"Your face tells me it is not good."

"The names of the dead will be read out this afternoon. There are many…"

"There was an engagement? When?"

"The Olynthian cavalry fell on our light-armed infantry–"

"Good fighters, those men. Lesser Spartiates and up-country volunteers. I knew them at Aigina." I recalled the change in the near-mutinous fellows, after Teleutias had given them back their pride as Spartans.

"When Teleutias saw it, he took up his own weapons and charged the enemy," Agesipolis went on. "You know Teleutias when he is angry. He pursued them all the way to the city walls. The Olynthians fired missiles from the towers and forced Teleutias to retreat."

"Teleutias can control his men. It would have been an orderly retreat."

"Please, Leo', let me finish. The Olynthian cavalry charged out then, and broke our line." He paused. I knew what he would say. "Teleutias is dead. The messengers said he died fighting like Achilles."

"He would. He loved his men. And they did him."

"I can't help thinking that had he kept a cooler head–"

"It has been years since Teleutias was a hot-headed young warrior, Ages'."

Had it been a deeper, futile anger that drove him to that fatal charge?

I rinsed my hands and face in the purifying spring, and entered the temple of Lykourgos. It had been my intention to sacrifice to the Law-Giver since becoming a citizen but, in the months that followed, other duties intervened.

A white-haired man was reading the inscription, on the pediment of the noble, bronze statue, to his grandson. The boy asked intelligent questions, and I recalled myself at the same age asking Pausanios why Lykourgos held no spear or club. Clearly, I recalled Pausanios saying, "He killed jealousy and greed in men, and those are the most fearsome monsters of all."

As the old man and the young boy left, I let my mind linger in those days when Pausanios was King, Teleutias a bold young soldier, and life simple. The priest came forward. The sacrifice went willingly. I stepped out of the penumbra into the sparkle of early morning.

I followed the stream in the temple garden to the shrine in back, where the Law-Giver's only son, the last of his line, lies buried. No, not the last of one who has a city for his posterity.

The old man and the boy were walking about the green, stream-fed grounds. The man turned. It was Chairon and his son. Chairon saw me and raised his arm in greeting.

I tried to conceal my amazement. The boy resembled neither Gorgo nor myself, but the man he had been named for. I reasoned that Gorgo's hair was dark, her mother's eyes grey, and Dorieus's complexion had been not unlike my own. But colouring and reason did not explain that astonishing likeness. As if Gorgo had willed his appearance.

"Father–"

"Go on, Dorieus. Ask him."

The boy's eyes were seemingly downcast before me. He stood without squirming or shifting his feet. "Sir, my cousin Dexippas says you won an olive crown in the Olympic Games."

Dexippas. That would be Kallias's son. "It was long ago, Dorieus, when I was a youth." I found myself telling him of Nikomedes and his warning, of other youths in Olympia, of the athletes' encampment, its comradeship and rivalry. Of the friendships of the flock. Why was I telling him stories of flock life? I had prepared Leonidas for what he must expect, but I had never spoken to him this way.

As I recalled some exploit of Sphodrias's, the boy's gravity was dispelled by a fleeting smile that explained the uncanny resemblance. Gorgo had been a frowning little girl. She was not a smiling woman. Perhaps she had learnt that smile from Doreius, and shared it only with her son.

"I must be the best runner in my flock." Determination steeled the young eyes. "Mother says it."

"Then it will undoubtedly be," Chairon said drily.

A pheasant cock landed on the grass, its proud tail-feathers shining green in the sun. The boy advanced a few paces towards the bird, and froze.

"Sparta will miss Teleutias, Leotychides." Chairon kept one eye on his son.

"I should reply that Sparta has many men as good, but it seems to me that war has an appetite for the best."

"Dorieus! Put that down." Chairon ordered, as the boy picked up a stone and took careful aim. "Everything here belongs to the Law-Giver. Even visiting pheasants."

The boy's eyes were guileless as he turned his head, "I'm sorry, Father. You told me he wanted us to share things like brothers."

"Share it with him by looking at it."

394

The boy sat himself on the ground. The fine-looking old man glanced back at the temple. "Like brothers...What shall I tell him, when he asks why I am rich when other men are poor?"

Most men of Chairon's wealth called themselves comfortable or well-provided. Chairon did not hide behind euphemisms.

"That it was none of your doing?"

"It was entirely my doing." He smiled wryly. "I am a survivor, Leotychides." I replied something vague. He went on "Most Lesser Spartiates claim that they were cheated of their kleroi or forced to sell, and later that is the way it was. But when the land law was first changed, men sold and exchanged readily. It was a site closer to the City, or one with a pretty stream, and so on. I had seen enough of foreign cities to know that, where there is buying and selling, a few men come to own a great deal of land and the rest none. I determined not to be one with none. So I sold my horses and everything of value in my house, except my father's shield and sword and my own panoply, to up-country traders. With the money, I bought land wherever men would sell it. When the land grew scarcer, the prices went up, and I sold off all but the best. I seem to have a gift for this sort of thievery. I almost came to enjoy it for its own sake. That is when I stopped buying and selling." He looked me full in the face. "If you want to know why I am telling you this, it is because, at my age, I don't know I will be alive when some youth calls him a rich man's son, and I want someone to tell him that I never pressed a man to sell land against his will."

"No youth in his flock will abuse him."

"Not in the flock, no. I think it is only in the flocks that the true Sparta lives on. Even you are too young to recall the real Sparta."

"I don't mean this as an impertinence, Chairon. But, in your youth, did elders ever say just that?"

He smiled. "I know it is the habit of age to sweeten its youth. Then as now. And, then as now, there were fools as well as wise men. And most something between the two. There were petty men and generous men. And greedy men, too. But there was balance. Sparta held the greedy and ambitious on a tight rein. So to answer your question; no, in my youth no elder recalled a different Sparta. For Sparta had been unchanged for four hundred years. He gazed into the distance. But now we are a city forsworn."

Agesipolis slammed his hands hard on the table, sending troops bouncing from Thrace into Attica and the Aigean Sea. "Must you have your way in everything, every way and always, Leo'?"

"I was promoted to lochagos shortly after I became a citizen. General now…It is too soon, Ages'."

"It's not preferment. It's the ephors, Hades take them! Don't you understand I am being sent to Olynthos to fail?"

Since Teleutias was slain, the army in the north had ceased to be an effective fighting force. The war against the Olynthian League was dragging on longer than it had ought to.

"They won't give me one Spartiate regiment." He went on. "It's Agisilaos, of course." He took a list and passed it to me. "You see the generals I am to include on my staff. All friends of Agisilaos. If I take Olynthos, he will claim the credit for them. If I fail, he can say, 'You see, all the boy's victories were flukes.'"

The cutting mimicry left no doubt that the bond of gratitude tying Agesipolis to Agisilaos had been severed.

"So you see, Leo', I cannot have the men I trust outranked by Agisilaos's lackeys. I have never been defeated in the field, and I won't be treated like an incompetent."

"Are you planning other promotions?"

"Only Sphodrias. Meleas is already a general."

"You are appointing Meleas to your staff?"

A touch of the goat look. "I still don't like the man." A slightly sheepish smile. "But I trust him. And it's time he does something more than teach his daughter the lyre."

I inspected the Lakedaimonian regiments Agesipolis had been assigned, and reported back to him, "The up-country volunteers are the best type of farm lads, Ages'. And the bastards are great fighters."

They were officially called regiments of illegitimate sons of Spartiate fathers. They promptly dubbed themselves "The Bastards." Like Chairon, they scorned euphemisms.

"And the foreigners?"

This regiment was comprised mainly of the sons of exiles living in Sparta. The young men had been reared Lakedaimonian fashion. A few were sons of distinguished foreigners, who had sent them here to give them the benefit of a Spartan upbringing.

"They looked good. Particularly that lad Gryllos."

"You must meet his father. A splendid man."

"He is a friend of Agisilaos, Cousin."

"So was I. You would like General Xenophon, Leo'. One could scarcely credit he is Athenian but for his accent."

Later I regretted not knowing that great soldier. If he sometimes distorted facts about men in Sparta, it was because he swallowed the deceits of Agisilaos whole. Being of such a direct and forthright nature, he could not believe a friend capable of falseness. He had a true appreciation of the law of Lykourgos, but he knew only the shadow of the old Sparta and took it for the substance.

"I am giving you command of the up-country men," Agesipolis said.

"I should prefer the bastard regiment."

"If you don't want the up-country men, take the foreigners."

"Ages' , the only possible justification for this promotion is to give me command of the bastards. I know many of them from the cavalry. I understand them."

"It is out of the question."

We argued it. He rose, stood looking out into the courtyard a long time and finally turned. "Very well. You win. You are Achilles again and I am Hektor. The bastards are yours and I wish you joy of them."

Olynthos is a difficult city to take. Situated on the isthmus of Pallena, westernmost of the three promontories of Chalkidiki, the surrounding countryside is rich in grain, and Olynthian stores sufficiently well-stocked to endure years of siege. (I should put this in the past tense, now that Philippos has destroyed that beautiful city).

We approached Olynthos by sea, to find the sprawling city surrounded by walls made of great, squared stones, levelled and smoothed so that they fit tightly together – against which Agesipolis's siege engines proved useless.

The Olynthians gathered on the walls of the citadel, a high hill to the right of the city; walls similar to those that had defied our attempt to breach them, reinforced by another wall of similar-sized stones: and shouted down abuse at us.

They had a strong cavalry. We were dependent on the Thessalians for horse, apart from the mounted troops Amyntas mustered – if those wild Macedonian chiefs, each leading his own tribesmen, could be so styled. Yet the Olynthians did not send their cavalry, or indeed any part of their army, out against us.

Cursing the impotence of his siege engines, Agesipolis decided to lay waste to the countryside, in an attempt to bring the Olynthians out from behind their walls to defend it. We were delayed by an outbreak of dysentery, which I believe to have been caused by some impure water from a trickle by the shore.

The colour was disguised by the colour of our drinking-cups, but the smell of the sediment caught in the lip of my cup was unpleasant. I ordered my men to go thirsty until we found a spring. We were not affected, but the rest were – as they had gulped it thirstily. Sphodrias managed to keep up the spirits of his suffering up-country lads. He was the only man I had ever known who could jest while he kept up an almost continual quick march to the bog.

We lost a few men to the bloody flux. By the time the rest recovered, the marsh-fever season was upon us. I had a touch of it myself, and I do not bear illness as well as Sphodrias. I was short-tempered with my men while it lasted, which did nothing to enhance my none-too-high popularity.

Every general would like to be an inspiring commander. What Brasidas had been for Sparta in the Long War, and Alkibiades to Athenians. To do what I had seen Teleutias do at Aigina. To be spoken of as Derkyllidas was by his men.

My bastard regiment was a grim tight-woven unit, its full Spartiate officers outsiders. It was known for its toughness, as if the men were proving themselves harder than any full Spartiate. Proud of its high casualties. Grimly jocular.

When I arrived to take up my command, one of the former

cavalrymen gave a shout, "Hades take us, Lads. It's the pentatarchos." Another replied, "Can't you see he's a general now. Well, he *looks* like a general in that armour."

I knew they called me "General Pentatarchos" behind my back. I presumed that meant that I was still the company commander they detested, now a general at thirty-two by virtue of being cousin to the King. I did not inspire them. Brasidas had inspired serfs to fight like Spartans. I was not Brasidas. Neither was I Agisilaos, to buy the favour of my men with contrived consideration and promises of rich spoils. I was not liked. So be it. I was obeyed.

We saw little action. A few skirmishes when some local lord would come out and fight. I did not like this sort of engagement. None of the Spartiates did, including the hard men of my regiment. Fighting in Hellas, I sometimes found myself pitted against eighteen-year-olds. In Sparta they would be eirens. Here lads fought at fourteen and fifteen. No more than melleirens. War is a man's concern. Not a boy's. As summer went on, we were still slaughtering barley and sending domestic fowl flying before the splendour of our swords. The up-country lads began to lose their enthusiasm. They wanted spoils and a good tale or two to take back to their villages. The Spartan-trained foreigners, waiting to show off to their teachers, looked as though they wondered what there was to live up to.

One evening, as Agesipolis and I took the evening meal with our tent-companions, Aristeas joined us to say that some of the Macedonians had gone off and the Thessalians were becoming troublesome.

The appointment of Aristeas as a liaison officer between the king and the foreign contingents was something that Pityas and Agesipolis arranged. The prominent citizen of Corinth may have been looking with nostalgia on the campaigns of his youth. Despite his luxurious living, Aristeas was still fit, and as lean as a Spartan.

One Macedonian tribe, he reported, had decided Amyntas was a lost cause, and gone over to the Olynthians. It was a small loss, but it persuaded Agesipolis that we might better spend our time whittling down the allies of Olynthos. He decided to start with Torone, on the south-eastern coast of the narrow promontory of Akte.

We were on the second day or the march east over low hills, scorched and yellow, when the higher hills of Aphytis in the distance presented us with a vision of green. I recall I was riding with Agesipolis and Sphodrias. None of us spoke, perhaps fearing superstitiously that it was an illusion that words would dispel. But the fruit-trees and laurel, casting cool shadows over green grasses, were true as the pink-blossomed corinilla. My cousin drew rein and halted.

Surrounded by willows stood a shrine. Marble-fluted columns supported a triangular roof, with statues of Zeus and Hermes in the pediments. A fine arbour ran the length of the shrine. Vines climbed the columns.

Agesipolis ordered a break for the midday meal. We dismounted as the order went down the line.

In the ground, a deep spring sent its waters into a thousand rock-bedded streams. Just beyond the shrine they converged and emptied into a clear, deep pool, with water-flowers on green pads floating on its surface.

The shrine sheltered a beautiful statue of Dionysos.

"I wish we could stop here," Agesipolis said.

"I thought we were."

"I mean forever. Pityas, see that the Thessalians tie their horses well away from the vines."

I went back to my own troops to give some order or other, and found myself having my midday meal with them. The enchantment of the place must have touched them too.

"How do you like the life of a hoplite, General?" a former cavalryman asked.

"I fought my first cavalry action on foot."

"I'll wager you didn't walk to it, sir."

"I'll wager he hasn't fought one on foot since," That man's face was familiar. Not cavalry. It went back before Lechion.

I was to know that I was included in their talks on their terms. One of the platoon leaders, a somewhat pompous young man, pointedly excluded himself from the meal. His lot was unenviable the rest of the campaign, although they never disobeyed an order.

Agesipolis did not give the order to resume the march. A sense of euphoria consumed us all. I saw Pityas and Aristeas walking hand in hand amongst the willows, like the striplings

400

they had been in Lechion ten years ago. Meleas sat by the edge of the pool playing his lyre. He was an accomplished musician, and Sphodrias, Kallias and Anaxandros listened enraptured. Night fell. The circle of tents was raised, weapons stacked in the centre. We took our evening meal amid the vines and the waters. At dawn we struck camp and moved on. The shrine of Dionysos behind us. Something out of war and time.

Mountainous Akte put heart into the Peloponnesians. Spirits were high as we stood in battle-order before the walls of Torone. I ceded my place at the right of Agesipolis to Chionis, rode back to my regiment, and dismounted to lead it on foot, catching the eye of the man who had thrown down the challenge.

Something sparked memory. The Monkey! Makarios, who disappeared from my patrol so many years ago. His eye registered that I had taken up his challenge, but no more. I withheld the secret of my recognition. In his place, I would not have wished it either.

We took Torone by storm. My cousin's face was flushed by the fire as the army celebrated, squabbles and complaints forgot in triumph and booty. Voices raised in the songs and accents of cities from the Peloponnesos to the far north. The Macedonians danced drunkenly.

"That's good meat you're wasting, Agesipolis," Sphodrias said.

Those small, spitted pieces of meat, taken from the sacrifice after the hind-portions have been given to the gods, taste of victory as well as the fires.

"You take it, Sphodrias. He held out the skewer. I'm not hungry. You know, I think we had ought to assault Olynthos now."

"Sit down, Sphod'," I said. "Agesipolis did not mean this instant."

Agesipolis moved closer to the fire. "Strange how cold the nights are here."

"Ages', have you been drinking your wine Skythian fashion? This is the hottest night of the year."

"It is the cold after battle," Kallias said. "It takes some men that way. Remember Lykortas at Aigina, Leo'."

We recalled other battles. Other victories.

We were on the march again, the baggage-trains heavy with booty. The donkeys could have had heavier burdens still, but that would have slowed us down. The troops knew that Olynthos would yield greater prizes yet. They had no doubt that Agesipolis was the commander who would take it.

When we bivouacked the night, Agesipolis would sit over his maps, planning his assault on Olynthos. "There is a key to every battle," he said once. "Sometimes commanders stumble upon it accidentally. I prefer to know it." One night, as the oil burnt low and our tent companions slept, interrupted his muttering. "The key, the key..."

"Ages', I want a man promoted."

He did not look up, "You have the authority."

"I want him raised to platoon leader."

He gave me his attention, "No bastard can be promoted."

"The man is capable, and the platoon leader is down with marsh fever."

He offered me an officer from his own staff. I told him the man was an ass. He replied the ephors had decreed that no Lesser Spartiate could hold a command, no matter how junior. "You command here. Not the ephors."

"Have done, Leo'."

"I won't suffer fools commanding my men. Promote him."

"I have said not," he spoke sharply.

"Your duty–"

"Nor will I be lessoned on my duty." He rose and abruptly motioned me outside. The sea brought a cool wind over the land. "Leotychides, no polemarch would dare order me as you do–"

"If you–"

"Be silent. It is the King who commands here, and I am King. Kindly remember it, or you will stand guard with your shield for disobedience." He ran his hand across his brow. "This accursed heat..." I assumed he meant it as an apology.

Two days' march from Pallena, Agesipolis collapsed and was carried into his tent. In the heat of day he lay wrapped in several cloaks, shivering as though it were midwinter. When dawn broke, my cousin threw off all his coverings and complained

402

that he was burning. Sweat poured from him, so that he looked as if he had oiled for games. He was lucid again. His eyes took in Sphodrias. Meleas. Me. The physician.

"I want to go back." He breathed the words. "Dionysos. The shrine. It is so near."

After three days amongst the arbours near Aphitis, Agesipolis recovered sufficiently to start talking about taking Olynthos anew. The fever ate so much of his flesh that he looked the thin youth again. His manner was that of the seasoned commander.

He called for his maps and for black broth. The cooks did their best. It was the first food he had taken for days, except a few bites of the dry porous bread soaked in water.

He grimaced as he took the broth, but it was an empty bowl he passed to his batman. "Black broth wants the taste of the spring water of Sparta... Leo', when I was ill I resolved to involve myself more in matters of the City. I know I have avoided it...It would be so much easier if one could fight Agisilaos openly."

"I think, Cousin, that as many men would follow you as follow Agisilaos." At least those who had campaigned with him.

"It's not that simple. He doesn't fight. It is hard to explain. When I was young, I noticed sometimes, when my mother wanted my father to do something, she would plant an idea in his mind, then pretend it was his and praise him for his cleverness. She never argued, like Aunt Timaia. It amused me then. But that is what Agisilaos does in Council. He uses the methods of a woman."

"Certainly the Elders are not deceived."

"He is clever in looking into the hearts of men. When I was a youth, he treated me as a man so that I would be a youth forever. He tells them what they want to hear, and uses their inner thoughts to turn them against one another, so that he is the only one they trust. They are all at odds with one another, quarrelling about every decision. Then it is Agisilaos who comes forward with the compromise, which is what he has wanted all along."

"I know Agisilaos, Ages'. I understand."

"I'm glad someone does. It seems so vague if I try to explain it. Leo', will you call my scribe?"

"Hadn't you ought to rest?"

"Rest?" he grinned. "I shall be up and about tomorrow. An invalid commander is bad for morale."

That night he took a turn for the worse, He had an unquenchable thirst, and it all poured out of him in sweat. His thirst extended to the sight of water as well as its taste. In the morning, when the fever subsided, he had himself carried on his pallet to lie beside the pool where water flowers floated.

"Leo'," he said. I am sorry I ordered you to be silent that day,"

"You were right, I was nearly insubordinate."

"You *were* insubordinate. But it was not my place to speak so to one who should have been a king himself."

He trod places the flock-bred know to avoid.

"The fact is I am not a king." I spoke too sharply. "You are, and a good one."

"Meleas is a hard judge of men. He respects *you* as an equal." He smiled weakly. The freckles on his nose stood out on his pallor. "Don't think you have commanded his loyalty all these years because of a futile infatuation he had for a boy of sixteen."

"Ages', is there anything you don't know?"

A shadow crossed his face. "I have always been over-curious."

On the sixth day, I found Sphodrias, Pityas and Aristeas gathered about Agesipolis at the side of the pool that had become his Court. They talked quietly, as Meleas played the lyre.

I joined them with Kallias and Anaxandros. Talk tired Agesipolis, and we fell into silence. Meleas sang Alkman's poem, "All things sleep, the beasts sleep, the bees, the mountain creatures that creep."

"Thank you, Meleas." Agesipolis spoke when it ended. "No one plays more beautifully than you."

"Alas, I am no Euagoras. It is my daughter who has been gifted by the Muses."

"Perhaps I can hear her when we take the midday meal some time in Sparta."

Pausanios would be pleased when he learnt his son and his friend had made their peace.

My friends sensed that Agesipolis wanted a word alone with

me, and left us.

"My men have sacrificed a cock to Asklepios for you," I told him.

"It was not for disdain of them that I wanted to withhold the command from you."

"I know. You didn't want it said that a bastard was leading the bastards."

"Not that alone." He asked for water. I gave it him. "Cousin, when you are thirty-five, you need only stand and you will be elected ephor. You will be chief ephor. When your year expires, you will be promoted to polemarch."

"Empty honours."

His thin hand clutched my arm. "Leo,' take them. The Council will think you reconciled and you will be left in peace.'

"Ages', I have told you. I have no wish to be king. But I'll not deny my *right* to my father's throne."

"You mean you haven't changed since the days when I had to be the Trojans every time we played war."

"You know my sentiments concerning unmerited promotion."

"You admire Aristodemos, but he would not have been a polemarch so young, had he not been very close kin."

"Aristodemos was never king."

"That is my meaning. Talk of plots surrounds you like clouds over a mountain-top. Even here, I have heard some of my generals say you are making the bastard regiment your own army. As I knew they would. That is why I did not want you to command it."

"That regiment doesn't love me, Ages'."

"It is what people *think* that matters. Even before you were a full citizen, your name came up in Council in connection with plots. That is why I insisted you come to festivals with me. There had been talk that we were plotting to depose Agisilaos."

"They accused you of this?"

"It's not done that way." His thin face assumed the lines and pomposity of a Lysandrian Elder. He still had his gift of mimicry. 'The boy is coming under dangerous influences, Agisilaos. We must protect him.' That sort of thing." He could even laugh now at that hated *the boy.* "But when we were seen publicly by all Sparta, they could hardly say we were involved in a secret conspiracy." He smiled weakly. "Rather the way the

Royal Heraklids defeated the secret police. By jesting openly about them."

"We haven't defeated them. Only made them useless in our own houses." My mother had demanded the return of Kallibios,when the police commander removed him. She found the fellow an efficient secretary.

"Leo', you have a good life. Between us, you have had the better. You had your flock. I had grey-haired tutors. I had false favourites. You had love…I'm sorry, Leo'. Does it grieve you to remember Dorieus?"

"It would grieve me more not to remember him."

"You have friends. I have suppliants."

"My friends are yours, Ages'."

"For your sake."

"For your own, now."

He grew reflective. "Something is troubling Aristokrates…" He closed his eyes. His face had a sunken look. "Your sons ... I have often wished for sons like yours."

"Well, Cousin, that is easily enough done."

"So says my mother." His eyes opened. Wide. Round, Bright Agiad blue. Their gaze was unswerving… "But we both know I have left it a bit late." It was no time for false assurances. "Don't hazard your good life, Take my advice."

"Ages', I cannot." The freckles stood out on his pallid face as he raised himself on his elbow. "Then take my army. Take Olynthos, Take Sparta."

I leaned against the trunk of one of those graceful willows, watching a streak of cloud pass across the pale blue sky. A figure in the distance made its way towards me. Sphodrias?

I could envision his grin if I said, "Sphod', we are going to take Olynthos. Then I shall fight Agisilaos for my throne."

A wild flame coursed through my veins.

Olynthos would not be a quick, fierce engagement, but a long siege. Could I succeed where Teleutias had failed? Return to Sparta with a strong army and a resounding victory. Seize my kingdom. Unlawful? Had I not been deposed unlawfully?

Agisilaos had not had a single outstanding victory since Koronaia. That was faded glory to many of the younger men voting in the Apella. And this time, as a full citizen, I could speak for myself.

I had been called persuasive. ("That mouth of yours will give you away if nothing else," Antalkidas had said when I was a rhodibas). I had taken it to mean to my speaking out of turn. He had been thinking of Alkibiades's wit. Had his powers of persuasion passed to me? I thrust the thought from my mind.

Let my army demand that the Council send to Delphi. Let spears proclaim that Apollo, not Lysander, names Sparta's king.

How many times had I felt the green eyes of Leonidas looking at me with reproach at some future time asking, "Father, why have you thrown away my heritage?"

"Leotychides!"

It was not Sphodrias who approached, but Meleas. Reflective, upright, lawful Meleas. "Agesipolis wants to see you."

I hastened to my cousin. He still rested by the pool, and I thought him asleep. His eyes opened.

"Leo', I don't want to be buried in foreign earth."

"I promise you will not."

"Stand by Kleombrotos."

"He will have my loyalty unmeasured."

The round, blue eyes looked into mine. "Will you take the honours?"

"You know better."

"Sparta?"

"I cannot."

"*Will* not..." His voice was weak. "Only on your own terms."

"It is not that, Ages'."

A thin smile tried to move his lips. "Always the Trojans, Cousin..."

Agesipolis died the next night.

We sent out the army to requisition honey from every farm and village in the area, to preserve his body for the journey back to Sparta.

King Agesipolis lies in the Agiad tombs. At the funeral banquet and afterwards, Agisilaos made a great point of praising him and showing grief at his untimely death. Sparta was full of the generosity of the Eurypontid in forgiving the

407

differences he had in the past with his fellow king. It is a pity the dead are not about to enjoy the kindness they evoke.

Agesipolis, my cousin, your friendship was so gentle I did not know its strength.

Chapter 18

Sparta throws off her shabby cloak of moderation to celebrate the accession of a new king.

The City becomes one vast festival for the six days of accession ceremonies. The emptied government buildings are festooned with flowers and tree branches. Men don their war jewellery, Women wear their brightest peploi. Horse bridles are decorated as though for war. Serfs fashion baked-mud beads for their goats.

Rich up-country men in fine apparel are carried in litters by their slaves. Farm families come down from the hills, riding donkeys or on foot. The fields of Lakedaimon are emptied. Serfs lay down their tools and join in the festivities. The olive trees marking the boundaries of kleroi become perching places for this vast throng.

It is one of the few times my mother's kanathrum is put to use.

This time she had no ceremonial duties, as there was a young queen to perform them. She took her place with the royal party, contriving to look most regal of them all, as Kleombrotos sacrificed to Demeter, ending the eleven days mourning for Agesipolis.

The new king, in his long heavy white robe with its wide crimson border, stood three fingers-widths shorter than his father and brother. My mother's side of the family had brightened the bronze lights in his garlanded chestnut hair. He walked with a soldier's step as he approached the temple of Demeter. With a sure hand, he offered the sacrifice.

"Kleombrotos uses the silver knife like a sword," Sphodrias said.

The king cut the animal's throat in one quick, efficient motion, rather as if he were gutting a deer after the kill. The sacrifice had gone willingly. A good omen.

Sphodrias joined the ranks of citizens following the ephors, who followed our royal party, who followed the Elders, who followed the King to the hollow of Artemis's sanctuary. The rest of Sparta followed, in no particular order. Kleombrotos laid a garland on the altar of the Huntress, as the finest girl dancers honoured the goddess with those graceful, deceptively easy-seeming steps, to the music of harp and lyre. The heavy old Agiad chariot waited on the level ground above the hollow. Kleombrotos lifted the hem of his robe to his calves, leapt in and started to take the reins. A young kinsman hastily mounted, and took them from him. The King never drives himself.

It was time to ascend the high path leading to the bluff. Halfway there, he stopped to sacrifice to the Twin Gods, Guardians of Sparta, at Polydeukes's sanctuary. A chorus of maidens sang a new poem about the Divine Brothers. I knew the poem. Kleonike had selected the girls for the chorus. It was led by Euagoras.

Kleombrotos declared it time for the city's meal, the repast given by a new sovereign to his people. It is fortunate we Spartiates eat simply. (Aristeas calls a Spartan feast famine). The up-country people bring fowl and dried fruit to supplement what we consider adequate at midday. The serfs drink their own strong wine.

Taking our places amongst the citizens, Sphodrias pointed to the royal party, "Isn't that your son, Leo'?" Agis was seated next to my mother, who gave the small boy food from her own plate. "You know, Leo', he looks just like you the year you came to the flock."

Something on Archidamos's plate caught my son's eye. He reached out and took it. "An omen...?" Hekataios breathed. Pityas and Kallias exchanged glances. Where the others saw omens, I saw only my son's bad manners.

Sphodrias saw his own son after the meal, when the youths danced. His cheeks were puffed with pride, as he pretended not to hear exclamations on the beauty and grace of Kleonymos. Then it was into our racing chariots (the only such vehicles we owned) to follow the king to the Bronze House.

We moved slowly at first, our horses growing restive.

"Leo', have you ever noticed that Agisilaos always has three friends amongst the ephors?" Kallias's eyes went to the backs

410

of those dignitaries.

"Men are easily flattered." We started to gather speed.

"Sometimes. Others can be—"

Kyniska, driving her own chariot, caught up with us and called out, "I'll race you to the temple of the Muses."

"Between two Games winners, I have no hope," Sphodrias laughed back.

She clattered on to Aristodemos, who took up her challenge. The two sped ahead, diverting through Lysander's victories into the colonnade.

"By the Gods, she is more of a man than Agisilaos," Kallias said.

"That is a small achievement," Sphodrias replied.

"How Agisilaos could be Agisilaos with such a sister and brother I can never fathom," Pityas opined.

"Ah, Teleutias," Sphodrias reminisced. "There was a man…"

"Kyniska is said to be like my grandfather," I told him.

Sphodrias flushed. He had forgotten that Agisilaos had two brothers. One a king in Sparta. Was my father already fading from Sparta's memory?

The next day the crowd was somewhat thinner when Kleombrotos visited the shrines and temples in the agora, that place being barred to Spartiates under thirty. Beginning with gifts to Zeus and Apollo, he went on to lay the garland on the statue of the People of Sparta.

Then came the games and competitions.

Kleombrotos awarded Euagoras's poem first prize. I took first in the boxing, and a second in the chariot race. Meleas was first. Aristokrates lost the wrestling to Sphodrias. Surprisingly, as he was acknowledged the best wrestler in Sparta since Thermon retired. Kallias said Sphodrias used some new skill the Theban Pelopidas had taught him on the Mantinean campaign, wherein an opponent's size and weight can be used against him.

The sixth day ended with that ceremony that moves me most. At the sanctuary of Lykourgos, Spartiates separate into groups of elders, citizens, young warriors and boys to sing the simple chorus Euagoras taught us as boys for the Leonidia. The voices are not as fine as the maiden's choruses, or even those of men chosen for good voices. The simple melody is not as beautiful

411

as the least of the poets in competition. But it is Sparta singing to her Law-Giver.

In the feeling evoked by the occasion, I quite forgot we had forsworn his Law.

A year after Kleombrotos ascended the Agiad throne, Olynthos fell to us. The Chalkidian league was dissolved. I do not believe Polybiades would deny Agesipolis's part in the victory. Before that, I received a message from Kleombrotos.

My aunt had sold the Agiad palace to her son, and taken a house without a great hall. The room where Agesipolis pondered over maps and markers was now strewn with scrolls. Kleombrotos kicked one aside as he came forward to greet me.

"Perhaps I wasn't cut out for an Elder at twenty-seven." He glanced at the clutter.

He wore a short-belted cloak on his sturdy pentathlete's body, like the young officer he had been six months previously, when the kingship was thrust so suddenly upon him. Unlike Pausanios and Agesipolis, he only donned the long cloak of a king when attending a meeting of Council, or performing ceremonial duties.

He came straight to the point.

"My brother kept campaign notes. There was something about offering you certain offices when you were thirty-five."

He ran his hand through his hair. "I thought it was Agesipolis being fanciful again. But an Elder approached me on the subject after the last meeting of Council."

"Agesipolis spoke of it to me."

"Why now? You are what? Thirty-two? Thirty-three?"

"I think he wanted to reassure them."

"Are you going to accept?"

"No, Kleombrotos. I am a free Spartiate."

"He says nothing of your refusal in his notes."

"He was too ill to write by that time." He frowned.

"Why would he wish to diminish you in this way? I've heard you spoken of as a man who makes his points well in the Apella. As well as a rising man in the field."

"Agesipolis thought of it as protection."

"From what?" He seated himself.

"My enemies. Your father's trials always haunted him."

"I heard less of it at the time." He gestured to a chair.

"Sit down, Leotychides. I always forget kings must invite people before they can sit. I was only about nine when Father went into exile. I think ours was the only flock in Sparta not to discuss it."

I recalled the polite discretion when I was deposed. "It would be."

Both flock-reared, we understood one another. Both flock-reared, it was unnecessary to say more.

"Agesipolis always saw sticks in the dark as snakes."

"Kleombrotos, he protected me when I was a young warrior with no voice in the Apella. I thought him heedless at the time."

I told him about the festival appearances.

He laughed and rose. I stood also.

"That would be his way. What was he like as a commander?"

"A brilliant tactician. Unorthodox. Brave, as you know."

He took a scroll from a box with a lid of the high-polished Lakonian wood that strangers mistake for marble.

"What of his staff?"

"Those he selected himself were loyal. Good officers, Good men."

"I'll have their names. Should I need a staff of my own." He ran his fingers through his hair again, as he scrutinised the scroll. "Can't make this one out. Can you?"

"Kleombrotos, it would be easier to read if I had the scroll."

He laughed and passed it to me, "And do stop sitting and standing like my shadow. Were you always so formal with my brother?"

"Ages' and I played with wooden swords as children. I only gave him king's honours in public."

He took the scroll from me. "Another time. Come into the great hall."

The high-backed chair that always brought back Pausanios to me still stood in its place. Little had changed since my childhood; but, in the days of Pausanios and Agesipolis, a large, covered object would not have stood in the centre of the floor.

Kleombrotos removed the soft, leather cover.

It was a memorial-stone inscribed, *My father Pausanios raised this stone for his beloved son Agesipolis, whose courage all Hellas praises. Kleombrotos.*

"He was an exasperating brother, but I loved him," Kleombrotos said.

"I, too. Although I think I was the exasperating cousin."

He covered the stone again. "I must take this to Delphi shortly. Will you accompany me?"

"Unwise. They would say we were consulting the oracle about my claim to the kingdom."

"Does that trouble you?"

"No. But I am a free Spartiate. You are a king."

"I shall try not to let that trouble me."

"Kleombrotos, in your lifetime two kings of Sparta have been deposed. Be secure on your throne before you court enemies." We started back to the small room where he had received me.

"That poet I gave first prize. Prothous said you were his flock-brother."

"Euagoras? Yes."

"Would he set down his best poems for me? My father thinks poetry is declining in Sparta. I should like him to read this man's verses."

"I'm certain Euagoras would be honoured. But Pausanios is right. Euagoras is an exception now. Poetry declines, like everything else."

"What do you know of Prothous?"

The question came as an irrelevance. I was not accustomed to Kleombrotos's habit of listening with one half of his mind, while he thought ahead with the other.

"I believe him to be his own man."

"That was my opinion. I wish Agesipolis had left as many notes on matters of the City as on his campaigns."

"He would have. In time."

"You must help me to decipher what there is. He used abbreviations." He closed the box with the scrolls. "When I return from Delphi."

"I think I shall stand for ephor."

The thought of being elected on merit after refusing the Council appealed to me.

"Not this year, Leotychides," Kallias said. "We have our man

414

chosen."

The Inspector of Boys had asked me to report to him on a battle between flocks. Some friends accompanied me. My kleiros was on the way back, and we stopped for refreshments. Now all sat or stretched out in the high grasses, growing sun-drowsy in one of the comfortable silences that exist only amongst old comrades. Occasionally punctuated by disconnected comments, and Sphodrias's snore.

"Already?" The election of ephors is held in autumn.

"And the year after it will be Meleas."

"He has at last agreed?"

"Mistress Argileonis agreed for him." Pityas yawned.

Aristokrates had spoken hardly at all. I recalled Agesipolis saying something was troubling him, and determined to fall into step with him along Hyakinthos Street some evening, as we set out for our halls.

"I shall stand when Meleas does. His election is assured. I won't rob his votes."

"There are other reasons to wait." Kallias picked a blade of grass.

"You think I am one of those asses who walk through the Apella only to have four or five voices raised for them."

"Your name did come up," Kallias said.

"We felt that, as both you and Meleas and a chance of being chosen chief ephor, you had ought to put yourselves forward in separate years."

I raised my head. "Where did my name come up?"

"Sorry," Pityas said. "You and Aristodemos were so taken up with Agesipolis's funeral arrangements you were left out."

We had been more taken up with preventing my mother from organizing the funeral. Eurydame used all her strength to keep a high head and dry eyes, and was able for little else. We diverted my mother to instructing Kleombrotos in the ceremony of his accession – which was perhaps not appreciated by the new king, but kept her out of the way.

"Hades take it, left out of *what*?"

"Kallias and Gorgo think we are dividing the vote into fragments with so many men of our own faction."

"Are we a faction now?" I directed the question to Kallias.

"Leotychides, we are a faction whether we would be or no.

415

But our purpose is to end factions."

The Magpie ran up and plopped himself in our midst. "Things that are started to end things have a way of becoming permanent." Being over thirty and unmarried, he was barred from the flocks.

Pityas turned to his cousin, "Convince the Cockerel that factions exist. He really should know, as he is considered a leader of one."

"I don't like this talk of factions, Pityas." I told him. "It has more the smell of Athens than of Sparta. What are we? Oligarchs? Democrats? Extreme Democrats?"

"Spartan factions take a different form," Kallias said. "When we were boys there was Lysander's faction and Pausanios's faction. Then there was the faction of Agisilaos and…" He hesitated.

"And the faction that held you were king," Anaxandros finished for him.

"Does any faction hold with the Law of Lykourgos?"

"I started to tell you during the accession celebrations, when Mistress Kyniska interrupted." Kallias slapped a fly.

"I'm still not certain what you are talking about."

"We have been meeting now and then, to discuss matters of the City."

"Thank you, Magpie. That is the first straight answer I have had yet."

"But we can't meet in your house or Aristodemos's, because they are full of secret police," Pityas added.

"Talking is not unlawful."

"Antalkidas says you can learn more from agora gossip than secret police reports," Anaxandros said. "His date palms always die. He is to marry."

"Who to?" Sphodrias woke, blinking sleep from his eyes. "The Great King's daughter?"

"Some Spartan maiden. A barbarian wife would disfranchise him. How did the mock battle go?"

"That is none of your concern," Pityas told his cousin.

"Get a wife in your house, and you can see for yourself," Kallias advised him.

"Stupid law," the Magpie said.

"It is not a stupid law." Sphodrias rose. "We were not there

416

only to judge the commanders and the boys, but to set an example." He walked to the stream to wet his face.

"I thought it was the Cockerel who judged," the Magpie called out.

"Any man going to the flocks must set an example, Cousin," Pityas informed him. "Marry."

"My brother can carry on our line."

"He can carry on his own line," Kallias said.

"Leave him alone." Aristokrates spoke for the first time. "If he doesn't want to marry, don't plague him." We knew the nature of his trouble with his words. And that none of us could speak of it.

Kleombrotos withdrew one of Agesipolis's scrolls from that elegant box. "What does 'ref. Leo. Prom.' mean?"

"Agesipolis refused me permission to promote a man unlawfully." I briefly sketched the history and quality of the bastard regiments.

After a silence, the King said, "That would explain some of the missing citizens."

"Missing citizens?"

He frowned. "Agisilaos proposed a decree in Council that would exempt every man with three sons from war duty, and every man with four sons from war taxes as well. Leotychides, Leonidas was concerned to perpetuate the lines of brave men…" He continued pacing. "I know I'm a tyro in Council, but it seemed to me that Agisilaos's proposal is designed to perpetuate the lines of cowards. Any faint heart can fornicate his way out of battle." Absently, he ran his fingers through his hair as he spoke. "The final absurdity was the reason he gave. It seems that Sparta is short of fighting men, and it was designed to encourage men to breed more. Any rhodibas who knows his sums could see that the more men you exempt from war duty, the fewer warriors the City will have. It defeats all logic!"

"I would hazard he has friends who have asked to be exempted. But remember, I am not unbiased." I smiled. "It could be something else. The mind of Agisilaos has a logic of its own."

He wheeled about. "Hades take his logic! In three

417

generations we would be over-peopled as Arkadia if men started breeding like rabbits."

"Breed like rabbits, fight like rabbits," I quoted our old jest about the Arkadians.

He laughed perfunctorily, his mind undeflected from the point. "We haven't kept our numbers small without reason, have we? Am I making sense, Leotychides?"

"When a city lives on foreign corn, it becomes uneasy if its sources of supply are threatened. That is often the cause of war. You make sense."

He sat down across from me. "I asked why we were short of fighting-men, and was given any number of vague replies."

Kleombrotos, six years my junior, had come from his flock into a Sparta in which the land decree of Epitadeus and Lesser Spartiates were simple facts. How swiftly men accept the unacceptable.

He motioned towards the clutter on the floor. "The Lakonian records. Copies. Some of the early ones were carved in stone." He rose again. "I decided to see how many fighting men we have." He searched amongst the scrolls and found what he was looking for "At the time of the Persian wars we had more than eight thousand citizens. And at the end of the Long War, slightly less than seven thousand. Five years *after* – and this is what confounds me, Leotychides. After five years of peace, we were down to four thousand! Does peace consume more men than war? What has become of our citizens?"

"I think you know that, Kleombrotos."

"The Lesser Spartiates. But they cannot all have been bastards. Or greedy or reckless men, as some of the Elders put it."

"Is that how they put it."

"Some of them mumbled about Lysander and coins and – by the Twin Gods, Leotychides, what were our fathers about to let this happen? We need more citizens. Not more people."

I told him what I knew. What happened to the Monkey. Dinon's kleiros. "Do you know any Lesser Spartiates, Leotychides?"

"Only the men I commanded. How would I know them? They had no vote in the Apella, although they are subject to war duty. I do not teach their sons boxing, because they are not in

418

flocks, and will undoubtedly grow up ignorant as rustics. Because they are Spartiate, if lesser, they must die before submitting, but they hold none of the land of Lakedaimon that they die for. No, Kleombrotos, I do not know them. Nor could you. For they do not open their minds to any full citizen."

"Waste…" His fingers ploughed through his hair again, leaving it standing upright from his broad brow. "A waste of men…I shall put forward a proposal that the private property of any man dying without an heir be claimed by the City, and given to a Lesser Spartiate."

"How will the men be chosen?"

"What does it matter. Let it be by lot." Kleombrotos was bored by details as Agesipolis had been fascinated. "And female heirs to inherit only half. The rest to the City, to enfranchise more men." He slapped his thighs and stood. "That should cut down the number of Spartiates marrying heiresses."

The sudden appearance of a servant cut him off in full spate. I recognised the man from Agesipolis's time. Kleombrotos stared at him; then, with a rueful smile, turned to me. "I think I am being reminded that I forgot to offer you wine." He rectified his omission.

When the wine arrived, he tasted it and grimaced, "Sweet sickly stuff." He called for more water to dilute it further. "My brother had terrible taste in wines."

Even Aristeas considered Agesipolis a connoisseur.

Kleombrotos's proposal was rejected. The Council approved Agisilaos's decree exempting men with three sons from war duty, and those with four from taxes as well.

I was in the hot baths with Sphodrias, sweating out the grit of the boxing-ground and discussing the latest news from Thebes.

The Theban exiles in Athens had devised an ingenious plan – one they have recounted so often all Hellas knows it – to get themselves back into their city and into power. Not a small part was played by those two lives – Pelopidas and Epaminondas – Agesipolis had so valiantly saved. Leontiades was slain. The new rulers dismissed the Spartan garrison in the Kadmea.

"We don't need a garrison there, with the war in the north over," Sphodrias said. "I wouldn't have thought Epaminondas and Pelopidas would have been mixed up in all that."

"I doubt whether they planned the blood-bath, Sphod'." I poured more water on the hot stones to raise the temperature.

"They had ought to have known. Theban politics are always bloody."

"Perhaps it is better to expect too much of one's countrymen than too little."

The door opened, letting in a flood of cold air, followed by Kleombrotos.

"Have you been wrestling?" he asked.

"Boxing," Sphodrias replied. "Leotychides likes winning."

Kleombrotos threw off his short cloak, unstrapped his sandals, sizzled the stones with more water, lay down on the empty bench, and closed his eyes.

"Agisilaos wants to make war on Thebes," he said.

"He has never forgiven the Thebans for not letting him play Agamemnon at Aulis," Sphodrias commented.

Agesipolis had invited Sphodrias to Kleombrotos's betrothal feast. They met again at my elder cousin's funeral. A few months later, Kleombrotos invited Sphodrias and other friends of his brother to the name-feast of his son, another Agesipolis. The young King and Sphodrias got on well. Kleombrotos spoke little, as we walked from the baths to the river.

"My head is cooler now," he said after our dip. "I persuaded two of the ephors that the peace could not be invoked in internal Theban matters, but the chief ephor is unconvinced. How do I convince him? You two sat with him in Assembly."

"I have never known him to be moved once he takes a stand."

"Except by his wife," Sphodrias added. "Polydora says she terrifies him."

"Who terrifies *her?*" Kleombrotos demanded.

Sphodrias smiled, "Will you speak to Mistress Gorgo, Leo'? Or shall I?"

Kleombrotos threw his cloak about his shoulders. "I think I shall talk to the other two ephors in the event that the formidable Mistress Gorgo fails. Assembly still must agree before we can war."

"There are a number of ways of putting matters before the

Apella," I warned him.

All five ephors refused to consider asking Assembly to vote
for war.

"By the gods, Leo," Sphodrias said. "I think we've got a king
to be reckoned with."

A cold wind swept the bleak Boiotian plain.

Kleombrotos won the skirmish in his contest with Agisilaos.
The more experienced man won the battle. Or rather Thebes
won it for him, by reasserting her old claim to the Boiotian
cities by force of arms – giving Agisilaos a clear breach of the
peace.

It was not a decisive victory for the old King. Sparta had not
made war on Thebes, as he wished. The ephors confined
themselves to ordering an expedition to protect the Boiotian
cities.

Having got his way, Agisilaos waived his right of command,
with the pretext of being over sixty – although the infirmities of
age did not prevent him from leading many more armies
subsequently. I believe that he hoped Kleombrotos would take
up his first command with the youthful exuberance of
Agesipolis in Argolis, and move on Thebes as Agesipolis had
attacked Argos.

Our march took us past Eleutherai, between Megara and
Thebes. There we encountered my old friend Chabrias, who had
arranged the ambush we fell into on Aigina. He was now a
general, and stood with a force of Athenian peltasts, blocking
the way to the town.

Eleutherai was not one of the places that had appealed to us:
so Kleombrotos did not engage the Athenians – much to the
disappointment of Sphodrias – but turned west, taking the hard
mountain road to go to the aid of Plataia.

The top of the pass was held by a band of Thebans, who had
more the look of criminals than soldiers, and probably were.
The returning exiles had opened the prisons. Sphodrias took
some of our peltasts, and went on ahead to engage them. He
returned from the skirmish looking quite pleased with himself,
and reported that the Thebans were dead to a man. His own

421

casualties were a few men with superficial wounds.

Whatever Thebans had been menacing Plataia departed, as soon as news reached them that we were on our way. We rested only a day or two after the hard march, and then proceeded north to the aid of Thespiai. Having accomplished our purpose, we turned to Dog's Head in Theban territory, where we set up our circle of tents and encamped sixteen days. Kleombrotos may have been a novice commander, but he was a seasoned soldier.

"Having seen so much flat country in Attica and Boiotia, I no longer wonder that small good has come of it," I said, as we warmed ourselves by the fire in front of our tent.

"What I wonder is what we are doing here at all," Kleombrotos replied.

Sphodrias stared.

Kleombrotos was known for his courage in the field – and to Sphodrias battle, like beauty, constituted its own reason for existence. There was something of the Bronze Age in Sphodrias. It did not matter greatly to him who the enemy was, or why we fought, so long as the occasion offered a good war.

"We are the arbiters of the peace," he protested.

"Within reason," Kleombrotos said shortly. "It is not in our interest to involve ourselves in every squabble in Hellas."

"Sparta is the shield of the Peloponnesos," Sphodrias argued.

"This is not the Peloponnesos," Kleombrotos replied.

"You mean we are not going to fight the Thebans?"

KIeombrotos could not contain his laughter at Sphodrias's fallen face, "Not if I have anything to do with it."

The King had ordered his army to behave as though it were in friendly territory when we reached Dog's Head. He made a short, incisive speech, saying that any man found guilty of plunder or rape would be executed. Behaviour was exemplary.

"Then why are we in Theban territory?"

"My orders are to protect the Boiotian cities. Not to make war on Thebes. Sphodrias, we could have long been reconciled with Thebes if we gave them a free hand in Boiotia."

"But the cities…"

"If they would be rid of Thebes, let them choose a war-leader from amongst themselves, and fight for their freedom."

"We fought for Corinth."

"Corinth is in the Peloponnesos, Sphod'," I reminded him.
"If we were meant to protect the whole of Hellas, Herakles
would not have given us a country in the south of the south."

"You wanted to fight for cities in Asia, Cockerel." Sphodrias
would not retreat. "Thebes is becoming entirely too thick with
Athens for my liking," He essayed diversionary tactics.

"There you have it." Kleombrotos jumped on the point.
"Thebes' ambitions are limited to Boiotia. Athens' ambitions are
limitless."

Sphodrias brightened. If Kleombrotos simply wanted a
change of enemies, it was all right by him. He allowed that it
might be best to war on Athens.

Kleombrotos smiled into his wine cup. His smile was all that
filled it. He had the habit of holding a cup long after he had
emptied it, as if he enjoyed the feel of it in his hand. Pausanios
had done the same.

"No, Sphodrias. All Hellas has had enough of war. But I
think we had ought to keep a wary eye on Athens. And we will
not do that by making bitter enemies of the Thebans. Look at a
map, my friend."

Sphodrias was not thinking of maps as he heated his wine
over the fire. I doubt that he took in all Kleombrotos said. Finer
points bored him. He attacked a concept much as he attacked an
enemy. With great verve and little heed. Generous as always, he
was pleased to leave Kleombrotos the undisputed victor in the
field of debate. On our sixteenth day at Dog's Head, messengers
rode in from Thespiai, saying that a Theban army was again
marching on that city. We struck camp and marched back, but,
if that Theban army had existed anywhere but in the fears of the
Thespians, it had departed by the time we arrived. Still, they
were uneasy and asked Kleombrotos to leave a Spartan garrison
for their protection.

It was while the King discussed the request with the city
leaders, that I saw Nikomedes. He stood alone, watching a
boxing competition between some of the younger officers. I
stood alongside him and said, "Let us show these fellows real
boxing, Nikomedes."

He spoke without turning his head. "A traitor is hardly the
sparring partner for a tent-companion of the King,"

"You over-esteem the memories of those lads in your regiment."

He turned. His eyes flashed. "You seem to forget that I, too, am Corinthian. Do you think I loved the Argives?"

"Nikomedes, I only know that it is simpler to be Spartan than Corinthian."

"Well, understand this. I hated them as much as any man. But those were my prime years. It is not like past times, when a strong man could take time out from war, enter the Games, and have a chance. Athenians have made it a trade. I simply hadn't time to go into exile. I took the laurel at Delphi. I was crowned at Nemea and the Isthmus. Only Olympia eludes me. And always will..."

"Perhaps not."

He laughed shortly. "You know better. Ask yourself whether you are the boxer you were two years ago. We are nearly of an age."

Two years previously I consistently bested Kleombrotos. Now we were evenly matched.

He let my silence reply. "For all I knew, the Argives might have stayed another twenty years. Or forever. Accept it. I sold my good name for an olive crown I shall never have."

"Then why did you volunteer for this campaign,"

"I had some mad notion of redeeming my name in battle." He had meant to die. He smiled wryly. "Like all my dreams, it was made of poor clay."

"Nikomedes, it will pass."

"You do not understand, You Spartans have never been conquered."

"Friendship is not beyond our limited understanding."

"I know that, Leotychides. It is friendship that keeps me out of your way."

"To ask a friend to despise you is asking too much of friendship. Someone came up and told me that the King wanted me. I resolved to argue it with Nikomedes another time. Kleombrotos sat at the table in his tent, looking none too pleased. "I think this false alarm was a ruse to get us back, in order to get their garrison," he said. "I have agreed to let them have one-third of each contingent of the allied troops. To defend their city only."

424

"They are not Lakedaimonian, Kleombrotos. They might disobey your orders and raid Thebes."

"I'm putting them under a Spartan military governor. That was part of the agreement with the Thespians."

He looked at me tentatively and then turned to Sphodrias, who fairly glowed at the prospect. Later, Kleombrotos told me that I had looked like a man waiting to be condemned. So he appointed Sphodrias governor of Thespiai.

The King gave the new governor all the money he had with him in the event of it being necessary to hire mercenaries. He admonished the incandescent Sphodrias that he would be held personally responsible if either the troops or the Thespians provoked an incident with Thebes. Sphodrias inflated with dignity, as he had whenever Dorieus put him in charge of some duty in the flock. Then Kleombrotos led us back to Peloponnesos and disbanded the army, having carried out his orders without causing war between Sparta and Thebes.

Chapter 19

Kleombrotos became a familiar sight about the city on his fine chestnut, his short cloak flying in the wind of his speed. Unlike Agisilaos, he used a king's prerogative to ride within the City. He had no time to waste on walking.

When Pausanios and Agesipolis wanted to see a man, they invited him to the Agiad palace. Kleombrotos rode out, found him at whatever he was doing, said what he had to say, and was off again.

I was teaching some nineteen-year-old eirens the dance to Apollo one day, when Kleombrotos turned up. He drew me to the side, without giving me time to wipe the sweat from my face.

"I put your proposal about flocks for the sons of Lesser Spartiates to the Council," he said.

"*My* proposals?"

"You told me they were given no training." He spoke impatiently. "They all agreed with me when we discussed it, but only seven voted for it."

"Agesipolis once said that Agisilaos privately sets them against one another."

"Agisilaos again."

About a month later, I was excused from Hall for hunting, and formed a party with Kallias, Anaxandros and some other flock-brothers. Just before dawn, the King came trudging up the mountain-slope.

"By Zeus, Leotychides," Kleombrotos said. "You can be a hard man to find." He took my hunting knife, and speared a piece of Kallias's bread, while his eyes took in the men with me and ascertained they were to be trusted. "I have been watching Agisilaos in Council, since we had that talk. What confounded me was how intelligent Members of the Council could be set against one another, without knowing it. That was why I almost missed it."

"I'm glad it was obvious to you, Kleombrotos," Anaxandros said. "Because none of this makes sense to me."

426

"It's a way he has of making himself unobtrusive. Not one of them would think of him, because he seems so...well... almost invisible. Does it make sense to you, Leotychides?"

I recalled the self-effacing Agisilaos waiting with the youths and women to present the leader with the ox and gown, the deferent Agisilaos walking in the shadow of Lysander.

"Yes, he can use insignificance as a shield."

The sky was paling. Kallias tested the shaft of his spear. Kleombrotos was deep in thought. "Before I went to my flock, I used to listen when Father was teaching Agesipolis about kingship. It was something to do. I think I recall him saying, once, that there were penalties for kings who tried to be greater than kings, but none for kings who tried to be less..."

"Why would a king try to be less?" Anaxandros asked.

"I think Ages' had asked him some idiotic question that he was answering." His words slowed, like those of a man speaking his thoughts aloud. "But if a king were trying to become greater by *pretending* to be less..." He leapt to his feet. "Give me a spear. We'd best get that boar before it gets us."

The ephors fined Agisilaos for trying to become greater than a king by appearing to be less.

There was the usual excitement of an election day. Any competitor stirs the blood. There are always a few people who come along out of curiosity to see who will put himself forward for election, although it is generally known in the dining-halls who the serious candidates will be; and the votes have already been decided in the gymnasium, the hot baths, and the racing courses.

On my way to the Assembly, I dropped into my armourer's workshop near the Babykon bridge. He was a great, full-bearded, up-country man, whom Etymokles had justly recommended as the best in Sparta. The armour had already been fitted to me, and he shouted to his apprentice to bring sketches of the designs from the decorations.

I approved the Twin Gods rescuing Helen from Theseus for the breast-plate, praised the fine work on Achilles's shield and Patroklos's sword on the back-piece.

"You haven't decided on the winged horses for the shoulders,

General," he reminded me. "Or will it be the winged lions?"

"Just a pair of winged cockerels will do," Euagoras said, as he came in with Anaxandros.

They had met in the ephors' building, after paying their unmarried men's fines yet another year, both having been born in the month of Geraistos.

"The shield for Master Euagoras!" the armourer shouted to an apprentice.

Euagoras was a commander of fifty, like Anaxandros, but he preferred his title of chorus-master. He had changed little over the years. With his slight build, he still appeared much like a youth of nineteen; if one overlooked his battle scars and the faint lines at the corners of his eyes. Anaxandros was still untouched by spear or sword.

"Do you think Meleas will be elected?" Euagoras asked.

"He could have been an ephor years ago."

"Then why have you been canvassing so hard? That black horse of yours has been seen further south than Amyklai."

"That was for Etymokles."

"But he is an Agisilaos man," Anaxandros protested.

"Three Agisilaos men will put themselves forward. He is the best." And he might feel he owed me a vote when the ephors discussed flocks for sons of Lesser Spartiates. "So I have been persuading men who will support an Agisilaos man anyway not to ruin his chances by dividing their vote."

"They listen to *you!*"

"How not? I have been arguing the contrary."

"You are becoming quite a politician, Leo'," Anaxandros said. "By the gods, Euagoras, you haven't had Muses cast for your shield?"

The question was rhetorical for, on one side of the lamda, Euterpe stood; on the other Erato.

"I am constant to music and poetry, in war as in the City."

"The only time you have been constant in your life," Anaxandros gibed.

"I loved only once. Vainly." We stepped out into the road. "But I am easily consoled."

A large number of people gathered around the mushroom-shaped roof that kept the light drizzle of rain off the otherwise open Assembly benches. Many were Lesser Spartiates.

Somehow word had reached them that this election could affect them, and they turned out to watch the voting.

At the end of the session, we had five new ephors. Meleas, Etymokles, and three men who were as yet uncommitted on what was becoming an increasingly open contest between the two Kings.

"I'm going to give you some advice," Anaxandros said, as we threw the discus.

"Please don't," Hekataios pleaded.

Shortly after the election for ephors, two Elders died, and we had to replace them next Assembly Day. Chairon asked me whether it was always necessary to replace fools with fools. I told him it was, if only fools put themselves up for election, and suggested that he stand if he wanted to change the pattern.

"You see, Cockerel," Anaxandros went on. "Men listen to you because they say, 'Leotychides is famous for discipline, but his men like him. He sits a horse better than any man in Sparta, but he goes on foot. His wife wears a linen peplos in summer, but it is honest booty and not a thing purchased from a trader. And if his armour is somewhat ostentatious...well, everyone likes the sight of a handsome general.'"

"I wasn't aware you thought so highly of me, Magpie."

"I haven't said I agree. But when you attack the new land law, they say you are immoderate."

"Is Lykourgos immoderate?"

"He is a god. You are not. It's your turn to throw. And if you are going to be immoderate, build a house in the City."

My discus went awry. Kallias burst into laughter.

News reached Sparta from several cities that Athens had approached them, in an attempt to replace Lakedaimon as arbiter of the peace.

The Athenians broke the terms of the peace immediately after signing it, by sending their fleet to Methymna and Byzantion, to coerce them into what they euphemistically termed an alliance. We overlooked it. We took no action against Athens when she intrigued with the Olynthian league. We could not disregard this

429

new affront.

The ephors sent an embassy to Athens to persuade her peacefully to put aside her old ambitions.

"I assume that if Kleombrotos wants war with Athens, Agisilaos will want peace," Hekataios said. "Or the other way about."

We had spent the afternoon visiting the flock where both Leonidas and the small son of Hekataios had been assigned. Leonidas, in his rhodibas dignity, ignored that lowly seven-year-old with the long, bright carrot hair.

"For once they are in agreement. Both want peace. Kleombrotos, because he knows that Hellas is bled by war. Agisilaos, because he is interested only in fighting Thebes."

"Cockerel, don't you exaggerate this Theban madness?"

"Hek', I was in the King's dining-hall the night he was told that Phoibidas had seized the Kadmea. He played the shocked and angry man, but his eyes were cool and knowing." I told myself it was not breaking the secrecy of Hall to describe a man's face. "I saw him at Piraeum, as you know." When Agisilaos had not recognised the mad-eyed young soldier behind the helmet. "Then he was truly taken by surprise." One never forgets the face of a man one intends to murder. "I tell you, he was playing a part in Hall."

"Sometimes I think that this peace has brought us nothing but war. Let Athens have our place and pay the price."

"Where we pay, Athens would profit."

Hekataios picked a mulberry from a tree without looking up. The flock was encamped near Sellasia, where ours had been so many years ago; each step of the path well-remembered. "I welcomed the peace. You opposed it. Now you defend it, and I question it. Does time change everything?"

"Only some things."

"Your father was right, Leo'. We should have destroyed Athens."

"He changed his mind, and Meleas insists that they have some good and reasonable men."

"They are very silent." We were on the main road to the City now, the trees at the side weighted with olives.

"Iphikrates leads the extreme democrats. Men who earn their living by war. And Timotheus, the son of Konon, is as

430

ambitious and tricky as his father was. If you want the subtleties of Athenian politics, ask Meleas." The approach of evening strengthened the scent of matthiola flowers. "Hek', I saw the Monkey at Torone..."

I told him of the encounter, as we took the turn that gave us a glimpse of the river-bridge before a curve in the road took it out of view again.

"Well, the Lesser Spartiates can rise to platoon leader in their own regiments now..." He was looking at something ahead.

Beyond the shrine of Hermes, a number of laurel trees stood. The shower of their silver-grey leaves created a roof over a soft, grassy place, where a stream took a wilful way from the river. The roseate sunset, turning blue-grey, played tricks with time and distance.

"That eiren will be in trouble with his commander when he is late back for the evening meal," Hekataios said.

What I had mistaken for shadows under the laurel trees were two youths, their heads close together, almost touching.

"He won't be late, Hek'. He will see a certain shadow lengthen on that rock, and then run to his flock as he would for an olive crown. And arrive just in time."

A breeze parted the tree branches, casting light on the hair of the younger lad. Hair the colour of an autumn leaf. His companion was a young man of fighting age.

"That is Sphod's son," Hekataios said. "And–"

He, too, had recognised the son of Agisilaos.

I stepped on to the narrower path, which led us out of the way of the two under the laurel tree. "Have I told you the Inspector of Boys has asked me to teach the Law in the flock?"

"Your wife and mother must be proud."

"My mother would be pleased only if I were asked to be King. As for Kleonike – my wife is a musician, Hek'. Had I been asked to teach the lyre, she might think me great as Euagoras."

My younger son Agis was a first-year rhodibas in the flock where I taught. Recalling the inspired lessons of Diopeithes, I called upon the boys for the meaning, as well as faultless recitation of the rhetrae. If any boy hesitated or stumbled over a reply, Agis supplied it for them.

I clouted him each time, to no noticeable effect. I cannot say with honesty that I was angered. There is that weakness in fathers that takes pleasure in seeing their own qualities, even the less admirable ones, repeated in their sons.

Of the eirens, Kleonymos, the son of Sphodrias, was by far the most outstanding. His ready comprehension put a sore temptation upon his teachers not to neglect other boys in the joy of giving knowledge to that eager, keen mind. He disturbed my dreams.

All his teachers exacted a higher standard from the brilliant youth. As we took our midday meal, it was the name of Kleonymos that came up most often, whether it was his excellence in the law, the lyre, poetry and games. I gave him the love that pretends not to be.

It was our duty to judge the boys as well as teach them. To recognize potential commanders amongst the patrol leaders, and to pass on their names to the Inspector of Boys. Perhaps even to find a boy worthy to lead the thieves, or the defenders, at the altar of Artemis Orthia. In Kleonymos we found such a youth. My love became the love of a teacher.

One day, as I left the flock encampment, Agis waited near the road. The shears had clipped his look of the child Dionysos, along with his long, fair, curls; but the shorn head revealed its perfect shape, and accentuated the flawless symmetry of his fine features.

"Have you no duties, Agis?"

"Gathering herbs, Father. I have done it."

"You must be very quick about it." I had seen him playing a ball-game, when I dismissed the melleirens.

"I take them from stupid boys when they are not looking." His sapphire eyes honoured me with the shared secret. "Father, why don't you ride a horse here?"

"Because my legs are strong enough to walk."

Another rhodibas came up and stood off hesitantly. The grey eyes under the dark stubble of hair were grave.

Agis scowled. "Go away, Doreius. He's *my* father."

Chairon's son was as quick to learn as mine, but he flaunted his knowledge less.

"Agis, if you know your rhetrae as well as you think you do, you would know that all the fathers of Sparta are fathers to all their sons. Doreius's father has as much right to thrash you as I have."

Agis smiled beatifically. "He's old and can't hit as hard."

I might have given him an example then, had a rider not galloped up, leading a second horse, and diverted my attention.

"What is it you wanted, Doreius?" I asked, as the rider dismounted.

"Sir, some boys called me a liar when I told them you talked to me about your olive crown. Did you? I was young then."

"You did not lie. It was at the Lykourgos—" The rider walked towards me. "If any boy calls you a liar for it, send him to me."

The boys admired the horses, while the rider asked a word with me.

"Sir, the King wishes to see you urgently. I have brought you a mount."

Kleombrotos sprang to his feet when I entered the room. "Sphodrias has invaded Attica."

The King paced the room as he talked; his finger ploughed hair standing at attention from his brow. "I trusted the man. My brother trusted him. I appointed a traitor."

"Sphod' a traitor, Kleombrotos? Impossible."

He wheeled about to face me. "Athens wants war." He took a spear from the wall. I thought he might hurl it like a thunderbolt, but he rolled it about in his hands. "We have refused to be provoked. Even now, we have an embassy there, trying to convince her of her folly. If Iphikrates's mob hasn't killed them, Sphodrias has given her precisely what she wants. The Athenians paid Sphodrias to invade."

"Wealth means nothing to Sphodrias. Could he not have misconstrued some order?"

"You heard me order him to defend Thespiai, and go to the aid of any other Boiotian city under attack. Eleusis is neither Boiotian or under attack."

"He attacked Eleusis?" An easy walk from Athens.

He marched by night. He reached Eleusis at dawn, and plundered the countryside. In broad daylight. So there could be no doubt it was a Spartan governor."

"Kleombrotos, there must be some explanation. Not

433

necessarily a logical one. Sphodrias is loyal. I have known him almost the whole of my life. There is no deceit in the man."

"Forgive me if I do not share your certainty. I can almost hope I am wrong." He sat down, his chin on his hands. I had seen a defeated Argive sit just that way once, his helmet on his shield. He had fought well, but we had simply been too much for him. The King looked up. "For whatever the truth of it, there is only one way to avert war with Athens. You know it, too."

The ephors ordered Sphodrias back to Sparta to stand trial for his life.

The horses ran free in the field. There is a poetry to running horses. My training-chariot lay idle where I left it, when one of the reins snapped.

Kleonike left off talking to the steward, and came to stand beside me as I watched the horses.

"Your mother is right, Leotychides. There are far too many."

A fine, black colt arrested my attention. I was partial to blacks. Perhaps because of Dancer. There had never been another like Dancer. Sheer fancy. Horse and rider had been young together.

"Why sell them? We want for nothing."

"It is a long way for men to walk here, to talk of elections and promotions."

"They need not. I can see them in the City."

"There is more dignity in inviting them to your house."

I glanced at her. "Those words have the ring of Mistress Argileonis. Not you, Kleonike."

"They are nonetheless true."

"Kleonike, it concerns Aristokrates that his line will die with him." He had at last spoken.

"He must divorce his wife. She bears him nothing but deformed offspring to be exposed. Everyone knows her two brothers had to be left at the Apothetas. That is why she is so great an heiress."

"He married her to please his father. Not for her wealth."

"His father did him no favour. Tell him to divorce her."

"He is too kind to put her aside for something that is not of her making. But he asked me whether I knew a fine woman

434

who would bear him a strong son. Such as ours."

"I know of no such woman. When desire is lacking, strong life cannot come of it." She put her hand to her hair, to protect it from the breeze. "I have been asked to lead the hymn to Artemis, so I must live chastely for the year. You will tell this to Aristokrates."

"Kleonike, it is a very great honour to serve Artemis, but the entire city will know soon enough."

She took the reins from my hand. "At the time your aunt approached my mother on your behalf, Aristokrates sent his mother to ask for me in marriage. Do not hurt a friend unnecessarily."

It seemed Aristokrates was fated to love in vain.

"You are wise, Kleonike. I am a fool."

"I am not wise, but sometimes you are a fool, Leotychides. Polydora asked me–"

"No, Kleonike. I will sell the horses. I will build a house in the City. But do not ask me anything on Mistress Polydora's behalf."

"I think I understand what Sphod' was trying to do," Anaxandros said. We were meeting at his house on the edge of the City. The wine-cups were filled again. "He intended to go further, but only got as *far* as Eleusis."

"Why decide to withdraw from Boiotia at all?" Pityas wondered.

"Sphodrias does not take decisions," I told him. "Decisions take Sphodrias."

"I doubt he was coming back to the Peloponnesos, Leo'. You know how he always admired Phoibidas. I think he was going to seize Piraeus, as Phoibidas took the Kadmea."

"Don't tell that to the ephors," Aristokrates said. "Or you will put the poisoned cup in his hand. How does Meleas stand, Leo'?"

"He had high hopes for the negotiations with Athens. He is not well disposed towards Sphodrias."

"Phoibidas was only fined," Anaxandros spoke hopefully.

"Phoibidas was successful," Aristokrates retorted.

"All this isn't helping Sphod'." Hekataios cut in. "Leo', you all but told me that Agisilaos saved Phoibidas."

"Sphod' has never made a secret of his hostility to Agisilaos," Anaxandros reminded him. "Don't look for any help from that quarter."

"I wasn't thinking of Agisilaos. Kleombrotos could speak for him. Sphod' might have misunderstood an order."

"Kleombrotos never gives imprecise orders."

"He may have, once."

"Hek'. I heard him give Sphodrias his orders. They were incapable of misconstruction."

"He could stretch a point. A man's life is at stake."

"The Athenians will only release our ambassadors, and accept our apology, if Sphodrias's life is the earnest of our sincerity."

"Hades take the Athenians!" Hekataios shouted. "Haven't they invaded foreign territory without cause?"

"It is not our way," Aristokrates interposed.

"All Sphod' did was plunder a bit of country and withdraw."

"Hek', you are talking wildly."

"Leo', only Kleombrotos can save Sphod'. He's your cousin. Sphod' is his friend. He is *your* friend. Kleombrotos is King–"

"And because he is King, he cannot set himself above the Law."

"The Law. Is that it?" He was on his feet. "Well, Hades take your Law and you, too, General *Rhetrae!* Sphod' was old enough to ruin himself when he went to Herea with you. When those boys whispered that you were involved in Kinadon's plot, Sphod' thrashed them. He is barely civil to Antal since he became friendly with Agisilaos. He has given you a lifetime of loyalty. A lifetime of loyalty to his friends, and all you do is spout the Law."

"Hek', there is nothing I will not do myself to help him, but Kleombrotos is not a private citizen."

The freckled face was grim. "Well, answer me this, General Rhetrae. Were it Doreius on trial for his life, would you stop at anything to save him?"

"Doreius would never have done such an idiotic thing," I shouted back.

He no longer listened. Hekataios's face had always been easy to read. It was not anger that propelled him from the house.

Recalling the evening we had stumbled on the pair under the trees, I knew precisely where he had gone. I let him go.

The Athenians released our ambassadors. Sphodrias's impending trial was the talk of the halls. To Sphodrias's friends, it was obvious that Hekataios had employed successful tactics in a futile strategy to save him.

All Sparta knew that Agisilaos, who doted upon his children, was avoiding his son, and that Archidamos avoided Kleonymos. It was not difficult to surmise that the king was unwilling to hear his son plead for his friend's father. Nor that Archidamos was ashamed to face the beautiful youth, having failed him.

I fell in with Etymokles, by the statue of the People of Sparta in the agora, one day, and we stopped to talk. He had been one of our three ambassadors in Athens when Sphodrias invaded.

"I can't conceive how Athenians are considered a clever people," he said "We were stopping in the Spartan consul's house when they came to arrest us. Did the fools think that we should have been in the first place they would look, had we been deceiving them with a peace mission to cover a surprise invasion?"

"At least you were spared the Pit."

He laughed shortly. "Okyllos thought that would be the next step. They kept us under heavy guard, until the order went out for Sphodrias's arrest. We were only released when the ephors agreed that the evidence of his guilt was unquestionable."

"Then his execution is a certainty?"

"By Zeus, not if Agisilaos has anything to do with it."

"Agisilaos!"

"Whenever the matter is mentioned, he says that, although Sphodrias is guilty beyond doubt, he has been an honourable man all his life, and that Sparta needs soldiers like him. It's the boy, of course. He could never refuse his son anything."

Sphodrias, being Sphodrias, did not appear for his trial. He was tried in absentia and acquitted nonetheless. Athens immediately declared war on Sparta, and signed an alliance with Thebes.

Agisilaos was criticized for having brought Lakedaimon to war for the whims of his son, but others praised Sphodrias for attempting to bring down a treacherous enemy. Sphodrias had always been popular. He returned to Sparta, quite pleased with himself.

As the Athenians prepared for war, Agisilaos induced the ephors to send him on a campaign against Thebes; his years lay less heavily on him than they had the previous year. Like an aged child, he sallied that he would be delighted to obey his orders.

"I wasn't afraid to die," Sphodrias said. "Had I been condemned in absentia, I would have died by my own hand."

I had taken the midday meal with Kleombrotos, who ordered that the remains not be removed from the sight of Sphodrias, who was pointedly told to come after the repast.

"Then why skulk over the border in Arkadia?" the King demanded.

"Because I didn't want Polydora and Kleonymos to see me lashed through the streets of Sparta. Or whatever death Agisilaos arranged for me." Had the spectacle of Kinadon's execution been the innovation of Agisilaos? "I'm sorry I bungled it. Kleombrotos. It was the allies. They can't night-march as we do. If I'd had Spartans, we would have been in Piraeus, and taken it before dawn. There are no gates on the port, you know."

"So you decided to plunder the countryside instead?" Kleombrotos's question was deceptively quiet. "To be certain, no Athenian could mistake your presence as transit to Attica from some other territory."

"That was the mercenaries, Hades take them! They got out of hand. They've no discipline."

"You dare to speak of discipline!" Kleombrotos exploded. "Can't you understand I am trying to fathom why you tried to seize Piraeus at all."

"It was the Thebans who suggested it. Good types. Rather like Epaminondas and Pelopidas, Leo'." He could have chosen a fortunate example. "In fact, they know them," he went on, to make it worse.

"What were they doing in Thespiai?"

"They came to see me. They had been members of Leontiades's party. Very friendly to Sparta. They warned me that Athens was intriguing...Well, you said that yourself, Kleombrotos."

"All Hellas knows that Athens always intrigues."

"They were very certain that, if we held Piraeus, Athens would be helpless. They had it very well thought out, and they felt I was the only man who could do it."

It was all too easy to envision the Thebans flattering Sphodrias, in order to incite an incident that would bring Athens to commit herself to the cause of Theban domination over Boiotia. Recalling that Pelopidas and Epaminondas had been with us in Mantinea, and observed Sphodrias there, I wondered whether they had sent the men to him.

"You see, after they had taken Piraeus, they were going to – do you mind if I sit down, Kleombrotos?"

"Whether you sit or stand on your hands is immaterial to me," Kleombrotos stated coldly. "By Zeus, Sphodrias, all I want to know is whether I appointed a fool or a traitor as Governor of Thespiai."

"Traitor...? You are jesting."

"Jesting? When you have plunged Sparta into war. The gods know I have tried to keep peace with Thebes. To avoid war with Athens, by negotiating from a position of strength. But you have played into the hands of our enemies, and set them in alliance against us. What am I to think? Don't look at Leotychides. He is neither your judge, nor your advocate. I asked him here, as a man well-disposed to both of us, should my anger unbalance my judgement."

I think only then did Sphodrias appreciate what he had done.

"Sire," he said. "I will swear, by any and all of the gods, I am no traitor."

After a long moment, Kleombrotos spoke. "I believe you. You have my permission to leave."

"Are you dismissing me?"

"Go and serve Agisilaos. He saved you."

"Agisilaos! Agisilaos saved me?"

"Agisilaos, and two young men, who are better, if no wiser, than their fathers. I would not have spared you."

"Then I owe Agisilaos my life and my gratitude. I shall acknowledge it freely and publicly. But I dislike the man, and nothing can alter that. It may have started because he robbed

Leotychides, but for years I have detested him on merit." It was difficult to remain angry with Sphodrias. "By the gods, those Thebans made a fool of me!"

"They hadn't much work to do," Kleombrotos muttered.

"Sir, if it will end the war, I am still prepared to take my life."

"It would accomplish nothing, and I would rather have you a live fool than a dead one."

Sphodrias turned his head into his cloak briefly, then faced his king again.

"Demote me to the lowest place on your staff, Kleombrotos, but do not dismiss me from your command."

Chapter 20

The Athenians sent their fleet to *invite* all the cities of the Hellenes to a conference in Athens, to appoint themselves arbiters of the peace they now claim always to have opposed.

They reaffirmed the rights of the Great King as overlord of all Asia, including the Greek cities that they now maintain they have always championed against the barbarian. Their proposal was a new alliance on the basis of the standing peace.

To calm old fears, Athens guaranteed that none of her citizens would be permitted to acquire land or houses in the new confederacy. She also renounced her old claims on her former possessions, but the confederation would be ordered by a Council, which could take no decision without the consent of their chief city. That was, of course, Athens.

The confederacy would maintain a large fleet, paid for by contributions to be fixed by the Council. It was not tribute, the Athenians insisted, although Athens was to have the management of the fund, and leadership of this not-empire in war. Defeat had taught the Athenians tact, if nothing else.

The Athenian fleet sailed about the Aigean. Paxos and its neighbouring islands immediately reacted. They had paid the price of resistance in the past. All the states of Euboia – that long island stretching from Lokris down to Attica – entered the confederacy, with the exception of the city of Oreos. It had a strong fortress that enabled it to defend itself, and its alliance with Sparta. With the return of her old subjects of Chios, Mytilene Methymna, Byzantion and Rhodes, Athens was again the ruling power of the Aigean, with a firm Theban hand keeping Boiotia subdued on the northern border of Attica.

Agisilaos led an expedition to Boiotia that accomplished very little. No, that is untrue. General Chabrias prepared his hoplites to meet the Spartan force, by ordering them to put one knee on the ground and firmly rest their spears on the other, as they covered themselves with their shields before the Spartan advance. Inducing the Athenian hoplites to stand firm was no mean achievement. Agisilaos had the gift of inspiring the enemy.

Kleombrotos wanted to strike at Athens. The Athenians maintained their powerful fleet at great expense. Their allies were unhappy about the magnitude of their contributions. Thebes simply did not trouble to pay her share.

Kleombrotos argued that we only strengthened the strained alliance between Athens and Thebes with our invasions of Boiotia. Agisilaos was pressing for yet another. That year's ephors turned a friendly ear. He was ordered to Boiotia with an army. He did the Thebans as little real damage as he had the previous year. Thebes captured the fortress of Oreos, and then took the town. Our last ally in Euboia fell to the confederacy.

The following summer, Agisilaos ruptured a vein in his good leg, as he was walking from the shrine of Aphrodite to the government buildings, to press the ephors for still another campaign in Boiotia.

Sphodrias mentioned that Kleonymos had it from Archidamos that Agisilaos lost consciousness when a physician bled him. He was confined to his bed well into the winter, but it did not stop him pursuing the matter through his followers.

The ephors ordered a spring campaign in Boiotia. It was left for Kleombrotos to command it, which suited Agisilaos well enough. Our allies were to meet in Sparta, for a conference concerning the conduct of the war, when Kleombrotos would be absent.

Kleombrotos ordered the main body of the army to halt at the lower slopes of Mount Kithairon. He sent the peltasts ahead to seize the heights above the road, while we took a short break for the midday meal.

Before we finished, the peltasts came running back, to say that Theban and Athenian troops already occupied the heights. Kleombrotos ordered a council of war to convene after the meal, and finished the last of his bread, saying "More Spartan lives wasted to ensure Thebes remains loyal to Athens."

"We shall be fighting Athenians," Sphodrias said. "The Thebans leave it to them when they see Spartans."

"I shouldn't count on it, Sphod'," I advised him. "Maro said that they encountered some good Theban front-line troops in the last campaign. Agisilaos always brings out the best in the enemy."

Sphodrias laughed. "You sound like Antalkidas. Maro told me that when Agisilaos was wounded last time, Antalkidas told him they had been well-paid for teaching the Thebans how to fight when they didn't know how, and didn't even want to."

Kleombrotos looked up sharply. "Antalkidas, too, believes that Thebes is reluctant to war?"

"You can't trust Antalkidas," Sphodrias declared.

"One can trust a man's judgement without trusting the man. Nor am I certain that he is unworthy of trust."

"Kleombrotos!" I must have spoken forcefully. The king started to rise, his hand reaching for his shield. "No. It's not the enemy. Just a thought. Lykourgos forbade us to war more than three times against the same enemy. To prevent foreigners learning our methods of warfare." I quoted the rhetra.

"General Rhetrae!" Sphodrias laughed. "Sorry, Leo'. The Magpie told me." Truly there was no man like Sphodrias. Not only was he without rancour towards me for having been prepared to sacrifice him, but apologised for the knowing of it.

Kleombrotos absorbed the implication more readily.

"So this fourth campaign is unlawful..."

Agisilaos was less than pleased to see Kleombrotos back in time for the conference. The ephors were less than pleased with Agisilaos for having manipulated them into giving an unlawful order.

The speeches of the allied delegates varied only in degree of dissatisfaction with strategy that was wearing them down to little effect. The ephors supported Kleombrotos's proposal to block Athens. It was a move not calculated only to disrupt Athenian trade routes, but to cut off the corn-ships coming through the Hellespont, on which over-peopled Attica depended.

Our allies supported Kleombrotos, and offered so many ships, that the alliance would man almost as large a fleet as the confederacy.

The siege of Athens was successful. With sixty Spartan triremes in the waters around Aigina and Andros, the Athenian corn-ships got only as far as the port of Geraistos in Euboia. Then Athens sent out her own fleet to break the blockade. The

443

two fleets engaged in an action, which the Athenians won.

Agisilaos leapt upon the Athenian sea-victory as a pretext to redirect the theatre of operations to Boiotia. Kleombrotos argued that sound strategy had ought not to be abandoned because of one setback. That the many Boiotian campaigns had failed to achieve a decisive victory. That, left alone, Thebes would abandon Athens. That the other member-states of the confederacy were becoming increasingly reluctant to continue paying the contributions Athens demanded of them, and that, the more Athenian ships we sank, the more Athens would exact from her allies.

The defeat at sea had frightened the ephors. Land is the natural element of Spartans at war. They ordered another expedition to Boiotia. Kleombrotos argued in vain that it was not only unlawful but foolhardy. Agisilaos maintained that, sometimes, the exigencies of war demand a certain leniency in the interpretation of the Law.

Enemies sometimes inadvertently help one another in war. Thebes and Athens sent out a fleet of sixty triremes sailing around the Peloponnesos, under the command of Konon's son Timotheos. With an enemy fleet in our waters, we could not spare enough men to mount the Agisilaosian expedition against Thebes.

Fifty-five Spartan triremes engaged the Athenian sixty. Kleombrotos claimed the victory for Sparta. The Athenians claimed victory, also. I think the battle was inconclusive, but it achieved a victory against Agisilaos and his all-consuming hatred of Thebes.

The next year, the alliance between Athens and Thebes came to breaking point. The Thebans still had not paid their contributions. More importantly, Thebes was becoming too strong for Athens' liking. Those well-disciplined front-line fighting-men Maro observed had been formed into a separate regiment, and given special training by Pelopidas. They were all pairs of lovers, and consequently would fight valorously to shine in one another's eyes. They were known as the Sacred Band, for the solemn vows they took to fight together and die rather than submit.

Epaminondas, too, was showing himself to be a fine general. With the whole of Boiotia under Theban control, Athens reconsidered her position, and sent a peace embassy to Sparta. An enemy was preferable to a rival.

Kleombrotos maintained that Athens was the true enemy, and that only a decisive defeat would secure peace. He favoured reconciliation with Thebes. Agisilaos responded like a madman, although the Agiad King advocated a confrontation with the stronger enemy.

The ephors considered the Athenian approach too tempting to disdain. Athens negotiated a separate peace with Sparta. There was a short-lived truce. Timotheos broke it as soon as it was agreed.

The war continued.

I noted a new fashion amongst men recently turned thirty. When I became a citizen, I had been proud to put on the cloak that meant young warriors would address me as *sir*, and youths stand at my approach. Now, many of the newest citizens only wore short-sleeved tunics or young warriors' cloaks. The same new citizens also wore their hair combed straight back up from their brows.

I doubt that Kleombrotos was aware that he had created a fashion. The energetic young King was popular with the men he commanded. They knew that, although he was always to be found in the most dangerous place in battle, he was not careless of their lives.

This imitation was more than just the popularity of a brave and good-looking young king. Kleombrotos was a new spirit in Sparta. Or rather something of the spirit of an old Sparta, which his admirers were too young to have known.

One regiment pooled funds to raise a statue of Kleombrotos to stand in front of its barracks. Some of Agisilaos's friends declared their intention of erecting a statue of the Eurypontid King. Agisilaos declined the honour, and forbade any statues to be raised of him anywhere. Perhaps he intended his modesty to be a rebuke to Kleombrotos. Or he may have been sincere. Beware of a man with no small vanity. Such men are monsters of ego.

I was sent on an embassy to our allies in Italy and in Sicily. They remained well-disposed to us, true to the alliance, but the wars of the mainland are distant to these Hellenic cities. In Syracuse, I was able to visit Anaxilas. For eight days I was a guest in the luxurious good taste of his fine house.

Megakles called. He had grown quite stout. His talk was of cargoes, the rise of the price of grain, and the fall of silver. Or perhaps it was the other way about. We found little to say to one another.

Anaxilas gave small dinner parties. His friends made sharp jests about Athens, but the Carthaginians were closer. They talked of plays, of horses, and of wines, and capped one another's wit as a girl softly played a pleasant flute. The food was exquisite in appearance as well as taste. The wine superb. Leaves of gold entwined with myrtle in our garlands.

Anaxilas's passion for the fair Daphne had turned on another fashionable hetaira, who sat on the end of his couch. The one who graced my own was hardly less beautiful. It was easy to understand how Gylippos had succumbed to such luxuries. Had I not the fortune to be born Spartan, I would be Syracusan.

The following year Anaxilas came to Sparta on a private visit. We raced chariots. He won. He was my guest in Hall, where he found Antalkidas the wittiest and most charming of men. I presented him to Kleombrotos. At some point in the talk, I recall him saying, "To have peace on the mainland, sir, you must teach Athens to like black broth. Else she will always steal delicacies from the tables of others."

As we walked back to my house from the Agiad palace, Anaxilas said, "King Kleombrotos must be on his guard."

"You have heard something?"

"I am Syracusan. I can smell intrigue."

"You talked long with Antalkidas."

"Would that Syracuse had a man like him."

Anaxilas took his son back to Syracuse with him. He was pleased with the youth's appearance and good manners, although he soon had him cloaked in finer apparel. Clearly this son was his favourite. I do not know whether he ever became an admiral or a Games winner, but if he was as fine a man as his father, he did well. Too soon I dismissed Anaxilas's suspicions.

Once more, greybeards outnumbered younger citizens teaching in the flocks. I gave over my lessons in the rhetrae to an elder, because too often a fresh campaign interrupted. In one

446

of the interstices between hostilities, I talked every day with an Elder who was greatly learned in the nature of law. The talks were abruptly halted by a general mobilization. When I returned to Sparta, he was dead. I continued with another Elder. Again, war interrupted.

"Tell me this before you go," he demanded, his anger piercing his wisdom. "When the men in their prime have no time to learn, who will pass on knowledge when my generation have gone to the hall of Hades!"

I cannot say these were bad years altogether. There was the comradeship of the circle of fires, on the hard campaigning with Kleombrotos and Sphodrias. There was the taste of victory after a well-fought battle. There was that first sight of the white peaks of Taygetos, on the return to Lakedaimon. There were my sons growing up in the flocks.

Whenever possible, I trained the young Lesser Spartiates. Some of these lads were less prepared for war than I had been at twelve. Kallias and Anaxandros offered to assist me, but if I needed senior officers I had them.

Kleombrotos was pressing for permanent regiments for Lesser Spartiates, and promotion to commander of fifty within their own regiments for the bastards. I used the platoon leaders of those regiments as senior officers, to ready them for command.

Once, in the Bellamina country, after I divided them into the usual two armies, I led the advance directly into the midst of a mock battle between two boys' flocks. Immediately I ordered a retreat to the heights above that lovely green country, and left the field to the boys.

The young soldiers became quite partisan, cheering one flock or the other.

A swift-running eiren rushed towards his lines, unaware that he was heading into an ambush. A platoon leader I had commanded at Torone started to shout a warning. I silenced him.

The boy was captured. He kicked and butted himself free from the two who held him. With a tremendous effort, he hurled himself against the third, shoving him against his flock-brothers, retrieved his blunted spear, and dashed towards his

447

own lines, his setting-sun hair blowing in the wind of his speed.

"By Apollo!" I spoke aloud as the men cheered. "Well done, Leonidas."

"Do you know the lad, sir?" the platoon leader asked. His name was Ainesios, I recalled.

"He is my son."

"And you stopped me warning him!" That grim face went back further than Torone. Cavalry days. Lechion. The man I ordered flogged!

I began to explain that one cannot interfere in mock battles, and then cursed myself silently for a fool. The man was two or three years my senior. He would have been reared in a flock.

"You know, general, we're aware of what you try to do for us. The flocks for our sons..."

I had visited one of these flocks. The boys' drill was as smart as ours had been, but their instruction in letters, music and the law was haphazard. They were being trained for war and little else.

"What do your patrol leaders tell them? You are the lesser sons of Herakles?"

"Be careful, general. Someone might mistake you for one of us."

I met the mockery in his eyes. "You are quite aware that I am one of you."

"No, sir. You are not." He laughed shortly. "Although when you were our pentatarchos, we called you the greatest bastard in Sparta."

Only then did I understand why I had been dubbed General Pentatarchos in their secret language.

Leonidas's flock celebrated with victory games. I told the men I would ask the boys' commander whether we could be onlookers, as it would undoubtedly please the boys to be watched by real soldiers.

"It might also please the general to see his son," someone called out. The word had gone around.

Leonidas had become a tall, handsome, wide-shouldered youth, his face perhaps a bit too broad for true beauty, but he would be a fine figure of a man. Fortune was kind to show him to me that day, as it was almost four years before I saw him again.

448

A large Theban army was marching on Phokis. Kleombrotos was exultant.

"The Thebans have given us what we want!" he cried. "With the best of their men fighting in Phokis, they will be of little use to Athens. The Athenians will sue for peace before the year is out."

The tired boxer was not as resilient as he had once been. He could still deliver the blows, but his legs were unsteady.

The Phokians appealed to Sparta to rescue them once more. The vote in Assembly was so narrow we had to have a division, but we voted to stay out of the war in the north.

Agisilaos was furious. He called upon the Council to set aside the Assembly decision as unlawful, arguing that Sparta was bound by the peace to protect Phokis. Kleombrotos retorted that the peace was a shambles, with most of its signatories at war with each other; two cities claiming the right to enforce it, and pursuing their claims by force of arms. If we were arbiters of the peace, then let us defeat Athens and prove it indisputably.

"How did Agisilaos win the vote?" I asked Chairon, after the lengthy Council meeting ended.

"Agisilaos kept repeating that we had sworn solemn oaths to protect Phokis," Chairon said. "He sat there mouthing 'solemn oaths' every time Kleombrotos paused to take breath."

"What arguments did he use?"

"The usual. Thebes had to respect the independence of cities, and so on. But it was those 'solemn oaths' that did it. Old men feel strongly about such things." Chairon smiled thinly. "We young fellows voted with Kleombrotos, but there were not enough of us."

He jested about his age, but Chairon seemed to have grown younger since becoming an Elder. Perhaps having a young wife and a young son contributed to his rejuvenation. At twenty, I had called him Old Chairon. At thirty-eight, I no longer found him old. Past seventy, he looked a fit and hearty sixty.

"So, Agisilaos gets another Boiotian campaign."

"It's not only that." Chairon frowned "I'm not certain what it is. Usually, he is jubilant when he had his way. Tries to hide it, but he is. This time... The man has something in mind,

Leotychides."

The ephors ordered a general mobilization. Once again, Agisilaos decided he was too old to go to war. Once again, it was a pretext, as he led many another campaign. Kleombrotos was ordered to lead the allied forces.

The expedition to Phokis would ordinarily have required no more than the King's honour guard, his staff of thirty Spartiate officers, and two regiments of freed serfs or up-country volunteers, as well as the allied contingents.

Kleombrotos was given command of two fine Spartiate regiments, and a rather sorry-looking cavalry. As most of our allies were Peloponnesians, it would have been reasonable for the army to assemble somewhere in the peninsula, as it did ordinarily. The ephors requested the allies to send their contingents directly to Phokis.

Kleombrotos thought it madness, and made no secret of it, but the ephors would not alter the arrangements.

"At least, with Spartiate regiments, we'll have a quick victory," he resigned himself. "And get back to the real work."

Kleonymos had just turned twenty. He wanted to accompany his father. Sphodrias assured him that he would not be offended if his son preferred to fight alongside Archidamos, but Kleonymos was adamant. I wondered whether the young man feared his father might get into trouble again, without his restraining presence.

He proved his worth in the engagement that sent the Thebans well back into their own territory. He had Sphodrias's courage, but not his rashness; his generous spirit, but not his exuberance. If Sphodrias was the Bronze Age, Kleonymos was the Age of Gold.

The Thebans fled. Kleombrotos would not dignify the action with the name of a victory. He made no move to disband the army. I began to wonder whether he thought the repulse of the Thebans had been too easy, and feared another invasion. When the weather started to turn, the polemarch drew me aside.

He made a few references to restlessness among the allied troops. We were in friendly territory. There was no plunder. There was also no enemy. As one of the King's tent-companions, I was meant to pass it on.

Kleombrotos invited the messengers to take the midday meal

450

with us. One told us that the new ephors had appointed Mnassipos grand admiral. Mnassipos was a pleasant fellow in Hall. Likeable and well-liked. Once he approached me, to hint that he would like to serve under Kleombrotos as a polemarch. When I was unhelpful, he asked Antalkidas for a command. Also vainly. No man in Hall would recommend a fellow who filled his stomach surreptitiously before dining. Obviously, he achieved his ambitions elsewhere. (I must remember to delete this. I am breaking the secrecy of what is said in Hall).

Kleombrotos went into his tent after our repast, to search out his own skytali, as the letters are only gibberish until the code is placed over its corresponding part. As he wound the papyrus about the staff, his face registered disbelief, and then flushed with anger. The chief ephor had ordered the King to winter in Phokis. It was thought in Sparta that Thebes might invade in spring.

I decided to use the time to get the cavalry into shape, but most of the men were well over fifty; disfranchised men who had long lost hope of improving their lot. In their way, they were quite content in Phokis – as they were certain of regular meals, and there was no enemy to bother them. I tried to convince them that regular drill could save their lives, but I doubt whether they cared that much for them. Perhaps Teleutias might have breathed spirit into them. I was not Teleutias.

Prostitutes of both sexes set up business near our encampment. Vendors of useless things hawked their goods to the troops. Quarrels broke out. A dashing general in his late thirties – brilliant in battle, but bored in our static situation – failed to keep order. Kleombrotos removed him from his command, and promoted Kallias.

"Older men are better with northern troops," he explained.

Kallias was fifty. I had still thought of him as the young cavalry officer who came to the flock, looking for the Magpie.

When summer turned to autumn, Kleombrotos wrapped papyrus about his skytali to send an encoded message to the ephors. The papyrus lengthened as he detailed his reasons for believing no Theban attack was imminent, how the remoteness of Spartiate regiments from Peloponnesos could only encourage Athens, and concluded by reminding them that it was contrary to Spartan custom to keep a large army in foreign parts.

451

After the passing of several weeks, three Spartan officers rode in. With reinforcements. One bastard regiment, and another of full Spartiates.

Kleombrotos shared the midday meal with the messengers. Listened courteously, as they told how Konon's son Timotheus had fallen into a disgrace in Athens, and hired himself out as a mercenary to a Persian satrap. How we had lost Korkyra to Iphikrates, because Mnassipos had become corrupted by luxurious living on the island, and behaved like a drunken tyrant. The moment the repast finished, the King asked Kleonymos to see the messengers to their quarters. Then he rose abruptly, and disappeared.

I found Kleombrotos near a stream Kleonymos discovered one day, when we were hunting. The two pieces of skytali lay beside him: his wooden staff, and the papyrus of equal length the messenger had brought; the latter looking somewhat battered, as if he had been rolling it over the staff, trying to make the spiral letters spell out another message by repeated attempts.

He sat hurling stones, one after another, across the stream. "Leotychides, there are more citizens of Sparta in Phokis than in Lakedaimon."

The regiment that raised the statue to Kleombrotos outside its barracks had been with us from the outset. In the other two Spartiate regiments were a number of those men who imitated his dress and hair. Not a few important citizens who had been known to oppose Agisilaos were in this last-to-arrive.

"I wonder that Meleas escaped notice."

"Meleas is useful in negotiations with Athens."

"Are we negotiating?"

"What would I know, but what they would choose to tell me?" He interrupted his barrage of stones. "I am as good as banished. At least they gave my father a trial."

"You command this army, Kleombrotos. Disband it."

He looked in the direction of our encampment, where huts had replaced tents, giving it a more permanent aspect. "Do you know that I am more powerful than any king of Sparta since ancient times..." In Phokis, as commander, his will was absolute. He commanded more than half Sparta's citizens. "But I am powerless to do the one thing I would." He picked up the two pieces of the skytali, and balanced them on his knees. "They have bound me so with orders this time that we must stay here till we rot."

His bitter mood persisted in the tent. Sphodrias tried to lighten it.

"Remember our first campaign in Boiotia, Kleombrotos? By the gods, I've never seen anything to equal the storm that blew when we crossed the mountains on our way back. That wind blew men over the cliff and into the river, as if they were thistle-down. Even donkeys with heavy burdens. It was a sight. Nearly went over myself," he concluded cheerfully.

Kleombrotos did not reply.

"You make it all sound quite jolly, Father," Kleonymos said.

"Amazing the way the Magpie hasn't a scratch to show for all his campaigns." Sphodrias tried again. "As if some god covered him in a mist."

Kleombrotos stared intently at a corner of the tent.

Sphodrias was not one to give up. "Some of the new men told me an amusing story about a mad Mantinean, Kleombrotos."

The King muttered something vague without shifting his gaze.

"Who is he, Father?" Kleonymos asked, and reached for his lyre.

"A merchant called Lykomedes. He is trying to persuade the Arkadians to come and live in some great monster city he intends building. All Arkadia, no less, is to be ruled from this city."

The howling wind replied.

Sphodrias continued, undaunted. "He put his plan to the Council of Tegea. They laughed him out."

I put aside my lyre. Kleonymos had a better touch. We fell into silence. Kleonymos. Played on. The lamp burned low.

Kleombrotos came out of his thoughts like a man from sleep. "Is it true, Leotychides, that you wanted to expose me?" he asked. How far back he had been. And how far away.

The King did not often give way to despair, and then only in the privacy of his tent with his close friends. Once, after he had

453

to execute a good soldier for raping a Phokian, and killing her husband. Another time, when he found it necessary to order one of his own flock-brothers flogged.

Usually, he was to be seen among the men, his head thrown back, laughing at this or that comment, exchanging gibe for gibe, shouting orders at a slack company, or competing in the games he organized to break the meaningless pattern of our days.

On the boxing-ground, the little between us turned to his favour. He was a fine runner and, had his duties in Sparta not taken so much of his training time, I believe he would have had a good chance of an Olympic crown.

In war, Kleombrotos was neither as flamboyant, nor as unpredictable as Agesipolis – although he had his brother's grasp of strategy and, whenever a situation called for it, his originality. He never overlooked a potential advantage, nor ignored a danger. His risks were calculated. He was wary about timidity. But, in games, he permitted himself the recklessness that he suppressed in the field; and either won gloriously, or lost hopelessly – sometimes ludicrously.

"Why does he wrestle?" Anaxandros asked, as a thoroughly defeated and mud-bespattered king struggled to his feet.

Like me, Kleombrotos was weakest at wrestling. Unlike me, he often chose to wrestle. I indicated the two hundred or so young Spartiates looking on, with their hair combed upright from their brows, feet planted in a Kleombrotos-like stance – who regarded him as the Myrmidons must have looked at Achilles.

"To remind them that he is only a Spartiate among Spartiates."

"And to remind himself." Kleonymos spoke the words so softly I doubt Anaxandros heard.

Here, where our peculiar banishment had rendered us something between a standing army and a city, Kleombrotos balanced his unique position finely. He was never less than a Spartan king, nor more than a commander.

"He is a great king," Kleonymos said. "Another Eurypon or Polydoros."

"I believe the Agiads pattern themselves on Leonidas," I told him.

"Leonidas found his greatness in death," he replied. "Kleombrotos must live."

I wondered at the intensity in the iris-blue eyes. Then I recalled that the beloved of Archidamos probably knew the secrets of Agisilaos's court better than I.

It is difficult to explain what Kleonymos meant to us during our exile in Phokis. His quiet intelligence, his gentle humour kept up the spirits of his tent-companions, as it settled disputes amongst the troops through those hard northern winters. Yet, as I write this, it seems I have made of him a waxen statue, and he was not that.

There could be a hard edge to his wry wit, and his sensitivity covered a core of iron. The freshness of youth clung to him like the scent of a spring morning, but I found myself talking to him of the ways of the gods and of men, as I would to a man of my own years.

Kleombrotos came to rely on his tact and good sense in managing the troops. Even the hardest of these rarely failed to smile when Kleonymos approached. Yet he could be hard in meeting out punishment when the situation demanded it.

One day he joined me as I idly played a song of Alkman on a lyre, as I rested under a tree on a rise facing the mountains. Phokis is green in spring and early summer but it is stark. One can see one is near the centre of the earth, even if it were not a known fact. It is grand. It is splendour. It is not Lakedaimon.

"I have won a night with the generals' whores," Kleonymos said, with his wry, gentle smile.

The prostitutes had settled themselves into more permanent accommodation, as the army showed no signs of leaving. The vendors became shopkeepers. Then came a better type of whore; beautiful, lettered and expensive.

There had been a pentathletic competition amongst the younger men. Kleonymos took the prize. He told me that he was in two minds about it. I misunderstood.

"No man is celibate on campaign," I told him, and recalled Doreius saying the same words to me on the bluff above Sparta, when I was an eiren, and talking about Asia. "There was a woman who had the walk of a woman of Lakedaimon, Leotychides, and a boy with the look of you," he had said. "But the woman was not Spartan, the boy not you; and it was the dry husk of love."

How memory assailed one here, where we lived on the dry husk of life, like the scent of the matthiola flower at evening in Lakedaimon.

"I have gone before with Father," Kleonymos said. "That is the trouble. I can go whenever I wish. Few of the young men can. It would mean something to them. But I won."

"The prize could have been won by some fellow here with someone he loves. Or a lad with a fine-looking widow in the town."

A breeze lifted his autumn-leaf hair. "It wasn't."

He would not shirk a problem, as many do, by assuring himself that others are troubled by it also.

"You are asking me whether it is right to keep something fairly won from someone who has nothing."

"And you are telling me to find the answer myself, as you did when you were my teacher."

"I cannot thrash you now."

"Only on the boxing-ground."

"Imbecilic prize! A prize should be something no one needs, and everyone wants for the honour alone. Who thought of it, Kleonymos?"

"A Sikyonian platoon leader."

"It would be a foreigner."

"Much longer here, and we shall all become foreigners."

Another lyre was playing a melody that sounded like early Euagoras. A flock-brother? Sphodrias? Anaxandros? Possibly even Makarios, who had been the Monkey. More of the matthiola scent of memory. Spartans are not created for long stays beyond the sight of Taygetos and the whisper of the Eurotas.

I recalled a duty Kleombrotos had placed upon me.

"Kleonymos, Kleombrotos would understand if you wanted to return to Sparta."

To Archidamos was understood. It was no longer simpler to be Spartan, I reflected, and the thought recalled Nikomedes. I had not spoken to him before we left Thespiai. There had been no time. When I looked for him on the march back, I was told he had remained. He had not boxed in the last Olympiade. Perhaps he trained one of the youths.

Kleonymos turned to me, and dispelled my surmises regarding Nikomedes. "There are few Spartans who would not follow the King if he chose to march on Sparta," he said. "All the young men are ready, and he knows it. He can only imagine what is happening in Lakedaimon in his absence. It is a heavy weight for one man to carry." He spoke softly and firmly "I shall never desert my King."

I could have told him that – however he was torn – Kleombrotos, like Leonidas, would obey his orders.

Chapter 21

I was boxing with Anaxandros when Kleombrotos sent Kleonymos to fetch me. I went as I was, oiled and sanded. Matters were never urgent. We had been in Phokis nearly four years.

The King sat on the ground in front of our hut.

"One of the new platoon leaders was kind enough to inform Kleonymos that there is to be a conference in Sparta."

Another Spartiate regiment had arrived a few days previously to swell our inactive army.

Kleombrotos took one of those hard, sour northern apples from a wooden bowl. "Athens is sending ambassadors."

"They risk losing the friendship of Thebes."

"All Athens' allies have received invitations. From Athens."

Clever and devious and Athenian.

"When they tied my hands with orders, they forgot to forbid me to send an observer to a conference I was not intended to know about." He bit into the apple without pleasure. "I am sending you to Sparta, Leotychides. Prothous has been elected an ephor. Ask him if he has seen my messages. You can trust him." He ran his hand through his hair. "When you see my sons – I had forgotten. Kleomenes will be with his flock now."

"There are not so many Spartiate flocks now that it will be difficult to find him."

"There is so much that is wrong in the City, Leo'. I feel my entire reign has been spent in war, or in trying to avert it."

"You have done what you can. And that is the first time you have called me Leo'."

A smile lighted his weary, angry face. "You were a patrol leader when I was a rhodibas. When I was a patrol leader, you were an olive-crowned games winner. I daresay I never outgrew my awe of you."

"From the time that you succeeded, I thought of you as king first and cousin second."

"How little we know those we know well?"

For an escort, he gave me as many Spartiates as he could

458

without overtly disobeying orders. Each one was a vote.

Kleombrotos came to see me.

"What do you want me to do after the conference?" I asked him.

"Stay in Sparta and try to get us ordered back. If you fail... return to Phokis. I will miss your company. The gods be with you, Cousin."

I dug my heels into my horses' flanks. Kleombrotos reached us, and seized the reins halting it.

"Embrace my sons for me," he said.

So long had I been out of Sparta that my memory played me tricks. Directly I entered the Agiad palace, I started towards what had been my aunt's quarters – and stopped stupidly, then called to a servant to announce me.

The King's nine-year-old elder son ran out. He manfully disguised his disappointment in seeing me, rather than his father.

"I saw soldiers ride in." The unspoken question was clear.

"Your father sent us. He entrusted me with a special mission, which was to see you and give you his embrace."

Clinging to my neck, he asked, "When is Father coming back?"

"When they let him." A soft, cool, voice replied with a note of bitterness. The neat-featured young Queen turned to her son. "Go back to your lessons, Agesipolis. You may talk later."

She ordered wine. The servants were dismissed before she spoke other than courtesies. "Yes, it has come to that." She lowered her voice. "Those two are new men allotted to us after Kleombrotos left. Men even speak carefully in their halls now. Well, Leotychides, do you think you can persuade them to recall my husband?"

"What pretext do they give for keeping him in Phokis?"

"Men who ask that too often are posted there themselves." She rose "I thought, two years ago, he would be recalled. Gorgo started the women jeering the ephors, for preventing men fighting for Sparta by keeping an army inactive in the north. The recall order was written, but the chief ephor delayed sending it until their terms expired. Agisilaos had Kyniska

459

praising his own friends for the next election."

"Kyniska and Agisilaos have been cool to each other for years."

"She will fight him on private matters, like her running-horses. In matters of state, she is with him. Your grandfather was a great king, Leotychides, but he did Sparta incalculable harm when he married Eupolia."

"Are there no men left in Sparta?"

The Queen was a literal-minded woman. "To be precise, two regiments."

With the four regiments in Phokis, it meant that the City had only six full Spartiate regiments altogether.

Agisilaos took no ceremonial view of his part in the conference. He seated himself on the dais with the ephors, rather than the Elders' benches where kings belong. His face was withered as a dry plum now; his grey hair matted, as if he seldom combed it. Although nearing seventy, he still wore it at warrior's length. His beard was neatly trimmed, revealing the stubborn set of the jaw, that grew more pronounced as age withered the flesh. The lips of the prim mouth, which sat so oddly with it, had become yet thinner, the old prettiness gone.

Before calling on the ambassadors to speak, the chief ephor gave the meeting apologies for the absence of Antalkidas, who was on his way from Persia with money from the Great King – making it clear that the King still regarded Sparta as arbiter of the peace.

After the usual formalities, one of the Athenians began a long-winded speech praising Sparta, her history and founders – in a way that was calculated to impress upon the hearers the distinction of his own ancient lineage.

My eyes and mind wandered, and I caught sight of Epaminondas leaning against a wall, smiling slightly to himself. He was now a Boiotarch; a title Thebans give to rulers of Boiotia, although its cities might rule themselves according to the terms of the peace. He wore his power casually. As we were much of an age, it occurred to me that I had passed into the years of my fifth decade in Phokis only half-aware.

A Corinthian replied to the Athenian's speech. It was less a reply than a vehement attack upon Athens for sending her warships to cities friendly to Corinth. Pityas informed me that he was a member of the mercantile party. The mercantile party of Corinth is unique among its kind in its hatred of Athens.

An Argive speaker followed him, advocating a union of cities in a wordy discourse, the point of which appeared to be that peace could best be achieved if all Boiotia were Theban; and Athens controlled, not only Attica, but also all those cities that had long been subject to her – which meant that Argos would do the bidding of Athens and Thebes, if they enabled her to swallow Corinthia.

An ephor rose, and said, "Larger states mean larger wars," and sat down.

The day's session ended.

I cleared my head of it by riding down past the river Tiasa to see Kleomenes. Like his brother Agesipolis, he had the chestnut hair and bright-blue eyes of the Agiads. Being but seven, he did not disguise his disappointment, but was more easily consoled by some tales of his father's valour more than three years stale.

As I was leaving, a beautiful, slender golden-haired youth rode across my path on an exceeding fine mount.

"Agis! Get off that horse. Return it immediately to my stables."

"A nice greeting, Father–!" He dismounted smartly, his lithe form agile. "I obey in as much as I can. As for the beast, it cannot return to your stables, as it was never in them. A gift from one of my admirers."

"I hope you are not frivolous in your attachments."

"My dear father, I took the gift, not the giver."

"Acquisitiveness is no better than frivolity."

"It was kindness, not greed. The fellow actually thanked me for accepting this rather nice piece of horseflesh." His sapphire-blue eyes sparkled. "And I am reliably informed that you broke a good many hearts yourself in your day. Understandable, as I am also told you looked like me when you were young."

"I rather thought you resemble me before I was in my dotage."

He laughed. A free, careless laugh. "Father, can't you come down from that horse. It has been four years since you have seen me." As soon as I dismounted, he linked his arm through mine as though we were contemporaries. I noted a fading ink

461

mark on his side, the size of a blunted spear-tip. The mock-battle wound would have been fatal in reality, and I hoped he knew it. "Has that great dolt of a brother of mine told you that he has become the best eiren boxer in Sparta?"

"I haven't seen Leonidas yet."

"You will find him in the gymnasium. We're going to enter the lists for the Pythian Games. I shall run in the short race, and he in the long, so we can each have a laurel crown." He shouted an order to another eiren.

"Agis, are you a patrol leader?"

"Today, yes. Tomorrow? Who knows? I have been appointed and dismissed so many times I lost count."

That meant once. "Why were you dismissed?"

"Some fool complained about me. If the dogs hadn't–"

Two youths ran up. One slender, one broad-faced and burly.

"Agis, are you in the competition or not? – Excuse me, sir." The burly eiren cast down his eyes.

"With me, there *is* no competition."

"Doreius is as good as you, if not better."

"Doreius tries. I haven't got to." He turned to me. "You must see me win, Father, and put the lie to this dolt."

The slender, dark-haired youth turned his head. Full-face, the resemblance was less striking than it had been. His lips were fuller – the shape of my son's – but, where Agis's were insolently pouting, or turned into that somewhat engaging lopsided smile, Chairon's son's were firmly compressed. Still, the look was there. And there was beauty. Doreius had an ink mark on his throat, twin to my son's side "wound."

"Who won the battle?" I asked.

"Hard to say," Agis replied, "as the two generals killed each other."

Doreius laughed drily. "I still say you threw that spear at me after you were dead."

"You couldn't convince the Commander." Agis threw a friendly arm about his shoulders, and motioned towards me with his head. "Go on. Ask him. Maybe you'll come up with another one to confound old Falcon Face."

"Falcon Face?" I asked. Agis went to choose a spear, leaving Doreius to give the explanation.

"It is just a name, sir. For the Elder who teaches the rhetrae,"

462

he finished lamely. I would have wagered Agis had named the teacher.

"In my day, the teachers gave the boys names. Was there something you wanted to ask me, Doreius?"

"If a citizen gave land to the City, could he insist that it be divided into kleroi and distributed amongst Lesser Spartiates, so that they could pay their Hall share? Sorry, sir." The fleeting smile. "Too many words."

It was not idle curiosity. There was too much urgency in the grey eyes that he forgot to keep cast down.

"I haven't the answer." That one would have baffled Diopeithes. "Does your father know your intentions, Doreius?"

"He says that, when his fortune is mine, I must do what I consider just."

Who had put it into his mind? Gorgo? Kallias?

"Doreius, did you think of this entirely on your own?"

"No, sir, You did."

"I?"

"When you taught us the rhetrae, sir. You said the Law—"

"Doreius! It's your turn," a youth called.

Agis gave a joyous cry as his spear flew straight.

(As I was setting down these last words by lamp-light, the tutor's shadow fell across my shoulder. His comings and goings are an accustomed thing now, and the servants let him in without question, although it occurs to me that he has not called for the past month. He confessed to me that he has recorded all the rhetrae for his own study, and excused himself on the grounds that it was only forbidden to *Spartans* to write them. Sophists can argue themselves out of anything. He asked me whether it was true that in Sparta Lykourgos was worshipped as a god. I assured him that it was.

"You do not do him sufficient honour", said this Aristotle).

The gloriously-descended Athenian ambassador had been at pains to show his love of Sparta. The second Athenian speaker attacked us, called us hypocrites, and recalled everything from Lysander's councils of ten to Phoibidas's seizure of the Kadmea.

463

Meleas said he was an extreme democrat, and he was certain the middle-party man would be more temperate; but I find the difference between a party dominated by the rich – who enhance their trade by conquest – and a party of the poor – who earn their wages by war – to be largely one of rhetoric. How much better it would be if we were all agrarian states, with cities of small numbers; but I digress again...

The third Athenian to speak was Kallistratos. Tolmiaos was not with him this time. Was he still alive? Kallistratos was by far the best speaker in that flamboyant Athenian way. He admitted to fault on both sides, and spoke of the good things of peace. As he went on, it became obvious that the two preceding Athenian contributions had merely been leading into this one.

I knew why Epaminondas smiled. The agreement between Sparta and Athens had already been struck.

Kallistratos went on. "Some cities oppose peace because Antalkidas is bringing more money from the Great King. Is this a reason for us, who are in accord with the Great King and who follow his lead, to be afraid? The Great King doesn't want to use his money making others strong. He wants his wishes carried out without spending anything at all..."

Would that those Athenians who call us the betrayers of Hellas been there to hear that!

Kallistratos raised his ringing orator's voice, and cried, "Spartans, if you were our allies, no state would attack us on land; and if we were yours, no one could threaten you by sea."

So that was the pact. Sparta was to be the leader on land. Athens on the sea.

The freedom of cities was reaffirmed – the only variant being that no state was obliged to defend the territory of another, although it might do so if it wished. That, at least, eliminated even the shadow of a pretext for keeping an army in Phokis.

If any doubt were left about that, it was removed when it was agreed that all foreign garrisons from either side were to be removed from foreign cities. Oaths were sworn, and the treaty signed. Agisilaos, who had stood with the Elders to come forward and sign for Sparta, returned instead to the dais with the ephors.

Epaminondas strode forward. There was a silence, as the tall, commanding figure halted before the dais. Quietly and courteously, he requested that the ephors alter the name of Thebes on the treaty to read "The Boiotians."

Before the chief ephor could speak, Agisilaos replied testily, "I am not prepared to alter anything."

Epaminondas's deep voice was controlled. "Our signator misunderstood his instructions. There are no other Boiotians here."

Agisilaos started from his seat. Veins stood out on his scrawny neck. Age had dried him like cracked leather. "Speak plainly. Will you or will you not leave each of the Boiotian cities autonomous?"

If Thebes signed for Boiotia, it could be interpreted as recognition of her suzerainty over all the cities of the territory. It could also be argued that, by signing, the Thebans recognised their independence as stated in the terms of the treaty. It was a matter that called for delicate handling. With his words, Agisilaos issued a challenge to Epaminondas.

"Will you leave each of the Lakonian cities autonomous?" Epaminondas replied.

It was still not too late. Agisilaos might have to come down from his haughty stance; to explain simply and truthfully that the up-country towns had their own elders who elected their own headmen, and that they lived by their own rustic law. – while the Boiotian cities had ancient constitutions distinct from Theban law and custom, and in many cases older.

He might have said and done any number of things to modify his ultimatum. Instead, he sat with his hatred of Thebes seething under his skin, like the breathing of a frog. Nervous coughs echoed here and there in the stillness. Agisilaos spoke again.

"I have asked. Do you not agree that Boiotia should be free?"

Epaminondas could be equally unreasonable when pressed. He might have replied that Sparta had signed for her allies, without prejudice to their sovereignty.

"Do you or do you not agree that Lakonia should go free?" he repeated.

His meaning was clear now. Boiotia was no more Sparta's concern than Lakonia was that of Thebes.

With a reddened face and throbbing neck veins, Agisilaos seized a stylus from the chief ephor, and struck the name of Thebes from the treaty – excluding the Thebans from the peace.

Leaving them unbound by his commitments.

Epaminondas walked out.

The ambassadors returned to their cities. The signatories to the treaty began withdrawing their garrisons according to the terms. The ephors ordered all the Spartan garrisons home. With the exception of the army on Phokis.

I spoke to Prothous openly, as Kleombrotos had advised me, regarding this senseless omission.

"Agisilaos is bent upon war with Thebes," he said. "I am going to take the question of recalling the army to the Apella."

There was the usual number of onlookers, as we gathered under the mushroom-shaped roof. Prothous put his case well. A loud mouth amongst the onlookers called out that Thebes was not bound by the peace.

I did not see who it was, but behaviour in Sparta had certainly declined when a bystander could interrupt an ephor's speech. Nevertheless, some citizens in Assembly followed it up by calling out, "What about the Boiotian cities?"

Prothous was prepared for it. He put forward a practical proposal that all cities party to the treaty contribute to a common fund, to be placed in the temple of Apollo in Delphi. If any state threatened a city's freedom, all cities that supported the cause of independence could join in a campaign against the offender, and draw on the fund.

We lost the vote.

"I cannot understand it, Meleas," I said in Hall. "There is hardly a man in Assembly who hasn't a close kinsman or friend in Phokis."

"Fear, Leotychides. When I was an ephor, I saw strong men break down and beg to be flogged or fined all but their kleroi, rather than be sentenced to banishment from Lakedaimon. Why do deserters never run away further than the forest of Taygetos, outcasts though they are? How has it been for you, four years in Phokis without a break?"

"I was so unhinged by the sight of Sparta that I forgot my aunt no longer lived in the Agiad palace."

"The men who voted to please Agisilaos have seen those who oppose him exiled to Phokis." He grasped the arm of the servant who refilled our cups, and spoke to his ear without lowering his voice. "I said that men who oppose Agisilaos are banished without cause. You may tell your masters that." He released the man.

"Careful, Meleas," a friend warned. "Agisilaos may no longer need a man who can talk to Athenians."

"Let him send me to Phokis with the best of Sparta," he smiled wryly. "Easy enough for me. I'm not that far off sixty."

"You mean to say the onlookers at Assembly were secret police?"

"Informers. Hirelings. Serfs and Lesser Spartiates. The secret police sit *in* Assembly." He raised his voice again. "And in the dining halls."

"Do you know who they are?"

"The monster has grown too large for that, Leotychides. That, too, is part of the fear. Men who would give their lives in battle without hesitation fear the watching of an unknown, unhealthy thing."

I see I am once more breaking the secrecy of Hall, and must remember to delete this conversation.

The orders I brought to Kleombrotos from the ephors were to lead the army directly against Thebes, if the Thebans did not free the Boiotian cities.

Chapter 22

The easiest route into Boiotia led through a narrow pass, where Kleombrotos (rightly) suspected that Thebans might be waiting in ambush. We went by way of Thisbai, a town between two mountains, and made a hard march over the mountains into Thespian territory, to the naval station of Kreusis.

In one of his swift, neat tactical moves, Kleombrotos captured the fortifications, and twelve Theban triremes as well. We rested a day; then, with spirits high after the successful action, we marched inland to the plain – where we raised our circle of tents near a village called Leuktra, between Thespiai and Plataia.

We were encamped on a slight rising in the monotonous countryside, where grazing cattle eyed us dully across the ditch in front of our camp. Kallias threw the discus with his son Dexippas, who had come with the last regiment to Phokis. Some of the men dug wrestling-grounds.

Kleombrotos remained in the commander's tent. He was composing his declaration to the Thebans, and had called me in to read out the draft, when the commander of this last Spartiate regiment stepped in. He was a man who had served on Agesipolis's staff in Chalkidi, spoke highly of him, and had become quite friendly with Kleombrotos while some of us were in Sparta for the conference.

"A number of my men are asking why we have not yet marched on Thebes, Kleombrotos," he said.

"They will go where and when they are ordered," Kleombrotos replied, without looking up.

"That is what I told them."

When he had done, Kleombrotos passed me the message to the rulers of Thebes. It requested assurances that they would quit the Boiotian cities they held and stated that, failing to receive such assurances, he had orders to march upon Thebes itself.

It was a masterpiece of diplomacy. By requesting assurances rather than immediate withdrawal, he allowed Thebes to comply without loss of pride. If anyone could avoid a pointless war with Thebes, it was Kleombrotos. Perhaps Thebans do not understand Spartan brevity. They sent an army in reply.

Our scouts reported seeing toque-shaped helmets the day after our heralds returned. The next day, the main body of the Theban army encamped on a hill opposite us. It was all flat plain between the two camps. They could see our movements as clearly as we saw theirs.

Pelopidas arrived, leading his Sacred Band. They certainly had a smarter step and formation than most Theban troops. Some of the men watched them, then returned to their games when the Thebans sat down to the midday meal. The Sacred Band ate apart from the rest.

A great cheer went up in the Theban camp when Epaminondas rode in. All that day, I noted Kleombrotos looking across the level ground from time to time, as the tall Theban strode out. Finally, his gaze held.

"I am going to talk to him," he said "He owes me a hearing. My brother saved his life."

"Shall I call the heralds, sir?" Kleonymos asked.

"No, Kleonymos. This is not a time for formal negotiations. I shall go alone."

"You can't, sir!" It was the general from the Olynthian war. "They might take you prisoner. Or even kill you."

"Then you have a polemarch to lead you into battle."

"Sir, you are the bravest of kings, but think as a soldier. How that would raise Theban morale!"

Kleombrotos was silent a moment. "You are right," he spoke finally "I shall ask a safe conduct from Epaminondas himself."

"But why, Kleombrotos?" Sphodrias objected.

"Did you not say that Antalkidas believes the Thebans do not want to fight us?"

"Agisilaos offended them at the conference."

"All the more reason to put an end to this madness."

The king stepped into his tent, and started writing the message in his own hand; then he discarded the papyrus, and began again, changing *Kleombrotos, King of Sparta* to *Kleombrotos, son of Pausanios and brother to Agesipolis.*

"I shall propose that they withdraw their garrisons from the Boiotian cities when I talk to him," he said. "I'll suggest that they put their case to a conference of all the Hellenes, and I will offer to withdraw my army and return their ships – as an earnest of good faith – if they agree. Agesipolis believed Epaminondas to be a man of honour..."

"I think so, too, Kleombrotos."

"Thank you, Leo'. Sphodrias, you look like a storm cloud."

"What if the ephors charge you with making political decisions?"

"Then they must charge Agisilaos, too."

"The Boiotian cities–"

"Sphodrias, if we fight the Thebans today, they will take the cities next year. Are we to keep a standing army in Boiotia? We are Peloponnesians."

Sphodrias smiled reluctantly. "I did want to test the mettle of those fellows Pelopidas commands."

Kleombrotos finished his letter.

"May I take it to Epaminondas, sir?"

"No, Kleonymos; it must be a general. And I need you here," he added, to soften the disappointment the young man tried to disguise. "Nor you, Leo'. Agisilaos would say you were conspiring with the Thebans to make yourself King."

Sphodrias started to volunteer, then flushed and broke off; I daresay recalling his performance at Eleusis.

"I will take it, sir," It was the general from Chalkidiki.

Kleombrotos smiled. "They could finish you as easily as me."

"A general is a smaller loss than a king."

Kleombrotos put his seal on the scroll, and handed it to him. Sphodrias motioned me out of the tent.

"Agesipolis didn't trust that fellow," he said, as we watched him make his way towards the Theban camp. "He claimed he was one of the men Agisilaos put on his staff."

"Sphod', it was a long time before he came to trust Meleas."

Looking across the even ground, we saw that – as yet – the Thebans had no allies except their fellow Boiotians, but it was a large army that had assembled. The baggage-carriers were light-armed army servants, who could fight if necessary.

"What is he doing now?" Our message-bearing general

470

stopped to speak to some men of his regiment.

"Probably naming his next in the chain of command, should the Thebans hold him. Or kill him. Sphod', Kleombrotos is a good judge of men."

Nonetheless, I conveyed Sphodrias's doubts to Kleombrotos.

The King was astute, but four years cut off from Sparta can unbalance any man's judgement.

"It is true that Agesipolis detested him," I added.

"He told me that," Kleombrotos said. "He always regretted that there was not enough time to change my brother's opinion of him." Kleombrotos smiled. "He is a good old fellow. Probably he criticised Agesipolis in his youth. We both know that Ages' was large-hearted about anything but that." The smile faded. "I hope I have done the right thing. If I have sent a man to be tortured and killed..."

Shortly after we began our midday meal, the incident occurred.

Some young soldiers ran up, and called on Kleombrotos to lead them against the Thebans, because the allies were saying that he conspired with Epaminondas. Young warriors closed on them from all sides. I think they would have torn them to pieces, had Kleombrotos not shouted at them to cease and save their fighting for the enemy.

The spectacle of Spartans confronting their commander left me speechless. I fear I simply gaped. One fellow had not done. He stood his ground, and shouted back that Kleombrotos had let the Thebans off before, when he was in their territory. Did he intend to let them off again?

Kleonymos seized him, and pinioned both his arms behind his back. He asked the King whether he wanted the man flogged. Kleombrotos ordered him to take the fellow to his own commander of fifty, who would teach him to behave as a Spartiate.

It crossed my mind that the disgraced warrior was no more than twenty-two. He could not possibly recall those sixteen days we had been encamped at Dog's Head. All the men who challenged the King were from the same regiment. That last to arrive. I must ask Dexippas about them when I saw him next. Or Meleas's son.

The suspicion hardened that these men acted for someone else. Spartiates simply do not insult a commander, let alone a king-commander. Unless they were acting under orders. Agisilaos had his agents here, as well as in Sparta.

Apollo, I prayed, speak to Epaminondas. Let his pride permit Kleombrotos to avert a war fashioned only to please Agisilaos, who would expend the life of every Spartan – as well as every Theban – to avenge his deserved humiliation at Aulis. There is no vengeance so great as that of a petty spirit.

The general came puffing towards us as we finished our meal.

"Kleombrotos," he said. "I heard what happened. I ask your permission, as his regimental commander, to have the man executed."

"Never mind that," Kleombrotos said. "Did you see Epaminondas?"

He replied with difficulty. "He saw me courteously. And permitted me to leave. Honourably..."

"Out with it," Kleombrotos snapped.

"He will not see you, Kleombrotos. He glanced at the scroll, tossed it aside after he read it, and said his army would reply."

Kleombrotos absorbed it expressionlessly, then said, "Sit down and eat while there is some food left."

"What did you ask him in the message?" Sphodrias asked.

"Only a safe conduct, that we might talk face to face."

"He must have changed," Sphodrias reflected. "At Mantinea, he had better manners."

We had just poured the libations to the gods, when the Thebans began amassing in battle-array on their hill. A number of men came running to tell us what we could see for ourselves.

I have always wondered if it were the aroma of the uncut wine, still fresh on the ground, that gave rise to the scurrilous rumour that Kleombrotos was in wine when he went into battle. No man was more moderate in his habits than Kleombrotos. Even in those long years in Phokis, where more than one good man was driven to excess by despair. The King's quick thinking on the battle-field proved his clear head that day.

As we formed up in battle-order, Kleombrotos turned to me and said. "You will fight at my right, Games Winner."

"There are younger and more recent games winners here."

"But none who is also my friend and cousin. Kleonymos to my left."

The young man's face radiated pride. Sphodrias started towards his regiment. Kleombrotos called him back. "I've given command to Kallias, Sphodrias. He hasn't had a chance to try his generalship in the field yet."

It was not the reason. He had seen Sphodrias eyeing the Sacred Band; with such ill-disguised exuberance that it was easy to imagine him breaking ranks, and leading his hoplites against it in an impulsive charge. There were three hundred men in Pelopidas's regiment.

Kleombrotos deployed his army in a long battle-line. The old deception of making an army appear larger than it is. Each Spartan half-company stood three files abreast, so that the phalanx was only twelve men deep; but the perfection of the bristling wall of *Lamda* shields made the Boiotian thousands, across the level ground, look clumsy and pointless.

As the army took up their positions, it became conclusive that the Thebans would be fighting with an entirely Boiotian force. Their baggage-carriers did not appear to like the look of us, and began to depart.

Kleombrotos deployed our cavalry in the van. We knew it for what it was worth. The Thebans did not. They imitated us, and placed their cavalry in front of their battle line.

There was a sudden movement down the line. Kleombrotos muttered an obscenity through clenched teeth. The Phokian peltasts, the Philasian cavalry and the mercenaries had broken ranks. They rushed out, and wheeled about the departing light-armed baggage carriers. They were attacking them; driving them back into the Theban lines, just in the event the enemy became short of fighting-men.

Our wayward allies returned, greatly pleased with themselves.

Kleombrotos raised his voice, leading us in the hymn to

Kastor. Pipes, flutes and lyre played, as the living wall of shields and spears advanced in deadly slow march. The hooves of the horses of the king's honour guard kept time with the Dorian march.

A thunder of hooves, as the Theban cavalry charged ours. The enemy horse was fit. Half our cavalry fell without damaging the Thebans. The rest fled the field in droves.

"Something wrong with us, Cockerel?" Sphodrias shouted. "They're more afraid of the Thebans than they are of us."

The shameless cavalrymen misjudged. I saw some of our hoplites strike them down, as they tried to escape. A shout of "General Pentatarchos!" carried from that part of the field.

It was the bastard regiment attacking the deserters. I knew why they called me the name they called me secretly. I knew they were reminding me of other days. I knew what they were asking.

"Many are seasoned cavalrymen," I told Kleombrotos.

He needed no more explanation. The flute sounded the order for the cavalry to regroup. I hoped they knew it was meant for them. That the older men recalled the notes of command. They did. Enough of them were able to seize horses to form three smart squares.

The Thebans advanced in an oblique line. Epaminondas sent his left wing forward, and kept back his right. An unexpected move, as it placed his Thebans directly in front of the Lakedaimonian section of our line. A place Thebans usually avoid. Did he lack confidence in the mettle of his fellow Boiotians? Or in their sympathies?

Kleombrotos ordered the charge. He led it himself; his high-crested helmet a pace in front of Kleonymos and myself. The Thebans fell back. I glimpsed Epaminondas. The tall Theban shouted an order that was soundless in the din.

Once or twice, my spear struck a shield. For the most part, the Thebans melted away – although there was no sight of those fleeing individuals that herald a disordered retreat. A chance turn of the head showed me what that unheard order given by Epaminondas had been. The Thebans were withdrawing to the left, to form an immense mass fifty shields deep!

Kleombrotos saw it at the same time. He sent the order down the line to right-turn, which enabled him to throw the re-formed

474

cavalry on the right wing of the Thebans. They fell back before the cavalry charge.

The earth shook. Not below us, but in front of us. I found myself fighting on foot. Pelopidas and his Sacred Band had charged us.

Kleombrotos, also, was unhorsed, and more than six paces away from me – when I should have been at his right. The impact of the charge broke through a part of the wall of shields of our hoplites. These Thebans were heavy-armed hoplites, too, but they moved swiftly and lightly as peltasts.

They fought in pairs. As they attacked the King's horse-guard, one man would dive under the mount, and thrust his spear in its belly – while his partner attacked the rider, as the animal sank. Then the first man would swing himself up like a weightless thing; and thrust his sword into the throat of the next rider, as his partner attacked the horse.

There was no waste in their movements. Swift, precise; two men fighting as one. I do not know when I noted all this; for I was fighting for my life, trying to hack my way to Kleombrotos. There was a poetry to their movements; a beauty, as there is in anything perfect.

They could also die. Sphodrias grinned as we dispatched two of them simultaneously. It is odd the things one recalls. That grin is as clear as if it were yesterday; but I do not remember how we separated, or how I found myself in the midst of another melée.

I saw Kleombrotos fall, still striking out with his spear as he went down. Kleonymos stood before his King, holding off the enemy. Kleombrotos rose again, his spear gone, his short thrusting sword in his right hand.

One of those brief, sudden partings opened my way to the King. Then two Thebans blocked it. A Spartan hoplite materialized as I attacked the Theban on the right. My sword-thrust found its mark, but not a fatal one. The man fought on. The two Thebans now stood back to back, both gravely wounded, but they fought on. To the death. Like Spartans.

Kleombrotos had fallen again by the time I reached him. Kleonymos stood off three, four, five of the enemy. I threw my spear at one, and brought him down. His partner brought

475

Kleonymos down.

Kleonymos rose, sword in hand, hacking at his assailants.

The Spartans around us rallied. Shields drew together. A Theban cry brought attention to the fallen King.

Kleonymos stood over his King, as if he were rooted to the ground. Another pair of Thebans rushed him. One brought him down. I killed the other. Kleonymos rose again, blood streaming from his beautiful face. O, brave lad!

Spartans were fighting their way through to Kleombrotos. I turned to deflect a spear. Just as the Spartan shield-wall was becoming a protective enclosure, Kleonymos fell the final time. There was no life in his iris-blue eyes, as I took my place over my cousin and King. For some time Kleonymos must have been fighting on spirit alone. His wounds were deep and ugly.

The ordinary Thebans, heartened by the success of the Sacred Band, advanced in great numbers. Such a fury filled the men around the King that we repulsed them long enough to lift Kleombrotos from the ground, and retreat in order back across the ditch that lay in front of our camp.

Retreat. The word hung in the air.

We sat in front of the tent, where Kleombrotos lay barely breathing. A brown haze of dust lay over the even ground between the two camps. The Thebans kicked up more, as they stripped the bodies, dancing and gloating like ill-bred boys. We had brought back our wounded during the retreat, at the cost of leaving our dead in the field.

"It was the right wing," an old general glared. "Why did the right wing give ground?"

"Because we saw you retreating," another regimental commander snapped.

The polemarch was dead. There had been prolonged argument as to who was in command until the King was able to speak. The oldest general. The general with the most victories. The King's cousin. The oldest general was too old. The King's cousin was too young, and had not commanded a *mora*. Which general had the most victories?

The names put forward as commander, including my own,

reached me as if from a distance. No conclusion was reached. They had turned to recrimination. Kallias spoke not a word through it all. Abruptly, he stood and walked away. Dexippas lay with the dead.

The physician came out of the tent. The King could speak.

Kleombrotos bit his lip whenever he breathed. A spear-tip stuck out of his side. The shaft had not been evident when we carried him back.

I sat beside the pallet. "When did you break it off?"

His voice was faint but firm. "Had to. Couldn't let the enemy see it." His lip bled. Why do we try to lessen great pains with small ones?

"Did we win the battle?" he said.

"We did not lose," the old general said.

"That means we did not win." A spasm of pain crossed his face. He did not bite his lip. "Losses...How many?"

"Not good, sir."

None of us could bring ourselves to tell him how bad.

"Men lost...never good." His eyes went to the physician. "Fool won't draw the accursed thing out."

"Can't you draw the spear?" I asked the man. A foreigner. "The King is in pain."

"If I draw it, sir, the King may die."

"And if you don't draw it?"

"He will live longer."

"If you draw it I shall die; and if you don't draw it, I shall die." Kleombrotos tried to laugh. The pain whitened his face.

"I said you *may* die, sir."

"Stop quibbling, man, and draw it. What use are a few days' life like this? That is an order.

There was not a sound as the physician withdrew the long, iron barb. No rush of blood followed it. There was an audible sigh of relief.

"You see," Kleombrotos said, his breathing easier and less painful now. "You were wrong. It did not touch the lung." The subsidence of pain heartened him, and gave him strength. It was hard to believe that a man with so many savage wounds could still sustain life.

"Kleonymos," he asked. "Where is Kleonymos?"

"His name will be written, Kleombrotos," I said.

477

The anger in his eyes was not for the Thebans.

"Someone must tell the men I am alive," he spoke again. "I want spirits high when we go into battle tomorrow."

"Tomorrow, Kleombrotos?" asked the old general.

"Can't leave a wounded boar."

"I must advise–" the physician began.

"Don't be such an old woman," Kleombrotos snapped. "We must isolate Pelopidas and his men. I'll deploy–" A stream of crimson rushed from his mouth, cutting off his words.

The physician bent over him. Touched him. Listened to something. His breathing?

"I told him it was the lung," the fellow said.

It was not for some moments that I understood I had watched another cousin die.

Ainesios waited for me outside the dead King's tent. Victory songs came from the Theban fires on the other hill. The stars seemed cold in the black Boiotian night.

"I found the man," he said. "Among the wounded."

"I want to question him."

"He is dead. Almost gone when I found him. But this was stuffed under his armour."

He passed me the scroll with Kleombrotos's seal still unbroken. Epaminondas had never seen it. Sphodrias was right about the traitor. It was too late to tell him. He would journey with his son to Hades's Hall.

"Who was the man?" Ainesios asked "Apart from a general. A traitor?" He had foregone the rough accent of the older men of the bastard regiment affected to copy from the younger.

"Of a sort. Where is Makarios?"

"Out there." With the bodies.

"He was my flock brother once..."

He looked out over the even ground, where a few drunken Thebans with torches danced among the stripped bodies. "They are all Equals now."

I brought the news of the King's death to the survivors of the regiment that had raised his statue. One man touched a silent lyre with his left hand. He was a gifted musician, and not a bad poet. The fingers were gone from his right.

The sound and the slightly wounded asked me to lead them,

then and there, to avenge their King.

"There are over one thousand Lakedaimonian bodies out there," I told them. The full Spartiates equalled the grim cavalry boast of the bastard regiment. The craven cavalrymen had perished, almost to a man. Were the wages of valour and cowardice the same? No, the significance of death is in the manner one meets it. "More than four hundred of the dead are full Spartiate."

Their commander understood. "And a boy of ten is Agiad King in Sparta," he said.

A lamp burned in Kallias's tent. I looked in. He held the still form of Anaxandros in his arms. His wounds had dried, but they were many. This single limp body chilled me more than all the dead and dying I had seen that day. Perhaps because we had joined the flock the same year. Perhaps because it came at the end of all the rest.

"I gave him a potion," Kallias said. "Sleep deadens the pain."

Tears of relief sprang to my eyes.

"We have asked for a truce to recover the bodies," I told him.

"'Sphod' would not like to come back that way."

"His shade will forgive us. We have also sent for reinforcements."

I destroyed the message from Kleombrotos to Epaminondas. It was the best work I have ever done. They would read it with the minds of malice. As it is, they have done everything they can to vilify his name.

The next day, a Boiotian exile from our ranks managed to slip into the Theban camp and mingle unnoticed. As we awaited his return, Dexippas wandered into the camp – apparently returned from the Styx. He had come into consciousness under a pile of Theban bodies, slipped away under cover of night, and fallen asleep at the edge of our encampment. The Thebans, he surmised, would be in no shape for fighting that day, after their night's drinking.

Our exile returned in the evening, and reported that Thebes also had called for reinforcements. From Athens and from Thessaly. On both hills, the hostile camps continued to watch each other, and do nothing.

Messengers from the Isthmus reached us during this period, bringing the news that the ephors had mobilized all Spartiates up to the age of sixty. In a break with custom, men holding public office were not excepted.

The Corinthians, Tegeans and Mantineans had already sent contingents, and other allies were on their way. Archidamos commanded the army. Spartans and Corinthians were manning the triremes themselves, to transport it.

The Thebans, also, gained support. Athens ignored their call, but Jason of Thessaly rode in with his army. Although he was allied to Thebes, Jason was our consul in Thessaly, and he paid a surprise visit to our camp. His purpose was to propose a truce.

He was a square, rough-looking man, with slightly bowed legs and a surprisingly soft voice. "The Thebans," he said, "owe their victory to the fact that they were fighting with their backs to the wall."

"Victory?" snapped a feisty old general. "Are we sitting here in Boiotia, or are they in Lakonia?"

The argument went on for some time. I was not listening. The Thebans had thought that they were fighting for their existence. Had Kleombrotos spoken with Epaminondas, it might all have been resolved without a battle that took such a toll of lives.

"I'm not here to quibble about words." Jason's sharp tone brought me back to the present. "If you go into battle with your reinforcements, you will be fighting for your own existence; because every Spartiate of fighting age will be engaged, and defeat means your destruction. If there is another engagement now, either Sparta or Thebes will perish. I would not wager on which one that would be."

The man was allied to Thebes. That meant they did not want to fight. But, with only slightly more than a thousand citizens in all Sparta, could we risk another fierce action."

"What do the Thebans want."

"They want a good deal. I think they would settle on having you out of their country."

I asked the shade of Sphodrias to forgive me, and voted to accept the truce. There was more important work to be done in Sparta.

We had withdrawn to Megaran territory when we saw an army marching towards us. For the first time since leaving Sparta, we broke in disorder. Their step told us who they were before we saw the lamda on their shields. Friend rushed to embrace friend. Brother to brother. Father to son, and son to father.

As Meleas examined his son's leg, I thought of that boy in Helen's courtyard stalking a butterfly. He would march again, but he would never take an olive crown in the long race.

Hekataios bounded up. We spoke at the same time, barraging one another with questions. Pityas embraced the pale Magpie, and took some of his weight from Kallias. Not far behind Pityas, I spotted the black head of Aristeas, touched now with grey at the sides.

Aristokrates held out blistered hands. "We turned rowers for you," he said. "Aristeas, show them your hands."

The Corinthian's elegant hands bled like a melleiren's after breaking rushes. "Herakles took an oar for Jason."

"Why didn't you leave it to the younger men?" I asked.

"Archidamos wanted them fresh in the van." The Corinthian's eyes went to the Spartan commander. Archidamos stood a bit apart from all the joy of reunion.

"There will be no fighting," Kallias said. "We agreed a truce. I'll explain it all later. Some of the men are saying the gods maddened us, but I would not blame it upon the gods."

"Kleombrotos?" Aristokrates asked.

"Certainly not Kleombrotos. By the gods, he was the best commander I ever had. Sphod' is dead."

"I know," Pityas said. "They read out the names of the slain in Sparta. What great pride you have in Dexippas, Kallias," he spoke formally "his name will be–"

"No. No. No." Kallias interrupted. "His name will not be written. That was all a mistake. Don't you see him over there, telling Anaxandros's nephew what war is all about?" And embellishing his own part, no doubt. How go things in Sparta?"

"Leonidas won the eiren's boxing in the Leonidia. Leo'," Aristokrates said.

"Antalkidas is going to stand for ephor," Pityas supplied. With each piece of news, the void that was Sphodrias intruded.

Kallias looked towards Archidamos. "Someone had ought to

tell him how well Kleonymos died. It is his right." And when no one moved, "Leo', you are the only survivor of the lad's tent companions."

I went to Archidamos. We sat down and talked quietly. The son of Agisilaos concealed his fox manfully.

"I went to the Gymnopaidia with Argileonis and Meleas," Kleonike said. "We were waiting for the men's chorus to come on." My wife's haunting, singing voice was quite ordinary, but pleasant in speech. Now she spoke in a flat monotone. "A bird flew on to the dancing floor, and started singing. Everyone smiled and looked at each other, the way people do in crowds when something amusing happens. Even the foreigners.

"Eurydame did not smile. She looked ill. She knew. We did not, but they told her. Your mother was with her. She is splendid, your mother. I could never be like her–"

"The gods are merciful. Sorry, I interrupted–"

"I asked Argileonis and Meleas to excuse me, and went to Eurydame to ask her whether she was all right. Then the men came on to sing. I thought she hadn't heard me, because she did not answer. When the men finished singing, the chief ephor walked on to the floor. He told us about the battle near – Leuktra, is it? Then he called for silence, so that he could read out the names of the slain. First. He said that the King was dead. Eurydame started to get to her feet. Your mother pulled her down, and said, 'Put a smile on your face, Sister. Show these foreigners how Spartans behave.' The foreigners started to leave, but the chief ephor told everyone to remain where they were. He regretted having to interrupt the festival. It would continue when he had done. He read out the names. Name after name. So many. Polydora looked as though she had been struck by a thunderbolt. Oh, Leotychides, Kleonymos! And Sphodrias too. That good, kind man. When they came to Dexippas, Gorgo called out, 'Doriska, what a proud woman you must be!' Doriska smiled and called back. 'Share my pride, Gorgo. For I know you loved my son as a nephew, although he was but your cousin.'"

"Dexippas was an error, and I wish they would stop all that, before he thinks he must get himself killed to live up to his

482

glorious death."

"Is it true that Kleombrotos might have lived if they had not drawn the spear?"

"A few days, perhaps. No more."

"When the chief ephor finished the list, people crowded about Eurydame, praising Kleombrotos."

"Where was the young Queen?"

"She sat a spears-length from us. There was a crowd about her, too. Eurydame still did not speak. I doubt anyone noticed. Your mother spoke for her, saying how proud her sister was."

I was certain everyone would have noticed, and said how splendid Queen Timaia was; but it was true my aunt's silence would have been forgotten, in all the praise of my mother. Few noticed my aunt when my mother was with her. Age may have finally defeated her beauty, but her presence she retained.

"She spoke about her pride in her nephew, and, when someone mentioned that you had been wounded, she looked shamed that had been all—"

"Wounded? I was not wounded."

"I could put an apple in the hole in your thigh."

"Well, don't. It is still painful."

Usually, Kleonike's smile was easily tindered. But the familiar laughter in the corners of her eyes, and the almost inaudible sound that accompanied it, did not materialize. Her face was expressionless as her voice.

"I went with Eurydame to her litter, and walked beside it back to Sparta after the festival. She kept saying 'Only boys, Timaia and I. Sons and grandsons.' I don't know what she meant. I doubt she did, either. We passed your mother on the road. She walked between Leonidas and Agis. She was smiling. Her eyes sparkled, so that her face reminded me how beautiful she had been. The next day, mourning for Kleombrotos began. I beat the cauldron lid, but kept to the house to hide my shame for having lost no one, and I thank the gods for that shame. I did slip out after dark to visit Eurydame. She was sitting in that chair of hers alone. When I came in, she said, 'Kleonike, Agisilaos murdered my son. Pray the gods not to let you outlive your sons.' Leotychides, why did so many die?"

"Let it pass, Kleonike. It is over."

Of course, it was not.

483

BOOK FOUR

Chapter 23

It was the day the Council meets.

Chairon detached himself from a group of his fellow elders, who stood near the agora shrine of Zeus. His straight back belied the pure silver of his hair. He wore his elder's gown as if it were a warrior's short cloak.

"Fancy a stroll, Leotychides?" he asked.

That meant that he wanted a private word. There were many ears in the agora these days.

We turned into Leaving Street, speaking of trivial matters, passed the Cattle Price House, and came to a dead halt. I looked towards the acropolis.

"What's the matter?" He laughed. "Think I'm too feeble to make it up that hill? Or is your leg giving you trouble?"

"It has healed well. If it weren't for the indentation, I'd be quite unaware of it." We started the ascent. "Did the Inspector of Boys ever decide who won that mock battle? Your son's army or mine?"

"He gave the decision to Doreius. I understand Agis argued that a fatally wounded man can still kill."

He was right. I wondered who had told him. "Well, the rules are, when you're stuck in a vital spot, you are dead. The Inspector was just."

It was high summer. The wild cherries were ripe, and the olives beginning to be tinged with purple. The rounded peaks of Taygetos stood guard over the City. Safe. Solid. Eternal.

"Pity that disputes between cities can't be settled by mock battles." Chairon reflected. "Accursed shame about Kleombrotos. He would have been another Archidamos."

"War is something of a gourmet, Chairon. It devours only the best."

He started to say something, but a number of people were coming from the Bronze House. We did not turn that way, but went past the temple of Aphrodite of War and the shrine of Zeus to stand at a quiet edge of the hill. Alone, Chairon became brusque and purposeful.

"Look here, Leotychides. I know that you and Kallias, and my wife are up to something..." I did an about turn, as if I were looking at the Victories in the western collonade. No one was within earshot. I turned back. "I don't know what it is," Chairon continued, "because I told them I did not want to know. But, by the gods, the man has gone too far."

"The man?"

"Agisilaos. Even his moderation is excessive."

I replied this or that. I would have trusted Chairon with my life, but we had agreed no one would be taken into confidence until all voted so.

"I should have joined you after the matter of the Leuktra deserters."

The men who retreated, when they saw us retreat in order to carry the King to safety, were lawfully deserters. There was a great number of them, and they had not fled the field in fear. The Council could not bring itself to condemn them to a lifetime as outcasts, and had passed the decision to Agisilaos.

"He made the right decision, in my opinion."

"I have no quarrel with that. But what sort of Council is it that delegates its decisions to a king? And one who made us the laughing stock of the Peloponnesos, at that?"

Athens was again showing two faces. She had refused aid to the Thebans, but she gave the mercantile party in Mantinea enough arms and money to put itself back in power. The first thing it did was to break the alliance with Sparta. Walls started rising about the four villages again.

Agisilaos led an expedition against the Mantineans. It was a failure. Were any state in Hellas in doubt about our weakness after Leuktra, he made it clear to them – by offering money to the Mantineans to rebuild their fortifications, if they would defer the work until it was less embarrassing to him. They refused.

"That was afterwards." I was still evasive. Chairon's eyes glittered. "He showed the weakness of his own position, as well as Sparta's, by that offer."

I returned to the safety of the original topic. "Agisilaos was right to suspend the law that once."

"I have said I have no quarrel with that. But it sticks in my throat to see him treated as a little law-giver. Leotychides, you are clearly bound by secrecy. Tell your colleagues, or your band, or whatever you call yourselves, that you can count on the support of twelve old men, who voted against giving that power to Agisilaos. Dare say I could tell Gorgo and Kallias myself – but, at my age, it is hard to climb down."

There were few citizens who came back from Leuktra without having resolved that something must be done. That something was a nebulous determination in my mind for weeks. When I clarified my thoughts, I spoke to Kallias. Who burst into laughter. "We considered you, Leo'," he said. "But we ruled you out as too lawful."

A group already existed. As well as Anaxandros, Pelles and the commander of a decimated regiment, there were men who had not fought at Leuktra; two Polemarchs, an immediate past ephor, and a former chief ephor. Several such groups existed, but it took some time before we discovered one another, and merged into a single movement.

The movement grew so large that it became unwieldy. Leaders were elected. We met in numbers of six, and not always the same, so as not to draw attention to ourselves. Our meetings took place in one another's houses at the midday meal. An early autumn made it seem natural to sit long over our wine, after dismissing the servants.

We were not seasoned plotters. Even after Chairon brought in the Elders, we sometimes found that what one meeting agreed was contradictory to a decision taken by a simultaneous gathering. Generals who had made rapid decisions, which won us victories in the field, argued about petty details barely relevant to the plan. Nor were we even agreed upon that. Some saw it merely as a way of ridding Sparta of Agisilaos – whilst others, like myself, saw the removal of Agisilaos as a step towards bringing back the whole of the Law of Lykourgos.

Events pressed. The Corinthian traitors failed in their attempt to return to power, but Athens promoted similar moves in Megara, Sikyon and Phlias. These were Peloponnesian cities;

and Sparta, citadel and shield of the Peloponnesos, must be prepared for the intriguer.

"We need Meleas, too, Leo'." Kallias said, after one particularly embattled session. "He's a good negotiator."

"With Athenians. I don't know whether he could manage Spartans, who are all on the same side."

I broached the subject with Meleas one afternoon, as we threw the discus.

"I know what you are going to say, Leotychides, and I do not wish to know."

"It will achieve more than shouting defiance at members of the secret police."

"Perhaps. But I draw the line at regicide." His throw went awry.

"Meleas, I am nearly forty-three. Not a hot-headed youth of seventeen. This is lawful. We are moderate men."

"You? Moderate?" He laughed. "Your nature is two wild horses that you kept in tight-rein all your life." he appeared to consider. "Well, perhaps that is a moderate man."

His fears were calmed when he saw a former grand admiral, and a distinguished member of our own hall, at his first meeting.

The rich Mantinean, whose activities had so amused Sphodrias, partially succeeded in realizing his monster city. Work on the public buildings of this Megalopolis was well-advanced.

The Arkadians are the oldest people in Hellas. Its cities the most ancient. Not unnaturally, they rejected the proposal of this madman to bring the whole of Arkadia under the rule of his upstart city.

Lykomedes responded by the slaying and abduction of rulers who defied him. Sparta, shield of the Peloponnesos, did nothing except give asylum to the exiles who fled to Lakedaimon in hundreds. Lykomedes called on Athens to crush the Arkadian cities that still resisted. Athens refused. He then turned to Epaminondas, who agreed to support him with Theban arms.

In a pathetic attempt to regain esteem, Agisilaos led another expedition against Mantinea, but did nothing more than waste some of the countryside. The ruse was unsuccessful. Everyone in Sparta knew he dared not waste Spartiate lives in a major assault. Nor was he in danger from the Mantineans, who were waiting for the Thebans to do their fighting for them.

"I wonder if we're not wasting our time," Kallias speculated. "Agisilaos may put the poisoned cup in his own hand."

"To pass to another." Anaxandros scoffed. "He is the withered tree that lightning never strikes."

Leuktra had changed Anaxandros. His wounds healed, but the careless rest he carried into this middle years was gone. He was no longer the Magpie.

"So we have agreed," the past grand admiral said. "It will be during the Hyakinthia, when most people are in Amyklai." We were meeting in the Menelaos House that day.

"Should it be during a festival?"

It was on this point that we dissented.

"There will be no blood shed. It is best done when the City is not full. Then, when Agisilaos has been abducted–"

"Not abducted." The polemarch cut in. "Mistress Gorgo will have a party of youths and maidens waiting outside his house with garlands, to accompany him to the sanctuary of Herakles; to honour him. Then Leotychides's men will respectfully escort him to his lands and detain him there, while the Council prepares the accusation."

The former chief ephor frowned. "The Council can try a king, but it is not empowered to *arrest* anyone."

"We've been through all that."

"Not while I was present."

"The emergency committee of the Apella will agree the arrest. Leotychides, you are not thinking of using Lesser Spartiates, are you?"

"He has already said he is not." Chairon snapped.

A servant announced Chief Ephor Antalkidas. A shocked silence ensued. Eyes swept about, searching for the traitor.

"Show him in." Meleas spoke, with his usual composure.

Antalkidas took his place amongst six people discussing the Persian wars, and exchanged a brief glance with the gods. His short ephor's cut hair broadened his now fleshy face.

"You know," he said. "If you were all trying to draw attention

490

to yourselves, you couldn't have gone about it better."

"I do not take your meaning, Antalkidas." Meleas put a slight chill in his voice.

"My dear Meleas, you have denied Sparta the sound of your lyre for months. Admiral, that bad leg of yours, that precludes your teaching, doesn't prevent you from walking briskly to your hall. Leotychides gave his training-chariot to his son. Mistress Gorgo no longer judges maidens' games, and so on and so on. No, you all forsake your usual activities for the pleasure of the midday meal in the company of friends."

"That is not unlawful." The polemarch barked.

"No," Antalkidas replied coolly. "But conspiracy is. Do you think prominent people go unnoticed by the secret police?"

"And what have they to report?" Chairon scowled his dislike of the man. "That we had black broth today and none yesterday? What is there to notice?"

"Only routine reports, sir. But it took little perceptiveness on my part to know the games you are playing. You should know that Agisilaos has his own men in the secret police. Do you understand the nature of routine reports? I think not. They are like the two pieces of a skytali. Only there are hundreds of skytali. And nobody knows which is the key to which. So, if something happens to arouse suspicion, my secret police start going through the records – as if it were picking up skytali at random, rolling papyrus over staffs. Usually, the letters spell nothing, but occasionally the spiral produces words. They may not be truthful words, but that is no matter. That's man's record becomes the object of careful scrutiny, and something more goes in it. Or the man is accused and brought to trial–"

"You condone this?" Chairon used his elder's prerogative to interrupt the chief ephor.

"Sir, I merely state what is."

"If Agisilaos thinks we are plotting against him, why haven't we been arrested?" Kallias challenged.

"I did not say he knows." Antalkidas supped the wine, and rearranged his long legs. "Although he might. He is far too clever to do anything about it if he does know. Nothing could ruin him more quickly than bringing such an illustrious group to trial. If you were acquitted, Agisilaos would stand condemned in the eyes of Sparta. If you were condemned, he risks a rising that could bring him down as quickly." He leaned forward. "You are moving too slowly. Epaminondas is marching south, with an army of seventy thousand. It is his intention to make the whole of Arkadia subject to Thebes, to pay back Agisilaos for his meddling in Boiotia."

"How can we save the whole of Arkadia, when we cannot even save Tegea?" the polemarch demanded.

"My proposal is this." Antalkidas. We remove Agisilaos, and send an embassy to Thebes with terms. We offer her a free hand in Boiotia, which she already has. We withdraw our objections to the Arkadian union, which we have no power to prevent. In return, we ask for freedom for Herea and Arkadian Orchomenos. We must appear to be prepared to defend Arkadia, but under no circumstances do so.

"You would give Peloponnesian soil to Thebes?"

"No, Admiral, we lend it. In four, five, six years we will be strong enough to restore the cities of Arkadia to their ancient constitutions."

"Why would Thebes barter for what she can take?" Chairon demanded.

"Lakedaimonian arms still command respect, sir. But we must act before Thebes knows the full extent of our weakness, or her own strength." He rose. "Don't be too long about it. Failed liberations are known as rebellions."

No sooner had Antalkidas joined our enterprise than he began to mould it into shape. He cut through the various approaches to our immediate aims, deferred differences regarding our ultimate objectives, and concentrated upon the trial of Agisilaos. The meetings became infused with a sense of urgency.

He appeared in the changing room of the gymnasium, one day, and glanced almost imperceptibly at the servant who was scraping the oil and sand off me. Something must have gone wrong. The complicity of Antalkidas in the plot had not renewed our broken friendship. We were as civil as in Hall. No more.

"You are becoming too old to box in the Leonidian Games, Leotychides."

"I am not too old to train my son."

492

"They say he is as good as you were."

Leonidas had great strength combined with a temperate and agreeable nature. Skill and determination outlast anger.

"He is better."

"I shall be in my sixties when my son is nineteen." Antalkidas had waited ten years for a girl of seven to come of marriageable age. She had a strain of Royal Heraklid blood, and a generous inheritance. "There is not a grain of sand left on you," he added impatiently.

I dismissed the servant, draped my cloak about me, and took my sponge and pumice.

"In other cities the gymnasia have baths." Antalkidas spoke without moving.

"There were baths in Olympia. We used the Kladaios."

"You always disliked foreign cities."

"I liked Syracuse too well."

He rose. "Perhaps it is I who dislike them. Athens is all hustle and hurry. Susa is suffocating."

"Only Sparta is all of a piece."

"The dignity of the old ways. We walk in their shadow."

"You say that!"

"A passing mood. I told you long ago I take things as they are." The pale eyes were weary. Kallias, senior to Antalkidas, still had the eyes of a young man.

I strapped on my sandals. We set off to the river. Antalkidas chose a deserted spot. As I bathed, he walked around the trees, to assure himself that no one was lurking unseen.

"Sit down, Leotychides," he said. How many times had I heard those words from him? Had he still been a friend, I might have jested with him. "There are matters of some urgency."

"Can they not wait until the next meeting?"

"Ephors receive idiotic complaints. Several men have reported seeing a youth escaping from their houses. All of them have beautiful wives. The youth is slender, tall, fair-haired..."

"By Apollo, I'll—"

"No, Leotychides. Thrashing Agis will not stop him. Advise him to throw some drugged meat to the dogs, to stop their barking. Be glad he is not risking a knife in his back with up-country girls, as Sphodrias did."

"Was there anything else."

493

He picked a pale, dark-veined crocus. "Agisilaos cannot be tried by the Council for treason."

When Antalkidas joined us, I assumed he had seen us as the winning side, and seized the moment. Apparently, for some reason, he had reconsidered.

"It is easily proven that he injured Sparta. He has already been fined once for taking on powers greater than a king, and has since assumed more."

"Men are often swayed more by passion than reason. Chairon thinks he has a majority in Council, and I dare say he has. *Now.* When the time comes, it will fall away. Too many of those old fellows served under Agisilaos in Asia, and at Koronaia to condemn him to death. It is a matter for the ephors."

"The ephors cannot try a king."

"The Council can set aside an unlawful king." He twisted the flower by the stem. "Then he is no longer a king."

"Agisilaos has reigned twenty-seven years."

"Demartos reigned a number of years, and reigned well. He was set aside. Agisilaos assumed the throne without consulting Delphi. Remember the oracle 'A lame king will bring wars of destruction to Sparta.'"

"After twenty-seven years?"

"The gods gave us time to rectify our wrong. They punished us at Leuktra. The earth has trembled many times this autumn. They are becoming impatient. Think also on this. If Agisilaos is executed, it merely makes a king of Archidamos, who has never been known to differ from his father."

"You have said the matter is for the ephors."

"The Elders who would shrink at executing Agisilaos will not hesitate to depose him. The ephors will banish him. Leotychides, the young men admire you; your contemporaries respect you, and the elders praise your respect of the Law."

"No, Antalkidas! I have not gone into this to make myself king. Let the kingship go to the best."

"Can you think how many disputes that would start?" He made an impatient gesture. "We need an orderly transition. Not a debate on the means of succession."

"I have said no, and that's an end to it." I rose.

He got to his feet with a swiftness surprising in a man of his increasing bulk. "By Zeus, you have a pride that would be

494

excessive in a god! Other deposed kings were provoked to take up arms by their pride, or driven into exile, but your pride was too great for anything like that. You could never admit what it cost you to lose the kingship, even to yourself."

"You may not believe it, Antalkidas, but being king never meant that much to me."

"Perhaps not. But you hate losing. Well, a man with too much pride is preferable to one with none, and you will be king–"

"I have told you–"

"You will tell me nothing. Doreius made you a good, obedient Spartiate, and you will obey your chief ephor. You will also obey the Apella when it proclaims you king. After we have mollified Thebes, and had time to regain our strength, you may attempt to restore the Law of Lykourgos, chop yourself up like Kleomenes, or whatever madness takes you. It is all the same to me."

"I still ask. Why do you want me as king?"

"People rally to a man quicker than to reason. Particularly when he is a handsome general with a good field record. And we have no time to lose. I should take little pleasure in being the most powerful man in a powerless City." The irony went out of his tone. "And I, too, am Spartiate."

Chapter 24

The cold bit as I stepped into the dark dawn, on my way to the river. A crust of snow covered the shadow-black grass. A few pale stars still clung to the sky. Not many birds heralded Apollo driving his chariot up from the east.

I collided with a running youth, He crumbled to the ground. I bent to help him up, and a sudden knife of wind stabbed between my shoulder-blades. He was not a youth, but a young man. A serf.

"Why are you lurking about my house?"

No reply. I shook him.

"I am Dromea's son, sir." he murmured, through lips blue with cold.

The fellow was half-frozen. I brought him into the house, and shouted to a servant to bring wine and sheepskins on the double. A swirl of skirts told me it was my wife I had spoken to with such unconscionable disrespect.

"Dromea's son died." I tested him.

"I am the son of her second marriage. My father is steward on the northern estate belonging to the queen your mother, may the gods give her long life."

Kleonike returned with servants carrying sheepskins and warmed wine, dismissed them and left us.

I recalled my mother telling me she had raised Dromea's husband to steward. "I had to know," I said.

"The queen my mistress has known me all my life." He was aware of the secret police.

"I believe you. Is Dromea well? What is wrong?"

He took the cup in both hands, warming them as he spoke. "I went into the village one evening, to a wine-shop, as there was little work." And much play, I thought. Coming unfrozen, the young man was quite good-looking. "There were some up-country men in the wine-shop. We know them as bad types. They were very drunk. I heard them boasting about how they tricked the Thebans. When I got back, I told my father. My mother said I must go to Sparta, and tell it to you – but I must

496

ask you to say that I am on the Queen's business, or I shall be punished for leaving the estate."

"I shall see to it. What about the Thebans."

"The up-country men said they went to the Theban camp."

Would any Lakedaimonian in his senses admit to that? This young fellow said they were drunk. The serfs like their wine and, if a serf considered these up-country men drunk, they were very drunk indeed. Past all discretion.

"What camp? Where?" Epaminondas had an army bivouacked near Mantinea.

"Over the border." Anywhere in Arkadia.

"Did they say how many troops were there?"

"A thousand thousands." A large force. "They told the Thebans that there are no guards in the passes in Lakonia, and that, if they gave them money, they will lead them in. The foreign officers said no army could go into Lakonia."

"I should think not."

"The up-country men were telling their friends that, if they go back with them, they can get silver, too."

"They were going back? I thought the Theban officers did not believe that they could invade Lakonia.

"These bad types told them that all the up-country people would make a great rising if they came in. The special Thebans took them to their own commander. Pel–Pel–"

"Pelopidas?"

"That is the name. He promised them great looting."

I told him I would hear the rest later.

Two up-country men, wearing sheepskins, stood in the room outside the chief ephor's room in the government buildings.

Several serfs, encrusted with several layers of winter's dirt, sat on the floor. They leapt to their feet when I came in. Antalkidas stepped out of his door, to see what the scuffling was about.

"So you have already heard," I said.

"Not from any responsible source. Until now. Where did you learn of it?"

"One of my mother's serfs. Not this sort–" I motioned about the room. "He's bright, and has been taught as a scribe. The son of her steward."

"Come into my office," he said. "I haven't had breakfast and I doubt whether you have, either. It might clear our minds."

The oil burned low in the lamp on the writing table. Antalkidas snuffed out the wick, as the sun gave us light but no warmth. Cold air poured in from the smoke-hole in the roof, defeating the efforts of the fire-pot to temper the chill.

"Where is Queen Timaia's estate in the north, Leotychides?"

"I wasn't aware she had one until now."

"Your mother has estates from Helos to Karyai. She understands the nature of power better than you–" He made an impatient gesture. "By Zeus, if Epaminondas had waited a month, Agisilaos would be gone, and we would be making peace, rather than resisting an invasion."

"Then you believe the Thebans *will* invade."

"I do not believe Epaminondas came to the Peloponnesos to invade Lakonia. But if the opportunity presented itself, I doubt whether he would throw it away. I would not, in his place."

"There must be a general mobilization. And a call for up-country volunteers."

"If the up-countrymen really are plotting to rebel?" The pale eyes were quizzical.

"Then we must garrison Gythion." Our port, with its shipworks, consisted of up-countrymen, as did the island of Kythera, just off the south-east promontory of Lakonia."

"We cannot risk Sparta to defend the port. As for Kythera, it will undoubtedly yield to the Thebans, as it did to the Athenians and the barbarians. Chion was right, when he said it would be well for that island to sink into the sea." An almost imperceptible glance to a god, and he added, "But Epaminondas is in the north. The south is not our immediate concern." He picked up the cup with the now-cold wine, and finished it. "I shall set my creatures to watching Agisilaos, and report to me if he so much as looks like thinking of leading Spartiate regiments out of the City. He is mad enough to attempt to take on an army of seventy thousand with six regiments. I must think on this...I shall talk to the Polemarchs when I know my own mind."

Antalkidas called all the generals of Sparta to a meeting after the midday meal. The Polemarchs were still with him. The other four ephors sat in stunned silence.

"Gentlemen..." Antalkidas began. "I have received reports that armed Arkadians and Argives have been sighted within the frontiers of Lakonia. The up-country men and the serfs, who brought me this information, came from places along our north and north-eastern frontiers.

"The armed foreigners were not the usual border raiders, looking for a Lakonian goat or two. We are all quite aware that neither the Argives nor the Arkadians would attempt to cross into Lakedaimon, unless they were assured of Theban support. "I must, therefore, tell you that Lakedaimon is under threat of invasion. Advance units of that invasion force may already be on our soil."

"They wouldn't dare!" It was the feisty old general from Leuktra. "Chief Ephor, you are misled."

Antalkidas smiled "Let us hope you are right, General. But we must assume the worst. Sparta does not guard her freedom by hoping for the best. That is why we have the finest army in Hellas. I have discussed the matter with the City's Polemarchs; and I'm convinced that Epaminondas will not repeat Xerxes's mistake, and throw his entire army against Lakedaimonians in a single pass. If he divides his forces, it will accelerate their mobility, and confound us as to where they are. It is my belief that they will rendezvous somewhere, and regroup to attack Sparta."

Silence greeted his words. Perhaps, like me, they felt it all to be unreal. Could we possibly be considering an enemy attack upon Sparta?

Antalkidas continued. "Where will they rendezvous, gentlemen? By what passes will they enter? The pass at Skiritis is unlikely."

"The Skiritis are good hill fighters," Kallias said. "They can defend the pass."

"If they are not too concerned with harvesting their olives," Antalkidas replied. "General Ischolaos, you are ordered to Skiritis. You may have a regiment of freed serfs and four hundred Tegean exiles. Give the Arkadians a good thrashing in the pass, but let a few escape to advise Epaminondas that invading Lakonia is not a very good idea."

There was some laughter then. My mind suddenly went back to that inadvertent "invasion" of the Argolid in flock days.

499

"Antalkidas, the pass at Karyai–"

A brief smile echoed his own remembrance. "It is a possibility I will bear in mind."

"Herea..." Another general began.

"Don't be absurd." the fellow beside him said. "They would have to go through Eleia. The Eleians are our allies."

"The truth of it is that we haven't got enough men to guard all the passes," Antalkidas admitted.

"Use allied troops," one man suggested. Jeers drowned his voice. Sparta did not call upon foreigners to defend her.

"General Alexandros," Antalkidas continued. "Stand by to await orders."

Alexandros was a brave, competent commander, who could be depended upon to obey orders to the letter. Ischolaos was one of Sparta's best generals, and believed to be the City's next polemarch. Neither man was of Agisilaos's faction.

There was another silence.

"The rest of you," Antalkidas said, "will remain in Sparta." He held up one hand to still the outburst. "The Spartiate regiments will remain in Sparta. Alexandros, I can promise you a regiment of Boiotian exiles, who will like nothing better than a chance to fight Thebans. Gentlemen, we defend the City. Sparta's walls are the spears of her men."

"There will be a general mobilization–" One of the generals began.

"Not at present." Antalkidas smiled. "No need to panic."

I tarried after the meeting broke up.

"Antalkidas, you did not warn them of an up-country rebellion."

"The artisans are the only up-countrymen about the City. They are unlikely rebels."

"You do not believe that the hill-men will rise?"

"Their lands have never suffered an enemy, because we protect them. Sparta is slow to war, and lays a light burden on them for war duty." It was as though he spoke his thoughts aloud. "If we move against them without cause, they could be driven to rebel."

"If we are invaded, they may feel they have cause."

"We shall act if need be. If you will excuse me, Leotychides, I must call upon Agisilaos, and convince him that his person is

500

too valuable to risk in battle."

Agisilaos was seen with crews of serfs, fortifying the heights. Antalkidas had thought of something to keep him occupied. General Ischolaos set out with his troops. Shortly afterwards, General Alexandros and the Boiotians marched out of the City.

All the activity occasioned little curiosity. The people of Sparta were taken by the snow. It fell in large flakes that children caught in their hands. It was not the usual snow that melts in the morning sun, but a heavy white blanket that muffled the usual sounds of the City.

Elders dared not risk their brittle bones on the icy streets. Women clung to the sides of buildings. Strong men plodded, placing one foot deliberately after the other. Sparta had become a white city of silence and isolated movement. Day after day, Apollo brought up a cold sun. The world was in suspense, as was the enemy. Wherever they might be.

As if Poseidon had been sleeping and woke, stretching and yawning, the earth trembled slightly. The skies darkened. With the clouding came heavy rain. It warmed the air, and sent the Eurotas rushing and overflowing its banks. The sanctuary springs atop the acropolis became small rivers rushing down the side of the hill. There was a mood of careless gaiety, as people were able to move about freely again.

With the thaw came the Thebans. Scouts sighted the van of a large force entering by way of Karyai. It was undefended, except by one sentry.

"You spoke of Karyai, Leotychides," Antalkidas said in Hall.

"It was a guess; no better than any other."

Antalkidas ordered the general mobilization. All the women and small children living on countryside kleroi were brought into the City. They crowded into Sparta with their personal servants, treating it rather like a festival. Visiting friends and relations. Exchanging gifts. Consuming food.

More than three-quarters of the troops Ischalaos led to Skiritis returned to Sparta. The Arkadians had invaded with a full division. Ischalaos ordered the young men back to Sparta. Then he made a last stand in the village, where he fell, with all the older men.

"If he had kept his force intact, and fought the Arkadians in the pass, he could have held it," I remarked to Meleas.

"With Spartiates. He had none. He did well. We need the men here."

"I cannot believe that Arkadians love Thebes."

"Have they any choice? As well as his own Thebans and other Boiotians. Epaminondas had come south with the eastern and western Lokrians, the Arkanians, the Thessalian targeteers and impressed Phokian contingents. "As for the mercenaries, they don't care where they fight."

Over-peopled Arkadia supplied Hellas with as many mercenaries as Athens does now.

The next day, we learnt that General Alexandros and two hundred of his men had been slain, by an Argive division that pushed its way into Lakonia. Antalkidas deployed the Spartiate regiments about the City, in strategic positions. The wall of spears was a thin one. Little more than a fence.

Antalkidas had been right. Epaminondas split his army. He divided it into four forces. They rendezvoused at Sellasia, and encamped at the entrance of the plain of Sparta – in the sacred groves of the sanctuary of Apollo, where I had given a small bird to the god and beseeched him to save Pausanios.

I was ordered to take a *mora*, and defend the bridge across the Eurotas leading into Sparta – and was given a Spartiate regiment, and one of the bastard regiments. I deployed them in the groves of Athena Alea, on the City side of the river.

A messenger rode up, with orders for one of the regiments to report to the Polemarchs at once. Leaving Pityas in command, I rode through the muddy streets to the government buildings.

"Antalkidas, the Polemarchs have commandeered one of my regiments."

"On my orders."

"I need that bastard regiment."

"I have received a message from Gythion, asking for troops." He looked up from whatever he was reading. "Do you understand? Gythion is loyal."

"Can they not fight for their own town?"

"They will. But they are artisans, not warriors. One regiment of Spartiates is little enough to send them."

"So the bastards are unqualified Spartiates when we are invaded."

"No orations, Leotychides," he snapped "Sorry..."His face looked quite grey. "Sorry I had to requisition your men... Sorry..."

"Never mind, Antal, just give me those Orchomenian mercenaries Agisilaos hired from Mantinea."

"I haven't seen a sign of them since the Thebans invaded. You must make do with what you have."

"Do you expect me to stand off the entire invasion force with half a *mora*?" I exploded.

"Leo', there is not a great deal between two hundred and fifty and five hundred, when you are facing seventy thousand..."

As I dismounted in the groves of Athena, Pityas pointed to the acropolis. "Agisilaos is in the Bronze House. I wonder why he has taken to the heights."

"The better to see the pass he has brought Sparta to."

In the distance, along the left bank of the Eurotas, came an endless train of marching men, like a monster sea-serpent. Its body twisted along the curving river-road from the north, its tail so many miles to the rear that it was not yet visible; its head a crested helmet two hand-spans higher than its neck.

I deployed my men in a long battle-line, placing the taller men in back to give an illusion of depth, praying to Athena that her olive trees might add to the deception. The hoplites watched the advance of the monster, resolution to die fighting written on their faces. It was not the time for one of those jests that go down so well before an action. Teleutias might have brought it off. Or Kleombrotos.

The scales of the serpent became columns, as the road broadened into the plain. Toque-topped columns. The crested helmet belonged to Epaminondas, making his superior height appear even greater. With a sinking feeling, I saw him turn, and lead his army directly towards the river-bank. The Polemarchs had calculated wrongly. They had been certain the enemy would not attempt the river in full spate, but would rush the bridge.

Never in memory had the water been so cold. Even we, who were accustomed to it, limited the evening dip to an instant's immersion, and omitted the morning one altogether.

Epaminondas waded into the river up to the tops of his soft leather boots, as if it were a summer day. The swollen Eurotas rushed on, overflowing its banks, as if trying to expel the alien body with all the force of its fury. There was something splendid about the man, who stood like Achilles fighting the Xanthos.

A few of his Thebans followed him. They ran back on to the river bank, as soon as the water touched their boots. Epaminondas gestured broadly, like a man inviting friends along for a swim, turned his back, and went in up to his waist.

I calculated. He was not within spear-throw.

He stood alone in the river. His men hung back. He laughed. He challenged. He cajoled. He threatened. He thundered at the troops huddling hesitantly on the river-bank.

They refused. Not for all the urging of their magnificent commander were they going into those icy waters. They disobeyed. They were not Spartiate. O, Dioscuri, Twin Protectors of Sparta, surely you cannot let her die!

A large detachment broke off from the main body, and marched towards the bridge. I thrust my arm into my shield.

"Leo'," Pityas said. "Don't lead them on foot. You will always be a cavalry officer. What will they do if you fall?"

"Obey their orders. They are Spartiate."

Their faces had altered. No longer were they going to die fighting a monster serpent, but preparing to engage an enemy who had already been bested by our Eurotas. Now was the time for the jest.

I fixed my eyes upon Dexippas, but spoke to them all. "You are not to die fighting, but to *kill* fighting. That is an order."

I brought up half the regiment close to the bridge, where we would be obscured by trees. The other half I deployed in full sight, shields locked, further back in the groves, as if they were the front columns of a large force.

The Thebans approached the bridge without hastening their steps. Not one must be permitted to step off. It would be like containing an enemy in a narrow pass. They began crossing in an unhurried manner.

When the lead men were within spear-throw, I ordered my hoplites to launch their spears. Thebans fell under the rain of iron and ash. The first oncoming men tripped over the bodies in the narrow confines of the bridge, and went flying into the river, screaming as the lethal cold closed over them. A few tried to float on their shields. The current carried them away.

The men behind hesitated. I led the charge. The enemy in the rear advanced steadily, unaware of the confusion.

"For Kleombrotos!" I shouted, as we fell on them.

My men fought with such ferocity that the superior numbers of the enemy fell back in disorder. When they tried to regroup, we charged again. More were hurtled into the water by the impact. Others died, trampled under the feet of their compatriots. The surviving Thebans saw the half-regiment of Spartan hoplites crossing the bridge. I called off the pursuit. The enemy fled to the main force, led by Epaminondas on the left side of the river. Bypassing Sparta, they headed south.

The overcast sky glowed brightly with a reddish haze. In the outskirts of the City, the Eurotas Vale was burning. The plain swarmed with foreign helmets. Thessalians staggered under heavy chests, spilling valuables. The Arkadians had found wine, and were already drunk. Theban troops hacked olive-trees, tore grape-vines from their poles, and pulled them out by the roots. Houses and outbuildings blazed.

The ephors sent me, with two companies, to quell a disturbance in the City.

The smell of smoke brought people out into the streets. A crowd starting at the Cattle Price House streamed on to the road leading to the acropolis. A large number of people were already gathered on top of the hill. Jostling and shouting, all dignity gone, as if the fire of their rage could quench the flames, they pushed past the Bronze House wildly, to better see their destruction.

I deployed my two companies of hoplites to form a cordon between the rush of people and the dangerous cliff. It was fury, not fear, which impelled them. Women, descended from twenty generations of women who had not seen the fires of an enemy, were maddened by the sight. Calling down the wrath of the gods upon the enemy, they set up a clamour to equal the Furies. Old men shook impotent fists, and shouted down to the looters that they would be dead men if they were still young. A hefty matron turned her anger from the enemy to the cordon of hoplites. A fistful of earth struck my face.

At some time, I found my mother standing beside me, looking towards the place where the outer reaches of lovely Kynsouria swell into the hills, sweeping up to Taygetos. She had built a second house there, where she spent the summer months; smaller than the palace, airy and beautiful. There she had taken many objects precious to her. It was a burning brand.

"It is good that you built that house in the City, Leotychides." The end of her peplos covered her white hair.

Had the day not been so unreal, my mother talking about houses, as I stood before my armed men, might have seemed an illusion.

Her eyes did not move from the leaping flames of her house. "I never showed you *his* portrait." She spoke with dead calm. "I kept all their gifts there, too."

"Whose gifts?"

"Agis and Leonidas. Their small gifts. Where are the flocks, Leotychides?"

"Leonidas is in Sparta. His commander brought them in during the snow. The boys are living in an old barracks."

Many barracks were empty, now that there were so few permanent regiments.

"And Agis?"

"Near Amyklai."

"The Thebans are marching south."

"Their commander will bring them into the town, if the enemy is sighted."

"Amyklai is a small town."

"It is a Spartiate town, Mother."

"Timaia!" A voice called. My mother turned.

Kyniska stood a few paces away, with the grey hair and deep lines none of her portraits show. My mother held her arms outstretched to her rival. They embraced. Together, they called upon the people to come with them to the temple of Artemis Orthia, to sacrifice. They led the way to the hollow. An example of serenity. Few people followed the straight backs of the two Eurypontid women.

A keening woman rushed up, and beat her fists against the shield of one of the hoplites. Her dash signalled a new

506

onslaught of the crowd towards the edge of the hill. I ordered my men to raise their shields, to block out the spectacle of destruction. The crowd rushed on, without ceasing its unearthly din. The hoplites retreated.

These soldiers, who had stood off an invading force at the bridge, fell back before the elders and women, doing no more than say, "Stand away, Mistress, Sir." It is something ingrained. The only measure that would halt the self-destruction of the mob would be a charge, bringing down the vanguard. I was as helpless as my men against my upbringing. I could not give the order.

I had them point their spears at the crowd. They retreated all the more quickly, in fear that the people might impale themselves. I ordered them to plant their spears on the ground at their sides. Which accomplished nothing.

A determined face broke through the milling mass. Gorgo spearheaded a file of young women. Her struggle through had knocked her hair loose from its high loop, and it tumbled loose and black down her back. She seized the keening woman who hammered the soldier's shield, and roughly slapped her face.

Her order to the young women behind her was inaudible in the cacophony. They understood what was expected of them. They broke into two groups, kicked and elbowed their way through to the extreme ends of the front of the crowd, and began beating them inwards. I divined their purpose.

The surprise attack of the determined women could only hold the throng a short time. It was long enough to permit me to spread my hoplites in a half-circle. A mindless mob can be turned as readily in one direction as another.

Slowly we turned the people back towards the Bronze House and down the hill, as the flames of the dying district sank into embers and smoke. The war-drunk, wine-drunk, triumph-drunk invaders were ravishing Lakonia the inviolate, while the people screamed their pain as the fox tore through the belly of Sparta.

507

Chapter 25

The abandoned barracks filled.

Every citizen under sixty again lived in barracks. Some of us two to a room. We had to double up, to give over a section of our own quarters to Lesser Spartiates, without permanent regiments.

Most of them were out of training. The youngest had not been properly hardened. These men, who were the same blood and bone as the men who fought at Thermopylai, were now but poor-baked brick sections, next to the stone of the full Spartiates in the living wall about the City.

Antalkidas offered freedom to any serf fit to fight.

The invaders continued their southward march. A messenger rode in from Amyklai, to ask for troops. The Thebans were besieging the town. The men who defended the bridge were sent to Amyklai. They went out under another commander. Some ass had put my name forward for polemarch after the action at the bridge.

The same day, Chairon reported for duty, accompanied by a number of other men over seventy. All were armed. The eldest was a nonagenarian. I accepted them, although I suggested that they sleep in their own houses. They refused this comfort.

"In any event," Chairon lowered his voice. "My house has become a barracks. My wife is drilling a regiment of women." So were Kyniska, the soft-spoken Mistress Argileonis, and other leading women of the City. "Please don't repeat it, my boy." He smiled wryly. "I have orders to keep it secret."

We both knew what it meant. If all the men died, the women would fight. And after they died...I had been a rhodibas and a melleiren...The boys would avenge their mothers and sisters.

There would be no Spartan slaves. No maiden would become some Theban's plaything. No proud woman do the menial work of an unlettered Theban mistress of the house. No Spartan boys be sold by mercenaries to traders. Sparta would live or perish fighting.

More old men took up arms again, their helpless rage of the day of the fires turned to resolution. Now, young men who had not been born when we took Lechion stood next to elders, whose fathers had fought in the Persian wars.

Over six thousand serfs came in, the first day, in response to Antalkidas's call. Hastily equipped, they were posted in the less vulnerable areas. Freed serfs had fought well against Athens and in Asia, but these men had never held anything more deadly than farm tools.

The siege of Amyklai continued. The enemy reached Gythion. The battle for the port began.

"The Philasians offer us troops." Antalkidas had moved a sleeping pallet into the chief ephor's office. A pair of dry boots stood in a corner.

"What they lack in numbers, they possess in loyalty." I forced the next words. "Accept, Antal; you must send to the allies for contingents."

"I already have." His smile was thin. "Messages went out this morning to the Corinthians, the Sikyonians. All the Peloponnesians." The shield of the Peloponnesos was calling upon allies for its own defence. "I cannot get a letter to Syracuse until sailing weather. Nor could they send troops before spring. By the gods, Leo', I have even sent to Athens."

The Orchomenian mercenaries reported for duty. Strapping up-country lads made their way in from the hills, to volunteer. Some reported that trouble-makers from their villages had joined the enemy to loot. Most up-countrymen remained on their own lands, to protect what they could. More serfs came in to volunteer. Pityas and I spent a day with each new lot, teaching them one end of a spear from another.

"I can remember when most of Hellas begged Sparta for an alliance," he said once, as we broke for the midday meal.

"Perhaps a city only has allies when it does not need them."

Eleians had been sighted amongst the enemy.

No longer was there game on the tables in Hall. With the enemy outside the City, men no longer hunted. Our club was crowded with citizens whose halls had been burnt down. Meals were meagre, but we kept up our jests and easy conversation. When no allied contingents arrived, a heavy gloom penetrated the hall, like a creeping fog.

509

One night, as Antalkidas made an amusing tale of the failure of his date palms. Derkyllidas looked about him, as though he was studying the terrain of a battle-field. Then, that great man made much of walking about the dining couches, looking for a seat. A number of young men rose, but he passed them by. With a glint in his eyes, he strode to Antalkidas's couch, and halted to force the chief ephor to rise.

A few members smiled. Antalkidas remained propped on one elbow, talking of new palms to come from Persia. Derkyllidas cleared his throat. After a time, he spoke. "Well, Antalkidas, will you not give your seat to an elder?"

Antalkidas looked up. "Most certainly not to one who has no son, to offer his to me when I am old."

There was laughter. I forget what Derkyllidas replied, but talk eased, and became almost merry, as lamp-flames reflected on the captured shields that hung on the walls.

After the libations, Antalkidas casually mentioned that Amyklai had driven off the enemy. The siege was lifted. The section of the invading army that failed to take the town had decamped, and was burning and plundering its way south again, on the road to Helos. Some speculated that they might turn west, and join their comrades in the assault upon Gythion. The port had not yet capitulated.

Everyone praised the Amyklaians. Someone said it was a pity about the eirens. Another commented that they had shown their mettle.

"What eirens?" I asked. Had eirens been involved in anything, Agis would be at the centre of it.

"Some eirens sharpened their spears, and fought for the town." Antalkidas said: evasively, I thought.

On leaving the hall, I set off to inner Kynsouria. This was not something my mother should hear casually.

Pale stars lit the cold night, as I rode towards the palace. Turning into a familiar street, I saw a division of armoured men, marching towards me in columns. The step was not Spartan. How had the enemy penetrated our defences so noiselessly? The beat of hooves warned me that cavalry followed them.

Cursing myself for a fool for coming out without armour, I reined in to the side of a house, and dismounted. The gate was barred. No gate-keeper appeared. The days of open gates had gone with the invasion. I stripped off my cloak and rolled it into a shield, drew my short sword from its scabbard, and pressed close against the wall.

The foreign regiments drew closer. "Seems deserted," I heard their commander say. "They never light their streets." Another spoke. "Spartans see in the dark like leopards." "Well, Hades take it, where are we?"

Corinthian accents! I stepped out. Threw on my cloak. Put myself at their disposal.

Pasimelos led them. "Could you think we would throw away the shield of Peloponnesos, and flee the field," he said. Corinthians always have a graceful turn of speech.

Aristeas was with the cavalry. He told me that Corinth had sent one of her most persuasive speakers to Athens to urge the Athenians to send us troops." (Eventually they sent Iphikrates. The shoemaker's son was still a mercenary at heart, and spent his time plundering Arkadia, without ever reaching Lakonia).

I took Pasimelos to Antalkidas, who always went back to his office after Hall. Aristeas and the rest I sent to Pityas, with orders to see them quartered comfortably in our barracks. Pityas told me later that Aristeas was amused by hearing anything in Sparta called comfortable.

It was near the late winter dawn when I reached the palace. I expected to find it in darkness. Lamps lit a number of rooms. A servant told me the queen had retired early to her chambers.

The room opening to her bed-chamber was brightly illuminated. My mother rested in a slant-backed chair, holding a cup of wine. Her head turned at my step. "Leotychides! Are we under attack?" She did not sound alarmed. "I hope you are not going to ask me to put anyone up. The house is full."

"Mother—"

"At least fifty sleeping in the great hall. Do sit down."

"And join us in a cup of wine, Father." I had not noticed Agis, reclining on cushions across from her, holding one of a set of cups painted with a boar hunt. "Grandmother's wine is always excellent."

"How did you come here, Agis?"

"On one of your running-horses. The only one, I fear, that

511

escaped the Arkadians." He sipped his wine. "Actually, I found the Thebans altogether better types."

"You are still standing, Leotychides." My mother observed. "Would you have room in your house for a few people?"

"I don't know." I seated myself. "I haven't been there since the invasion. Ask Kleonike. Why are you in Sparta, Agis, when your flock is at Amyklai?"

"Father, I have passed out."

"You are based with your flock. Where is it?"

"In the town, I dare say. The commander took us in when the Thebans arrived."

"Why are you not with it?"

"Some of us went out again."

"Agis, I knew eirens were fighting. It is all right. You can tell me."

"I have already told Grandmother. It would bore her to hear it again."

"Agis—"

He looked apologetically towards my mother, and smiled his charming lop-sided smile. "The Thebans looked like settling in. We could see them from the town. They were cutting down trees and stacking them one on the other, as a barricade in front of their lines. The Arkadians were too busy looting the countryside to help. A detachment of Thebans broke off from the main body, and made for the town. It was quite annoying, because our troops were lined up in battle-order, ready to advance on the Thebans in the stockade. The Theban detachment assaulted the town, and people began throwing rocks, knives and anything that came to hand down on them. I am boring you, Grandmother. To cut it short, we sharpened our spears and decided to have a go at them. The commander only gave permission to those of us who had passed out, poor fellow—"

"What I asked you is why you are not here, when your flock is in Amyklai."

"Leotychides, you are not sending him back now."

"No, mother. I am not ordering my son into a countryside infested with enemy troops. But I should rather like to know how he came to be in Sparta."

"I know your horses quite well, Father. When I saw an

512

Arkadian riding one, I killed him and rode the beast to Sparta."

"Could you be more specific?"

He sighed in an exaggerated manner, and emptied his wine-cup. "We were standing off the Thebans with spears – swords being somewhat impractical, as we had no armour. Somehow I became separated from the rest. It is like that in battle."

"I shall bear it in mind."

"I dispatched a few Thebans–"

"A god must have covered you in a mist, for you are remarkably untouched for someone fighting without armour."

"I was coming to that. Three of them came at me. One knocked the spear out of my hand. The other seized my shield, and pinioned my arms behind my back. His friend was about to run my own spear through my throat. The officer just watched, so I said to him.' Sir, would you ask your man to run my spear through my chest, as I have been told I have rather a beautiful throat.' He laughed, and said, 'By the gods, he's barely more than a boy, but he is more of a man than Agisilaos.' I told him I considered that no praise at all, as Agisilaos was not man enough to be compared to a boy. He asked 'Have you so little liking for your King?' 'He's hardly my King,' I replied, meaning that he is a usurper–"

"I never said that, Agis."

"Others do." He replied. My mother averted her eyes. "Anyway, the Theban officer misunderstood, and asked, 'Are you not Spartan?' That gave me the idea."

"What idea?"

"I told him I was Athenian. He said I had a Dorian accent. I replied that my father had sent me here to have a Spartan upbringing, and I had been reared in Lakedaimon. He looked doubtful. I asked him whether I did not look Athenian. He agreed that I had the high Athenian looks, whatever those are. Then he asked me the name of my family. I told him the Alkmaionid." My mother had been filling him with stories of Alkibiades, as I suspected. "He ordered the two ruffians to release me, which was a relief. Every time I spoke, that spear pricked my throat. I thanked him. He wanted to know why I had been fighting for Sparta. I told him his soldiers had attacked my comrades, and any man would fight for his friends. He found my sentiments laudable and advised me to tell my father that

513

Sparta was no longer a safe place to be. I said his men might keep my spear, but I should like my shield back, as it would be quite humiliating to lose it. Very agreeable fellow. He gave both back, and expressed a wish to see me one day in his city." Again, the lop-sided smile. "I assured him it would be my greatest pleasure."

It was hard to restrain a smile at the retort. "Why did you not return to your flock?"

"I saw that damned Arkadian riding your horse, and lost my temper. In any event, our men had seen what was happening, and come to the rescue of the town. The eirens were no longer fighting. Half the enemy army looked like crossing the river at a narrow part, and heading north. I thought I should cut quite a figure if I rode in and gave the warning."

"Why didn't you? Give the warning?"

"I did. Antalkidas already knew."

"What are your plans now, if I may ask?"

He pulled himself up. "To show you my shield, my trusting Father." He seized it from behind the cushions. "And my spear. Are the blood-stains fresh enough to satisfy you that I have been in battle? The scratches on my throat? If so, I shall wet the inside with another cup of wine. I am rather tired."

"I, too," my mother said.

"You do too much, Grandmother." Agis took her cup and refilled it. Bending over her shoulders, he returned it to her. "Let Kleombrotos's widow do her share."

For once, I agreed with my son. My mother and Kyniska continued their rounds of the shrines and sanctuaries, as much to calm the people as to appease the divinities. The young Queen, barely thirty, was better able for it than these two ageing women.

"She will not leave the palace. Agesipolis went out in the cold, and took a fever."

"Boy's fevers are nothing," I told her. "That first winter in the flock, I no sooner ended one cold than I started another. Agesipolis is eleven."

"Nonetheless, a worried-faced queen is of little use."

I left, not quite convinced by my son's story, but the return of

Theban troops in the morning appeared to confirm it. They raised their tents just outside the City. Although they were in large numbers, they made no concerted move to attack. Sometimes a detachment would break away and press closer. Sorties went out and drove them back.

Shortly after the first Corinthian contingent came in, the Sikyonians arrived. They were followed by the Philasians, the Poleanians, and contingents from other small cities. It is only in danger that one knows true allies.

From the Theban fires, one night, a chant arose.

> "Agisilaos, Agisilaos,
> King of the Bronze House,
> Prowling dog in Boiotia,
> Afraid to fight in Lakonia..."

There were more verses. All scathing. Many ribald. Each night, the chanting grew by many voices, and new verses were added.

"Agisilaos is becoming more difficult to control," Antalkidas confided one day.

"I wonder that you have kept him in the Bronze House this long."

"I told him that, by not responding to the Theban jibes, he showed greater mastery of himself than any king in history. Remember Megabates?" His smile faded. "Now Phrixus is with him all the time, and only the gods know what the two fools are planning. By Zeus, Leotychides, he could destroy us if he provokes an engagement now."

"Perhaps better now than when the divisions in the south return."

"We must await our allies."

"I doubt there will be any more contingents, Antal."

"Not those allies. Cold and hunger. When Epaminondas laid waste to the Vale, he destroyed his supply base." Our own stores were running low, but it is impossible to effectively besiege an unwalled city. Night runners brought in what they could from the hills. And Spartans are hardened to endure hunger. "He doesn't know the Arkadians as we do," Antalkidas went on. "They have had their amusement, and they have their

515

booty. They are already slipping away at night."

Our Orchomenian mercenaries did not return to Arkadia. They were hired men doing the job they were paid for.

"He may attack while he is still in strength."

"He will wait for his Thebans in the south. Gythion is still holding. The enemy suffered heavy losses. They will suffer more before it falls. He was a fool not to have thrown his precious Sacred Band on you at the bridge. Now cold and hunger can save Sparta, Leo'. But not if Agisilaos precipitates an engagement before they have had time to do their work."

A group of men seized the sanctuary of Artemis on the Issorian Hill, by the simple means of saying they had been ordered to defend it. Antalkidas made contact with them, and learnt that they were Spartiate officers. They demanded that Agisilaos be deposed, and tried for causing war with Thebes. When he was brought to trial, they would surrender the sanctuary.

Antalkidas refused. It was his belief that Agisilaos would not surrender himself willingly. That he still had a few supporters; Kyniska had more, and Archidamos had his own circle. We dared no risk war within the City when the Thebans bivouacked outside. He smiled slightly then, and added that no attempt would be made to dislodge the men in the Issorian.

He also told me that my son Agis was among the rebels.

The Thebans withdrew from Gythion. That brave city of up-countrymen had stood them off. The bulk of the widely dispersed invasion force was assembling and returning north.

The people of Sparta did not appear unduly perturbed. It was as if they were beginning to regard an enemy presence as part of life. Or simply to accept having lost all the certainty of their lives.

I was ordered to the sanctuary of Poseidon, with one hundred of my best men. Pityas waited as I stepped out into the cold, dark morning to strap on my armour. My batman had developed eyes like Lynkeus in recent years, and I had posted him as a lookout.

"Your hair has turned nearly brown," Pityas said, as I put on my helmet. "Mine grows grey."

"The truth is, Pityas, that we are both older than our sons." I glanced at the regiment, standing smartly, spears planted on the ground.

"Take two hundred and fifty to guard the bridge."

"How can I? You are taking one hundred to the sanctuary."

"Use Corinthians."

An order calling for the best men meant a dangerous action. All my men were the best. I called for volunteers. A youth, with curly black hair, fairly flew in front of me. He looked so much like the young Aristeas, in Olympia, that I almost started.

"Nikandros, the son of Aristeas," Pityas said.

I explained to the eager youth that I had need of Spartan hoplites. Aristeas and his son were both cavalry.

"I have the straightest spear in Corinth, sir. Pityas will tell you."

I heard some of my own men say that the youth had the look of luck on him. Perhaps it was simply Corinthian charm, but men fight best when they feel luck is with them.

"Eighteen." Pityas said, as I wavered.

"Ask your father's permission, exchange that *kappa* shield for a *lamda*, and fall in," I said.

"Eighteen..." Pityas repeated.

"Eighteen is fighting age everywhere except Sparta."

Meleas was waiting, as we marched up. On the racing course, near the sanctuary of Poseidon, stood a very sorry-looking cavalry unit. In front of the Tyndariae House stood more than two hundred fine-looking young Spartan hoplites.

"By Apollo, Meleas–"

"Sorry, Leotychides. I need at least three hundred, if this is to work. I squeezed a hundred and fifty from Archidamos, and picked up fifty volunteers."

"Volunteers? Every Spartiate is under orders – Eirens?"

"They have all passed out. I need every man. An enemy cavalry force is going to try to break into the city this way."

A young voice remarked in soft, sibilant Doric. "What a fine house! It looks like an ancient palace."

Meleas eyed the Corinthian with disapproval.

"It is, Nikandros." I said "It belonged to the Twin Gods. Go back with the others." With a sparkling smile, he left the conversation of his elders. "The men think he is favoured by

517

Fortune," I explained.

"We can do with her help," Meleas replied quickly.

"You know that cavalry will scatter like quail before the enemy."

He smiled grimly. "They are bait. I was thinking that a wooden horse would be of more use, when it occurred to me that I had one. The Twin Gods' House. The owner's family are in mine. The cavalry will draw the enemy like flies. The hoplites will be hidden inside the house." He turned to the young hoplites. "Gentlemen, when some of you dozed through your poetry lessons, I daresay you never considered their use."

I caught sight of sunset-gold hair, almost entirely covered by a helmet. Leonidas! His green eyes pleaded with me to keep my silence.

Meleas integrated my hoplites with his own. "Do not make a sound once you are inside the house," he instructed them. "When I order the charge, come out as if the Furies were after you. If the enemy stand their ground, you know what is expected of you." His eyes went to the Corinthian youth. "Does he?"

"Spartans fight on discipline, Corinthians on passion – but they fight."

"Discipline is more dependable." He addressed the men again. "If the enemy retreat, pursue only far enough to scatter them. That is an order."

He sent the eirens first into the house, so they would be the last out. Aristeas's son he placed with the eirens. The Corinthian boy asked to be allowed to pour a libation to the Twin Gods in front of their own house.

"I see what you mean," Meleas admitted.

All was quiet. The only enemy in sight were the usual Thebans on the far outskirts of the City. They showed no signs of grouping for an attack.

"Meleas, how do you know the enemy will attempt a breakthrough here? Did Mistress Argileonis tell you?"

"Loyal up-country men slip into the enemy lines and mingle with the looters. They pick up useful information. Leotychides, do you think you might smarten up that cavalry a bit. The way they look, the ruse might be too obvious."

I shaped squares from sloppy rectangles, and returned to

Meleas. He called to his batman for food, passed me a piece of bread and a drinking cup. The wine and water were already mixed in the flask.

"I hear our hall is to boast another polemarch," he said.

"It would still have one more, had you not declined."

"Didn't decline..." He cocked his ear, listening to an almost inaudible throbbing from the south. "Enemy cavalry. Quite some distance. No, I didn't refuse. Just reminded them that there was little point in promoting me when I would be sixty next year, as they seemed to be dithering between the two of us. I had quite forgotten that, by then, you will have a polemarch serving under you."

I, too, had not given a thought to our enterprise since the invasion.

"So Antalkidas talked you around."

"His reasoning cannot be faulted. And I think you will be a good king. I didn't always, although I considered you had been unlawfully deposed. Once, I thought you might take Kinadon's way."

"Once, I thought you would *not*."

He laughed, then sobered. "We may have little to do. Everyone is saying that Sparta was supreme when Agisilaos became king, and he has brought her low." The throbbing became discernible as hoof-beats. He downed the last of our scanty meal.

"Meleas, let me lead the cavalry. I might keep it in formation when the enemy is sighted."

"Take my mount." He smiled "Sire."

No dust rose from the muddy ground, as a column of enemy horse advanced towards the racing course. Men of the north. Thessalians and Lokrians. Good horse country. Good horsemen. They were followed by a detachment of hoplites, in toque-shaped helmets.

The enemy cavalry was close enough to see the horses breathing cloud into the cold air. Meleas ordered the charge. The door of the house flung open. Hoplites ran out. Cavalry and foot attacked simultaneously.

The horses carried our reluctant cavalrymen forward into the enemy ranks. The northerners were caught up in a tangle of men and mounts. By the time our cavalry was routed, the young hoplites were on the enemy, spearing the horses, and falling on the riders before the beasts sunk fully to the ground. Unaccustomed to foot-fighting, the men from the north fled in disorder.

When the Thebans lost the protection of their cavalry, they turned their backs and fled, chased by our hoplites. Meleas ordered them to halt. Another attempt to break through Sparta's thickening wall of spears had failed.

I stepped quietly into the darkened barracks. With the arrival of the foreign contingents, we were crowded three and four to a room. A voice from the past spoke in my mind, saying, "Go to sleep, Leotychides. And don't wake the other boys."

"Leo'? Pityas whispered. "Niko' did not ask Aristeas's permission to accompany you today."

"Nor did Aristeas ask his father's permission to go into exile. The lad fought well." So had Leonidas, but I did not want to boast.

"My son fought at Amyklai, Leo'... a number of eirens were slain."

"Pit', why didn't you ask sooner? Antalkidas sent to the families privately." With invaders in the country, it was not time for public readings of dead youths. "If you heard nothing, he is safe...Leonidas fought today, too. He and Nikandros get on well."

"Those were good days at Lechion when we were young. Pity we didn't know it at the time."

"There will be other good days..."

Days when we would ride to battle with our sons beside us, as Aristeas rode with his. Not in far-off meaningless places, but in our own Peloponnesos. Agis was a rebel in the Issorian sanctuary, but already citizens whispered praise of what the men inside had done Agisilaos had brought on the invasion, and Agisilaos must pay. The rebels would come out to cheers.

The enemy forces were becoming disorganized. That vast army lacked cohesion, and looked to the Thebans for direction. Those Thebans were the same we had defeated at Nemea, Koronaia, and sent running to the roof-tops at Lechion.

The Sacred Band alone were fighters equal to Spartans, and there were only three hundred of them. At Leuktra, their quality had taken us by surprise. Thebans fought in their own country then. Now this vast amorphous mass was in a land unknown to any enemy. And faced with a disciplined, determined defence.

I let the years ahead unfold before me. Lakedaimon returned to the Law of Lykourgos. Sparta again the citadel of the Peloponnesos. No more. No less. My sons and the sons of my friends winning honours in games and in battle.

Pityas was right. Youth had been sweet. But the autumn years held something too.

The death of young King Agesipolis stunned Sparta. Silent people lined the streets to watch the funeral processions pass. Gorgo, with her women, stood ready should the bier provoke another mad outburst, but the mood of this crowd was dazed and dull-eyed.

People saw the boy King's death as an omen. I attributed it to the soft rearing of kings' heirs. Both Kleombrotos's sons had been sturdy as their father. The new, rhodibas-shorn King Kleomenes headed the Agiad men, oblivious to the cold wind.

I followed the bier with the Eurypontid men. Not far from me limped slight, gnarled, white-haired Agisilaos. An Elder with the loud voice of the deaf pointed to him, and remarked to a companion, "The oracle warned us not to pass over the sound for the lame. We did a sure wrong when we set aside the son of King Agis."

The words omen and oracle were on many lips, as the young Agesipolis was placed in the Agiad tombs, with his namesake. Men looked towards the Issorian with open admiration.

The ceremonies ended. We turned back towards the Agiad palace for the funeral banquet. A glance at my mother's face told me she knew her favourite grandson had joined the rebels. I started towards her with Leonidas.

Someone cried out, "Look at the youth! He might have sprung from the loins of Herakles himself."

Another concurred. "He is certainly the great-grandson of Archidamos. Hades take it, you can't make a king of a kinglet." Several men gave me the royal salute.

521

The people on the streets slowly began to disperse. I passed Gorgo. Greeted her. Stopped. Chilled by some prevision. Or was it simply an unusual lustre in those great, dark eyes? I told Leonidas to go with my mother.

I closed my mind to those eirens at Amyklai, who sharpened their spears. Apollo brought out the sun from behind a cloud. Forgetting Kallias, forgetting Dexippas, forgetting everything, I beseeched him, let it be a cousin, Apollo, a friend...Chairon...

I looked into the full depth of her eyes. They were bright with pain, like a soldier dying from a spear-thrust in the belly. Her head was high. She smiled and spoke resonantly in that rich voice.

"My son had the honour to die for Sparta."

I buried my pain in the pain of her eyes. Heard myself saying, "His name will be written, Mistress Gorgo."

Chapter 26

Collective anger is a wind. It blows this way. It blows that. The enemy units returned from the south, and reinforced those already encamped around Sparta. The eleven days mourning for the boy King ended.

On the twelfth day, the Regent sacrificed to Demeter in the new King's name, and the new reign began. With it, the wind of anger turned from Agisilaos to the rebels in the Issorian. Those who had praised their efforts to remove the cause of the invasion now abused them, for plotting rebellion, while others defended the city.

Agisilaos did not return to the heights after the funeral. Nor after the mourning period. Nor after the sacrifice.

"I had heated words with Agisilaos," Antalkidas confided, as we walked to our hall. The blue light set in early these winter days, and it was almost dark; the slopes of Taygetos white against the coming night. "He claimed command of the army. I reminded him that in the city the ephors give the orders. He insisted that Sparta was a theatre of war. I told him it was he who made it so. The gods know what is in his mind." Lines were etched deep in his face. He was becoming thin, as he was in his youth. "Leo', I have considered killing him. I cannot. I scoff at custom, but four hundred years are too strong for me."

Since Lykourgos had brought the Law to Sparta, no man had been condemned without trial.

Agisilaos turned his attention, not to the Thebans, but to the Issorian.

Unarmoured and wearing only his shabby cloak, the old King limped up the hill, accompanied by one servant. He called out to the men inside that they had mistaken their orders. It was not the sanctuary that they had been told to defend. It was strong. No guard was necessary there.

The rebels knew it was strong. That is why they seized it. Sparta had not risen. They were losing hope. The King's words led them to believe that no one was aware of their plot. Or more likely, like the Leuktra deserters, their action was to be overlooked. Despairing men clutch at straws.

A few came out tentatively. Agisilaos ordered them to take up positions elsewhere. More left the sanctuary. He deployed them in another area. When they saw their comrades walk off safely, the rest came out. The King ordered twenty here, thirty there, until they were all deployed in separate parts of the City. In dispersing, they surrendered their strength as a body, as well as their stronghold. One can never afford despair in desperation.

When they had been successfully disbanded, Agisilaos ordered them arrested. All but fifteen, who were an entire dining-hall. I believe they were the leaders. A number of them had won prizes for valour, and were senior officers.

Agisilaos's standing rose. He was praised for his single-handed ending of the rebellion. The King was in control, it was said. Although Thebans were still encamped outside the City, and Sparta's women and children were learning to live with the sight of the enemy's fires.

Antalkidas fell into step with me, as he often did, as we were leaving the hall. The smoke from the Theban fires blew towards us. The wind carried snatches of foreign songs.

"Agisilaos has become uncontrollable," Antalkidas said. "Sometimes he wants to go out and fight the Thebans. The next day, he will be despondent, and say we are doomed. He asked for a regiment to clear out the Issorian. When I refused, he went alone."

"You were right to let those fifteen men go free, Antal. They are all good officers."

We stepped off the path to let others pass.

"Do you mind if we sit down a moment, Leo'?" He mopped his brow.

"Antal, are you ill?" The night was bitterly cold. Or had he to tell me that Agis was to be punished severely. Disfranchised? Surely not executed. A youth...

Antalkidas turned his back and vomited. Then he sat leaning

forward, his face in his hands.

"The bodies of those fifteen officers are lying in the Kaidas, with the bones of condemned criminals, Leotychides."

"I heard they were not arrested."

"They were not arrested." He raised his head, and leaned back against the tree trunk. "They were not tried. Agisilaos had his own guards placed in their barracks. When the officers went to their rooms that night, they were slain."

"Antal, there are always rumours–"

"One of the ephors asked me what to tell their kin. I thought he was mad, as you think me. I confronted Agisilaos. He said it was necessary. That is all. With that prim, priggish mouth of his, as if he liked the taste of the word."

"What became of the other officers? The men he *did* arrest." And a youth. I could not ask that. There are things a man cannot ask another to put into words.

"The gods know. He will treat them leniently to show his generosity. Or savagely for slighting him."

"The ephors decide the charges."

"I tell you the man has taken the power of life and death into his hands. You would have him tried for treason. By Zeus, I would condemn him for hubris. I am frightened...not of my life...I have never feared for my life. Nor for what is not...Sorry, Leo', I hadn't intended to trouble you with all that. I only meant to tell you to hasten to Queen Timaia."

The gate-keeper had to rouse a servant from sleep to unbolt the inner door.

The room opening to my mother's bed-chamber was in darkness. Only the flicker of a lamp illuminated the chamber itself. It was an empty silence. Serfs are as superstitious as foreigners about the dead and dying. I thought, "Dromea would not have left her."

As if a phantom replied to my reflections, my mother's voice floated from the bed-chamber, saying. "I wish you hadn't got Dromea freed. She could be trusted."

My mother stood in the entry-frame, solid and mortal. Her fingers were blackened up to the knuckles. With a darkened forefinger, she beckoned me in. On a table, lit by that single

525

lamp, stood a bowl of some sticky, darkish stuff. "I'm not certain I'm doing this well."

"I'm certain I don't know what you're doing at all."

She walked to the small room behind her bed-chamber, where her personal woman-servants slept, looked in and said softly, "It's all right, Agis. It's only your father."

My son walked out, hair tousled, rubbing sleep from his dark-fringed blue eyes.

"Are you all right, my dear?" My mother asked him.

"Yes, Grandmother. I think I have slept it out of me. Antalkidas tricked me. He came to the sanctuary, and offered to negotiate with us. We were getting damned hungry in there. He called for me to be spokesman. He gave me food and wine. The wine had something in it. I don't know how I came here..."

"I know, my dear," my mother said.

"Have I told you? When I woke before? What a bore. Hades take Antalkidas! They will think I deserted them."

"Be quiet, you silly child." I had never before heard her speak sharply to him. "Antalkidas saved your life. Your friends in the sanctuary have all been arrested."

He leapt to his feet. "They will think I betrayed them. My men–"

I stepped in front of him. "So they are your men. After how many days?" I shook him "What of the comrades of years you left lying dead at Amyklai?"

"As they were already dead, I could do little to help them."

"They were dead when you rode to Sparta?"

"They were dead when that Theban bastard pinioned me. I told them they were going about it the wrong way, but they had to show how well they knew their drill. Standing there in cloaks, in columns, as though they were a company of heavy-armed foot."

"*They?* Were you not with them?"

"When they wouldn't listen to me, I left the Commander and fought on my own. Like a peltast. I accounted for more Thebans than the rest together. Ask any boy in the flock who watched it from the town."

"I am asking you."

"The Thebans cut down the others before they could do them any damage. Barely a dead enemy to their credit. You will be pleased to know that Doreius brought down two. The second when he was half-dead himself. Pity his wit didn't match his spirit."

I struck him with what I had forgotten was a boxer's hand. My mother seized my arm, as Agis collapsed to the floor. He rose, shakily ignoring the blood that trickled from his right temple. The look in the eyes facing me, across the slant of lamp-light, I had faced on the battle-field.

"You may beat me all you like, Father." He spoke with deadly calm. "But nothing you do will remake me into Doreius."

"Leotychides–" My mother began.

"My Lady Mother, this is between my son and me." Had he inherited her jealous nature? Or had she instilled him with her jealousy? "Have I ever asked you to be other than yourself, Agis, unless it was yourself better?"

"You know well, Father, that Leonidas and I have always had to make do with what fondness you could spare from Doreius."

"Agis, love is not something finite, that is taken from one and given to another. By Apollo, for all your insolence, I have loved you more than Leonidas – who is far more deserving – and I love him greatly. But I would not have loved him more had you never been born, nor you more or less had Chairon never had a son." I crossed the divide of lamp-light, and examined the cut on his temple. It was not deep. "Jealousy is not akin to love, my son. It is its murderer."

"Sit, down, Agis, My mother said in the silence. "I am going to darken your hair."

"What is that, Grandmother?"

"Soot and oil. Men used it in Athens when it was the fashion." She slapped the mixture on to the golden curls.

"Grandmother, I rather like my hair the way it is."

"The black will rinse away when you reach Tegea. You must leave Lakonia, Agis. It was Agisilaos who arrested your people on the Issorian. Not Antalkidas."

"I'm glad. I always liked Antalkidas. How will I go to Tegea?" It was already becoming an adventure.

She looked directly at me. "Your father will put you in armour and a crimson cloak, give you a horse, and send you out with a message under his polemarch's seal."

"Mother, Tegea has been swallowed by Megalopolis."

"The allies of Epaminondas will not turn away a Spartan exile, Leotychides." She snapped impatiently, as she finished the hair-blackening "I do not think I have done this properly, but it must do."

His curls stuck out like small snakes. Under a helmet, it would not be apparent. She wiped her hands, and went rummaging through a chest. At last, she brought out a man's travelling cloak and wide-brimmed hat. My father's? Or *his?*

"Discard the armour, and wear these, when you cross the border." She searched through another chest and brought out jewellery I had never seen her wear. She spread out the travelling cloak, and tossed the jewels in the centre. After adding some familiar pieces, she began stripping the rings from her fingers. You will need enough to set yourself up as befits your station in Athens."

"Athens!"

She hesitated before removing her necklace. "You surely don't expect him to live as a suppliant at eighteen, Leotychides. I think it best, Agis, if you use another name. I never liked yours anyway. We shall call you back to Sparta when it is safe. If you must live abroad, remember that Lakedaimonian swords are highly valued. Do not sell yours cheaply."

"Agis," I said. "Promise me that you will never become an Athenian citizen."

"By the Twin Gods, no, Father. Exiles are far more distinguished than metics."

I had to content myself with that. No Athenian swore by the Dioskouroi. "Do you think you might confide in me the reason you joined the revolt in the Issorian."

The lop-sided smile. "I rather fancied making you king."

My mother reached up to the gold lions clinging to her ear-lobes. Agis caught her hand. "Not those."

She held him, and rested her cheek on his head. "How well you know me."

"Grandmother, will you give me my jumping stones to Leonidas. Tell him I'll see him in the Pythian Games...whatever..."

With an effort, she released him. Her cheek was smudged where it had lain on his sooty hair. She smiled. "Beware of jealous husbands. I have heard Athenians can enter their wives' quarters at any time. Revolting custom."

"How dreary." He never smiled back. "I have heard Athenian women are dull. Tell the pretty wives of Sparta I loved each one best."

They embraced again.

"Take him, Leotychides," she said "Quickly."

Antalkidas brushed away all thanks, and shied from the subject of the Issorian revolt altogether. I think his moment of weakness on the path-side embarrassed him. Agisilaos was more in evidence about the City. The Arkadians were decamping at night in droves. We had deserters, too. Antalkidas was baffled.

Up-country men and serfs, who had made their way in from the further reaches of Lakonia to fight for Sparta, now melted away almost as quickly as the Arkadians left the Thebans.

My batman told me the reason.

Often servants know what great men do not. He was the same batman who had been with me since I was a young warrior in Sikyon. I was certain he gossiped about me freely. I trusted him implicitly.

The fifteen murdered officers also had batmen. These army servants had kin who were fighting men in the freed serf regiments. They talked. Some of these regiments were deployed in the same areas as the up-country volunteers. Word spread. Few Spartiates were aware of the killings that were common knowledge to serfs and up-countrymen.

"Why are they deserting, Theoklos? The men in the Issorian were all Spartiate. No suspicion attaches to freedmen and up-countrymen."

"They still fear, Master."

Had the serfs feared battle, they would not have volunteered. Sudden death in the night is another matter. Death that stabs without warning, sanctioned only by a single man.

The desertions continued. My batman told me that the King sent his men to search the troops' quarters. They hid the arms of the deserters, so that the greatness of their number would not be known. Spartiates were more easily deceived by Agisilaos than serfs.

Epaminondas did not attack the City. The Arkadians had disbanded. Before the rest of his forces became totally broken in spirit by cold and hunger, he withdrew from the country. Agisilaos, in one of his turns of despair, sent Phrixos to Epaminondas with ten talents of gold – to pay him to leave – when Pelopidas was already decamping with the best of the Theban army.

"The old fool! I thought he had learnt his lesson when he tried to bribe the Mantineans." There was a touch of the old mockery in Antalkidas's pale weary eyes. "By Zeus, Leo', we must remove that man, and agree a truce with Thebes, before they come back."

"You believe they will?"

"All the Hellenes know the frontiers of Lakonia are no longer inviolate. No good hunter leaves a wounded boar alive."

"Kleombrotos said much the same thing." But he referred to the Thebans.

The soft breezes of spring came. Barley pushed up from the earth that had known the tread of enemy feet. Eirens returned to their flocks, and the flocks to the countryside. A few wistful-eyed youths and maidens recalled handsome faces in the departed allied contingents. My mother and Kyniska resumed their hostility. Leonidas danced for Apollo, turned twenty and became a warrior.

I stood at the edge of the acropolis with Anaxandros and Kallias, watching serfs in the distance plant saplings where olive groves had stood. The sounds of hammering and sawing reached us, as houses and outbuildings rose to replace those burnt by the enemy. The sweeter sound of a chorus of garlanded maidens came from the sanctuary grounds.

Kallias looked at the sun. It was nearly overhead. "We had best go."

"Chairon looks eighty now," Anaxandros commented, as we passed the statue of Aphrodite Who Keeps Off Old Age.

The death of his son had broken everything in the Elder but his determination.

"When will Pit' be back from Corinth?" Kallias asked.

"In time for the liberation," I told him.

The bickering at our meetings had ceased. In a sense, the invasion acted as a cleansing fire. Even the greatest landowners amongst us agreed to again divide the Eurotas Vale into equal kleroi, and thus restore the Lesser Spartiates to full citizenship.

The coins, at last, would be sent out of the City. Many of them in exchange for grapes and olives. It would take some years to renew the groves and arbours the Thebans destroyed. Sparta would be restored to the whole of the Law of Lykourgos. There could no longer be any doubt that the only lasting power is that of excellence.

I remember that, that day, we were meeting at Aristokrates's house. Reluctantly, he sent his small daughter out of the room. She was a charming child, not the blood-daughter of his wife – but she was as much a prattler as her name-mother.

The former chief ephor, who was still a hair-splitter, had just asked me whether Lesser Spartiates could vote to have their lands restored before they actually had the lands to pay their Hall portions and vote, when the present chief ephor burst in and sat in the nearest chair.

"You must disperse immediately," Antalkidas said. "Agisilaos went into the government buildings last night, and seized every document concerning every one of you. Quit the city. Visit guest-friends abroad. Go into sanctuary. But *go*."

"Let him bring us to trial," Gorgo challenged. There were permanent dark shadows under her eyes now, making them seem even larger. "And condemn himself."

"Agisilaos does not believe in trials," Antalkidas stated. "I beg you, postpone this enterprise of yours." It was no longer his. "You are in danger."

"By the Gods, Antalkidas," the admiral said. "We're not fifteen young officers to be slain quietly during an invasion."

Antalkidas listened, as several voices spoke at once. He broke in. "I have warned you. I can do no more."

"One really wouldn't expect you to." The former chief ephor spoke coolly. "An ephor who uses his powers to send his children to safety on Kythera. Who would have them survive the City." I recalled that brief exchange with a god, when we spoke of Kythera at the start of the invasion.

531

"My children are young–" Antalkidas looked about the room.

Meleas glanced at Aristokrates. "Others have young children, too."

Antalkidas rose. "Very well. I have been less than a father to all Sparta's sons. So I shall leave you in all your Spartan purity. You need not fear that I shall interfere in your conspiracy. You just might rid us of that madman before you cut your own throats."

When he had gone, I told them I had sent Agis out of Sparta. I would withdraw if they wished.

"Don't be an ass," the admiral said. "We all know that. The lad was escaping the vengeance of Agisilaos. Not the Thebans."

It was in the admiral's house that we were arrested.

There are some things that can only be set down simply. Anything more would debase the telling.

When dark covered the City, we were taken from the house to a derelict barracks, at the very edge of the barracks quarter. There we found the rest of the leaders. We were held in a guarded room, where only the differing shades of night broke the blackness.

We talked amongst ourselves of everything but what was. Old friends spoke of things that only old friends remember. At some time, a guard, an up-country man, brought us bread and wine; and water, and a small piece of cheese. He told us the King was kind to feed traitors. In this way, we learnt that we were accused of treason.

I wondered whether Agisilaos planned a spectacle similar to the death of Kinadon for us. I did not speak of it. As the night went on, our talk ranged from great things to small absurdities. The guard who brought us food left a battered oil-lamp to light our meal. It smoked. Kallias did something to it that cleared the air. Odd the small things one recalls. Chairon had fallen asleep on the single bench.

The admiral and an elder tried to sit on the two broken chairs, gave up, and joined the rest of us on the floor. The cry of a night-bird, oddly clear, made me aware of a small aperture between the ceiling and the roof. It might have been from there that the night sent us its dark lights.

The guard appeared again, and Euagoras was hurled into our midst. Anaxandros and I hastened to him. He stood and brushed the dirt from his cloak. At festivals and competitions, his small, light frame gave him the appearance of a youth. His face was a young man's, superimposed with lines of middle years.

"Bastard broke my lyre," he said.

"Why are you here, Euagoras?" Someone asked him.

"Agisilaos does not like my music."

Surely mocking songs could not be treasonous.

Meleas whispered. "Deny it. There is no proof you composed those things. Poets are worth more than ordinary men."

"Alas, they caught me passing the words of my latest to Hekataios, to take south. They must have been watching me."

"Hek'? Where is he?"

"He was riding away like the Furies were after him. I think it was me they wanted, anyway."

Hekataios was brought in later. "I think I was a mistake," he said. "My crime was in seeing a chorus-master arrested." There was a pale echo of the old grin. "Sphod' would say our patrol has done well."

They took the former chief ephor and an Elder first.

"Questioning," Meleas said.

Outside, the silence gave way to a number of voices. I stood one broken chair upon the other, to reach the aperture. It was still too high. Gorgo and Kallias lifted Chairon from his bench, and added it to my perch. The others held it steady.

"What are they saying?" Anaxandros demanded.

"I suggest each of us implicates only himself." The admiral.

"Where are they taking them?" Aristokrates. "Leo', can you hear them? Leotychides!"

By then it was over. The serfs wiped the blood from their axes. I climbed down. Told the others.

"How many of them are there?" asked the admiral.

"Two, with a regiment of armed serfs standing by."

"We can take them on. Go down fighting." The polemarch.

"Agisilaos would like that." Meleas spoke calmly. "Proof that we were lawfully slain trying to escape."

"I was preparing a fine speech for my trial," Anaxandros sighed.

The admiral and Meleas were next. I embraced my old

533

friend. There was neither time nor need of words.

"Witness my death," the admiral ordered me. "I'd not have that filth outside the last to see me alive."

Meleas coolly addressed the Spartiate commander. "You have been with the police long enough to know that political offenders are punished with the poisoned cup. We are not common criminals."

"Iron is a warrior's death." The admiral turned to the commander. "Tell Agisilaos that we are honoured to die for Sparta and her gods."

The guard noticed the stacked chairs when he next came in. I had forgotten to remove them. He laughed, and widened the aperture with his spear.

I watched no longer. Aristokrates's name was called out, with that of Kallias. Wordlessly, I tugged him back by his cloak to let Anaxandros go in his name. Gorgo stood and went to her cousin, embracing first Kallias and then Anaxandros.

They walked out hand in hand.

In the dim room, we spoke our last farewells, and said the rest in silence. Aristokrates broke the quiet to ask, "Will my daughter remember me as a traitor?"

"Your wife will teach her to honour you," I assured him. I doubted whether it would be long before the frivolous heiress married again.

He was deep in thought when the name of Anaxandros was called. We had to remind him of the personation.

"Farewell, Leo'," he said. "Poor liar. Good friend. My King."

As I embraced him, Gorgo laid a finger across her lips.

"Let him die for his King. He has always looked on you that way," she said, after they had taken him.

Some walked out jesting. Some defiant. Some silent.

"Will you push me into the Styx, Hek', as you used to shove me in the Eurotas?" Euagoras asked.

The reply was inaudible, as the door was slammed and bolted behind them. Gorgo and I were last.

Three will fend off doubt, to keep up the spirits of the others. One wears solitude as armour. Two give an ear to voice those doubts that words give solidarity.

"Were we right, Gorgo? It is not death that gives me doubt."

"It is failure."

534

"All my life I obeyed my orders. I lived the Law. But I die a conspirator."

"So men will say." That unbending strength of hers that allowed no compromise. No misgiving.

"I envy your certainty, Gorgo."

"Certainty? *Certainty?*" A harsh, dry laugh. "There is only one certainty, and that is that there is none." The room's emptiness replied, but she raised her arm, as if for silence. "Listen – the birds – It is nearing dawn."

Then they came for us, and took us out into the paling night. The peaks of Taygetos reminded me that all the mountain things were coming awake.

Serfs turned the blood-slippery earth. Anaxandros lay slanted over Kallias's legs. Euagoras's face had smoothed in death, until he looked truly a youth. The song-bird stilled. Hekataios, his carrot hair still without a strand of grey, lay beside Chairon, who had been stolen from the arms of gentle death, to be thrown to his raving brother. They were dragging Meleas away by his feet.

"It is good to die," Gorgo said.

I was not accused of treason.

There had been no plot. No conspirators. I could not be tried, as nothing had taken place. I was declared a bastard, but illegitimacy is not a crime. It made me a Lesser Spartiate. The City reclaimed my kleiros. My retroactive bastardy acted as the basis of other crimes. For marriage to a woman of Spartiate family, the fine was equivalent to the value of my house in Sparta and my running horses. For commanding Spartiate regiments by posing as full Spartiate, my service and honours were struck from the Lakonian records. The penalty for paying my Hall share from a kleiros unlawfully held was banishment for life.

In brief, I had ceased to exist from the time Agisilaos was proclaimed the heir of King Agis. The price of my silence about the killings was the citizenship of Leonidas. My son, in respect of his strain of royal blood and being of good character, was to retain his full rights as a Spartiate. It was a decision that could be reversed if I shouted abroad fancies about unlawful killings.

The ephor who sentenced me had eyes that glittered in his expressionless face. Perhaps he was an Agisilaos man. Or perhaps he disliked me because I had not voted for him. At least, I thought, they cannot conceal the killings forever. I was wrong.

They had planned it carefully. Meleas was in Athens, on secret negotiations, when footpads robbed and murdered him in a side street. Euagoras threw himself over a cliff, in despair at unrequited love. Aristokrates died when a wild boar charged him, and so on, until war could account for the rest.

The police commander who escorted me from the government buildings was known to me. I had commended him for valour in the field. The citation brought him his invitation to join the law-keepers. I had not known, until then, that he had been absorbed into its secret body.

"What of Mistress Gorgo?" I asked him.

"The fools bungled it. It was the woman to have been executed. Not the Elder. The City is giving him a fine funeral. Too much talk, if hers were the same day."

"Why was I not slain?"

"They are afraid Herakles might punish them. Many men believe you to be the true son of Agis." He unbound my hands. "I have always thought so myself."

"But you serve Agisilaos."

"I serve whoever commands. Had your plot succeeded, we would have served you as loyally as we serve Agisilaos."

"Had we succeeded, there would be no secret police."

"Our work may not be pleasing, but the City needs us."

"No city has need of vermin."

His face darkened. "Do you want your bones to lie in the Kaidas?"

"They would be in better company than in the government buildings."

"Be gone from Sparta in three days." He snapped.

"No, Leotychides. No," Kleonike pleaded. "Don't ruin Leonidas."

"I won't be silent."

"They are dead. Leonidas lives. Leotychides, don't do this to your son. Not Leonidas. Agis was always more your mother's

536

than mine. But Leonidas–" Her voice broke.

"Kleonike is right," my mother said.

"I have heard that the Athenians have a statue of two men who struck down a tyrant, and that they esteem it above all others."

"The mob killed one on the spot. The other was lawfully tortured to death."

"Their deaths brought the tyrant down."

"Sparta brought the tyrant down. He ruled for years after your liberators died. Now every demagogue who would be a tyrant himself makes speeches about the statues." She rose and laid her hands on my shoulders. "If you speak, a way will be found to make you ridiculous. Your friends died in dignity. Let their dignity stand."

She turned, and busied herself in what I remembered her doing since childhood. Rummaging through a chest. It was a great chest that had to be unlocked. I noted this for the first time, perhaps because I was seeing the familiar room for the last time.

She brought out a shield. "It belonged to Agis. I hid it, so that Agisilaos could not claim it. Old men will recognize it. Go in your fine armour."

"It would not be seemly."

"There are ways other than words to say a thing. Ride out a king." With a swift transition to practicality, she added, "Splendid armour will raise the fees for your sword. Oh, Leotychides, I have never understood you, but I have loved you."

She had given up her dreams. Had she been younger, she would have told me to return with an army at my back.

The river was becoming pleasant as I had my morning dip, on my last full day in Sparta. Birds greeted the sun as I dried myself. I walked to the sanctuary of Lykourgos and then to the top of the acropolis, to view the City below. Eirens ran on the racing course in the distance, in front of the Twin Gods' House.

537

Two women, walking in opposite directions, stopped to pass the time of day, as their servants gossiped. The agora was filling.

I descended the hill and walked to the Babykon Bridge. It was Assembly Day, and I crossed paths with some men I knew, near the shrine of Zeus. They neither looked at me nor away, but through me. Only a member of my hall averted his eyes. Sparta was all around me, but I was apart. I now understood Nikomedes, and regretted that I had neglected to search him out again at Thespiai.

The sounds of hammering rang out from the street of artisans. Feeling the need for the talk of a fellow creature, I made my way to my armourer.

I was a favourite of that talkative up-country man, who regarded his customers as objects on which to display his skill. He found my measurements adequate for his hero-gods, fine-winged lions, horses and chariots. Aristokrates was his ideal. He had always distressed the artisan by his simple taste.

We exchanged a few pleasantries. He was courteous. I felt my presence embarrassed him, and took myself away. Those I would have approached avoided me. Those who would have extended friendship I avoided, lest I implicate them. Nikomedes would have understood, if they did not. I walked to the agora.

On a sudden impulse, I entered the temple of Dionysos. There, in its place, was the portrait of the god as a boy of twelve. Had I forgotten the leopard at his feet? Or had Apelleas added it later? Beautiful Dionysos stood proud, yet at ease, in his arbour of rich grapes – the folds of his shoulder-cloak hanging gracefully from the extended arm, the insolence of innocence in his dark blue eyes. I left the young god in the arbour as he had been, is, and would always be – gods, unlike men, being unchanging.

The wild cherry trees were in full bloom. Iris pierced the rushes. I had a quick midday meal by the river, took a horse, and rode to Amyklai at fast pace. Vast time contracted so little.

I tied the horse to a tree, and walked up the rocky path to the plateau where the temple of Apollo stands. The purifying water of the sacred spring was cold on my face and hands. In the penumbra of the temple, the god stood on his throne of beaten gold. The Eurypontid ring was at his feet. A priest must have moved it from the offering table. The gold shone. The carnelian of King Polydoros's face was immaculate as the day my father gave it to me.

"Apollo, the ring is yours forever. My father's sword I keep, to fall upon." Agisilaos would not drive me from my city.

I do not know whether it was the god who spoke silently in my ear, or if it was my father's shade. "Do you leave the dead unavenged, Leotychides?"

"Shall I slay my father's brother? Command! I obey."

"Command an impiety?"

"What do you want of me?"

"You know."

"If I may not end his life, I offend no god by ending my own."

"Die then," the god said, or did not say. "Give Agisilaos untroubled sleep. By your death, make him lawfully King."

Apollo had taken the sun westward when I rode back north. On the high bluff above the City, the blue and white parapet of the tomb of Helen and Menelaos reached towards a blue and white sky. My waning, precious time lost meaning.

The waters of the Messeis Spring flowed through moss-lined rocks into a clear stream. Iris flowered on its banks. Anemones of every hue were scattered in the soft, green grasses. The City, and the river far below. I followed the stream to the shade of a plane tree, where I rested. Ants crawled about its trunk, oblivious to the affairs of men.

Scarlet anemones sprang up like drops of blood. I rolled on my back, and gazed through the broad-leafed tree. The sun picked its way through the branches. The blood-drop anemones spread and ran. Hekataios, Aristokrates, Euagoras, Kallias, Anaxandros...

It was not autumn-yeared Anaxandros whom I saw lying dead amidst the carnage, but the little Magpie, offering me the first friendship of my life with a half-eaten apple. Hiding with me in the tall grasses to watch a melleiren's competition, when a beautiful dark-haired youth raised his arm like Apollo, and threw his spear with faultless grace.

I turned and pressed my face into the damp, fresh-scented, red-brown earth. Grasped it in handfuls with the grass. Soaked it with the bitter tears the fox tore out of me in racking sobs.

The roseate glow was settling over the City when I left the bluff. There was one more visit to make.

The sun passed over the rounded lower peaks of Taygetos, and hovered over the mountain heights. I went into the temple of Artemis Orthia. The blue prelude had set in when I came out into the still hollow, to walk beyond the laurel trees that bound the sacred groves. Amongst the graves, I found the one I sought, and rested beside it.

"We shall not know one another in Hades' Hall, Doreius, but can your love fail to know mine?"

The cicadas could not tell me, nor the butterfly that passed in flight.

"I haven't shamed you, have I, Doreius?"

Doreius was not there. Only a marker with marching warriors, that had been twenty-one years standing. I had said my farewell to Sparta.

"You must divorce me, Kleonike."

"Never."

"The wife of a Lesser Spartiate cannot teach the maidens singing, nor lead the hymns at festivals. Your friends will turn their backs on you."

"I will not divorce you. Will you go to Agis in Athens?"

"Agis does not need a banished father in autumn years, without an obol to his name."

"Your mother says mercenary pay is good in Athens."

What had happened within Sparta we had brought on ourselves, but it had all started in Athens.

"It will not be Athens for me, and you are changing the subject. Kleonike, you are still lovely. If you do not want a man in your bed, take an old husband who will ask nothing but your sweet presence, and the sound of your voice in his house. I no longer own this house we sit in, and I shall never be back."

"I shall go to my father."

"Divorce me. I order you."

"I am not one of your officers, to be ordered. I will not divorce you, and that is an end to it."

A servant appeared to say that there was a lady to see the mistress. I started to take off.

"Kleonike, please tell your husband to stay." Gorgo stood in

540

the entry frame; a tall, straight, stark figure. The shadows under her eyes were dark, her handsome face drawn and white. Deep lines cut across her brow and the sides of her mouth. The end of her peplos had half fallen from the thick, dark hair. "I cannot stay long, Kleonike. I must leave Sparta by night. I am judged guilty of corrupting the youths and maidens of Sparta. I have been forced to swear by Artemis not to speak to any of my associates in a certain enterprise."

"At least you were spared," Kleonike said.

"Spared! It was either swear or banishment. I asked them to let me die like my friends. I am condemned to be confined to my furthest estate, to neither visit nor be visited, to live surrounded only by my servants – but I have not come to talk about that–"

"Surely exile would be better..." Kleonike almost whispered.

"I am Spartan. I was born in the City. When I die, I shall lie in the earth of Lakedaimon – with my son, my cousin, and one who died long ago." She pushed back that wayward strand of hair. "But that is my concern." She dropped a cloth, tied in four corners, into Kleonike's lap. "Here are enough jewels to buy you another house." I noted Gorgo wore no adornments, except the slim, silver arm-ring.

"Gorgo, my kin will have me."

"No woman can live with her kin, having been her own mistress. I shall have no use for baubles where I am going." Her great eyes met mine, then fastened again on Kleonike. "I would give you one of my houses, but I am certain Agisilaos will find a means of seizing them for his kin." She rearranged the peplos end, and covered her head.

Kleonike put out her hand to stay her. "It is a moonless night, Gorgo. Too dark to travel."

"It will be an easy journey." Kleonike did not understand. She had not been meant to. "For one thing more have I come," Gorgo continued. "Kleonike, tell your husband that, although there are no certainties, there is a truth; that truth being that it matters more to be right than to win." Her head lifted, the dark eyes above the shadows fierce and radiant. Her face exultant. Her spirit already went out to the dark river. She was the most beautiful woman I had ever seen. "Farewell, Kleonike," she said. "And farewell. No tears – I detest them. Sing the songs of

541

Euagoras. Men die, but poems live."

She turned without another word, and was gone.

"She will wither and die alone in the country," Kleonike said.

"She will not wither."

"Go with her." Kleonike spoke suddenly in the silence. "Go after her. Take her into exile with you."

"Nothing would induce Gorgo to leave Lakedaimon."

"You could persuade her. She's strong. She's rich. She could live abroad. She loves you. You have always loved her–"

"Kleonike–"

"Don't argue with me. I tell you I have known it for years. It was her love of you that made me like her. I was never one of those maidens who was so soppy about her...Oh, go, Leotychides. Hasten. I will divorce you as you ask."

"Have you done? Then listen. Of course, I love Gorgo. She is the bravest and most noble of women. But it is not the love you speak of." My wife's lips parted in a slight smile. "If anything passed between us, that was not love. Nor does Gorgo love me. Her love was given once, and to someone other than me. Now, if you wish to compose any more poems of great loves, I suggest you make them into a song."

"You mock me."

"I mock your fancies."

She looked up. "It pleases me that you would not have preferred her to me."

I sat quietly that last evening, looking into the courtyard as men walked to their dining-halls, smoke rose from the cooking fires of flocks in the countryside, and the matthiola sent up its sweet scent as Sparta plunged into its living night.

The morning struck the bronze scabbard of my father's sword. The sword returned its salute. I savoured the citron-blossom-drenched breeze like a returning soldier, as the City came awake. Sparta sang with spring.

My batman waited with the horses. I mounted and rode towards the bridge, with my father's shield slung across my back. He fell in behind me. I looked back, once, across the City, to the white-capped peaks of Taygetos – then crossed the bridge, and followed the curving bends of the road to Arkadia.

542

Chapter 27

No Spartan has told it. No Spartan will. Let poets sing the tears of Troy. Sparta's fox is her own.

I give the woman all this scribbling, and tell her to destroy it.

"It is for the King," she objects.

"Burn it."

The scrolls fill both her arms as she balances them against her sagging bosom. She will not read them. Like all women here, she is unlettered.

"Why write more of that, if you are going to burn it?"

The scribe talked less. His mother was a serf, and his father an up-country man; he told me. Or was it the other way about? They followed Epaminondas to Thebes, but fell on hard times and sold themselves into slavery. I gave the scribe back to Philippos. No, I freed the scribe, but he sold himself to someone else.

It was the house I gave back to Philippos, when I stopped writing that thing I have given to the woman to burn, and returned to my room in the barracks. I wanted to be with my own kind. Soldiers.

Philippos is in Thrace. The tutor has gone. The King's son acts as regent. He has golden hair like Agis. Like Agis! I think of my son as a youth. His sons, if he has any, will be grown men.

Hades takes these wounds! The one in my thigh confines me to my bed. I attract thigh wounds. When I turn, my shoulder screams violent protest. Had I been five years younger, that Illyrian bastard's spear would not have caught me.

The Macedonians talk of nothing but crossing into Asia. That is not the thing that makes them drop their voices when I am present. No matter.

Although I have lived amongst these men for one and twenty years, they are shadows. I can barely recall the face of the woman who has just left with my scribbling, although I have shared her bed whenever I wished for near twenty years. Reality leaps up in bright flames, jagged as a plane leaf. Reality turns

543

brown at the edges. Curls and crumples into black ash.

Reality is the waters of the Messeis Spring, clear and cool; and Doreius beside me, in the roseate glow of the afternoon. The City bathed in blue-grey, as we return. Sphodrias in the changing room, importantly relating the latest news. Anaxandros and Kallias spearing boar on the slopes of Taygetos. Gorgo, with her grape-dark eyes and proud step. Euagoras, singing and playing his lyre by the river bank. Pausanios walking in the colonnade. Kleombrotos with his short cloak flying, as he rides about Sparta. Meleas. Pityas. Hekataios. My sons. My wife. My Hall. All so fresh in memory that I see that light spray of freckles across Agesipolis's nose, as he moves armies on maps.

Some shadows come in. I close my eyes, and let the stylus fall.

"He is sleeping," one says.

"You wouldn't think such a dried-up old fellow would have that much blood in him to lose."

Some Illyrian tribes seized upon the King's absence to revolt. His son put down the rebellion. He is only sixteen, but he is a promising commander. It was his first campaign.

"He's not a day under sixty-five." A shadow speaks. I am seventy-three.

They go. There are more voices outside. The King's son has arrived.

"I don't think the old Spartan will last much longer," I hear one tell him.

"He is strong. It comes of being temperate in his habits."

Uniquely among Macedonians, the King's son drinks his wine well-watered.

The Prince stands by my bed. "Is there anything I can do for you?" My pretence of sleep does not deceive him.

"Yes, Alexandros. See that I am buried decently."

"So you have decided to die."

"An Illyrian decided for me. That Tegean officer here... Will you ask him to buy pure white animals to sacrifice at the shrine of Brasidas at Amphipolis?"

A curious look passes over his face. I remember the Tegean

was slain ten years ago. Few Greeks here now.

"You really are set upon it," he says. "Well, if you do not change your mind, rest easy; it will be done."

"Another thing. I know that it is the custom of your people to burn the dead. Our bodies prefer the earth."

"Have no fear. You will be buried honourably in your armour."

"No! No! No! In my cloak alone. Nothing in the grave with me. Bury me as befits a Spartan. My armour will buy goats for Artemis and Apollo in my name. If there is anything after the sacrifices, give it to the men I commanded."

I cannot remember them all, but he will. He knows all the men by name.

He tilts his head slightly to the side. "May I ask you something?" Without leave, he proceeds. "What happened to that youth who was passed over to make Agisilaos king in Sparta?" I go by a different name here.

I know why he asks. There had been talk that he is not his father's son.

"The youth died at Lechion. The man died later..."

"Why didn't he fight for his throne?"

"He was Spartiate. He obeyed."

"I would have fought."

"If you fight, *win.*"

"That is good advice," he says.

I could have been fond of the boy, had he not been a shadow like the rest. In my end, as in my beginning, only shades are real. I finish this account for no better reason than that I have started it.

*　　　　　*　　　　　*

I sold my sword to Athens after all.

In the first summer of my exile, the Thebans marched south again. This time, Athens seriously joined Sparta in league against them. I gathered an assortment of Peloponnesian mercenaries from the wine-shops of several cities, formed them into a regiment, and offered our services to Chabrias.

Despite its fine decorations, my shield looked bare stripped of its *lamda.* My own shield. My father's sword and shield I

545

sent back to Sparta, to Leonidas. To fill the empty space, I had my own device fashioned. The head of a cockerel. The self-mocking jest was an offering to the shades of my murdered flock-brothers.

Having joined the Athenian forces with my own band, I was spared the carrying of an Alpha shield. At the end of the campaign, cockerels began to appear on the shields of my men. I had become what I had always aspired to be. An inspiring commander. Perhaps the trick of it is not caring.

A number of my motley lot had served under Iphikrates the previous winter. They despised the shoemaker's son for keeping them in Arkadia while he plundered, when they had been paid to fight. A mercenary has his honour, I learnt, although an Athenian ruler may not.

Chabrias was something else altogether. He understood discipline. He knew how to get the best out of his men. I respected him as a commander and a man.

We were with the Corinthians in a fierce engagement, in which our joint forces cornered an Argive army. Argos had allied herself again with Lykomedes, who was allied to Thebes. I thought I saw Aristeas, but perhaps it was someone who resembled him.

I kept my distance from the Corinthians. They would have heard of my disfranchisement. I could easily, like Pityas, have lived in exile with guest-friends in Corinth, or gone to Anaxilas in Syracuse: but I wanted them to remember me as they had known me; a citizen and polemarch of Sparta. Not as a man without a city, like some of the old Theban exiles I had seen in Lakedaimon, living out their days planning a return that would never be. I did not indulge in the indignity of hope.

The Thebans withdrew from the Peloponnesos when Thessaly made war on them. Lykomedes attempted to set his Megalopolis over the peninsula, with his Argive allies. Under Chabrias, we fought in the ranks of the combined forces that defeated the Arkadians.

In the same year, Archidamos commanded an allied army of ten thousand, which defeated the armies of Argos, Arkadia and Messenia without loss of a single Spartan life. Agisilaos burst into tears when he heard the news. What dignity! What mastery of self! When Praxitas sent the message "Lechion taken," the ephors told him that the single word *taken* would have been sufficient.

It is said that all the Elders joined in Agisilaos's joyful tears. The Council room must have been flooded. Few maidens in Sparta could not have set them an example of manly self-restraint.

I left Chabrias's service the next year, to offer my sword to Thessaly. The Thessalian war drew enemies away from the frontiers of Lakedaimon. As for Chabrias, I still respected the man, but who knew where Athenian intrigues would take him next.

Most of my men chose to accompany me, although Athenian pay was better than Thessalian. I had not reckoned in the devotion of mercenaries to their general. They fight for him as citizen soldiers fight for their city.

In Thessaly, my band of mercenaries grew. A number of up-country men, and some serfs who had departed Lakonia with Epaminondas, had found Thebes and Thebans not to their liking. They came over to me in the midst of a battle. If they were going to be ordered to die, they preferred to hear it in Lakedaimonian Doric.

We took what horses we could from the enemy. I bought more, in that good horse country. We took the rest in raids. I trained the men to fight mounted, and again became a cavalry commander.

Whilst I was with the Thessalians, Thebes sent Pelopidas to Persia. He convinced the Great King that Sparta was broken, and persuaded him to name Thebes arbiter of the peace.

It was about this time I heard a strange tale. Antalkidas was dead. He had died by his own hand, because he failed to prevent the Great King turning from Sparta. Baseless rumour, I thought. The man who first told me it was Athenian, and did not know that Sparta does not punish failure. The story was confirmed by better men. Soon it was common knowledge.

Something did not set right. Antalkidas never owned failure; to him its name was delay. He was not yet a great man when his first mission to Persia came to little, but he sharply set about

547

planning a second attempt. Would he, in all his fame, be disheartened now? It was years later, here in Macedon, that I came closer to the truth of the matter.

A noble Persian exile living in Pella had been at the Great King's Court when Pelopidas arrived.

"Antalkidas was present also." This Artabazos told me. "The King heard the Thebans, turned to Antalkidas, and once more gave him his own garland. We Persians took the meaning, although the Theban did not."

"Nor do I."

"Why, that nothing had changed."

"Your King named Thebes arbiter of the peace."

"It is my belief that Antalkidas advised him to do so."

"Antalkidas was loyal to Sparta."

"How not? It was for that loyalty, as much as his wit and courage, that we honoured him."

"No loyal Spartan would give to Thebes what is Sparta's"

"You reason like a Hellene. Antalkidas could think like a Persian. What better way to end Thebes's pretensions, than by showing that Hellas would have none of her? Sparta was too weakened to defeat Thebes by arms. Antalkidas would bring her down by contempt." He went on. "Had he, like so many great Hellenes, chosen exile in Persia, the King would have given him an island or a province to rule. When news of his death was brought to Susa, the King wept, as for a lost son."

Antalkidas was Spartan. He returned to the City. No doubt, with any number of schemes to make her great again. Perhaps the only man who could do so. The only man clever enough to outwit Agisilaos. And Agisilaos knew it.

Antalkidas did not die by his own hand. He died as my friends died. As fifteen officers died. Struck down stealthily in the night. May the gods of the underworld avenge them all!

On the return of Pelopidas from Susa, the Boiotarchs called a conference in Thebes. The cities of Hellas sent embassies, but loudly objected to meeting in that crude city. One of the loudest was Thebes's old protegé, Lykomedes of Megalopolis. The Corinthians flatly stated that they wanted no more exchanges of oaths with the Great King. They were followed by other cities. The conference broke up.

Thebes had wrested power from Sparta, but could not replace her. The cultured centres of south and central Greece would not accept her leadership. Had Thebes retained the slightest hope of leading the Hellenes, it was shattered when Orchomenos was destroyed by Theban mobs.

A Thespian who served with me in Illyria was present when Epaminondas heard of it. It was many years later, but he still recalled the Theban leader's fury when he vowed that, had he been present, the atrocity would never have occurred. Epaminondas was a man far above his compatriots. Perhaps that was the tragedy of Thebes and Sparta. A great leader of an unworthy people, pitted against an unworthy king of a great people, in mortal combat, cracked the foundations of Hellas.

By the time our work in Thessaly was done, I was leading a sizeable army. We moved on into gold-rich Thrace, where those endless wars between savage kings kept us in work. We always chose the highest bidder; and, if any king or lord cheated us of our pay, we took his town and put him to the sword.

Sometimes we wintered in one of those towns. Usually, we sacked them and moved on. My troops were disciplined in battle. Afterwards they could do as they pleased. I was glad Agesipolis was not there.

I imposed two rules. No man was to take more booty than could be loaded on to a donkey. Heavy baggage slows an army down. The other was that we would take service with no state or ruler allied to an enemy of Sparta. The Lakedaimonians understood. The others looked upon it as a quirk of their general. Mercenary generals are permitted their quirks. Indeed, the men take a perverse pride in what they consider their commander's eccentricities.

The men regarded themselves as citizens of our army. We were, in effect, a city on the move. It occurred to me, at one time, that I had more men in my army than Sparta had full citizens. The thought did not gladden me.

It was one of the up-country men who put it to me that we go to Sicily, and found a city of our own. He was educated; the son of a ship-builder at Gythion. He had fought the Thebans in the heroic defence of his town; and only followed Epaminondas to Thebes because his father insisted that he follow his trade, and was a born soldier. Yet his roots longed for earth, and his spear a city of its own to fight for.

A number of the men had taken Thessalian women, and had small sons who followed the army. They were eager when word of the Sicilian plan got about. They wanted me as their ruler, king, tyrant; whatever I wished to name it. I considered it; but such a venture wants a leader to whom it matters. Or something matters. Or anything matters. I felt that, if a fox clawed through and gnawed my innards, it would get a mouthful of dry dust.

Disguising my intent, I encouraged the enterprise; I planned a constitution with the ship-builder's son, and contented myself that he had the qualities of a leader. By the time I told them of my decision to stay behind, their hearts were already across the water.

I believe I gave hem good law.

It was based in the justice of Lykourgos, but diffused with enough up-country customs for it not to be alien to them. I do not know what became of them in Sicily; whether they were slain by Carthaginians, or their city thrives. I wish them well.

With the departure of the Lakedaimonians, I lost my fine cavalry. Again we sold our swords to the highest bidder, but I chose the losing side. Our numbers were depleted. We were no longer an army, but a band once more.

Iphikrates was in the north, aiding King Perdikkas of Macedon in his war against his kinsman Pausanios, who had seized the throne. Both needed men, The Athenian offered higher wages, but I could not stomach the thought of serving under the man.

I sent the oldest of my troops home with their booty while they still had it, disbanded the regiment, and let my men go wherever the pay was best. I was going to offer my own sword to Pausanios, when I was offered command of the army of a Thracian prince.

The Prince was a louse-covered, red-haired tribal chieftain, who had become great locally by conquering all his neighbouring tribes. He claimed descent from Theseus. (All these far northern lines have pretensions both Hellenic and divine). By commanding his army, he meant training his tribesmen. Later I learnt that he made his offer to me not, as I thought, on the strength of my reputation, or even the fame of Lakedaimonian arms, but because he admired my armour.

He was open-handed with his gold. I used it to lure some good Greek officers from Iphikrates, by doubling their pay. One of these officers, a Philasian, told me that he had gone abroad because the Peloponnesos was in chaos since Sparta's leadership had ended.

Almost every town was at war with another. Some had been completely destroyed in the strife. The gods were given no sacrifice, because men murdered one another at the altars. Rebellion and insurrection were everyday occurrences. There were more exiles from a single city than there had formerly been from the whole of the Peloponnesos.

"The rich," he said, "would rather throw their possessions into the sea than give to the poor."

"And Sparta herself?"

"There is always good order in Sparta. It is just that no one heeds her any more."

I having made the Prince's force into something resembling an army, he found a man with armour even more splendid than mine, and dismissed me.

"Bad luck, sir," the Philasian said. "I shall be moving on myself soon. I don't fancy my chances under that Syracusan fool he's hired. I hope you kept back a fair share of the savage's gold for yourself."

I had not. I had spent it building his army. Still, my pay had been good, and I was leaving better of than I came. I was getting my gear together. Preparing to leave, when the Thracian boy appeared.

I had seen him about, feeding the horses, and running errands for the troops. He threw himself at my feet and begged me to take him with me. I told the boy I had a servant. My words fell on deaf ears. Perhaps my speech was as nearly incomprehensible to him as his was to me. His desperation thickened his accent.

He told me the Prince had bought him from pirates for a trifling sum, along with his mother, and had probably forgotten he owned him. He would sell him to me cheap, if only I would not let the Prince see him. I understood. He was one of the dark-haired Thracians. His eyes were wide and blue, and his features good. He was about thirteen or fourteen, and would fetch a good price from the barbarians, if the Prince did not keep him for his own pleasure. I bought the boy and took him with me. I was going to buy him a mount. He had already stolen one.

When we were out of the Prince's territory, I set him free.

"You no want me? Your slave ugly." He tried to mimic the face of my ageing batman.

"He is not a slave–" I began, and then knew the futility of explaining serfs, let alone freed serfs, to a Thracian.

"You no want me." His eyes filled with tears. "I ugly? I old?"

"*I* am old. I have sons with sons your age."

"You not old. Like Greek."

"Even Greeks grow old. And my sons *are* old enough to have sons half your age." Had Agis and Leonidas sons? Were my sons alive? Or had their bodies been carried off some battlefield? "I will give you silver coins, and take you to a town where you can find work. Or send you to your village."

"I no want silver." Slavery had not taken all pride out of the boy. Weeping, he tied his few possessions in a small cloth.

I told him he could stay.

I travelled for two years with the Thracian boy, selling my sword where there were takers. When my batman died of marsh fever, he cleaned my weapons and prepared my food. When the booty was good, we ate well, and slept in the inns of large sanctuaries. When times were bad, our only shelter was my tent, and our food whatever the countryside yielded.

A small tribal war brought us some trivia to trade in the nearest large town, as well as enough for a good meal in a wine-shop. It was there that I learnt that Epaminondas was dead.

He had been wounded in a battle near Mantinea, where Thebes involved herself in a Peloponnesian affair that began with a quarrel between the Arkadians and the Eleians, and eventually involved almost the whole of the peninsula. The sort of thing Sparta had once settled with a single mediator.

Epaminondas was carried from the battle-field, with a spear still jutting out of his body. When news that the Thebans had won the battle was brought to him, he had said, "Now is the time to die," and pulled out the spear himself, releasing the fatal

552

flow of blood.

I remembered the young Theban officer another time at Mantinea, defending his badly wounded friend. I remembered the splendid figure battling against the icy river. A man who might have spent his energies raising his people in emulation of his own excellence, had Agisilaos not set him off on the road to conquest.

"You sad," Teres remarked. "Good friend die?"

"A good enemy."

After the death of Epaminondas, Thebes fell back into insignificance. Athens was weak, drained by war, over-peopled, and the flotsam of that once-great city saturated the market with Greek swords. Our lean times grew in frequency and duration.

We were in bare country that game ignored, and the larger birds disdained. Teres went out with his bow, a quiver of arrows, and hope. When he returned empty-handed, I had bread, cheese, barley and olives.

He gazed at the spectacle with wide-eyed admiration. "You steal better than me."

"I learned young."

We finished our meal, and he started cleaning my shield. He burnished my armour and weapons daily, even when they were not in use. "Fine shield. Like Greek."

I was not certain whether he used the word Greek to describe everything admirable, or whether it implied a certain excellence.

We heard of a town where soldiers were being hired, and followed the rumour. Teres asked permission to do the bartering.

"Send slave talk for you. Make you look big. Also, I think, maybe you don't understand money."

I knew the rate of pay. It embarrassed me to discuss it. When I left it to him, not only my wages increased. It seemed I was also entitled to a stipend for my servant. The boy was not venal. Our pay was kept in the same coffer. We feasted or starved together.

He noted my eagerness for news of Sparta when I encountered other Greeks, no matter how stale the news. It was after I came to Macedon that I heard of my mother's death. A newly arrived Corinthian mercenary casually mentioned that he had been in Sparta the day of Queen Timaia's funeral.

Kyniska followed my mother to Hades's Hall only little more than a year later. She did not long stay there, but took up residence with the hero-gods in the Elysian Fields, when Spartans set up altars and worshipped her.

One night, my foraging produced some meat. As Teres cut it into small pieces, and stuck them on spits to rest between forked sticks over the fire, the sight and sound brought back nights on campaign. I played my lyre, and sang a song of Tyrtaios.

"Good song," he said. "Teach me."

"Only Spartans sing that song. I will teach you another."

I found the melody on my lyre, as I sang a song I had picked up from an Arkadian mercenary.

"If I were a lark,

554

I would soar
into the blue,
never to return,
to earth,
where men sow corn,
where men reap corn,
where they sow
and they reap,
without knowing why..."

He had a pleasant voice, and memorized the words with the rapidity of illiterates. I taught him a few of the songs of Gitidias, when he asked for more.

"What you like best?" he asked.

"The Lark," I lied. Too much of Sparta is in Gitidias.

We found steady work, protecting towns from the Athenian mercenaries who terrorised them, extorting money and valuables. Sometimes they captured territories, and divided them amongst Attic colonists, with the tacit approval of their city.

"These people pay no good." The Thracian boy spoke contemptuously.

"They pay what they can, Teres."

He never complained when we were without shelter, and living off the country. Not even when our tent was stolen, and we had only each other to warm us under a rainy sky. He felt it beneath my dignity to fight for insignificant towns.

We returned to the part of Thrace where I had found him. Teres learnt that the Prince had been slain, along with his Syracusan general, by another chief, who styled himself king. The Thracian boy again negotiated the pay. The King, he told me, already had a commander; but, although I would be subordinate to him, I would receive the same pay as the other general.

"How did you arrange that?"

"I tell the King that you are King in your own country. Other King make plot against you to drive you out. But King cannot take less money than common commander."

"By Apollo, who gave you leave to say these things?" I nearly struck the boy in my anger.

I started packing my gear. When he would have done it for me, I thrust him away. "You had best stay here. You know enough of arms now to make your way."

When I rode out, he followed me a spears-throw behind.

I sheltered from the rain that night, in a deserted peasant's hut. Silently, he cooked the remains of our food, and brought it to us. Silently, I gave him half. He put it aside, and laid his cheek against my hand, warm tears spilling on it. "I not know it true when I say it."

"I am not a king."

"You Prince. You King."

"I was an Equal. That is something beyond your comprehension. Eat and be silent."

He huddled in a corner. It was not the boy's fault. My anger was unreasonable.

"Teres, come here." He left his untouched bowel and ran over. "I'm sorry I spoke harshly. But never again tell anyone that tale."

"Never. I tell it like it happen to the Greek."

"Who is this mysterious Greek you are always talking about?"

"He most beautiful god-man. He come to Thrace with the most beautiful woman in the world, and they live in his citadel. Then the ships come and there was big battle."

"You have mixed it up. His name was Paris, and he was Trojan. The ships were Greek." These people worship some of our gods, as well as their own. "And it happened in Troy. Not Thrace."

When we had no money to go into the wine shops, Teres learnt where swords were being hired, by picking up gossip in the market-places of towns. We were in Illyria the time he came running back to our bivouac, out of breath.

"King of Sparta dead!" He shouted.

"Which King?"

"King of your country."

"We have two Kings." I thought of the ill-fated Agiads. There had been six in my lifetime. Kleomenes was only seventeen. "What is his name."

"Greek men only say King of Sparta dead in Egypt."

I knew then the boy had confused it.

556

"You go wine-shop." He gave me some small coins. Enough for a jar of wine. I did not ask how he came by them; I was unable to teach him the difference between living off the land and theft.

The Greeks in the wine-shop were Boiotian mercenaries looking for hire. They had the full story.

The Egyptian Kings Tachos and Naktenabo revolted from Persia. Agisilaos marched to Egypt at the head of an army, to fight their battles for pay. Egyptians are even worse soldiers than Persians. He arrived expecting to be appointed commander-in chief of the combined armies. The Egyptians made him captain of mercenaries.

He failed even to engage the Persians in combat, and died on his way back to Sparta at the age of eighty. Too late for the dead of Leuktra. Too late for my murdered comrades. Too late for my exiled son. Too late for Lakedaimon.

As Teres lighted the cooking-fires, and set about preparing our meagre fare, I wondered what had sent Agisilaos into Egypt. Was it his old vindictiveness? Hatred of the Persians for turning from Sparta to Thebes? Or was it an old man's attempt to relive the glory of his triumphs in Asia? Whatever it was, he could have spared Sparta the indignity of his end.

"Why are you laughing?" Teres asked. "Something comical you hear in the town?"

"Comical? No..."

How could I explain the irony of Agisilaos ending his days, like myself, as a mercenary?

There were rumours that swords were needed in the south of Thrace.

Riding south, the country became very rich. Although barley still stood in the fields, the green olives clinging tightly to the trees already had a purple tinge. The storerooms of farms were richly stocked.

"My country," Teres said, as we neared the Hellespont.

"You never told me you were from the Chersonese."

"Chersonese...? Is Greek word?"

"Where is your village?"

"Near the fort." There were a great many fortresses.

557

When we came to a town consisting of four or five huts, and a wine-shop built of warped greyish wood, he exclaimed that his village was but a half-day away. I told him to go and see his kin, while I asked the owner of the wine-shop where there was fighting.

Two other Greek mercenaries occupied one of the establishment's two tables. One was in his fifties, the other about thirty. Both looked as if they had seen better days.

As I started to sit down, the younger called out, "That stool is broken. The table is safer."

His accent was Peloponnesian and Doric, and pleasant to my ears, although it was Argive and slightly rustic. The elder man was Athenian. They had been lured to the Chersonese by the same rumour that had brought me. They undeceived me as to the call for swords.

The Athenian introduced himself as Aristedes, and his companion as Euphron. I told them that my name was Leon. It is the name of one of my ancestors, and sufficiently like the familiar Leo' that I remembered to answer to it.

"Did you leave Lakonia with Epaminondas, like the rest of them?" Aristedes laughed.

The Argive laughed shortly. "This one is no up-country Lakedaimonian. He has Spartiate written all over him. Excuse my friend. He is Attic and ignorant."

"If I am so dense, get us to Macedon." Aristedes turned to me. "They say King Perdikkas is desperate for men to fight the Illyrians."

"They say! They say!" Euphron drained the last few drops from his cup. "*They say* brought us here to the end of the world. You boasted we would become rich by our swords–"

"Don't start that again. Things are harder now. Iphikrates dead... Chabrias dead... Too many soldiers looking for hire–"

"That *young* Athenian made a fortune. Not yet thirty. Younger than me."

"He was lucky. And he's not Athenian. He's Spartan, like our friend here."

"He's got an Athenian accent."

"To Argive ears. His accent is slight, but it grows more Lakonic when he is in wine."

A name would mean nothing. Agis would not be using his

558

own.

"Speaking of wine, the jar is empty."

"You have had enough."

"I'll judge that."

The Athenian got to his feet. They left the wine-shop before I could ask them more.

Teres returned, and told me his kin would be honoured to have me on their farm. They were forever in my debt for returning him from slavery. It was a fine farm, and so on.

I replied that I was a soldier, not a farmer. The boy was torn two ways. I ordered him back to his people. He reminded me that he was not a slave. I asked him to stay with them a year. After that, he could return to me. If he wished.

In a year, many things could happen. He could form an attachment to some young man who was not stuffed with sawdust. His kin would marry him. He might have a son. It was a relief when he was gone. I missed his presence.

The two Greeks were again in the wine-shop. I brought the talk about to those men who had made fortunes as mercenaries. It is a favourite topic of mercenaries.

"That young one you mentioned—"

"The foreign bastard has one of the best houses in Athens. I am a citizen, and I have nothing. Everything we owned was on Aigina..."

"How did he make it? Is he such a great soldier?"

"He's good. But no better than many another man. Charmed his way into the best circles. That's how he did it. Claims descent from kings. That's the way with exiles. The further from home, the more distinguished their ancestors become."

"I think I may have seen him. Is he fair and slender, with a lopsided smile?"

"That's him. That's Polydoros, Hades take him!" I suppressed a smile. Agis had appropriated the name of Sparta's greatest king for himself. "Spends a fortune as soon as he makes it – then goes off on another campaign before his creditors catch up with him, and comes back with so much booty they fawn on him again. Too many foreigners in Athens."

I wanted to ask more, but they were questions a father would put. If this flotsam made his way back to Athens, I would not have him throw at Agis that he had seen his father, looking to sell his sword to the first savage who would pay him a few obols.

The proprietor set a jar brimming with wine on the table.

"For you, sir." He addressed me.

"I ordered no wine." And doubted I could pay for so large a jar.

"From him." He gestured towards a very old Thracian in a shadowed corner. "He says you are the Greek, and wishes to honour the god with wine."

"Take it." The Athenian said.

The old man looked poor. "Tell him I am not a god, and return his money."

The proprietor removed the wine with ill-grace.

"That was enough wine for all of us." The Argive whined.

The proprietor was back with the jar and the old man, who looked at me closely and made beseeching gestures, mumbling in his own speech.

"He says he has seen the god," the proprietor interpreted. "When he was a boy tending his goats, the god passed him and asked to water his horse. If you do not take the wine, he will believe he has offended the god." The old man looked truly frightened. More Thracian babbling. "He says the god loves wine."

"This is accursed nonsense. I am no god–"

"You won't convince him." The Athenian laughed. "Best take it."

"I cannot take wine intended for a god."

"Don't worry," the Athenian said. "It's no true god. The old bumpkin thinks you are Alkibiades. Some of these savages worship him. You have his height and build."

So Alkibiades followed me here. As it transpired, I had followed him.

"Very well, I will accept his offering – but as a man, not a god."

The proprietor translated something too brief to be accurate. The old man tottered off happily.

"Where are you lodging?" The Argive asked.

"I have been sleeping in the old fortress."

"So are we." The Argive said.

"Why don't you and that pretty Thracian boy of yours join up with us?" Aristedes suggested. "Four riding together is safer than two."

I explained that Teres had returned to his kin. The Athenian emptied his cup and refilled it. I left them with the rest of the wine.

I had found a place in the ruined fortress, where the straw was dry, if not fresh. A foraging expedition produced some bread and hard cheese. I washed it down with water. To put the thought of steaming black broth from my mind, I went to walk along the ramparts.

Below, a black sea sparkled with moon-touched waves.

The Athenian Aristedes appeared, reeking of wine. He swayed as he stood. "Euphron fancies you. He's no good, but he is all I have. You take my meaning?"

I told him I had no interest in his Argive, and I was not afraid to ride alone.

"He will leave someday...I am fifty-five. In ten years or so you will know what that means." I was fifty-three. Had my life continued its normal course in Sparta, in seven years time citizens would have addressed me as *sir*, and hastened to offer me their seats. "Have you thought of what becomes of a mercenary when he is too old to fight?"

"Spartans are never too old to fight."

"When they hire a man's sword, they look at the lines on his face, and the white in his hair. In the end, you starve or sell yourself into slavery. Hades take him, that Polydoros has Athenians amongst his slaves. I'll not sell myself to a foreigner...What was I saying?"

"That the people who made slaves of cities now become the slaves of foreigners." I wished that he would take his fear and his self-pity elsewhere.

He looked down into the water. "That is where our fleet lay, before your chaps sunk it. Now Sparta and Athens are both sunken ships."

"That is Goat River?"

"Did you not know?" I no longer troubled to ask the names of places that mattered nothing. "Alkibiades built this fortress.

561

All of them around here." He seated himself unsteadily on the edge. "He must have known Athens would turn on him someday. Athens loves brilliance and hates the brilliant. Mine is a fickle city."

"I hear he returned her love in kind."

"Have you ever hated one you love?"

"My love and hate do not share a common table."

"Perhaps Doric passions are simpler than Ionian."

"Or less confused."

"My father knew him well. Alkibiades. I was born a gentleman... everything gone when we lost Aigina in the Long War... What was I saying? Oh yes, Alkibiades... The leaders were jealous of his brilliance, his youth, his high birth... If we had Alkibiades today, no accursed Polydoros would own Athenians..."

"You surely can't remember Alkibiades."

"My father took me to see him return in triumph. Then, after he won the first victories we had had in years, the accursed fools dismissed him again. And still he rode down from these heights to warn the fleet. Generals mocked him and sent him away, and we lost the empire and everything on Aigina." He shook his head, as if to clear it. "He was the proudest of men, but his love of Athens was greater than his pride. And you say he returned her love in kind! By the gods, he must have ridden back here with the rage of Achilles..." He tilted on the ledge, staring into the sea. "Remember him? To see him once is to remember him always..."

"I saw his son once, long ago in Olympia. He entered nine chariots."

"That was Axiochos. He was killed in a drunken brawl. Alkibiades's sons never came to much."

"I understood he had only one."

"There was another from a Milian woman. A by-blow, of course. He recognised the boy, and brought him up as a gentleman." There was a story that he lay with a Spartan Queen, and has a son in your city."

"It would have been before I was born. There is no such man in Sparta. The local people here say he brought the most beautiful woman in the world to Thrace. I thought Teres spoke of Paris and Helen."

"He probably meant Timandra. The one he was supposed to have abducted in Asia. She was a black-haired Thracian. Exquisite, as they say. Educated and trained as a hetaira in Corinth. Nothing like these red-haired sows here. He could have any woman he wanted for a smile. They were all passing whims. He only seduced that Queen because he fancied founding a line of Spartan kings."

"He admitted to it?"

"He dined out on it. But Timandra had something for him. Brought her here. Took her to Persia with him. I suppose that is how that story started. She saw him slain. Sold her jewels to bury him. After all these years, we talk about the man. Or rather, I have talked. I have been here too long without the conversation of civilized men. Forget what I said earlier. The wine made me demean myself for an Argive peasant. Ride with us to Macedon. What say you?"

"I say that, after all the wine you drank, you are likely to fall into the sea."

He laughed, and got to his feet. "Think on it. As we are both the guests of Alkibiades for the night, I dare say we shall meet in the morning."

I stayed on the ramparts, where Alkibiades had watched the Athenian fleet meet its doom. It was the sole time I felt akin to this man, who had cast his shadow across my life. He, too, had choked on the dry dust of exile, and thirsted for his native springs. He, too, had seen his city bent on destroying herself, and been powerless to halt her.

I rose at dawn, rode west, and gave my sword to the Illyrians, who were warring on Macedon.

The Macedonians were in as bad a way as when Sparta rescued them for Amyntas. We raided their flocks with impunity. The Paionians pressed down on them from the north. Thurians and Triballi also raided regularly. It was time to move in for the kill, and simply a question of who would make it. The Illyrians were determined the prey would be theirs.

Perdikkas, the eldest son of Amyntas, was King of Macedon. There was a sad dignity to him as he rode out at the head of his army, wearing his father's gold-inlaid armour. Most of his men were poor tribesmen in their sheepskins, each following his own tribal chief. All looked hungry.

This was the host that faced us as we crossed the frontier.

The Illyrians were no better disciplined, but they were well-fed and in high spirits. Shouting war-cries, they rushed the enemy, each man at his own pace. A disciplined force could have made quick work of them. It was the Macedonians who fell back.

A few Greek officers tried to rally the scattering tribesmen. One succeeded in making ten or twelve of them stand and fight. I brought him down. His armour, weapons and mount were the only booty worth taking. His Macedonians fled. I moved in for the kill. He was tough.

A cry went up. Illyrians swarmed like insects about a riderless horse. The Macedonians were in full rout. Perdikkas had fallen. My sword bit deep in my enemy's neck. He crumpled.

I placed my foot in the Greek officer's chest to free my spear. It was embedded in bone. I gave it a sharp twist, freed it, and began stripping the body.

There were horses running riderless. A horse and this fellow's panoply would bring more than enough to take me some place that paid real wages. I cut through the armour straps with my short sword. The armour bore the dents of many battles, but it was good. Fitted to the body's shape. Not bought cheap, ready-fashioned.

The body moved. I ceased abruptly. Hades take the man! I could not strip a living Greek.

The Illyrians were going after the horses. I glanced at my prisoner. He would not last long enough to sell. If I left him, some savage would have the armour. If I did not, the Illyrians would seize all the horses. A horse, or the armour? Die, you bastard, before the savages have every last nag.

"Take the fucking armour!" The fellow forced the words through clenched teeth. "Illyrian pay...food...booty...no wages..." The accent was Doric. Argive or Corinthian, overlaid by the gods alone knew how many cities and armies.

"Don't be a fool, Man." Just die.

He groaned. I removed his helmet to ease him.

The ground roared. The sky fell. The sun spun, black as death.

564

Apollo! Hermes! Zeus! Gods of Olympos. Let this not be. Take time back a day. A cloud's passing. Stay my hand, so that which is done rests undone.

I knelt by the dying man. "Nikomedes... Oh, my friend..."

"Stop weeping, Leotychides, and take the fucking armour."

"I'm not weeping."

"Dry tears. Spartan tears."

"Don't call me Spartan. I'm nothing. A scavenger. A jackal of savages."

"Heard something about you..."

"Do they know the truth of it in Corinth?"

"Haven't been in Corinth since I turned mercenary at Thespiai. Forget who told me."

I rolled up my cloak, and placed it under his head. "Be still while I see to your wounds."

"Waste of time. Take the armour."

"You will need it."

"You know better."

"Then I'll bury you in it."

"Don't you call that superstition, Spartan?"

"I'll bury you in your superstition."

"You think I wouldn't kill you?" He challenged. Still game.

"What I'm paid to do." I gave him wine. Colour touched the pallid face. "Per– Perd–" Blood frothed his lips.

I wiped them clean. "Perdikkas is dead."

A chain of Illyrians began their victory dance in another part of the field.

"Won't be Amyntas." He mumbled. "General Philippos. First Regent. Then King. Strong, but needs Greek officers..." His hand gripped my wrist. "Go to Philippos."

"Anything, Nikomedes. I'll give my sword free to the bastard, if you think so highly of him."

"Highly? Another savage. But a clever savage. I could have set myself up well in Macedon." He tried to raise his head. "Take my place. Make dying matter that way. Something for a friend. Make something matter anyway... Another thing..."

"My life. Or my death." The same thing.

"The truth."

"That is harder."

"Truth." Insistently. "Swear..."

565

"By Apollo. The truth."

"Olympia... If I had fought on longer... a little only... Would you have submitted?" He raised himself on his elbows, to hold my eye with his. "Was I good as you?"

I looked back into those eyes that had challenged me across the boxing-ground so long ago."

"Nikomedes, it was Artemis who gave me the victory."

He fell back. "Nothing can be done against the gods."

The chain of jubilant Illyrians grew larger, longer, closer, louder, then turned and changed direction.

Nikomedes closed his eyes against the glaring sun. His breathing became hoarse and strained. The wine I gave him poured down his chin, and into his grey-flecked beard. I set aside the flask.

He blinked. His eyes opened.

"Artemis..." he said, as he died.

O, Fox, I thought I had done with you.

Dublin-Sparta-Dublin

In 338 B. C., at the battle of Chaeronea, Philip of Macedon made himself master of Greece, extinguishing the freedom of the city-states forever.

Only Sparta refused to accept Macedonian hegemony.

In the following two centuries, the Spartans attempted, valiantly and vainly, to return their city to the laws of Lykourgos, as Hellas struggled to throw off the yoke of Macedon.

Notes

All words and actions of real persons on public occasions are factual. Where sources are contradictory regarding historical events, I have attempted to reconcile; where there are lacunae, I have fallen back on the novelist's prerogative of imagination.

The chronology is that of Xenophon, rather than that of Diodoros.

The strength of the Spartan *mora* is a matter of debate. Xenophon gives it as six hundred men; but, as Spartan military thought manifested itself in terms of fifty, I have treated the *mora* as consisting of five hundred, accompanied by one hundred light-armed auxiliaries.

I have translated *strategos* as general. It is a temptation to give the rough British equivalents of other military ranks as well, but it would be misleading. I have, therefore, endeavoured to let them explain themselves in the text.

The grand admiral is the *nauorchos*. The up-country people are the *perioikoi*. The serfs are the *helots*.

I am aware that those birds in the Alkman poem are long-winged, but I have deliberately translated them as swift. A literal translation of poetry cannot always convey mood. The Arkadian's song is a folk song one has encountered in varying versions, in many parts of the Middle East and North Africa, where Greek armies have passed and Greek colonies settled. I haven't the slightest idea whether it is Greek in origin.

My views regarding transliteration are not dissimilar to those of T. E. Lawrence, although I have kept it consistent in the text. For the most part, it is as close to the original as possible, without being a phonetic nonsense. Place names, such as Corinth and Piraeus, that are very familiar to the reader in the Latinized spelling, I have employed in that form. It is, of course, an absurdity for a Greek to refer to the Erinyes as the Furies, but I have had my narrator do so for the same reason.

Modern historians still draw upon Xenophon in assessing the characters of Agisilaos and Kleombrotos. However, if one judges them by their actions, the picture is altered considerably. Kleombrotos emerges as a man of great intelligence and foresight, who exerted every possible effort in trying to prevent

568

Sparta from taking the disastrous path that led to Leuktra. There can be no doubt that Xenophon's friendship with Agisilaos biassed his thinking. Indeed, some of his comments concerning Kleombrotos are uncharacteristic of his own straightforward, colourful prose, and have the somewhat waspish tone of the recorded quotations of Agisilaos.

The letter from Kleombrotos to Epaminondas is my own device, although Xenophon hints at some form of communication. Agesipolis's rescue of Epaminondas and Pelopidas is recorded by both Plutarch and Diodoros.

We know that Antalkidas was the eponymous ephor during the first Theban invasion. Plutarch records that he sent his children to safety in Kythera. This would have been contrary to all Spartan tradition. We cannot know whether his term of office had expired when Agisilaos ordered the murder of the prominent Spartans. It is doubtful whether the King would have confided his intentions to him, whether he was or not. It is my firm conviction that Antalkidas did not die by his own hand. The advice to Artaxerxes that I have put into the mouth of Artabazos is only a guess. The presentation of the garland is from source.

Leotychides drops out of history after the succession dispute, but the life I have ascribed to him is a not unlikely one for a number of reasons. The Spartan who went inside the walls of Lechaeum with Pasimelos and Alkimenes is not named, nor is the first messenger to Agisilaos at the Piraeum. In both instances, I have given the job to Leotychides.

We are not given the names of either the polemarch or the cavalry commander of the 390 B. C. disaster. I have called them, respectively, Hipparchos and Anakos.

The Dionysos relief – and that of Apollo and Artemis – described in the text, can be seen in the Sparta Museum. All that remains of Kyniska's statue is the inscription, which is in the museum at Olympia. Pausanios mentions the statue of the boy with the fox, but does not leave us a description. The memorial stone to Agesipolis is still extant.

In portraying historical figures, I have taken into account incidents not described in the text. If I have been unjust, may their shades forgive me.

M.N.J.B.

Select Bibliography

Thucydides

Xenophon   Hellenica

Plutarch   Life of Lykourgos
                                Life of Alcibiades
                                Life of Lysander
                                Life of Agesilaus
                                Life of Pelopidas

Pausanias

Diodorus Siculus

Bommalaer   Lysandre de Spartre
MacDowell   The Origins of the
                                Peloponnesian War

Printed in Great Britain
by Amazon